D0586200

BLADE OF FORTRIU

Also by Juliet Marillier

THE SEVENWATERS TRILOGY
Daughter of the Forest
Son of the Shadows
Child of the Prophecy

Wolfskin
Foxmask

THE BRIDEI CHRONICLES
The Dark Mirror

www.julietmarillier.com

BLADE OF FORTRIU

BOOK 2
THE BRIDEI CHRONICLES

JULIET MARILLIER

TOR

First published 2005 in Tor by Pan Macmillan Australia Pty Limited

First published in Great Britain 2006 by Tor
an imprint of Pan Macmillan Ltd
Pan Macmillan, 20 New Wharf Road, London N1 9RR
Basingstoke and Oxford
Associated companies throughout the world
www.panmacmillan.com

ISBN-13: 978-1-4050-4108-9
ISBN-10: 1-4050-4108-0

Copyright © Juliet Marillier 2005

The right of Juliet Marillier to be identified as the
author of this work has been asserted by her in accordance
with the Copyright, Designs and Patents Act 1988.

Map by Bronya Marillier

All rights reserved. No part of this publication may be
reproduced, stored in or introduced into a retrieval system, or
transmitted, in any form, or by any means (electronic, mechanical,
photocopying, recording or otherwise) without the prior written
permission of the publisher. Any person who does any unauthorized
act in relation to this publication may be liable to criminal
prosecution and civil claims for damages.

1 3 5 7 9 8 6 4 2

A CIP catalogue record for this book is available from
the British Library.

Printed and bound in Great Britain by
Mackays of Chatham plc, Chatham, Kent

This book is sold subject to the condition that it shall not,
by way of trade or otherwise, be lent, re-sold, hired out,
or otherwise circulated without the publisher's prior consent
in any form or binding or cover other than that in which
it is pubished and without a similar condition including this
condition being imposed on the subsequent purchaser

Acknowledgements

My thanks to all who assisted in bringing this book to publication: Brianne Tunnicliffe of Pan Macmillan Australia, Claire Eddy of Tor Books and Stefanie Bierwerth of Tor UK for their editorial work; Julia Stiles for her excellent copyediting; and Bronya Marillier for her work on the map. I also thank Cate Paterson of Pan Macmillan for her ongoing support and encouragement, and my agent, Russell Galen, for his professionalism and his genuine enthusiasm for this project.

When researching Faolan's and Ana's journey my base was the Loch Maree Hotel in Wester Ross, where I was looked after with true Highland hospitality. The Groam House Museum in Rosemarkie provided me with the opportunity to play a replica Pictish harp, and with excellent information on the early history of the region.

Last but not least I thank my family for their expert advice on topics from sixth-century medicine to the tricks of unarmed combat, for their readiness to brainstorm plot developments whenever required and for their love and support.

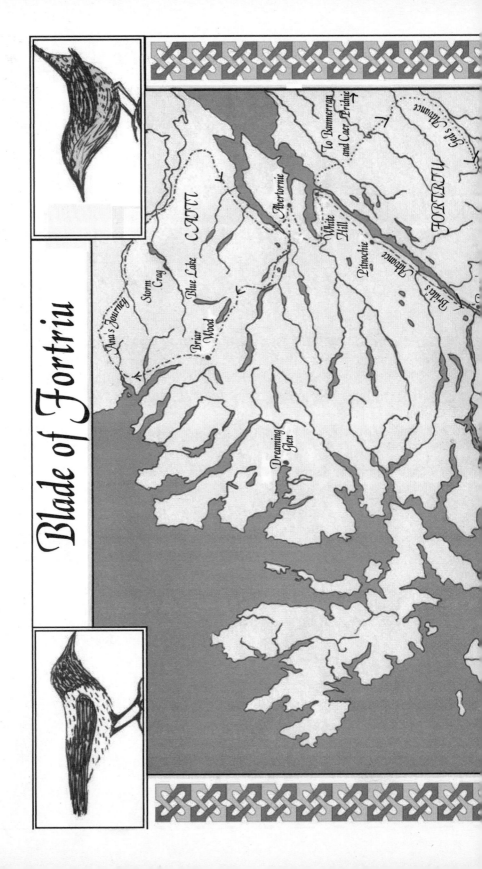

Blade of Fortriu

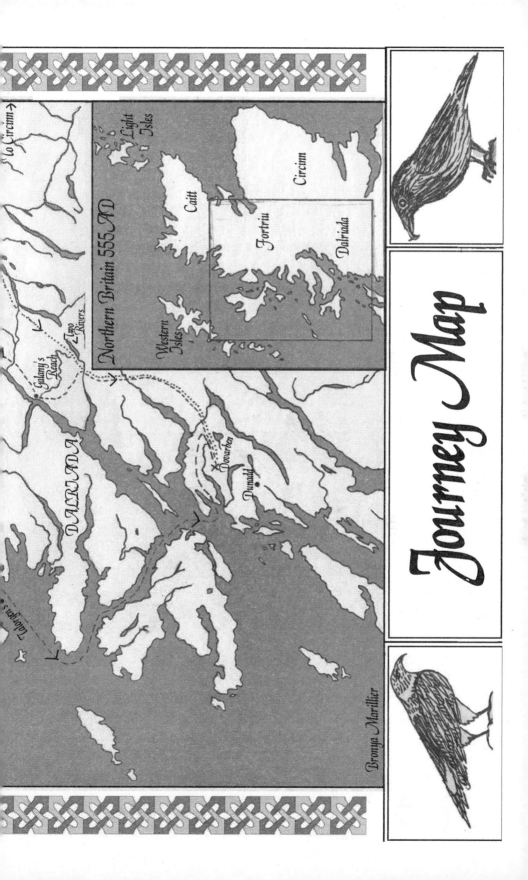

Journey Map

Bronya Marillier

Northern Britain 555 AD

to Circinn →

Light
Isles

Caitt

Fortriu

Circinn

Dalriada

Western
Isles

DALRIADA

Galany's
Reach

Two
Rivers

Dovarben

Dunadd

Talbot's...

Character List

White Hill (Court of Fortriu)

Bridei son of Maelchon	King of Fortriu
Tuala	his wife
Derelei	their infant son
Broichan	druid, foster father to Bridei
Ana of the Light Isles	royal hostage
Breda	her younger sister
Aniel	councillor
Tharan	councillor
Faolan	Bridei's principal bodyguard; a Gael
Breth	Bridei's second bodyguard
Garth	Bridei's third bodyguard
Kinet	
Wrad	men-at-arms
Benard	
Elda	Garth's wife
Darva	serving woman
Orva	nursemaid
Garvan	royal stone carver

| Snowfire | Bridei's horse |
| Ban | Bridei's dog |

Pitnochie

Mara	housekeeper
Uven	
Cinioch	men-at-arms, now attached to
Elpin	Bridei's forces
Enfret	

Banmerren

| Fola | senior wise woman |
| Derila | her assistant, tutor in history and politics |

Abertornie

Ged	chieftain
Loura	his wife
Aled	their son
Creisa	serving girl

Raven's Well

Talorgen	chieftain
Ferada	his daughter
Bedo	his elder son
Uric	his younger son
Sobran	Talorgen's bodyguard
Brethana	a comely widow

Caer Pridne

| Carnach | chieftain of Thorn Bend, head of Bridei's armed forces |
| Gwrad | Carnach's bodyguard |

Briar Wood

Alpin	Caitt chieftain
Drustan	his younger brother
Deord	Drustan's minder

Suneda	Alpin's sister, now living elsewhere
Erdig	
Goban	men-at-arms
Mordec	
Lutrin	
Orna	housekeeper
Ludha	maidservant
Dregard	Alpin's adviser
Sorala	Erdig's wife
Foldec	archer, Ludha's sweetheart
Gerdic	serving man
Cradig	owner of fighting dogs
Erisa	Alpin's first wife (deceased)
Bela	old nurse
Dovard	kennel hand

Blue Lake

Dendrist	Caitt chieftain
His son (unnamed)	
Domnach	
Omnist	men-at-arms

Storm Crag

Umbrig	Caitt chieftain
Orbenn	messenger
Hargest	stable hand
Berguist	druid

Other warrior chieftains of Fortriu
Uerb
Fokel of Galany
Wredech

Gaels

Gabhran	King of Dalriada
Odhar	Gabhran's emissary to the Caitt
Pedar	an informant
Brother Suibne	a Christian cleric

Dubhán	Faolan's brother
Áine	Faolan's sister
Echen	a chieftain of the Uí Néill
Brother Colm	
(Colmcille)	a Christian cleric

Court of Circinn

| Drust the Boar | King of Circinn |
| Bargoit | councillor |

Chapter One

In a draughty passageway below the Dalriadan fortress of Dunadd, two men met in shadow. The place was well away from the eyes and ears of the Gaelic court there, and thus suited to covert exchange. The information to be passed was dangerous; in the wrong hands it could be deadly. The future of kingdoms depended on it.

'What do you have for me?' There was a pattern to such exchanges; the younger man, a lean, dark individual with a shuttered expression, fell into it with the ease of long practice.

'A name,' said the other, a tall fellow clad in the russet tunic of King Gabhran's household retainers. 'Bridei must move quickly and cleverly if he is not to be hemmed in from north and south.'

'Spare me the analysis,' the dark man said. 'What name?'

'And in return?'

The dark man's lips tightened. 'You'll get your information.'

In the little silence that followed, the tall man glanced left and right along the shadowy way. All was quiet; moonlight, slanting in from the distant entry, allowed the two to read each other's features dimly. Under such a light it can be difficult to know if a man lies or tells the truth; it is hard to tell how far to trust.

1

Both of these men were expert in such judgements, for a spy's existence is all calculated risk.

'One of the Caitt chieftains,' whispered the tall man. 'Alpin of Briar Wood. He commands an extensive personal army. The alliance could be sealed before next spring unless your people act to forestall it.'

The dark man nodded. 'Which of the other northern chieftains would support him? Umbrig?'

'In my judgement, no. But they are kinsmen. Alpin has a natural son fostered in Umbrig's household. As for the others, I can't say. The chieftain of Briar Wood has both allies and enemies amongst his own.'

'I see.'

'Your king would be well advised to make a speedy approach to Alpin,' said the tall man. 'You'd best have a quiet word in Bridei's ear.'

The dark man's expression did not change. 'I'm hardly in a position to do that,' he said levelly. 'I'm only a bearer of information. I'm not the king's confidant.'

'That's not what I've heard.'

'Then you've been misinformed,' the dark man said.

'Now give me what you have.'

The dark man's eyes had grown colder. 'Gabhran should look to his eastern defences,' he said. 'Should this matter of the Caitt not impede him, Bridei could be ready to make his major push against the Gaels next spring. There's a council planned for Gathering, with high hopes Drust the Boar will fall in behind Bridei at last.'

The tall man grunted acceptance. The exchange of information was fair. What each man did with it was his own business.

The two parted without farewells. The dark man had a long way to go; the tall man was closer to home, and he walked back along the passageway and out under cover of trees with his mind on supper and a warm night in the bed of a certain accommodating woman.

A boy out fishing found him a few days later, his body swollen and distorted from immersion in a stream and bruised by the rocks under which it lay partly wedged. It was just possible to

2

ascertain that he had not died from drowning but had been expertly strangled by something strong and thin, such as a harp string.

As for the dark man, by then he was long gone from Dunadd, headed back across the border out of the Gaelic territory of Dalriada and into the lands of King Bridei of the Priteni. The bag of silver he had received from his Dalriadan masters had been hidden away. There would be another payment when he got to Bridei's fortress at White Hill. Considerable wealth now lay in his secret place, a resource he would surely never use, since he had neither wife nor children, brother nor sister to spend it on; at least, none he was prepared to acknowledge, even to himself.

He travelled with the speed and efficiency of a man who does not allow anything to distract him from his goal. It was unfortunate that his contact had required removal, but not unexpected. Pedar had not been stupid, and Faolan had known he would start to ferret out the truth about his own close relationship with Bridei eventually. He'd let his informant live until the danger of exposure was no longer outweighed by the value of what Pedar was able to supply. It was necessary that his Dalriadan masters believe Faolan entirely loyal to their cause. One must hope Pedar had kept faith with the delicate codes of covert intelligence and had not shared his suspicions with anyone. At any rate, Faolan would need to stay clear of Dunadd awhile, just to be sure. Perhaps Bridei would despatch him to serve with Carnach's fighting men, preparing for the great war to come. Perhaps he might be assigned to Raven's Well, where another army readied itself for the final push westward into Dalriada. A little honest fighting would not be unwelcome. He had been dancing on the fringes of kings' courts for too long now and was growing weary of masks. Ah well; good speed, clement weather, and he should be back at White Hill before the moon reached full again. Perhaps, Faolan mused as he made his way up the track by the lake's edge, heading northeastward under the clear skies of a crisp spring day, he might simply return to his old role as personal guard. In the five years since Bridei had been elected to the throne in somewhat unusual circumstances, nobody had got close enough to lay a finger on him or his wife. Faolan had made sure of that. Whenever he went away, he installed an infallible system of deputies to cover the period of his absence. All the same, nothing was quite as effective as his own presence by Bridei's side. He found, to his surprise, that this felt almost like going home.

Ana had been a hostage at the court of Fortriu since she was ten and a half. After eight years, she recognised that what had once seemed a kind of prison, albeit one where the captive ate at the king's table and slept in fine linen and soft wool, had become more like a home. When Bridei built his new fortress at White Hill and moved the court of Fortriu, Ana moved with the rest of them. Bridei's wife, Tuala, was one of her closest friends. That, thought Ana as she guided the tiny, tottering figure of the king's son, Derelei, across the sheltered garden that lay within the fortress walls, presented a problem for Bridei. The whole point of taking hostages was leverage against their kinsfolk. She was here as surety against a possible revolt by her cousin, who was monarch of the Light Isles and a vassal king to Bridei. In those eight years there had been no sign of unrest in her home islands, so it seemed her captivity had had the desired effect. On the other hand, there had been little interest shown by those at home in her welfare; her family seemed to have forgotten her. These days, it was White Hill that felt like home, and she could not imagine Bridei hurting her in any way, should her kinsmen suddenly take against him.

'Oops!' Ana exclaimed as Derelei's infant knees gave way and he collapsed abruptly onto his well-padded posterior. He looked momentarily surprised, seemed to ponder whether crying might be in order, then reached his arms towards her, offering a sound that meant 'Up!'

'Come on then.' Ana lifted the child to her hip; he was small for his age and had something of his mother's fey looks, the skin pale as milk, the eyes wide and solemn. His hair was Bridei's, brown as a nut and already curling tightly.

Who would have thought it, back in the Banmerren days when they were students together? Tuala was married and a mother, and Ana was still here in Fortriu, unwed. Carrying the royal blood of Fortriu often felt more like a curse than a privilege, especially if one were a woman. In the lands of the Priteni, the royal descent came through the female line: kings were selected, not from kings' sons, but from the sons of women like Ana, those descended from an unbroken line of royal females. It made her a prize piece in the great game of political strategy. Whoever wed her could be the father of kings. Bridei, as king of Fortriu, would be the one who eventually made the decision as to where she would go and when. There might be a token consultation with her cousin, but with both her parents long dead, and her kin far away in the islands, she knew it would be Bridei's choice. When she was a little girl with a head full of stories, she had hoped for love. She knew now how foolish it was to expect that.

And yet, for some people, love could be everything. Look at Bridei and Tuala. Their marriage had seemed impossible. It had been frowned upon by the powerful Broichan, the king's druid and Bridei's foster father. Ana looked down at Derelei, who had a strand of her long hair clutched in his fist and was exercising his new teeth on it. He gazed back, eyes solemn as an owl's. He was his mother's son, all right; the legacy of the Otherworld was plain in the tiny face, the delicate hands, the unusual gravity. Bridei had done the unthinkable: he had married for love and, as a result, Fortriu now had one of the Good Folk as its queen. Ana smiled to herself. A fine queen Tuala was, strong, courageous and wise. People had accepted her for all her difference, and her husband loved her with a devotion that was plain every time he set eyes on her. Nonetheless, Bridei was king and conducted his business in a realm of powerful and dangerous men. When it came to it, Ana was just another useful piece in the game, kept in reserve for the moment when she might be deployed to best advantage.

'Mama!' Derelei stated with emphasis, releasing Ana's hair and turning his head towards the archway at the far end of the garden. It was a sunny spring day; the light touched the creeper that twined up the stone wall, making a pattern in shades of subtle green. There was no sign of anyone; no sound save the distant voices of men-at-arms about their business, and nearer at hand the chirping of small birds hunting for nesting materials. The child was intent on the archway, his body jiggling with

5

anticipation in Ana's arms. She waited. A little later Tuala appeared through the archway with another woman behind her.

'Mama!' the small voice proclaimed, and the infant leaned forward at a perilous angle. Ana relinquished him into Tuala's arms.

'He knew you were coming,' she said. 'He always seems to know.'

'Ana, see who's here!' Tuala said, settling herself on a stone bench with her small son on her lap. The other woman moved forward and Ana realised belatedly who it was.

'Ferada! How good to see you! Tell me all your news!' Ferada, daughter of the influential chieftain of Raven's Well, had shared part of her education with both Ana and Tuala back in the days before Bridei became king. Unfortunate circumstances, kept largely from public knowledge, had enforced her return home to oversee her father's household and raise her two young brothers, and it was a long time since she had visited Bridei's court at White Hill. Ferada looked older; older than she should, Ana thought. A mere two years' advantage over her friends should not be enough to have caused the weary lines that bracketed Ferada's mouth, nor the unhealthy pallor of her complexion. One thing was unchanged: Ferada's gown was immaculate, her hair carefully dressed, her posture fiercely upright.

'News?' Ferada echoed, clasping her hands together in her lap. 'Nothing very exciting, I'm afraid. I've learned how to keep household accounts. I've managed to instil a little wisdom into Uric and Bedo with the help of visiting scholars – yes, Tuala, I took a leaf from Broichan's book on that score, knowing what an excellent job your old tutors did with you and Bridei. The boys are well; Bedo is good at his lessons and Uric has made steady improvement. Now, of course, they think themselves men and beyond such sedentary pastimes. It's all horsemanship and weaponry these days. Father seems to believe a stay at court will be educational for them.'

'I always thought they were good-hearted little boys,' Tuala said. Derelei had settled in her lap, fingers grasping a fold of her tunic; she stroked his curly hair with her small, white hand as she spoke. 'So, does this mean Talorgen is seeking suitors for you,

Ferada? You know there will be a major assembly before long; many chieftains will gather at White Hill to debate strategy for war. It is an opportunity . . .'

'I expect anyone who expressed interest in me when I was sixteen will be wed by now,' said Ferada. 'If Father is looking about, it'll be amongst the older ones, those who are not so desperate to father large broods of children as rapidly as possible.' She glanced at Derelei, then met Tuala's searching eyes and mildly amused expression. 'Don't take offence, Tuala, you know I don't mean you and Bridei. Didn't the two of you wait an agonising two years from betrothal to formal handfasting? The fact is, women like Ana and myself are viewed principally as breeding stock, and by twenty we're considered past our best. On that subject, I'm surprised to see you still here, Ana. Pleased, of course; I've missed you both terribly. But I would have expected you to marry years ago. There was certainly no shortage of interested suitors. You were a beauty at thirteen and you still are.'

Ana looked down at her hands. 'I understand Bridei does have someone in mind; a chieftain from the north, he said. Perhaps next summer. I do feel as if I've been waiting forever.' The comment about *past our best* had disturbed her, but she did not want her friends to see this. As a daughter of the royal line, one must always put duty first, as indeed Ferada had most admirably in returning home to five years as glorified housekeeper. During that time numerous opportunities had passed her by. At this rate they would be toothless old crones together, with not a husband nor babe between them.

'In fact,' Tuala said, 'there have been some developments on that front. Faolan's back, and Bridei wants to speak to you later today, Ana. I understand it's to do with this chieftain, Alpin. I didn't press him for details; he wanted to talk to Faolan alone.'

Ana shivered. 'That man! I always wonder, looking at him, whose blood he has on his hands this time; what dark corner he's been lurking in. I don't know how Bridei can trust him.'

Tuala gazed at her. 'I've never known Bridei's judgement to be faulty,' she said quietly. 'Misinformation, deception, sudden death, those are the essence of Faolan's work. He is of great value principally because he does those things so expertly, and without qualms.'

'He turned against his own people,' Ana said. 'I don't know how anyone could do that.'

'No?' Ferada lifted her brows. 'What about you, living contentedly at the court of the folk who took you hostage when you were too young to know what it meant? Making yourself at home amongst people who have denied you the chance to grow up with your family? That's not so different from Faolan gathering information in Dalriada.'

'Shh,' Tuala said. 'Ferada, I admire your outspokenness, I always have. But you're at White Hill now; you should moderate your speech a little, even amongst friends. Ana should not judge the king's assassin, and you should not judge Ana. A great deal has changed at court since Drust the Bull took her hostage. Indeed, she can hardly be called that any more; I view her as something more like a sister.'

'All the same,' Ferada said, 'I notice Bridei hasn't sent her home.'

Home, Ana thought as a cloud of misery settled over her. The Light Isles. In the early days she had longed to go back to that realm where the lakes held the pale light of the open sky and the green hills folded gently down to pasture land. The place of her childhood was full of ancient cairns and mysterious stone towers, sudden cliffs and drifts of wheeling seabirds. Yet now, if Bridei sent her there, she thought it would seem like another exile. As for the other option, the one that now loomed as real and immediate, it made her cold with misgiving. The Caitt were of Priteni blood, as were her own island people. She thought of the only Caitt chieftain she had seen since her childhood: Umbrig of Storm Crag, a man like a big bear, fierce and uncouth. Umbrig had appeared unexpectedly at the election for kingship and had cast his vote for Bridei, helping him win out over Drust the Boar, monarch of the southern Priteni realm of Circinn. Folk said the Caitt were all like that, huge and ferocious. Ana shrank from the notion of sharing such a wild man's bed.

'Derelei walked all the way along the path today, holding my hands,' she said, changing the subject. 'He'll be doing it on his own soon. He's a credit to you, Tuala.'

'I catch Broichan looking at him from time to time, no doubt searching for eldritch talents, seeking to discover how much of my own blood our son bears and how much of Bridei's.'

'Broichan doesn't fool me,' Ana said. 'He dotes on the child, to the extent that a king's druid may unbend enough to show affection. You watch him some time when he thinks you're not looking. Derelei's like his own grandchild.'

'And does he?' Ferada asked, scrutinising the infant, who was sitting quietly on his mother's knee, examining his fingers. 'Have any eldritch talents, I mean?'

Ana opened her mouth to answer, but Tuala was quicker. 'I would be happy if he could conjure a charm to alleviate the pangs of teething,' she said. 'We're all short of sleep. Ferada, I see a look in your eye that tells me you have more news. I did hear a rumour that Talorgen has made the acquaintance of a certain comely widow. Or is that merely gossip?'

It was interesting, Ana thought, how deftly Tuala managed to avoid discussion of any special abilities her son might exhibit and, indeed, of her own talents in certain branches of the magical arts. As queen, she seemed determined to avoid those matters, as if they might be in some way dangerous. Ana knew Tuala's power at scrying; it had become the stuff of legend at Banmerren, the school for wise women. And there was a very strange tale of a time when Tuala had run away, and what had befallen both her and Bridei in the forest of Pitnochie, a tale neither of them had ever told in full. Still, one must abide by the queen's wishes. If she wanted to be ordinary, if she preferred her son to be unexceptional, one must pretend, outwardly at least, that this was so.

Ferada shifted a little on the bench. 'Father plans to seek permission to dissolve his marriage,' she said grimly. 'We don't know if Mother is still alive, or where she is, only that she travelled beyond the borders of Fortriu. Father has good grounds to do this. I understand it's the king's druid who makes such decisions. I think Broichan will allow it.'

'And?' Ana prompted.

'Father wishes to remarry. The widow's name is Brethana; she's quite young. I like her, inasmuch as a girl can like her father's second wife. The boys don't care one way or another. At that age their own activities are all that matters in the world. Once Father marries, there'll be nothing to keep me at Raven's Well.'

There was a pause, during which Tuala and Ana exchanged a meaningful glance.

'You know,' Tuala said, 'I feel quite certain the next thing Ferada wants to tell us has nothing to do with suitors and marriages. I see a certain look on her face.'

'Mm,' Ana mused, 'the look she always used to get just before coming out with something outrageous.'

'I'm not sure if I should tell you yet,' Ferada said. 'I need to talk to Fola.'

'Fola! You mean you're going to return to Banmerren and become a wise woman?' Tuala's tone expressed the incredulity Ana felt; whatever their friend's abilities, and these were many, Ferada had never seemed destined for a future in the service of the goddess.

Ferada's cheeks reddened. 'I am going to Banmerren. Or, if Fola comes for the assembly, I will speak to her here at White Hill. And no, of course I'm not planning to become a priestess. I have a proposition for Fola. It troubles me that so many young women of noble blood receive, at best, half an education, and more commonly none at all save in the domestic arts. I know Fola provides places for them at Banmerren, as she did for Ana and me. But what's offered is lacking in structure and depth; no sooner does a student start to get interested than she's whisked off back home, or to court to be paraded before the men, or into some fellow's bed to have his heirs put in her belly. Don't look like that, Tuala; I know your own experience has been somewhat different but, believe me, for most girls it's a brutal and arbitrary business. If there was a place where young women could stay just a little longer, learn a little more, gain some wisdom before they are thrust out into that world of men, I think we might equip them better to stand up for themselves and play a real part in affairs. So that's what I want to do. Start a school; or rather, expand the one Fola has already to include a whole branch for girls who are not to become priestesses but to live their lives in the world. I plan to ask Fola if she will let me organise it; let me be in charge of it. I have done quite well with Uric and Bedo. And I learn quickly. What do you think?'

Tuala was smiling. 'A bold idea, entirely typical of you, Ferada,' she said. 'I'd be surprised if Fola were not interested. What about your father?'

'He's not entirely comfortable with it, but his new marriage is foremost in his mind. Besides, he owes me. I've done a good job of managing his household and the boys; I've given five years to it.'

'You will encounter some opposition, that is certain,' said Tuala. 'Broichan is unlikely to support such an idea; he does not believe in education for women, save for those destined to serve the goddess. Many of the men will think it unnecessary, a waste of time. Some will consider it dangerous. Not all men are as open-minded as your father, who always encouraged you to express your opinions.'

'What of your own marriage?' Ana asked. 'How would you achieve this plan if you had a husband and family to look after? Surely you don't intend to sacrifice that?'

'Sacrifice?' Ferada's tone was scathing. 'Oh, Ana. Can't you entertain the possibility that a woman might reach deeper fulfil-ment in her life without a man?'

Ana felt the heat rise to her cheeks. 'I –' she began.

'I'm sorry,' Ferada said in a different tone. 'I've upset you; I didn't mean to. It's been so long since I was able to speak openly, and my head is so full of ideas. I want to teach. I want to make a difference. I want to be sure I don't waste my life.'

'I don't intend to waste mine,' Ana said, unable to ignore the implication.

'Then you must hope whatever suitor Bridei has in mind for you is a paragon of male virtue,' Ferada said. 'Tuala, will you speak to Bridei about my intentions? His support for the general idea of it would help me immensely.'

'Of course,' Tuala said. 'And you should ask him yourself, as well. I feel certain he will approve. He admires you, Ferada.'

Ferada fell unaccountably silent, and at that moment the baby began to squirm, drawing several deep breaths that seemed to presage a storm of some kind.

'We should go in,' Tuala said, rising and hitching the child expertly to her hip. 'He's getting hungry; it must be all that walk-ing. You're good with him, Ana.'

'I like it,' said Ana. 'Seeing him grow; watching all the little changes.'

'All very well when it's someone else's,' Ferada observed, 'and you can give it back when it yells or dirties itself or gets a fit of the midnight terrors. Count yourselves lucky you don't have five or six of them milling around your ankles. If they'd married us off when they first started speaking of suitors, we'd each have a brood by now.'

'I'd love another child,' Tuala said with a smile. 'If the Shining One blesses me with a daughter, Ferada, I'll be sure to send her to you for her education.'

'That's if Fola doesn't get in first,' Ferada said.

The king's court at White Hill was built on the site of an ancient fortress fashioned of stone laced with fired wood. Traces of those walls still remained deep in the undergrowth that clad the steep slopes of the hill. Here and there under the shade of tall pines a crumbling fragment of shaped stone would suggest a rampart, a wellhead, a stretch of paved way; the stream that made its circuitous course down the flanks of White Hill flowed into basins and pools both natural and constructed. The place was considered impregnable. The steep pitch of the hill itself, the sheer, strongly built fortress walls, the views allowed by strategic gaps in the screening cover of the trees, gave the occupants great advantage in defence. From here, one could see both northward to the ocean and southward to the changeable waters of Serpent Lake and the dark hills of the Great Glen. The natural supply of fresh water and the broad expanse of level ground at the summit of White Hill, now covered with the halls and dwellings, the gardens and workshops of Bridei's establishment, all within the massive new walls, would allow the occupants to withstand a siege for as long as it took for attackers to tire of it, or for reinforcements to arrive.

To the east, along the coast, lay the old defensive fort of Caer Pridne, which had housed the royal court of Fortriu under Bridei's predecessor and many other kings before him. Bridei had been young when he came to the throne, but possessed of a powerful will for change. At one and twenty, two years into his reign, he had completed the construction of White Hill and shifted his headquarters there, breaking with tradition. The first celebration in his new court was his marriage to Tuala, then barely sixteen years of age. Other changes followed. The most risky was Bridei's decision to alter the practice of a certain ritual that marked the year's descent into the dark. The last time that had been attempted, the offended god had exacted a terrible retribution. But the chieftains and elders accepted Bridei's decision. It was known that both he and his druid, Broichan, enacted personal rites in place of the old observance, and that these were demanding in nature. Folk did not ask for details. Their trust in their new young king was strong indeed. There was a quality in the man that swept others along, a passionate dedication and blazing energy, tempered by caution, subtlety and cleverness. After all, Bridei had grown up as Broichan's foster son, and Broichan was a powerful mage, chief adviser to both the old king and the new.

There had been whispers in the early days. Broichan was not well liked; many feared his power and distrusted the esoteric nature of his knowledge. Some had said that having Broichan's foster son as king would be just the same as having the druid himself on the throne. Was not this his carefully created puppet, set up to conduct the affairs of Fortriu to Broichan's plan? From the first day of his kingship, however, it was clear Bridei had a mind of his own and intended to make his decisions independently. He formed a council composed of a clever balance of the older, more experienced men and those younger chieftains who were prepared to countenance new ideas and consider calculated risks. He weighed druids against war leaders, scholars against men of action. On occasion he included women in his group of advisers: not only the senior priestess, Fola, who ran the establishment where girls were trained in the service of the Shining One, but also the old king's widow, Rhian of Powys, and sometimes his own wife, Tuala.

While the decisions were largely made at White Hill, Bridei maintained strongholds elsewhere. Caer Pridne still housed a garrison, stables, training yards and an armoury. Raven's Well in the southwest and Thorn Bend in the southeast were strategic outposts under the leadership of influential chieftains loyal to the king. All knew Bridei's plan was to strengthen Fortriu sufficiently and then move against the Gaels. All knew the time was drawing ever closer. Exactly when was a matter for the laying of wagers.

The day after Faolan's return to White Hill, Ana was called to the royal apartments. Derelei was out in the garden with the nursemaid; within the chamber used for informal meetings, the king and queen were waiting quietly. Their serious faces alarmed Ana. She had a fair idea of what was coming, but she had expected Bridei, at least, to present the news as positive. The little white dog, Ban, who was Bridei's constant companion, arose from his place beneath the king's chair, stance alert, then, seeing a friend, settled once more. Moving forward into the chamber, Ana saw that there was a fourth person present. Faolan, Bridei's assassin, Bridei's spy, Bridei's right-hand man, was leaning against the wall by the narrow window, his form in shadow. His eyes travelled over her as she went to sit by the table. Ana saw in his face not the open admiration that other men offered her, but a cool assessment: plainly, the Gael was calculating her value as marketable goods.

'You know why we have called you, I imagine?' Bridei said as Tuala poured mead.

Ana was suddenly tense with nerves. She gave a tight nod. These were her friends. She dined with them every day. She played with their son. Nonetheless, Bridei had such power over her future that, for a moment, she was afraid. 'I understand Faolan has news of this Caitt chieftain, Alpin,' she said, keeping her voice calm. 'He has, perhaps, shown an interest in marriage?'

A brief silence. Evidently her guess was wrong.

'We find ourselves in rather a difficult situation,' Bridei said, 'and, as a result, we're about to ask for your help, Ana. What we need you to do is difficult. Awkward. It will mean great change for you.'

Ana had no idea what he meant.

'We've called you here now, just the four of us, so that we can give you this news in private and allow you some time for consideration,' Bridei went on. 'There's to be a formal council this evening, at which our decision must be made on this matter. Faolan's news has made this urgent. Critical.'

14

'Bridei,' Tuala said, 'I'm sure Ana would prefer it if you just set everything out for her. This is a great deal to ask. She needs all the facts.'

Faolan cleared his throat.

'You know, of course,' Bridei said, 'of the great venture we plan against the Gaels in the near future. Gods willing, our old foes will be swept from the shores of Priteni lands once and for all, and their Christian faith with them. In this endeavour we need whatever allies we can get. Circinn has been invited to an assembly before full summer, as you'll be aware. We have high hopes of securing Drust the Boar's cooperation this time, for all he let the missionaries of the cross into his own kingdom. I also intend to set in place what alliances I can with the northern realms of the Priteni.'

'My kin in the Light Isles?' Perhaps, against all expectations, he was sending her home.

'I've sent a request to your cousin for armed men. The message also sought his formal consent to my bestowing your hand in a particular quarter.'

'I see.'

'Ana,' Bridei's tone was kind, 'you've known this was coming for a long time. You are in your nineteenth year now, well past the age when you might have expected to be wed.'

'Just tell her, Bridei,' said Tuala with uncharacteristic sharpness.

'I'd planned to investigate the chieftain we have in mind for you, Alpin of Briar Wood, more thoroughly before approaching him,' Bridei said. 'Thus far, Umbrig is the only Caitt chieftain to pledge support against the Gaels. The Caitt are a strange breed, full of pride and aggression. Alpin is probably the most powerful, and he's also the hardest to get to, his territory being both remote and situated in the middle of an impenetrable forest. Messages travel slowly.'

Ana thought hard. 'Don't the Caitt usually stay outside other people's disputes?' she asked. 'They crossed to the Light Isles from time to time in their war boats; I can remember them at my cousin's court. He used to buy them off with gifts.'

'They are of our own kind,' Tuala put in. 'They share the same blood and the same tongue as the Priteni everywhere, in Fortriu,

Circinn or the Light Isles. And if Umbrig can pledge warriors, so could Alpin. That could make all the difference.'

Ana waited. She felt she might be missing something.

'Faolan,' said Bridei, 'tell the lady Ana what you have discovered; at least, that part of it we agreed is safe to tell.'

Faolan folded his arms and stared into the middle distance. He was an unexceptional-looking man, of average height and wiry build, the sort of man who could blend into any crowd. His only distinguishing feature was the lack of facial tattoos which, since he was plainly neither druid nor scholar, marked him out as not of Priteni blood. Ana wondered if, as a spy, he worked assiduously on being instantly forgettable.

'I heard talk of a second territory,' he said. 'On the west coast, with a sheltered anchorage. If this information is accurate, the place is ideally situated for access by sea to the Dalriadan territories. That's the first piece of information, and it means we're not likely to be the only player trying to woo this Caitt leader with incentives.'

An incentive. She had never been called that before. 'And the second piece of information?' she asked him coolly.

'You understand,' Faolan said, 'that you cannot be privy to all the details; in the wrong hands, information can be dangerous.'

Ana was outraged. 'I may be a hostage,' she said in her most queenly tone, 'but I can be relied on to be unswervingly loyal to Bridei. I don't much care for your implication.'

Faolan looked through her. 'The strongest man's loyalty can break under torture,' he said flatly. 'You'll be told what you need to know, no more. Alpin is a powerful player, far more so than we realised. I heard that he may be on the verge of agreeing to an alliance with Gabhran of Dalriada. We have to move swiftly. We cannot afford to have that western anchorage in Gaelic hands, nor Alpin's private army ranged against us in battle. It's simple enough.'

'I see.' Ana struggled for calm. 'So you plan to offer him a royal bride?' she asked Bridei. 'To render this powerful player still more powerful by offering him the opportunity to father a king?'

'Alpin is wealthy,' Bridei said. 'He has land, men, cattle, silver. We can't tempt him with any of the usual things. Our leverage rests on two facts we've gleaned from Faolan's investigations. One, Alpin craves respectability and status. Past history has rendered him less than well regarded by the other Caitt chieftains, such as Umbrig, for all his natural son is fostered out in that household. Two –'

'He isn't married,' Ana said.

'Exactly. He is a widower with no legitimate children. You see what an opportunity this is.'

'Bridei understands how difficult this is for you, Ana.' Tuala's small, clear voice was apologetic. 'Although you have been anticipating this for so long, that makes it no less daunting to face the reality, I know. Please ask any questions you like; I imagine it will be far easier to do so now, informally, than at tonight's council.'

Ana swallowed. 'Why a council?' she asked. 'Is not this Bridei's decision?' One thing was certain: her own choices did not come into it at all.

'My advisers and war leaders need to hear Faolan's news at first-hand,' the king said. 'It's significant.'

It seemed to Ana that all of them were holding something back. 'There's more, isn't there?' she said, looking from Tuala's big, troubled eyes to Bridei's honest blue ones to Faolan's dark, closed-off stare. 'What?'

'Time,' Faolan said. 'There's no time. You need to go now. That's what it amounts to.'

Ana stared at him.

Bridei sighed. 'In effect, that is what we must ask you to do. The nature of Faolan's information is such that this has become of pressing urgency. I've despatched a messenger to Alpin advising him of our offer. However, it's in our best interests not to wait for a written response, but for you to set out for Briar Wood right away. We need you married and an agreement signed by summer. We must move before Alpin commits himself to a Gaelic alliance.'

'Go now – but –' Ana was speechless. Suddenly she was ten years old again, full of excitement to be visiting the court of Fortriu, then being told she was a hostage and would not be going home again. 'But Bridei – Tuala – how can you do this? It means I'll be on the way there not even knowing if he's agreed! What if I turn up on his doorstep and . . .' She could not quite put it into words. *What if he doesn't want me?* There was a terrible shame in it.

'Ana,' said Bridei, 'the man would be a complete fool to be displeased with such a bride. Believe me. He need only take one look at you. Put such doubts from your mind. It is our belief that your physical presence at Briar Wood will be one of our most telling bargaining points.'

This did not make her feel better. 'Surely this could be approached a little more gradually,' she protested. 'Even if your advance takes place as early as next spring, couldn't we wait for the messenger to come back with Alpin's answer?' Alpin might even travel to White Hill in person to fetch her. That way there would at least be a little time to make his acquaintance before the formal handfasting. 'There'd still be plenty of time for me to travel to Briar Wood before next winter,' she said.

'It has to be now.' Faolan's tone was final. 'Strategic reasons. Reasons it's best you don't know in full.'

'I see.' Ana was shaking; she clenched her fists, wondering if what she felt was anger or fear. 'When is *now*, precisely?'

Bridei's eyes were full of compassion. 'As soon as you can be ready,' the king said. 'There are certain arrangements to be put in place; someone from court will accompany you and assess the situation at Briar Wood before any final agreement is made between yourself and Alpin. I'll see to it that you have an appropriate escort. You'll wish to take a little time with preparation of clothing and personal effects. Tuala will make sure you have any help you need. Faolan will speak to you later; he'll let you know what's required. The terrain's difficult in parts, so the baggage must be kept to a minimum.'

There was a silence. Ana looked down at her hands. 'Someone from court,' she said eventually. 'That is to be Faolan?' It was not possible to keep the note of distaste from her voice.

'Correct,' Bridei said. 'He's well equipped to assess the risks when you reach Briar Wood, and expert in matters of personal security.'

She looked up then and saw on the face of the king's assassin an expression that must surely be the mirror of her own. It gave her some little satisfaction that to him, too, this arrangement was less than welcome.

'You look tired, Ana,' Tuala said quietly. 'This is a great deal to take in.'

Her friend's kindness was, somehow, the last straw. Ana knew she was on the verge of bursting into tears or uttering some ill-considered protest. 'I'm fine,' she said brightly. 'This council – what is expected of me there?'

'Your formal consent to the handfasting. Some council members may have questions for you, or you for them.'

'I see.' And she did see; she saw a future in which things happened regardless of her own choices; a future in which she was completely powerless. Duty: so this was what it amounted to. She hoped Alpin of Briar Wood was a kind man. 'Excuse me.' Holding her head high, she managed to leave the room with her dignity intact. She waited until she was in her chamber alone before she let the first tear fall.

'I don't like this,' the King of Fortriu said to his wife a little later, when Faolan had departed and the two of them were alone. 'I had always hoped, not only to find the right strategic match for Ana, but also to select a man whom I knew would be kind to her. I hate this need for haste.'

'She's very upset,' said Tuala. 'She was doing her best not to show it, she's been well trained, but it was obvious she was on the verge of tears. If there is some way to make this easier for her, we should do our best to find it.'

'I know.' Bridei reached down to scratch Ban behind the ears; sighing, Ban laid his head on the king's foot. Since the day the dog had mysteriously appeared by the scrying pool at Pitnochie, in the momentous winter of the election for kingship, he had scarcely left Bridei's side. 'It's a great deal to expect from her, I'm well aware of that. But Ana is a grown woman now, and she's made no secret of her wish for children of her own. At least this did not happen when she was fourteen, fifteen, as it could well have done had the right offer come at that time.'

'All the same,' said Tuala, 'any woman in her situation would be thinking, what if I reach Briar Wood and discover my betrothed is a monster: pox-ridden, or a drunkard, or a wife-beater? It would be so much better if Alpin could come here first, so we could find out what manner of man he is. Ana is our friend, Bridei.'

He opened his eyes a little. His wife sat, slight and upright, in the chair opposite his. Her dark hair, which was escaping its neat braids, curled in becoming wisps around her face. Her eyes were like Derelei's, wide, light and clear. 'I know,' Bridei said. 'Were I only that, her friend, I would advise her to refuse our request. I'd caution her against making a long and perilous journey to place herself in the hands of a chieftain of Alpin's reputation. But I am the king. My decisions must weigh what is best for Fortriu.'

'Bridei, you know I don't blame you for this choice,' Tuala said softly. 'I understand, as you do, that it's necessary for the greater good. Ana knows that too. But she's shocked and afraid, as anyone would be in the circumstances. Is it really essential that she leave before we receive Alpin's answer?'

'According to Faolan, yes. I've consulted Broichan, and he is in agreement. We've been preparing for this final assault against the Gaels for years. Everything is falling into place. To the extent that it's possible, we've taken steps to cover every eventuality. Or so we thought. It seems Alpin is the unpredictable factor, the element that could tip the balance one way or the other. Until now, we had not realised just how much influence he could wield. Nor did we know how seriously he was considering an alliance with Gabhran. Ana is our solution, Tuala, and though it hurts me to say it, we need to deploy her now. Each day that passes while we keep her at White Hill is one too many.'

'It's dangerous, isn't it? This journey?'

'Faolan will make sure she is safe. He'll assess Alpin and the overall risk; we'll lay out terms that require a certain period between their arrival at Briar Wood and the handfasting. That will at least allow Ana time to get to know her betrothed a little.'

'She despises Faolan. It is odd; Ana's such a sweet, good creature, with not an ill word to say of anyone, but in his case she cannot see past the nature of his work.'

Bridei grimaced. 'The feeling seems to be mutual; Faolan would not refuse a commission, of course, but he made it as plain as he could to me that nursemaiding spoiled princesses and their bride chests over the fastnesses of Caitt territory was not the kind of task he relished. Indeed, he set out with some cogency all the reasons this was a job best suited to some other man.'

'Spoiled?' Tuala smiled. 'He doesn't know her very well, does he?'

'He's planning to put her through her paces on horseback every day until they leave. It's plain he believes she'll barely be able to trot from one end of the yard to the other without pleading exhaustion or a sore back.'

'I don't like this at all, Bridei.' Tuala's tone was sombre. 'The whole situation is fraught with uncertainty. You could surely have trusted Ana with the real reason why this has to be done in such a hurry.'

'I acted on Faolan's advice,' Bridei said. 'In his opinion, the less she knows, the less she can tell if things go awry. It's in Ana's own best interests.'

'Mm,' said Tuala. 'Of course, she's clever. Men tend to overlook that when a woman is as beautiful as Ana. I expect she's already worked it out for herself.'

It was evening. Ana had dressed plainly, in tunic and skirt of blue-dyed wool with cream borders embroidered in a darker blue, and had plaited her thick fair hair into a single braid down her back. Now she made her way down through the garden, past a pair of tall guards, along a stone-lined passageway where torches burned in iron sockets, and up to the oak door of the designated chamber. Outside the door stood a large man with a spear: Breth, one of Bridei's personal guards.

'They're ready for you, my lady,' he said, and swung the heavy door open for her.

The proceedings appeared to have been under way a good while; jugs and cups stood on the table, and several people who had been talking ceased abruptly as Ana came in. She held her chin up and her back straight in an effort to quiet the nervous churning of her stomach.

'Welcome, Ana,' the king said, rising to his feet. From his position by Bridei's chair, Ban gave a token growl. 'Please be seated.'

Ana looked around the circle of faces. It was a small council and a select one, comprising the most powerful of Bridei's advisers. Tuala was seated by her husband and gave Ana an encouraging smile. The wise woman, Fola, who had arrived earlier in the day, regarded Ana quizzically down her beak of a nose. She had always reminded Ana of a small, ferocious bird. By the hearth stood the king's druid, Broichan, a tall man in dark robes, his hair in a multitude of tiny plaits twisted with coloured threads. His face revealed nothing; it was ever unreadable. Bridei's councillors, Aniel and Tharan, sat sober-faced; the chieftains Carnach and Morleo, with Ferada's father Talorgen, were also present. Behind the king's chair stood Faolan. Ana met his gaze and looked away.

'Now,' said Bridei, 'I've set out the situation for the members of this council, and Faolan has given an account of his travels and the intelligence he has gathered. I regret very much that we could not give you more time to consider this, Ana. If you agree to it, the kingdom of Fortriu will be very much in your debt. I wonder if, after reflection, you have some further questions for us?'

Ana cleared her throat. She had spent the afternoon wrestling with questions that could not be asked, questions that had nothing at all to do with strategy, but concerned her personal inclinations. 'I wondered if any of you had actually met Alpin of Briar Wood. If there was someone who could give me a picture of him.' She glanced at Talorgen, at Carnach. Warrior chieftains travelled widely and encountered many folk.

'May I answer that?' It was the grey-haired councillor, Aniel. Bridei nodded. 'Unfortunately, we must answer no, Lady Ana. We know Alpin only by reputation. He's feared and respected amongst his own kind. His stronghold is isolated; it lies in a tract of dense forest. Such a setting can easily give rise to the type of rumours that feed on men's natural unease.'

'Choosing to live in a forest is not necessarily a bad thing,' Tuala commented. 'The territories of the Caitt are full of such wild places, or so we are told. I suspect every chieftain wears his own particular cloak of tales.'

'There was a mention of past history,' Ana said, who had found little of reassurance in Aniel's words. 'What history?'

'Nothing specific,' Aniel said. 'Some of Faolan's sources hinted that Alpin liked to go his own way, that was all. Isolation breeds such men; they can be dangerous in times of war, for their allegiances may alter with a change in the wind. Hence our pressing need to make a friend of this one. A marriage by summer, an heir within the year, that will be our best way of forging a bond that is strong and lasting.'

'It's that or eliminate the fellow.' Faolan spoke with no particular emphasis.

'You would not wish to do that,' Ana retorted, 'if you needed his fighting force on your own side rather than the enemy's.'

Faolan's eyes met hers for a moment and she shivered. They were dead eyes, the eyes of a man who has forgotten how to feel.

'Precisely,' Talorgen said. 'In fact, it's vital that we prevent him from throwing his forces behind the Dalriadan resistance. We can't afford to have him allied with Gabhran.'

'I understand that,' Ana said. 'Broichan, may I have your opinion on this matter?' As king's druid, Broichan had the ear of the gods. When it came to it, if it was their will that she should agree to this, she must do so without hesitation.

'Prior to Faolan's return I cast an augury,' Broichan said in his deep, commanding voice. 'My interpretation revealed a threat from the north. Unfortunately, reliable intelligence on the Caitt is very difficult to obtain. The region is a fastness, stark and mountainous, subject to extremes of weather that would test the most seasoned traveller.' He studied his long, bony fingers; a silver ring formed like a tiny snake with green jewel eyes glinted there. 'The misgivings my vision aroused have now been reinforced by Faolan's news. As a Gael, he may travel where others cannot. We must take swift action.'

Ana clutched her hands together behind her back. 'I know I have to do this,' she said, holding herself straight and striving for dignity. 'That doesn't mean it's something I'm happy with. What am I supposed to do if I get to Briar Wood and Alpin refuses? It's a long way to go for nothing.'

'He won't refuse,' Aniel said, echoing Bridei's sentiments of earlier in the day. The other men in the chamber nodded or murmured assent; Ana could feel their eyes on her golden hair, her

23

figure in the blue tunic, her face, which one ardent suitor had assured her resembled a wild rose in bloom. She felt a flush of humiliation rise to her cheeks.

'You do understand,' said Talorgen, 'that if you are wed to Alpin, and he becomes our ally, it eliminates a very dangerous possibility that could otherwise greatly weaken our battle strategy. I won't bore you with the details, but I'm sure you realise a seaborne force led by Alpin in support of Dalriada could spell ruin for our plans. On the other hand, should we gain some measure of control over this anchorage ourselves, that would be significantly to our advantage.'

Ana looked at him. One would have thought that, as Ferada's father, he would have better insight into how she was feeling. At least he did not think her too stupid to be given strategic details. 'I understand that,' she said. 'I understand about the war, and why it's important to secure Alpin as an ally. It just seems such a rush. I hardly have time to prepare myself . . .'

'The journey is long.' Faolan's tone was neutral, detached. 'You'll have more than enough time to think about it on the way.'

'How long?' She frowned at him.

'For a party with women, more than a turning of the moon, even if the weather's favourable. Quicker for warriors, or messengers.'

Ana turned back to Bridei, addressing him formally. 'In your message, my lord king, did you tell Alpin I was coming?' she asked. 'So he will have had a number of days' notice, time to consider this for a little before I arrive?'

'That was my intention,' the king said.

She had run out of questions. Everyone seemed to be waiting for her to speak. The wrong words were on the tip of her tongue, angry words, hurt words, the words not of a princess of the Priteni, but of a frightened girl who finds herself given to a stranger. She swallowed them.

'My consent to this is, of course, a formality.' She could hear the tight, sharp tone of her own voice, and worked to moderate it. 'I will begin my preparations in the morning. I hope this proves a significant help to Fortriu's cause. I would hate it to be wasted.' For all her best efforts, her voice shook.

Nobody said a thing. Ana saw tears in Tuala's eyes, and a

resigned compassion in Fola's. 'Goodnight,' she said. 'I will retire now. May the Shining One guard your dreams.' Even the king rose to his feet as she made her way out.

'She doesn't want to go,' Tuala said to Bridei. 'It's plain in her every word. She's frightened. Who knows what kind of man Alpin might prove to be?'

Bridei was sitting by the fire in their quarters with his small son drowsing on his knee. The council was over. The royal bride would be despatched as soon as Faolan had the escort ready. As king, Bridei had become used to making decisions on a balanced assessment of risks and advantages. This decision had been harder than most.

'That's one reason I'm sending Faolan,' he said. His head was starting to thump with persistent pain; he closed his eyes, leaning back in his chair, the warm, relaxed body of the infant a comforting presence in his arms. 'He may see this mission as somehow beneath him, but I trust him to make certain Ana will be safe before he leaves her at Briar Wood. He has the skills to assess Alpin's true intent, to predict his future moves.'

'But not those to recognise whether he will make a good husband,' Tuala said quietly.

'Ana understands the situation,' Bridei said. 'She'll be as well protected as we can manage. If for any reason this goes awry, the escort can see her safely back to White Hill. Faolan's taking ten men-at-arms. You know how capable he is.'

'Capable isn't enough. This is worrying me, Bridei. It just doesn't feel right. Here, give me Derelei. He should be in his bed.'

Bridei lifted the sleeping child and placed him in her arms.

'Ana will miss him,' Tuala said. 'She loves him.'

'I suppose she'll have one of her own soon enough.'

Tuala bore the child away. When she returned some time later, Bridei saw the glint of tears in her eyes. 'You're crying,' he said, alarmed. For all her delicate, fey appearance, Tuala possessed an inner strength that had impressed him even when she was a child of five. She did not often let him see her tears. 'For Ana? I'm sorry – here –' He gathered her into his arms, his cheek pressed against her dark hair. 'I do regret the manner of this bitterly, Tuala. At the same time I know I must do it. If I don't take steps to win Alpin over, and promptly, I put the lives of hundreds of men at risk.'

'It just seems so unfair,' Tuala said, leaning against him and putting her arms around his waist. 'That she, and others like her, must endure these loveless bargains while you and I . . . We broke so many rules to be together, Bridei. We let love be our lodestone. We defied Broichan's dictums and all the usual protocols of court. Yet we're not allowing Ana any choice at all. She's one of my dearest friends, and has been since those days when we were first learning what love was all about.'

'At Banmerren?' Bridei smiled. 'I think I learned it long before that.' A memory of a tiny Tuala, her hair wild in the breeze, turning in place on a perilous pinnacle of rock, came vividly to his mind, and his arms tightened around her. 'Besides, the gods smiled on our marriage. Even druids must yield to that higher authority.' And, when she did not reply, 'Tuala? I am truly sorry. I will give Faolan a strict set of instructions. If anything goes wrong, he will bring her home. He's never yet failed to execute a mission with flawless efficiency.'

Tuala disengaged herself, holding his hands and looking up at him. 'I hope your faith in him is justified,' she said. 'He's a good friend, I acknowledge that, and excels in his various trades. But he doesn't know the first thing about women.'

Chapter Two

Faolan's lengthy morning drills, conducted in rain or shine, seemed to Ana excessive. She learned to mount and dismount at a click of the fingers and to rein her pony in instantly at a near-inaudible whistle. She strongly suspected he was taking out his annoyance on her; it was plain the man thought he should be elsewhere, perhaps in the thick of a battle shedding other people's blood, or more likely lurking in the shadows somewhere with a big knife in his hand. Wasn't that what assassins were supposed to do? This one, however, possessed a singular talent for standing about with eyes narrowed and lips tight, emanating a hostility that was almost palpable.

It took only one day of the journey for Ana to realise the necessity of what he had done. Dismounting at the edge of the clearing where they were to set up camp, she felt dull pain spreading across her lower back. She could walk, but her legs felt like jelly. Faolan was issuing crisp orders to the men of the escort, and Ana caught his eyes on her, assessing. She met his gaze coolly, then turned to attend to her mount. It had not been possible to bring her own pony, Jewel, from White Hill; Faolan had pronounced the creature insufficiently strong to endure this particular ride. He had allocated her a shaggy, sturdy animal with a certain stolidity of temperament, and Ana had said nothing. She had vowed to herself that she would not utter a single word of complaint; she would not give him the satisfaction. It was plain enough what he thought of her: that she was pampered and weak and knew little of the world outside the sheltering walls of court.

Nearby, the serving woman whose job it was to attend to Ana was standing immobile, grimacing, hands pressed to her back. She had shared a horse with one of the men and looked considerably the worse for wear. Ana kept her thoughts to herself. They'd insisted she have a female attendant. It was regrettable that none of those considered capable of looking after her wardrobe could ride. They'd better have allocated her a farm girl; no matter if she could not clean and mend a lady's fine garments, as long as she could make herself useful when it really mattered. 'Never mind, Darva,' Ana said grimly. 'You'll get used to it.'

Darva responded with a whimper. Sighing, Ana led her pony over to the others, hobbled it, and began to rub it down. One of the men had the process of feeding and watering in hand. The fodder would not last long, but these stocky creatures were used to gleaning what they could from the woodland tracks and the bare fells, and would weather the journey well enough.

'One of us can tend to the creature, my lady,' the man said, indicating the sacking she was using on the pony's damp coat.

'I'm almost finished,' she said.

'Best if one of us does it.' He took the cloth from her hand and she sensed that she had broken the rules of the encampment. She smiled and backed away, not wanting to argue.

A couple of the men set off with bows in hand, evidently to procure supper. The camp had been speedily made: a small, tent-like shelter for herself and Darva, a fire amongst stones, a place for the provisions and packs. The men would unroll a blanket apiece and sleep in the open.

A question occurred to Ana, one that would be a little delicate to ask. Before she had the time to consider it further, Faolan appeared by her side so abruptly he made her start. Another one of those things that spies were good at, she thought sourly.

'You'll want somewhere to perform your ablutions in private,' he said. 'Down there between the trees there's a stream. I've a man on guard some thirty paces further into the woods. Go now while there's still light.'

'Do you ever make polite requests, or do you only give strings of orders?' She regretted these words as soon as they were spoken; she had sounded discourteous and lacking in self-control. This man seemed to bring out something she had not known was in her. 'I'm sorry,' she muttered.

'Go now,' Faolan said, as if she had not spoken. 'Take your woman with you. That's if she can walk. Make it quick.' He turned away, striding across the clearing to supervise some other task. The men-at-arms moved obediently to his command.

Scooping out a makeshift privy in the bushes, quickly washing face and hands, roughly tidying up clothing and hair was all that was possible. Darva had to hobble along leaning on Ana's arm; she would be hard put to climb into the saddle in the morning. There were to be three days like this, then a respite, for the fourth morning should see them arrive at the stronghold of Abertornie, home of the chieftain Ged; there would be beds and warm water. Ana doubted very much that Faolan would allow a stay there of more than a single night.

He was taking no chances, even so early into the journey. It was evident a watch was to be maintained through the night, on every side of the camp. Ana could not imagine what danger they expected a mere day's ride from White Hill; it seemed to her they'd be better to get a good night's sleep while they had the opportunity.

They ate their meal around the fire; the bread and cheese brought from White Hill were supplemented with hare cooked on the coals. There wasn't much talk. Faolan watched her as she took out a clean napkin from her bag and wiped the grease from her mouth and fingers. Then she and Darva retired to bed, if bed it could be called; there was little more than a folded quilt between her and the hard earth, and her body, protesting from the day's ride, seemed to have no corner that was entirely free from pain. The exhausted Darva fell quickly asleep.

Ana looked out between the folds of the shelter's opening.

29

Five of the men were lying by the fire while five had gone to keep watch. Faolan sat staring into the flames, his sombre features transformed to a flickering pattern of red-gold light and shadow in the night. As Ana tossed and turned, restless and wakeful, he maintained his still pose. From time to time she looked out as the night wore on, but did not see him move; the eyes, perhaps. There was something there, a look she did not understand, a bleakness that chilled her.

She drowsed fitfully, waking now and then with a start. In the middle of the night, when creatures came alive in the woods, hooting, screeching, crying, rustling about the campsite, she saw him get up in a fluid movement, stretch, and wake the others. The watch changed; five men came in to settle in their blankets and five went out, knives or spears in hand. Faolan remained by the embers, standing now, his face in shadow. Ana realised that his particular task must be guarding her. She found that deeply unsettling. Close to dawn, she fell asleep to the sound of Darva's steady snore.

They travelled north and inland. The third day saw them ford a substantial river, the water rushing about the horses' legs and soaking the riders' boots. Faolan rode downstream of Ana, keeping a close watch on her pony. At the far side, she dismounted to wring the water from her skirt and, seeing him nearby, said testily, 'I can ride, you know.'

'Just as well,' Faolan said. 'That's only the first.'

She climbed back on the pony and the journey continued. Another woman might have demanded a fire to dry herself by, she thought, or a rest, or food and drink. Another woman might be deciding, already, that Abertornie was as far as she was prepared to go, and that if Alpin of Briar Wood didn't want her enough to come and fetch her, he could do without. Ferada, for instance, would already have put her foot down, Ana was sure of it. Ana would not do so. Eyeing the straight, somehow disapproving back of Faolan as he rode ahead to assess the safety of the track, Ana felt she had something to prove, not only to him but to herself. She had been brought up with a strong sense of duty. There was her duty to Bridei and Tuala, who had provided her with a home and family of sorts. More importantly, there was her duty to Fortriu. As a woman of the royal line she was bound to marry and produce children: sons who could contest the kingship in future years, daughters to make strategic marriages such as her own. Her family in the Light Isles would expect this of her. Her family . . . She had hardly seen them since she was a child. Her cousin, vassal king to Bridei; her older brothers, who had been distant presences in her childhood world. The aunt who had raised her after her parents died. A little sister, Breda; her she missed most of all, remembering summer days at the tide's edge, the two of them gathering shells under a wide, pale sky; winter afternoons by the hearth fire, embroidering linen kerchiefs; Aunt pretending not to be snoozing in her chair, and Ana surreptitiously fixing Breda's wobbly stitches. Breda would be sixteen now, old enough to have a husband of her own. It was not so very far from White Hill over to the isles. Yet, when you were a hostage, it was a whole world away.

Ana spent most of the day trying to distract herself from the chill of the wind through her damp clothing and the aching in her bones with stories of heroes and dragons and strange forest creatures. She sang songs under her breath so her mind did not dwell on her misery. She went through the repertory of little tunes she had sung to Derelei: counting rhymes, lullabies, songs for seeding or harvest or hauling in nets. The isles were full of such melodies, each with its particular purpose.

The ride continued; the path was steeper now, the horses picking their way on stony ground. A vista of pine-clad slopes opened to the west. Beyond the forest she could see high, dark mountains, snow-capped and lonely. Ana began to hum a longer piece to herself, the ballad of a traveller in faraway lands and the strange and wondrous folk he encountered on his journey. With luck, its dozens of verses would last her until they reached level ground and Faolan decided they could stop.

A considerable time later, as Ana reached the part where the hero slew the dragon, they came to the foot of the hill and the men reined in their mounts, gathering around Faolan. As Ana rode up, she heard him speaking.

'. . . made good progress. I judge there's time to reach Abertornie before dusk if we keep up a brisk pace. That way we'll avoid the need to make camp again. It means we can be on our way across the borders while the weather still holds.'

The men were nodding. Ana glanced across at Darva, who sat white-faced behind a tall man-at-arms on a broad-backed pony. Darva's eyes were shadowed with purple; she looked barely conscious.

'We must rest a little,' Ana said firmly. 'We're cold and tired. We need to stretch ourselves and have something to eat and drink. It needn't be long. I understand we must reach our destination while it's still light. We're doing our best, but not all of us are warriors.'

Faolan looked at her, looked at Darva, who was swaying in the saddle, then back at Ana. 'You prefer to camp here?' he asked, surprising her. 'To add a day to the journey? Surely you're eager to have this over as quickly as possible.'

Ana blinked in surprise. It was a long way to Briar Wood: a journey of more than a full turning of the moon, he had said. 'Are you offering me a choice?' Ana asked, raising her brows.

'If we go on today, we'll be ahead of time.'

'And you, I'm sure, are anxious to be relieved of this particular duty.'

Faolan's expression did not change. 'Your musical repertory could begin to pall if repeated too often,' he said.

To her profound annoyance Ana felt herself flush scarlet.

'Don't let it trouble you,' Faolan said. 'Who am I to judge? Now what's it to be? Camp or go on?'

'Go on,' said Ana grimly. 'As long as we rest first. The prospect of civilised company makes Abertornie look better by the moment.'

'I'd get you extra men if I could,' said Ged of Abertornie in apologetic tones, reaching to refill Faolan's cup from a jug of good ale. 'Never know what you'll come up against in those parts. Clan against clan, friend against friend, brother against brother. Sometimes they seem to fight for no better reason than because they can. Think what Bridei could do with some of that manpower behind him. But Umbrig's the only one to show any real interest in cooperating. The others are like a pack of wildcats.

Or would be, if they moved in packs. Up there in the north it's every man for himself; a land of solitary hunters, each with his own little domain to protect. Only in Alpin's case, it's more of a big domain. Big and well manned. That's a meagre escort, Faolan. The girl's vulnerable.'

Faolan studied his goblet, saying nothing. The two of them were seated in an antechamber off the hall of Ged's house at Abertornie, after supper. The door was secured, with a guard on the other side.

'As I said,' Ged went on, 'I'd have helped you if the timing had been different. I've men here who know the territory quite well, though none who have travelled all the way across to Alpin's holdings. Reliable mountain guides. You need one of those. But I can't do it now. Headed south within days. Those few not coming with me, I need back here to keep watch on the house, the women and children.' He sighed expansively and took a mouthful of ale. Ged was a man of robust build, and was dressed tonight in a tunic and trousers woven in a startling pattern of squares and lines, vividly dyed in scarlet, green and blue. His men, who had been in evidence in the yards of Abertornie, busy with preparations for an expedition of warlike nature, had all been clad in garments of similar brilliance. If his mountain guides wore the same kind of uniform, Faolan thought, at least they'd be visible at a distance. The only place where it would provide good camouflage would be a riotous flower garden.

'It was my choice to travel with this number,' he said. 'They're all hand-picked. She'll be quite safe.'

'Don't underestimate the importance of what you're conveying, lad,' Ged said, regarding him thoughtfully.

'When it comes to it,' said Faolan, unable to keep a certain tightness from his voice, 'she's just a woman. We're all expendable.'

'Nonsense. Taking that young lady from White Hill to Briar Wood is just like escorting a cargo of gold pieces or a chest of precious jewels. In fact it's even more important, and certainly more perilous. If what you tell me is true, Alpin's a major threat to our cause. The ties of kinship conferred by this marriage will give the fellow a status he could never have dreamed of. In addition, Ana's personal charms are – let's say, well above the run of the mill. There's no doubt in my mind that this'll win Alpin over. The girl's literally worth her weight in gold, Faolan. More, in fact, since she's a slight thing. Expendable? Hardly. The job's vital. That's why Bridei gave it to you, no doubt.'

Faolan took a deep breath. His personal feelings about the commission were irrelevant. He had expressed them to Bridei in private; to speak of them elsewhere would be disloyal. He'd agreed to it and he would do it. Perfectly. 'He did, and he trusted me to judge what security was required. Ten men are sufficient. I anticipate being back at White Hill by Midsummer at the latest. The return trip, without the women, will be considerably quicker, of course.'

'Of course.' Ged was still watching him closely, as if not quite convinced by any of it. 'And you'll be eager to get back. Tell me, does the young lady know what's planned for the autumn?'

'It's safer for her not to know. Strategic reasons, Bridei told her, requiring us to move in haste. She does understand that Alpin could swing either way. Wisely, she asked very few questions.'

'Hmm,' said Ged. 'I find myself somewhat in sympathy with young Ana. She's a good girl. She deserves better than this.'

Faolan said nothing.

'We can supply you, at least,' Ged said. 'Dried meat, cheeses, whatever your pack animals can carry. You do know you won't be able to ride all the way? Parts of the track will require your men to lead the horses, and the women will have to walk. If things had been different, you could have taken her the low way, along the lakes and over by Five Sisters. Still, you wouldn't want to run into someone's army coming in the other direction. A momentous season, this should be. Who'd have thought Bridei would make his move so soon, eh?'

Faolan did not respond; there was nothing to say. Within two turnings of the moon, he would be at Briar Wood settling a new bride into a stranger's home, and Bridei would be about to lead his forces down the Great Glen towards the confrontation of their lives. That Bridei had planned it thus, had intended all along that Faolan should not be by his side at his moment of truth, only made the whole thing harder. Best concentrate on facts. He was a hired man and he would give value for the silver they paid him.

34

The door creaked open; the guard looked in. 'The young lady wants to speak to you, my lord.'

Ana stood in the doorway. She had been wan and bedraggled when they rode in to Abertornie some time before. Now she wore a clean, pressed tunic and skirt in soft blue, and her fair hair was dressed in a circlet of braids, shining in the lamplight. It hardly seemed worth the bother, Faolan thought, since they had to go on in the morning.

Both men rose to their feet, Ged springing up, Faolan moving more slowly.

'Please, don't get up,' Ana said. 'This won't take long.'

Ged settled her in a chair and poured ale, his eyes frankly admiring. Married man or no, he was known to delight in the company of comely women, especially quick-witted ones.

'Thank you.' Ana sipped politely, set the goblet down, turned her gaze on Faolan. 'It's Darva,' she said. 'She can't go on.'

This was simple truth. Faolan had seen the serving woman when they arrived; she had more or less fallen from her horse and been carried inside.

'She's not up to this,' Ana went on. 'Best if she rests here, then goes back to White Hill when it's convenient.'

'We can certainly accommodate her here at Abertornie,' Ged said. 'But –'

'I hope,' Faolan said to Ana, 'that you're not about to suggest we delay our departure because of this. I had assumed you would select a companion who had at least some riding ability.' He watched the pink rise in Ana's cheeks; she seemed to be able to do that at will.

'Forgive me,' she said, 'I thought it was you, not I, who was in charge of this expedition. You drilled me thoroughly enough before we left. How was it the most reliable of escorts neglected to check the qualifications of my companion?'

She was right, of course. This was his responsibility, and he had made an error of judgement. He watched her face; observed the little frown between the elegantly shaped brows. It had been plain to him from the first that this royal bride did not want to go to Briar Wood any more than he did.

She was ignoring him now, addressing herself to Ged. 'I was

hoping,' she said, 'that there might be a girl here at Abertornie who could come with us in Darva's place. It doesn't matter so much about her skills as a serving woman; I can teach her those in time. She needs to be able to ride, I mean really ride, and she must be able to smile no matter how annoying things are.' As if to press her point, she turned her head towards Faolan and graced him with a smile of calculated radiance, which somehow managed to convey both warm approval and total insincerity. He could not keep his mouth from twitching in response. Ged roared with laughter.

'I did ask your wife already,' Ana told the chieftain, 'and she promised to try to find a willing girl, one who likes the idea of an adventure. We just need your approval. The only thing is, we're leaving in the morning. She'd have to pack up quickly; she wouldn't have much time to make up her mind.'

She had surprised Faolan again. He had expected, at the very least, a request to stay and rest for one additional night. The men would have welcomed that.

'Setting yourselves a hard pace,' Ged grunted. 'I'm sure Loura can find you a girl. We breed 'em tough around here.'

'Thank you,' Ana said. 'It's not as if I really need a serving woman, I can manage quite well by myself. I don't have many belongings to look after, since I was ordered to leave as much as possible behind. I need this girl principally for reasons of propriety.'

Ged grinned. 'What, with this fellow in charge? None of them would dare to set a foot astray, nor cast a glance where they shouldn't. But you're right. I already told him the escort's too small. Three or four women to attend you, twenty men-at-arms, that would be more like it. Some ladies would demand a washer-woman, a seamstress and a court bard for good measure.'

'She doesn't need the bard,' Faolan found himself saying. 'The lady provides her own entertainment.'

Ana glared at him; he made sure his features showed nothing in return. Her singing voice had been small, but pure and true-pitched; he had found that after he had silenced her with words that had come despite him, words that he had known were cruel, the tunes remained in his head, following him even into his brief snatches of sleep. They conjured memories of older songs in another tongue, a music that belonged in a different life, one he should have forgotten. He would have begged her not to sing, but the codes he imposed upon himself forbade such honesty.

'I'm right, aren't I?' she asked him now. The blush had faded; her grey eyes were calm and cool as she gazed at him. 'We should go on as soon as we can, since bad weather might slow us later.'

He inclined his head. 'Tomorrow,' he said. 'You'll be eager to meet your new husband.'

Something flickered in her eyes. 'Eager,' she echoed. 'That is not the way I would express it. I have a duty to perform, and since I have been told speed is important, I will adhere to whatever timetable is considered appropriate. That's all there is to it.'

Faolan did not respond. Her voice had become tight and cold, a different voice from the one that had kept weariness at bay with music. Duty he did understand, as far as it went. Duty, for him, was quite a complex issue.

'It may not be so bad, lass,' Ged said, putting a hand on Ana's knee and, with a glance at Faolan, removing it again. 'This fellow Alpin is wealthy, at least. And youngish. You may do very well for yourself.'

It was difficult to tell if the new girl, Creisa, would be a help or a hindrance to the expedition. She came with her own pony and a shawl woven in the rainbow hues that set Ged's household apart wherever they travelled. Creisa could certainly ride, and she did not snore. It was her effect on the men of Ana's escort that gave cause for concern. She was young and had a freshness about her like that of a spring primrose: red cheeks; full lips; wide, long-lashed brown eyes. Her figure was generous and showed to advantage when she sat astride her pony, back straight and shoulders square, with the unconscious grace of a natural horsewoman. In the evenings she engaged the men in conversation around the fire, keeping them from their sleep. By day she joked as they rode along, and the hand-picked escort responded, vying for her attention, until Faolan silenced them with a curt command. Then there would be a period of peace and order, until Creisa made a throwaway comment or a giggling suggestion and it all began again.

Faolan developed a little line between his brows and a corresponding tightening of a mouth already less than relaxed. Ana found the girl's banter and the men's responses amusing, harmless; all of them knew that on such a journey it could not go any further. She was sorely tempted, after Faolan's snarls at the men, to comment that surely this pleased him better than her singing, but she held her tongue, not wishing to let him know that the jibe had hurt her. She had sung Derelei to sleep more times than she could remember, and she missed his infant warmth, his trusting smiles. Long ago she had taught the same songs to her little sister. Music was love, family, memory. She did not know how anyone could dismiss it thus.

Abertornie had been the last friendly house, the last overnight stay within the shelter of walls. It was deemed too dangerous to seek accommodation with the unknown inhabitants of the wild northern valleys, few as they were. An unplanned visit to the stronghold of a Caitt chieftain, especially when one traveller was a young woman of particular strategic value, might just as likely end up with the whole party being seized as hostages or worse. That risk was not worth taking for the sake of a night's shelter, clean clothing or a better quality of supper.

So the travellers went on, maintaining a good speed as the moon went from new to half to full and began to wane again. Each day the way seemed to be steeper and the forests darker, the undergrowth thicker and the hillsides more precipitous. The weather assisted them, remaining mostly dry, though cold. At night Ana and Creisa slept close under their shared blankets, keeping one another warm.

'Better than nothing, my lady,' Creisa whispered as, outside their small shelter, the men who were off watch settled around the fire and the night creatures began their mysterious dialogues in the forest beyond. 'Not that I wouldn't rather be snuggled up with one of the fellows, that Kinet, for instance, he's got a good set of shoulders on him and a lovely smile, or maybe Wrad, have you seen the bold way he looks at me? When we get to where we're going, I've a treat in store for someone. Can't make up my mind which, so far.'

'Shh,' Ana hissed, torn between the need to reprimand her serving woman as a lady should, to silence such foolish talk, and a kind of envy that the girl could speak so openly, and with such evident relish, of matters that were still a mystery to Ana herself, even at nearly nineteen years of age. 'You should not speak thus, Creisa. It's unseemly.'

'Sorry, my lady,' Creisa said in a small voice. She was silent for a little, then began again. 'Of course, the quiet, closed-up ones can be the most exciting, if you can get them interested in the first place. I know which one I'd really like to spend a night alone with. That Faolan, I reckon he'd be a stayer.'

There was something in the quality of the silence beyond the opening of their tent after this speech that told Ana she must produce an answer that was both quick and quelling. 'Faolan is King Bridei's personal emissary. He's the king's trusted friend. You will not speak of him thus again, Creisa. I hope I do not have to tell you twice.'

'No, my lady.' It was evident in Creisa's tone that she was smiling in the darkness. 'All the same –'

'Enough!' Ana snapped, loudly enough to be heard by anyone outside who happened to be listening. Creisa fell silent at last and, not long after, the sound of her breathing told Ana she had fallen asleep.

Ana herself did not sleep. She pondered Creisa's life growing up on Ged's home farm, working in the kitchen and vegetable gardens and, from the sound of it, forming casual alliances with any number of lusty young men. Questions came to her: wasn't Creisa worried she might conceive a child? Would not such wanton behaviour damage her chances of attracting a reliable husband? Above all, amongst the confusion of thoughts and feelings Creisa's whispered foolishness had awoken in her, Ana recognised that she was envious: envious of the ease with which Creisa spoke of the congress between man and woman, and still more envious of the fact that, if Creisa were to be believed, such congress was for her not brutal, arbitrary, a thing to be endured, but entirely pleasurable, easy and natural. For a woman of her own status, Ana thought, it could hardly ever be so simple. To wed for love, as Tuala had done, was an opportunity rarely afforded those of the royal blood. Ana could almost wish she had wed kindly, courteous Bridei herself, as many people, the king's druid Broichan amongst them, would have preferred. She had, indeed, considered that prospect seriously for a little, but only until the moment she first heard Bridei utter Tuala's name, and Tuala his. From then on, Ana had recognised the inevitability of things, for there was a bond between those two that transcended the ordinary. A tiny, hidden part of Ana still longed for a love like that in the grand tales of old – powerful, tender and passionate. Before they got to Briar Wood, she told herself grimly, she'd best quash any trace of that yearning, for such a foolish fancy could only lead to grief.

As the journey wore on they all became progressively dirtier, wearier, quieter; even Creisa. There was no opportunity for clothing to be washed, and scant facility for personal ablutions. For Ana, who was accustomed to bathing in warm water with reasonable frequency and to other folk bearing her tunics, skirts and smallclothes away for regular cleaning, the days were spent in an uncomfortable awareness of the layer of dirt and sweat clogging her skin, the itches and crawling sensations, the mud stains around the hem of her skirt and, worst of all, the lank, greasy texture of her long hair; the only way to wear it now was plaited tightly and coiled atop her head, fastened with pins, for she could not bear the touch of it against her neck.

They stopped late one afternoon close to a deep forest pool set amongst rocks, and Ana was seized with the urge to bathe. Creisa was all for stripping off and plunging right in. Faolan would not allow it. When Ana tried to argue, he cut her off sharply.

'It may be springtime, but the water's cold. What if you came down with an ague? We can't take that risk. Besides, this would leave us vulnerable. If we were attacked while the two of you were disporting yourselves, we'd be at a disadvantage. The men have enough to attend to. Don't make their job any harder.'

'The men could do with a bath themselves,' Creisa muttered in a mutinous tone.

'*Disporting?*' Ana echoed. 'All I want to do is get clean. What sort of impression do you think I'll make if I walk into Briar Wood looking like this, not to mention the smell?'

Faolan's mouth twitched; he controlled it before it became a smile. 'I imagine you have a set of clean clothing in reserve, somewhere in that bundle that's weighing down the packhorse,' he said. 'Since we're unlikely to encounter washerwomen between here and Briar Wood, and since we have still many days' travel ahead of us, I suggest you wait until we're nearly there. At that point, ask me again. You're right, of course; this is a commercial enterprise, a fact I was in danger of forgetting. As leader, I'm responsible for delivering the goods in prime condition.'

Creisa giggled. Anger made Ana's cheeks hot; the man's rudeness and her own frustration made her want to scream at him like a fishwife and spit in his supercilious face. To her horror, her voice came out wobbly and pathetic, as if she were on the verge of tears. 'There's no need to be so unpleasant about it. I have tried not to make things any harder for you. This didn't seem too much to ask.'

There was a brief silence while Faolan regarded her, his dark eyes assessing, and she did her best to meet his gaze steadily. As usual, she could glean no idea of what he was thinking. Her own face, she suspected, was flushed, filthy and in no way evocative of new roses.

'I'm sorry,' Faolan said tightly and, turning on his heel, moved away to busy himself elsewhere. Ana stared after him. An apology was the last response she had expected.

'We could do it anyway, my lady,' Creisa whispered. 'Don't know about you, but I'd endure a tongue-lashing from that long-faced Gael for the sake of clean hair and a chance to wash my smallclothes. I could rinse a few things out, hang them over a bush –'

'We must do as he says.' Bad manners or not, there was no doubt in Ana's mind that Faolan was an expert and reliable leader, and that they must trust him to know what was best. 'All the same, I do have another change of undergarments in my big bag, the one on the packhorse. I may even be able to find something for you, if you have none for yourself. Let us at least wash out our smallclothes; we'll dry them where we can. Perhaps by the fire . . .'

Creisa exploded in a new fit of giggles. 'That'll give the men something to think about, my lady. I'll fetch your bag and we can see what's what.'

'And, Creisa?'

'Yes, my lady?'

'Please don't refer to Faolan as a long-faced Gael. It may be the truth, but it sounds less than respectful. Just because he has forgotten his manners, there's no need for us to do the same.'

Creisa's white teeth flashed in a charming grin. 'Yes, my lady.'

They managed to wriggle out of shifts and drawers while keeping reasonably covered. Faolan must have had a word to the men, for they remained up the hill making camp, out of sight save for a guard with his back turned. The two women washed their faces, their arms, waded in up to their knees, came as close to bathing as was possible without quite disobeying Faolan's orders.

Creisa would not let Ana launder the smallclothes; she performed the task herself, pounding the soft linen with a smooth, round stone, working her fingers along the cloth, rinsing with such vigour that she did a good job of drenching both herself and Ana into the bargain. Ana sat on a flat stone, watching Creisa work her magic on the sweat-soaked garments. At length the small biting insects that inhabit such places in spring and summer began to swarm, droning, around the women's exposed flesh, and it was time to retreat.

In the newly made encampment, a meal had been prepared and someone had strung a piece of rope between bushes in readiness for drying their apparel. Creisa draped shifts and more intimate garments over the line without a shred of embarrassment. The men tried hard not to look at them. Ana supposed it must be usual on such long journeys for men-at-arms to wear the same set of clothing day in, day out, and think nothing of it. She wondered if Faolan had ever travelled with women before. Indeed, she wondered if he understood anything at all about them. He must have had a mother once, maybe sisters. A wife? A sweetheart? Perhaps he had left her behind when he turned against his own. When he decided to become a traitor. It was almost impossible to imagine him with a family. Ana pictured a tiny Faolan, the size of Bridei's little son Derelei to whom she had sung her lullabies, whose hands she had held secure as he learned to walk. Faolan would not have let anyone hold his hands. He would have learned to walk all by himself.

Tuala had been giving instructions for the refurbishment of White Hill's guest quarters; she had called in the formidable Mara, Broichan's housekeeper from Pitnochie, to oversee preparations for the anticipated influx of visitors. With the assembly now close, it was important to get things right. Some royal wives would have placed the preparation of accommodation, provisions and entertainment for such an event before all else. But Tuala knew her own principal duty was to be a support and sounding board for Bridei. He was strong, capable, possessed of a remarkable maturity of outlook for a man of his years. But he had his vulnerabilities; Tuala, who had known and loved him all her life, was aware of every one of those. She had promised she would always be there for him, and Tuala never broke her promises. Next in importance was her son, Derelei. Because the royal succession came through the female line, Derelei would never be king, but he must still be raised in love and wisdom, balance and judgement, as any child deserved. He came second only because, for now, there were others who could provide what he needed. Derelei was universally adored in the king's household. The women vied for the opportunity to play with him and tend to his small needs; the men made a pet of him, and often it was difficult for Tuala to get her son to herself so she could talk to him, sing to him, whisper secrets or simply sit quiet with the child in her arms, pondering the wonder of this new blessing the gods had granted her.

It so nearly hadn't happened, her and Bridei. She'd been on the point of stepping, or flying, beyond the margin into a world without pain or sorrow. If she had not hesitated a moment, if Bridei had not called out to her, she would have travelled there and remained immortal. That was what they had told her, the Otherworld folk who had shadowed her steps and whispered in her ears all through the dark days and troubled nights of that difficult time. She would have lived forever. She would have left Bridei on his own. And there would have been no Derelei.

It was unthinkable now. In the event, Bridei had come for her, had saved her, and matters had taken their true, god-ordained course. The Shining One was content with their choices, Tuala thought. Derelei had made his arrival into the world on a night of full moon, which seemed entirely apt, since this goddess had taken a particular interest in Tuala's life from the very start.

As for Bridei, he had made a strong beginning as King of Fortriu. Already, only five years into his reign, he was massing his forces against the Gaels. Who would have thought it would be so soon? The Flamekeeper, too, must be happy. As god of men, of courage, of virtuous struggle, he must indeed see his own earthly embodiment in this strong young leader whose bright eyes and forthright words kindled the spark of inspiration in every man's heart.

For all that, a question remained unanswered for Tuala, worrying at her. She had never found out who she really was. Her Otherworld visitors had not enlightened her as to who, precisely, had decided to abandon her, as an infant, on Broichan's doorstep at Pitnochie in the middle of winter. And she wanted to know. Certainly, she had made a decision not to employ her magical talents of scrying and transformation, of conversation with the creatures of the forest, of conjuring light and shadow. When such sources of information had provided answers in the past, they had often been cryptic, difficult ones, more like further questions. That did not mean she felt no urge to employ her arts; but she would not use them. She knew how perilous a path a woman of the Good Folk trod as Queen of Fortriu. There would always be those who sought to undermine Bridei's authority, and she was determined they would not employ her as a tool. That did not stop her from needing the truth, a truth her son, in his turn, would want to hear when he was grown.

Tuala did not speak of this, not even to Bridei. She whispered it in her prayers sometimes, thinking the Shining One might help her, for this goddess had ever looked on her with kindness. So far the Shining One had provided no revelations. As for the two strange beings who had teased and cajoled Tuala, bullied and tested her, the girl Gossamer with her fey eyes and floating garments and the youth Woodbine of the nut-brown skin and ivy-wreathing locks, they had never come back. As soon as Tuala had made her choice to be human, to live in this world, the two of them had vanished as if they had never been. At times Tuala wondered if the whole strange sequence of events had been a kind of crazy dream.

It was early afternoon and Derelei would be in the garden playing in the care of one of the young serving women. Instructions complete, Mara had more or less shooed Tuala away, as if she were five years old again and a queen only in her own imagination. Mara had changed little since the early days; she preferred to be in sole charge and did her job with dour efficiency. Mara was quite undaunted by the responsibility of a royal household many times bigger than the one she managed at Pitnochie. Already she had folk scampering in all directions to fetch fresh rushes, scour floors, brush down high cobwebs and hang blankets to air.

Tuala walked through the hallways of White Hill, past the closed door of the room where Bridei was in consultation with his chieftains. They were preparing for the arrival of the delegation from the southern kingdom of Circinn, always a challenge and, under the current delicate circumstances, this time a particular test. She made her way out along a flagged path between patches of grass and beds of grey-leaved herbs: wormwood, chamomile, lavender. There were stone benches here, positioned to catch the afternoon sunshine, and little figures of gods and creatures were set about pools and in niches in the stone wall that surrounded the garden, sheltering it from the fierce northerly winds. It was a place of repose. Ana had liked it; she had spent many happy times here chatting to Tuala, playing with Derelei, doing her intricate embroidery. Tuala missed her. She wondered how far Ana had travelled on her journey by now, and what she was making of it. Perhaps they were already at Briar Wood. Maybe Alpin would be a kind man, a man like Bridei. Ana had wept when she said goodbye, despite her obvious efforts at control. For all her understanding of duty, she had been sad and frightened. Tuala knew how that felt. She wished with all her heart that it had not been necessary to do it so quickly, so cruelly. But it was necessary. It was vital. Alpin must be won over before Bridei's forces went into action against the Gaels of Dalriada. And, contrary to the word that was being put about, that would not be happening next spring. The council would not be at Gathering but at the feast of Rising, when spring was turning towards summer. The men of Fortriu would move in autumn, two seasons earlier than their enemies anticipated. They would surge westward in great numbers; by the time Gabhran of Dalriada received word of their advance, it would be too late for the Gaels to mount a strong counteraction, too late for Gabhran to summon his kinsmen from Ulaid and Tirconnell to back up his own armies. This time the Gaels would be defeated. They would be driven out of Fortriu. Even if Circinn refused to aid him, Bridei would make it so.

They should have told Ana, Tuala thought. Not to do so was to act as if this royal bride were too foolish to keep her mouth shut on matters of strategic importance. Not only that, it made the decision to despatch Ana to the lands of the Caitt seem cruel and unnecessary. What bride wants to confront her intended husband before he has agreed to wed her? That is to court humiliation. What young woman wishes to marry a man about whom she knows nothing beyond the fact that there is a question in his past? An arranged marriage was one thing; this went far beyond that.

Tuala came through the archway and halted. The serving girl was nowhere to be seen. Seated bolt upright on the grass, his infant hands waving in the air, was her son Derelei, engrossed in some kind of game. Opposite him, cross-legged in his dark robe, sat the king's druid, Broichan. It was a mark of the power the man carried with him that, even in such an undignified pose, with a little child as his only companion, the druid looked remote, grave and intimidating. Tuala had never lost her fear of him. She stood watching them, herself unseen. For once, Derelei had not sensed her approach. Both druid and infant were deep in concentration, and now she could see, as Broichan moved one hand before him, the fingers curving in a particular way, that her son was not, in fact, waving his arms about somewhat randomly as little children do when discovering how their bodies work. Derelei had his eyes fixed on Broichan's, and he was copying the druid's gesture. The tiny, plump-fingered hand formed itself into a shape graceful as a gull's wing; mimicked Broichan's long, bony fingers as they flattened, stretched, came up before his face. A bird flew down to settle on the wall beside them, ruffling its feathers. Another, smaller bird arrived an instant later, alighting alongside the first with a puzzled look. Derelei gurgled with pleasure.

Broichan bent his head, his long plaits falling forward, streaks of white hair amongst the black, coloured threads woven through to bind the braids, and spoke softly to the child in his deep voice. Derelei did not reach and grab as he usually did when something interesting came so close. He stayed where he was, looking up intently, and said something in his mysterious infant language. Thus far he had few recognisable words.

'Circle, thus . . .' Broichan was telling him, and using his fingers once more to demonstrate, making a subtle sign a handspan above the grass. Derelei copied him, small hand stretched just so, circling before him. The grass flattened obediently, making a neat little ring on the sward.

Tuala was shocked. She was angry. Her first instinct was to march forward and confront the druid, *Who gave you permission to teach my son? How dare you?* For all her terror of the man, she would have done it. Derelei's skills were no surprise to her; she had seen already what he could do, what her own blood had given him, and if she had wished to see his talents developed so early she would have taught him herself. For Broichan to interfere without her blessing or Bridei's was not just unfair, it was alarming. This was their child, not his. He had done enough damage to Bridei. In his assiduous efforts to form his foster son into the perfect king, Broichan had created a young man who was, in essence, desperately alone. Of course, Bridei was unswerving in his devotion to the ancient gods of Fortriu, steeped in learning, strong in courage and entirely equipped to lead his kingdom. In that, Broichan had done exactly what he had set out to do. He was unable to see that he had erred at all.

Tuala remained in place, mute, held by something she could not name. The two of them matched gesture for gesture. They turned flowers into glowing, mysterious insects; they made shadows creep across the grass and retreat again. A toad hopped onto Derelei's knee, then vanished. A mouse ran up Broichan's arm and disappeared into the hood of his robe. It was not the magic, the facility of it, that held Tuala spellbound. It was the uncanny resemblance, the exact echo of stance, posture, movement, expression, for all the stark contrast between tall, robed mage and short-legged, bulkily swathed infant. This was uncanny. It was unsettling. What she saw had a strange beauty, an odd symmetry; it was the stuff of an impossible tale or a disturbing dream. Tuala felt an eldritch prickling sensation in her spine, almost like the feeling she had experienced in the forest by the seeing pool, the Dark Mirror, when she first encountered the Good Folk.

'Mama,' Derelei said, turning to look at her, and the spell was broken. The birds flew off and Broichan rose to his feet, not quite as easily as he might once have done. Tuala found herself able to move forward, to kneel beside her son and speak to the druid in civil tones.

'Where is the serving woman, Orva?'

'Not far off; she's sitting over there by the long pond. I gave her leave to go, but she won't let him out of her sight.'

Derelei was tired now; he wilted in Tuala's arms. Such concentrated practice of the craft was draining. It was too much for a little child. Tuala drew a breath to tell Broichan so; even now, it took all her courage to confront him.

'It's as well,' Broichan said before she could speak, 'that he cannot be a candidate for kingship. The child has a future, perhaps an exceptional one. He should be raised in the nemetons.'

'He's not going anywhere,' Tuala snapped, clutching her son so tightly he began to whimper in fright. 'There, there,' she muttered, patting him. 'It's all right.'

'There's time,' Broichan said. 'He need not go until his sixth or seventh year; the training is arduous and should wait until he is strong enough to endure it. You cannot deny his natural talent, Tuala.'

'I don't,' she said. 'But he's only a baby, and he can be anything he wants, a scholar, a warrior, a traveller, a craftsman. A druid, if that's the path he chooses.'

'Will he choose wisely at six years of age? Will it not rather be the path chosen for him by his elders?'

Tuala thought of the child Bridei and the choices he had not been given. 'It will be up to his mother and father to guide him,' she said as firmly as she could. 'I do not think Bridei would be happy to see his son sent away at so tender an age. Family is precious to him.'

Broichan did not answer for a moment. He was twisting his silver snake ring around and around on his finger and frowning. He would not meet her eyes. After a little he said, 'I would teach him. With Bridei's permission. And yours. There would then be no need to send him away, at least not until he was old enough to make up his own mind.'

Tuala was startled, as much by his seeking of her sanction as by the proposal itself. There was no doubt in her mind that her son was destined for a future in which his particular talents would find a use. She did not, in fact, want him to become a warrior. She had seen the pitiful, ruined survivors who limped or were carried home from Fortriu's encounters with its enemies, and she did not see how any mother could be content for her son to become a fighting man. A druid, a scholar, a craftsman, those were good occupations. There was only one problem. 'He is the king's son –' she began.

'Yes,' Broichan agreed gravely, 'and he is your son, and we both know my opinion on that issue, although I do not express it publicly, having kept a promise I made to Bridei long ago. There is no reason why the king's son cannot enter the service of the gods. There are precedents. And if his talent in such arts as the child has demonstrated here today is a little . . . Otherworldly, shall we say? . . . what better way to avoid drawing undue attention to your own origins than for you to pass responsibility for guiding the boy into my hands? I can ensure he learns to harness his power, to channel his abilities to right ends. I can teach him to control what he has and turn it to the good of Fortriu. In doing so, I will protect both your child and your own reputation.'

Tuala did not reply. He was taking over, as he always did; he would steal her son, make Derelei his own. His project; Bridei all over again.

'You don't trust me. That is nothing new; the feeling is mutual.

It has long been thus between us. Talk to your husband. Set terms for this if you will. It's important, Tuala.'

'I want my son to be happy,' she told him. 'I want him to grow up with his family around him; with brothers and sisters, if the goddess grants it. Children don't just need education and guidance. They need love.'

There was a little silence. 'I'm aware,' Broichan said stiffly, 'of your opinion of my deficiencies as a foster father. I cannot take that seriously. Bridei is everything he should be.'

Tuala nodded. 'Yes,' she said. 'He's grown adept at concealing how much it costs him. You robbed him of his own childhood. I won't allow you to take away his son as well.'

'Allow?' Broichan hissed, and Tuala flinched at the look in his eye. The air seemed to spark around him and his shadow grew larger. Derelei began to cry.

'He's tired; he needs his afternoon sleep,' she said, feeling a sudden weariness in her own body. The serving woman, Orva, came hurrying over now and made to take the infant, but Tuala dismissed her with more briskness than was her habit. 'No, Orva, I don't need you. Go on, I'm sure Mara can put you to work with the linen. I'm taking him inside now,' she added, frowning at Broichan.

'Baw-ta,' Derelei enunciated clearly, reaching out towards the druid. He had learned a new name. Tuala shivered as Broichan raised his own hand and placed it gently over the child's head of fuzzy brown curls, not quite a caress, but as close as such a man could come to it.

'I do not request this because of a desire for power, Tuala,' the druid said quietly. 'Please speak to Bridei.'

'Tell me,' Tuala said, 'why did you approach me first and not go to Bridei direct?'

'Because I know he will not agree to it if you are unwilling. You prefer that I do so?'

'No. He has enough to concern him right now. And so do I; he must ride to war soon enough. I share the common fears of all women at such a time.'

'Yes.' Broichan's voice was like a shadow made sound, like a deep well of secrets. 'Will you not be tempted to follow him, to seek reassurance in the scrying bowl? They will be gone a long time: a season or more. Surely this calls you strongly.'

'Not so strongly that I cannot resist,' Tuala said grimly. 'Contrary to what you imagine, I never forget how lucky I am that these folk accept me as Bridei's wife. I don't plan to give them any cause to doubt my suitability for the job. My husband needs me. My first loyalty is to him and to what he must be.'

'Then you would be most wise to agree to my request. You cannot train the boy yourself unless you begin once more to exercise those secret arts. I, however, can do so without exciting any comment. Such practices are a druid's daily bread.'

'There's no hurry. He's a baby.' She turned to go.

'Tuala.' Broichan spoke very softly behind her. There was something new in his tone, something that made her halt where she stood. 'I don't have as much time for this as I would wish,' he said. 'Let me give the child what I can.'

And, looking back at him over her shoulder, Tuala saw the pallor of his long face, the way the bones of nose and cheeks jutted under the skin, the lines that had not always cut such grooves between mouth and nose, nor bracketed his lips so severely. It seemed to her there was suppressed pain in the dark eyes and that he leaned on his staff as a far older man might; that he used it, not so much as the major tool of his craft, but as a simple support.

'I –' she began, and fell silent at the look in his eyes.

'As you said,' his voice was only a whisper, 'Bridei is much occupied with the forthcoming endeavour of war and with the assembly, which will be challenging. We will not burden him with other concerns at such a testing time. Speak to him only of his son, of what is best for Derelei.'

Chapter Three

Faolan was following a map he had in his mind, constructed from what little he himself had observed of the territories north of the Great Glen, and from what several informants had told him. It was enhanced by his sensitivity to warning signs in weather and terrain. He could read the moisture in the slightest of breezes, could sense the portent behind a shifting shadow, a cooling of the air. At Abertornie, he and Ged had sat up late with one of the expert guides and discussed the path this expedition would need to take through the mountains. They talked about the narrow defiles, the precipitous slopes where riding was not possible, the places where the track was all too easy to lose. Thus far the preparation had served the travellers well.

There were certain shadowy places on Faolan's map, places he could not see clearly in his mind. Fords that had claimed lives. Hillsides with a reputation for rockslides. Hemmed-in valleys perfect for ambush. Lastly, there would be the forest itself: Briar Wood, a place with a reputation for oddity.

He pushed his party on as quickly as he thought they could manage. The men were good, and the servant, Creisa, was at least more capable than her predecessor. She could ride, and her brisk competence in camp was some compensation for her busy tongue and flirtatious manner. One could hardly expect a royal bride to travel alone amongst men.

He did not quite know what to make of Ana. Sometimes she challenged him, showing wit and strength. More often she was quiet, docile, so accepting of her fate that it would have irked him, had such matters been of any interest to him. She was like a creature led to the slaughter, all big eyes and golden hair and fastidious attention to cleanliness, when she was about to be handed over to a warrior of dubious reputation who would probably use her as roughly as he might any filthy creature by the wayside . . . He was letting his mind wander; he was breaking his own rules. Faolan rode ahead of his party, fixing his thoughts on the here and now. He had not mistaken it, that slight hint of moisture in the air. Rain was coming, if not today, tomorrow; if not tomorrow, a day or two later. They had made good progress, and he judged they might reach Briar Wood close to dark of the moon or a little after, a matter of eight or nine days more. If he had imagined his map right, there was a river to the northwest, and a ford of which Ged's man had spoken in troubling terms. By the time the rain set in, Faolan wanted to be on the other side of it.

He called Wrad and Kinet to ride closer; consulted briefly. Judging by the thickly wooded country they were passing through, the chain of small lakes to the south, the hazy contour of the distant mountains, they agreed on an estimate of two days' ride to the place in question. Perhaps the rain would hold off long enough. Perhaps the horses would make sufficient speed. Had Bridei been here, he would have called down the aid of the gods to see them safely across the water and on to Briar Wood. Faolan did not believe in gods or in luck, only in good management. He gathered the full party around him on the forest track. The pines were tall here, and in the shadows beneath there was a strange quiet, as if the woods were listening; breathing; waiting. He would be glad when this mission was over.

'We'll ride on until the light fails,' he told them. 'No hunting today; we'll eat after dark, from what supplies we have. Straight on in the morning as soon as the sky lightens.'

'But –' Creisa began, and fell silent at his look.

'It's important that we move on quickly,' Faolan said. He would not explain why; no point in getting the women alarmed. The men would work it out for themselves.

'Is there a risk of ambush here?' Ana asked, surprising him.

'Why would you suggest that?'

She hesitated before speaking. 'It's densely wooded; good cover, I would think. And they do speak of rival tribes here, warring chieftains . . .'

'If he has his wits about him,' Faolan said, not believing his own words, 'Alpin will be anticipating our arrival and will have taken what steps are necessary to make our way safe. He should have received the king's message by now, advising him of our intention to travel to Briar Wood.'

'Of course.'

There was something in Ana's tone that alerted him. He looked at her more closely and observed that she was paler than usual; she looked tired. 'Did you understand?' he asked her. 'We must keep riding until nightfall, make what progress we can.'

'Of course I understand!' she snapped, surprising him again; she had the good manners of a lady, and rarely let them slip even when tried severely, as with the bathing episode. 'I'm not a fool. Rain's coming and we have a ford to cross. A child could understand.'

Creisa made to speak again. This time it was Ana who silenced her, making a sharp gesture.

'On, then,' said Faolan. 'Let us make what way we can while the light still holds.'

When the sun was hanging low in the sky, and the dark trees stretched long shadows across the narrow, needled path, they came down to the bank of a river. The track followed its course, winding between alders and willows. The riverbed was broad and stony, the water flowing fast. Faolan sent Kinet to wade in with a staff in his hand; they watched him take two cautious steps, three, and go in up to his waist, struggling to balance against the pull of the current. Faolan and Wrad helped him out.

'The ford's almost certainly downstream,' Faolan said, trying to fix this spot on his imagined map. 'Keep up the pace; we must cross before dusk.' This could not be the river Ged's man had warned him of. They had made good speed, but not as good as that. He was sure the major obstacle was days ahead and situated in a broader valley than this wooded divide. 'Move!' he snapped, seeing how the women were holding back, seemingly reluctant to start off again. They had disappeared into the woods while Kinet was testing the water and now, returned, were slow to remount. They conferred in low voices, then Creisa helped Ana up into the saddle before getting on her own pony. 'Don't fall behind,' Faolan warned them. 'We can't afford to be trapped here after dark. We must find the crossing. Make sure you keep up.'

Creisa scowled at him. Ana rode forward without a word. Was he imagining how white she looked? Curse this mission. Already he had slowed the pace to accommodate the women's weakness. In the world of men, the journey would have been relatively simple, its principal hazard the chance of ambush.

Faolan could deal capably with difficulties. He had learned early that alongside the stunning blows fate could deliver, the practical matters of day-to-day were trivial. Once there had been people, pastimes, ideas that had possessed significance for him. They were gone. In the space of a single moment's decision, a single instant's action, that part of him had died. For a long time, until he met Bridei, there had been nothing at all save the requirement to take the next breath, to set one foot before the other and move on. Bridei had given him a purpose, had offered a friendship Faolan did not have it in him to return. Instead, he gave what he could manage: loyalty and perfect work. Hence this mission. It might not be to his taste, but he would execute it perfectly. The women were doubtless weary of living rough, but they could not be allowed to endanger the party by lagging behind.

They followed the river bank as the sun slipped lower and the valley darkened. Here the familiar trees were joined by other, stranger ones whose twisting branches and clawing twigs stretched out across the path, scratching at horse and rider, seeking to slow their progress. The ground became slippery, the sward giving way to a slick, muddy surface; here it had already rained. Faolan pushed them on. They must cross this valley and get to higher ground. Only a fool would halt for the night in such a spot.

Once or twice the women fell back, and Faolan sent a man to

hurry them forwards. He held his tongue with some difficulty. If his anger showed in his face, so much the better. He hoped he would not need to spell it out for them: rain, a river in spate, a narrow defile in darkness. A well-defined track, wooded hills providing cover, a perfect spot for travellers to be ambushed. 'Move!' he called again, and at the same time heard a shout from further ahead. Wrad, who had gone forward to ensure the path was clear, was yelling, 'The ford!'

Around a bend the river broadened, dividing into four channels across a wide expanse of flat ground covered in stones. On the other side, the track snaked away up the hill under trees. They halted. Kinet, the tallest man, dismounted and waded across, one, two, three, four small rivers; he reached the other side wet only as far as his knees. Beyond the pines, the sun was setting. The sky was darkening towards dusk.

'Forward,' Faolan said. 'Take it slowly. Once you're over, straight up that track to higher ground.' He looked around and saw the women's ponies standing together; their riders had disappeared. He swallowed an oath. 'Where –?'

'Just slipped into the woods,' a man-at-arms called Benard offered. 'Think the young lady has a pain in the belly. Might be that hare we had last night; thought it was on the rank side.'

'By all that's holy,' Faolan muttered, making himself breathe slowly. 'Wrad, you wait with me, the rest of you get on over and up, then find a campsite for tonight, it will be dark soon. Get a fire going.'

He and Wrad waited for what seemed an interminable time. Men, ponies, pack animal crossed efficiently and disappeared up the track. The light dimmed still further. The stones of the ford were a pale gleam amongst shadows. By the time the women reappeared, Faolan was holding onto his temper by the merest thread. 'Your sense of timing leaves a great deal to be desired,' he said. 'You want to be left behind in these woods? Get back on your ponies! We must cross now, without delay.' As he spoke, Ana swayed, buckled at the knees and collapsed onto the muddy ground beside her mount. Creisa, exclaiming in alarm, crouched down beside her, putting a hand to her brow.

Faolan dismounted, addressed the serving woman sharply. 'Is she sick? What is this?'

Creisa's tone was accusatory. 'You shouldn't have made her go on. You can't treat a lady as if she were just another of your men-at-arms. She has cramps. And she's tired.'

'Cramps?'

In the fading light Creisa's face could be seen to flush red with embarrassment. 'Women's business. She's one of those gets taken bad when her courses come on; at home, she'd likely be two days in bed at the very least. Delicate. A real lady. The pain's fierce, not that you'd know. You shouldn't have made her ride.'

Ana lay limp, her head on the serving woman's knee, her face a pale oval in the dusk.

'She should have told me,' Faolan said.

'How could she tell you?' hissed Creisa. 'A lady doesn't speak of such matters before men. I'd have said, but she wouldn't let me. And now what, since you seem to have the answer to everything?'

Faolan looked at her. 'Now you make yourself useful,' he said. 'Wrad, over here. The lady will have to go across with me. Help me lift her – careful – that's it.' Ana was returning to herself slowly, but they could not wait for that. They lifted her onto Faolan's horse, sitting sideways, and he mounted behind her, balancing her against him with one arm, holding the reins in the other. 'Go!' he barked. 'Wrad, lead the lady's pony. Creisa, follow him closely and keep your mouth shut. I'll need to take it slowly. Don't wait for me, go on up to the others. I want us out of this valley.'

They obeyed him in silence, their horses moving steadily away across river channels and gravelly shoals. Using his knees, Faolan guided his own mount forward.

As they moved into the water, Ana stirred in his arms, reaching out a hand. 'What –?' she murmured groggily, her eyes closed. Faolan tightened his grip; he must ensure she did not topple the two of them in her confusion. Cramps. So she had been bleeding, and he had made her ride all day. He remembered how pale she had looked; how he had chosen not to ask what was wrong. He recalled how easily he had dismissed it as contrived, insignificant. He knew little of such matters. But the evidence was there for him to see: her face ghastly white, her eyelids purple with shadows, her cheeks hollow with exhaustion. Her hair had come partly unplaited and spilled down across his chest and over his knees, a waterfall of silvery moonlight. 'How –?' she muttered.

'It's all right,' he said. 'We're nearly there.' Her hand came up and fastened itself on a fold of his cloak as a child clutches its father for reassurance, an infant its mother as surety against the dark. No, not like that at all. He felt her shift against him, turning her head into his shoulder; heard her sigh. He sensed the quickening of his own heart; its beating was a music of warning, of unexpected danger. So, holding her safe, he guided the horse on in the half-dark and reminded himself that he was a man who could not afford to feel. His job was to convey this woman to Briar Wood. When that was done, Bridei would give him another job. One foot in front of the other, step by step. Just like crossing a ford. There was room in him for exactly that and no more. And yet, as they moved forward in the dusk, and her body, pressed close against his, was the only warm thing in the chill of the wooded valley, there was a song in Faolan's mind, a whisper of melody from long ago, from the time he thought he had managed to forget . . . *Like summertime her flowing locks, like spring's first blush her skin . . . Away from Fionnbharr's dazzled mind fled home and craft and kin . . .* That was a tale of a fairy woman, of course, one of the *daoine sidhe*. Ana was real, she was alive, he could feel her gentle breathing, smell the scent of her, sweet and pleasing for all the rigours of the journey. She was real, and there was a small part of him that wanted to be crossing this river forever; something deep inside that wanted this moment to be the only thing there was.

Ana stirred in his arms.

'Hush,' he said. 'Keep still. We are nearly safe.'

'What –?'

'You fainted. I didn't know you were ill.'

'Oh – oh, gods, oh, I'm sorry –'

'Shh.' He shifted his position, balancing her slight weight as the horse scrambled out of the last stretch of water and began the ascent of the steep path on the other side. There was barely enough light left to show the way.

'You were singing,' Ana said quietly, as if unsure whether she were dreaming or waking.

'Me?' Faolan retorted, wondering if he had indeed uttered

those words aloud. 'Hardly. You're the one who does that.' He glanced down; met her gaze, the grey eyes coming back to awareness, steadfast and clear for all the weary shadows that encircled them. He wondered if he would be able to see them even when it was dark.

'I'm so sorry,' she said, trying to sit up. It was distasteful to her, Faolan supposed, to find herself in his embrace, as if they were a pair of lovers sharing a horse just so their bodies could touch, press close, feel the heady warmth of it like fine mead, promising good things to come. 'I've slowed us down,' Ana went on. 'I'll try to keep up tomorrow. I know it's important.'

'Shh,' Faolan said again. He had heard the tightness in her voice, the pain not far below the surface. 'The men are making camp now. Time enough for decisions in the morning. And if there's an apology to be made, it's mine to you. I was unobservant. As leader, I cannot afford to be so. I regret that.' As apologies went, it was perhaps somewhat lacking. He had not said what he wished to say. This, however, was safe. It was what he would have said, before they crossed the river.

'We're both to blame,' Ana said. 'And both not to blame, for it's clear to me neither of us truly wishes to be here.'

To that, Faolan had no reply. It was no longer clear to him what the answer was.

Night. The men were weary, the strain of the journey beginning to tell. He divided them into three shifts to allow more rest. Those off duty fell asleep the moment they lay down by the fire. Faolan himself would rest before dawn, while Wrad and Kinet, the men he judged most reliable, kept watch. His plan had been for an early departure, a quick ride to the next river. This must now be changed. In the darkness he felt the cool in the air, the taste of rain. Ana lay in the shelter, a warmed water-skin against her belly. She was only pretending to sleep; he could hear in her breathing that she was wakeful and still in pain. Creisa was dead to the world.

The night wore on. The first shift came back in and settled to sleep. The second shift went out into the darkness. There were many birds in this part of the forest; what kind they were, Faolan did not know. Something that hunted at night, owls maybe. Their cries were hollow and deep, making the hair rise on the back of his neck. There were other sounds in these woods, odd sounds he could not place for all his knowledge of wild realms: cracklings, hissings, whisperings. He fixed his mind on the immediate dilemma: the rain, the ford, the woman who could not be asked to go on in the morning. He regretted greatly that he had no gods in whom to put his faith, no deity or spirit who might be offered a polite request to hold back the rain, just for a day or two, so they could get safely to the edge of Briar Wood.

He had made up his mind as they crossed the ford. They must wait here for at least one day and let Ana rest. Rain or no rain, he could not let her ride on until those spasms were over. His job was not simply to travel to Alpin's stronghold within a certain margin, it was to convey there a treasure of great worth and some delicacy. Getting there on time but with that cargo damaged in some way was failing to execute the mission perfectly, and was therefore not to be considered. They would wait. By doing so, they would narrow the options. If one river rose, so would others. If the rain came they might find themselves trapped, unable to go either forward or back. The prickling of Faolan's skin, the vague unease in his mind, told him they were not alone in these woods. He placed little credence in tales of Otherworld presences. Far more likely was an acquisitive local chieftain accompanied by his war band, tracking the travellers to a point of ambush.

'What's that smell?' The voice was Ana's; she was stirring. He saw her reach for a shawl, wrap it around herself and make her way out of the shelter, moving to sit quietly by the fire amongst the huddled forms of the sleeping men. Her pale hair shone in the light of the waning moon. The fire's glow touched to a false rosiness a face that was drained and wretched.

'One of the men had herbs in his pack, a mixture to dull pain,' Faolan told her, lifting a small pannikin from the edge of the fire where it had been cooling. 'I thought this brew might help. Is it bad?'

'I'm used to it. I don't know if I can drink. Sometimes the pain makes it hard to keep anything down.'

Faolan poured the brew into a metal cup. He said nothing.

'I'll try it if you want,' Ana said. 'I can't sleep. Maybe it will help.'

He passed the cup across. When his fingers touched hers, he felt a shiver run through his body. He breathed slowly, trying to keep his gaze on the fire. Whatever had happened to him, crossing the ford, it was not just unwelcome. It was intolerable.

'I'm sorry to be such a nuisance,' Ana said politely, sipping the drink. Her fingers were white-knuckled, one gripping the cup, the other clutching the shawl around her. Her hair was loose now, escaped entirely from its customary controls, a shimmering flow that gave her the appearance of something not quite real: a figure from a dream. He had been travelling in her company for the best part of a turning of the moon. He had seen her often enough at court over the years since he came to Fortriu, and had thought nothing particular of her. She'd been a hostage; a girl with fair hair; Tuala's friend. Nothing more. No concern of his. Suddenly, now, he was finding it difficult not to look at her.

'You do a lot of apologising.' This came out despite him.

'What do you mean?' She did not sound affronted, merely weary. She held her voice low, as Faolan had, so as not to wake the men.

'It would have been perfectly reasonable to ask me to halt the party so you could rest, under the circumstances. But I didn't know. A man can't guess these things.'

Ana gazed at him. Her eyes seemed to him deep, secret, yet clear as a tidal pool in summer, full of mysteries. A man would be a fool to keep on looking; he risked drowning. 'You think me foolish and pampered,' Ana said. 'I'm well aware of that. You made it clear from the first, when you decided I needed riding lessons without asking me if I were already capable. I haven't lived the life of a man. I have little understanding of the existence of a person like you, one who follows his own rules and makes his own choices. But I do possess some intelligence and a modicum of common sense. I know why we need to keep moving on. I smelled the rain coming two days ago. I've heard the sounds in the forest. To tell you I was . . . indisposed . . . would have been unreasonable. Selfish. It would have lost us valuable time.'

Faolan regarded her. 'It will do so anyway,' he observed.

'I can ride on in the morning –' She broke off, wincing, set the cup down and put a hand to her belly.

'Nonsense,' Faolan said. 'I won't allow that. You're plainly not up to it. You'll need at least a day's rest here, maybe two. You might as well have told me and saved yourself a day of discomfort.'

Ana did not speak for a little. 'What did you mean,' she said eventually, 'about apologising? I've been taught good manners, something you'd do well to make more use of.'

Faolan felt his lips twitching with amusement. He made himself think ahead to Briar Wood, to Alpin of the Caitt. The urge to smile left him. 'I didn't mean to offend you,' he said. 'It concerns me how readily you seem to accept your lot, no matter how inconvenient, how – distasteful. You dislike the path others choose for you, but you follow it meekly anyway. You express regret at slowing the journey, when any reasonable person would have demanded that I halt earlier today and make camp.'

'I'm a woman,' Ana said simply. 'I'm of royal blood; a tradable commodity. I owe it to my kinsmen, to Bridei, to the future of Fortriu to do as I'm bid. I owe it to the gods.'

Faolan considered this answer awhile. 'What would you do,' he asked her, 'if you were not constrained by those things? By birth, by duty? What choices would you make? What path would you follow?'

Ana was silent a long time. Faolan busied himself with the fire, setting on sufficient wood to keep it going without creating too much of a blaze. When he looked up he saw the glint of tears on her cheeks.

'I don't know,' she said in a whisper. 'Not this one.'

'But you don't seek to change your direction.'

'I'll do what is required of me.' She blinked a few times, scrubbing her cheeks, and squared her shoulders. The royal blood, Faolan thought, was never more evident than now; it shone through the tears, the drawn pallor of her face, the undressed hair and hastily donned shawl. 'In my case, there is no choice,' Ana went on. 'I imagine it's different for you. You can determine your own future. You are answerable only to yourself.'

There was no possible response to this. He could not tell her the truth. To do so was not within the rules by which he survived, the strictures that allowed him to go on. This conversation should never have begun. He thought he had crossed the river successfully. Now it seemed that crossing had plunged him in over his head.

'What is it? What did I say?' She was quick. Even in the dark she had seen something change in his face.

'You should try to sleep,' Faolan said. 'There's more of this brew; pass me the cup, I'll refill it.'

They sat on awhile in silence, save for faint snoring around them and, beyond the safe circle of firelight, the mysterious noises of the forest. Ana held the cup in her elegant, pale hands; even after the riding, the living rough, her nails were glossy, perfect ovals. His own were broken, filthy, gnawed to the quick. A killer's hands. There was a time when it had not been so. Once, his hands had plied a different craft.

'Who was Fionnbharr?' Ana spoke after a long silence.

Her question took Faolan unguarded and he answered without thinking. 'A traveller. He was enchanted by a woman of the *daoine sidhe*, a fairy woman, and journeyed out of this world for nine and ninety years.' Too late, he realised what question and answer had revealed.

'I see.' That was all she said. As women went, this one was remarkable in her restraint. For that he was deeply grateful.

'You know Gaelic?' he asked her, thinking that he must guard his tongue more carefully in future.

'A few words only. We spoke the Priteni tongue at home but there were Christian monks on our home island. They were of the same origins as yourself.'

'You should sleep,' he said again. 'If you need to go into the woods before you retire, I'll keep watch for you. No need to wake the girl.'

Ana nodded. 'She sleeps soundly, doesn't she? Thank you. When will you sleep?'

'That needn't concern you.'

'I disagree. After all, you're supposed to be leading this party; our safety depends on your being alert.'

After a moment he realised that she was teasing him; there was a little smile on her lips, a dimple at one corner of her mouth. Her face was still streaked with the marks of her tears. The sight was incongruous. It made him feel very odd. Possibly she was right. What but extreme weariness could play such havoc in his head?

'I'll sleep when the last shift goes out. As we won't be riding on for a day, there's plenty of time.'

'You are human,' Ana said. 'You should remember that sometimes.'

'Are you giving me orders?'

'Didn't you call me meek? The meek don't give orders. I merely point out what may be useful. You're the one who is in charge here. Shall we go?'

They walked a certain distance into the forest. He waited while she disappeared to perform her private functions. At one point he flinched as a bird passed close by his face, its appearance so sudden he had no time to evade it. The creature alighted in a tree nearby, a blur of feather and shadow. Its beak was inimical; its strange, wild eye like that of a seer in trance.

When Ana came back she said, 'Did you see it? The bird, a crow or something like that. It flew so close. This place is full of presences. And we're not even at Briar Wood yet.'

'If a bird is the worst we encounter, I'll be content enough.'

Back at the shelter, she thanked him in the courteous way she had and retired to lie on her blankets while Faolan remained by the fire. He was reluctant to wake Kinet and Wrad, who had worked hard for him and were bone weary.

'Goodnight,' he said quietly in the general direction of the shelter.

'Goodnight, Faolan.' Her voice was soft but clear. He liked the way she said his name. 'May the Shining One guard your dreams.'

He knew the right response. One did not live at Bridei's court long without becoming aware of the full pattern of formal greetings and farewells, the conduct of ritual observance among the folk of Fortriu. The correct response was, *May the Flamekeeper light your waking.* But he did not believe in gods, neither those of Bridei's people nor the arrogant, elusive deities of his homeland. Such blessings were not appropriate in his case. No god had the power to cleanse the dark visitations of his nights. They were with him forever, a hell of his own making. He should curse Ana, not bless her. She had awoken something within him that he did not want, a thread of memory he had spent long years crushing with all his strength. He did not need this. He could not allow it. All he wanted were the orders, the task, the flawless execution of it. Then the next orders.

'Sleep well,' he said despite himself, and saw her curl up under the blankets, her fair head pillowed on one hand. He waited until he knew she had fallen asleep. Then he woke the third shift and sent them out to watch. Above them, from the branch of a gnarled and twisted tree, a hooded crow, bright-eyed, watched every move.

Next day, Ana lay in the shelter listening to the pattering of rain on the oiled cloth and the sounds of the camp going about its orderly business around her. Not a moment of the unexpected respite was wasted. Game was caught, butchered, cooked. Weapons were sharpened. Water-skins were filled and horses tended to. Some of the men slept, but only after gaining Faolan's permission. Ana herself drifted off to sleep from time to time; the acrid herbal draught that Faolan kept brewing had a decidedly soporific effect. In the dusk they cooked oats into a gruel for her, and she found she was hungry. The next morning they struck camp and rode on to the west.

Her cramps had subsided. She still felt faint and tired, but she could see the look in Faolan's eye and did her best to appear confident and strong. The rain was not heavy; not yet. Not here, at least. But the river was still some way off, if Faolan's estimate was correct, and in this increasingly grim high country many streams rushed down the valleys, tumbling over rocky shelves, gurgling through secret chasms, spreading here and there to sucking swamps that lay in wait for horse and rider. To the north, dark-bellied clouds massed. In the air above the riders rang out the alarm calls of many birds. So many birds; this place was full of them, those Ana knew well – kestrel, buzzard, skylark – and some that were quite new to her. From time to time she saw a bird like the one that had startled her in the woods by the ford, something akin to a hooded crow, but not quite as it should be, for there was a singular look to the eyes. They were wary, knowing. By the time the travellers moved out of the denser regions of the forest and onto a narrow track across steep bare fells, she had sighted a bird of this kind three times, and was beginning to wonder if it were but one bird, the same bird, that followed them, here winging high above, there perched on a great stone by the wayside, observing the travellers with its piercing eyes as they passed. One of the men took out a slingshot, palmed a stone.

'No,' Faolan told him. 'We've meat enough for a supper or two. Leave it.'

They heard the river before it came into view. At first it was a whispering, then a murmuring, then an insistent drumming that sought to drown their voices. Ana's skin grew clammy with trepidation.

'Don't be alarmed.' Faolan had ridden up beside her. 'If the water is too high we'll camp somewhere on this side and wait. I won't attempt a crossing unless I'm certain we can do it safely. It's not worth risking our lives for the sake of getting there on time.'

'Isn't it critical that we do just that?' Ana asked.

'Let me be the judge of what is critical,' Faolan said. He had the old guard back on his expression now; she could not tell what was in his mind. That strange conversation, the two of them alone in the dark, seemed increasingly like something from a dream. 'According to Ged's man, this is traversable as long as appropriate safeguards are put in place. Trust me.' Without waiting for a response he rode away to the head of the line.

'I've a word for men like that,' Creisa observed from her place behind Ana. 'But you would frown on it, my lady, so I'll keep it to myself.'

'He knows what he's doing,' Ana said. 'If we go on, it will be because that is the best choice, after all considerations are taken into account.'

'Yes, my lady.' The tone suggested Creisa was far from convinced. She had hitched her skirt up somewhat higher than was strictly essential for riding astride. The men who rode nearby had their eyes on the interesting length of shapely stocking-clad leg that was thus revealed; if their horses kept sure footing on a path that was stony, narrow and increasingly steep, it was little thanks to their riders. Ana felt a deep longing for all this to be over. Her back was hurting and she felt dizzy and sick. Her mind was on a warm bath, clean hair, fresh clothes and a comfortable bed in which she could sleep out of the weather. Alone. Once she got safely to Briar Wood, she would never take those simple things for granted again. A little voice inside her whispered that once she was married to Alpin, sleeping alone wouldn't be an option. She closed her mind to that. It did not bear thinking about.

The track wound around the flank of a valley; here the countryside was wooded again, dark pines on the upper reaches, a mixed clustering of smaller trees down near the river, screening it from sight. Its voice was insistent; somewhere down there, there must be rapids. Ana heard Faolan shouting an order and, behind and before her, the men picked up the pace. Her own pony surged forwards, taking its lead from the larger animals.

'Black Crow save us,' Creisa exclaimed, 'I'm going to have bruises in places I've never even thought about!'

Then Faolan yelled again, sharply, and there was no breath left to spare for complaints; keeping up on the narrow track took all their energy. Ana's head swam. She clenched her teeth and made her back straight. Now was no time for weakness.

A final corner, a sharp, sliding descent down a perilous, gravelly incline and the ford came in sight, fringed by willows. Birds darted across the water, their paths crossing and recrossing in an elaborate dance. There was a single broad channel here, unbroken by visible rocks. The water's surface was smooth; the flow did not seem unduly swift. Ana thought it seemed safer than the shingly, treacherous waterway of their first crossing. Rain was falling, gentle but persistent. If they wanted to go over, now was probably the time.

Kinet dismounted, took staff in hand and, at Faolan's nod, waded carefully in. It was immediately evident that the current here was stronger than appearances suggested. He staggered, thrust the staff in hard and regained his footing. The water came to his thighs.

'Keep going,' Faolan called over the noise of the flow. 'Test it right across, if you can.'

It was difficult. Three times Kinet came close to falling, and he was a big man. Creisa was biting her knuckles. At length Kinet staggered out on the far side, wet almost to the waist. Faolan gestured him back.

The men conferred in low voices while the women waited. On a bending branch, half concealed behind the delicate foliage of a willow, a bird sat, bright-eyed and uncannily still amid the forest shadows. Ana stared back; she was becoming sure it was the same creature following them, tracking them. If she had had Tuala's abilities, she might have been able to tell what it was thinking; to interpret its cries. She remembered what the girls at Banmerren had said of their Otherworldly fellow student, how Tuala had taught them to listen for the voices of marten, eel, beetle and dunnock; how to understand the deep, slow thoughts of an oak. Ana had no such skills. The bird was bothering her. 'What do you want?' she found herself whispering. 'What are you, some kind of spy?' The gaze remained on her, intense, unblinking. It was disturbing.

She saw Faolan beckon, and rode over to the men, Creisa behind her.

'Very well,' Faolan said, his expression stern. 'We –'

Ana never found out which he had decided, to go on or to wait. There was a whirr and a thump, and Kinet, who had waded out of the river once more, toppled to the ground, his eyes bulging and a blue-fletched arrow protruding from his neck. Creisa screamed. The men moved in a flash, forming a protective circle around the women while two of their number dismounted to crouch by the fallen man. Ana heard Wrad say, 'He's dead,' and Creisa utter a stifled sob. A moment later another arrow came, from the opposite direction, and lodged itself with a thud in Faolan's upper arm. He glanced at it and, with a cold-blooded detachment that impressed Ana even through her terror, gripped the shaft in his hand and wrenched it out. The tip glistened scarlet. The men held their circle, weapons pointed outwards. There were sounds of movement in the woods around them now, twigs cracking, bushes rustling, footsteps; a force of some considerable size was closing in from many directions, unseen, deadly. There was only one way out.

'Over!' Faolan snapped. 'Wrad, take Creisa behind you. Ana, with me. Move!'

Someone had thrown him a length of cloth and he was winding it around his arm even as he spoke. In a matter of moments Ana was on Faolan's horse once more, this time behind him as he guided the animal one-handed. They moved into the river. As if to mock their decision, the dark clouds rolled over them and the rain turned from a persistent drizzle to a deluge.

'Hold on tightly.' Ana could just hear Faolan's words above the voice of the river and the drumming of the downpour. 'The bottom's uneven and the water's rising.'

Ana glanced over her shoulder. Behind them, some way back, Wrad had ridden into the ford with Creisa clinging on behind him. Benard led the pack pony; another man walked beside a horse across which the limp form of Kinet had been hastily laid. The others were still on the bank, weapons at the ready, scanning the expanses of the forest. The attackers had not yet appeared. She looked ahead again, through the curtain of rain to the shadowy darkness that was the rise on the western side. Might not more men be waiting there to pick them off one by one as they rode out of the ford? She hoped Faolan had thought of that. Shivering, she hummed under her breath, hardly aware of what the song was, only hoping it might help her be brave. *One two three four, chickens pecking at the door. Five six seven eight, corbies perching on the gate . . .* It had been useful when she was little and lying alone in the dark, waiting for sleep to come.

She looked behind her again. They were all in the water now. She thought there were dark-clad figures under the trees on the eastern side, emerging from cover onto the bank. They seemed to be wearing blue headbands. Through the downpour she thought she could make out a man lifting a bow, fitting an arrow.

'They're right behind us,' she said. 'On the bank.'

Faolan gave a tight nod. At some signal Ana could not detect, the horse moved forward more quickly. It stumbled, and water surged up. Tension ran through Faolan's body as he struggled to help the animal balance. The current felt like fierce hands

69

clutching, like an enemy force seeking to drag them down. Then, all of a sudden, the animal staggered out onto a pebbly shore and up to a grassy rise, and they were safely over.

Faolan swung down, awkward with his wounded arm. Blood was seeping through the makeshift bandage; the sleeve of his shirt was red. 'Lead the horse. Go higher,' he said. 'The water's coming up fast. Here.' He took something from his belt, slapped it onto her hand: a knife, unsheathed, a serious-looking weapon with a serrated edge. 'Take it. If you need it, use it. Get out of sight and wait for us. Go!'

'What are you –?'

'Ana, go!'

The look in his eyes made obedience the only choice. Over his shoulder she could see the long line of riders stretched out across the breadth of the ford. They were slow; already the water was visibly deeper and the horses were in obvious difficulty. She watched Faolan make his way back to the edge, waiting in full view of anyone who might seek to loose another arrow. Waiting until he saw all his men safely across. Then she took the horse's bridle and began to climb the hill.

Ana had not gone far when there came a sound that froze the blood in her veins. She did not know what it was, only that it was the voice of catastrophe. She turned on the path, edging out from the cover of close-growing bushes to get a clear view towards the ford. The noise was a roaring, a rolling, a huge, tumultuous growling as of an approaching monster. The men in the water were looking upstream; she saw their faces in the moment before it struck them: white, stunned, eyes full of the recognition of death. Then the wave came, a flood that had been trapped some- where in the higher reaches of the river and released all at once as a barrier gave under its pressure, sending the mass of water hurtling downstream. Its power snatched up everything that stood in its way: massive tree trunks with roots like reaching fingers, rocks, earth, bushes, broken creatures, all in a tumbling turmoil. It was a scouring of the land that would be a long time mending. The wave moved across the ford before Ana's disbeliev- ing eyes; in an instant men, woman, horses were caught up in it, their screams lost in its ferocious music, and borne away in its churning madness. The rain had eased a little; she could see clearly across the water to the other side. The far bank had been gouged out. The river had taken a monstrous bite of it. There was nobody there. From side to side, the valley was full of rushing water.

Ana could hear the high, gasping sound of her own breathing. She could feel the thunderous drumming of her heart. For a moment she stood paralysed by the terrible finality of what had happened. Then she looped the horse's reins over a branch and, hitching the hem of her skirt up into her girdle, ran back down the path. The water had obliterated the river's old boundaries. It surged around tree trunks, it coursed through thickets and splashed over rocky outcrops. The things it carried made a new peril: logs came hurtling down to smack into the trees that still held fast against the flood, and loose boulders rolled haphazardly in the powerful current. She couldn't see anyone. Not anyone. Out in the middle, caught on a protrusion, something small and bright moved crazily in the swirling water: a scrap of Creisa's multicoloured shawl.

She couldn't go on without a search, unlikely as it was to bear fruit. The banks were a nightmare, all crumbling earth and shifting stones, slippery foliage and snapping branches. Ana picked a way downstream, counting landmarks as she went: here a solitary oak on the hillside above, here a white rock in the shape of a goat, here a deep scar gouged in the earth where a stream had made its own contribution to the devastation. She called, her voice feeble and lonely above the triumphant song of the river: 'Faolan! Wrad! Creisa! Is anybody there?' She wouldn't think of where she was; of those men with arrows; of being all alone, cold, wet, with no supplies and little idea of the way. She would search until she had just time to get back to the ford and find the horse before dark. She wouldn't think beyond that.

Time ceased to have any meaning. She found a way where there seemed none. She ignored the scratches and bruises inflicted by thorny, broken bush or jagged stone. Her throat ached from shouting; tears bathed her face and made her nose run. She went on until, ahead, there loomed an obstacle there would be no passing. The swollen river plunged down in a white, foaming fall, and to either side high rock walls made a formidable barrier. There was no point in attempting a climb. What she sought would be found on the river bank or not at all. If anyone had been sucked into that whirling chaos of white water, if anyone had lived so long, they had journeyed now beyond her reach. It was time to turn back.

The knowledge of defeat was overwhelming. Ana sat down on a rock, staring blindly at the river. If she had not fainted, if Faolan had not allowed her a day's rest, they would have crossed safely. Creisa would be alive, and Wrad and Kinet and all those young men. They had died because of her. Because she was weak. And Faolan, who had crossed safely, who could have lived, had died because he cared about his men. He had waited for them, and the river had borne him away. His devotion to duty had cost him his life, and it had saved hers.

No choice now: she must go back. There was nothing more she could do here. Grimly, Ana began to consider the practicalities. Faolan's horse wore saddlebags; perhaps there were some basic supplies there. She was still bleeding. She'd need to rip up her shift, wet as it was, to use for rags. Everything had been on the pack pony: her bags, her personal items, the clothing she had packed for the wedding, the little things she had embroidered, over the years, against the time when she might have children of her own. All gone. All swept away.

'Ana, go,' she ordered herself, sniffing and wiping the tears from her cheeks. She rose shakily to her feet, and at that moment the crow flew across, so close to her face that she flinched back with a gasp. It winged away down to the water's edge, calling a harsh summons, and as she stared after it, Ana saw what she had not noticed before as she scrambled her tortuous way along the river's flank. There was something partly submerged amid a jumble of flotsam caught against jagged rocks. The river made a frothing surge around this protrusion, as if angry that anything should think to hold fast against it. On the river bank a great tree that was half toppled by the flood leaned out towards the rocky islet, maintaining a precarious hold on the earth. Beneath it the water had scoured the bank away, exposing a twisting mass of roots. More debris had been washed against them, snapped-off branches, broken bushes, sticks and leaves. Ana looked out again towards the rocks. Almost under them, she could see something dark in the water: a man's tunic, sodden and stained. And something pale: a drained, semi-conscious face. A hand gripping, gripping a wedged branch for dear life against the violent pull of the current.

She ran, stumbling on the stones, heart in her mouth. Faolan was alive. He was holding on. Out of the nightmare there was still something to be salvaged.

The bird perched in the upper branches of the leaning tree, its eyes on the man in the water. Ana scrambled down below the angled trunk and edged along the slippery, disintegrating bank, her head awhirl. The place where Faolan's desperate hand clutched onto that length of branch was twice her own body's length out into the swirling water; she could only reach him by wading in herself. It was deep; he had obviously not been able to touch the bottom with his feet and get out that way. The moment his fingers released their grip he would be gone. There were more rocks downstream of him; he would likely be dashed to pieces on these before he had time to drown. The water surged around him, tugging at his clothing, ripping at his hair. His eyes were closed, his face sheet-white. The jaw was set tight; the hand clawed grimly around the branch. If she called out, would she startle him? Would he let go? Above her, the bird cried shrilly, and Faolan opened his eyes.

'Faolan, I'm here on the bank! I can reach you!' Ana shouted with false confidence. 'Just hold on!' She cast her eyes over what was to hand, something, anything with which she might bridge that gap. There was a jumble of items washed up under the muddy overhang: branches, roots, small bushes, dead things that she did not want to examine. And . . . yes! A piece of wood that had once been part of a shed or a barn or a house; shaped wood, a strong plank perhaps a handspan wide. She thought it might be long enough. If she could wedge one end up between the roots that still held fast in the crumbling bank, and move the other out to form a kind of bridge to the place where he was, she had at least some chance of getting out there to help him. She saw in her mind how she would reach down her arms and grasp his; how the moment he loosed his grip to hold onto her, the force of the water would topple the two of them. It wouldn't work. She could not hold him against the current, nor would he have the strength to scramble up on his own even if she could. Right now Faolan looked even weaker than she; she thought she could see his fingers slipping, his eyes starting to glaze and roll back into unconsciousness. The plank would be strong enough if she could get it in the right place. But nothing was stronger than the river . . .

She had it. They must use that destructive current to help them. She had to lay her bridge over to the rocks downstream of Faolan. If only she could do that, the pressure of the water would hold him firm against the wood while she hauled him up. She scanned the river once more, her heart in her mouth lest, in the instant while her attention was elsewhere, he should disappear quietly below the water's surface, gone without a word. The image came, the picture of how it could go wrong. She did not allow it to linger.

'Faolan!' she called, pitching her voice to be heard above the rushing water.

He was too exhausted to speak; his head moved in an attempt at a nod.

'Don't move!' she yelled, knowing how foolish that sounded. 'I'm coming out to get you!'

Easy to say. The plank was heavy; she could not believe how heavy. Balancing in the shallows, she came perilously close to slipping into deep water before she succeeded in lifting and turning it. Sliding the end between the higher roots by the trunk, getting the angle right so it would hold, left her arms and shoulders fiery with pain. There, it was done. Now the other end; she must swing the wood around, keep it out of the water, keep it away from Faolan's head at all costs . . .

'Ah!' Ana gasped as her foot slid in the mud and she went down on one knee, jarring her hip against the wood. The clutch of the river was terrifying; her heart pounded. She fought her way back to her feet, gripped the plank again and manoeuvred it until the far end rested with what she hoped was reasonable security between the smaller rocks about which the water seethed and foamed not far below Faolan's position. She tested the makeshift bridge. It wobbled, but held.

'I'm coming out now!'

Rain was still falling. Everything was wet. She clambered up onto the plank, hands clenched around the sides, skirt hitched as high as it would go, and crawled out from the bank. The wood was barely clear of the water, and her weight dipped the plank lower the further she crept. The current teased at her, pulling, and she felt her heart pounding fit to burst. She tried not to look down. Behind her she could sense things shifting and groaning and creaking under the strain; she did not think this would hold amongst the tree roots for long. A little further, a little more, hand, knee, hand, knee . . . Her heart was a drum now, beating a music of sheer terror. Still, somewhere deep inside her, a fierce will burned. She would save him. She would do this.

She was there. Perched perilously on the far end of her bridge, the water surging around her, she was not far downstream of Faolan. His face was barely clear of the water; he looked half drowned already. How could she ask him to release his grip? He would likely be swept straight under her plank and away down the river. Her rescue seemed doomed from the start. She would not think of that. There was only one chance, and if she did not take it soon, there would be no chance at all.

'Faolan,' she called briskly, 'listen to me! I'm just downstream here, two arm's-lengths away from you. I have a length of planking across the water from the bank. Don't let go yet. If you can get to the plank and hold on, I'll be able to haul you up. Wait for my count. Can you use your left arm at all?'

The wounded arm moved sluggishly in the water; the hand came up, fingers blanched and wrinkled, to grasp feebly at the roots.

She needed to keep the instructions simple. 'Good. You'll have to be quick. Be ready to grab on with both hands. Never mind if it hurts. You'll have to help me all you can.'

'You . . . fall . . .' His voice was a thread.

'Don't be silly!' She teetered as she struggled for a better balance; the bridge provided the narrowest of purchases, and there was nothing else to hold on to. She stuck one foot into a crack between the rocks, under water, and balanced with her stomach on the wood, leaving both arms free. The water coursed on every side. 'Now, when I say, you're going to take one deep breath and let go, then grab with both hands. If you can stretch out your arms as you come it's going to be easier. Do you understand?'

A flicker across the blanched features; she had to take that as a yes.

'Good. I'm going to count to three.' Her breath was coming as if she had run a race. The water roiled around her; she was more than half submerged. 'One, two, three, go!'

He let go. An instant later his body smacked into the plank and his arm came up to hook on. Ana snatched and held; it was a battle, herself against the river, with the prize a man's life. She prayed, a silent, screaming cry to the Flamekeeper, straight from the heart. Her arms felt fit to spring from their sockets; her leg was ready to snap where it was jammed between the rocks. She held on. It was a moment that seemed to last forever. She hauled, and felt Faolan's desperate effort to help himself with his final, ebbing strength. It seemed as if he might be swept beneath the makeshift bridge, for the swirling water washed over his head as he sought to get both arms around the wood. Ana held him by whatever she could, a fold of cloth, a handful of hair, her grip shifting frantically as he moved, and then he was pulling himself along the bridge, seeking a foothold amongst the rocks and debris of the smaller islet, a tenuous refuge that was crumbling now even as Ana took him by the arm and somehow hauled him up beside her. He sprawled across the plank, his eyes closed, his chest heaving. Ana's own breath was coming in wheezing gasps; she felt the warmth of tears on her cheeks. Her back hurt. Her legs were a mass of bloody cuts. Her shoulders were aching and her arms felt numb. Above, the light was starting to fade from a sky already gloomy with clouds.

'Faolan!'

He lay limp, hands open in the water, held only by his own body weight and her weakening grip. Fresh terror arose in Ana. If he fainted now they were as good as lost.

'Faolan, wake up!'

He did not respond. Close by, something cracked and subsided. A rivulet ran across his body.

'Faolan!' Ana reached over and slapped him hard on the cheek. 'Wake up immediately! You're on duty, remember?'

A feeble groan; a slight stirring. Her heart bled for him even as she summoned her most regal tone. 'Come on, Faolan! It's nearly dark. I need you!'

They crept back across the fragile bridge, Faolan going first, Ana behind, goading him to keep moving. Faolan's greater weight made the plank bow ominously low into the water, but it held firm. When they set foot on the mud of the scoured-out bank, he fell to his knees. Ana pulled him up, setting his good arm around her shoulders. Above them, the tree now leaned towards the river at an impossible angle. It greeted its impending doom with a creaking, groaning song of anguish. Ana heard the sound of wings; sensed rather than saw the crow as it arose from this tenuous perch and flew away. Its mission, if such it had been, was complete. Ana wished she could say the same for her own.

'You can't lie down, not here,' she snapped. 'Not unless you want a tree falling on your head. We have to walk. Walk, one, two, come on! We have to fetch the horse, find a dry place to shelter, make fire.' Gods, she hoped so much that the horse was still there. That there was a flint in the saddlebags. That Faolan would last the distance. 'Come on, move!' she ordered. 'I'll help you, but I can't do it all. I'm just a spoiled princess, remember? It's you who are supposed to be the leader. You're meant to be looking after me. Careful, there's a boggy patch there . . .'

Perhaps her prayer had been heard. Perhaps it had reached the ears of the Flamekeeper, a god who valued courage and tenacity. The light held until they staggered back onto the track by the place where, only that morning, there had been a ford. Dusk was falling as they climbed the hill to find Faolan's horse still waiting patiently where Ana had left it. Dark held off while they made their slow way higher, each on one side of the horse, comforted by its warmth, its solidity in a world where all was gone awry. They found a place where a rock wall formed an overhang; where, within, there was a dryish expanse of level ground with sheltering bushes to either side and a stand of pines in front. Waves of violent shivering racked Faolan's body. When Ana unstrapped the saddlebags and brought them over, he could not still his hands sufficiently to help her unpack them. There was a rolled blanket behind the saddle. She fetched this as well, then hobbled the horse and left him to find what fodder he could. There were grasses aplenty; he would eat better than they.

By now Ana was hardly thinking about what she was doing. Her body was simply going about the necessary tasks in what seemed to be the best order. Faolan was white-faced and trembling, with a look in his eye that worried her more than she was prepared to admit. She untied the twine that bound the blanket; where it had been tightly rolled it was tolerably dry, most certainly the driest item they had between them. Every piece of clothing they wore was saturated. And the night was growing cold.

'Here,' she said. 'Get that shirt off, and the tunic. Wrap this around you. And tell me there's a flint in these bags somewhere.'

'You –?' Faolan managed as she passed the blanket.

'I need to get a fire going. Take your things off. We're not at White Hill now. If you're to be any help to me at all, you must get warm.'

He stared at her, eyes shadow-dark in a face still drained of colour. He made no attempt to remove his wet clothes.

'Do I have to undress you like an infant? Let me put this in plain words. I can't get to Briar Wood on my own, Faolan. I need you. Now do as I say. If I can make a fire, we have some hope of drying our things. Flint? Where?'

He gestured, hand shaking. 'Wood . . . wet . . .' he muttered, wincing as he tried to slip his tunic over the damaged arm.

'Oh, shut up!' Ana said, finding the flint and, to her immense relief, a bundle of dry tinder compressed into an oiled bag. 'There happens to be a supply of old wood up there under the rock shelf; others have been here before us. I'm not stupid.'

Making the fire required a number of attempts; her own hands were less than steady, and her arms were so weary it was hard to summon even the force required to strike a spark. As the Flame-keeper sank below the rim of the world and night fell, her own small flame flared and caught, and the dry log she had dragged to the centre of the open space began to burn. She rummaged for anything else that could be used for fuel: along the shallow cave lay twigs and thin boughs and needles, perhaps hastily stored by others for just such a makeshift camp.

Faolan had scarcely moved. His sodden upper garments lay in a heap; he sat with the blanket around him, staring into the fire. Ana wondered if she would ever be really warm again. Faolan hadn't said a word about what had happened. There was no need to say it, Ana thought. It was all there in his eyes.

His saddlebags were those of a seasoned traveller. Ana took out what would be immediately useful: a full water-skin; a packet containing strips of dried meat, dark and leathery; a shirt, plain of design, made in what felt like very fine linen. A pair of trousers in dark wool. They had been well wrapped in protective coverings and were almost dry. His good clothes, for Briar Wood. He was, after all, the king's personal emissary.

'You,' Faolan said. 'Wear those. Dry.'

'Me?' Ana stared at him. 'These are your special things. Besides –' There was an argument somewhere in her mind, an argument that had to do with what was proper for a lady, and what people would think. After today, it seemed meaningless. 'You should wear them,' she said. 'You're freezing.'

'Put them on,' Faolan told her. 'I have the blanket. Go on.'

'I don't think –' she protested.

'Put them on, Ana. I won't look.'

So she did, and very odd it felt to be clad like a man, though the trousers did allow a freedom of movement that made the tasks of fetching wood and draping the wet clothing near the fire a great deal easier.

Ana settled by the blaze with her sodden shift in one hand and the knife Faolan had given her in the other, and proceeded to rip the garment into short, serviceable lengths. These, at least, could be dried quickly. Faolan was watching her, a question in his eyes.

'Women's business,' she said, thinking that what, yesterday, had been too awkward and embarrassing to mention was now no more than commonplace. 'I'll need these for a day or two more.'

There was a little silence. 'I'm sorry,' Faolan said so quietly she could barely hear him.

'For what? Because we must speak of such matters openly now? Because I'm reduced to tearing up my fine clothing for such a mundane purpose?'

He said nothing. The unspoken loomed between them, a dark shadow.

'This is not your fault, Faolan,' Ana said in a different tone; the brisk, authoritative voice she had maintained for so long had suddenly deserted her. 'It happened. I could just as well blame myself for causing the delay. There's no point in that. We're here. For some reason known only to the gods, we've survived. We must go on. There's nothing else to be done. Here.' She passed a strip of the fine linen across to him. 'Hold this up to dry. We'll need to bandage that arm properly.'

'It's nothing. A flesh wound.'

'All the same, I would prefer to see it kept reasonably clean. I imagine you want the best chance of using your arm to its full capacity again. If you let ill humours into the wound, anything could happen. I'll dress it for you when the bandage is dry.'

There were things to be done, small tasks to stave off the time when there would be nothing but the dark and the images of today. They forced themselves to eat a little of the dried meat, though neither had any appetite. They drank from the water-skin. Rainwater had pooled here and there amongst the rocks; between this and the grasses, the horse would be adequately provided for. Ana bandaged Faolan's wound, despite his protest that he could do it himself.

'What is this?' she asked him as she wrapped the cloth carefully around the muscular arm and saw that above the ripped skin and oozing flesh of the new wound there was an older scar, that of a deeper injury long ago healed.

'That? The first time I met Bridei, he put an arrow through me. Fortunately he wasn't aiming to do serious injury, only to slow me down.'

'Bridei? Why would he do such a thing?' Ana could not imagine this at all. Faolan was Bridei's most loyal supporter. In the past, she had considered this his only redeeming feature.

'He didn't like the sound of my voice.' Faolan's tone was curt; the tale would have to wait until she could ask Bridei himself, or Tuala. No; that was not going to happen. For a moment she had forgotten where she was and where she must go. It could be years before she saw her friends again. Abruptly, it all came flooding back: Briar Wood, Alpin, the long future among strangers. The fact that her own family had consented to the marriage, without even finding out what she thought. It was as if she had ceased to exist save as a playing piece. Yet today, in the face of grief and terror, she felt more real than ever before.

'What is it?' Faolan's eyes were intent on her as she knotted the ends of the linen together and sat back on her heels.

'Nothing.' She could feel tears close now: such a foolish thing to start them off, after everything.

'It was something. You're distressed.'

She would not tell the truth; it sounded weak and pathetic. 'Those men, the ones who attacked us – what if they find us here?'

Faolan seemed to consider this before he answered. 'I could reassure you with a lie,' he told her, 'but I know you would see through it. In truth, I am too weak at present to defend you adequately, even against a single armed man. I would do the best I could. Tomorrow I will be stronger. It's more than likely they don't have folk on both sides of the river. Ged's man identified it as a border between the territories of rival chieftains.'

'Oh.' Ana pondered this. 'You mean we're in Alpin's domain now? In Briar Wood?'

'We must be close. Ana, you should try to sleep. You're worn out.'

'So should you. But the fire – we must keep watch –'

'I never sleep much. Here –' He was taking off the blanket, holding it out to her. Ana told herself that, under the circumstances, the sight of his naked chest was nothing to be concerned about. She could imagine what Creisa would say. Creisa . . . so vibrant, so full of life. So young . . .

'Lie down,' Faolan said. 'Try to rest.'

She gazed at him, the blanket in her hands, and he looked back. The firelight flickered on his skin. He was making a disciplined effort to suppress the shivering.

'Faolan,' Ana said.

He wrapped his arms around his upper body; in that moment she glimpsed a different man, one who was young, weary and desperately alone.

81

'I don't imagine you're feeling any better than I am right now,' she said. 'It's freezing cold. It would be stupid to die of a chill just because of propriety. I think we can agree to share the blanket. Nobody need ever know.'

'I don't need to sleep.'

'If you believe that, I can't imagine why Bridei ever entrusted this to you. Look at it this way. I'm cold to the marrow, and I need both you and this blanket to keep me warm. Unseemly and distasteful as that may be, if you want to complete the mission and get me to Briar Wood, you'll do it.'

'Spoken like a true princess.'

Ana felt a blush rise to her cheeks. 'I'm just doing as my friend Ferada would if she were here. The old Ana, the meek one who likes to do fine embroidery and sing songs, she's the real one.' She felt the tears spilling from her eyes and reached to scrub them away.

'I'm prepared to obey orders if they're sound,' Faolan said. 'Here.'

It amazed Ana how good it felt to lie with him behind her, curled to accommodate her, and the blanket over the two of them. The ground was hard. The shallow cave was full of whispering draughts, for all the sheltering trees and glowing fire. Unwelcome images jostled for space in her head, making the tears run hot and fast. Nonetheless, it was good. His arm across her, his heartbeat against her seemed protective forces of great power.

He was saying something.

'What?'

'How did you do it? How could you have the strength to pull me up to safety, against that current?'

'I prayed. The gods helped me. The Flamekeeper does not easily let go a man of great heart. It was he who saved you, not I.'

A silence. She could feel his breathing, not entirely steady; she suspected the visions that haunted him were even darker than her own. She knew already that the mission was foremost in his mind; had, indeed, used that to spur him on when his strength was flagging. He must believe he had failed bitterly. Failed his king. Failed his friend.

'I put no trust in gods,' Faolan said.

'That does not stop them from helping you. From loving you.'

'Then the gods are foolish. Their judgement is faulty. I'm not a man of great heart, Ana. I'm not a man like Bridei.'

'I hope some day you come to realise how wrong you are. This was an accident, a terrible conjunction. It was not your doing.'

'There are no gods,' he murmured, rolling onto his back. 'Not for me. They cast me aside long ago.'

'But –'

'What happened today was my responsibility, nobody else's. A cursed touch; a darkness.'

Ana held her tongue. It was clear to her that he did not speak just of today, but of the past, of something he brought with him, perhaps the same thing that had kept him awake by the fire all those nights, watching over her while his men slept. She did not ask him to explain.

'I'm cold,' she said after a little. 'Would you mind moving closer again?'

When he did so, wrapping the protective arm back over her, the confusion of feelings that flowed through her was too much to bear. She began to weep like a child, sobbing without restraint.

'It's all right,' Faolan said, and she felt his hand come up to stroke her hair. He spoke again, but it was Gaelic and her limited knowledge of the tongue meant she understood only a word here and there. Perhaps he was telling a tale; the soft, rhythmic flow of it soothed her even as it made her tears run faster. In time there seemed to be no more tears in her, and she lay still, the warmth of his touch, the lilt of his voice a ward against the uncertainties of the night and of the morning to come.

Still later, when perhaps he thought her asleep, he sang a snatch of the same tune she had heard from his lips as they crossed that other river, the song about a traveller and his Otherworld sweet-heart. Ana had heard the best of bards in her home, at the king's court of the Light Isles. She had listened to the offerings of accomplished musicians in Bridei's household at White Hill. But never in her life had she heard a voice like this, so sweet and so full of sorrow. It did not matter that she could not understand most of the words. She knew he sang of hopes dashed, youthful ideals quenched, the bonds of love cruelly severed. And yet, his song was a beguiling thing, like a tune from beyond the margin, calling her into a different world. The clear, sad sound of it wrapped her like a soft cloak, and she fell into sleep.

Chapter Four

'King Bridei must think me a fool,' observed Alpin of Briar Wood, leaning his florid cheek on one hand as he stared into his ale cup. 'Doesn't the manner of his offer arouse your curiosity as to the reason for such haste?'

His companion pursed his lips and frowned. 'There's no doubt this is in response to some information that's come his way,' Odhar said. 'Word from Dalriada, most likely. I wonder who's been talking? I had not thought any man privy to our negotiations save ourselves and the lords of the Uí Néill. Can there be a Priteni eye in the heart of Dunadd? Is King Bridei a mage that he ferrets out secrets where no other can penetrate?'

'The tale is that he was raised by a mage,' Alpin said heavily. 'Fellow called Broichan; powerful and devious. That suggests there's more to this than meets the eye. Is it possible they plan to move early? Perhaps before next spring's thaw?'

'Or still earlier,' suggested Odhar, a thin man in the tattered clothes of a wayfarer. He was the kind of person nobody looks at twice. It was a semblance he had worked hard to achieve.

Alpin's dark brows rose in disbelief. 'Before the winter? Surely not. Fortriu has a council planned for Gathering, so I've heard. They're expecting the King of Circinn himself. What purpose can there be in such a grand meeting, save to plan for a concerted assault on Gabhran in the west? Bridei can hardly be planning that for autumn if Drust the Boar isn't to be consulted until harvest time.'

Odhar gave a nod. He was drinking little; he had a long road ahead of him. 'You speak sense, Alpin. Still, you must consider that this may be a deliberate attempt to lead you astray. A ploy devised by Bridei's coterie of advisers: druids, mages and wise women, the lot of them. They make difficult enemies. The fellow even took a woman of the Good Folk for his wife. What kind of king does that? It sounds like the action of a young fool.'

'But?'

'You know what's being whispered. That this new king has awoken something in Fortriu, something old and dangerous. That his people are flocking to his banner. That he may be the one to do what no king of the Priteni has managed to do thus far: achieve a comprehensive victory over the Gaels of Dalriada.'

'And he offers me a bride, just like that. Holds out a choice morsel to tempt me away from the alliance with Gabhran. Eighteen years of age and a rare beauty, that's what the message said. Gross exaggeration, no doubt. If she's a rare beauty, why hasn't she been wed these six years or more?'

'You will refuse, of course,' Odhar said, making it not quite a question. 'Send her back forthwith.'

Alpin's fleshy lips curved in a smile. 'Not necessarily,' he said. 'I'll look her over first. After all, I am unwed, without legitimate heirs, and if the message is accurate this girl has an impeccable blood line, no less than the royal line of Fortriu. I may decide to keep Bridei's generous gift.'

'But –' Odhar began, then thought better of speaking.

'Don't leap to conclusions, my fine Gaelic friend,' Alpin said. 'I am a subtler man than this boy-king. If I play this right, I will achieve my goal and acquire, into the bargain, the right to father a future king of the Priteni. If I like the look of this girl, I'll try her out and see if she breeds boys. Should she not please me I'll despatch her home with a message to Bridei to mind his own business. I don't see how I can lose. Once I've bedded the girl, Bridei can hardly ask for her back when he decides he doesn't care for some new friend I may make.'

'Does his letter state a requirement in relation to Dalriada? Is the offer contingent on your keeping out of the conflict entirely?'

'It was implied rather than specifically laid out. If Bridei had not despatched this bride already –'

A sharp rapping at a small inner door made both men start. Their conversation had been private, with a guard posted outside the chamber where they sat over their ale. Odhar's visits to Briar Wood took place covertly; few in the household had ever seen his face.

'I'm not to be disturbed,' growled Alpin.

The knock came again.

'I said, no interruptions!' Alpin rose to his feet, a formidable bear of a man, his fine head of hair and luxuriant beard adding to the effect. He fished a key from his pouch, strode across to unlock the little door at the rear of the chamber and opened it a chink. Behind him, Odhar drew his hood forward to conceal his features. 'Make this good!' Alpin snapped. 'I'm in council.'

'I regret the interruption, my lord.' The man who stood outside was short, bald and possessed of broad shoulders and a barrel chest. He wore a long dark robe, slit at the sides to reveal loose trousers, and carried a staff. 'Your brother wishes to see you. He says it's urgent.'

'My brother can wait,' hissed Alpin, glancing over his shoulder at his visitor. 'You know not to come and seek me out at his every whim, Deord. I'll see him after supper as I always do. It can wait.'

Deord gazed up at him. He was a man whose relaxed grace of posture and calmness of eye made him seem far taller than he was. 'He says it cannot, my lord. I would not have disturbed you otherwise. He's seen something he says requires immediate –'

'Didn't you hear me? Later!'

'Travellers,' Deord said quietly as the door began to close in his face. 'A man and a fair-haired girl of unusual beauty. Their escort set upon by the Blues at Breaking Ford.'

The door stopped moving. 'And?' queried Alpin.

'Drustan can tell you,' said Deord. 'It was not I who saw this. They're in trouble.'

Alpin cursed under his breath. Deord waited, silent and still. 'Tell my brother I'll be there shortly,' the chieftain growled.

Deord bowed and moved away. The door closed.

'Confounded servants,' Alpin said. 'I must leave you, I'm afraid. Are we done here?'

'Whether we are done or no, I must be gone,' said Odhar. 'I want to be on the way south before nightfall. Your message, then, is unchanged? This offer from Bridei makes no difference to your decision?'

Alpin smiled. His eyes were cold. 'None at all, save that I will consider making my men available somewhat earlier than I intended. The fleet will be ready; they'll work on the boats over summer. I expect there will be more information to be had before long. Indeed, its sources may be closer to home than I ever imagined.'

'I don't suppose we will meet again soon,' Odhar said, rising to his feet. 'My sphere of influence is not the battlefield.'

'Who knows?' Alpin's tone was light. 'Farewell. Safe journey.'

His guest dismissed, the chieftain of Briar Wood made his way in long, impatient strides to the distant part of the fortress where his brother Drustan was housed. It was a lengthy walk through outhouses and narrow ways, all behind the locked entrance that opened from his own private chamber. Nobody was going to find Drustan's quarters by chance. The final approach led Alpin down a deep path between high stone walls which were pierced by chinks of windows. Through each of these could be seen a glimpse of the world outside: a sliver of dappled green, a dark swathe of needled pines, a flash of water under the spring sun. Above the walls, Briar Wood's tall elms presented their crowns to a pale sky. Birds passed over, crying. The sound of them made Alpin's flesh crawl. He hated coming here. It filled him with memories. His hands began to tremble, and he clenched them into fists. If only he could do it; if only he could put an end to this. Move on, start anew. A wife. A beautiful young wife. That would be a powerful tool for change. But not with his brother hanging around his neck. Not with Drustan immured here, forever dragging him down. Why was he thus cursed? What had he ever done to anger the gods so?

The walls curved around, carrying the path between them, and the iron gate came into view, the chained and bolted gate that led to the place where Drustan lived with his keeper. Alpin thought he had done well for his brother, all things considered. The indoor quarters were clean, private and of reasonable size. Outdoors there was a patch of grass, a bench, a small pond. This area was securely walled, of course, and roofed with iron grille-work. That made the little garden dim. Drustan would never again see the Shining One in her perfect fullness, save quartered by the bars of this open cell. And just as well. At full moon he was at his most unreliable.

Alpin knew he could have been far less generous. There were those who would have thrown his brother into a dungeon, never to see the light of day again. The crime he had committed warranted that. But Alpin had not done so; Drustan was kin, for all his ill-doing and his strangeness. Let him see the sky, as long as he could not fly away.

Deord unlocked the iron door at Alpin's call, and locked it again behind the chieftain.

'Where is he?' Alpin was already restless. 'I don't have long.'

'By the wall, there.'

Alpin peered into the shadowy corner of the enclosure, following Deord's pointing staff. 'Is he chained?'

A flicker of expression passed across the shorter man's face. 'We comply with your requirements, as always, my lord.'

Alpin glanced at him sharply, suspicious of the blandly obedient tone, but Deord appeared calm and relaxed, as ever. For a man of such muscular build, a man whose every move spoke of harnessed power, Drustan's guard displayed a remarkably even temper. Alpin considered this combination ideal in a keeper for his brother. He wondered, sometimes, if there were more to Deord than met the eye, but the fellow never gave much away.

Alpin advanced towards the corner where, now, the figure of Drustan could be seen in the shadows, a tall man, as tall as his brother, but lean and wiry with none of Alpin's bulk. A shock of tawny hair fell across Drustan's shoulders. His hands were tightly clenched; he leaned against the stone wall, head tipped back, eyes closed. Nearby, up in a niche, three birds perched in a row, staring down at Alpin unwinking: a hoodie, a crossbill, a tiny wren. Alpin glared back. He loathed the creatures that seemed to haunt this place, coming in and out through the impossibly small openings in the grille; their preternatural stillness unnerved him. Drustan stirred as he approached, and there was a shiver of metal.

'At last!' Drustan exclaimed, eyes snapping open to fix his brother with the bright wildness that never failed to send a chill down Alpin's spine. 'She's in danger – lost and frightened – she needs help –'

'Now, now,' Alpin attempted a placatory tone such as one might use with a distressed infant or temperamental horse, 'let us take this slowly, Drustan. Come, sit here on the bench, take a deep breath and –'

'The ford – Breaking Ford – they were caught by the Blues, and a man fell, and then the river snatched them away –'

'Drustan!' The tone had changed; now Alpin spoke as to a disobedient hound, sharply commanding, and pointed at the bench. His brother moved; a metallic music followed him as the fine chain that linked the iron bracelets around his wrists, then ran to a ring set in the stone bench, snaked along beside him. Drustan would not sit down, perhaps could not, for a vibrant energy, a deep restlessness possessed him, and he shifted from one foot to the other, moving his hands, jangling the metal.

'Stop it!' Alpin snapped in irritation. 'Now, what did you see? Tell me in simple words, as if it were a story. Who was there? A woman, Deord said. What woman? I need all of it. Slowly, Drustan.'

'A party of travellers. An attack. I couldn't help them. I couldn't warn them, I tried but I couldn't – the Blues came. One man dead, another wounded. A flood – a terrible, sudden wave, like the anger of Bone Mother – so many fallen, broken, scattered . . . all swept away, swept away down . . .'

'And then?' prompted Alpin with a sigh.

'She was brave. So brave. So beautiful. Like a princess in a song. She saved a man. Bone Mother nearly had him. The river nearly took him. She saved him. All gone, horses, men, baggage . . .

nothing left. Cold . . . wet . . . lonely . . . You must help her, Alpin. Go now. Now!'

'This woman. You say beautiful, like a princess. Was she young? Richly dressed?'

Drustan had fallen silent. His eyes changed, warmed.

'Drustan!'

'A princess.' His voice was quieter now. 'Hair like a stream of gold; eyes full of courage. Young, yes. And sad.'

'Where are they now?'

'Coming to Briar Wood. Along the old path. A man, a woman, a tired horse. A little fire by night. You must go, Brother, go and find her. She's cold.'

'A man. What man?'

Drustan said nothing.

'What man, Drustan? Black Crow save us, you have enough to say when it suits you, why can't you give plain answers?'

Deord shifted slightly. He was watching from a distance, expression impassive, staff in hand. Alpin welcomed that. He was never quite sure what his brother would do or which way he would move. And Drustan was quick. He had always been quick.

'A dark man,' Drustan said. 'Her companion.'

'A guard?'

'Her companion.'

'Well dressed? Armed? A warrior? A courtier?'

'A dark man,' Drustan said again. 'Go now, Alpin! Help her!'

'Oddly enough,' said Alpin, rising to his feet, 'for once I agree with you. This must surely be the bride chosen for me by King Bridei of Fortriu. Young, beautiful and headed this way – I can think of no other explanation. I'll send a party to meet them. Or . . . why not? I'll go and fetch her myself.'

Six nights they spent camping rough, six nights warmed by little fires and each other's bodies under the shared blanket. Faolan had begun to regain his strength. His arm was healing well, assisted by the fresh bandages Ana insisted on applying each morning. That he no longer felt the sapping, draining despair of that first night was, in one way, an inconvenience. Once the exhaustion was gone, physical desire began to make itself apparent, and his efforts to conceal this from Ana as she lay half asleep curled up against him kept him long awake. He could hardly refuse to lie close to her; the nights were chill. He could most certainly not explain to her. For all her nineteen years, she was an innocent, and would be shocked and frightened, he thought, if she knew the truth. Under the circumstances it would be all too easy to take advantage of her. That he needed to consider such a thing at all showed how far his self-discipline had slipped.

There came a morning when neither of them felt the compulsion to move on. The shocked numbness that had followed their losses at the ford had been gradually replaced, as they travelled, by a tolerance between them, an acceptance that what had befallen them had altered the rules and constraints of their mission entirely. There was a new easiness to their talk and a new trust in their sharing of the day's responsibilities.

They had camped in a grassy hollow above a small stream, and the sun had arisen on a day already full of spring's promise: birds were noisy in the trees fringing the water; small, bright flowers bloomed in clumps here and there amid the grass, and the air was fresh with the scent of renewal. Yet Faolan's heart was full of a new heaviness, a thing he did not wish to put into words, even for himself. By his calculations, they were close to Alpin's stronghold. Within a day or two they should be there, and the major part of his mission would be achieved. He could never call it a success, not with such grievous losses. But he would deliver this bride to her husband. He would seal this alliance for Bridei and take the news of it back to White Hill. Looking across at Ana as she sat by the fire working the knots out of her long hair with the small bone comb he had carried in his bags, he recognised within him a powerful wish that he need not do so. He did not want to deliver her up to a man unknown to her, and leave her to live the rest of her life among strangers.

She looked up, perhaps conscious of his scrutiny. 'Faolan?'

'Mmm?'

'How long do you think it will be now? We are near the edge of Briar Wood, aren't we?'

He attempted a smile. 'Getting hungry?'

Ana looked at him. 'I would welcome a meal other than those pieces of leather, most certainly. But that's not why I ask.'

'Perhaps two days,' he said. 'We must travel through dense woods; the paths may elude us and make the journey longer. I'm sorry about the food. If I'd brought a bow –'

'It wouldn't be much use with that arm the way it is,' Ana said crisply. 'I never expected you to provide me with sumptuous meals and a soft feather bed, Faolan. I grew up in the islands. It wasn't a pampered existence.'

'All the same,' he said, 'I would wish to provide for you, at least. I've done a poor job thus far.'

'If it helps,' Ana said, 'I will tell you that, of all the people I know, you are the one I would choose to walk by my side and be my protector on such a journey as this. I would have no other.'

He was mute.

'It wasn't like that when we set out from White Hill. I resented those riding lessons. You had such a disapproving air about you, and I dislike being judged by people who haven't made the effort to know me. I'm sorry you cannot stay long at Briar Wood.'

'I'm not sorry,' he said, feeling a strong distaste for the prospect of seeing her wed to a man who valued her only for her blood line; thinking that perhaps this journey had sent him somewhat crazy, since such thoughts had no place in the head of a hired guard. And, having chosen to put his past entirely behind him, that was indeed all he was.

'Oh,' said Ana, her head drooping like a wilting flower.

'I didn't mean – I meant –'

'I understand, Faolan,' she said with careful courtesy, picking up the comb again. 'You must get back to White Hill. You must take Bridei the news of our terrible losses, and tell him the alliance with Alpin is sealed.'

'I'll stay for one turning of the moon at the very least. Bridei's instructions were precise. He doesn't want a formal handfasting until I'm certain of Alpin's loyalty.'

To this, Ana had nothing to say.

'Or if you . . . should you . . .' No, he would not put this into words.

'If I don't take to him? I don't think that was ever a factor,' Ana said tightly.

'Ana –'

'What?'

Faolan had a leaf between his fingers; he twisted and twirled it. 'I've asked you this before, but I'll ask it again. If you . . . if there were no duty, if you had free choice, what would you do now?'

She was silent a little, pondering the question. Then she said in a whisper, 'I can't lie to you. I would ask you to take me home. Back to White Hill. I think I would rather grow old as a maiden aunt to Derelei than go through with this journey. At heart I'm a terrible coward. What about you?'

'Me?'

'Given free choice, what would you do?'

'I can't tell you,' he said. 'Besides, I can't have free choice. I sacrificed it long ago.'

'You mean, to serve Bridei?'

He shook his head. 'Oh, no. That was a liberation of sorts. This was far earlier. When I was a boy.'

'Will you tell me that story?'

Her voice was very sweet to his ears; he felt the danger in it and drew himself back from the brink. 'It's not worth telling,' he said. 'We have two days; then you become Lady Ana once more and I melt into the anonymity of Alpin's household to do the work Bridei pays me for.'

'I'm glad you will be staying,' Ana said, 'if only for a little. Bridei said you were a good friend, and I told him I found it hard to believe. I believe it now.'

'Bridei is all too ready to bestow the status of friend on those who are no more than loyal servants.'

'That's rubbish and you know it,' said Ana. 'He relies on your good counsel, your strength, your support. He sees through the walls you build around yourself. And you, I think, have stood by him in his own times of self-doubt.'

Faolan remembered the winter when he had first been assigned to Bridei; himself and his fellow guards keeping vigil with a shattered and sickened young nobleman after his first and only observance of the Gateway sacrifice at the Well of Shades. He recalled a desperate ride through the snow from Caer Pridne to Pitnochie, and a valiant old horse that had carried him to Bridei's side in time for him to fish the future king, half-drowned, from the seer's pool. Ana was perceptive; she saw what he had believed well concealed.

'I want to ask a favour,' Ana said.

'What?'

'If we're going to arrive there in two days, I should make some effort to clean myself up. I'd like to appear presentable when Alpin first sees me. There's a pool downstream, and it feels as if the day will be warm. I want to bathe and wash my hair and put my old clothes on. You can have these ones back; they're cleaner than what you're wearing. You could do with a wash yourself.'

He looked across at her then, imagining himself in Alpin's shoes as the travellers walked out of the woods and up to the gate of the fortress. She was lily-pale and her face was smudged with ash from the fire. In his tunic and trousers, with his belt tied around her narrow waist, she looked every corner a woman. The too-large garments failed to conceal the graceful curves of her body, the high, round breasts, the swell of her hips, the shapely thighs. She was replaiting her hair now; the dust of the journey had darkened its ashen flow to the colour of honey and subdued its floating exuberance, but still it was a thing of rare loveliness, a silken waterfall, a swathe of living light, a cloak of springtime. He looked into her eyes, the honest, clear grey eyes that seemed to speak straight to his heart. 'Your misgivings are groundless,' he said. 'Alpin will be satisfied, believe me.' And he wanted to tell her, *You are beautiful*, but he silenced those words before they left his lips.

A delicate blush rose to Ana's cheeks; she held his gaze as if seeking to ascertain if he were, indeed, capable of lying merely to please her. 'I would like to wash, all the same,' she said. 'For my own sake as much as Alpin's. To look my best – or at least to make a small effort towards it – would give me courage.'

'You need courage for this, after all you have done? After what you did at the ford? You risked your own life to save me.' He was incredulous.

Ana looked down at her hands. When she answered, her voice was like a child's. 'I'm very afraid of this, Faolan. I need all the help I can get.'

They lingered by the stream. They spoke little, but rested quietly, content in each other's company. The horse grazed unhobbled; here in this gentle cup of the land the grasses grew sweet and lush, and the beast found no reason to wander. It was, Faolan thought, a day he would put away in his memory and keep like a precious talisman to sustain him when this was over. He knew that, for him, there could never be another such day, a brief span of time that seemed to stand outside the ordinary life of a man or woman; a day that was not part of the turbulent flow of affairs but, quite simply, a gift.

By midday it was warm enough for him to discard his boots and tunic and lie on the grass in his travel-stained shirt and trousers. Ana was sitting on the rocks by the stream, dangling her bare feet in the water and humming to herself. Faolan got up, intending to tell her that if she insisted on bathing, now would be a good time. He had taken one step towards her when a sound made him freeze in place. Ana went very still; she had heard it too. Movement in the woods beyond their small sanctuary: voices, hoof beats, a jingle of harness.

They had rehearsed this, weary as they were those first days after the disaster at the ford. By the time the riders came into view between the pines on the hillside above them, Faolan was standing strong and defiant, a throwing knife in his left hand and his short sword in his right, and Ana was behind him, gripping the weapon he had given her.

The riders advanced in single file. These men did not wear the blue headbands of the earlier attackers. Red seemed to be their colour; it was blazoned on their tunics in the form of a scarlet dog, marking them out as members of a household whose chieftain bore this kin symbol. They were big men, as was the nature of the Caitt, tall, broad-shouldered and distinguished by flowing hair and full beards, some plaited, some left to their natural bushiness. They came down the hill and halted, moving so their leader was flanked by a man on either side; both of these bore thrusting-spears, and the tips of their weapons were pointed with accuracy at Faolan's heart. He stood relaxed, calculating the required trajectory for his throwing knife and knowing he would not use it, not with Ana here. To attempt a defence was to ensure his own demise and her capture.

'Well, well,' drawled the man in the centre, grinning, 'what have we here?' He made no attempt to dismount. 'Your name and business?' This came in a different tone, sharp and dangerous.

'I might ask you the same,' Faolan said evenly. 'As you see, I have a lady with me, and we are in some difficulty, having suffered a serious mishap at the ford some distance from here. The lady is weak and distressed. We require your assistance, not an inquisition.'

The Caitt leader eyed him closely. His expression was less than warm. 'Only a fool traverses that path in time of spring thaw,' he said. 'What is your errand? Where are your warrior markings? You have the semblance of a Gael, and the accent to match it. And what's this about a lady?'

'I am –' Faolan began, and then Ana stepped out from behind him, the knife in her hand, and all eyes went to her. The Caitt leader's gaze passed up and down her body, measuring, assessing; his brows rose in disdain and his nose wrinkled as at an offensive smell. A black rage possessed Faolan; his fingers tightened on his knife.

'My greeting to you,' said Ana sweetly. 'I am a kinswoman of Bridei, King of Fortriu, and am on my way to Briar Wood. The accident that befell us had nothing to do with spring thaw. We were attacked and had no choice but to attempt a crossing at the ford. There was a . . .' She faltered.

'A flash flood,' Faolan said. 'Our escort was swept away.'

The Caitt leader dismounted; his two guards maintained the position of the spears and, behind him, others moved in with weapons in hand.

'I prefer to speak with the lady,' the leader said with a slight emphasis on the final word that was deeply insulting. Faolan's fingers itched to silence the man with a quick blow to the throat. It would only take a moment. 'Your name, my dear?' the fellow enquired.

Ana took a deep breath. 'You offend me,' she said calmly. 'I am nobody's "dear". My name is Ana, daughter of Nechtan, princess of the royal blood of the Light Isles. I journey to Briar Wood as the intended bride of the chieftain Alpin. I need your help. An escort as far as his stronghold, if you can provide that. We've travelled from the ford under some difficulty. Our baggage was lost and my companion is wounded.'

'Your companion. And who is he, precisely?'

Faolan and Ana replied at the same time.

'I am –'

'He is –'

Their eyes met. Faolan read in Ana's the doubt he himself had begun to feel. These could not be Alpin's men; they would have known travellers from White Hill were expected. There was danger here. Ana had identified herself; she was, at the least, a potential hostage, a trade item of significance. And Faolan was a source of information. He knew from past experience what that could mean.

'My court musician,' said Ana smoothly, sending a jolt of pure horror through him, followed by a reluctant recognition of her cleverness in thus rendering him instantly harmless. 'His name's Faolan. The only one of my escort to survive the flood.' The wobble in her voice owed nothing to artifice. 'You're not to harm him. He is no threat to you.'

The Caitt leader eyed the weapons in Faolan's hands, the stance he had adopted, legs apart, shoulders square. 'Doesn't look much like a bard to me,' he grunted.

'I have no other protectors left,' Ana said softly. 'Faolan's doing his best. Please remove the spears. You're frightening us.'

It was uncomfortable to be so neatly emasculated in a few carefully chosen words. However, Ana's ploy seemed to be working. The leader gave a curt nod and his men withdrew their weapons a handspan or two.

'If you will not help us,' Ana said, 'you will allow us to pass unhindered, I trust. We will make our own way to Briar Wood. If this is the right path?' She attempted a placatory smile. Faolan could see how frightened she was, and how angry.

The Caitt leader grinned suddenly, white teeth flashing in a face covered, above the lush beard, with intricate tattooing. His arms, solid as tree limbs, bore rings of the same decoration, spirals, twists and running creatures, battle scenes and flying birds. 'Goban! See if you can find a horse for the lady. Erdig! Help her gather up her gear, such as it is. You,' looking at Faolan through narrowed eyes, 'don't move. Drop your weapons.'

'I won't take orders from a man who will not give his name,' Faolan said quietly, knowing this was not the right answer from a hired musician, but unable to summon a more servile response.

'How unfortunate,' the leader said, taking a step closer and putting his hand to his own sword.

'Faolan!' said Ana sharply. 'Do as he says!'

With bitterness in his heart, Faolan dropped his knife and short sword to the ground and put up his hands.

'That's better,' said the Caitt leader. 'Mordec, put these knives away somewhere safe. We wouldn't want our bard here cutting himself, would we? I expect we'll all enjoy some fine entertainment later – the harp maybe? I've heard the Gaels have a talent for that.' There was a rumble of laughter. 'We don't get much of it in these parts.'

'He's wounded,' Ana said. 'There will be no playing yet awhile. Not until . . .' She fell silent. One of the men was leading forward a pony from the back of their line, a well-groomed creature of pearly hue, whose saddle and bridle were of fine leather decorated with ornate silverwork. The mane was plaited, the long tail combed to a fine sheen. It was unmistakably a mount for a lady. Faolan saw her look up at the Caitt leader. Her eyes were accusatory.

'You knew we were coming,' she said. 'Who are you? Why are you playing games with us?'

The leader grinned anew, as if mightily pleased with himself, and strode over to seize Ana's hand in his own huge paw. Faolan forced himself to remain still.

'Ah, you see through my little joke! I am Alpin, my dear, and these are the men of Briar Wood. You are safe now. We thought it possible you might be close to our borders by this time and took it upon ourselves to ride out and welcome you. We did not expect to find you without your escort and in such a state of disarray.' His eyes ran up and down her figure again. Now that he stood closer, their expression was somewhat altered. Faolan liked it even less than the disgust the fellow had shown before. 'Your bard has been forced to lend you his own clothing, I take it. Just as well he is a harmless musician. As your intended husband, I might well take offence at such a gesture of familiarity.'

'Such games as these do not amuse me, my lord,' Ana said. 'Once you have heard the full story of my journey here, you will see that jesting is not appropriate. Such small matters as the need to wear inappropriate clothing count for little when one's companions have been drowned before one's eyes. Of course I would have wished to appear before you dressed like a lady. The gods did not permit that. I thank them that my life was spared, and that of Faolan here. The river took ten souls that day, and the men who ambushed us killed another. Against that, what is the loss of a bride chest? What is a little humiliation?'

'Our humour is too crude, perhaps, for the kin of King Bridei,' Alpin said, not smiling now. 'You will become accustomed to it in time. As for the other, the amenities of my household will be available to you, of course, and more seemly attire. We are not barbarians. It is as well we came out to meet you. The inner reaches of Briar Wood are not easily traversed by strangers. The paths can be deceptive. Let me assist you to mount. That is one advantage of men's clothing, of course; it makes it easier for you to ride astride.'

Faolan heard one of the men joke to another under his breath, something about the lady being an expert rider thanks to having a tame bard to practise on at night. He saw Ana flush crimson with mortification, and felt his own hands ball into fists. A moment later Alpin was by the offender's side, hands on hips, glaring up at the man. 'Get down!' he ordered.

The fellow obliged; he, too, was a big man, but he was dwarfed by his chieftain. 'Repeat what you just said,' snapped Alpin.

'My lord, I –'

'Repeat it!' A fist thudded into the man's right cheek; he reeled back against his horse's side.

'I'm sorry, my lord. I –'

'Are you deaf, Lutrin? Put your filthy words forward for the gods to hear. Are you afraid now you realise that's my wife you're spreading your poisonous gossip about?' Another thump, this time to the left; it seemed Alpin was equally adept with either hand. Around them the Caitt warriors sat silent on their horses, watching with what seemed to be a degree of appreciation.

'I made a filthy suggestion about the lady and her bard, my lord,' Lutrin said faintly, staggering back. 'Clearly untrue. I regret it.'

'Not good enough,' Alpin growled, and let fly once more. This time his victim was sent sprawling with the force of the blow to lie motionless on the sward. His horse lifted its feet nervously.

'Take this horse, bard,' said Alpin. 'And remember that's the only piece of flesh you'll be putting your leg over in future. Leave him!' he barked as a couple of his own men made to tend to the fallen Lutrin. 'Let him make his own way back, if the forest allows it. And take heed, all of you. Insult my wife and you'll find yourselves in the same state.' He turned to Ana, whose face was still flushed red with embarrassment, as much from Alpin's own words, Faolan knew, as from Lutrin's ill-considered jest. 'Come, my dear,' Alpin said. 'Let's get you home.'

There was a sickness at White Hill. It had made itself apparent soon after the festival of Balance, and did not seem in a hurry to leave the royal household, despite the recitation of prayers, the burning of healing herbs and the brewing of time-tested remedies. In the men and women it manifested as a few days of fever along with an inflammation of the throat that made swallowing difficult. In the children it was more deadly.

The small daughter of Bridei's chief gatekeeper died on the fifth day of the illness. Bone Mother returned three days later for the infant son of a kitchen woman. This ailment gripped the young fiercely, testing the small bodies with racking, painful spasms of coughing. There were eight children under the age of ten living at White Hill, or there had been until the sickness came. The twin sons of Bridei's man Garth and his wife Elda were afflicted and recovered. They were sturdy boys, built like their father. Two small girls had been sent away to Banmerren at the first signs of illness in the house. Now Derelei was sick.

A few moons over one year old and slight of build like his

mother, Derelei looked a little flushed one day, and the next day was prone on a pallet, burning with fever and struggling for breath. He didn't cry much. Tuala wished he would cry. She wished he would fight. Bone Mother could take him all too easily, a scrap of a child the goddess could slip in her pocket and spirit away in the blink of an eye.

There were certain things that could be done, and Tuala did them with her mind in a daze, her heart paralysed with terror. She brewed curative potions. She kept a brazier supplied with soothing herbs and sponged her son's small body with cool water. She sang to him and stroked his fevered brow. When he could not breathe, she carried him about against her shoulder, for that seemed to ease his chest a little. She sent desperate prayers to the Shining One, prayers not of the formal kind: *Don't you know how much we love him? He's only little! Stop hurting him!*

When Bridei was there, which was as often as he could get away from the final preparations for his great council, Tuala tried to conceal from her husband how frightened she was. There was a bevy of serving women to help, but there were few to whom Tuala was prepared to trust Derelei's care at such a time of risk. Mara, the housekeeper from Pitnochie, was still at White Hill. Mara did not offer to help nurse Derelei, small children never having been her preferred companions. She simply took over most of Tuala's other responsibilities, seeing to the management of the household in the same dourly efficient manner she had applied to the running of Broichan's domain in the years when Bridei and Tuala were themselves children. In the evenings she would appear at Tuala's door with a spiced drink or wedges of bread and cheese on a platter, and order the Queen of Fortriu to put her feet up. 'You'll be no good to anyone if you're worn out from lack of sleep.'

Bridei, too, was reeling from exhaustion. By day he was closeted with his advisers, preparing not only for the imminent assembly – contrary to the word put about by his spies, it would not be at harvest time but before Midsummer – but also for the major undertaking they all knew would come in the autumn, whether the King of Circinn chose to support it or not. The assembly would be vital. It was the first time Drust the Boar had been persuaded to visit Bridei's court since Bridei had defeated the Christian Drust in the election for the kingship of Fortriu. Drust had hoped to extend his rule over both realms; this would have had the long-desired result of seeing Fortriu and Circinn once again united, but under Drust's Christian faith. That would have been an unthinkable catastrophe, a gross denial of the ancient faith of the Priteni, a faith to which Bridei had maintained unswervingly loyalty since the days of his childhood in Broichan's house.

In the five years of his kingship, Bridei had worked assiduously towards a wary peace with Drust the Boar. Obtaining the southern king's consent to travel to this assembly had been a coup and was generally taken to indicate Drust's readiness to support the armed struggle against Dalriada, a common foe. Others would attend with the King of Circinn, notably his influential adviser Bargoit. The chieftains of Fortriu were planning what might be said, and by whom, down to the finest detail. They worked long hours. Even Tharan was looking tired.

At night, when Derelei struggled with the cough, Bridei and Tuala stayed awake with him. Bridei walked up and down with his son in his arms, patting the child's back. Tuala rocked Derelei on her knee as she sat near a basin in which aromatic leaves, calamint and fennel, had been set to steep in hot water. The steam aided the child's breathing. When Derelei's eyelids did close at last for a brief spell, neither of his parents dared to sleep, lest he slip away from them unobserved. They listened for the small sound of his breathing, and held each other's hand, and knew that, whatever tests the gods had set them in the past, nothing could ever be as hard as this.

On the third day of Derelei's illness it was necessary for Bridei to ride to Caer Pridne; he would be gone a few days at least. The coastal fortress was now the headquarters for the king's military endeavours, overseen by his kinsman and war leader, Carnach of Thorn Bend. It was here that the great endeavour against the Gaels of Dalriada was in preparation. It had become necessary for the king himself to put in an appearance to hearten, inspire and challenge those who would all too soon be shedding their blood in his cause. Tuala knew Bridei did not want to go, not now. And she knew he had to go. She reassured him as best she could.

'Derelei seems a little better this morning. He's breathing more easily; the herbs help. Try not to worry too much, dear one.'

Bridei bent to kiss her on the brow; to touch a finger to his son's cheek, where the soft skin was hectically flushed. Then he left. His face was drawn and pale; it seemed to Tuala that he had reached that point of weariness where one scarcely understands what people are saying, and where one's own words, too, seem to have little sense. At least at Caer Pridne he might get a few nights' sleep.

The matter of Broichan had not been raised between them. Broichan, being a druid, was steeped in learning and skilled in herb lore. He had kept the old king alive for many turnings of the moon beyond what had seemed to all others the appointed time of his passing. Thus had he ensured that his foster son Bridei would be ready for the kingship when the opportunity offered itself. Tuala knew Broichan had been tending to other victims of this malady. He was a powerful seer and had the ear of the gods. Why not ask him for help? But Bridei had made no such suggestion, even with his little son burning in his arms. There was no need for him to say it. Tuala was afraid of Broichan. There were reasons for that, old reasons and new ones. She could not bring herself to trust him, especially with her son. She would not ask him and, knowing this, Bridei would not ask either.

With Bridei gone, Tuala felt very much alone, even though White Hill was full of folk. She longed for Ana. Ana's presence was restful; she went about her business quietly, spreading a feeling of warmth and calm, and she loved Derelei as if he were her own son. If Ana had been here, Tuala could have let go and wept, and not felt as if she were somehow letting everyone down. She wished with all her heart that Bridei had not sent Ana away. And she wished he had not sent Faolan either. Breth had travelled to Caer Pridne as Bridei's bodyguard, but Tuala did not think her husband's personal safety was ever really assured unless Faolan were somewhere near at hand. With the assembly almost upon them, she feared knives in the dark, sudden arrows, poisoned chalices. Even the best-loved king has his enemies.

It was a bad day. Derelei would not feed, and Tuala's breasts were aching and engorged with milk. She used a rag to dribble a few drops of cool water into the child's mouth, but what he swallowed came back up again not long after in a retching, painful spasm that left him limp and exhausted. Mara came and this time stayed, keeping up a supply of cooling cloths and tending the fire while Tuala paced with Derelei in her arms. The chamber had a sick smell, the smell of despair. From time to time Tuala tried the child on the breast, and from time to time he snuffled and moved his head as if he were hungry, and hope arose in her, only to be dashed as his head rolled away, the little mouth too weary to suckle. They tried the water again. They sponged him down, Tuala holding him while Mara patted the damp cloth over the hot skin. Tuala could see how her son's features were changing, the eyes growing sunken and distant, the skin taking on a greyish hue, the plump cheeks hollowing. He looked like a ghost of a child. The water in Mara's bowl rippled as the housekeeper dipped in her cloth. Quickly, Tuala averted her gaze. Mara said nothing at all, but it seemed to Tuala there was a message in her eyes. *Ask him. You're a fool if you don't, for you've nothing to lose.* And it came to Tuala that, if she did no more than this, the patient walking, the baths, the herbs, her son would not see another dawn.

'I'm going to fetch Broichan,' she said. 'I'll go as soon as we've got Derelei wrapped up again.'

'Aye,' said Mara. 'You do that. Chances are he'll be ready for you. Go now; I'll tend to the child. You've waited overlong. I never thought you'd be foolish enough to let pride rob you of your only son.'

And when Tuala stared at her, cold with shock, Mara said, 'Open your eyes, lass. You're not the only one who loves the little lad. Bridei would have had Broichan in here two days ago if he hadn't known you'd be set against it. Don't look like that. Go on, fetch him. Maybe there's still time.'

It was the longest speech Tuala had ever heard Mara make. Swallowing the tumult of feelings that arose in her, she made her way from her own quarters to Broichan's private chamber without being aware of moving at all.

105

It was not necessary to tap on the door. It opened as Tuala approached, and there stood the druid, tall and sombre in his dark robe, with a flat basket over his arm in which various items were neatly packed: a sheaf of herbs, candles, birch sticks, small vials and stoppered pots. Tuala looked up at him and saw on his features the selfsame look of exhaustion and anxiety that had shadowed Bridei's face in the moment of leaving. She saw that Mara was right. Broichan had been waiting for her to ask for help, waiting in despair that she would leave it too late for him to be able to save Bridei's son.

'I need your help.' It came out in a whisper.

Broichan nodded without speaking and fell in beside her as she turned to walk back to her own quarters.

'I've done everything I can,' she said. 'Everything. And he's still no better.'

'Everything?' Broichan's tone was mild. 'You have looked into your scrying mirror to examine his future? You dared that?'

Tuala shivered. 'No. Not that. You know I do not use those arts now; it is not fitting, as queen, that I draw attention to myself in such a way. Besides, I could not. Not for this. Not if I might see . . .' A terrible thought came to her. Was this why Broichan had not appeared before? 'You . . . you have done this? You have seen –?' She would not say it aloud. *You have seen my son's death and will not pit yourself against the will of Bone Mother.*

'No, Tuala.' Broichan's voice was a dark music, deep and resonant. 'I am not so strong. If I am to fight a battle for this child, I will go armed with hope. My scrying bowl is covered; thus it will remain until this scourge is gone from White Hill.'

'Can you save him?' Tuala heard her own voice shaking. They were at the door of her chamber; within, Mara could be heard moving about, muttering to herself. There was no sound from Derelei.

'The question is not so much can I save him,' Broichan said, opening the door, 'as will you allow me to treat him so that he can be saved? What lies in our past has been the cause of deep distrust between us, I know that. Why else would you leave this so long, until the ill is almost past mending?' He was standing now beside the pallet where the infant tossed in restless half-sleep. Mara, wringing out a cloth, watched with carefully neutral eyes. Broichan laid his hand on Derelei's brow. 'This is beyond herbs and potions,' he said. 'The flames of this fever scorch him; his heart is pushed to bursting point. Will you trust me?'

'Yes.' A whisper.

'Very well. I need to put the child into a deep sleep, a sleep so profound it may seem to you that Derelei is on the point of slipping away from us. Don't be alarmed. I will remain by his side and retain control. This will allow his small body the rest it so desperately needs, Tuala. He has almost exhausted his strength fighting this. I will pass him into the hands of the Shining One for a little. It can be difficult to watch. You may wish to retire and seek a period of rest for yourself. Mara can provide what assistance I need.'

'No,' Tuala croaked. 'I'm not leaving him.'

Broichan regarded her soberly. 'Very well. You will see a shadow pass over. You may feel a chill. That is to be expected. Trust me, Tuala. I will not let him go.'

She looked again at his shuttered features, the dark impenetrable eyes, the stark planes of cheek and jaw. Broichan seldom revealed what he felt. He laid his long hands, now, on either side of the child's flushed face and spoke in a voice that was soft and low, almost like singing.

'Derelei. Sleep now, little one. Dove and owl fly with you; salmon and otter swim by your side; deer and hare show you the secret pathways. Sleep now, Derelei. The Shining One watch over you and give you good dreams.' His thumbs moved against the little face; his eyes were different, soft with love yet bright with the power of the charm. Watching him, Tuala knew how cruel she had been to shut him out. She saw that her child was, indeed, as dear to the druid as he was to her and to Bridei. What the reason was for that she did not know, but she knew it had nothing to do with power or ambition or the playing of games. It was a true thing, an honest thing, and she had no right to stand in its way.

'Sleep now, valiant one. Rest from your great battle. Rest now, sheltered and secure. Save your strength. There will be good times ahead.'

Derelei was relaxed, lids shut, neat mouth slightly open. His arms were outstretched, the small hands closed on themselves as if he held secrets there. Broichan began to make signs in the air above the infant's face and to chant rapidly in a tongue unknown to Tuala. The room seemed to darken and the air grew chill as if an icy breath had penetrated the solid walls. Tuala clenched her teeth, remembering a night of Gateway, when the dark thing she saw in her scrying bowl had been almost too much to bear. Broichan was not infallible. What if he were wrong about this? She could almost feel the clutch of Black Crow's claws in the quiet chamber; she could almost hear the beating of her dark wings. Lying defenceless on the pallet, Derelei looked very small. His face seemed to pale, as if the life were being sucked away before her eyes, and she saw the laboured rise and fall of his chest slow until his breathing was hardly discernible. One by one, the candles set about the room guttered and died of themselves. In the gloom, Derelei's skin looked grey and dead. He seemed now not so much relaxed and peaceful as sprawled like a victim awaiting the knife. Mara poked the fire, whose fitful light barely touched the dark corners of the chamber.

Broichan's chant went on, weaving its way into Tuala's head, filling her mind with its insidious power until she, too, felt an overwhelming weariness, a profound wish to give herself into the goddess's keeping, to rest, to heal, to enter a time of darkness that was like a little death. Her legs would no longer hold her.

'Here, lass,' Mara said, pushing a stool into place at the foot of the pallet, and Tuala collapsed onto it as the invocation continued. Now, as he chanted, Broichan was performing a ritual around the deeply sleeping infant: scattering herbs on Derelei's chest and groin and over his hands, anointing his brow with a pungent oil and setting a single small flower on each of his eyelids. Tuala shivered, thinking of death. She had to trust; she had seen the love in Broichan's eyes.

Now the druid opened a tiny pot and, taking out a pinch of a reddish powder, made an outline all around the child's sleeping form, a ward against intruders, a safe barrier. The smell of the herb made Tuala want to sneeze. Derelei did not stir; he lay as if he would never move again. In the half-dark Tuala could not see the tiny rise and fall of his breathing. She reached out to touch him for reassurance, for he seemed like a discarded toy, limp and helpless. Broichan's hand came out, fastening on her wrist, holding her back. His chant flowed on without pause. Tuala felt hot tears slipping down her cheeks. She closed her eyes and sent her own prayer to the Shining One. The goddess had always watched over her, always, even when she had believed herself quite friendless. How could the Shining One do less for Derelei? *Hope,* Broichan had said. *I will go armed with hope.*

The chant slowed, taking on the rhythm of a lullaby, and Broichan, his ritual complete, settled on his knees by the child's side. Mara touched a taper to the fire and began to light the candles, one by one. In a little while there was a warm glow in the chamber, and silence.

'We must let the child rest now,' Broichan said. 'Do not touch him; see, he breathes still, but slowly. This is a sleep deeper than man or woman knows, a sleep on the very margin of death. We must wait. I will watch over him. You should rest. There is nothing you can do here. Not until he begins to stir.'

Angry words were on the tip of Tuala's tongue, but she bit them back, swallowing the hurt. 'I will stay, all the same,' she said quietly. 'You need not keep vigil alone.'

Broichan glanced at her and away. There was no reading what was in his eyes.

'How long?' Tuala asked.

'I cannot tell you. You look exhausted. It has been a testing time. Rest while you can.'

'You, too, seem weary,' Tuala said. 'I think it is not only I, and Bridei, and our son who have been put to the test. I will stay with you. Mara, will you ask one of the women to bring mead and some food for us? And thank you for being here. For being so patient. You must go to your bed now.'

'Patient?' Mara echoed. 'Don't know if I'd call it that. I know when to speak and when to keep my mouth shut, that's all. I'll be away then. Some of us know better than to refuse a rest when it's offering. I'll send someone with a bit of supper for the two of you.'

Deep below the fortress of Caer Pridne, ancient seat of the kings of Fortriu, there was a place of dark ritual. The god whose power inhabited this chilly cave had no name, or none that might be spoken. He stood beyond the pantheon of deities who ruled the daily lives of Bridei's people: the Shining One, whose journey across the night sky governed the tides in all living things; the Flamekeeper, who loved men of courage and loyalty; the fair maiden All-Flowers and Bone Mother, keeper of dreams. This god had his small reflection within every man, hidden away in a part of them few would acknowledge. He was the Flamekeeper's other side, the shadow without which the substance cannot be, the chaos beneath the order, the turmoil at the very heart of existence. Year upon year, the Well of Shades had witnessed the death of a young woman in recognition of the Nameless One's hunger. Year upon year, the head priestess of Banmerren had prepared the victim and the King of Fortriu, with his druid by his side, had enacted the sacrifice. Until Bridei became king.

He had witnessed the ceremony only once. He had seen it, had taken part in it, and had known he could never let it happen again. The Gateway ritual took place at White Hill now, and there was no spilling of blood, no waste of young life, no terrible requirement to place duty before the most desperate clamouring of the human heart. That this change would have its cost, few doubted. Once before a king had defied the dark god. A shocking retribution had been exacted, a punishment that came close to extinguishing the Priteni forever. Bridei, steeped in lore and faultlessly loyal to the gods of his ancestors, nonetheless knew in his heart that his choice had been right. If there were consequences, then he would bear them.

The Well of Shades was closed up now and an iron gate set across the precipitous, narrow pathway that plunged down into the hill. Bridei waited while Breth unlocked the gate for him. He walked through with the little dog, Ban, at his heels and waited again while Breth closed the grille behind him.

'Will you wait?' he asked his bodyguard. 'I don't know how long I will be.'

'I'll be here.' Breth settled by the gate, a solid, reassuring presence. Higher up the path, atop one of the rising banks, a torch had been lit. The fresh breeze from the sea made it sputter and flare. Bridei descended the steps, a smaller brand held in his hand. The well was set deep into the hill and could only be reached by this single, improbably steep entry. The lower reaches were pitch dark; a preternatural cold arose from the cave below. Ban halted on the steps, shivering. Bridei glanced down at him.

'Guard!' he commanded, allowing Ban the dignity of performing a duty. The small creature was not lacking in courage; his long history proved that. Entering the chamber of the well, however, was more than should be expected of any creature. Ban settled, a white shadow on the dark stone steps, keeping faithful watch. Bridei went on down.

He could not come here without remembering that first time: the inky water, the torches, the dark-clad men and the solitary girl like a pale flower in her ceremonial robe. The old king, who had been deathly sick, his iron will struggling to rule his failing body. Broichan, tall and grim, a vessel for the terrible power of the nameless god. And the moment when King Drust had asked for aid and he, Bridei, was the only one who stepped forward. The moment when he had helped to drown a girl . . .

He set his torch in the iron socket by the entry and moved to kneel beside the water. The rectangular pool was bordered by a narrow stone shelf a handspan above the black surface. There was a cold breath here, a deathly thing that hummed and whispered into the corners of the chamber. Bridei closed his eyes and stretched his arms out to the sides in pose of meditation. He made himself utterly still. As the sky outside the sunken chamber turned to the violet of dusk and the dove-grey of a spring night, he knelt in silent vigil. Both Bridei and Broichan kept this observance each time they visited Caer Pridne, believing that the silent obedience of king and king's druid might ease, in part, the deity's anger that his dues no longer came in hot blood and living flesh.

Bridei was practised in the conduct of rituals. Broichan had kept him up on Midsummer Eve since he was barely four years old, and had ensured that his foster son was as thoroughly steeped in lore as any druid. Tonight, however, presented a particular challenge. Derelei was dying; Bridei knew it, for all Tuala's reassuring words. There were particular prayers to be offered here, forms of words suited to this most perilous of gods, but Bridei's heart was full of an incoherent kind of prayer that had nothing to do with ritual practice. He fought to suppress it, pacing his breathing, maintaining his still pose, fixing his mind on the sequence of statements Broichan had taught him as the appropriate ones for the time and place:

I breathe into the dark
I breathe into the stillness
I breathe into the centre of the dark
I bend as the wheat stalks before the wind
I bend as the birches before the gale
I bend under the flail of his breath
Oldest of all . . .

But under the solemn words, others clamoured to be heard; under the steady rise and fall of his chest was the chaotic breath of panic; under the even beat of the meditative heart was the wild, thumping lament of impending loss, the rending, the wailing, the things a king did not give vent to, not even when he was a young father and his little son was a hair's-breadth from Bone Mother's long embrace.

Beneath the earth lies the great stone
Beneath the stone lies the fire
Beneath the fire lies the ash, the dust
Beneath the dust, the breath
Rise and fall.

The words came freely, steady and sure; he had been expertly trained. The tears that were rolling down his cheeks were not part of Broichan's teaching.

Cleanse, Fire
Strip to the bare bone
Drown, Flood
Deeper than whale's way
Scourge, Wind

Score away kith and kin
Swallow, Stone
Silence all story
Way for him: Shadow-Master,
Oldest of all.

The words helped him. Their patterns had been so well learned they flowed almost despite him. He had become aware, over the years of his childhood, that such discipline held firm against the most powerful assaults. At length the words had all been spoken and there was only the chamber, and the water, and the silence. Bridei held his pose, back straight, arms outstretched; the torchlight threw his shadow across the cave, an eagle, a sword hilt, a cross. The little cold draughts moved around him, murmuring in his ears. *Gone. Gone. He's gone.* And he heard his own voice replying, its tone not the steady, even chant of formal prayer nor yet the anguished scream of his heart, but a whisper.

'I do not seek to bargain; I understand that is not possible. Know only that I am loyal. I love the gods of Fortriu and have sworn to keep my people true to the ancient ways. I do not ask for favours. Why should my son's life be of any greater value than the lives of other children already taken by this plague? I tell you simply that he is my son, and that I love him. And that he is innocent. He is not only mine, but Tuala's; in this she, too, is mortally wounded, she who has always been a treasured daughter of the Shining One.' In his head, Bridei heard in answer to this: *She knew from the first that you would be king. She understood what it would mean to love you.*

Bridei swallowed and went on. 'I tell you that if this is the punishment you have chosen for my failure to keep tradition, then I must accept it. And I tell you that it rivals in cruelty the sacrifice itself, for each sees the crushing of a life new-minted, fresh and good. Such obedience as you require of me is a heavy yoke to bear. But I am king, and I will bear it.'

Chapter Five

She'd been foolish to identify Faolan as a bard, Ana thought. The king's personal emissary was supposed to put Bridei's terms to Alpin and secure the Caitt chieftain's firm agreement not to ally himself with the Gaels. He was meant to smooth the way for her and ensure the handfasting did not occur unless the treaty was signed. Now he would not be able to do any of that. She hadn't liked the look in those men's eyes, for it had seemed to spell either a summary execution or the extraction of a confession by whatever means they fancied. She'd only wanted to protect Faolan. Now they were almost at Briar Wood and, with a sinking feeling, Ana realised she was going to have to do the negotiating herself.

The pines here were as tall as towers, the slopes erratic and the ground studded with bizarre clusterings of rocks that resembled creatures found only in tales: grinning goblin, earth-dragon, padfoot, crouching monster. Sometimes Ana thought she saw them move, extending a clawed finger, a stubby tail, a pair of unlikely furred ears. Sometimes she heard things flying overhead from tree to tree, things that were most certainly not birds, for they creaked and whined as they passed. There were birds as well, many, many birds, all kinds. Crows perched beside the track, greeting the travellers with derisive cries. Pipits and wrens hopped amongst the undergrowth. Higher up, from time to time, could be heard the calls of siskin and crossbill. In the bushes were constant rustlings, and Ana saw furred creatures streak up and down the pines, their small bodies arrow-swift. In the air countless insects buzzed and whined; no wonder birds congregated here.

The paths were certainly tricky. Often the men paused to confer before going on, even though they must be familiar with this forest. Sometimes there seemed no real track at all, just a precipitous, stony incline, or a wide patch of bog choked with fallen trees, or the narrowest of gaps between twisted, thorny bushes. The place had a wild beauty, a dangerous beauty. Ana wondered how she and Faolan would have found their way.

She couldn't see Faolan now. Alpin had insisted she ride near the front of the line, just behind him, and her bard had been relegated to the rear. At White Hill, as at the court of her cousin in the Light Isles, skilled musicians were held in high esteem, for were they not weavers of dreams and tellers of inmost truths? The best were considered to have the ear of the gods. Attitudes at Briar Wood were evidently different. The Caitt were known as a wild and warlike people. Perhaps they had no music. Ana shivered. The broad, leather-clad shoulders of her future husband were constantly in view as she rode after him. His dark brown hair, long and thick, hung down his back, not unkempt exactly, but suggestive of a certain quality she had seen already in his questioning of Faolan and his crude attempts at humour. He did not seem a particularly refined sort of man. Ana wondered how many women there might be at Briar Wood and who they were. Perhaps Alpin had sisters, a mother. Some of these warriors would have wives. Perhaps they could tell her how it might be possible to tolerate living amongst such men.

The forest clung thickly around the stone walls of Alpin's stronghold. Thatched roofs came into view as the travellers crested a rise, and near them was the sudden glint of a lake, glimpsed then lost as they began to descend again. Nearer to the fortress, pine gave way to dark oak and tall elm, new leaves fresh under the spring sunshine. An image came to Ana: Faolan lying relaxed on the sward in his shirt sleeves, and herself dipping bare feet into the stream as if she were a child set free from lessons. She marvelled that it belonged to the same day as this ride, these alien warriors, these high, forbidding walls. This coarse stranger whom she must somehow train herself to tolerate. With whom she must, all too soon, share her bed.

They reached the gates, which were swung open from within at Alpin's shout, and entered a courtyard surrounded by stone buildings: a substantial dwelling house, a barn, places for stock and supplies and, Ana supposed, everything needed to maintain a large household in what seemed an extraordinarily out-of-the-way place. The high walls encompassed all, shutting out the forest, though here and there elms stretched their heads above the topmost row of stones.

Alpin helped her down. Ana did not care for the way his hands lingered on her body as he did so, nor the way he grinned at her discomfiture. She stood very still, waiting for him to take his hands away. She tried not to meet his eyes. She looked past him to the other riders, no longer in a line but gathered close. Her gaze met Faolan's. His expression struck a chill of unease through her, for this was a man who had ever schooled his features expertly. Ana knew, because Tuala had explained it to her, that a man whose trade was spy and assassin must learn to be invisible. He may have feelings, but he learns not to let them show. Faolan was not abiding by those rules now. His eyes were bright with fury.

Ana looked away. He must learn to play the game differently. He would need to adapt to the new rules she had set when she named him her bard and took away his authority. She had nobody to blame for that but herself.

'I am quite weary,' she said. Alpin had finally let go of her waist and was regarding her a little quizzically. Dirty, unkempt and exhausted as she was, not to speak of her male attire, it seemed important to take the initiative early. 'If it's possible to have the assistance of a serving woman . . . a quiet chamber . . . some hot water . . .'

'My own apartments are at your disposal, of course,' Alpin said smoothly. Beneath the silken tone there was a note of mockery that made Ana deeply uncomfortable.

'Thank you, but that would not be appropriate. Later I will set out Bridei's terms for you. But not until I have bathed, changed my clothes and rested. I require my own apartment. A chamber of reasonable size. A door with a bolt. And I expect my man to be well looked after. He was wounded and nearly drowned. I want your reassurance that he will be not merely safe, but well fed and comfortably housed.'

'You are solicitous for his wellbeing.'

'My lord Alpin,' said Ana, 'I set out from Bridei's court at White Hill with an escort of twelve. This man is the only one I have left. Of course I am solicitous. I will be seriously displeased if you cannot, or will not, accommodate my wishes on this matter. And on the other.' She had not expected it would be necessary to lay down the law to him, and she found her hands were shaking. Fear and anger made it increasingly hard to maintain a calm demeanour.

'A bolt, is it? That would be on the inside?' Alpin looked around the circle of men. 'Lads, she's only known me an afternoon and already she doesn't trust me!' A ripple of laughter came from the warriors. 'Ah well, chances are I have forgotten how a lady should be treated. Once you've had your bath and we've consigned that outfit to the midden, perhaps I'll find it easier to get back into the way of it.' There were serving men and women coming from the house now, and Alpin snapped his fingers in their general direction. 'Orna! This lady needs your assistance. Take her inside and see to her needs; find her a maidservant. The lady will be wanting a chamber of her own. Put her next to me.'

'Yes, my lord.' Orna was tall and broad like the men, with features every bit as forbidding. Her hair was caught back under a linen kerchief of dubious cleanliness.

'Thank you,' Ana said politely.

'It pleases me to please you, my dear.' Alpin's tone could only be described as uxorious, and it made her skin crawl. Finding nothing to say, she turned her back and followed Orna into the house.

Some time later, sitting on a bench as a nervous girl combed her newly washed hair for her, Ana was forced to admit that her future husband had indeed provided everything she had requested. Demanded. She felt embarrassed, now, at how sharp she had been. Once inside the house, which proved to be many-chambered and grand in scale, though dark and smoky, Orna had rapped out a series of orders and folk had scampered to obey them. Ana had been led to a chamber furnished with a sizeable shelf bed, an oak chest for storage and two benches. The only window was a tiny slit and there was no hearth, but it was tolerably warm, for there were dusty woollen hangings on the walls, their patterns faded to a uniform dun colour.

An iron tub was fetched, and a copious supply of water, hot and cold. Coarse soap; coarser cloths for drying. A comb, scented oils, candles in heavy holders. Herbs for the bath: chamomile and peppermint. Lastly, this handmaid, shy and stammering. Ludha had proved adept with jug and ladle and had scrubbed Ana's skin until it tingled. It was wonderful to be clean at last, but not quite as wonderful as she had imagined it through the weary days of travel, when the thought of warm water and a soft bed had helped sustain her. How could she give herself up to the pleasure of the steady combing, the feeling of fresh linen on her skin, the sweet scent of lavender against her temple where Ludha had dabbed a drop of oil, when there was so much to worry about? The treaty; the lie she had told; Faolan. And Alpin. How could you marry a man when his touch made you cringe in disgust?

'Ludha?' Ana asked.

'Yes, my lady?' The little voice was whisper soft. The comb moved gently, teasing out the knots.

'The man who came here with me, Faolan, my bard – do you know where he is?'

'No, my lady. Do you wish to send for him?'

'No, Ludha.' Ana tried for authority. 'Of course he cannot come here to my private apartments. I simply wish to be sure he is safe.'

'Safe?' Ludha sounded astonished. 'Oh, yes, my lady, he will be quite safe here. Briar Wood is very well defended. My –' a blush, 'my friend, Foldec, says nobody could get near us here. Lord Alpin has the biggest army in the whole of the north.' Ludha fell abruptly silent.

'Tell me more,' Ana said. 'This Foldec, he's a warrior?'

'Yes, my lady.' Proud now, Ludha gave a charming smile. 'An archer in my lord's forces. He's away just now in the west. Foldec's had his warrior marks three years already; he earned them when he was just fifteen.'

'He must be very brave,' Ana said with a smile of encouragement.

'Oh, yes, my lady.'

'And what do you do while you're waiting for him to come home, Ludha?'

'Sewing, my lady. There are plenty who can do the plain jobs, hemming and mending, tunics and other gear for the men. But I was taught by my mother; she was seamstress to a lady. They give me all the fine work.'

'Did you make this?' The clothing Ana had been given was plain but of good quality, a tunic and skirt of fine wool dyed russet, with borders of embroidered flowers. There had been smallclothes as well, and soft kidskin slippers.

'No, my lady. Orna found those in store. They're from a girl who used to live here, a maidservant to Lord Alpin's first wife.' Ludha faltered. 'Sorry, my lady,' she muttered.

'No need to apologise,' Ana said. 'I know Lord Alpin was married before. Tell me, has he any family, apart from the natural son they speak of, who I understand does not live here at Briar Wood? I know there were no children of that first marriage, but perhaps Alpin has sisters or brothers?'

Unaccountably, Ludha flushed scarlet. 'I don't rightly know, my lady.' She busied herself with the comb once more; this time she was less careful, and Ana winced.

'I'll finish that, Ludha. I'm used to doing it for myself. I hope you'll show me your work some time; I have a particular interest in embroidery. I had a collection of little shirts and other garments for a baby. They were all lost at the river crossing when my escort was swept away. It shouldn't matter; against the loss of so many lives, such a thing becomes quite trivial. But it made me sad, all the same. There was a great deal of love in those stitches.'

Ludha nodded in sympathy. 'Yes, my lady. Still, a mother loves her child even if she has only rags to put him in. At least, that's what I think.'

Abruptly, Ana found herself on the verge of tears. 'Yes, well,' she said briskly, 'perhaps you and I will do some sewing together. As you see, I have nothing at all to wear. Nothing of my own.'

'It would be a pleasure to help, my lady,' Ludha said.

'Where would I begin finding out about bolts of cloth and suchlike?'

'Talk to Orna,' Ludha said. 'She seems fierce, but she'll help you all she can. All of them will. All of them are saying . . .' She hesitated.

'What are they saying?'

'It's not my place to repeat it, my lady, but they're saying a new wife for my lord Alpin might be the best thing that's happened here for years. Orna does everything in the house. She gives all the orders. But even she would rather be working for a lady. And we could see that was what you were from the first glance.'

Ana thought about this. 'Were you here when Lord Alpin's first wife was alive, Ludha? Can you tell me about her?'

'I came here after she was gone, my lady. Had to find a new place for myself when my mother was taken by an ague. Orna hired me, seeing the fine work I could do.'

'I'm sorry about your mother. Are there many people here who knew her? His first wife?'

Ludha was suddenly busy with tidying the accoutrements of the bath, folding cloths, anything she could set her hand to.

'Ludha?'

'Folk don't talk about it much.'

'How did she die?'

No reply. Ludha began to dip the bathwater back into its jugs and buckets for ease of removal.

'How did she die, Ludha?'

'I don't rightly know, my lady. She was expecting a child, that's what they say. The two of them died together. It was a long while ago, six or seven years at least.'

'Oh.' This was the most likely explanation, of course. Such a death, though doubly sad, was common enough. Ana was able to summon a twinge of sympathy for Alpin. He must have loved her a great deal, and grieved long, to wait so many years before seeking another wife, another chance for children. But then, he had not exactly sought Ana. It was more the other way around.

'You'll be wanting to rest,' Ludha said. 'I'll call a boy to take away these things and then leave you to yourself, if that suits.'

'What?' Ana had not been listening. 'Oh, yes, of course. Will you come and fetch me when it's time for supper? You're right, I am very tired.'

Sleep did not come, for all the soft mattress and good linen. At the back of her mind was the ford, the wave, the broken bodies and the heart-clutching terror of being all alone. Ana suspected that would be with her every day for the rest of her life. Then there were the immediate concerns. She rehearsed, over and over, what must be said to Alpin and how she would do it. The marriage was contingent upon his forming an alliance with Bridei, not Gabhran of Dalriada. Bridei was not asking him to fight alongside the men of Fortriu, although another Caitt chieftain, Umbrig, had pledged a band of warriors to that purpose. That particular piece of information, Ana thought, was probably not to be passed on. But Alpin had to understand that a sworn agreement was required, written down if possible, that he and his men would not take up arms against Bridei, either by land or by sea. It was the 'by sea' part that was most important; it was his access to the western sea route to Dalriada that made Alpin such an important player. If Alpin agreed to Bridei's terms, Faolan would take the news of it back to White Hill and the handfasting would go ahead.

Ana wished very much that she could discuss this with Faolan in private before she needed to broach the subject with Alpin. What she knew of it was the broad framework only. There was a lot more detail, which Bridei's personal emissary held in his head, and which was almost certainly terribly important. The fates of armies depended on getting this right and doing it quickly. The more Ana thought about it, the angrier she was with herself for her ill-conceived attempt to protect Faolan with a lie. She had really messed things up. She must make quite sure she did this perfectly from now on.

She tried to imagine what Alpin might wish to know. Questions about strategy: she would have to answer truthfully and say she knew little of such matters. What if he asked her about the alternative? If he refused the offer, what was she going to do? She could hardly ride out of Briar Wood with Faolan and attempt the long journey home with only one horse between the two of them and the ford washed out, not to speak of those blue-clad attackers. She would have to stay here at least until the rivers went down, and she would have to ask Alpin for an escort through the places of danger.

Perhaps the best course of action was to tell the truth: confess that she had lied and why, and let Faolan do the job he had come here to do. Ana considered this. It was undoubtedly sensible; it was probably what her friend Ferada would suggest. *Don't be so silly, Ana, just tell the man the truth. He won't bite your head off.* Yet she hesitated. Quite apart from the fact that Alpin would think her wayward and stupid, his manner filled her with unease. There was danger here, she sensed it.

A little sound from the slit-like window interrupted Ana's thoughts. She turned her head. There on the sill was a tiny bird, a wren, neat in its plumage of brown and cream. It perched there motionless, head tilted to one side, bright eye fixed on her. Ana was charmed. The creature seemed so fearless; surely no wood-land bird would venture so close to human habitation and stay there so calmly. Indeed, this habitation was a particularly unlikely place for birds to linger: on the way from the front door to her chamber Ana had seen no fewer than nine cats in the house, most of them made in a similar mould to the men and women of Briar Wood, sturdy and muscular.

Ana sat up in bed, arms around her knees, regarding her small visitor. She gave a soft whistle. The wren shifted a little; its eye did not leave her. Now that Ana thought about it, she had seen that look before, intent, watchful, as if the creature had some purpose of its own in seeking her out. Had not the hooded crow at the ford turned its penetrating eye on her with just such con-centration? That had unsettled her. But the hoodie had proved a friend. Without its help, she would have lost Faolan.

'What are you?' she murmured, getting out of bed as slowly as she could so as not to frighten the tiny bird away with a sudden movement. 'Where have you come from?'

The wren hopped along the sill; not far, since the window was so narrow. Ana had not looked out before. She came closer. The wren stayed where it was. She could have reached out and touched its soft feathers. Ana wondered if it had once been a lady's pet. Probably not; the look in its bright eye could scarcely be called tame.

'Who sent you?' she whispered, looking out the window at the sliver of view it offered. The chamber was high; she had climbed stone steps to reach it. From here she could see a stretch of forest, oak and elm, a scrap of pale sky and, if she edged to one side, part of the long, high wall that appeared to encircle the fortress. Ludha had said Briar Wood was very safe. This appeared inarguable; without Alpin's say-so, there would be no coming in and there would be no getting out. Ana felt suddenly cold.

The wren gave a warble and, as quickly as it had appeared, launched itself out of the window and away. Ana craned her neck to watch as it flew along the wall, arrow-straight, and downward out of sight. Wherever it was headed, it had not gone into the wildwood but to a place inside Alpin's fortress.

'Odd,' Ana said to herself. 'Very odd.' She wondered if Alpin had druids or wise women in his household. That could explain it. Such practitioners of the crafts of healing, divination and magic could be very close to their creatures. Fola had once had a huge cat, Shade, which had not seemed particularly magical, but with whom the wise woman's bond was clearly strong. If these birds were indeed the companions of Alpin's druid or priestess, Ana hoped she would get an explanation of why they seemed to be seeking her out.

By suppertime Faolan had acquainted himself with the layout of Alpin's stronghold. The fortress at Briar Wood had three levels: cellars for storage, living and working areas at ground level and a few higher chambers which included the chieftain's own apartments. Ana had been housed next to Alpin. Faolan had been given a pallet in the serving men's quarters. As soon as he'd been announced as a bard, Alpin's men-at-arms had begun to treat him as an amusing novelty rather than a person of genuine interest. Sharing his quarters with grooms and cooks might prove useful; such company was often a source of good intelligence.

The central courtyard was fringed with buildings backing up against the huge wall around Alpin's fortress. There was a smithy, a tannery, a bakehouse, a kennel packed with hunting hounds of fearsome appearance, a grain store, an armoury. Further down were barns and stables; it seemed little of this household's business was conducted outside the protection of the wall. In his mind Faolan made a new map: the run of the wall, the buildings each in its turn, the points where trees were tall enough to be seen above the barrier, reminding those inside that they were only a stone's throw from the great wood. He looked for entrances and exits; somewhere there must be a lesser opening in the wall, a back door, so to speak. A drain perhaps? A place where goods might be brought in without the need to heave open those great gates?

The questions he asked aloud did not concern such matters. His queries were carefully structured to seem innocuous, to be soon forgotten. They were designed to encourage people to give him what he needed without knowing they had done so. Faolan had been a spy a long time and he was good at it.

It was not possible to go far afield that first day. They had reached Briar Wood in the late afternoon, the last part of the ride having been quicker than he anticipated with Alpin's escort showing the way, and by the time Faolan was settled and had visited the stables to check on his horse and exchange a word or two with the men who worked there, it was growing dark. He would save night explorations until these folk grew accustomed to his presence amongst them.

There was a corner of the fortress that caught his attention, a place where it seemed to him the wall doubled, creating a narrow space bordered on both sides by high stone barriers. There was no apparent entry point to this area, but the wall showed a slight curving inwards for the length of perhaps fifteen strides; beyond it, Faolan judged, there might be sufficient room for a hidden courtyard or chamber. What might one value so highly that one set it away thus? A store of arms? A cargo of spices or silks that might be offered to a powerful enemy as a bribe? Or perhaps there was something of a different nature behind that odd contour of construction. Perhaps it was not a bulwark against intrusion but a barrier to keep something in, something too dangerous to be housed in ordinary confinement such as the barn, kennels, cellars. A prison? Surely not. What captive requires such elaborate concealment? Shackles and a big guard or two were all a competent chieftain required to keep men confined. True, once or twice Faolan himself had made an escape from that kind of security, but he did not count himself as an ordinary prisoner. It was his job to be one step ahead, one level better; it was one of his codes for survival. Ah well, there was time to discover the truth about this and other matters of interest. There was time, as long as Ana could get the message across to her intended husband that he could have her only on Bridei's terms. She must summon the strength to insist on a delay, and fend off any attempts by Alpin to bed her until Faolan could verify the fellow's promises. As bard, he'd have no problem ferreting out information. In that respect Ana had done him a favour. He just hoped nobody would ask him to play.

What he could not do was step in to help Ana with the initial negotiations. Faolan had planned with Bridei exactly what information he would present in response to Alpin's inevitable questions. Some of it would be false and misleading, designed to reinforce the intelligence he had already passed on at the Gaelic stronghold of Dunadd, before he had met a man called Pedar and had been obliged to silence him. Bridei wanted the Gaels to be aware of the likelihood of an early strike: he wanted them to believe the council with Drust of Circinn was called for the harvest festival of Gathering, and the advance itself planned for Maiden Dance, celebration of the first stirrings of spring. This rumour was to disguise the true timing of his venture, which was much earlier. Dalriada would feel the teeth of Fortriu the day the leaves turned to gold; the campaign would be over before Bone Mother fastened her icy grip on the hills of the Great Glen. The strategy had been good: there is nothing better designed to conceal the truth than intelligence that is very close to that truth but inaccurate in one crucial particular. Faolan doubted greatly that King Gabhran of Dalriada had an inkling Bridei was almost ready to strike.

Ana was a dangerous player in this game for she could not be relied upon to withhold information whose strategic importance she did not understand; the names of Bridei's existing allies, for example, including the Caitt chieftain Umbrig. Faolan was glad they had kept the full truth from her; he was under no illusions as to the methods that might be applied to both men and women to extract information. She did have one advantage in the negotiations. It was clear from that wretch Alpin's hot eyes and roaming hands that he wanted her. The thought of it made Faolan sick.

He had washed under a pump and dressed in the plain attire one of the kitchen men had found for him, homespun in dun and grey, coarse and serviceable. His own boots had been left in the forest; they gave him a pair of ancient shoes with cracking leather and ragged stitching, and he put them on without protest. Since the lie had been told and could not be withdrawn, he would use it to his advantage. The less he looked like a royal emissary the better. In these garments he should blend in without much difficulty. It would be good for him. It would remind him that women like Ana lived in a different world from men like himself.

At supper they seated him near the opposite end of the long table from the place where Ana sat at Alpin's right hand, wan and drawn-looking in her clean clothing. She had her hair plaited in a crown on top of her head and was holding her neck straight, aiming for a regal carriage. Alpin hardly took his eyes off her. Faolan, who never drank ale when he was working, drained his goblet in one draught and allowed a woman to refill it. Alpin was laughing; he was patting Ana's hand with his big, rough paw. Faolan saw her flinch. He focused his gaze on the platter of roast mutton before him; speared a slice with his borrowed knife and began to chew. He watched the folk around him; he observed, also, the corners of Alpin's hall, the doorways covered by loose hangings, the broad hearths at each end. They said the winters were perishing cold in the realm of the Caitt.

These were loud folk and seemed to like their jests, many of which concerned their own exploits in the beds of buxom women or their besting of some other fellow in a brawl. They ate and drank with robust appetite and at first plied Faolan with questions: what was his name, where was he from, did he have a wife, and what was a Gael doing living at the court of Fortriu? He made his answers brief, polite and entirely without interest, and was rewarded when the talk turned to other matters. He counted the number of men-at-arms present, estimated those who might be on watch and compared the total with the capacity of the sleeping quarters set aside for warriors, a realm he had investigated quietly some time earlier. There was room in Alpin's house for a complement of eighty men. There were perhaps thirty present now, including those on guard. Alpin was known to have an outpost on the west coast, where his ships were maintained, but there was no current information as to its size or resources. This, Faolan needed to know. He would find a weak link somewhere at Briar Wood; he was expert at spotting them – a fellow with a grudge, a lonely woman with a loose tongue, a child who had overheard what should have been secret. He'd have it out of them all in good time.

He glanced up the table at Ana; at the same moment she looked at him, her eyes conveying an apology. He allowed himself a little nod of reassurance; saw her lips curve in the slightest of smiles.

Ana had turned back to Alpin now, gesturing, her expression serious. She was working hard on her own mission: to trade away her future for the sake of kings who had held her hostage for half her life. It was wrong, bitterly wrong. She was like a princess from an ancient tale, who surely should find her happiness in the gaining of her own kingdom or in a transcendent triumph over adversity. This was no triumph. With every tilt of her lovely head, with every gaze of her limpid grey eyes, with every expressive movement of her hands, she moved one step closer to committing herself to that oaf sitting there beside her. Not one of these folk had the capacity to recognise her true worth . . .

'So,' someone said, 'you're a court bard? There's an old harp around here somewhere; used to be a fellow played a bit, long while ago, what was his name? A few tunes after supper, that'd be good.'

A harp. Faolan turned cold. 'Some time, perhaps,' he said non-committally. 'I was injured on the journey here; my arm. It will be a while before I can play again. And I imagine the instrument will need attention if it's been unused awhile.'

'I'll get a boy to hunt it out; you can take a look. Not much diversion here, you understand. Bards don't make a habit of wandering this way. The women'd like a song or two.'

'I work for the lady,' Faolan said. 'If she agrees, of course I will oblige. But it will take time. Some fellow in a blue headband winged me with an arrow. Thought I was a warrior, I suppose. Must've been short-sighted.'

His companions at the table guffawed with laughter.

'Show us your scar,' someone said.

'It's bandaged.'

'Show us.'

There was no choice but to oblige. Faolan took care to roll up his sleeve only as far as the new wound, and not to reveal the other, older scar above it. For a musician to sustain one such injury was just about plausible as an unfortunate accident. To bear the marks of two must arouse suspicion.

'The Blues, huh?' commented an elderly man whose left cheek was adorned with row on row of faded warrior marks. 'Folk are saying they attacked your lady's party by the ford. Alpin won't let such an affront go without retaliation.'

'The Blues?' Faolan feigned ignorance. 'Who are they? Neighbours?'

'You could say that. Dendrist's territory, Blue Lake, runs to the east of Briar Wood. He's a man who never seems content with existing borders.'

'Ah.'

'Not the safest way to ride in here, over Breaking Ford,' commented a sharp-eyed man. 'Whoever was leading your party must have been a fool. You'd have best gone down the lakes and up by the western tracks.'

'I know nothing of such matters,' said Faolan, whose constant scanning of the riotous hall for anything that might be of significance had at last been rewarded. There were serving dishes on a stone shelf at the side, and amongst the servants who bore platters to the table and away, a man was quietly loading items onto a small tray, enough food and drink for perhaps two. This in itself was nothing surprising; he was probably taking supplies to some of the fellows on watch, or tending to the elderly or infirm. It was the man himself who caught Faolan's eye. He was shortish, with a powerful chest and extremely broad shoulders, his build accentuated by the ankle-length robe he wore. His head was completely bald and, unlike the hirsute Caitt warriors, he was clean-shaven, his face decorated with battle counts but not with kin signs; a seasoned campaigner, then, and of Priteni blood, but not high born. His stance breathed power. In that contained energy there was a control that stopped Faolan's breath. What was such a man doing bearing little trays of roast meat and ale as if he were an ordinary servant? The bald head turned, and Faolan noticed a mark behind the right ear, a small, crudely executed tattoo in the shape of a star. A pair of light, inscrutable eyes met Faolan's briefly, then the fellow took up his tray and went out. Faolan noted the exit he used; it was the doorway closest to Alpin's private quarters.

'Bard!' the chieftain called.

With a pang of misgiving, Faolan got to his feet.

'Come here!'

He walked to the top of the table, bowing low and obsequiously as he reached Alpin. 'My lord.'

'No music tonight?' Alpin asked with a grin. 'No ditties to divert us?'

'My lord –' Ana began.

'Let the fellow speak for himself, my dear. He has a tongue; I've heard him use it.'

'I hope to entertain you in due course, my lord Alpin,' Faolan said, aiming for a subservient tone. 'It would be little enough recompense for your consideration in riding out to meet us. Unfortunately, my arm is damaged and I cannot play. Besides, my instruments were lost in the accident that befell us.'

'You don't need your instruments to sing, nor your arm,' Alpin growled.

'Indeed not, my lord. But I am weary tonight. I do not think the Lady Ana will require music of me when our losses are so recent. It is hard to summon fair tunes when the heart is full of sorrow.'

'Of course you need not sing for us tonight, Faolan,' said Ana. 'Later, perhaps.'

'Not planning to keep the fellow permanently, are you?' challenged Alpin. 'I don't have Gaels in my household; it only makes folk suspicious.'

Ana's cheeks had turned pink. 'Faolan is entirely reliable, my lord. A musician stands outside political loyalties. I'm hoping he will remain here for some time. At least until our negotiations are concluded. I had hoped he might play . . .'

'At the wedding,' Faolan said through gritted teeth. 'After that I will return to White Hill.'

There was a brief silence, then Ana put a hand up to shield a yawn. 'Will you excuse me, my lord? I am very weary and wish to retire now.'

'By all means.' Alpin's eyes were all over her; Faolan could read his mind, see the image there of Ana lying on her bed, relaxed in a soft nightrobe, the curves of her body enticing, the candlelight playing on her pale skin and shimmering fall of hair. 'Sweet dreams, my dear.'

'There's just one thing,' Ana said, rising to her feet. 'I need your assurance that we will have an early opportunity to discuss Bridei's terms for the marriage. I wish to have that settled before I make any decisions. I would prefer to have Faolan present during our negotiations, since he is the only man left from my escort. While he has no expertise in such affairs, I imagine it is he who will bear the account of our dealings back to King Bridei. It would be foolish to send another messenger when Faolan will be travelling that way in any case.'

Alpin regarded her, full lips twisted in a sardonic smile. He seemed torn between amusement and irritation. 'I'm not accustomed to women giving me orders,' he said.

'It's not an order, my lord,' said Ana. 'The flood robbed me of my skilled negotiator, along with many friends. You would not want King Bridei to hear that you took advantage of me in these dealings because of that unfortunate event, I am sure. Of course you will make some allowance for the very awkward position in which I find myself.'

Faolan suppressed the urge to applaud; it had been neatly done. She possessed an infinite capacity to surprise him. The conversation had drawn the attention of all the men and women seated close to Alpin; their heads were turning from one speaker to the other with the avid interest of folk watching a skilled combat. Faolan, still on his knees, made his expression blank.

'Discussions, negotiations, what need of those?' Alpin spread his hands. 'I know what I want.' He winked at the men seated near him. 'I don't think you would have made this long journey, my dear, without a pretty good idea of what would happen at the end of it, escort or no escort. All we need is a day or two to get to know each other, and a druid for the handfasting, and your man here can be back off to White Hill before he's had a chance to set finger to string.'

'Faolan,' Ana said, 'get up, please. My lord, I am too weary to assemble my thoughts. What I do know is that Bridei made precise terms for this arrangement. I am duty-bound to set them before you. If you cannot accommodate that, I – we – have no choice but to return to White Hill forthwith.'

Silence again. Alpin was picking his teeth with a shard of mutton bone.

'Really,' he said at last. Behind the word stood the flooded river, the attackers, the long, lonely road back to the southeast. A woman travelling with only a musician to protect her. The fact that, here at Briar Wood, Alpin was master.

'Yes, my lord,' said Ana. Her courteous tone was belied by her tightly clenched fists.

'Ah, well,' said Alpin, 'it's late. You've had a long journey. Wise to retire; don't forget that bolt, my dear. You can't trust a bard, their minds are all on the impossible events of story, the ones in which swineherds become kings and slaves bed princesses.' The men laughed. 'Goodnight, my dear. Don't look like that, I'm only joking. Bard, you're dismissed. I hope you have songs in our own tongue and not just in that wretched Gaelic.'

'I'll do my best to oblige, my lord, should the opportunity arise.' Faolan returned to his lowly place at the board as Ana departed with her waiting woman behind her. He hoped she did remember the bolt. This fellow was clever, a deal more clever than his boorish manner suggested. He must be watched. Now Alpin got up and, with a word or two to his men, followed Ana out through that door leading to the family quarters. *Put her next to me.* If the man thought she would let him in tonight he was deluded.

'My lord retires early,' Faolan murmured a little later to Gerdic, the serving man who had helped him earlier with clothing and shelter and now sat by him at table.

'He'll be back,' Gerdic said.

So Faolan waited, watching the comings and goings in the hall, listening to the gossip. Some of the men brought out game boards – so they were not all uncouth oafs – and he observed and made helpful suggestions, but did not play. Later, bouts of wrestling took place before the hearth, the men laying wagers on one another's prowess. Faolan joined in the betting and made sure he lost, not that there was anything to lose, since he had no worldly possessions in this place beyond a horse that was not his to trade.

'I saw a fellow here before who would make a sturdy opponent in such a combat,' he observed at one point; Gerdic seemed friendly, and he thought this casual comment worth risking. 'Bald man with big shoulders. Looked like a fighter. Don't think he's here now.' He glanced around as if seeking the man.

'That'd be Deord.' No more was offered.

'Deord? What is he, a warrior?'

'Not exactly.' Gerdic seemed ill at ease. 'Alpin's special guard. We don't see him much. Keeps himself to himself. You wouldn't take Deord on in a fight unless you had a death wish.'

'Mm-hm.' Faolan did not ask, *What does he guard? Where did he come from?* He knew when to push and when to hold back. There was a reticence here. In the morning he would go further afield; he would find the information Bridei wanted. He supposed, also, that he must attempt to mend a harp.

Sleep evaded him. It was strange that he, who had for so long spent his nights alone or kept vigil by a wakeful Bridei, now lay in the darkness feeling Ana's absence as a sharp ache somewhere in his chest. Six nights he had held her in his arms, had sheltered and warmed her, had cradled her strength and her gentleness against his heart. Then, he had longed for journey's end so that he might not have to confess how much he wanted her. At the same time he had wished the journey to be endless, to fade into a song, a tale, a memory of piercing joy and deepest regret. It was over now, and the loss of her made this pallet the loneliest bed he had ever lain on. No, perhaps not quite. There had been a night, once, when he would have begged the gods to let him die, save that he had already learned the bitter lesson that such choices are always beyond the scope of men. He did not want to die now. There was still work to be done.

The sun climbed higher in a clear, pale sky, and as the rising tide washed in a gentle, insistent murmur around the base of the great coastal fortress, the warriors of Fortriu began to assemble in the open space on Caer Pridne's topmost level to hear their king. Men had come in from many outposts for this occasion. The place was brimming with fighters and bristling with weaponry. Some were accommodated in tentlike shelters beyond the walls, and many riders could be seen on the tidal flats between the fortress and the house of the wise women at Banmerren, along the bay. The visit had been planned a long time; there had been no way Bridei could disappoint them.

The King of Fortriu had not slept. After the vigil he had lain quietly on his bed awhile, Ban curled at his feet, while Breth snatched a brief period of exhausted slumber. Faolan had once commented that the primary qualification for Bridei's bodyguards was the ability to do without sleep, and Bridei was uncomfortably aware that the three of them did just that; they were loyal friends who went far beyond the call of duty in their care for him. With Faolan away and Garth staying with his wife and sons at White Hill – he had offered to come to Caer Pridne and Bridei had said no – Breth had only the backup of the Pitnochie men, none of whom were trained bodyguards, and the big man was weary. Bridei wondered how Faolan was managing his own task; whether the Caitt chieftain was prepared to accept the rare gift they had sent him. Faolan; ah, Faolan, his mystery, his reluctant friend . . . There was no way he could take Faolan with him down the Glen, no way he could require a man to ride into battle against his own people, whatever his declared loyalties. Faolan knew, of course; he'd seen through it instantly, the man missed nothing. And he'd accepted the mission anyway. Having chosen to set himself up as no more than a hired guard, he could hardly refuse his king's order. By the time Faolan and the others got back from Briar Wood, Bridei would be gone. The army would be streaming to the west, and the great endeavour would be under way. By the time the leaves were turning to the russet and crimson and gold of Measure, the blood of the Gaels would stain the land they had stolen. By the time another Gateway came around, the war would be over. He must make this a victory worthy of all those who had put their trust in him. The gods had given him this mission and he must carry it out according to their will. He must believe, in his heart, that he could do this; that the Priteni could triumph, at last, over the Gaelic scourge that had lain across their western lands for three generations now. That they could push back the creeping threat of the new religion. The human cost would be great. He must pray that it would not be too high.

Bridei sighed, thinking of Ana and the cruel necessity of sending her away. He hoped her new home would be welcoming and her husband delighted with his lovely young wife. His mind shied away from the fact that, once the war was over, he was going to need a new hostage to replace her.

He lay still while outside the sun came up and the songs of birds turned from solitary piping to busy chirrups to a swelling chorus of greeting. He thought of Derelei: the wondrous morning of his birth, his first small cry, his tiny clutching hands and bright unfocused eyes. The thatch of damp, dark hair. The fragility of the little skull beneath. Tuala's smile of exhausted triumph, and his own tears. He could feel the warm weight of his son in his arms; he could smell the sweetness of Derelei's breath and hear the little snuffling noises he made at night. He remembered Derelei's astonished yelp when he rolled over for the first time; his wide-eyed wonderment when Bridei carried him outside to watch the full moon sailing across the night sky; his stumbling, valiant efforts to walk. His face in repose, his small form curled asleep on Tuala's lap. His body racked by fever, his cheeks flushed hectic red, his voice turned to the harsh cry of a crow. So small on the pallet; so very small.

When it was fully light outside, Bridei arose and washed the signs of weeping from his face. Breth woke quickly from long habit and fetched the good clothes the king would need, along with some soft bread, dried fruit and a herbal drink Broichan had ensured all Bridei's guards knew how to brew and when to administer. Bridei had no appetite, but ate and drank all the same, knowing Breth would stand there waiting until he did what was required.

'He might pull through it,' Breth remarked quietly. 'Garth's boys did.'

Bridei said nothing. Garth's boys were big for their age, strong and robust. Even they had hovered close to death.

'You all right for this morning?' In private Bridei's bodyguards did not observe formalities when they spoke to him.

'I must be.' The bread tasted of ashes; the drink was bitter in his mouth.

'If we get away quickly after,' Breth said, 'we've a chance of being home before nightfall.'

Bridei managed a smile and slipped the remains of his bread to Ban, who was under the table. 'We'll see,' he said. 'Come, then, I expect they're waiting for me.'

At that moment the tall chieftain, Carnach, was at the door, clad in the formal attire such an event required: a tunic of fine dark wool belted in leather and silver; a shirt underneath of pale linen well-pressed; woollen trousers, polished boots. The tunic had a border of embroidery, black on red, a pattern of tiny warriors on horseback, and the penannular brooch that fastened the chieftain's short cloak was decorated with a rearing stallion in silver. The cloak was a particular deep blue, his family colour. Like Bridei, Carnach was descended of the royal line of Fortriu. Carnach's red hair was neatly plaited down his back; his face now bore an impressive pattern of tattoos, for he had led Bridei's men and his own in numerous skirmishes against their enemies, both Gaels and troublesome neighbours from closer at hand, over the time he had been the king's chief war leader.

'The men are assembled, my lord king,' Carnach said in the formal manner required by such an occasion. 'They've been somewhat dispirited since the news came that a party of Fokel's men was ambushed in the north, with nine warriors lost. Some had friends amongst the slain. Your visit will give them new heart.'

Bridei nodded as Breth helped him fasten his own cloak with

the silver eagle clasp the old king had given him, years ago, in recognition of courage. He wondered how one might give new heart when one's own heart felt torn and aching. How could he step out and rally men in the cause of Fortriu when, in truth, he was asking them to march out and die for him? He closed his eyes.

'Come on then,' Breth said quietly. 'The sooner you make a start the sooner we'll be on the road for home. My lord.'

Ban was sitting on Bridei's foot. The king bent down; anxious eyes looked up, and a small tongue came out to lick his fingers.

'I'm sorry to hear about your son, Bridei,' Carnach said in a different tone. 'They told me this morning how ill he is. A terrible thing.'

'Yes.' It seemed to be all Bridei could manage right now.

'We'd best be going. They're waiting for you.'

'Yes.'

'Men of Fortriu!' The king's voice rang out strong and clear across a courtyard packed with warriors standing shoulder to shoulder. All along the raised walkway that circled this topmost level of the fortress, more men stood in silence, gazing across at the stone dais where Bridei stood with their leaders by his side, a square-shouldered, handsome figure in his plain, good clothing. He was a warrior amongst warriors; his young face bore its share of battle counts, foremost amongst them the marks of the first great encounter at Galany's Reach, where his exploits had formed the foundation for a number of epic poems and stirring songs. He was their king, but he was also one of them, and they liked that. 'I stand here amongst you today to bid you prepare for the greatest endeavour of your lives. I greet you as your leader and as your brother. We are all sons of this fair land of Fortriu, bred of its soil, raised in its clear air, sustained by the sweet water of its many springs and inspired by the living fire of the Flamekeeper, whose light burns in the heart of every man of courage. The god looks down on you in love and pride, my brothers. I see his strength in your eyes; I see his steadiness in your bearing; I see his valour in your hearts.

'Very soon now we set forth on an undertaking that will stretch us to our utmost limits. The creeping parasite of Dalriada has set its alien presence on our land for too long now.' A small chorus of supportive whistles broke out. 'Too many of our best and finest have fallen in conflict with that enemy; too many brave spirits have perished in the struggle.' At Bridei's feet, Ban stood very still, tail stiff, legs planted, eyes on the crowd. 'It is time to make a final stand; to say, no more. It is time to sweep this invader from our homeland once and for all. Men, this is the season of our greatest battle and of our greatest victory.'

The courtyard reverberated with shouts; feet stamped, hands clapped, voices were raised in acclaim.

'I have the utmost faith in every one of you,' Bridei went on, 'and in your leaders. Carnach will ensure that you are prepared in every respect to take this fight to the enemy's door and to overcome; he will stand by you while there is breath in his body. Make no mistake: neither he, nor I, nor any one of the chieftains of Fortriu will suffer the Gaels to darken our lands beyond next Measure. The west will be ours once more, and the banners of our great houses will fly anew above the territories plundered by our enemy. We will see them streaming in the wind: the colours of Longwater and Raven's Well, Thorn Bend and Abertornie, the star and serpent of the ancient holding of Galany and the brave white and blue of the kings of Fortriu. Gabhran of Dalriada will kneel before me; he will renounce his claim to the territories he has taken. He will quit this shore forever.'

'That's too good for him!' someone shouted, and there was a swell of angry agreement.

'Maybe so,' Bridei said. 'But I will not let the tale be told that the men of Fortriu lacked magnanimity towards their enemies; that they would slaughter in cold blood a foe already surrendered and helpless. Those who meet us on the field meet their own deaths. Make no doubt of that, warriors of Fortriu. We march to battle with the names of our slaughtered fathers, our lost brothers, our maimed and ruined comrades on our lips, a song of blood and of victory. We ride with the voices of our ancient gods in our hearts, chanting us into the great tale of the Priteni. And if we die, we die with our spirits full of courage, loyalty and love, for we are the very embodiment of the Flamekeeper's will, and each one of us, young and old, grizzled warrior of many scars or bright-eyed lad with battle skills new-learned, is the god's own son.'

A roar of acclamation. Some men clapped their friends on the shoulder; more than a few wiped their eyes.

'You've worked hard,' Bridei went on more quietly, so the crowd was forced to hush to hear his words. 'From your leaders I hear good reports of the conduct of this camp and of our other gathering places. You are a fine band, united in friendship, in competition, in the will to excel and to succeed in the great mission to come. For that I offer you my heartfelt thanks. And I say to you, for every skilled swordsman, for every valiant spear holder, for every keen archer there is a husband with a young wife left behind, a father with a brood of growing children, a man with a field of barley that needs seeing to or a fishing boat that needs refurbishing. Those things are real; they are your lives, men, they are more part of you than any heady charge to war can ever be. But you must set them aside for now. Put them away in your hearts; they will be there waiting for you when this is over. I ask of you a season; a season of heroism, of struggle and of blood. Some will die. You will see your comrade struck down beside you, your brother in arms pierced by a Gaelic spear, your childhood friend choking in your arms and begging for a quick end. Men, we are warriors. We are the Flamekeeper's loyal army, and our courage will not fail us. We will close the eyes of our fallen and lay them quietly down, and then we will run forward, our weapons in our hands, and on our lips the cry of our forefathers: Fortriu!'

The king raised his fist high and, as one, a forest of arms came up before him. The cry from a thousand voices was like the shout of the god himself in the clear air of springtime: 'Fortriu!'

It became plain that a quick departure from Caer Pridne and a speedy ride back to White Hill would not be possible. Men crowded around the dais, sending Ban into a frenzy of barking and causing Breth to shoulder forwards, interposing his own body between Bridei and those who sought to come too close.

'Let them come,' Bridei said. 'They want to talk to me, that's all.' He moved down into the crowd, shaking a hand here, touching a shoulder there, admiring a fine weapon, recollecting a shared meal, hearing of a marriage or a feat of arms or a lame horse with all the interest and attention each man needed. Breth did his best to keep space clear around the king; Ban growled at knees and nipped at ankles. By the time the men of Caer Pridne were satisfied and were beginning to disperse from the courtyard, the sun was well past its midpoint. There would not be time to reach home before nightfall; not with the fittest horses in all Fortriu.

'Perhaps it's for the best,' Breth muttered as they made their way indoors with Carnach. 'At least you can catch some sleep.'

Bridei nodded. He could not speak what was in his mind. *It seems to me, foolish as it sounds, that if I close my eyes for an instant he will slip away forever.*

'It suits me much better if you don't go until tomorrow,' Carnach said. 'I want to run through some ideas with you, a few new tactics I've been working on. And the men were hoping you'd watch them go through their paces later; they've planned a bit of a display for you . . .'

While Bridei had kept his solitary vigil by the Well of Shades, others, too, had been maintaining a night-long watch. In the king's apartments at White Hill, Broichan and Tuala had remained by Derelei's bedside, every sense alert for the slightest change in the child's condition. But the only change was in the patterns on the stone walls, images of light and shadow conjured by the fire's flickering and the draught-stirred candle flames. Two or three times folk had brought food and drink, and Broichan and Tuala had coaxed one another to eat. Once Tuala had fallen asleep, to wake sitting on the floor by the bed, her head against the straw mattress, her neck stiff and aching. Broichan had not slept. He had stood or sat or knelt where he could keep Derelei in view, and sometimes he had recited prayers or told snatches of stories, the kind of tales a tiny child might enjoy. But most of the time the druid had held a pose of extreme stillness, a stillness that had seemed beyond the abilities of ordinary man. He'd been silently praying. Tuala had felt the power of it in the chamber.

There were questions she could have asked. How could a little child survive when he had taken no milk for a day and a night? The aching fullness of her breasts had told her how hungry her son must be. Why didn't Broichan cover Derelei up, fever or no fever? Night had brought a chill to the room. Shouldn't they sponge the baby, or rock him, or hold him? Without the reassurance of touch, would not her son lose his way on the dark road he followed? Would not Bone Mother beckon, smiling, and this small traveller stumble towards her with hands outstretched? Tuala had not asked. To do so was to doubt not only Broichan himself, but the gods in whom he put his trust.

Light came at last, a pale dawning visible through the smoke hole above the hearth, and with it came Mara, bearing a basin of warm water in her hands and a clean cloth over her arm. She said nothing, simply placed these items by the fire and came over to look at the child. Broichan and Tuala stood one on either side of the bed, their gaze on Derelei's shadowed eyelids, his rosebud mouth, his little outstretched arms. Mara reached past Tuala and put her rough and reddened hand to the infant's brow, and Broichan did not try to stop her.

'The fever's broken.' Mara's tone was commendably steady. 'He'll be a hungry boy when he wakes. You'll welcome that, no doubt; it can get painful when they're weaning. I've seen it with Brenna when you were a wee scrap of a thing yourself.'

Broichan let out his breath in a long sigh and turned abruptly away. Whatever was in his face, he did not want Tuala to see it. She looked again at her son, and saw his eyelids flutter, his arms move, the starfish hands closing and unclosing. He squirmed, kicking, and the line of coloured powder that Broichan had traced around him was broken. The flowers fell from his lids, their delicate blue replaced by a still sweeter colour, that of the child's eyes, dazed with sleep but clear and bright. Derelei reached for his mother, and as he began to cry she scooped him up in her arms. In the time it took her to move to the bench by the fire, to unfasten her bodice and put the famished child to the breast, Broichan was gone.

He had watched a lively display of single combat with staves, and an archery contest, and a demonstration of horsemanship. He had visited stables, armoury and smithy and commended those who plied their trades there. He had taken supper with Carnach and his captains, and listened to a group of warriors with a talent for singing. Now the long day was over and the Shining One hung sickle-thin in the shadowy field of the night sky. Bridei stood on the walkway outside his quarters, the same quarters he had shared with his guards during the momentous visit before his election to kingship. Memories crowded this place; the shade of his foster father, Broichan, was particularly strong. Broichan, without whom he would never have become king; Broichan who, at the end, had almost made it not happen. Broichan, who was the closest thing he had to a father; Broichan, who had never truly understood the man he had made. And Tuala . . . gods, he had been away only a day or so, and already her absence was a fierce aching in his chest. How could he have left her to deal with it all alone? *Derelei* . . .

'My lord.' It was Carnach's bodyguard, Gwrad, coming down the steps from the upper level. 'A messenger. From White Hill.'

Within Bridei's belly something clenched in on itself, tight and cold, in preparation for a mortal blow. He could not speak. Behind Gwrad's stocky figure was another; it was one of the Pitnochie men, Uven, who had been in attendance at White Hill. All at once Breth was standing at Bridei's shoulder. Carnach's appointed guards kept their distance.

'Tell us, then,' Breth said in carefully level tones.

'Your son . . .' Uven was breathless.

Bridei stood very still as the cold thing inside him stretched slow tentacles towards his heart.

'For pity's sake,' Breth snapped, 'spit it out, man!'

'My lord, your son's fever has broken,' gasped Uven. 'He's a great deal better and should recover . . .'

Bridei's knees felt suddenly weak; his head was reeling. He put out a hand, seeking the support of the parapet wall, and felt Breth's arm around his shoulders.

'The Flamekeeper be praised,' said Breth quietly. 'This is welcome news. You'd best go and recover yourself, Uven. That must have been a hard ride. If there's more, perhaps you can come back and speak to the king again later.'

When the messenger had been shepherded away by Gwrad towards a fire and sustenance, Breth took Bridei's arm and made to steer him indoors.

'No,' Bridei said. 'No, I will stay out here awhile, under the gaze of the Shining One. There should be prayers . . .'

'Maybe you're a king, but you're still a man,' Breth said bluntly. 'Let it go. Laugh, weep, shout, do what you will. I'm the only one here to see you. I have no sons of my own, but I can imagine how it feels.'

'I'm fine,' Bridei said, subsiding abruptly to a sitting position on the ground, his back against the parapet wall, his hands shielding his eyes. 'Fine . . .'

Ban put his front paws on his master's shoulder and attempted to lick his face.

'The way I've always seen it,' said the big bodyguard, settling beside his charge, 'the gods know what's in your heart without needing to be told. Yours more than most, I wouldn't wonder.'

Chapter Six

On the morning after Ana's arrival, not long after she had risen, washed and dressed with Ludha's help, the tall figure of the housekeeper appeared at her door. 'My lord wishes you to breakfast with him in his apartment,' Orna said. 'With your maid in attendance, of course. Ludha, you'll go with the lady and sit quietly in a corner. Take your sewing with you.'

It was a reasonable enough request; Ana wondered if Alpin intended to sort out the issue of Bridei's requirements over a quick bowl of oatmeal. She very much hoped not. She had slept badly and was fighting a headache.

Alpin's quarters were spacious, with two narrow windows similar to the one in her own room next door. There was a bed of generous size, its covers still rumpled, and an oak table with two long benches. Here, it would be possible for eight people to sit in council or over a meal. A fire burned on a hearth; there were hangings on the walls with scenes of battles and hunting, their colours vivid in the light of oil lamps set on two massive oak chests. By the hearth was a small door which Ana assumed led to a privy or storage area. She was relieved to find Alpin up and fully dressed; he stood by the table in conversation with two other men. They fell silent as she entered.

'Ah, Ana, my dear! I trust you slept well?'

She forced a smile. 'The chamber is very comfortable, my lord. I'm still not quite myself after the journey, but that is through no fault in your hospitality.'

Alpin laughed heartily, setting her head throbbing. 'No faulting your manners, either,' he said. 'Mordec, Erdig, you have your orders. I'll meet you in the courtyard when I'm finished here. Be ready to ride out straightaway.'

The two men gone, Alpin ushered Ana to the table. 'Sit down, my dear. Of course you will be weary. I should have left you to sleep in peace.'

'I've been awake since dawn.' She would not tell him another small bird had come to her windowsill with the first rising of the sun: a crossbill resplendent in its deep red coat, eyeing her with the air of bold assessment she was coming to expect from these avian visitors. She had watched it fly away; had seen it vanish in the same spot as the other, down within the wall on the northern side. 'I do have a slight headache; perhaps if I eat something it may fade.'

There was oatmeal porridge on the table, as well as fine bread and a dish of honey. Alpin's big hands, ladling the porridge into a bowl for her, were steady and capable.

'Try that,' he said with a sidelong glance. 'Hope it puts the pink back in your cheeks. I thought maybe an apology was in order.'

'Oh?'

'I can see you're a lady and not used to our ways. It's a long time since we had a real lady here. I've become accustomed to living amongst men. To talking a certain way; not guarding my tongue as perhaps I should.'

In the corner, Ludha had seated herself on a stool and was pretending to sew.

'But,' Ana said, 'there are plenty of other women here at Briar Wood. Not just the serving people, but the wives of your warriors, some of whom sat at table with us last night. And what about your own kinsfolk?'

Alpin took a while to reply; he was frowning as he attacked his porridge. 'I've just the one sister,' he said eventually, 'and she married a chieftain in the far north; haven't seen her for years. As for the wives, I suppose we've got into a way of doing things and they just put up with it. They're not like you. You're a gem, a star, something rare as fine silk.'

His hand came over hers on the table, and Ana suppressed the urge to snatch her fingers away.

'I'm accustomed to pretty words,' she said, 'and I'm expert at judging the sincerity of the men who offer them. You don't know me, Alpin. Don't feel obliged to say these things just because you think they may please me.'

Alpin grimaced and withdrew his hand. 'You forget,' he said, 'a small matter of a marriage.'

'A possible marriage. There are details to discuss before the decision is made as to its viability.'

'Oh, it'll be viable all right.' Alpin tore off a chunk of bread and used his knife to smear on honey. 'I'm rushing you, I suppose. Forgetting, again, what a princess you are. Never lain with a man, have you?'

Ana felt the flood of heat to her face. She was speechless with mortification. From her corner, Ludha gave a little shocked gasp.

'I see you haven't,' Alpin said in tones of satisfaction. 'Gives you greater bargaining power; you probably didn't think of that. Blush easily, don't you?' His hand came up to cup her cheek; she closed her eyes and held herself very still, like a creature trying to avoid a predator's notice. Her heart was thumping. Alpin's fingers moved against her hot skin, stroking. 'I like it,' he murmured. 'There's passion in you, for all your proper ways. No need to be wary of marriage. You're old enough to be bedded; old enough to take great pleasure from it. Are you afraid of me?'

This was difficult to answer. It was not fear she felt at his touch but disgust. She could hardly tell him this. 'After what we went through on our journey,' she said, 'I'm not sure I can feel fear any more. Besides, I came here as a bride; it would be foolish to have qualms about it now. But I do need time to settle in at Briar Wood. And, to be quite honest with you, I find your open talk of such . . . intimate matters . . . not altogether appropriate. It seems a little

145

soon for that.' Gods, she hoped Ludha was not a gossip; this conversation would make fine fare in the servants' quarters.

'It's a long time since my first wife died,' Alpin said, removing his hand from her face and resuming his breakfast. 'I like a woman in my bed; I don't enjoy waking up alone. Perhaps I've grown rather uncouth over the years.' He grinned ruefully; it made his broad features into those of a boy caught out in a piece of petty mischief. For a moment he looked almost likeable. 'It seemed to me that, as you are not a young bride of twelve or thirteen, we might progress more quickly. If I'd my choice we'd be handfasted today. I'm impatient. You're a fine-looking girl now you've been cleaned up. And I like the way you dismiss me so coolly, as if you were the queen and I the lowliest of kitchen boys. Just as long as you understand who is master here at Briar Wood.'

Ana cleared her throat, struggling to find the right things to say through a maelstrom of emotions, of which the foremost seemed to be irritation.

'I do have a piece of news that will please you,' Alpin went on. 'The attack on your party at Breaking Ford offended me. Folk who offend me pay a price. I'll be riding out this morning on a retaliatory mission; five or six days ought to cover it. That should make you happy.'

'I . . .' Ana struggled for words. 'You are warlike neighbours in Caitt territory,' she observed.

'I pride myself on swift decisions and swift justice. I'm doing this for you; for the losses and hardships you suffered. Take it as a token of my genuine regard, pretty words or no. I value you. I want you. I can't be plainer or less pretty than that.'

Ana could not look at him. 'I'm not accustomed to bride gifts paid in human blood,' she managed.

'Here in the north,' Alpin said, 'we are real men.'

Her appetite was gone. She sipped at her mead and tried not to think too far ahead. With Alpin and many of his men out of the house, she would surely be able to talk to Faolan alone. He could advise her; she could make her apologies for telling a foolish lie to protect him. With the chieftain of Briar Wood away, Faolan would have a better opportunity to gather information covertly.

'Oh, and by the way,' Alpin said, wiping his mouth with the

back of his hand, 'I'm taking that bard of yours with me, what's his name, Finian? This could be the making of him.'

Ana tried to conceal her alarm. 'I don't think that's a good idea at all,' she said hurriedly. 'Faolan put up a reasonable pretence when you came upon us in the woods, I know. But he's no warrior. His presence would only hinder you –'

'I'll be the judge of that.' Alpin rose to his feet and proffered a hand to help her up. 'Thank you, my dear, I've enjoyed this. You blush beautifully. Make yourself at home while I'm gone. Look around the place, decide what changes you'd like, get to know the folk here. Orna's very capable; she'll find you anything you need.'

'But –' A last plea came to her lips.

'We'll be leaving shortly,' Alpin said. 'I'd like you in the courtyard to bid us farewell. Make sure your goodbye kiss is for your betrothed and not for that puling bard of yours. You seem altogether too attached to the fellow.'

'Oh, there's nothing like that –' Ana pulled herself up. Why was she apologising to this boor?

'I'm pleased to hear it. Then let your behaviour in front of my household reflect that and we'll have nothing to worry about, will we?'

Ana stood on the steps as the men made their farewells and, when Alpin bent his head towards her, she gave him a prim peck on the cheek. Alpin seemed to find her effort most amusing and, judging by the grins and winks, so did the assembled household. She tried very hard not to look at Faolan any more than might be considered appropriate. He sat astride the horse they had allotted him, his eyes giving nothing away. He appeared to be completely without weapons. Amongst the heavily armed Caitt warriors with their flowing locks, their bristling beards and their fierce tattoos, he was like a sheep amongst wolves. When they circled the courtyard and rode out between the great gates with Faolan in their midst, it seemed to Ana that her bard looked more like a prisoner under armed escort than a visitor on royal business. Still, she reasoned, if anyone knew how to look after himself it was Faolan. And in his absence she had a job to do. Since he had been robbed of the opportunity, she would turn her own hand to a little spying.

'Orna,' Ana asked casually, 'where does that little door lead to, the one by the hearth in Alpin's chamber?'

It was customary for the women of Briar Wood to spend the afternoons in a long chamber set aside for sewing and spinning. This workroom was a free-standing structure that opened to a secluded courtyard where stone benches had been placed to catch the cool northern sunlight. It was nothing like the well-tended gardens of White Hill; here, little grew beyond lank grasses struggling up here and there between the flagstones and a sad-looking pear tree in a meagre patch of soil. On one side rose the great outer wall of the fortress. A lesser wall, still too high to permit a view beyond, curved around from this to meet the stone exterior of the sewing room.

Ana found the atmosphere of the workroom dispiriting. These women were slow to trust and that made extracting useful information hard work. It was the third day after Alpin's departure, and she had learned that within the fortress certain paths were guarded and certain barriers kept locked. She had slipped into Alpin's chamber very early in the morning, before the household was stirring, and tried the little door, but without a key it could not be opened. That pricked her curiosity. The place where the birds had vanished within the wall lay somewhat beyond the family area of the house, and lower down. The door in question seemed to lead in the same sort of direction.

'There's nothing to interest you in there.' Orna's lips were tight as she worked her way along a seam. 'Storage places, outhouses; every dwelling has such an area.'

'Who has the key?' asked Ana.

Orna's fingers stopped moving. 'Alpin,' she said. 'Believe me, it's not a part of the house you'd want to be seeing.'

There was something in the quality of the other women's silence that told Ana she was treading on dangerous ground.

'And one other person, surely,' she said, using her most queenly tone. 'I've seen that short, bald man, the one who wears a long robe, going into Lord Alpin's chamber with a supper tray, even though Alpin is away. That seems rather an odd thing to be taking to an outhouse. What is that man's name?'

'Deord, my lady,' someone offered.

'Deord,' echoed Ana. 'Perhaps I'll have a word with him. Alpin did suggest I make myself known to everyone in the household. Orna, perhaps you would request that this Deord comes to see me.'

There was a charged silence, during which nobody looked at anyone else. All eyes were on distaff and spindle, needle and thread, weaving tablet or carding comb, but not much work was being done.

'Orna?' Ana asked quietly. 'Is there someone living in that part of the house?'

'You'd be best to ask Alpin, my lady,' Orna said heavily. 'He'd be planning to tell you in his own time.'

'Tell me what?'

'It's best coming from him. He'll be back in a few days; he'd have been going to tell you.'

'Then I will speak to Deord in the meantime.'

'Yes, my lady.' Then, after a little, 'Deord doesn't have much to say for himself at the best of times. I doubt he'll be able to help you.'

'What is he? A warrior? He walks like a fighting man.'

'A guard, my lady. A special guard.'

'What does he guard?'

'He guards what's best kept where it is, out of sight and away from questions.' Orna's tone was almost angry. 'I'm sorry, my lady, but sometimes it's better not to ask. Now, I was meaning to say to you, there's a roll of good fine wool we found set away, in a very pleasing shade of celandine blue. It would look well on you. I thought we might ask Sorala here to make up a tunic and a skirt or two, and Ludha can do the finishing touches. What do you say?'

If they thought she would be so easily distracted, they thought wrong. 'It sounds ideal,' Ana said. 'Thank you; you've all been most generous. I'd like to see Deord before supper today, Orna. Could you arrange for him to come to Alpin's chamber? Ludha, I'll need you there as well.'

'I'll do what I can,' Orna said. 'Deord keeps his own timetable and makes his own rules. Sometimes he can't come.'

'All the same.'

At the appointed time she waited, but Deord did not appear. Questioned later, Orna said that yes, indeed she had asked him, but that he was unavailable today.

'Tomorrow then,' Ana said, finding herself quite put out by the consistent lack of answers.

'If he can, my lady.'

'This seems odd,' Ana said, looking the housekeeper straight in the eye. 'Don't the guards here answer to their master? Isn't it reasonable that, as Alpin's intended wife, I expect the folk of Briar Wood to attend me on request? I'm giving him a full day's notice.'

'My lady,' said Orna, 'believe me, we're all glad you've come here. We've been hoping Lord Alpin would wed again and start to put his life back to rights; it was a dreadful blow to him, what happened to the lady Erisa. You mustn't feel ill at ease or unwelcome amongst us. But we've our own ways here, and they may not always be what you've been used to at King Bridei's court. Believe me, this is just a wee door and a few dusty old sheds, and anything you need to know about it, or about Deord, is for my lord to answer. And he will, I'm sure.'

'Very well, Orna. Thank you. I know you're trying to help.'

'Yes, my lady.'

It was not yet dark. The days were lengthening and the high crowns of the elms, studded with rooks' nests, stood out against the cool pallor of the evening sky. Ana stood at her window combing her hair and watching the forest birds fly in to roost. Perhaps it didn't really matter: the little door, the jealously guarded keys, Deord and his supper tray set for two. It was like something in a tale, the small mystery, the detail out of place that worries at the mind, making it hard to let go. She would appear foolish indeed if she insisted on going through that door and found beyond it exactly what Orna had said: dusty storage rooms, neglected outhouses. And Alpin would be back in a few days. In the tales, young women who allowed curiosity to get the better of them generally came to quick and unpleasant ends. She was being silly. She should concentrate on the sorts of information Faolan might want to take back to Bridei, observations about men and armaments and positions, and not concern herself with what this household plainly wanted kept secret.

There was a whirr of wings and there on the sill before her, not two handspans away, was a hoodie, surely the same one that had aided them at Breaking Ford and shadowed their journey through the forest. It seemed to be on the hunt for nesting materials, for a wisp of something soft and bright dangled from its sharp beak.

'So you're back,' Ana said softly. 'You're late building a nest; those rooks have had theirs ready a long while by the looks of it. Now what do you want, I wonder? What is it you're trying to tell me, you and your friends?'

The bird took a hop and a jump and came into her chamber, alighting on the storage chest near the window. Its neat grey cape gave it a demure appearance; its eyes were piercingly bright and seemed to Ana to have a question in them. 'I've got no answers for you, even if I knew what you wanted,' she said. 'All I have are questions of my own.'

The bird dipped its head and laid its burden on the chest by its feet, then looked at her again.

'What is it you have there?' Ana bent to look more closely; the bright-eyed scrutiny did not waver. She picked up the small item and held it up to the fading light from the window. Strands of hair; such hair as she had not seen on any head here at Briar Wood, for it was of an unusual tawny shade, wavy and strong, and took on a fiery glint in the light. The threads were long and curled around her fingers. 'Whose is this?' Ana asked, knowing there would be no answer, not until she went out to find one.

The hoodie was looking at her, head tilted; it was waiting. It came to Ana that there was only one response to this strange challenge. She plucked three hairs from her own head, pale gold and twice the length of those others, and held them out on the palm of her hand. Lightning quick, the hoodie snatched the strands from her hand and took wing, flying off out the window. Ana's palm stung; the bird had a businesslike beak.

That night her dreams were full of dark corridors and lurking presences around corners, of steps that went down to nowhere and bolts that could not be unfastened. She woke at dawn with her mouth parched and her heart racing. She resolved to spend the day in domestic tasks and not to meddle further.

Much to her surprise, when she returned to her chamber after a morning spent talking to the many craftsmen who plied their various trades in the household – Orna introduced her to each – and an afternoon being fitted for her new clothes, the man Deord was waiting for her in the hallway outside Alpin's apartments. Ana had already dismissed Ludha and was unattended.

'You wished to see me.' Deord's tone was level; he was the calmest-looking man Ana had ever seen. At the same time he seemed dangerous. His build was as powerful as a fighting boar's, his body muscular and hard under the loose robe.

'Yes, I did.' Now that he was here, she was not at all sure where to start. Without Ludha present, she could hardly interview a man alone in Alpin's chamber. She would have to question him here in the hallway. 'I wished to meet everyone who lives here at Briar Wood. You know, I suppose, that there is a possibility I may wed Lord Alpin. Your name is Deord?'

He inclined his bald head a little, not speaking.

'I hear you are a special guard.'

'A custodian, yes, my lady.' His eyes were pale and serene; his air of self-possession had something in common with Faolan's usual manner. It made Ana feel awkward and uncouth.

'I notice your place of work seems to be through the little door in Lord Alpin's private chamber. Is that correct?'

'Yes, my lady.'

Ana cleared her throat. 'Orna tells me that's a storage area. Old outhouses. I'm wondering if there may be some birds in those outhouses?'

A flicker of expression passed across the well-governed features. 'That's possible, my lady.'

'Yours?'

Deord smiled. 'No, my lady.'

'Deord,' Ana said, 'I'm finding it very difficult to get straight answers to my questions about that door and where it leads to. Are you able to give me those answers?'

He regarded her levelly. 'When I cannot tell the truth,' he said, 'I remain silent. There are outhouses. Also living quarters, my own included. And my place of work. Alpin hired me to maintain the security between that part of his house and this, and I've done that work well throughout the seven years I've been at Briar Wood. That's all I can tell you. If you want more, you must ask your husband.'

Ana flinched at his tone. 'That's what Orna said. And he's not my husband.'

'Not yet.'

'Not yet, and perhaps not at all. The arrangement is conditional.' Why was she telling him this, justifying herself to a serving man? 'Very well, Deord, since you make it clear that is the extent of what you're prepared to tell me, you may go. I expect you have a supper tray to deal with.'

'Yes, my lady.' He turned and was gone.

'Come inside,' Deord said. 'You must eat something. There's barley broth here and good cheese. Come on, Drustan. What's keeping you out there?' He had laid the simple meal out on their small table. The living quarters were made up of two chambers, this with its hearth, its bench, its storage chest, and another behind it with two shelf beds. It was basic in nature; there were no hangings and only a single lamp. Rushes blanketed the earthen floor. A small alcove in the inner wall housed a privy dug deep into the ground, with a bucket of ash and a scoop set on a stone. Deord maintained everything in a state of scrupulous cleanliness. This was part of his personal discipline, hard-learned and never forgotten.

'Drustan!' he called again. 'The soup's going cold.'

His charge appeared in the doorway, moving soundlessly, the hoodie on one shoulder and the crossbill on the other. The wren perched on his head, almost hidden in the exuberant bright hair.

153

Drustan's eyes alerted his keeper; they were full of suppressed excitement.

'What?' Deord said, scrutinising him.

'Nothing,' said Drustan, thrusting a hand into his pocket and moving to sit at the table. 'Deord?'

'Yes?'

'I need to go out. Tonight, tomorrow. It's like a flood in me welling up, a fire catching and spreading. It's like a shout trying to break free. When can we go out again?'

Deord regarded him calmly. 'You've been building up to it, that's been plain to see,' he said. 'Not tonight. I'm wary of excursions in the dark and the moon is waning. It's too easy to lose sight of each other in the woods; you know what can happen if we don't abide by our agreed rules. Tomorrow, maybe, if the weather holds fair.'

'Have you seen her?' Drustan asked. He held a piece of cheese between his fingers but did not eat. The hoodie edged down his arm.

'I don't fetch good food only to see those creatures gobble it up,' Deord said mildly. 'Eat, Drustan. You must maintain your strength.'

'For what?' The mobile mouth was suddenly solemn; the brightness in the strange eyes faded.

'For the future. Some day, something will change. This is not for ever.'

'Alpin will not change. I will not change. How can I ever be other than a prisoner?'

Deord chewed on a crust of oaten bread. 'Life is change,' he said. 'Yes, I've seen her and the fellow who came with her. They're trouble, the pair of them, her with her golden hair and her questions, and him . . .'

'And him what?' The hoodie had snatched the cheese and retreated to Drustan's shoulder to eat it.

'He is of a kind I had not expected to see here at Briar Wood,' Deord said.

'What kind? A sorcerer? A priest?'

'No,' Deord said. 'He is the same kind as I am.'

Drustan regarded him in silence. After a little, he began to eat his soup.

'What it can mean, I don't know,' said Deord. 'Alpin's taken him away on a raiding party.'

'You saw her,' Drustan said. 'Is she better now? Happy? You said questions. What questions?'

Deord's expression was quizzical. 'Come now, Drustan,' he said. 'Aren't you in a better position than I to answer that, with your spies there? They've been especially busy on their errands these last couple of days.'

'Tell me,' said Drustan. 'What questions?'

'She called me in for a brief interrogation. It was reasonable enough, since she's to be your brother's wife and mistress of Briar Wood. Asked me about doors and keys and who lived in this part of the fortress. He hasn't told her yet, obviously, and nor did I. Oh, and she threw in a casual enquiry about birds.'

Drustan smiled. It lit up his features and set a dazzling brightness in his eyes.

'Drustan,' Deord said quietly, 'I must warn you. Don't get involved in this; don't get tangled up in the situation, Alpin and this woman, the marriage, the treaty they're after, that fellow who quite clearly isn't the bard they call him. For you, this is perilous ground. Your brother did do as you bid him. He did go out and rescue the girl. Be glad of that, and stay out of it from now on. Think of her, if that will help. She's young and full of hopes, and she knows nothing of what happened here in the past. She's your brother's best chance of a decent future. Don't endanger that with your meddling.'

'What is her name?' Drustan asked softly.

'Ana. She's from the Light Isles, by way of Bridei's court. Impeccable pedigree, royal blood and, I'm forced to admit, not only beautiful and apparently virtuous but perceptive as well. Her only fault seems to be excess curiosity. Once Alpin tells her the truth, that should cease to be a problem. Let's hope he does so swiftly.'

'Ana . . .' Drustan's fingers, inside his pocket, toyed with the little thing the hoodie had brought him the night before.

'So,' Deord said, 'let us hope for good weather tomorrow. Now eat the rest of that supper or you won't have the strength to walk over to your bed, let alone out into the woods.'

✲

Alpin's party rode to the northeast, and when they crossed the river it was not through a ford but by way of a precarious plank bridge set high above a place where the water narrowed between rocky banks. The horses were blindfolded and led across each in turn. It seemed an ideal spot for an enemy to spring a surprise, but Faolan did not comment on that. He kept his ears open and his mouth shut.

The pace was swift. By the third sunrise the anticipated engagement with the Blues was imminent. Alpin's men were not saying much, but there was a look in their eyes that Faolan recognised: these hunters had scented blood. Nobody offered him a weapon with which to defend himself, and he did not ask for one. Instead, he devised strategies against the very real possibility that Alpin had brought him along so he could dispose of him out of Ana's view. *Your bard fell in battle, my dear. His fighting skills were, as one might expect, somewhat less than adequate.*

They came upon the Blues in a clearing by a stream. The approach was on foot, in silence. In this terrain a mounted attack would be chaotic, the advantages of height and speed outweighed by the enemy's ability to flee into thickets and copses, to dodge and weave where the horses could not readily follow. They had left their mounts at some distance. Faolan had rather hoped to be given the job of keeping an eye on them but Alpin, with a savage smile, had bid him come on with the men. 'We'll give you something to make songs about, bard!' Still no offer of dagger or knife.

Once it began, there was no time to think of songs. The attack was swift and bloody. The party of Blues, caught off guard in a makeshift encampment, put up a spirited defence, but they were no match for the swords and clubs, the thrusting spears and knives of Alpin's troop. The forest clearing was full of alien sounds: the grating of metal on metal, the gurgle of a man choking to death in his own blood, the scream of another who had lost a hand. Faolan did his best to follow the action while pretending to cower behind a tree, grateful that his drab servant's clothing made him unobtrusive.

The sounds changed after a while, with less of the screaming and grunting of injured men, and more of the systematic sound of sword or spear driving downwards as Alpin's warriors finished off the stricken remnants of the foe. Faolan saw the chieftain of Briar Wood lift a fist high in the air and call out a victory shout of some kind; and then came a sound that made the hairs rise on his neck. From all around them came the sound of running footsteps. The clink and jingle of metal closed in under the trees. Reinforcements had arrived.

There was only one way to go: upwards and out of reach. Faolan jumped, gripped a branch with both hands and swung himself less than gracefully into the beech tree that had furnished his cover. He was only just in time. A shrieking battle cry broke out on every side as a new party of Blues, he estimated twenty or more in number, charged from the woods with spears at the ready.

Alpin's men had already formed a tight circle, weapons held outwards. They were no barbarian rabble, but a disciplined fighting force; it was no wonder the Gaels sought him as an ally. Faolan shifted on his perch, peering out between the delicate new leaves of the beech. He freed a hand; one must be prepared for whatever might come. If necessary he would climb higher. There was no reason why a bard should not possess a modicum of athletic skill.

For some time Alpin's small band held off the attackers, but the men of Briar Wood had nowhere to go; any of them who broke from his comrades and ran at the circle of Blues would be mown down instantly. The Blues were angry. The clearing was strewn with the bodies of their comrades, slaughtered in the first attack. They would not leave off until they had had their recompense in blood.

Under such circumstances, a bard should remain quietly in the tree and let things unfold. He should wait until Alpin's men grew weary and started to make mistakes, then watch them being butchered in their turn. Do nothing; watch Alpin die. Take Ana home . . . It was not possible. The treaty must come first. So, take action. Save Alpin. Win himself approval, and with it the freedom to seek out information, which was, after all, his job. He did have one small tool at his disposal . . .

Unwittingly, Alpin assisted him. The chieftain of Briar Wood, red-faced and sweating, was holding his heavy sword before him two-handed and shouting taunts at one of the Blues, a thickset, ginger-bearded fellow.

'Taken to assaulting innocent travellers now, Dendrist? That was my wife you nearly killed down at Breaking Ford! That was her escort your thugs set upon! You'll pay for that miscalculation, and pay dearly! Nobody slights Alpin of Briar Wood!'

The Blues leader was standing a little behind his men. His own sword was sheathed. It seemed he was content to let his under-lings do the dirty work for him. 'Wife? What, another one?' he mocked. 'Lucky she drowned then. Better a quick death in the water than the sort of fate wives meet in that godforsaken pile you call home. You can save your rhetoric, Alpin. I lost ten men of my own in that flood. By the way, I heard there were two girls in that party of travellers. Who was the other one, a wife for your brother?'

Dendrist's men greeted this with derisive laughter. Alpin gave a snarl of pure hatred and lunged forward with the sword. One of the Blues jabbed with a spear; Alpin moved back out of reach. Thus far, his anger had not overruled his common sense.

'That what you're teaching your son there?' Alpin challenged, eyeing the young man with the spear. 'How to send innocent women to their deaths, how to fight battles with cheap taunts? No doubt he's growing up in the image of yourself, Dendrist, a black-hearted coward with nothing in his head but a petty greed for what's not his own. A weasel of a father, a stoat of a son.'

The young man thrust again, this time somewhat wildly. Alpin was standing quite still now, and the men had hushed as well, awaiting a response. Faolan seized the moment. He drew out the item he had hidden in his boot before they left Briar Wood, narrowed his eyes and threw.

The young man sagged to his knees, dropping the spear. In an instant, Alpin's sword was in the hand of the man next to him, Mordec, and Alpin himself had Dendrist's son pinned in front of him, a knife across his throat, while blood seeped from a wound in the young man's shoulder to dye his tunic crimson. The youth's face was grey with shock.

'How about a deal?' Alpin asked calmly. After one brief, aston-ished glance up towards the beech tree, he had not looked at Faolan.

Dendrist took a step closer; his own countenance was somewhat pale. 'Let him go!' he commanded. 'Your men have nowhere to run to! You're outnumbered and outplayed. Let my son go!'

'Now why would I do that? Notice how he's bleeding. You'd want to get a physician for that, or at the very least a bandage to stem the flow. And you wouldn't want to take too long about it.'

'Alpin, you scum –'

'I'll finish him off quickly if you prefer. I have the means here, and I've a knack for this. See?' The knife scored a thin red line on the boy's neck, and he drew a shuddering, squealing breath.

'You wouldn't dare!' Dendrist's voice was distorted with rage and fear.

'Try me, Dendrist. Am I known for holding back? No, don't order your men to attack. Do that and I'll be obliged to slit the boy's throat right away so I have both arms free to defend myself. Gods, this is an untidy business; I'm all over blood. Now, about that deal.'

'You swine, Alpin,' Dendrist muttered. 'Set your terms, just let the boy go. By all that's holy, you'll pay for this.'

'You take him, you leave, you go off and see that he's tended to,' Alpin said. 'You don't send half your men back to slaughter us the moment our backs are turned. You don't start running my men through as soon as I let the boy go. You don't have time for that, not at the rate he's bleeding. Have I your word?'

'You have my word,' Dendrist said through gritted teeth. 'Now release him.'

'Order your men to put up their arms and take five paces back. Give us clear passage out of here.' Alpin's grip on the young man had not slackened, nor had his troop's defensive ring of weapons lost its discipline.

'Do as he says.'

The men of the Blues muttered oaths and flashed furious looks as they sheathed their weapons.

'Release my son!'

'Not quite yet,' Alpin said. 'I don't think I trust you, Dendrist. Give me two of your men. We'll take them and the boy with us as far as Beacon Rise; then we'll move on for home and your fellows can bring your son to you. That limits the opportunity for dirty tricks on your part.'

'He could be dead by then!' Dendrist shouted, his eyes on his son's face, from which the colour had drained alarmingly.

Alpin smiled. 'And then won't you regret that you took so long to make up your mind? Now, how much longer do you want to continue this entertaining interchange?'

'Domnach, Omnist, go with him. My son's safety is paramount. We'll wait for you at the Deeprill crossing. I'll send a man ahead for healers. Now go, you!'

The circle of Blues drew back still further. Alpin and his men moved out, maintaining a defensive formation, the injured boy supported by two of the Briar Wood warriors. He would not bleed to death. Faolan knew that, and he suspected Alpin did as well. The position of the injury meant a spectacular amount of blood initially, but as long as it was staunched soon the boy would likely make a full recovery.

Now the Blues were on one side of the clearing and the men of Briar Wood on the other, heading off under the trees, their rearguard backing away with spears still pointed at the enemy. Faolan cleared his throat; all heads turned towards him and a Blue with a bow reached for his arrows.

'Ah,' Alpin said easily, 'we almost forgot our bard. Come down, Finian. It's all over now.'

Faolan swung down and walked across to Alpin's group, assuming the unsteady gait of a man in a state of shock after witnessing his first battle. He was somewhat relieved that nobody laughed. As Alpin's party, accompanied by the designated Blues, headed off in the direction of home, Dendrist's men were beginning the grim task of gathering up their fallen comrades. Alpin's act of revenge would surely spark retaliation later, forcing the chieftain of Briar Wood to respond in kind once again. Folk said it was in the nature of the Caitt to feud thus; today, Faolan had seen for himself that it was true.

At the place where the horses were tethered Alpin called a halt, and they cut away the young man's tunic and shirt to examine the wound. Erdig pulled out the weapon still lodged in the lad's shoulder, and a man who seemed to know what he was doing applied a pad of linen and a tight bandage. The boy gritted his teeth, making no sound. It seemed they bred them hardy in the north.

Alpin was holding the bloodstained weapon in his hands and frowning. He looked up and his eyes met Faolan's.

'That's one of our own kitchen knives,' Mordec said in surprise. 'See your mark on the handle, my lord?'

'Given to me for use at table,' said Faolan, making his tone a little tremulous. 'I didn't expect to be using it thus.'

'It's somewhat sharper than we usually keep them,' Alpin observed.

'I'd no tools for mending the harp, my lord,' Faolan said. 'A musician can't keep his instruments in order with a blunt knife.'

'And where does a bard learn to throw with such accuracy?'

Faolan attempted a nervous laugh. 'I surprised even myself, my lord. I'm astonished that my contribution was of service. To tell you the truth, I just shut my eyes and . . . well, threw.'

There was a ripple of laughter from the men. Alpin grinned but his eyes were shrewdly assessing. 'Well, you've given yourself something to make a song about when we get home. Now, is the lad strapped up? Erdig, he can ride in front of you to Beacon Rise. These fellows will have to run if they plan to come with us. Then it's on homewards. I've a comely young woman waiting for me now, and an itch that's demanding to be satisfied.'

Faolan felt a profound wish that he had aimed a little differently and sent the knife straight into Alpin's throat. Save for the unfortunate fact that, had he done so, they'd probably all have been slaughtered, the thought of that had great appeal.

'Good throw, bard,' one of the warriors said. 'Eyes shut? Hardly.'

'If that was sheer luck,' Mordec said, 'I'll eat my horse blanket. It was quite a distance.'

'I hate to admit it,' said the other man, 'but the mealy-mouthed musician here just saved all our lives.'

They reached the place called Beacon Rise before the sun was at its peak. Dendrist's two men, on foot, had been left far behind as Alpin's party rode on. Dendrist's son was unceremoniously dumped from Erdig's horse and staggered away to collapse onto the rocks by the track. He was sheet-white, tight-lipped, silent.

161

'Tell your father,' Alpin said, 'that it's time he learned to keep his hands off what's mine: land, stock, women. He should know by now that I'll take payment in kind.' His dagger was in his hand now; he dismounted and strode over to the young man. 'If my wife-to-be had indeed drowned, your father's men would not find a wounded boy here, but a lump of meat with the name of Alpin of Briar Wood carved into it. She survived, therefore you live. This time.' The knife was a handspan from the lad's face, and rock-steady. Faolan held his breath. 'As it is, you'll be waiting alone. I hope they get here soon; you're bleeding through your bandage. Come, men! I want to be halfway to the bridge by night-fall. I won't lie content until we're back across our own border.'

'We could wait,' Mordec suggested. 'Make an example of those two fellows when they get here.'

'Not this time,' Alpin said. 'We've had our due payment. Not that I wouldn't have enjoyed stringing the two of them up and indulging in a little target practice. But I've no great wish to add more fuel to this fire. All too soon we'll have bigger things on our minds. Dendrist and his kind will keep.'

Faolan pondered this as they headed for home. Bigger things. An active part in the war to come? On which side? The key lay in those western holdings, he was sure of it. With the terms of Bridei's treaty still to be laid out before Alpin, Faolan suspected double-dealing, lies and treachery. Time would tell; the longer he could maintain this guise of harmless musician, the better chance he had of unearthing the truth before it was too late.

The day after Ana spoke to Deord, the hoodie brought her a key. The bird came early, waking her soon after dawn with tapping, scraping sounds as it hopped from windowsill to chest, then a little thump as it dropped its gift on the polished wood for her inspection.

'What –?' Ana rubbed her eyes, half asleep. Her visitor uttered a cry in its harsh crow voice. Sitting up in bed, Ana glanced across and saw what it had carried to her. She was instantly wide awake. There was no doubt in her mind which door this would open.

She reached for her shawl, her mind racing ahead. 'Someone

wants me to go and look at storerooms today.' The hoodie had its head on one side. Its pose seemed expectant. 'I'm supposed to send a message back? I can't think what.' She'd end up bald as an onion if exchanges of hair were the only means of communication with this unknown entity. She should shoo the bird away and give the key to Alpin when he got back. A sensible girl brought up in a king's court should have no hesitation in doing just that. Ana reached out and took the key in her hand. 'There,' she said. 'I can't promise anything.' As if satisfied by her words, the hoodie hopped back to the sill and, with a strong beat of its dark wings, was gone into the morning.

Now, Ana thought, her heart drumming. Right now was the time. It was so early even the kitchen men and women would barely be stirring. As for Deord, he was a servant, however intimidating. If she went in there and encountered him, she would simply demand to be shown his place of work. She had met every craftsman at Briar Wood. This was no different, she told herself, not quite believing it. She could get there and back before anyone missed her. Alpin was away, and so was Faolan. It occurred to her, as she dressed quickly and put on the soft indoor boots she had been given, that Faolan would not approve. What lay beyond that door might be genuinely dangerous.

She picked up the little key once more and slipped out of her chamber, realising that before the journey to Briar Wood she would not have dreamed of attempting this. Something had shifted within her, something deep and vital. She walked quietly along the passageway to Alpin's door, opened it and went in. She tried to look as if she had every right to do so. The last thing she wanted was for her future husband to hear she had been sneaking around his house, spying out secrets and breaking rules.

The key turned noiselessly in the lock of the little inner door. Taking a deep breath, Ana pushed the door open and walked through.

She was in a stone chamber holding piles of sacks, old leather buckets and rusting iron tools. It was dim; shadows crept out from the corners and cobwebs festooned the roof beams. A black cat slept on the sacks, its tail twitching as it dreamed. Another could be glimpsed under a broken bench, a pair of gleaming eyes, a hint of stripes. Ana felt a stab of disappointment. She was not sure what she had been expecting, but it was certainly not this.

From somewhere beyond the storeroom a bird chirruped and there was a flutter of wings. The black cat lifted its head, suddenly awake.

'No, you don't,' Ana whispered and, following the sounds, threaded her way through the clutter into a second tiny room holding little more than empty shelves and piles of dust. The light brightened; she reached an open doorway leading out onto a steep flight of stone steps plunging down between looming walls. There were little windows set in the outer of these; Ana counted them as she passed. One: a distant view of water, a silver mirror in the dawn light. Two: the trunks of elms, warmed to gold by the rising sun. Their rook-tenanted crowns could be glimpsed above the stones. This was the outermost wall of the fortress, that was clear. But what was this inner wall, so tall, so solid? What need for that, and this strange narrow space between? Three: she was rapidly descending, and here she glimpsed the dark green shadows beneath the pines where the forest grew closer to Alpin's stronghold. Ana judged she was approaching the same level as the buildings set around the courtyard – the dining hall, the sewing chamber, the places of cooking and brewing, the armoury and smithy. Four: deeper still, the window level with the ground outside, thorny bushes pressing against the wall, their sharp fingers seeking entry to this lonely path, their strong hands clutching at the stone as if to test how well Alpin's defences might stand against the power of the wildwood. This opening would be invisible from the outside. Five: a secret kind of window, set in a depression of the land. The foliage was softer here, curling tendril and subtle frond and delicate leaflet. The crossbill waited on the sill, a splash of red against the lush green. The cats had not ventured beyond that last doorway.

'I'm here,' Ana said softly. 'Where are you taking me?'

At the foot of the steps the path went on, following the curve of the outer wall and sinking deeper still, the barriers on either side formidably tall. Ana thought of certain ancient stories; of captives held in high towers or behind impenetrable hedges, of heroes scaling walls or hacking through briars and brambles to liberate true love. For every such tale of quests fulfilled, she suspected there was another peopled by forgotten, lonely prisoners and fair ladies grown wrinkled and faded as they waited for a deliverance that never came.

The crossbill was leading her on, a short whirr of flight, a pause to wait, look, assure itself that she was still following. At length they rounded another curve of the path and there before them was a gate of iron grille-work, higher than a tall man, as broad as the path and, from the look of it, locked fast. Beyond it was some kind of court or garden.

The bird alighted on a crosspiece of the gate, looking back at her, then flew away within, a streak of scarlet. A moment later the wren appeared in its place.

Ana weighed the key in her hand. She moved up to the bars and peered inside, and the wren hopped onto her shoulder. There was a little sunken courtyard, bordered by the curving outer wall and roofed with close-set iron bars. It was gloomy within, for the place was set low in the ground and little of the early morning light penetrated there. Dimly, she could make out a patch of struggling grass, a stone bench, flagstones. On the inner side there was a building of some kind, its doorway shielded by a rough woollen hanging. Was this subterranean dwelling Deord's home? If so, why did he need such a gate, such a roof? It was like a cage. Ana thought of wild animals. Perhaps Alpin was one of those eccentric men who kept exotic creatures for pleasure, seeking to enhance their status by apparent mastery over such beasts. A wildcat, a dragon, a manticore . . . Surely not. Would these birds fly in and out so freely if death lay within one snap of the jaws? On the other hand, to unlock the gate, supposing she could, and march right in was perhaps over-bold.

'Is anybody there? Deord?' she called, not sure how she would respond if anyone answered. Her voice sounded odd in here, hollow and ringing, as if the place saw few visitors and could not quite accommodate her presence. 'Hello?'

There was no reply. The wren was preening its plumage close to her ear, and the crossbill had flown out of sight.

'Hello?' she called again, but nobody came. She tried the key in the lock. The iron gate opened smoothly and Ana went in, closing it behind her.

It did not take long to walk the perimeter of the sad little enclosure. All there was sorely bereft of sunlight, the grass limp and yellowing, the pond choked with slimy weed, its borders cracking into cavities where black mosses crusted the surface. Where there was stone paving, the place was swept clean. Ana moved over to the bench, stumbling as her foot caught in an obstacle. Metal chinked, and both birds cried out together as if in answer. Ana looked down. A long chain was fastened around a heavy iron ring set into the bench. The chain lay across her foot and over towards the outer wall where the smallest of openings was set through stone as thick as the length of a man's arm. The chain ended in an iron bracelet of cunning design. At a glance she could see how it might be tightened to fit a man's wrist or ankle snugly, and locked in place with a pin; how it might be loosened by another man so its captive could be freed. Ana felt a chill run through her. Who lived here? Who was it Alpin held under such security? And where was he now? She had been stupid to come here, utterly stupid . . .

She wondered at the position of the shackles, lying below the window chink as if the prisoner had stood there watching the world beyond his cell. What did he see? She stood on tiptoe and peered out through the tiny aperture. The place was so low that the bottom part of this window was underground. Through the narrow space above could be glimpsed, on a sharp upward rise, a single, beautiful oak, its spring foliage touched by the light of early morning to the purest of greens. A chorus of birds sang in its branches; their music was an anthem to freedom, and as Ana watched she saw them rise in a great flock to the open sky, winging out into the new day. Had a man wept here, raged, pleaded with the gods, watching them? She was being fanciful; putting her own thoughts into someone else's head. And time was passing. She would have a quick look inside, then hurry back to her chamber before Ludha arrived to help her wash and dress.

A table, a shelf, a bench. A container for water. On the wall, another iron ring set at the height of a man's waist; did this captive eat his meals chained? A millet broom, a bucket, folded cloths, all stored in orderly fashion. No supplies, only an empty tray, a platter, two bowls, two cups, two spoons. No knife. Ana ventured into the inner chamber, the wren on her right shoulder now joined by the crossbill on her left. There was so little light in here that she returned to the outer chamber to loop up the door-hanging before she investigated further. A lamp on a stone shelf, unlit, with a crock for oil beside it. Two rudimentary beds with straw mattresses and blankets of good woollen weave, sadly worn. All was neatly stowed, and the floor was strewn thickly with fresh rushes: Deord's doing, no doubt. Above one of the beds was yet another of those rings. It made her shudder to see it.

'It's a man they keep here,' she said to the birds. 'One doesn't house a wild beast in a blanketed bed, nor feed him his scraps on breakable earthenware. Imagine it: sleeping fettered, so that even in his dreams he can't run free . . . Surely he'd go crazy with long-ing for open skies and the wind on his face.' This neat apartment was, in its way, as sorry a place as the shadowy enclosure outside it. The key she had been given had revealed nothing but more unanswered questions. Time to retreat. Ana made to turn and the two birds flew down together to the rushes in the corner, where they began to peck about busily.

'What –?' Ana took a step towards them. Suddenly, the ground beneath her foot was not there. Teetering, she stepped back, then knelt and pulled aside the rushes, her heart racing.

Boards lay across an opening of some kind. She moved them aside, peering deeper. It was a tunnel; no hastily scooped hole, but a well-formed exit large enough for a strongly built man such as Deord to pass through without difficulty. The opening and its cover had been entirely concealed by the generous rush carpet. From the look of it, this had been here a long time. Its walls were stone-lined, not part of the fortress's original construction, she judged, but made afterwards by someone who knew what he was doing. Light was entering the underground place from the far end. It was a passage to the outside world; a way under the great wall of Alpin's fortress with, more likely than not, an exit amid the thick cover of the wildwood. Bold indeed. The prisoner could escape when he chose. This was becoming odder by the moment.

Ana hesitated on the edge of the drop. It was still early, but not so early that a servant or two might not be about quite soon, lighting

167

fires, tending to horses or dogs. She did have the key. Perhaps this should wait for another day. But . . .

The wren's tiny form darted down to vanish into the sub-terranean way. The crossbill fidgeted, ruffling its wings.

'Just to the outside then,' Ana murmured. 'Just to the other end, no further. I suppose these folk must have good reasons for such strong walls.'

She was quite a tall girl, but this had been made for big men, and passing through was easy. The bird flew ahead of her, and before long they reached the outside, emerging into a hollow at the foot of the fortress wall, a place well grown over with briars and creepers and concealed still further by a tumble of stones, perhaps remnants of some earlier construction now fallen to ruins. Ana was breathing hard, as much from anticipation as exertion. It was not far past dawn and the light was gentle on the foliage above her. Crossbill and wren perched side by side on a thorny branch at the lip of the hollow, apparently waiting. There was no way she could simply turn back as she had promised herself she would do. These two were surely leading her to the answers she sought.

She clambered up, glancing to the top of the wall as she did so; there might be guards patrolling there on an upper walkway with a wide view of the forest. Just now, nobody was in sight. 'Very well,' she whispered. 'Take me to wherever it is, but be quick about it or I'll be in trouble.'

If there was a path into the forest, the feet that travelled it walked lightly, for it was scarcely visible. Ana picked her way between the sharp-thorned bushes, the snagging briars and perilous brambles, following the bright splash of red that was the crossbill. The wren could hardly be seen amid the restless, changing tapestry of leaves and sunlight. Before long the way fell into deep shade. They were going under oaks and the light was filtered through a canopy of burgeoning green. The prickly undergrowth turned to moss and fern, through which small watercourses threaded a meandering way. Myriad tiny, damp-loving plants spread small blankets over fallen branch and trunk. The leaf litter of last autumn had left a rich, dark mixture underfoot, and Ana sensed the working of creeping creatures in its depths, bringing the soil to teeming life. A mob of siskins darted through the trees above her, squabbling amongst themselves.

The path took a turn uphill between great stones over which brambles had spread, knotting themselves into tight cages. There would be good pickings here later in the season. If she was still at Briar Wood in summer, she would come out with Ludha and gather berries. If she married Alpin . . . Ana's mind veered away from that possibility. Frowning, she hitched up her skirt and clambered to the top of the rise.

The birds were waiting again, side by side on a branch. Ana paused to listen. The forest was full of little sounds, chirping, calling, rustling, the murmuring of water. But there was something else there now, a shuffling, a grunting that was not made by the small creatures of the woodland about their business. Ana thought of wild boar, and considered what she would do if such an animal appeared, tusks, bristles, a driving force of sharp-footed muscle. Scream? Run? Scramble into a tree and wait for rescue? She blushed to imagine what Faolan would think of her wandering out here all alone. She had not even brought the knife he had given her.

The sounds were coming from further along the path, where the way dipped down on the far side of the rise. It was a place well out of sight of Alpin's sentry posts. The natural contour of the land and the close-set tree cover made this prime territory for secret movement. The men of Faolan's expedition had been full of tales they had heard, of travellers lost in the forests of the Caitt and never found; of sudden inexplicable deaths; of ways that started broad and straight and ended in twisting nightmares, leading a fellow in circles until he perished from cold, thirst or sheer terror. They had indeed lost their lives, every one, but only the Blues and the inclement season could be blamed for that. Still, Ana had seen for herself how far Briar Wood lay from other settlements. She had heard Alpin speak of the changeable nature of this forest and she had believed him.

She stood still, trying to interpret the sounds, until the birds flew off again, leading her down the hill. She trod carefully. Whatever lay ahead, she did not wish it to see her until she had a chance to assess the danger.

She emerged to a clearing encircled by smaller trees: here grew elder and willow, and the gurgle of a hidden stream sounded from somewhere beneath their shade. Ana took a step further, then halted abruptly. Two men were wrestling on the open ground, their bodies locked in a fierce embrace, muscle holding hard against muscle, heads down like those of sparring stags, legs planted firmly as each sought to topple the other. Stripped to the waist, their bodies gleamed with the sweat of exertion. On the sward nearby lay a homespun robe and other items of clothing, belts, shirts. One man she recognised, for he was stocky and bald, broad-shouldered, barrel-chested: Deord. Perhaps this was a time off duty for Alpin's special guard and one of his fellows. That was Deord's robe, and the belt that lay half concealed by it had borne his keys, almost certainly including the one now safe in her pocket. The hoodie was perched on a low branch not far from these possessions, as if guarding them.

As for the second man, he was tall, she could see that as the two of them released their hold and, in a flurry of agile limbs, circled and came to grips once more. The second man was graceful, wide of shoulder and narrow of waist, long-legged and supple in his movements. He was quick; his skill in ducking and weaving kept him out of Deord's powerful grip until he was ready for him. This man had a strong-boned face that seemed vaguely familiar. The skin was unmarked; he bore neither kin signs nor battle counts. Like Deord he was clean-shaven, but he had a head of luxuriant hair the tawny hue of an eagle's feathers, or sun on autumn oaks, or the pelt of a red fox. His eyes were bright; whether it was the fair morning or his enjoyment of the fine sport, or whether he was a man naturally given to laughter, those eyes captured all the brilliance of the dawn, rendering his features radiant with light. Ana had to remind herself to breathe. He was, quite simply, the most beautiful thing she had ever set eyes upon.

Suddenly the need to avoid being seen was urgent. She had come where she should not; she had intruded on something deeply private. She edged back towards the cover of the bushes.

The hoodie cried out harshly; wren and crossbill took flight in the same instant, winging towards the men. There was a sudden stillness. The combatants unlocked themselves and straightened, turning towards Ana as the wren alighted on the tall man's head and the crossbill on his shoulder. Too late to flee; she must brazen this out, account for herself somehow. She was breathing too fast and her palms were clammy. Deord was starting towards her now, saying something, but she did not know what, for the other man was looking at her, and the expression in his eyes stripped away all but the need to look back, to look and look until she thought she might drown . . . Oh, how he stared! His eyes were like stars, like pools under moonlight, like deep wells full of dreams, and she could not turn her gaze away, but must stand like a foolish girl unable to summon a single word to say, unable to collect herself and behave as a woman of royal blood should. She could feel his gaze deep inside her, making her burn and melt and tremble. What was he, a sorcerer, that he could wield such power over her?

'My lady,' Deord was saying as he reached her side, 'you should not be here. How did you –?' He had himself well under control, but Ana could hear both anger and alarm in his tone.

'I . . .' Still she could not find her voice. She clasped her hands tightly together, struggling for self-control as the tawny-haired man walked over to stand behind Deord, not three paces from her. His gaze had never left her. For all the light in those bright, wonderful, terrifying eyes, his mouth was sombre, his manner guarded.

'You found us,' he said quietly.

Deord stiffened. 'Drustan,' he snapped, 'what have you been doing?' Then, to Ana, 'How did you get out here? Why have you come?'

His manner was not at all that of a servant to a lady; however, Ana was all too aware of the rules she had broken this morning. She drew out the key from her pocket, holding it on her open palm. Deord reached for it, and she closed her fingers.

'How did you come by that? Surely Alpin didn't give you –'

'I think it's yours,' Ana said. 'Delivered to me at dawn by a small visitor. Someone wanted me to come here.'

'Back inside.' Deord's tone was sharp, a command. 'Drustan, get your things on. I told you not to meddle. Your folly has cost you time in the sun today, and may yet bring down a far harsher penalty. The lady must return to the house immediately.'

His companion made no move. His eyes were on Ana. 'Not yet,' he said.

'Now,' said Deord. 'Make haste. No argument.' As the other man moved to pick up his clothing, surprising Ana with his acquiescence, Deord addressed her once more. 'As you have come this far, no doubt you will have questions. I will answer them if I can, but not here, and not now. If we are discovered outside the wall, or if you bear the tale of this meeting to Alpin, we lose what little freedom we have made for ourselves. You've done us a grave disservice through your curiosity. Drustan and his birds are equally to blame. We must return within our enclosure straightaway.'

'But –' Ana did not finish. The man called Drustan had thrown his shirt on roughly, not bothering to fasten it, and now he was picking up a length of chain attached to an iron bracelet; the other end trailed along the ground to end in a second such manacle. As she stared, horrified, the tawny-haired man set one of these rings around his wrist, then stood quietly while Deord tightened it and locked it in place. Then the guard shrugged on robe and belt and settled the other bracelet around his own arm. Ana stood mute. This was the wild beast, the dangerous captive, this lovely young man with his open face, his shy voice and his eyes bright as stars. A prisoner who went willingly, it seemed, out of fresh air and sunlight to his dark confinement, his place where high walls shut out the morning. She had seen the way his eyes changed as he submitted to the shackles.

'Not yet,' she said, putting a hand on Deord's arm. 'Please. Let him enjoy the sunlight a little longer. I didn't mean to . . .'

Deord's mouth tightened. 'This isn't a game for highborn young ladies. You were foolish to come here. To anger Alpin is to risk much.'

Suddenly she was able to lift her head high, to take a deep breath and to speak as a royal daughter should. 'Alpin is not my husband yet,' she said coolly. 'I am my own woman. I mean no harm here; in fact, Alpin told me to make myself at home in his absence. To explore as I pleased.'

'You will not please him by wandering alone in the forest, nor by unlocking private doors,' Deord said. 'You meddle in perilous matters. You could cause great harm. We must go now.'

'Deord.' Drustan spoke quietly still, but there was a note in his voice that gave Ana pause. Where did the balance lie between these two? Surely a man who was a prisoner did not use such a tone to his keeper. 'A few moments only. There is time.'

Deord was silent. After a little he turned his back to stand staring out into the forest. 'Be quick,' he said. 'You know my opinion. What in the name of all that's holy did you think you were doing? And don't tell me one of your friends there took my key without your knowledge; I see in your face that it's not so.'

'I was opening a door,' Drustan said.

The chain was taut between the two men. Deord held a loop of it in his free hand, as if ready to jerk Drustan away if he moved too close to her. Ana looked at the prisoner and he looked back at her. His eyes were changeable, their colour reflecting the many hues of the forest, leaves dappled with sunlight, distances of shadow-grey. He said nothing more. Perhaps, like her, he had momentarily lost his words. She thought his manner something akin to that of a wild creature poised for flight, fascinated yet wary.

'I'm sorry,' she managed, her racing heart making her voice unsteady. This was all so strange; it was as if the usual codes of behaviour had been suddenly swept away. 'If I've put the two of you at risk, I very much regret . . . I didn't know . . .'

'Are you well?' Drustan asked. His voice was under no better control than her own; he cleared his throat and tried again. 'It was a terrible thing when your companions were lost at the ford; a dark day for you.'

'You know about that?'

There was a moment's pause, then he said, 'Deord and I spoke of it.'

'Did you send them?' Ana asked him. 'The birds?'

A nod, a fleeting smile that revealed a dimple at the corner of his mouth.

'Why would you do that?' Ana was struggling for clues as to what questions to ask, for there were so many she did not know where to start.

173

Drustan made no reply. Indeed, Ana began to wonder if he were somewhat confused in his wits. For all the keen intelligence in his eyes, his manner was more than a little odd. Had long captivity caused him to forget the conventions of a household such as Alpin's, so that he spoke as and when he chose, without the constraints of accepted behaviour? Or was it that Drustan existed on some level outside those patterns and cared nothing for convention?

'Are you angry, Ana?' he whispered.

As he spoke her name she felt something stir deep within her, in the place where the blood surged most strongly. 'No,' she said. 'Just confused. Are you a druid or a sorcerer, that you make such use of creatures? Why are you locked up here?'

He dropped his gaze; his fingers fiddled with the shackles. His shoulders were no longer set square. 'From necessity,' he said. 'To do otherwise is dangerous.' Then, after a moment, 'Are you afraid of me?'

How might one answer honestly? She could not tell him his eyes made her hot and cold and faint, that they captured her and swept her into a dream. If there were anything here to frighten her, it was that. 'I can't answer that, Drustan – that is your name?' she said, and saw his body tense as she spoke it. 'I know nothing of you save what I see.'

He looked up once more. 'What do you see?' he asked.

These were deep waters indeed. 'I can't tell you,' said Ana.

They walked back to the tunnel in silence, a strange procession. Deord made Ana go first; he followed, and his captive came behind with the full length of the chain between them. It seemed to Ana, glancing back, that the two of them had done this so often they adhered to certain codes of behaviour without much conscious thought. It was evident to her that Deord preferred Drustan not to come too close to her. Given the shackles, the locked doors, the secluded enclosure, she must assume that this prisoner was dangerous, but for the life of her she could not imagine him as a violent man. Would that tiny wren nestle in his hair and the other creatures perch trustingly on his shoulders if he were given to bouts of rage or frenzy?

Back in the dim enclosure, Deord fastened his charge to the

shackles set in the bench before releasing the bracelet and chain that linked the two men together. Drustan was not looking at her now. He stood in the shadows by the wall, his head bowed, and said not a word.

'Come,' said Deord. 'I'll escort you as far as the door and ensure you are not seen. Give me the key.'

Ana looked at him.

'Without it,' Deord said calmly, 'the two of us are imprisoned here and cannot so much as fetch our meals or fresh water. We do not go out often. These trips beyond the wall are covert. Perhaps you did not understand that.'

'You asked me not to tell Alpin,' Ana said. 'I suppose you expect me to hand over the key and keep my mouth shut, as if I had seen nothing here. I won't do that, Deord.'

His manner remained untroubled. 'I will take the key from you if I must. I would prefer that you gave it willingly. He requires protection. You're interfering in a matter of which you have no understanding.'

'Then explain it to me,' Ana said. 'Tell me who he is and why he's shut up here. Tell me why nobody out there has mentioned this. What sort of crime must a man commit to deserve such incarceration?'

'Not here. You must leave now.' Already he was ushering her towards the grilled gate. Behind them, Drustan had not stirred. To see him thus defeated, the light in his eyes quenched, troubled Ana greatly. Deprived of the sun and the wildwood, he seemed a shadow of the man she had watched in the clearing, a creature lovely as a bird in flight.

'Very well,' she said. 'I will go, but you must tell me the story later. And you must let me return here.'

'Folk don't come here,' Deord said flatly. 'It's not safe. Alpin's rules. If you want to change it, talk to him. Now move.'

Ana was not accustomed to being addressed thus and it offended her, but Deord was right to urge haste, for the sun was creeping up the sky; she had been here far too long. 'Give me a moment,' she said, and without waiting for a response she walked briskly across the enclosure to stand beside the silent Drustan, close enough to touch.

'No!' Deord said sharply, but Ana closed her ears to his voice. She reached out and took the shackled hand in hers. The touch sent a thrill through her body, startling and heady.

'I must go now,' she said, looking up at the prisoner. 'I'm sorry I cut short your time of freedom. If there's anything I can do to help you . . .'

'Enough,' said Deord, and he seized Ana's arm to draw her away. Drustan's hand came up so quickly that Ana gasped, the captive gripping his guard's wrist until Deord's fingers opened and he released her. She recognised in that moment Drustan's fearsome strength.

'Don't touch her,' Drustan said quietly. 'She will go with you of her own accord; no need for force. Goodbye, Ana. It made me happy to see you.'

Ana felt a curious sense of bereavement. She could not understand it; they were strangers to one another. 'Farewell,' she said. 'I hope I will speak with you again. No matter what you did, surely you do not deserve this.' She made to withdraw her hand; Drustan lifted it instead, touching it to his lips and closing his eyes a moment. Ana felt the blood surge to her cheeks, and saw a flush rise in Drustan's features, a perfect reflection. Then he released her, turning away. The strange meeting was over.

'I cannot speak to you now,' Deord said quietly as the two of them reached the little door to Alpin's chamber and, with a sigh, Ana placed the key in his outstretched hand. 'It will be noticed if I deviate from the expected pattern of my day. I will attend you before supper.'

'With my maid present, I will be unable to seek the answers I need,' said Ana.

'That is your choice.'

'No,' she told him, 'it seems it is Alpin's choice: to lock this prisoner away and conceal him further behind a web of secrets. Whatever it is he has done, Drustan could still have visitors, surely. He does not seem a dangerous man.'

'No, he does not,' Deord said mildly, opening the door and going through in front of her to check there was nobody about. 'But I know him. You are a stranger here.'

'Very well,' Ana said. 'I will speak with you later. You can rely on my discretion. Please tell Drustan that. I'm truly sorry the two of you had to come back inside because of me. I understand how precious those escapes must be to you.'

Deord inclined his head politely. A moment later he had vanished back through the door and closed it in her face.

Chapter Seven

It was afternoon. Ana sat in the sewing room with the other women and tried to concentrate on hemming, but she was finding it difficult to fix her mind on anything save Drustan's light-filled eyes, his quiet voice, his powerful hands. The memory of his touch brought the blood to her cheeks once more. Her hands trembled and she almost dropped her needle.

'Are you unwell, my lady?' Ludha asked in an undertone, eyes anxious.

'I'm quite well, Ludha, just a little tired. I slept poorly last night.'

'I could finish that for you –'

'I can do it!' Ana heard the sharp note in her own voice. It was not fair that her little maid should suffer because she could not keep her mind on her job; because she was behaving like some foolish lass who cannot look at a comely man without her knees turning to jelly. Ana straightened her back and spoke to herself with the voice of a royal daughter. *They don't chain people up for nothing. Drustan must have done something terribly wrong.* It didn't seem to help much; her body was still restless, her mind filled with his image. She tried again. *I'm here to make an alliance for*

Bridei. I shouldn't allow myself to be distracted. Then she said to herself, *Faolan would be shocked by what I did. He would think very badly of me.* After that, it was possible to turn her attention back to her work for a little and to observe how crooked the last few stitches had been. Sighing, she began to unpick them and found the garment removed gently from her hands.

'Please,' Ludha said. 'Let me help. This is such a sweet little gown, it would be a pity to spoil it.'

Ana nodded. 'I thought I'd begin replacing the baby clothes, the ones that were lost at the ford. But my stitching is awry today.'

'No matter, my lady.' Ludha was already whipping out the spoiled work, lips pursed in concentration, eyes narrowed. 'I could finish this with a worked border, if you approve. I have some fine-spun coloured thread, russet, blue, a heathery green. Flowers, maybe?'

Ana smiled absently. 'How about birds?' she said.

'Birds? What kind of birds?'

A wren, a crossbill, a hoodie. 'I'll leave that up to you,' Ana said. 'I'm sure you'll do a beautiful job, Ludha.'

'Thank you, my lady.'

Drustan's hands were white-knuckled on the grilled gate, the fingers threaded through the ironwork. The rhythmic clang of the metal filled the small enclosure, a drumbeat of pain; the birds were hiding up high, huddled in a tiny niche below the barred roof. Each time Drustan struck his head against the iron, the birds shuddered as if they felt the blow in their own frail bodies. On the far side of the enclosure Deord was calmly sweeping. He kept a close eye on his charge.

The gate was rattling on its supports; Drustan was strong. One day he would wrench it free. It was unlikely to do him much good. Deord had seldom been required to exercise his full strength, but he had been hired for his ability to deal with such a situation and deal with it he would, if it came. He hoped it would not. There were other ways of controlling this captive, better ways of keeping his mind and body reasonably sound during the long imprisonment. Deord swept and watched, and after a certain length of time the slamming sounds slowed and ceased and there was only Drustan's breathing, a gasping like that of a child who has wept all his tears.

The broom stopped moving. 'Drustan?' Deord asked quietly.

Drustan turned. His eyes were wild. The pain in them struck Deord like a blow to the chest.

'Out!' Drustan's voice was hoarse and uneven. 'I want out! I want it to be over!' He strode towards Deord, hands raised before him as if to seize the other by the throat.

'Come,' said Deord, setting down his broom and moving to the bench. 'Sit by me. Breathe slowly.' His arms came out to take Drustan's and he guided him to sit. 'You're frightening the birds.'

Drustan buried his head in his hands. His fingers clutched tight into the fiery strands of his hair. His whole body quivered with tension.

'Breathe slowly, as we practised,' Deord said again. 'This will pass.' He had made no attempt to shackle his charge; the manacle and its chain lay slack beneath the bench. 'Sit quiet; let your breath calm you. Trust me, Drustan. It will pass.' He continued in this vein awhile, his tone soft as he sat on the bench beside the other man.

After a time, Drustan's breathing became less laboured, less ragged. It was clear the red-haired man was making an effort to regain his self-control. After a longer time, Drustan raised his head, sat upright and took his hands from his hair to wrap his arms around himself as if he were chill to the bone. Without a word Deord got up and fetched a blanket from the sleeping quarters. By the time he came back the birds had flown down to perch one, two and three on Drustan's head and shoulders.

'Here,' Deord said, wrapping the blanket around the other man; the birds arose with a small flurry of wings and settled once more. 'This girl has upset you. You should not have encouraged her curiosity. All that's likely to achieve is to bring down your brother's anger, not just on the two of us, but on her as well.'

'She will not tell him.'

'Your trust is childlike, Drustan. She may not intend to do so. But I saw the look in her eye as she handed back the key. A righteous look; she believes your imprisonment unjust and will be hard put not to tax her husband with it. How can she explain that to Alpin, when he believes she knows nothing of your existence?'

Drustan regarded him soberly. 'He's not her husband,' he said.

'He will be,' Deord said. 'He wants her. They say he makes no attempt to conceal that. She's more than usually comely. And she's here to seal a treaty between Alpin and Bridei of Fortriu. It will happen.'

Drustan reached up and the wren hopped onto his finger. With his other hand he stroked its plumage gently. 'Deord?'

'What is it?'

'Ana should not marry my brother.'

'Should not? What is this? You know such decisions are all to do with strategy, alliances, territorial advantages. Clearly both Bridei and your brother think it entirely appropriate that this go ahead. You should not have involved yourself with her.'

'She should not wed him. Her light will be dimmed; her spirit will be quenched.'

Deord regarded him curiously. 'It was you who sent Alpin to fetch her from the road,' he said.

A flicker of his earlier anger made Drustan's features suddenly dangerous. 'How else could we help her?' he challenged. 'Had I been free to go myself, I would have told her . . . I would have warned her . . .'

'Hush,' Deord said. 'You go too far. Your brother has an opportunity. He and this girl should do well enough together. I agree, she seems a little too much of a lady to be quite at home here, but she's not lacking in her wits and she's demonstrated that she can stand up for herself. Besides, your opinion and mine count for nothing at all in such matters. You should not have meddled.'

'She will not tell.'

'In fact the lady asked me to convey a message to you to just that effect,' Deord said diffidently. 'That we could rely on her discretion.'

Drustan smiled, the anger gone.

'Her intentions are good,' Deord went on. 'It's her ability to maintain that discretion once Alpin starts to tell her the truth that

181

concerns me. Your brother will want to keep Ana as far away from you as possible. You can hardly expect otherwise.'

Drustan made no reply. The smile had faded quickly. After a little he said, 'I would never hurt her.' His voice was constrained. 'Never. She knows that.'

Deord's eyes were full of compassion as he regarded his charge. 'She is naïve,' he said, 'if she makes her assessment of men so quickly. Perhaps she believes she knows. But you cannot know. You can never be sure, and nor can your brother. For that reason you must stay out of this. You must leave the two of them to live their lives, and to make and mend their own errors.'

Drustan looked his keeper straight in the eye. 'And what do you believe?' he asked quietly. 'Do you believe I would hurt her? What do you see in me?'

'A man of many good qualities.'

'But you still don't trust me.'

'You don't trust yourself, deep down. You did what you did. Alpin believes it can happen again. If you hadn't been his blood kin he would have put you to death seven years ago. There would then have been no need for my services.'

Drustan gazed down at his hands, open on his lap, and the tiny wren nestled trustingly on his palm. 'This is a kind of death,' he said. 'Had I a knife, I would be a hair's-breadth from ending this imprisonment today, from opening my veins and letting Bone Mother take me. I've endured seven winters. I can't do this forever.'

'You'd be surprised what a man can weather,' Deord said. 'You're strong. You'll get through it.' After a moment he added, 'Don't think I haven't been tempted, at full moon in the woods. Don't imagine I haven't thought of turning my back a moment too long and letting you disappear.'

'Then he would punish you. He would kill you.'

'I'm not without certain physical resources. That's why he hired me.'

'My brother has many loyal men, and all of them love to hunt. Even you could not escape.'

'The question's irrelevant,' Deord said. 'You would return. You always do.'

'A hundred years would not be long enough to compensate him for what I did.' Drustan's voice had shrunk to a whisper. 'I cannot risk repeating that deed.' Drustan lifted his hands and the tiny bird flew across to perch on the iron gate. 'Why don't you leave, Deord? Even the heaviest purse of silver is inadequate pay for such an existence. Guarding me condemns you, too, to lifelong imprisonment.'

'Hush,' Deord said, rising to his feet. 'I do what I do and, like you, I dream of an end to it some day. An end that has nothing to do with knives and veins.'

Drustan sat quiet for a long time. Crossbill and hoodie kept vigil, one on each shoulder. Deord busied himself within the living quarters. The sun passed over. Its pale light glanced briefly across bare flagstones, dark water, stone walls, gone almost before it had time to touch this sunken space. At length Drustan got up and went to stand by the little window, staring out at the tree framed by walls made to withstand the assaults of siege weaponry. The oak's broad canopy was brushed with light; the colour glowed.

'A flower plucked carelessly and left to wilt,' he said softly. 'A forest bird tethered to a perch and forced to sing. How can we stand by and see that? She should not wed him.' But there was nobody to hear him but the two birds, and if they had any opinion on the matter, they did not voice it.

As Alpin's party rode back to Briar Wood, Faolan worked at his bardic character: a little shaken, but surprised and pleased that he had been able to assist them in their skirmish. They made rudimentary camp for the night, then rode at speed along the ill-defined tracks that threaded, mazelike, through these tangled woods. When they stopped to confer before crossing the difficult bridge that marked the border of Alpin's own land, Faolan noticed that the water level, though still dangerously high, had gone down since their previous passage four days earlier. Soon enough Breaking Ford might provide safe crossing once more, if the flood had not scoured too many holes in the riverbed.

Ana was waiting for her husband-to-be as the party rode

through the gates of the fortress. She looked distracted as she greeted Alpin, as if her mind were somewhere else entirely. She did not glance Faolan's way at all. He let a groom take his horse and made his way to the sleeping quarters.

Someone had found the harp. It lay on the pallet he had been allocated, a sorry-looking instrument whose broken pegs and missing strings spoke of long neglect. An image of another harp was in Faolan's mind, one whose curves and lines a bard's hands knew intimately, whose strings recognised his touch like that of a lover, whose frame trembled in his arms as the instrument sang of passion or death or delight. This poor remnant of the past would never play such a tune.

'Can you fix it?' Gerdic was passing by, a bucket in each hand, heading out to the pump.

'Given the materials, I might make something of it.' The desire to offer a negative was strong, but one must be mindful of Alpin and how much rode on winning his trust. 'Need to replace at least three of the strings and fashion a couple of pegs as well. If there's a supply of suitable wood, and tools I can borrow, I'll make a start in the morning. Where would I find sheep gut?'

Faolan could not speak to Ana alone at suppertime, nor afterwards. He sat in his place amongst the serving men of Briar Wood and watched her unobtrusively as she partook of the meal. She was listening to Alpin and his favoured men as they recounted the tale of their victory over the Blues. She seemed a small island of tranquillity amid the raucous company of the Caitt with their rowdy jests, expansive gestures and robust enthusiasm for their ale and meat. Faolan wondered if she could ever be at home here. He pictured her as an old woman; she would still be beautiful. She would sit quietly as the household belched and shouted and guffawed around her. She would watch her children and grand-children in turn become part of this riotous, undisciplined company. Undisciplined: no, that was inaccurate. On the field of battle these warriors were no rabble. Their leader was astute and decisive, the men courageous, controlled and skilful. They could be a threat to Bridei or a significant asset. He must not lose sight of that.

Faolan's attention moved to the broad-shouldered form of the bald serving man, Deord, who had come in with his little tray and was filling it from the side table. A small loaf, a squat jug, roast meat on a platter, something steaming in a bowl. Deord was efficient and methodical; his task did not take him long. For a moment, as he turned to retreat once more to the family quarters, his eyes met Faolan's and there was recognition in them, acknowledgement of something shared. A moment later he was gone.

When the meal was over, the tables and benches were moved and there was wrestling, and after it dogfighting. Faolan made himself stay in the hall and watch. He pretended to drink his ale. He did his best to shut out the gurgling, snarling screams as the stronger hound slowly tore the other apart. He joined in the applause for the victor's owner, a pugilistic-looking fellow with a thick neck and a network of scars on his face overlaying his warrior markings.

Ana had remained in the hall. She was ashen white, her features pinched with horror. Most of the other women had left before the dogfighting began, with only one or two staying to join the men in their avid, howling circle around the combatants. Faolan had seen Alpin's hand close around Ana's arm as she tried to excuse herself, and it had turned him cold with fury. The lord of Briar Wood was not just a boor, he was cruel.

The entertainment concluded, folk set about clearing away the mess of bloodied straw. Faolan sat awhile with Gerdic and the others, pondering what it was in a man that such harsh sports awakened. He thought of Bridei and the god of the Well of Shades, a god who required an annual sacrifice as demonstration of his people's obedience: a sacrifice not of a chicken or lamb or goat, but of a young and innocent woman. Bridei did not speak of it much; discussion of this particular deity and his demands was forbidden under the laws of Priteni ritual observance. But Faolan had seen Bridei's face on the night a girl had died at the hand of the old king and his druid to appease the Nameless One. And Bridei had told him that what men felt when that god awoke in his dark power was not only awe, terror, revulsion, but also excitement, a thrilling sensation that was both pleasure and deepest shame. All men possessed that sense within them, Bridei said, though it was generally hidden deep, and few were prepared to acknowledge its existence. Privately, Faolan doubted very much that Bridei himself had ever gained enjoyment from shedding the blood of the powerless. Bridei was the embodiment of all that was just and good, balancing the authority of a king with kindness and generosity. Indeed, he had called a halt to that most extreme form of the Gateway sacrifice. For him, once had been more than enough.

As for other men, Faolan already knew the darkness that resided within them, the desire not merely to shed blood but to twist the knife while doing so. His personal lesson in man's inhumanity had been unforgettable. Tonight, watching as the folk of Briar Wood bayed and roared at the slow death of a hound, he felt a profound desire to be back at White Hill. He wanted quiet. He wanted time to think. In particular, he did not want to be sitting here watching Ana's distress, and himself not able to do a thing to help her. As for the harp waiting for his expert attention, he tried to put it from his mind, for that, in its way, was the most troublesome thing of all.

'Bard!' barked Alpin suddenly.

Faolan walked up to the place where the chieftain sat by Ana's side and bent his knee in show of deference. 'My lord.'

'Your presence will be required in the morning,' Alpin told him. 'The lady wants you to be in attendance when we hold our formal discussions on the subject of marriage. I don't see the need for it myself, but we must humour the womenfolk, mustn't we?' He patted Ana's hand and winked.

Faolan kept his expression impassive. 'As I will be the bearer of your reply to King Bridei, the lady's request seems appropriate.'

Alpin scowled. 'We don't require your opinions, bard. That's all. You'll be summoned when it's time.' It was plain that any gratitude the chieftain of Briar Wood might have felt for the gift of a strategically thrown knife had evaporated now he was on home soil once again.

'Yes, my lord.' Faolan retreated; he felt the eyes of Alpin's men on him as he did so, not hostile exactly, just interested. They were perhaps more interested than was altogether desirable. Never mind that. It was pleasing that the negotiations would be so soon.

186

Get this thing done and he had some slight chance of being back at White Hill before Bridei departed. He had planned to stay and see Ana settled, if not happily, then at least securely. His enthusiasm for that job, never strong, was fading by the moment. What he really wanted was to remove her from Briar Wood straightaway, to head for home and never come back here. That was a wild dream, impossible for so many reasons he could hardly believe some part of his mind still entertained it. If he could not separate his own feelings from the situation, she was surely better off without him.

They met in the small council chamber that was part of Alpin's sleeping quarters. Faolan did not much care for the venue; he could not look at the capacious bed with its luxuriant fur covers without imagining Alpin disporting on it with his new wife, and this made it difficult to maintain the demeanour he had calculated best suited to this meeting: calm, quiet, perhaps a little overawed, for what does a mere musician understand of weighty strategic matters? At least, that was the way Alpin would think. Such an oaf would not make the logical connection between a bardic repertoire and a knowledge of the great flow of affairs. And that, thought Faolan, was just as well. When they finally forced him to sing, he'd offer some rollicking ditty full of hunting, drinking and nubile women, and with luck it would satisfy them.

A guard let him in. Alpin, seated at the table, acknowledged his presence with a grunt but did not invite him to sit. Faolan stood relaxed, hands behind his back, gaze on the middle distance. There was a second guard standing behind the chieftain and another man seated at the table.

They waited. Ale was poured; Alpin did not offer Faolan a cup. After a considerable time there was a tap on the door and Ana came in accompanied by her maid.

'You won't need the girl,' Alpin said crisply. 'Ludha, that'll be all –'

'Stay, Ludha.' Ana's face was pale, her eyes shadowed from a night either wakeful or haunted by unwelcome dreams. Her firm tone was that of a princess. 'A simple matter of propriety, my lord. It's inappropriate for me to attend a meeting of men without my maidservant. I am accustomed to certain standards of behaviour, and I do not intend to let them lapse now that I am in a new home.' She forced a polite smile.

'Very well, my dear, mustn't let our standards slip, must we?' Alpin blustered. 'You're late. I forgive you that; I can see you haven't been wasting the time.' His eyes travelled with admiration from her elaborately plaited hair to her neatly pressed tunic and skirt to her soft kidskin slippers. It was quite plain to Faolan that the fellow was assessing the sweet curves and lines of the figure part concealed by the demure dress. He saw the self-satisfied look on Alpin's face. The chieftain was sure of victory here and made no secret of his desire for the prize. Faolan turned his gaze away.

'You can sit on the bench by that little door, Ludha,' Ana said, coming to join Alpin at the table. 'Are these men to remain here, my lord?'

'Only fair,' said Alpin, grinning. 'You get your bard, I have Dregard here to advise me. We can't have the Gael running back to Bridei with a report that things were conducted improperly.'

'And the others?' Ana glanced at the guards.

'You must be used to minders,' Alpin said. 'Haven't you been a hostage since you were a child? That much was conveyed to me in Bridei's cryptic message. I took it as a veiled assurance that my bride would reach me in pristine condition.'

A protest rose to Faolan's lips, to be swallowed as Ana frowned at him.

'What danger could possibly threaten us in such a stronghold, my lord?' she asked Alpin, casting a casual glance towards the inner door as she spoke.

There was a little pause, during which Faolan detected a tension in the chamber which he could not put a name to, something unspoken and deeply dangerous.

'The guards are for your own safety, my dear,' Alpin said. 'And mine. We don't like surprises here, but at least we know how to prepare for them. Now, where were we?'

Ana cleared her throat. 'As you know, Bridei's official spokesman was drowned at Breaking Ford. He had some written messages with him; those were all lost –'

'What was this man's name?' The question was sharp.

'Kinet,' said Faolan before Ana could answer. 'Kinet of the house of Fortrenn. He fell to a Blues arrow.'

'If I want you to speak I'll tell you so,' Alpin snapped. 'The lady doesn't need your assistance to respond to simple questions. Was this emissary Bridei's blood kin? A warrior?'

'This is a meeting to discuss terms for an agreement,' Ana said quietly. 'It is not an inquisition. Kinet was a good man, both fighter and courtier, a friend to the king and to me. And he is dead. I will set out Bridei's terms as well as I can, my lord. I would ask that you allow me to do so uninterrupted. It will be necessary for Faolan to help me with some details; we did travel a good part of the way in company with the king's spokesman, and we talked of certain matters with him. In addition, I am Queen Tuala's personal friend, and –'

'We?' Alpin's dark eyes were suddenly stony, his full lips compressed into a dangerous line.

'A bard's job is to entertain his lady, my lord,' Ana said. 'To hearten and cheer her. We were a party of thirteen in all; not large. It was inevitable that Faolan became privy to certain information.'

'I see.'

'May I proceed with the terms?'

'By all means.' Alpin leaned back in his chair and folded his arms. His adviser, Dregard, put his elbows on the table.

'Faolan, you may sit down,' Ana said, and for a brief moment the full warmth of her eyes was on him. He sat, not speaking.

She did a very passable job considering there were aspects of the situation she had not been advised of. She explained that Bridei, as a long-time enemy of the Gaels of Dalriada, was anxious to secure Alpin as a sworn ally; that he wished to ensure the allegiance of Briar Wood was with himself and not with the invaders in the west. The king understood, Ana said, that the location of Alpin's territory, so close to the furthest reach of the Gaels within Priteni lands, would likely make him a target for overtures from Gabhran. However, as the Caitt and the folk of Fortriu were both of Priteni blood, descended from the same ancestry and sharing the same language and the same faith, Bridei thought it likely Alpin would be amenable to an approach from White Hill.

'How many of the other Caitt chieftains has he persuaded to this?' Alpin asked. His gaze had sharpened; Faolan was struck once again by the feeling that there was a good strategic mind behind the brash exterior. *Don't mention Umbrig*, he willed Ana. There was no safe way to warn her. Alpin was following their every glance.

'I cannot tell you of that,' Ana said.

'Cannot or will not?' Alpin's tone now verged on the outright discourteous; Faolan saw Ana flinch and spoke quickly.

'Lady Ana is unlikely to be able to provide that sort of information,' he said. 'It's been a long time since any of your fellow tribesmen visited White Hill. You can hardly imagine –'

'Be silent!' Alpin rapped out. 'You're here under sufferance, and if I want you to open your mouth, I'll say so. The question was simple enough, even for a woman. Well?'

'I can't tell you because I don't know.' Ana's voice was less steady now; her features were pinched with distaste. 'Nothing was said of this by Bridei's messenger. And, after all, there was only one bride to send.' She summoned a smile, answering Alpin's rudeness with wit and charm. After a moment's startled silence, the chieftain of Briar Wood broke into laughter.

Faolan sat rigid lest fury overwhelm the need to continue playing his part. He was within a whisker of leaping to his feet and telling Alpin the truth, for how could he look on while this man insulted and belittled his future wife thus? Couldn't he see what Ana was, as rare and lovely a woman as had ever walked the glens of Fortriu, so fair and honest and good that she deserved the finest of kings as a partner, not some crude wretch who couldn't even attempt to be civil? Faolan's hands balled themselves into fists; he took a deep breath and relaxed them, wishing he had a few of Bridei's druid tricks at his disposal.

'I've a question.' It was the man Dregard who spoke; he wore a grey woollen robe rather than the tunic, trousers and boots of a warrior, and had the look of one whose trade is plied indoors, for he was pale of complexion and a constant small frown had worked a double wrinkle onto his high forehead.

'Go on, Dregard,' Alpin said. 'I'm sure Ana is keen to tell us all she knows, little as it seems to be.'

'Is Bridei after an addition to his fighting force?' the grey-robed man queried. 'It's well known that the Caitt armies are formidable, Lord Alpin's in particular. Such overtures as this are hardly new to him. So, is this a request that we offer men and arms in support of a venture by Fortriu? A major advance against Dalriada, for example? When might such an expedition take place?'

Ana drew a deep breath. 'That is four questions at least,' she said. 'To the best of my understanding, and you are right, my lord, it is limited, I believe Bridei seeks only your assurance that the men of Briar Wood will not take up arms against him. He does not anticipate any contribution by the Caitt to his own forces. I cannot tell you what venture is planned, nor when it might come about. I did, in fact, attempt to ask some questions on those matters when I learned I must travel to Briar Wood. I obtained no satisfactory answers.'

This was close to the truth; Faolan had not thought she would play such a dangerous game.

'You're well endowed with curiosity,' Alpin commented with a little smile. 'But then, that's perhaps not so surprising in a young woman.'

Ana did not reply.

'If I'd been in your position,' Alpin said, 'I'd have been asking Bridei why he didn't wait for a reply to his message before despatching you on your journey. Why such haste? Unusual, that. Unusual and not particularly kind to you. Isn't this young king generally referred to as a model of all that is just and good, as if he were indeed a human embodiment of the Flamekeeper or some such?' He scratched his beard. 'Or is that just a tale put out by his cronies, the druid Broichan and the others, to remind the rest of us who holds the real power in the Priteni lands now? The druid worked the election rather cleverly, so I was told.'

Ana looked at Faolan, an appeal in her eyes.

'May I speak?' Faolan addressed the question directly to her.

'Please do, Faolan,' Ana said. Then, turning to the others, 'Faolan has spent some time at Bridei's court; he's had opportunity to observe the king in the company of men.'

'What they say of Bridei is true,' Faolan said quietly. 'It is not for nothing they call him the Eagle; he possesses a far-seeing strength and a heart-deep devotion to the old gods of the Priteni. Of recent times men have been giving him a new name, one in keeping with his plans for the future of his people.'

'And what name is that?' Alpin was interested despite himself.

'They're calling him the Blade of Fortriu, my lord; the one who will sweep the lands of the west clean of the Gaelic invader.'

'I see.' Alpin regarded him closely. 'You announce this in the manner of a man who thinks little of it one way or another. And yet you're a Gael, and a Gael of high birth unless I'm very much mistaken. Why aren't you plucking your strings and blowing your pipes at the court of the Dalriadan king in Dunadd, or back over the water in Ulaid? The lords of the Uí Néill would value your services, I expect.'

'I'm in Lady Ana's employ, my lord, until she is settled at Briar Wood. At that time, lacking another messenger, I will convey the news of what transpired here back to White Hill for her. My past is of no relevance. I left the west long ago and I have no plans to return.' Alpin had come close to the mark, painfully close; this line of questioning must be shut down swiftly.

'As for the other question,' Ana put in, 'I was disconcerted by the requirement that I ride here before the king received your response. You can imagine, I am sure, how a young woman feels in such a situation.' She was blushing. Faolan was struck, for a crazy moment, by the belief that she had seen his own confusion and spoken up to divert Alpin's attention from him. 'A woman prefers to know she is welcome,' Ana went on. 'She prefers to wed where she is sure of her future husband's approval. That we had no idea of your feelings on the matter troubled me greatly on the journey here but, of course, when the flood came and we lost so many . . . I realised then how unimportant such petty concerns were . . . I'm sorry . . .' She reached up a hand to brush tears from her eyes; an instant later the little maid, Ludha, was there with a clean handkerchief and a murmured word. 'Thank you, Ludha. I apologise, my lord.' Ana squared her shoulders, lifted her head. 'As you see, I am still not quite recovered from that experience.'

'You should give the lady more time.' Faolan was unable to remain silent. 'Surely this discussion can wait –'

'No, Faolan,' Ana said. 'We must at least set out Bridei's terms now. We owe it to those who perished to complete the mission.'

'Mission?' echoed Dregard. 'Since when does a bridal journey become a mission?'

'It becomes one when the marriage is dependent on a written and witnessed treaty,' Ana said firmly. 'That's what Bridei requires. The terms are to be set down by a scribe and overseen by an independent party such as a druid; since you'll need to summon a druid for the handfasting anyway, that should be easy to arrange. Lord Alpin agrees that Briar Wood will not take up arms against Bridei nor ally itself with the Gaels. That's what it must say. In return, the marriage between myself and Lord Alpin will go ahead.'

Her voice had suddenly lost its confident note, but she went grimly on. 'I did not think to have to present my own case here, but it seems I must. I am of the royal line of the Priteni, through the branch that furnishes the kings of the Folk, who are subject to the overlordship of the King of Fortriu. My cousin is king in the Light Isles. I come from a healthy and fruitful family. I am in my nineteenth year and have lived at the court of Fortriu since I was a child of ten. As for Bridei's reasons in despatching our party when he did, I was never told them. As a royal hostage of long standing I have learned to obey the king's orders and not to ask too many questions, my lord. Perhaps I do possess an excess of curiosity, but I would never allow that to endanger other folk's lives, nor my own.'

There was a moment's silence, then Alpin put his hands together in slow applause.

Ana's blush deepened to red. 'You mock me, my lord?' Her voice was shaking now.

Tension filled every part of Faolan's body, though whether the urge to take her in his arms and comfort her or the desire to wring that hairy thug's neck for him was stronger, he could not tell. He sat perfectly still, keeping his demeanour calm. In his line of business, the skill of not drawing attention was a primary tool. There wasn't a lot he could do about the maelstrom in his heart, but he could at least ensure it remained there, invisible.

'Not at all, my dear,' Alpin said. 'Let me give you some ale; you seem distressed. My admiration is entirely genuine. You find yourself in a particularly awkward situation and, I'm sorry to admit, there's a certain entertainment to be had in watching you struggle with it. You deal with it ably for a young woman; of course I do not expect you to have much knowledge of the games men play, your Bridei amongst them. Any education you have had was all fine embroidery and preserving fruit in honey, I expect.'

Ana regarded him in silence a moment. Faolan recalled that she had been educated in Fola's establishment at Banmerren, along with an exceptional group of young women, including both Tuala and Talorgen's daughter, Ferada. Fola was revered for her scholarship and intellectual rigour.

'Fine embroidery is one of my particular interests, my lord,' Ana said coolly. 'Now, concerning the treaty. Do you require a certain time to make up your mind? Have you any questions?' Her brows lifted in queenly fashion, and in that moment Faolan admired her most of all, for she made humiliation into a triumph. Her eyes caught his a moment; he allowed himself a little nod, a hint of a smile.

'May I speak, my lady?' he asked her again.

'Most certainly, Faolan.'

'I believe there's a point that needs to be clarified,' he said, hunching his shoulders a little in the demeanour of a man uncomfortable at having to speak out in a company of his betters. He hoped he wasn't overdoing it.

'What point?' Alpin snapped.

'Go on, Faolan,' Ana said softly, playing the game. 'You may well have heard something of significance at White Hill, something I was not privy to. Men will discuss these things in more depth when women are not present, I know that.'

'It was something Kinet mentioned,' Faolan said, thinking quickly. 'Something about my lord Alpin's other property on the west coast and the need to be sure the loyalty of both households is secured by this treaty.'

'On the west coast?' mused Ana, who knew very well the significance of that. 'Now why would – oh, I see. It would provide a sea route to Dalriada . . . yes, I'm sure Bridei would want to be certain the agreement extended to all your territories, my lord. I was not aware that you had another tract of land besides Briar Wood. It is a long way to the west coast, is it not?'

'Long enough,' said Alpin shortly. His tone had grown cold. 'The place there, Dreaming Glen, is not mine, it's my brother's.'

Faolan managed to conceal his surprise. Back at White Hill there'd been no talk of any brother; if this had been known, Bridei would have been sure to investigate further before setting out his terms. He was still searching for the right question to ask when Ana spoke.

'You have a brother? You didn't speak of him when I asked you about your family. Or perhaps I misheard. He's in the west, I presume. Alpin, the marriage must wait until this brother can be consulted. Clearly Bridei will need the consent of you both to the agreement. I regret to say this, but it appears he views each of you as a potential threat or, one would hope, a significant ally.'

She was bold. Faolan hoped she had not overstepped the mark, for if Alpin reacted with anger he thought he might not be able to control his own response this time. But the answer, when it came, surprised him. The chieftain of Briar Wood erupted into bitter, self-mocking laughter.

'Consult my brother? I think not. All you'd get out of him was nonsense. I speak for him on all such matters.'

There was a silence. Ana and Faolan looked at him, waiting for more. For the first time Alpin looked uncomfortable. His broad cheeks had flushed and he was not meeting anyone's eye but fiddling with his ale cup, a fine piece with red stones set near the rim and a pattern of dogs in wire work.

'I don't understand,' Ana said after it became apparent Alpin was not going to offer a further explanation. 'You say you speak for him, but if this place, Dreaming Glen, is his, then surely he must control whatever forces are there. What do you mean, my lord?'

'Briar Wood was our father's land,' Alpin said. His reluctance to elaborate was obvious; he was ill at ease, restless on the chair, fingers in constant movement. 'The other place was passed to my brother direct from our maternal grandfather, a special arrangement.

But, alas, my brother is in no fit state to take responsibility for lands or men. He is . . . deeply unwell.'

'I'm sorry to hear that,' Ana said. 'I hope he will be better soon. Perhaps a messenger could be despatched to the west so we can obtain his consent to the agreement. I understand that he cannot travel, of course. Such a long way, and difficult . . .'

'I could go,' Faolan offered helpfully.

Dregard cleared his throat as if about to speak.

'This is not something of which we talk openly here at Briar Wood,' Alpin said heavily. 'It would have suited me better to wait and give Ana the information in private. It's a family matter and quite delicate in nature.'

Ana and Faolan maintained their silence, waiting for more.

'The fact is,' Alpin said, 'my brother is not at Dreaming Glen, he's here, and has been for all the years of his . . . illness. His affliction is a lifelong condition, and incurable.'

'Your brother is here?' Ana exclaimed. 'Then why . . . is he too ill to be in company? How sad for you!' She was not playing a game any longer, but spoke in genuine sympathy. 'What is it, the falling sickness?'

Alpin gave a grim smile. 'Would that it were a malady so easily accommodated, my dear. I'm afraid Drustan has a condition that renders him a threat both to himself and to others. It's been necessary to keep him in . . . confinement. He's . . . I don't know how to put it for you. He's just not right in the head, and he never has been.'

Faolan's attention was drawn to Ana's face, for during this last speech something had changed in her expression; she seemed to him unaccountably dismayed by Alpin's speech. 'Excuse me,' she said abruptly. 'I'm feeling a little unwell. May we resume this later? Ludha, come with me.' She turned her back and left the chamber, and the maid scurried after.

For a little, none of the men spoke. Then Alpin took the ale jug, refilled his own cup and Dregard's and, after a moment's hesitation, poured a third and pushed it in Faolan's direction. 'I've upset the lady,' the chieftain said. 'Such news is never well received, and certainly not by a young bride. What girl wants to learn she's marrying into a family with a streak of insanity?

There are ways of telling people these things, and that wasn't the best way.'

'I'm sorry,' Faolan said quietly, and meant it. Not that he cared at all for Alpin's sensitivities, but he would have done much to avoid distressing Ana. Her reaction had surprised him. She had handled Alpin's veiled insults with the judgement of a councillor and the good manners of a lady. But this news had shaken her.

'She'll come to terms with it, my lord,' Dregard said.

'I hope so,' Alpin said, sipping his ale, 'for I confess to a strong desire – a bard might say a burning desire – for this marriage to go ahead. This woman can provide me with fine sons, and a great deal of pleasure in the getting of them. I can see she's livelier than her demure manners suggest. I had hoped we might conclude this speedily. I've already sent for a druid, I did so the day you arrived,' glancing at Faolan. 'The fellow should be here within a turning of the moon, possibly sooner if the weather allows. There are not so many of that kind in the northern lands, and they tend to favour inconvenient places to live: caves halfway up cliffs, or barely accessible islets, or hidden clefts in deep woods. There's a small community of them in the far north of Umbrig's land; I sent my message there. Let's hope we get someone who can write. I don't keep a household scribe here. Word of mouth is a good enough pledge of faith amongst the Caitt.'

'I understand King Bridei's terms were quite specific, my lord,' Faolan said. 'A written, witnessed agreement, to be conveyed back to White Hill.'

'Who would sign on Bridei's behalf?' Alpin's eyes narrowed.

'I think you'll find the lady knows Latin and can write.' It gave Faolan considerable pleasure to watch Alpin's face as he said this. 'She's had an extensive education. For a woman.'

'I see. A scholar, is she? All the same, I expect I'll be able to teach her a few new tricks.'

'Yes, my lord.' Faolan spoke through gritted teeth.

'You are close to her,' Alpin observed.

'I've worked for the Lady Ana awhile, my lord. But I am, after all, no more than a servant.'

'Hmm. Very well, you're dismissed. I don't have the inclination to discuss this further now. I'll consent to the agreement on

Drustan's behalf. He hasn't the capacity to make such decisions. The value of the lady to me is far above some petty matter of alliances. If Bridei wants us to leave his forces alone, we'll do so. We've enough territorial problems of our own without getting embroiled in the south as well. Once the druid's here we'll conclude the matter and you can be off home, lad. Get that harp in working order and you can keep us entertained while we're waiting for him to arrive. New song every night, keep you on your toes.'

'Yes, my lord.'

Alpin rose to his feet. He towered over the other men in the chamber. 'Stay away from the lady,' he said, and his voice had a note in it that was new. 'No private conferences. *No more than a servant* isn't good enough for me. She's mine, and any man who lays a finger on her, or looks at her in a way I don't like, will find himself dangling from a rope above my front gates with his personal parts stuffed in his mouth. Do I make myself clear?'

'Yes, my lord.' Faolan was seething.

'Go now.'

Faolan managed to maintain a servile demeanour as he quit Alpin's chamber. A whole turning of the moon, he thought as he passed the door to the room where he knew Ana was lodged. It was going to be quite a test. Perhaps it was just as well he was forbidden to see her alone, for his heart might get the better of him, causing him to speak words he would bitterly regret. He might beg her to come home with him; he might do his best to convince her she must not wed a man who could never make her happy.

Faolan found a place alone, up on the walkway behind the parapet wall, and stood there thinking as the sun passed overhead and the shadows changed in the vast pattern of greens and browns and greys that was Briar Wood. The treaty was almost secured. The mission was all but accomplished. Why, then, was he full of this ridiculous longing to go back, to be tired and cold and hungry, sitting by a tiny fire in the midnight dark with only Ana for company? The feeling gripped him so powerfully it was a physical hurt. *You can't have it,* he told himself. *You can't now, and you never could. Let her go. Do your job. Do the only thing that you can do.*

After a while he returned to his quarters, sought out the material he needed and set to with knife and wood to fashion tuning pegs.

Ana spent the day in her chamber with only Ludha for company. She had no desire to hear Alpin's explanations, though he had knocked on her door three times to enquire how she was. His brother. Drustan was Alpin's brother. How could that be? How could that lovely man with his lambent eyes and gentle manners be kin to an uncouth chieftain whose tastes ran to crude blood sports and the baiting of women for amusement? Even if Drustan was suffering from a sickness of the mind, how could Alpin keep him chained like a savage dog, shut away from the light? Besides, Drustan did not seem sick. He did not seem mad. Though a little odd in his manner of speech, he had appeared quite rational to her. As she paced the length of her chamber, torn between confusion and indignation, it came to her that being incarcerated for a long time would inevitably have the effect of turning a man's mind somewhat strange. Wouldn't Drustan be hurt, angry, resentful, afraid? She had seen how his eyes lit up when he was out in the woods, free, able to feel the sun on his face and to stretch his body to the full. She had seen the shadow that fell on him like a dark cloak when he re-entered his subterranean enclosure. Perhaps there was not much wrong with him at all. Why wasn't Alpin trying to help his brother instead of pretending he didn't exist? Why wasn't he seeking a cure?

Deord could have given her answers, should have done, as he had promised when he took back the key. Thus far he had evaded her, muttering something about Drustan needing him, and no spare time. And now that Alpin was back, Ana had lost her opportunity to question Drustan's keeper.

'What is it, my lady?' Ludha asked for the tenth time, eyeing her mistress with growing alarm. 'Are you unwell? It distresses me to see you like this.'

Ana opened her mouth to say yet again that it was nothing, then hesitated. It was unfair to involve Ludha in such a matter, but there was nobody else who could help. Faolan was beyond her reach; it was clear to her that Alpin would not sanction any private meetings between his lady and her bard.

'Ludha,' she said, 'I suppose you heard what Lord Alpin told us about the prisoner, his brother, Drustan.' To speak the name aloud gave her the strangest feeling, a warmth deep in her breast.

'Yes, my lady.' Ludha was not meeting her eye; she worked industriously at her embroidery. An exquisite garland of forest green and violet blue now flowered across the hem of the tiny garment Ana had passed on to her maid for completion.

'You already knew of this captive? That Alpin's own brother was shut away here at Briar Wood?'

'Everyone knows, my lady. We were told not to mention it until Lord Alpin had the chance to explain it to you himself. So you wouldn't be upset or frightened. It's quite safe. That man, Deord, looks after him.'

'It's not my safety I'm concerned about, Ludha. I'm shocked and distressed that Alpin would treat his own brother thus. That he would shut him away in such a . . .' Ana fell silent. She would not reveal what she had seen, not even to Ludha. There was a conspiracy of silence here and the maid had been party to it. Who was to say she might not now go running to Orna, or to Alpin himself, to pass on anything Ana might tell her? 'It's cruel for a man to be a prisoner his whole life. I suppose he is kept in that place where Deord goes, behind Alpin's sleeping quarters.'

'That's what they say, my lady.'

'What is he like, this man Drustan? Alpin said he was . . . incapable. That he could talk only nonsense.' And since that had already been demonstrated to be untrue, perhaps the rest of the story was a lie as well.

'I don't know, my lady. They never let him out. They say he's crazy. Violent. He has fits, turns, as if a kind of frenzy comes over him. Deord is the only one strong enough to handle him. That's what they say.'

Ana felt cold. 'But you've been here – what – six years? You mean in all that time Alpin's brother has never been out of his cell? Not once?'

'No, my lady. Orna says it's too much of a risk. I couldn't say myself. There aren't many folk here who knew him before.'

'Before what?'

Ludha had fallen silent. She bent, lips pursed, over her handiwork.

'Before what, Ludha?' Perhaps, Ana thought in exasperation, if she simply went on asking, eventually these folk would tell her what she needed to know. 'Speak up!' Too late, when Ludha looked up and was revealed to have tears in her eyes, Ana realised how sharp her tone had become. 'I'm sorry, Ludha. I'm not cross with you, just angry that they would treat a man like that when his condition is hardly of his own making. I'm not used to people having so many secrets. Please, just tell me what you know. I would like to help Drustan if I can. Indeed, if I am to stay here as Alpin's wife, I believe it is my duty to do so.'

'He did something bad when the fit was on him,' Ludha whispered. 'So Alpin had him put away. Most of the folk who lived here in those days are gone. Hardly anyone really knows what happened, and people don't talk about it. But it was terrible enough that Lord Alpin's brother can't be allowed out, ever. That's all I know.'

Ana pondered this. 'What about earlier?' she mused. 'When he was a child, a boy? Who would know about that?'

Ludha shook her head. 'Nobody. Only Lord Alpin and his sister, who never comes here. And . . .'

'And who?'

'There's an old lady they speak of, who lives all alone out in the forest somewhere. Bela, her name is. She used to be their nurse when they were children, Lord Alpin and his brother and sister. But nobody really knows where she is, or even if she's still alive.'

'I thought these woods were dangerous. Full of eldritch presences, not to speak of combative neighbours. Why doesn't this old retainer live within the safety of the fortress walls?'

'I don't know, my lady. Old folk can be quite pig-headed. My grandfather got very difficult at the end. He was always bringing chickens into the house. It drove my mother crazy. Maybe this old lady is just tired of being among folk.'

Ana reached a decision. 'Ludha?'

'Yes, my lady?'

'I need to know if I can trust you. I must be sure you won't speak to Orna behind my back, or to Lord Alpin, or to anyone else I tell you not to. You're working for me now. Maidservant and friend. What do you say?'

'My lady –' Ludha stopped short, staring past her mistress to the narrow window opening. A fluttering of wings and, as Ana turned, the crossbill flew over to alight on her shoulder. It carried a small blue flower in its beak.

'Oh,' Ludha said softly, making a sign of protection with her fingers. Her rosy cheeks had turned pale. 'They say – that is –'

'That the birds come from Drustan?' Ana queried.

Ludha nodded, round-eyed, as the crossbill preened its feathers and settled, making itself at home.

'This is not the first such visit to my chamber. Do these creatures go freely in the household?'

'No, my lady. People speak of them. Of him and his birds. I've never seen one before. There are lots of cats here, and they're all good hunters.'

'Now, Ludha, answer my other question. I need to know if you can hold your tongue. If the answer's yes, I want you to help me. I know you're a good girl, a kind girl, and I hope you will agree, for I have nobody else.'

Ludha put her embroidery down. 'Yes,' she said. 'What must I do?'

'Nothing dangerous. First, I want you to let Orna know I have a headache and I'll be keeping to my chamber for the rest of the day. You'll fetch me a tray for supper. I particularly don't want to see Lord Alpin.'

'Yes, my lady.'

'And then, while the household is at supper, I need you to keep watch for me.'

'Keep watch? Where?'

'Outside Lord Alpin's chamber. It's all right, Ludha, don't look so shocked. All I'm going to do is ask a couple of questions I should have had answers to long ago.'

Deord had not got his job as special guard without good reason. As he opened the little inner door and stepped out into Alpin's bedchamber, supper tray in hand, Ana moved from the shadows to stand in front of him and found herself spun around with both arms pinioned behind her in a bone-breaking grip. The tray clattered to the ground, spilling its contents. Deord had moved so fast she was his captive before she had time to draw a single breath. A moment later his hold slackened and he released her. Ana rubbed her wrists, wincing. The bird had flown through towards Drustan's quarters the moment the door was opened.

'That was foolish.' Deord's voice was calm. 'I'm obliged to react to any possible threat immediately. There wasn't time to identify you. You should not be here.'

'In the bedchamber of my future husband? Are you obliged to react to that as well?'

Deord regarded her steadily. 'I perform a duty as a custodian,' he said. 'A protector. By now Alpin will have given you the explanation you sought. I must go. My duties are by the book, precise and timely.'

'It was you I wanted answers from.'

'Drustan was distressed that evening; unwell. I told you. I could not be absent long.'

'Perhaps it is his captivity that distresses him. I believe such long periods in the semidark would render the sanest man unwell.'

He said nothing, but bent to gather up the fallen objects, platter, bowls, spoons.

'Please,' Ana said. 'Alpin hasn't told me anything yet, only that Drustan is his brother and has some malady that renders him unable to live a normal life. I want you to tell me why. Why is he locked up? Is he really dangerous? What was it that happened to begin all this?' She scooped up the two cups and set them on the tray. 'Please, Deord. I want to help Drustan. I can't believe his illness is incurable; he seems so courteous, so . . . so good.'

'He's a comely man,' Deord commented without any particular emphasis.

Ana's cheeks flamed. 'That has nothing to do with it!' she snapped. 'Now answer my questions.'

'What orders I take, I take from Alpin.'

'Answer me, or I'll tell him I saw you outside the wall.' Her voice was shaking. She hoped he would not realise she had no intention of doing any such thing, not if telling would mean the end of this captive's snatched moments of liberty.

'Here.' Deord set the tray down, opened the little door, drew Ana through by the arm and closed the door behind them so they stood in the darkened storage room beyond. 'This must be quick. By meddling thus you risk our safety and your own. Alpin knows everything there is to know. He's the one you're marrying; his answers are the ones you need.'

'I want yours.'

'Why?' he asked flatly.

'Because I believe that if you tell me anything, it'll be the truth. Because I think you are Drustan's friend. Is he really ill? Mad?'

Deord hesitated. 'His mind is not like yours or mine,' he said. 'Some folk see it as madness.'

'And how do you see it, Deord?'

'I'm a hired guard. My opinions are irrelevant.'

It was just like talking to Faolan at his most difficult. 'Do you think Drustan is out of his wits? Is that plain enough for you?'

'Out of them, or more in them than us ordinary folk. He and I have shared these quarters a long time. Being shut away – it changes a man's outlook on the world and the people in it. Maybe nobody's sane. Maybe there are only different degrees of craziness. You shouldn't interfere. This goes deep, with him and with Alpin. The way it is now may be the best that can be managed. Best for both of them.'

'The best?' Ana was outraged. 'Shutting that man up in a shadowy hollow, forbidding him the sun and the open, keeping him away from other folk as if he were a dangerous beast – that is a very poor best.'

'You know little of such matters,' Deord said, 'if you think that a cruel form of captivity. Ask your bardic friend what he knows of prisons.'

'Ask Faolan? What do you mean? You know him?'

'I had not met him before he came to Briar Wood. Nonetheless, we have a shared past. I am certain Faolan understands that, given the circumstances, Alpin's arrangements for his brother are as generous as they can be. Speak to your bard about a place of incarceration known as Breakstone Hollow, in Ulaid. A place both he and I know intimately, from the inside.'

'I can't speak to Faolan,' Ana said flatly. 'Alpin won't allow him to see me in private.' She was bitterly disappointed that this was all Deord could offer. It had seemed to her, that morning in the forest as she watched the play of light on naked flesh and the sport the two of them made together, that there was a bond between keeper and captive beyond that of mere familiarity. She had thought he and Drustan were friends. As for the talk of incarceration, she found herself unsurprised there was such a tale in Faolan's past.

'I can't help you,' Deord said flatly. 'You'd best leave us alone. Your arrival stirred Drustan up; awakened dreams he can't afford to entertain. It only makes things more difficult –'

The door crashed open. Alpin stood in the entry, hands on hips, face distorted with fury, and as she flinched back, Ana glimpsed Ludha across the bedchamber, cowering against the far wall with the mark of a blow red on her cheek. The Chieftain of Briar Wood took a stride into the narrow way, reaching out as if to grab Ana by the shoulder. In an eye-blink Deord was between them, his sturdy figure standing with one hand flat against each wall, forming a barrier between Alpin and his wife-to-be. Ana's heart was pounding. A clammy sweat broke out on her skin. Deord had moved in total silence.

'What is this?' roared Alpin. 'What are you doing here with him? Who gave you the key?'

Ana swallowed and spoke from beyond the protective line of Deord's muscular arm. 'I wished to ask your special guard a question,' she said. 'This is not Deord's doing; he did his best not to speak to me, my lord. He said you were the one to provide me with answers. Perhaps you will do so now. It would be a great deal more comfortable over there at the table. And we can allow Deord to go about his duties. Your brother will be hungry.' Gods, she was shaking like a leaf. Alpin was opening and closing his fists as if he were about to attack Deord or herself or both of them at once. She couldn't think of anything to do but act as if this were all quite normal. 'Thank you, Deord, I will be safe now. You can go.'

Deord lowered his arms very slowly, his calm eyes set on Alpin's angry ones. The Chieftain of Briar Wood stepped back a pace.

'Come, my lord, I still feel somewhat unwell and would prefer to sit,' Ana managed, making her way to the table. 'Ludha, go and put a cold cloth on that bruise; ask Orna to help you. I'll be all right here until you get back.' Ludha fled; Deord, tray in hand, moved quietly from the chamber, a whisper of long robes on the flagstoned floor. Alpin stood in the centre of the room, legs apart, glowering.

'Did you strike my maid?' Ana asked, seizing the upper ground. Her teeth were chattering; she clenched her jaw tight, raised her brows, tried for the queenly expression that had often aided her confidence in the past.

'What were you doing in there with him?' Alpin demanded, ignoring her question. He made no move to join her at the table. 'My wife doesn't spend time alone with any man except me, *any* man, bard or courtier or servant, understand? If the fellow wasn't so valuable I'd have him horsewhipped for breaking that rule –'

'Alpin, sit down.' Ana fought back her anger and summoned a smile. 'Please. I was upset earlier today when you spoke of your brother and his illness. I would have asked you to explain but . . . I felt awkward. So I asked Deord, since I could not fail to notice his routine as a particular kind of guard. I'm sorry if I have transgressed some rule I did not know of. You must trust me very little if you think it necessary to set such restrictions on my freedom. I'm not accustomed to being treated as if I were untrustworthy.'

Alpin sat down opposite her, his big hands on the tabletop, features set in a thunderous scowl.

'I do want you to explain it all to me,' Ana went on. 'But first I need to tell you that now Ludha is working as my personal maid, she answers to me, not to you. That means if any rebuke is required, any . . . discipline . . . I will mete it out myself. I do know how to govern servants, Alpin. I grew up in a royal household, and spent many years at the court of Drust the Bull at Caer Pridne, and later with Bridei at White Hill.' Where, she did not add, the servants were treated with courtesy and fairness at all times. She could not recall a single instance of physical violence.

'It's not you I don't trust, my dear,' Alpin growled, 'it's men. You don't see your own charms, but they do, every one of them. There's a hot look in your Faolan's eye every time you wander by, and the fellow's a Gael, after all; I wouldn't put anything past him. As for Deord, I imagine he experiences a degree of frustration, as any man must who spends most of his time out of female company. I won't have any of them alone with you. Not now. Not ever.'

Ana refrained from pointing out that the marriage was not yet signed and sealed. There were questions to be asked, and she must tread carefully and keep him placated if she were to get answers.

Ludha slipped back in, a square of cloth pressed to her cheek. Ana gave her a reassuring smile. The girl was brave. Alpin was a big man, and his anger was frightening.

'You spoke of your brother's affliction,' Ana said. 'I should tell you that, while you were away, I observed Deord with his trays, and was informed by the women that he is a special guard. It was apparent to me that the little door must lead to a place where prisoners were confined; perhaps only one prisoner, since the trays were set for two. I tried to question Deord before, but he would not talk to me. Orna told me I should wait and seek answers from you.'

'Orna gave you good advice. A pity you did not follow it. You could have saved us all some distress.' Alpin's gaze flickered over to the silent maid and back to Ana herself. 'Why did you go into Deord's area? Why were you in my bedchamber? It was a lie, wasn't it, that you were indisposed today? You look perfectly well to me. What are you playing at?' His anger was rising again; it was there in the tight jaw, the clenched fists, the voice threatening to become a shout.

Ana reached out a hand and laid it over his. It had the effect of quieting him instantly. 'I did play a little trick on you, my lord,' she said, making her voice hesitant. 'I thought you enjoyed such games, the kind men and women play. I was indeed most upset this morning. A girl does not welcome that sort of news about her future family. But I have to confess, I did put Ludha at the door to keep watch, and then I waylaid Deord, thinking to ask if it were indeed true that your own brother was incarcerated here at Briar Wood, and all because he had the misfortune to be subject to an illness for which nobody had thought to seek a cure. I'm sorry if I have offended you, Alpin.' She curled her hand around his, putting her head on one side and smiling in what she hoped was a placatory way. It seemed to her quite likely he would see the insincerity of this straightaway and erupt once more into fury, but instead Alpin placed his other hand over hers and spoke quietly.

'Will you ask your maid to send for some mead and a little supper? You haven't eaten since this morning.'

'Of course. Ludha, will you get one of the men to bring us something? Thank you.'

They waited. It was evident to Ana that he was not going to speak until there was no chance of interruption. He simply held her hand and smiled, and this she found almost more difficult than his anger, for his touch was less than pleasing to her even when offered gently. The knowledge that this time she had invited it made her most uncomfortable, as if she had somehow sullied herself.

A servant brought food and drink. Not long after, Deord walked back through the chamber with his supper tray, full now, and vanished through the little door without a glance at either of them. Ludha resumed her place.

'I'm not surprised that this has upset you,' Alpin said. 'You'll be thinking of our children, how such a dark streak may run in a family. You fear your own pure blood line will be tainted by something wild and unpredictable. It is possible. I cannot deny it. I was married before, as you are aware. I would have had a son. He did not live long enough to be born. I never knew what he might have been, future leader or raving madman.' He bowed his head.

'I'm sorry,' Ana said. 'I did hear you had lost a child, and your first wife as well. That is terribly sad. And – forgive me if this is awkward for you – I understand you have a natural son?'

Alpin nodded. 'Fostered away. He can't inherit, of course. You need not concern yourself with him. He's adequately provided for. No sign of madness, if that's what you're getting at.'

'I must admit it is not so much the prospect of a flawed heritage

208

that troubles me,' said Ana. 'It is – it is the thought of your brother locked away here, all those years, with not even the slightest hope of freedom. What exactly is wrong with him? Can't anything be done for him?'

'He's beyond help.'

Alpin's tone was crushingly final, but Ana went doggedly on. 'Have you sought advice from expert healers? The king's druid, Broichan, is renowned for his ability –'

Ana's words were cut short as Alpin smashed a fist down on the table, setting cups and knives rattling. 'Don't talk to me of cures and advice! Drustan's a threat to anyone who lives and breathes! He can never be let out!'

Ana drew a deep breath and waited until her heartbeat had slowed a little. 'I see,' she said, although he had as yet explained nothing.

'Takes him worst at full moon,' Alpin muttered. 'Wild as a mad dog, totally unpredictable. Unreachable. And he's strong. Full moon, he needs to be tightly confined so he can't see the sky. Other times, the fit's not so severe, but it still makes him difficult. And it strikes without warning. Letting him out would be irresponsible. There's no saying what he might do. Who he might harm.' He took a long draught of his mead. 'Didn't want to tell you at all. Didn't want to go into detail. Less you knew, I thought, happier you'd be.'

Ana did not contradict him. Her heart was heavy. She thought she saw truth in his eyes at last, and found that she did not want it after all. 'But . . .' she ventured, 'you could at least seek to make his confinement more tolerable. While it is day, surely he could be housed where he can see the open sky, the forest . . . where the sun can reach him, without bars between. To be shut up forever in that dark place for a malady visited on him through no fault of his own is . . . it's cruel, Alpin. It's barbaric. He is your brother.' She faltered to a stop. His eyes were fixed on her, iron-hard, and the expression on his face terrified her.

'But you know nothing of his quarters.' His voice was menacing in its quiet. 'You told me yourself that nobody would give you answers. Why do you speak of a place where the captive cannot see the forest, a place where the sky is visible only through bars?

209

All you have seen is a door and a passageway to storerooms. Or have you been lying to me?'

'I . . . that is . . .' The ready words she needed deserted her.

'Answer me!' Alpin snapped, half rising to his feet. He lifted a fist.

Words came: the wrong ones. *If you strike me, Faolan will kill you.* 'I'm obliged to say to you,' she fought for her most ladylike tone, 'that if you raise a hand towards me you will have destroyed any chance you have of my agreeing to the marriage. I've no intention of being the butt of your anger at the injustices of the world. Please sit down.'

'Tell me the truth!' Alpin shouted, but he had lowered his hand. 'Who let you in there? You've seen him, haven't you? You've been with him!'

Unaccountably, Ana felt a warm blush rise to her face, perhaps the worst thing that could happen at such a moment. Blessed All-Flowers aid her, she was a hair's-breadth from destroying Bridei's treaty and putting herself and Faolan in a still more precarious position, not to speak of poor Drustan and the loyal Deord. 'I have not,' she said, 'but I do have a small confession to make. I hope you will forgive me, my dear.' She managed not to choke on the words.

'What?' Alpin snarled.

'While you were gone, I did venture through the little door and along the way to the place where your brother is confined. I looked through the iron gate. Nobody was visible. Your brother and his guard must have been indoors that day. I retreated quickly, not wishing to go where I should not.'

'You're lying,' Alpin said flatly.

'No, my lord.'

'How could you get in? Deord keeps one key and I had the other. Don't tell me he left the door unlocked.'

'N-no, my lord. It was very strange. A bird brought me a key. It came in my window and left it by my bed. I don't expect you to believe that, but it is the truth.'

Alpin picked up the meat knife and speared it violently into the oak tabletop. 'That devious freak!' he muttered. 'How dare he meddle!'

'I left the key just by the iron gate,' Ana said, 'where Deord would be sure to find it. I hope I did not do wrong.'

Alpin looked at her. 'Just as well it was Deord who found it,' he said, 'and not my brother. It's plain to me you have no conception of the danger involved here.'

'I'm sorry, my lord. Blame feminine curiosity. I won't do it again.'

'What's this "my lord"?' Alpin blustered. 'Think I preferred the other.'

It was becoming harder and harder to force a smile. 'I need time to become accustomed to it, my dear. I have never addressed a man thus before. This is all new to me.'

'Mm,' Alpin grunted. 'You'll need to curb your curiosity here at Briar Wood. This is not a game, it's a tragedy, and the dangers are entirely real. Let me be quite open with you. If Drustan hadn't been my blood kin, I'd have strung him up before the gates for what he did.'

'Wh-what he did?' There was a prickling sensation in Ana's spine. She felt the certain knowledge that she did not want to hear what was coming.

'He killed them,' Alpin said in a voice that now sounded calm, numb, beyond anger or sorrow. 'My wife, Erisa. My unborn son. In a fit of frenzy he drove the two of them to their deaths. He pursued Erisa through the forest. She fell from a place where a cliff towers over a waterfall. She broke her neck. It took us three days to retrieve her body.'

A chill ran through Ana. 'But . . . why?' she whispered.

'With a madman there is no why.'

She struggled for words. 'Were there any witnesses? Are you sure he –?'

'Only one. An old woman was there, our childhood nurse. Bela's no longer with us. But there was no doubt about it. He admitted what he'd done.'

Ana was mute.

'I locked him up the day we brought my wife's body back. Our son would have been born within one turning of the moon. I wanted to drive my dagger through Drustan's heart and make an end of him. But a man doesn't kill his brother. Instead, I had the enclosure built and I hired Deord as keeper. The ties of blood are strong. I will bear this burden all my life.'

Ana was horrified. She wanted to protest that it wasn't true, it couldn't be, Drustan was incapable of such an act of callous violence. But she remembered Deord's words: *Given the circumstances, the arrangements are as generous as they can be.* Deord's veiled references to danger indicated this tale was true. And somewhere there was a witness. Alpin was absolutely right, she had meddled where she should not have, and all she had done was stir up a tangled mess of anguish and loss.

'I don't know what to say,' she whispered. 'I'm more sorry than I can tell you.' Over by the wall, Ludha sat transfixed. It was clear from her expression that she had never heard the full story before.

'I imagine Bridei would not have despatched you here so eagerly had he known our sad tale,' Alpin said. 'I'm in no doubt you had plenty of better offers from chieftains with no such dark secrets.'

'I did indeed,' Ana said. 'However, I am here at Briar Wood and I suppose we must make the best of it. Thank you for telling me the truth. I prefer honesty, no matter how unpalatable the facts may be. I will not interfere in this matter, my lor– my dear. In return, I hope you will not keep secrets from me; not when I am your wife.' She spoke through gritted teeth. The fact that Alpin had at last been straight with her had done nothing to quell her physical revulsion. He had struck Ludha, and he would have hit Ana herself. The prospect of sharing his bed made her shudder.

'Let's drink to that,' Alpin said, pouring more mead. 'To marriage; to the future. By next spring, if the gods smile on us, we'll have a son.'

Ana smiled and tried to ignore the image that would not leave her: Drustan in the forest, his fine, strong body, his exuberant flame of hair, his eyes bright with the joy of living. The birds nestled so trustingly close to him. His soft voice. That man was a frenzied murderer. She would give anything for it not to be true. But she could not make it a lie just by wishing. Alpin said his brother had confessed. Drustan had, in effect, done so again when Ana asked him why he was locked up, though at the time she had not understood. 'To do otherwise is dangerous.' So it must be true. Her heart, all the same, shouted that it could not be so. Ferada had always said the heart was an unreliable guide, and that sensible people followed the dictates of the intellect. She wished Ferada were here now.

'To marriage,' Ana said grimly, and raised her cup.

Chapter Eight

On the eve of the festival of Rising, Drust the Boar, monarch of the southern kingdom of Circinn, came to White Hill with his advisers and a modest escort of men-at-arms to attend Bridei's assembly. By the second day everyone in the household knew that the negotiations had failed. Drust had no intention of providing support against Dalriada, either in the form of a significant fighting force or in some less practical, more symbolic way. Never mind that he had exchanged messages with Bridei over the course of the last two years, working slowly towards common ground. Someone had had a word in his ear, someone influential, and now the King of Circinn was immovable.

The territorial disagreement with the Gaels was a local problem, he told the assembled chieftains of Fortriu. They needed to sort it out for themselves. His forces had more than enough to keep them occupied on home soil without being summoned to march all the way to the west. Besides, it was a fool's errand. The Gaels were too well established to be moved. They were breeding a third generation in their settlements. Drust's adviser, Bargoit, twisted the knife in the wound by offering the opinion that those inhabitants of the western regions who had ceased to resist and allowed the invaders to settle, to marry women of the Priteni and to father half-breed children, had shown sound common sense. It was time to accept that the Gaels were here for good, and the Christian faith with them.

It was outrageous, and Bridei had been hard put to hold on to the composure his position demanded of him. Others had been more outspoken. Broichan had come close to pronouncing a curse; Talorgen had raised his voice and his fist. The council was in effect concluded almost before it had begun.

Drust the Boar would stay awhile at Bridei's court nonetheless. His gesture in making the long trip from Circinn must be recognised, even if the decision he brought them was unfavourable. His company must still be accommodated at White Hill and entertained, and there were other matters to discuss, issues of trade and borders. But the truth was, with their primary objective lost to them so quickly and so emphatically, Bridei's councillors scarcely had the heart to continue the assembly's business.

By day, the representatives of the two kingdoms met at the council table and went through the motions of diplomacy. Other activities were organised: hunting, riding, sports. In the evenings there was feasting and music. At the same time, behind closed doors, the King of Fortriu met with his inner circle to make a crucial decision. The advance had been planned for the time of Gathering, the harvest ritual. The sheer scale of the undertaking meant the forces must soon begin to move. This was not to be a massed march down the Glen, nor yet a bold advance by boat. The Priteni army would be composed of several large forces, each with its own leaders, and when it was time for the assault, Dalriada would find itself attacked from many quarters at once and pressed ever southwestward. It could not be set up quickly, even if secrecy were not an issue.

To go ahead without Circinn's support would be a gamble. Failure would not only cost Bridei in the lives of men and perhaps in more territory lost to Dalriada. It would set back his long-term cause, his dream: to see the Gaels swept out of Fortriu entirely, and all the lands of the Priteni united under the old gods. Failure must tarnish his shining image amongst his people, and so lessen the chance of future success. The question was whether, if they delayed a year, two years, Drust the Boar might be persuaded to change his mind and come to their support. With the armies of Circinn arrayed alongside those of Fortriu there would be a far greater promise of victory.

'He won't back down,' Talorgen said flatly. They were meeting in a small council room without windows; lamps were set about the chamber, showing the men's faces as flickering masks, Bridei's well governed, Talorgen's angry, Aniel's thoughtful. Broichan's features were impassive, his eyes unreadable as always. Aniel's fellow councillor, Tharan, was restless, folding his arms, crossing his knees, picking things up and putting them down again. Bridei's war leader, Carnach, stood with hands on hips; for him, this decision meant a choice between a season on the march and a bloody confrontation at the end of it, or the disbanding of the forces he had put his heart into readying for Fortriu's cause. Had matters been different five years before, Carnach might have been king now, and Bridei living a quiet existence as a scholar. The gods, however, had chosen to smile on Bridei in that season of change. What the gods were up to now was anyone's guess.

'Bargoit is behind this.' Tharan's tone was bitter. 'That weasel has long been able to swing Drust's opinions one way or the other. Besides, there are Christian missionaries swarming all over Circinn now, if our intelligence is accurate. Drust's religious advisers will have lent weight to Bargoit's arguments. They'll have put pressure on Drust to hold back from conflict with the Gaels, followers of the same misguided faith. I had hoped the King of Circinn might finally summon the strength to make his own judgements. Would that he might at last break free of the poisoned web of false counsel that draws ever tighter around him.'

'Something has shifted,' said Bridei. 'He was on the point of agreement not two seasons since; I had his message of provisional support. A verbal one only, I regret to say; it would be difficult to hold him to it now. Is a new influence come to bear on him, I wonder?'

'We'd do well to look into that when there's the opportunity,' Aniel said. 'Meanwhile the question is, dare we risk going ahead without them? There is much to be lost here.'

In Bridei's mind were the shining eyes and eager, determined faces of those soldiers he had addressed at Caer Pridne, every one of them ready to fight and die in their king's great cause. Some were little more than boys, some young fathers, some scarred veterans of many conflicts. If he calculated this wrong, he was asking them to pay the ultimate price for the sake of his own pride. But if he called off the advance he might be throwing away the best opportunity to secure the future of Fortriu. It was common knowledge that Gabhran of Dalriada aspired, in time, to conquest of all the lands of the north. Gabhran as king meant a foreign yoke around their necks. With the Christian faith spreading fast in Circinn under Drust's weak rule, and the Gaels planting their crosses in the west, Fortriu was squeezed tight already. Let Gabhran encroach further and it would not just be territory that was lost. Gaelic rule spelled the death of the old gods. 'The season is passing,' he said. 'We must make our decision quickly, one way or the other.'

'If we call a halt now,' said Carnach, 'not only do we lose the momentum gained by a season of dedicated preparation, we may also sacrifice the element of surprise that our spies and our tight security have ensured. Wait a year, and the enemy has a year of opportunities to glean information as to the timing, manner and scale of our operation.'

'True,' said Talorgen. 'We can't afford to keep the men on this knife edge much longer. They anticipate a move within one turning of the moon to take them to their various points of readiness. They expect the full assault by Gathering. They're already straining at the leash. If we don't move as planned, we've no real choice but to disband the armies and send the men back to their homes. It will be doubly difficult to sharpen the tools of war next time, if this ends in nothing.'

'If we send them home, they live to plant crops, father children, ply a trade another year.' Bridei's tone was calm; he had been well trained in the concealment of what he felt. 'If we proceed and our great endeavour fails, how many of them will return whole to settlement or farm or chieftain's hall? It is possible that the force we have assembled, impressive as it is, may not be sufficient to do its work.'

'We have Caitt support,' Aniel pointed out. 'Umbrig has promised a sizeable force, and you know his reputation.'

'I'm beginning to regret I didn't ask Alpin of Briar Wood for a commitment in armed men instead of restricting my terms to an assurance of truce,' Bridei said. 'It's too late for that now, unless Faolan's party gets back here with remarkable speed. We must simply hope the agreement's been signed and sealed. If we delayed our move until next year or the year after we'd have time to secure practical help from that quarter. By then, gods willing, Ana will have given Alpin a son.'

'I spoke to Ged this morning,' said Talorgen. 'Morleo, too. Neither was overjoyed to be missing this meeting, but I pointed out that someone did need to keep Drust the Boar and his lackeys occupied while we consulted in private. I understand they've taken him fishing. Ged is in favour of proceeding as planned. He believes the men's enthusiasm is our greatest strength, and that a delay would make it difficult to generate the same momentum. Morleo was more cautious, but he believes we have the numbers.'

'I do not wish to lead them to certain death, whatever their enthusiasm,' Bridei said. 'We know the strategic arguments; we've weighed them over and over during the long period of our preparation. We need something more now, some guidance beyond our own knowledge of risks and opportunities. Perhaps Broichan is the best one to advise us.'

They looked at the druid, a tall, pale figure in his dark robes. He had been unusually quiet through their debate.

'An augury should be performed.' Broichan's voice, ever the deepest and most commanding at White Hill, was today almost hesitant. That in itself suggested omens that would be less than favourable. 'We must seek the gods' wisdom. Thus far their guidance has steered us towards this conflict; the Flamekeeper's light has shone over Bridei and the whole endeavour. It is difficult to believe their will would change direction merely because the King of Circinn has not the courage to stand with us.'

'Will you cast the birch rods here?' Bridei asked him. 'That way all of us can observe the pattern of their falling and be party to your interpretation at first hand.'

Broichan did not answer for a moment. The others were

nodding assent, for such an augury could generally be relied upon as a powerful means of understanding the intentions of the Flamekeeper and the Shining One, whose desires governed every step in the long history of the Priteni. 'Not now,' the druid said. 'This is too weighty a matter to be determined by one seer alone, king's druid or no. It would be best performed under the gaze of the Shining One, with Fola in attendance. I believe the goddess will show the path more clearly if her senior priestess assists with the ritual. After supper, when Drust the Boar is occupied with White Hill's best mead and finest music, we'll cast the rods in the upper courtyard. Let us hope the gods show us clear answers, for we have sore need of them.'

Clouds passed across the bright face of the Shining One, obscuring the pattern thrown out on the stone table. The goddess was taxing both druid and wise woman to the far reach of their considerable abilities. Broichan had served as personal druid to two kings and was known throughout all the lands of the Priteni as learned, adept and dangerously powerful. Fola headed the school at Banmerren where women were taught all the skills required to serve the Shining One as priestesses. She was clever, subtle and had a reputation for unswerving honesty. If these two old friends, between them, could not read a message from the gods, it must be assumed the gods were deliberately withholding their wisdom.

Tuala had already looked at the pattern and formed her own opinion as to its meaning. It had taken her only a moment. This was something at which she had a natural ability, similar to her ease with scrying: the answers seemed to spring to her mind fully formed almost before she asked the questions. She held her silence. Later, when she and Bridei were alone together, she would tell him what the gods had said.

A select group looked on as Broichan and Fola circled the table, peering closely at the lie of the rods. Each short length of birch was carved with ancient symbols; each had its own range of meanings. For every casting there was a wealth of possible interpretations. The true skill of the seer lay in teasing out which of these was right for the question being posed. The gods of Fortriu were complex creatures and their counsel seldom came in plain, unambiguous terms.

Fola had brought her assistant, Derila; it was fortunate that both had already been in attendance at White Hill for the councils. Apart from these two, the druid, Tuala and Bridei himself, the only other people present were Bridei's bodyguard Garth and the old scholar, Wid, who leaned on his staff as he squinted at the rods in the fitful light. Wid had never claimed to be a conduit for the voices of the gods. His expertise was in worldly skills such as the reading of men's eyes and their gestures, the interpretation of the silences between their words. Both Bridei and Tuala had learned from him. In time he might teach Derelei; Derelei who was now spending part of every afternoon in Broichan's company, and who had a tendency to fall asleep at night singing to himself in a manner that set shadows dancing oddly in the corners and frogs hopping out from the wood basket.

'It's quite obscure,' Fola said. 'A pair of pathways, by my interpretation, each of which then branches further. For the life of me I cannot decide which is predominant. It is all dogs and birds; not an army in sight. What do you say, old friend?'

The moonlight had turned Broichan's face ghostly pale. Tuala could see the lines there, more lines than a man of his age should have. He was not yet old. 'I see death in this,' he said. 'But that is to be expected. Our question dealt with war, and wars are not won without the loss of life. I agree, Fola, birds do seem to the fore. The eagle is lying from east to west; that can only be taken as a positive sign. The shadow lies behind him. Ahead is . . . ahead is a choice of paths, and here the message becomes a challenge to interpret.'

'It is chaotic, perhaps, simply because wars are ever thus.' It was the young priestess, Derila, who spoke. She had risen quickly through the ranks of Fola's wise women and was well respected for her scholarship. 'I see both sun and moon in the west. Despite the fact that the eagle is hemmed in by these other rods, I would take that placement as a sign that both the Flamekeeper and the Shining One favour a move on the Gaels.'

'I agree with your interpretation, Derila.' Bridei bent to examine the pattern more closely. 'But I see nothing here that clarifies whether the endeavour should take place now or later.' He glanced at Tuala over his shoulder. He would not ask her to comment.

'Tuala,' said Fola, 'in this company of friends, won't you give us your opinion? You're young and keen-eyed. Perhaps you can see something we can't.'

Broichan opened his mouth, then shut it like a trap.

'I'm too close to this,' Tuala said, suppressing a shiver. She kept her voice calm, for she had learned under Queen Rhian's tuition to school her tone and her expression. 'What wife, given the opportunity to pronounce on such a question, would not offer the interpretation most likely to keep her husband at home and away from harm? You are adept. Perhaps all that is needed is some time for thinking.'

'There is no time!' snapped Broichan. His display of irritation was uncharacteristic, and Bridei glanced at him in surprise.

'There is tonight, at least,' the king said quietly. 'If we can find no more answers here, then let each of us seek the wisdom of the gods alone awhile and see what comes to us. Tomorrow, after we speak together again, I will make my decision.'

Later, when they were alone, Tuala told Bridei what she had seen: a sure sign from the Shining One that he must go now and, to balance it, the undeniable indication that in doing so he would be taking a risk far greater than any of them could calculate. 'There was something hidden,' she said as they stood before the fire in their private quarters, 'something we were not meant to see. Perhaps it is still obscure even to the gods. But whatever it is, it's perilous beyond the dangers inherent in the nature of armed conflict. I wish you could take Faolan with you.'

'You think this sign means personal danger for me? That surely is preferable to the kind of peril that might strike my forces: a great storm, perhaps, or a plague, or the leaking of critical information to our enemy.'

'Don't sound so pleased,' Tuala said drily. 'You may care little for your own safety. Others place a higher value on your life.'

'If I thought it would win back the west for Fortriu,' Bridei said, 'I would lay down my life with a light heart.'

'Without you they could not succeed,' said Tuala. 'You are their heart, Bridei. You are the Blade of Fortriu. I know there are other strong leaders, men who would step up in your place, Carnach in particular. But it is you whom these men love. It is you they will follow to the death. The goddess sets you a difficult test here. She wishes you to place yourself in peril. By doing so, you may win back our lost territories. Or you may lose all and be remembered as a king of five bright summers. I could not say this in front of the others. But it seemed to me the rods did show two possible paths, and that each of them begins the same way: with a movement to the west by summer's end. You asked the gods the wrong question. They are not offering any choice in the timing of your venture, only the knowledge that, before the leaves fall from the oaks, you will triumph or you will die.'

The moon waxed and waned again; the days began to rush by, each blurring into the next. With every sunrise Ana knew with sinking heart that her handfasting to Alpin was one day closer. She found herself thanking the goddess for every day on which the druid yet again failed to arrive; she found herself praying he would never come.

Alpin was trying to make her feel at home. He presented her with gifts, breakfasted with her every morning and made an effort to moderate his language, not always successfully. Ana tried to conceal the fact that his touch still turned her cold and that his conversation either bored or offended her. With grim determination she endured his kisses, averting her face so they did not reach her mouth. She listened patiently to his rambling accounts of great stags hunted and fierce enemies routed. She ate sparingly of the enormous meals and took steps to improve the comforts of the sewing chamber and of her own quarters. It would be essential to retain some private space once she was married: without a retreat from Alpin she would surely go mad. She determined to put Drustan and Deord and that whole sorry mess to the back of her mind and make the best of things.

There had been no opportunity to speak to Faolan alone. The only time she ever saw him these days was at the supper table, and since Alpin had threatened any man who so much as looked at her, Ana made an effort to avoid her bard's eyes. So far he had not been commanded to sing. She began to think Alpin had forgotten about him, and was glad of it, though she would have welcomed a chance to seek Faolan's advice, had it been possible. On their shared journey he had become a friend. She knew she could trust him, rely on him. She suspected that, at Briar Wood, she was going to be short of friends. And she wanted to ask him about Breakstone Hollow.

She tried to forget her unfortunate foray into spying and its distressing aftermath. It wasn't as if there were nothing else to keep her occupied. A wedding outfit must be made, along with other garments for herself and a fine new tunic for her future husband, with an embroidered border of dogs which Ana had undertaken to fashion with her own hands. Ludha was doing the fine work on the wedding dress, having completed the baby gown. The look in her maid's eyes as she handed over the tiny, exquisitely finished garment told Ana, with no need for words, that Ludha understood her mistress's ambivalence about the impending marriage.

The birds kept coming. A series of tiny gifts came with them: a delicate flower; a wispy grey feather; woollen threads from a blanket, intricately plaited into a small circle like a ring. Ana resisted the temptation to send something in return. The man was a murderer, and she had sworn to keep out of this. Sometimes the hoodie or the crossbill or the wren simply flew in to perch on windowsill or chair back and watch her awhile, bright-eyed. Sometimes, when Ludha was absent, Ana caught herself talking to these visitors and made herself stop, for it seemed to her that such conversations amounted to speaking to Drustan, and that she was playing with fire if she did so.

The design for Alpin's wedding tunic would not come right. Ana worked a series of samples on small squares of linen in order to perfect the dog motif, but the stitches would not flow and the small hounds came out snarling and repellent. Ludha observed and held her tongue, though it was plain that she was bursting to offer assistance. This bride had offered to fashion her husband's outfit with her own hands. The symbolism in that gesture was quite clear, and Ana must not be seen to fail in the task. Grimly she continued to produce one unsatisfactory design after another until, on a particularly warm afternoon a full turning of the moon after her arrival at Briar Wood, she and Ludha took their handiwork out to a small, secluded courtyard on the upper level of the fortress, a place reached by a flight of stone steps whose narrow, precipitous nature meant most of the women did not go there at all, despite the attractions of a vista of trees and a sheltered, sunny space in which to work and talk.

The two of them settled in a companionable silence, each claiming a stone bench for herself and her work basket. The songs of a multitude of birds could be heard from the reaches of Briar Wood, over the walls. Ludha began to hum under her breath, a tune Ana recognised as a tale of lovers parted long and delightfully reunited at the end; no doubt the girl had her absent archer, Foldec, in mind. Next time Ludha reached the chorus Ana joined in, singing a lower voice. Ludha smiled with delight and launched into another verse.

For a little it became possible to set it all aside: the marriage, the appalling prospect of sharing Alpin's bed, the whole future spent by his side, in the company of his oafish friends. Drustan and his malady, the murder of the innocent, the shutting away behind stone walls and iron bars. Bridei and his vital treaty. Faolan, whose safety was much on her mind; Faolan to whom she was forbidden to speak alone. Ana sang on, and as she sang her hands plied needle and thread and she fashioned another small motif on another minute square of cloth. This time the image was not that of a dog. The threads were scarlet and dark brown, and the bright-eyed creature looking back at her from the linen, when song and embroidery were done, was a crossbill carrying in its beak a strand of russet hair. Ana stared at it; she had shocked herself. Her instinct, as Ludha glanced across, was to thrust the little square into her basket, to hide it as if it were incriminating evidence. She suppressed that. She had nothing to feel guilty about, nothing at all.

'What a sweet design!' Ludha exclaimed, coming closer to look. 'That would be lovely on a little shirt for a child. It could go on the breast, and you could pick up the red in the border.'

'Mm,' said Ana noncommittally, selecting a pale thread to hem the edges of her tiny creation. Her mind was not itself today; it was playing dangerous tricks, for the infant she had instantly pictured in such a small shirt had a head of flaming auburn hair and eyes bright as stars. 'I should be making dogs, but I just can't get them right. And time's passing, Ludha. It's passing all too quickly. That druid could be here any time now.'

'The bird is lovely,' Ludha said quietly. 'You have such a gift, my lady. May I show you something I've been working on?'

'Please do.'

Ludha took a neatly folded strip of cloth from her own basket. 'I did this at night, by candlelight. Of course, you need not use my design, but I thought it might help. It's not my place, I know, but . . .'

And there it was, the dog design, perfectly executed and entirely pleasing, with a noble regularity to it that would be exactly Alpin's preference for this depiction of his kin symbol. Spirals and cross-hatching linked the small canines into a balanced and flowing border. It was a sample only, two dogs, three links, but it could be plainly seen how well this would look on the red-dyed fabric of the bridegroom's new tunic.

Ana let out her breath in a sigh.

'I hope you're not offended, my lady, it's just . . . I could see how this was troubling you. It happens to me sometimes. I know I can do something, but I just can't get started on it.'

Ana smiled. 'I'm not offended, I'm most grateful, Ludha. If you are prepared to let me use your design, I'll start working on the border tomorrow.'

Ludha gave a nod. 'You know how there are three birds?' she said, watching as Ana's needle turned a corner on the tiny square. 'You could . . . that is, if you wanted to . . .'

'Mm,' said Ana, thinking it was just as well the two of them were alone today in this out-of-the-way part of Alpin's stronghold. 'Just for my own enjoyment, of course. You realise that, matters being as they are, such designs could never appear on the garments of any infant at Briar Wood.'

'No, my lady. Although it seems a shame, doesn't it?' Then, as Ana completed the hem and bit off the thread, 'Do you know the song about Big Fergal, who was a sort of giant, and how he tamed the Monstrous Worm?'

'I used to sing it with my sister, a long time ago. You start and I'll see how much I remember.'

What with the singing and the sunshine and the privacy of the upper courtyard, Ana's mind grew calmer as her hands began to fashion a second little square, this time in hues of black and grey. It was towards the end of the third ballad, the tale of a girl who fell in love with a toad, that her spine began to prickle and her needle stilled. She looked at Ludha, frozen on the opposite bench. Their voices faltered, leaving only that of the third singer whose deeper, more hesitant version of 'The Maid of the Mere' was reaching them, impossibly, from somewhere beneath the flagstone flooring of their sanctuary. As they stopped singing, this voice went on a little, '"And so she sighed, alas for me! My love lies in the shadowlands."' Then, as the singer realised he was the only one left, he too fell abruptly silent.

Ana cleared her throat. Ludha had both hands over her mouth, as if too shocked to let herself utter a word. Rapidly, Ana performed some calculations relating to the position of various apartments at Briar Wood and the movement of the sun. She looked out over the wall once more and saw, framed by the upper branches of the elms, a vista of rising ground crowned by a single majestic oak. Birds rose and settled in its spreading canopy. She swallowed. 'Ludha?' It was a whisper.

'Mm?'

'What apartments lie beneath this court?'

'Just storage rooms, my lady. A closed-off part of the house. And . . .'

'And Deord's quarters. Just beneath us.' It must be so; even had her quick estimates of distance not made this evident, she knew whose voice that had been, a voice she heard nightly in her dreams. The grilled roof of Drustan's enclosure must lie below and to the west of them, concealed by the high parapet wall on that side of the courtyard. The sleeping quarters must be almost directly under them. Some quirk of construction made it possible to hear quite clearly, for all the considerable difference in height. Ana's heart was making a nuisance of itself, pounding as if she had run a race. She felt the flush in her cheeks. Common sense said quite clearly, *Pack up your work and go; do so in silence.* In her hands she still held the little square on which the form of the hoodie was half stitched, its neat plumage glossy in her best silk thread. She stroked the bird image with a finger that was not as steady as it should be.

'My lady!' hissed Ludha, jerking her head towards the steps. She had gone pale; fear was in her eyes.

'Not yet, Ludha,' Ana said. 'We are safe here a little longer. Let us finish the song, at least, and reunite Linia with her warty sweetheart. Where were we?'

'"So she went out on a fair spring morn . . . "' Ludha sounded as if she was singing through clenched teeth, but she had picked up her work again and begun to sew with grim determination.

'"When birds flew swift from tree to tree . . . "' Ana sang, wondering why there was a lump in her throat and tears in her eyes.

'"And pricked her finger on a thorn . . . "' came the hesitant voice from below, not a resonant, well-formed tone like Faolan's, but that of a man who has almost forgotten how to make music, so long has it been since he had either the inclination or opportunity.

'"And shed her blood so all could see,"' sang the three voices together, blending in a sweet sound that rang across the sunny court. The ballad went on to tell how Linia won back her lover by a little self-sacrifice and a smidgeon of well-directed hearth magic. As they worked their way through it, Ana pinpointed the spot where the third voice could be most clearly heard, a crack between flagstones and inner wall, and when they were done she moved to kneel by this narrow aperture.

'Drustan?' she asked softly. Ludha was staring, either aghast or impressed, Ana could not tell which.

'Ana?' His tone was uneven. Perhaps he had believed she would run away, would never return, once she knew he was there.

'Where are you?'

A pause. 'Where would I be but here?' he said.

'Where exactly? Is Deord there?'

'I am in the sleeping quarters. I heard you singing. And talking. I'm sorry if I have offended you . . .'

'Deord?'

'Fetching water. I will know when he returns. The gate creaks.'

Then, abruptly, Ana found herself lost for words. The only question in her mind was, *Did you do it, did you really kill them?* This could not be spoken, not so baldly. Not at all.

'You are well?' Drustan whispered. 'Deord told me Alpin was angry. That he would have hurt you.'

'Deord did a good job of stopping that,' she managed, 'though not before your brother had struck my maid. Your guard is a very capable man. Alpin did have cause to be angry with me, though not with Ludha. I had disobeyed a rule. More than one. He told me your story, Drustan.'

No reply at all to this. Glancing across at Ludha, Ana surprised an expression that was more fascination than terror. This was too far gone now; she would have to hope her maid could be trusted. 'He told me something terrible. About what happened all those years ago.'

Silence again.

'Drustan, talk to me.'

'What can I say?' The tone was weary.

Tears pricked Ana's eyes again. The truth burst out despite her best efforts. 'I suppose I'm hoping you will tell me it was a lie. That you didn't do it. It is something I do not want to believe.'

After a little he said, 'You are distressed. Better if you do not talk to me. That's what Deord says.'

Ana felt anger stir. 'It's not up to Deord or to anyone but me to decide that. Unless, of course, you don't want to talk . . .'

'I do not wish to make you sad. I do not wish to frighten you. That was a dark day. It set a shadow over Briar Wood that will never be lifted.'

Ana's heart was still racing. She made herself take a deep breath. 'Will you talk about it? Tell me? Is it true, what Alpin said?'

'What did my brother tell you?'

Ana gritted her teeth; she did not want to utter the words aloud.

'Ana? What did he say?'

'He told me you . . . you are subject to some kind of frenzy. That it grips you from time to time, and you act as if you were

228

mad. He said you killed his wife. That you . . . drove her to her death.'

'A man does not lie about a matter so close to his heart.' The tone was flat now.

'Wh-what are you saying, Drustan?'

'I would give much to be able to tell you my brother is wrong. But I cannot.'

Her heart was a leaden weight. She closed her eyes, unable to speak. Why this mattered so much, she could not imagine. She hardly knew the man. Yet it seemed the heaviest of blows. 'Thank you for being honest,' she said when she found her voice again. 'This grieves me. I did not believe it could be so; you do not seem to me like a . . . a . . .'

'Monster? Madman? They give me many names, some far worse than those. My brother has treated me better than I deserve.'

Ana was gathering up her work, packing linen and needles into the willow basket. On the other bench Ludha did the same. The silence stretched out.

'Your singing gave me light,' came Drustan's whisper. 'Thank you. I had forgotten such fair sounds.'

Ana quashed the strong inclination to ask further questions. Something within her was unwilling, still, to accept the truth about this captive, even now he had confessed to her. She must not allow those thoughts to get the better of her common sense.

'We must leave now,' she told him. 'It's late and it's getting cold up here.'

'Will you come again?' There was a forlorn note in the question that told Ana he knew the answer must be no.

'I – I don't know,' Ana whispered, hating the weakness that would not allow her to grant him a firm response, *I cannot come.*

'Say it.' Drustan's voice had changed: this was a challenge. 'Tell me the truth. You will not come because you despise me. Because you shrink from me. Say it!'

'That's not true! I don't despise you!' Sudden tears filled her eyes.

'Then will you come?'

'What about Deord?' Curse it, why couldn't she shut her mouth and walk away as any sensible woman should?

'Sometimes he is here, sometimes out in the house; he must fetch what is needed. If you sing, I will know you are there. If I speak, you will know it is safe.'

Ana looked across at her maid. A great deal depended on Ludha's loyalties. The girl gave a little nod.

'A friend advised me once,' Ana said to her unseen listener, 'to rely on the intellect before the emotions. It was wise guidance. If I heeded it, I would tell you I cannot return here. Your brother has promised immediate and cruel punishment for any man who so much as looks at me in a way he dislikes. I can imagine how he would view our meeting thus. To do this again would be foolish, risky and entirely inappropriate.'

Silence indicated Drustan was waiting for more.

'I'll come if I can, Drustan.'

'I'll wait for you,' Drustan said. 'Farewell, Ana.'

That night Ana gave the crossbill its portrait in fine silks and received in her turn a gift of a small chip of stone on which, roughly scratched, was the outline of a heart. If she had refused to acknowledge to herself, before this, that her interest in Drustan went beyond curiosity, compassion and a need to see justice done, she was forced to do so in the moment when the bird laid this token on the small table in her bedchamber. Ludha had retired for the night; the creature had flown in the window from the darkness outside and waited at a safe distance from the candle, watching as Ana put the gift under her pillow.

When it was gone she lay on her bed thinking of Alpin, who had pressed her up against a wall after supper and given her a kiss that was unabashedly persistent. She had endured it, imagining all the while how it would be if another man held her, a man whose kiss would be as gentle as this was rough, as tender as this was brutal. Alpin's embrace chilled and frightened her; she knew that the other kiss would send a fiery warmth through her body, making her limbs weaken and her heart pound with excitement. It was a thing that was never going to happen: the stuff of foolish fancy. She wanted it more than she had ever wanted anything before.

The druid was taking a long time to come. As one turning of the moon stretched into two, Ana recognised the delay as a gift of sorts, and began a delicate kind of dance, a dance with an invisible partner. Each step, each measure, each move was fraught with danger. Often the patterns of it were interrupted, for Ana could not disappear to the little courtyard every day without attracting undue notice, and when she did go there, often Drustan remained silent, which meant Deord was with him. Ana thought it likely Deord already had suspicions, for if he had ever been within the sleeping quarters when folk sat conversing up above, he must surely know the building's secret. But Alpin's special guard went to and fro with his supper trays and kept his tranquil eyes discreetly away from his chieftain's bride-to-be. In no way did Deord indicate anything was out of the ordinary, and Ana's heart beat more calmly for it.

All the same, her days formed themselves around those brief times, those brief, magical times when she could speak to Drustan, could whisper to his unseen ear and crouch by the wall to catch his soft replies. She finished the second little square and despatched it with the hoodie when the bird came visiting. She planned a third but did not start on it, since she had not quite the right colours to render the smallest bird's plumage exactly. Besides, she had Alpin's wedding clothes to finish, and now that Ludha had provided the design there was no excuse for not getting on with it. It was this piece of work she had with her the afternoon Ludha forgot to pack a particular length of ribbon in her work basket and had to go down to the sewing room to fetch it.

It was the first time Ana had been alone with Drustan. She had been careful, thus far, in what she said to him. Not a word had been spoken of their encounter in the forest, nor the fact that he and Deord had the means to escape their confinement. If Ludha had suspected anything unusual in Ana's rapid befriending of her prospective brother-in-law, she had not spoken of it. Often they sang songs together, the three of them, and once or twice exchanged old tales and childhood rhymes. On one occasion Ana asked Drustan about the birds, how they came to be so close to him, how it was they stayed safe in a house full of cats. He answered cryptically; it was hard to interpret his words. She told him a little about her childhood in the Light Isles, and about becoming a hostage and how it had felt.

As summer advanced, their talk became easier. She asked him about his childhood, and learned of a boy who had been often alone but never lonely. Creatures had been his companions; dreams had sustained him. He had lived at Briar Wood with his brother and sister until he was seven years old. Then he had gone away to the west, to his grandfather's house, a house that had later belonged to Drustan himself, before he was shut away.

'That place is called Dreaming Glen,' he told her with a shy pride. 'It is full of soft light, a light not seen anywhere else in Caitt territories. It's like a blessing from another world; I always thought the touch of the gods was on those sheltering hills, that still water. There are two lakes near my house; I had my own names for them, names I gave them when my grandfather first took me back there with him.'

'What were the names?'

'The first lake, near the house, is fringed by trembling birches. It seems to give back a brightness beyond that of sun or moon, as if it made its own shining. I called it Cup of Sky. The other is a place where mist lies over the water even in the heat of day. Broad-leaved plants float on its surface, with white flowers in summer, and long-legged birds move in and out of the vapour like visitors from another realm. That lake was Cup of Dew. A child's names.'

'Those names paint a picture for me. I would love to see Dreaming Glen one day. Drustan, why were you sent there to live when you were so young?'

'There was no place for me here. I was a source of shame to my parents; my brother and sister shunned me. My grandfather made me a place.'

He asked her about the wedding and she gave guarded replies. She did not know if the tumult of feelings inside her, the longing to see him, the desire to touch him, an impossible, ridiculous thing, was evident in her voice. She thought she heard an echo of it in his, but Ana put it down to a craving for company to while away the endless days of incarceration.

Now, today, Ludha was not here, and all of a sudden she felt quite different.

'Drustan?'

'Yes, Ana?'

'Ludha's gone to fetch something from the house. We have a little while alone.'

A pause.

'A little while is scarcely long enough to begin,' came his voice. 'To find the first words.'

'I know,' Ana said softly. She had moved to sit on the flagstones by the base of the wall, her knees drawn up under her skirt. Even on this summer day the stones were chill. Down below it would be bitterly cold. 'I wish I could talk to you properly. I wish I could see you.'

'That cannot be.'

'I know that. I know what happened here; I've heard it from Alpin's lips and from yours. I suppose . . . I suppose I want to remake the past. But not even the gods can perform such a task.'

'You wish you had never come to Briar Wood? Perhaps, that you had wed a man of the Light Isles or of Fortriu and never set eyes on these two benighted brothers of the Caitt?'

'No,' Ana told him, clutching her arms around herself for comfort. 'I don't wish that at all. Only that somehow what happened here can be mended. I know it's foolish, but I still long to hear that what you've told me isn't true. But even if it is, I could never be sorry I met you, Drustan. If you did do that ill deed, it seems to me you have paid for it. It seems to me you have changed. I cannot believe the man I know now is capable of performing such an act.' She felt the heat rise to her cheeks and was glad that he could not see her.

'My gifts are poor things,' Drustan said. 'If I could, I would give you treasures woven of light and laughter, of colour and shadow, of life and breath. I would wrap you in a cloak of moonlight and set slippers of rippling water on your feet. I would . . .' The voice faltered. Ana sat motionless, spellbound. 'I would touch you and awaken joy,' he whispered. 'I knew this from the first moment I saw you, alone by the swollen river with your face full of terror and courage. I knew it when I watched you sleeping by your little fire, with another man's body to warm you. I wanted to be that man; to hold you as he did. I knew it when you came upon us in the forest, the day you had to learn what I had done. It was a forlorn hope. And yet, I was not able to kill that longing; it remains with me every waking moment. It walks with me in my dreams.'

Ana could not speak.

'Your friend will return soon,' Drustan said. 'Don't waste this with silence. Speak to me; say anything. Let me hear your voice.'

Ana's head was full of all she wanted to tell him, the messages of the heart, but the habits of a lifetime spent in royal households died hard. She could not say what she felt; she was betrothed to another man, and there was the treaty. 'I – how did you see me, by Breaking Ford?' she asked. 'The hoodie was there, but . . .'

'Sometimes I see through different eyes,' he said. 'We are linked, my friends and I. We help one another. Without them, without my little ones, I would have perished here for all Deord's patient care. I send them out; they let me travel beyond my cage.'

'Do your birds have names?' Gods, she was wasting time, precious time.

'Hope,' Drustan said. 'Flame. Heart.'

'That's beautiful, Drustan.'

'They are part of me. And you are part of me, Ana. I don't want you to marry my brother.'

She sucked in a sudden breath. 'You shouldn't say such things,' she told him. 'The marriage seals a treaty. That's why King Bridei sent me here. I have no choice.'

'Don't marry him, Ana.' The tone was not soft now, but conveyed a warning. 'If you were a bird I would bid you fly away while you still can.'

'Drustan, I'm sitting here with your brother's wedding tunic half sewn beside me. A druid is on the way to perform the hand-fasting and set the treaty in writing. If he'd come when he was supposed to, we'd be married by now. Alpin met all the terms the king put forward. I can't change that.'

'This is what you want? To see your light quenched, your heart constricted, your freedom lost? To wed a man you cannot love?'

Ana closed her eyes. 'What I want has nothing at all to do with this,' she said. 'I have always known this would be my future. The blood I bring with me is of too much value to allow me freedom of choice. A woman of the royal line does not wed for love.' Her voice shook on the last word. 'I think I hear Ludha coming back. We must stop this.'

'Ludha is still in the sewing room looking for her ribbon,' Drustan said calmly. 'There is time to tell me what you think, what you feel. There is time to tell me the truth.'

'How can you know – oh. A bird. That unsettles me. Your little wren has perched on my windowsill and watched while I undress at night. While I fall asleep. Your crossbill has attended my waking with gifts. It seems I cannot escape your gaze wherever I am, whatever I do. That is . . . it is another form of captivity.'

'Not so, Ana. I would never watch if I thought it made you unhappy. I do not employ this often. Only when there is a need. Are you saying you would not wish to undress before me?'

'I . . .' The bold question, spoken in a tone of extreme delicacy, stirred every part of her. She felt the blood rush to her face and could not answer.

'That would not please you?'

'I can't answer such a question, Drustan. It's . . . improper. There are countless reasons why I should not conduct a conversation about such matters with you, even supposing I wanted to.' She drew a breath, forcing herself to stop before she said something utterly inappropriate. 'I wish to ask you a question in your turn. You will find it even more difficult than I did yours. But since you speak of telling truths, I need you to tell me one.'

'I have never lied to you. I know you wish that I had.'

'Then tell me what happened that day, the day Erisa died. Tell me why you did what you did.'

A silence. Then he said, 'If I answer your question truthfully, will you answer mine?'

'That is only fair,' said Ana, shivering in anticipation, for she was on the brink of hearing the truth, the whole truth at last, and she did not know if it would make sense of things or merely break her heart. 'Quickly now. Ludha cannot take all afternoon to fetch a ribbon. It is hard for you, I know. Just tell me the facts.'

She heard Drustan take a deep breath and let it out in a shuddering sigh.

'I don't know where to begin,' he said.

'Just start on the day it happened and tell me what you did.' Ana's heart was pounding; in effect she was asking for a first-hand account from a murderer. This bargain was the most unfair she could imagine.

'I must explain first that . . . that when I go there, I cannot always remember afterwards. Sometimes it is clear in my mind, sometimes it is lost and never regained.'

'What do you mean? I don't understand. Go where?'

'To the other place.'

'What place?'

'Where I go when the . . . the frenzy, my brother calls it . . . comes over me. He is wrong to give it that name. I would not call it a frenzy, but a journey. Still, I am at its mercy, whatever it is. If it renders me mad, as folk say, then I am the last one who can argue otherwise, since my every word must be doubted.'

'How does it happen? What does it feel like?'

There was a long silence.

'Drustan? Can you tell me?'

'Like coming alive,' he said in a whisper. 'Like waking from a long sleep. Like fresh water to a man dying of thirst. Like the first touch of the sun. Like being set free. But it made me do a terrible thing. It makes me dangerous. They tell me I would kill again if I were let out. I must believe them. Why would they lie about such a thing?'

Ana was mightily confused. 'But Deord did set you free,' she said. 'You were out in the woods, without fetters, when I saw you.' *When I saw you and thought you the most beautiful man in the world.*

'Deord is very strong and very quick,' Drustan said. 'He walks a fine line. He knows I would indeed run mad without those short flights into freedom. He trusts me to return within, and I have never failed him, not in seven years. He understands what it is to be a prisoner. Without him, despair would have claimed me long since.'

'I . . .' Ana made herself wait and regain her composure.

'I don't pretend to understand all of what you've just said, Drustan. It disturbs and perplexes me. Do you remember what happened on the day she died? Can you give me an account of that?'

'I had come from my own home in the west to visit my brother. I was in the forest. I went out in the morning. There was a mist; it swirled cold around the trees, creeping into the lairs of wolf and badger, obscuring the paths of marten and hare. It was almost winter. She was screaming. She was running. She fell. I went away. When I came home from my journey, they had found her body.'

Breathe slowly, Ana told herself. 'This is the account you gave of yourself after you returned? Just this?'

'It is what I remembered.'

'What about before? Why was Erisa screaming? Alpin said you . . .' No, she could not say it.

'My brother said I drove his wife to her death. Caused her to fall. That is his account.'

'What is your account, Drustan? That's what I want, and it seems difficult for you to put it in plain words.'

'I suppose my brother's tale to be true.'

'What are you telling me? That you can't actually remember what happened?' Impossible hope had awakened, alarmingly, somewhere inside her.

'I was in the other place. What I remember is . . . different. When I am there, I do not see in the same way. I cannot explain in words that will make any sense to you, or to Alpin, or to any man or woman who asks me for an account. I cannot say with certainty what action I took before I heard Erisa's screams, before I saw her fleeing through the woods. I do not remember hurting her. But there are other things I do not remember, from other journeys. They say I killed her. They say the old woman saw it and was so distressed she fled away into the forest not long after. What Alpin told you is true.'

Tears made hot paths on her cheeks. 'Drustan,' she said, 'how can you do that? How can you tell me with one breath that you want to . . . to touch me, to be close to me, and with the next breath say you are too dangerous to be let out? What do you expect me to do? How do you expect me to respond to that?'

237

'I don't know, Ana,' he said quietly. 'Perhaps it is another sign of my insanity that I tax you thus. Will you answer my question now? I hear the creak of the gate; Deord is coming in.'

'Oh, gods, Drustan, how can you expect an answer to that, after . . . Very well, the answer is, if I were not betrothed to your brother, what you suggested would please me well enough, once I got used to the idea of it. But since I am to wed Alpin, I can in no way even imagine such a thing happening, let alone take the discussion of it any further. We must stop this. Farewell, Drustan.'

'Farewell, my light.'

Ana closed her eyes; it was too much. It was too hard. She wanted to go home to White Hill and for all this to be a bad dream. And yet . . . and yet, what she had told him was true. Murderer and madman that he was, she could never wish that she had not met Drustan, even if all of it were to end in sorrow. Until she had met him, she did not think she had been truly alive.

'Goodbye, my dear,' Ana whispered, making sure it was so quiet that Drustan could not possibly hear, and then she got to her feet and went back to the bench. When Ludha came up the steps not long after, her mistress was busy sewing the little dogs on her betrothed's fine new tunic, and if Ana's eyes were looking rather red, her maid had nothing at all to say on the matter.

Chapter Nine

T he weather was set fair. The summer forest cloaked Alpin's fortress in a soft garment of many greens, and the chieftain of Briar Wood announced over supper that in the morning his household would be going hunting.

Faolan had been busy. The druid's non-appearance had given him more time for investigation than he had anticipated, and he had gained the confidence of several members of Alpin's household. He made sure the harp was difficult to mend, and escaped the requirement to sing by developing a lingering chesty cough, which was generally put down to his lengthy immersion in cold water at Breaking Ford. He spent a great deal of time listening, and still more thinking. The folk of Briar Wood were like hazelnuts: hard to crack, and not especially rewarding even then. Faolan could not remember a time when he had taken so long to extract so little useful information.

Ana was unhappy, edgy, nervous; he saw it in her face and, under Alpin's keen eye and stated intention to punish any man who so much as looked at her too hard, was powerless to help her. At the supper table, watching her without being seen to do so,

Faolan deduced that she was asking Alpin if she could be excused from the day's hunting. She was saying, perhaps, that blood sports had never been her first choice of outdoor pastimes, explaining that other tasks would keep her at home. Bitterness welled in Faolan as he watched Alpin roar with laughter, set a heavy hand on his bride-to-be's delicate shoulder and shake his head; he was telling her she must come, she'd enjoy it, and besides, what better opportunity to view the extent of her new husband's domain?

'Take care, friend,' Gerdic advised from the bench by Faolan. 'You're sticking the knife into that cheese as if it's about to attack you. Watch your fingers, fellows, our bard's not in his best mood tonight.'

'Only got one mood,' someone else commented. 'Surly. Typical Gael.'

Faolan made no reply and the talk turned to other matters, notably the proposed hunting expedition. There'd be game for the pot; Gerdic and the other kitchen men could expect a long day. The men-at-arms, seated further up the board, were exchanging theories on what might be tracked so early in the season. Not deer, for certain, but the dogs might take a boar or two, and with the help of hawks, there might be capercaillie or other game birds to be flushed out, though they'd likely not have much meat on them at this time of year.

Faolan made a show of cutting cheese, tearing bread, slicing an onion. He watched out of the corner of his eye as Alpin's arm crept around Ana's narrow waist then slid up so his hand could brush the lower curve of her breast through the fine dove-grey wool of her tunic. A little spot of red appeared in each of her cheeks.

'Hunting, eh?' Gerdic said meditatively. 'Not an occupation for bards, I imagine.'

'Oh, he'll expect me to go.' Faolan's tone was as grim as his mood. 'You wait, he'll give it a little longer then call me up to grovel, and he'll let me know he's kindly including me in the expedition and that he'll expect a song about it when we get home.'

'Shh,' hissed Gerdic. 'Don't let him hear you speaking like that, nor any of his warriors.'

'He won't hear me. And you won't repeat it.'

Gerdic glanced at him nervously. 'Not when you glower like that, I certainly won't. But watch yourself.'

'I do.'

'What if he does that, what you said? You got the harp ready?'

'As ready as it'll ever be,' said Faolan sourly. 'I just need to stay out of the way of boar spears tomorrow, and to use this cheese knife cautiously tonight, and I may have sufficient fingers left to play a tune or two about our chieftain's exploits on the track of the biggest boar in the north. The voice, now that's another matter.'

'Put in a good chorus,' Gerdic advised, his expression serious. 'Make it one of those tunes that are easy to remember, the kind that keeps on going in your head, you know? That way, we can all join in and give you a bit of help.'

Faolan came as close to a smile as he ever did. 'Thank you,' he said. 'I'm going to need all the help I can get.'

It was all part of the well-practised game, of course. Faolan performed his missions with no help from anyone; it was far simpler that way. He preferred to rely on nobody but himself. It minimised the risks. If it suited his purpose to humour Gerdic, who occasionally let slip morsels of information not available elsewhere, he would summon a friendly demeanour. Since it was necessary to be a bard tonight, he would be one. Ana could never have imagined the ordeal she was confronting him with when she told her expedient lie out in the forest. He would rather stand naked and unarmed before a circle of Alpin's fiercest warriors than set his hands to that harp and make music in a crowded hall. It would be like hanging his heart from a meat hook. It would require every scrap of his considerable control to survive the experience with his mask intact. It was not Ana's fault. How could she know such exposure must excoriate his very spirit? He'd done his best, at White Hill, to be a creature of cold detachment, an efficient tool, a man whose only alliance was with whichever master offered the heaviest bag of silver. He had come to believe in that carefully cultivated persona himself over the years. The mask had kept him safe; safe from his memories. The harp would bring them flooding back.

Ah well, that was for tonight. Today was the hunt, and an opportunity that must be seized. He was outside the wall, and he had a horse, his own this time, and the nature of hunting was such that he might slip away unseen if he played it right. There was one quarter he had not yet investigated, and today provided an opportunity to do so. He could not pack up and head off home to White Hill without being completely sure of Alpin's loyalty to Bridei. A mark on parchment, a sworn promise, these were without value when the man who made them had no concept of honour.

The oddity of Alpin's family arrangements intrigued Faolan and stirred his suspicions. Two brothers, two estates. One brother accused of a heinous crime and locked up for life under decidedly bizarre conditions. The other brother thus in control of both landholdings, including one with a strategic anchorage. That had to be cause for doubts, and Alpin's behaviour did little to allay them. Since nobody in the household was prepared to discuss Drustan, Faolan must go straight to the source.

Then there was Deord. A Breakstone man; like himself, one of the very few survivors of the dark cesspit that was the Hollow. If a man got out of that place, as Faolan himself had done, surely the last occupation he would choose was prison guard. He considered it as he rode down a steep incline under tall firs, following the strung-out line of Alpin's hunting party. Seven years, they said the fellow had been here. Seven years of dark memories; seven years of evil dreams. Why hadn't Deord settled down somewhere, found a comfortable woman and raised a family? Why wasn't he plying a trade in a safe settlement as far away from the touch of the Uí Néill as he could get? Going back under lock and key was the action of a madman. Well, Deord was guarding a madman, if what folk said was true. Maybe they were good company for each other.

The forest was playing tricks today. The tales Faolan had heard suggested presences beyond the human, beyond the animal: creatures of bone and darkness, long-fanged monsters with reaching arms, crones bearing little bags of perilous charms, fell warriors armed with deadly, invisible weapons. Then there were the trees themselves, the tortuous pathways and the eldritch mists. To hear folk talk, one would think the very stones had legs and eyes and a capacity for mischief. Faolan discounted such tales, for he knew the propensity of men's fears to build on themselves, making a mighty monster out of a creak in the dark, a furious demon from a darting shadow. In his own opinion, the ill deeds of men were a great deal more alarming than the phantoms that could be concocted from a bad dream and too much mead. Nonetheless, these pathways were tricky. At more and more frequent intervals the hunting party halted in a clearing or on the banks of a stream and held a consultation as to which fork to take, which path to follow.

Ana rode at the front with Alpin; Faolan himself was far down the line with the last riders of the party, mostly household servants leading packhorses, whose task would be to carry today's kill home in triumph. Faolan rode quietly, making himself as unobtrusive as possible and memorising each turn, each branching of the way as they went. With luck, it would scarcely be noticed if he disappeared for a while; once the hounds scented boar, the last thing on anyone's mind would be how many men were currently in the party and exactly where they were. He hoped they would not ride too far before his opportunity came. His own quarry was not out here in the forest but back at Briar Wood. He intended to find Deord and extract a few truths from him. Their kind had a bond, forged through adversity and survival. They were bound to aid one another whether it suited them or not. If the guard would not talk, maybe Drustan would.

When the party halted again he caught a glimpse of Ana, mounted on her horse, waiting quietly while Alpin explained something to his men. The hunting dogs milled around the horses' legs, turning their heads at every rustle in the bracken; they were long-legged, shaggy creatures, taller at the shoulder than the White Hill hounds, with an implacable look about the eyes and jaw that suggested a boar might be easy prey for them. Ana was looking pale and tired.

As they moved on, Faolan gradually allowed one, then another rider to pass him until he was behind the packhorses. Before long the hounds erupted in a baying cacophony of noise and Alpin's chief huntsman released them. The dogs vanished into the forest, each one a battering ram of sheer muscular power. The riders set off in pursuit. The ways were narrow and overgrown; within the space of a few breaths the party was spread out so far one could see no more than one or two other riders, and the dogs were well ahead, driving their quarry to a point where it must turn and face them in its last desperate stand.

The men with the packhorses found a small clearing and settled to wait it out. While they were unloading their gear and tethering the creatures to graze, Faolan slipped away under the trees, his mount obedient to his touch. He made quietly back the way he had come. So far, so good. He'd no desire at all to be in on the kill. He had seen enough violent deaths in his career, had indeed inflicted many of them with his own hands; the battle of a wild boar against that rapacious pack held no appeal whatever. He'd his own hunt to execute today, and it needed to be quick, for he must rejoin this party as invisibly as he'd left it and then obtain the account of its successes, for the fashioning of a song.

Once he was far enough from Alpin's hunters he began to hum under his breath, the beginnings of one of those tunes that kept going through a man's head. Gerdic was right; these folk would be best pleased with something simple, and this musician would be far safer with such a ditty to deliver, a trifling thing devoid of high emotions or grand themes. But the song that dogged him, insinuating its own form into the tune he hummed, was the ballad he had sung when he carried Alpin's bride across a ford: the tale of a man bewitched by a fairy woman, a man who could never be the same again.

Deord was weary. When Drustan had a bad night there was no sleep for either of them. This had been one of the worst, his charge raging up and down the enclosure in darkness, beating at the iron gate, punching tight fists into the stone walls until his hands were raw and bleeding, crouching with arms over his head, leaping up to hang from the grilled roof of their cage as if he would breach the barrier by sheer force of will. Later Drustan had torn a blanket into strips and begun knotting them together with grim purpose, and Deord had been sorely tempted to put the shackles on him to keep him from self-harm. But he had not. Maybe the bad nights were the product of a disordered mind, but it was incarceration that provoked them; to bind Drustan while he was in this mood would be particularly cruel. The madman's prison at Briar Wood was spacious and comfortable by Deord's standards. Any man who had endured the hellhole of Breakstone Hollow must see Alpin's provision for his brother as generous and fair. But Drustan was no ordinary man, and this confinement was, for him, every bit as hideous a torture as those dank, malodorous cells in the secret prison of the Uí Néill chieftains had been to Deord himself. Denying Drustan the sun, the sky, the freedom of the wildwood was as bad as the beatings, the strippings, the humiliation and debasement Deord had endured at the hands of his Gaelic captors.

A man never forgot such experiences. They had taken away the light, so that he lost track of day and night completely. They had kept him awake, endlessly, with torches and noises and sudden deluges of chill water. They had strung him up by the hands; by the feet. They had done other things, which he had put away in a deep part of his memory with impenetrable barriers around it. If one were strong enough to survive, to escape, one could not then afford to be eaten up by bitterness. There were few enough of them who wore the Breakstone mark out in the world again. One lesson he retained, and that was how easily evil could rise in any man if he gained too much power over another. He had seen it in the guards at the Hollow; how they started as ordinary, well-intentioned individuals and how quickly they changed. After a while Deord had stopped making the effort to befriend new prisoners; he had ceased trying to help them survive. Watching his comrades fall apart, one by one, had begun to weaken his own resolve. In the end his mind had had room for only one thing: a fierce and selfish will for survival. He forgot the past; he did not think of a future beyond the single thought, the talisman: *escape*. He made himself blind to the present, which was full of blood and screams and quiet despair. In the end a chance had come his way and he had seized it. He knew that if he had squandered his flagging energy on helping the others, neither he nor they would have lived to see freedom. He did not allow himself any regrets.

So, Drustan: poor, beautiful, benighted Drustan, shouting and punching and weeping through the night, Drustan who could not be left alone for more than the briefest time in case he made an end of things . . . What was to be done for Drustan? All the compassion Deord had suppressed as a captive, he let flow through him now he was a prison guard. He knew what his charge had done, a heinous, unforgivable deed. He knew Drustan's wildness, his difference, as perhaps nobody else did. Deord had learned to be strong in body and mind; he had learned a truly fearsome self-control. He used his strength, now, to give his prisoner what freedoms could be managed. He broke Alpin's rules, but carefully so no harsher punishment would descend on this unhappy prisoner who, for all his malady, was a man of rare talents, great charm and considerable intellect. He wondered if Alpin had ever considered, in seven years of nightly visits, consulting Drustan on issues of trade, alliances, war or the management of the two sizeable estates the elder brother now controlled. He had never heard them speak of such matters. It seemed Alpin had decided his brother's frenzies meant an addled mind, a degree of idiocy despite the soft-spoken manner and generally rational speech. He had become blind to Drustan's humanity.

Before dawn, Deord had managed to talk Drustan into a state of reasonable quiet; to coax him indoors, put a blanket around his shoulders and persuade him to drink a cup of water. In order to achieve this it had been necessary to promise a venture outside the walls, a brief flight into freedom. Alpin would be away hunting, and most of his men with him. It would be as safe as it ever was, providing they kept it short and adhered to their self-imposed rules. After that promise, Drustan had calmed considerably, to the extent that the birds came down from their hiding place high in a corner of the roof to perch close to the red-haired man once more. That was an infallible sign that the fit was over, for this time.

The sun was warm today. Deord had folded his robe neatly on the ground, set his staff down by it and was rehearsing the preparatory moves for a particular form of unarmed combat he had learned from a bronze-skinned sailor in a southern port, long ago. Such exercise was essential to keep his body ready for action and to maintain sharpness of mind; in his job, one never knew when trouble might strike. He had taught Drustan the moves, and other skills too, for he knew how soon a man lost hope when he let his body become slack and weak in confinement. It was no wonder Drustan could move so quickly, fast enough to terrify his brother. It was unsurprising, given the strength in his limbs, that the prisoner could leap and grip the iron grille of the roof, then haul himself up towards it. Perhaps it had been an error, allowing Drustan to tune his body so effectively. When frustration made him crazy, the captive's strength allowed him to damage himself all the more. As with all his decisions, Deord had weighed this one. Without the disciplines they practised together, Drustan would have died from despair before he'd been shut away three summers. That was Deord's considered opinion.

As for himself, there had been times, many times in the early days, when he had come close to walking out, to telling Alpin he could no longer do the job. After Breakstone he'd only been home once. He'd tried. A man had to try. But he just couldn't do it. That time of darkness had leached something out of him, something a man needed to be a husband, a father, a brother. For a while he'd wandered. Then came Briar Wood and this strange, mercurial charge, and he'd never quite been able to take that step away. Drustan needed him and, to his surprise, he seemed to need Drustan. After the blood and death and despair of Breakstone Hollow, his duties here gave him something to prove. Quite what it was, he was not sure. Perhaps that there could be compassion even in a place of shadow. Perhaps only that every captor need not lose his capacity for kindness, nor every prisoner his ability to hope.

Deord spun, kicked, blocked with an arm. Now the other way, ducking low, rolling, coming up with a twist to evade his imaginary opponent. Today he would not spar with Drustan, for it was Drustan's time of freedom. The shackles lay on the ground beside the folded robe, the precisely coiled chain. Two birds perched side by side on an elder branch, watching as Deord rehearsed his graceful combat sequence. Of Drustan there was no sign at all. He would return. That was their understanding. The prisoner recognised the danger he posed to others. Before long, he would come back of his own will to the fetters and the darkness.

Faolan was not sure which of them saw the other first. He was leading his horse, going with extreme caution now he was back within sight of the high walls of Alpin's fortress, for a number of men-at-arms still kept lookout there. His plan was to make use of a certain aperture he had discovered, a stone-lined drainage conduit that pierced the wall on the southern side. From there, he would do a little climbing to emerge, he hoped, above the iron-barred roof of the quarters Alpin's brother shared with his special guard. After that he'd play it by ear and hope Deord didn't spike him with a thrusting-spear before he got the chance to identify himself. It was risky, but not too risky; Faolan was well practised at weighing danger against opportunity.

For a moment, as he moved forward under rustling birches, the sun blinded him. He put up a hand to shield his eyes and saw it, a flash of movement in the clearing down the track and a sudden stillness as the other, in his turn, realised he was no longer alone. Three steps forward and Faolan recognised the man who stood there in the sunny hollow between the trees: Deord, clad in serviceable loose trousers with his upper body naked, and a long-bladed knife in his hand that had not been there a moment ago. Faolan continued to approach him but put up his hands, one still holding the horse's reins, to show he meant no harm. The knife did not waver. The serene gaze held Faolan's, the look of a man so sure of his own ability that he fears very little.

'What do you want here?' Deord asked as Faolan halted beside the staff and folded clothing. 'Is the hunt returned so quickly?'

'Alpin's still out there in pursuit of boar,' Faolan said, looping the horse's reins around the branch of a bush. 'The only one who came back is me, and I'll rejoin them as soon as I may. Sooner than I planned; you've saved me a crawl through fetid water and a spot of wall-scaling. You can put the knife down.' As he said this, Faolan pushed his hair back and turned a little so the other man could see the tiny star-shaped tattoo behind his right ear, twin to the mark Deord himself bore in the same place.

Deord lowered the knife and stuck it in his belt. He reached for the robe. 'I spotted that already,' he said. 'Looked for it, once I saw the way you carried yourself and a certain expression in the eyes. When were you in?'

'Long ago. I was young. You?'

'Not long before I came here; eight years ago. Must have been after your time. You've done me no favours today. What if Alpin sees you're gone and sends a party after you?'

Faolan regarded him calmly. 'Why would that concern you?' he asked. 'A man can take a walk in the woods on his day off, can't he, without a need to keep looking over his shoulder?'

'You don't know the half of it,' said Deord. 'Quick now; I've no desire at all for you to be here, but it seems you've come back to speak to me. Or to Drustan. What is it you want?'

'I won't place you in danger. As a Breakstone man, I'm hoping you'll help me. What you can give me, I will repay in kind if I can. I want information. My questions concern your master, Alpin of Briar Wood. I need to establish whether he is a man of his word.'

'Master? That's not a term I use, bard.'

'My name is Faolan.'

Deord's eyes narrowed. 'I know that. And you're a Gael: the same breed as those who man that living hell we've both experienced. Indeed, you've a strong look of one or two individuals whose throats will be neatly slit if ever I get the chance to come near them again. That bothers me, Faolan. And it interests me that you've come here as a court musician. If those hands ever employed a length of gut, I think it more likely it was to strangle an enemy than to produce fair music.'

'My talents are various,' Faolan said. 'As for my lineage, it's irrelevant. My only allegiance is to the man who pays me, and currently that man is Bridei, King of Fortriu. You said you were in a hurry. Was I wrong about days off?'

Deord gave a grim smile. 'I don't have those. There's nobody to take my place.'

'I see.' Faolan's glance moved to the discarded shackles, the neatly stowed chain. 'You don't have them, but your prisoner does?'

'I know what I'm doing,' Deord said. 'He's not far off and will return in time. That's if you haven't drawn half of Alpin's men back after you. Our chieftain has his eye on you, Gael. You must have seen it.'

'I have. I will attempt to divert that gaze tonight by presenting my bardic credentials.'

Deord smiled. This time he appeared genuinely amused. 'That'll make for an interesting suppertime. Tell me, where does the lady fit into this?'

Faolan felt a scowl come onto his face despite his best effort to suppress it. 'She is exactly what she seems,' he said. 'And I'm the one with urgent questions here. No doubt you know of the treaty on whose strength this marriage depends. You're the only Breakstone man I've ever met outside those walls. The only one I know survived, apart from me. Can I rely on you not to talk? In particular, not to speak of this conversation to Alpin?'

'You surprise me,' Deord said. 'If I learned anything in that place, it certainly wasn't selflessness.'

'We got out. We survived. We owe it to each other to go on surviving.'

There was a silence; then Deord said, 'You have my word.'

Faolan acknowledged this with a nod. He was getting an increasingly odd sensation, as if the grove around them had eyes that were fixed intently on him. One might dismiss the local tales of witches, monsters and evil charms. Nonetheless, there was no doubt Briar Wood was an unsettling place. He would be glad to be gone. 'It's my job to ascertain for Bridei that Alpin will adhere to the terms.'

'He agreed to it, didn't he?'

Faolan did not respond.

'You're asking me if he's a liar? Me, a hired guard? You'll have seen how seldom I mingle. I've scarcely had the opportunity to find out if the fellow prefers meat to cheese, let alone to be privy to his political leanings. How can I judge such a thing?'

'Maybe you can't. But what about Drustan? A brother has a pretty good idea of his brother's mind; his trustworthiness, his ambitions, what matters to him. Doesn't Alpin visit Drustan every evening after supper? Surely that's provided you with some clues?'

'My job's security,' Deord said. 'What's between them is their own business.'

Faolan sighed. 'Unfortunate,' he murmured. 'If you'd had some answers, I could have left here speedily, and given myself a better chance of getting back to the hunting party before they notice I'm gone. I've no desire to attract undue attention, for reasons I'm sure you will understand, hired guard though you are. But it seems I'll have to wait here until your prisoner comes back. If he comes back. I want to hear what he can tell me about the Chieftain of Briar Wood.'

Deord was a man whose expression and stance were ever a model of control, even in those moments when he was called to action. Now, for the first time since Faolan had appeared, he looked uneasy. 'You can't stay here,' he said. 'How long since you came to Briar Wood? Getting on for two turnings of the moon, by my calculations. Long enough for a man of your calibre to get Alpin's mettle. You're a fool to think your absence today won't be noticed. You'll be a suicidal fool if you stay away any longer than you must.'

'How inconvenient, then, that your charge is not here, that his shackles have so fortuitously been loosed on the very day his brother is absent from home.'

'I hope you're not threatening us, bard.' Deord's tone was very quiet. 'The lady's already tried that method of extracting information from me and I didn't much care for it. Tell tales to Alpin as to where you found us today and you'll be breaking your own rule. You just held up Breakstone as a reason for me to help you. Now you're suggesting you'll betray me.'

Faolan had heard none of it past a certain point. 'What did you say about the lady?' He heard the edge in his own voice. 'How could she –?'

'Did a bit of her own spying,' Deord said. 'I thought she'd have told you, that's if ladies and their bards are as close as folk say. Still, Alpin's a jealous man. Don't clench your fists, Gael; I have your measure. The two of you should keep out of Drustan's life. She's stirred him up enough already, made him restless and unpredictable. Don't you step in and make things worse. Now I want you to go.'

'When?' demanded Faolan. 'When was Ana spying? Where did she go? You're saying she met the prisoner? What did she ask you?' By all that was holy, how could he have missed this?

'She acquired a key to our quarters not long after the two of you first arrived. She came out here early one morning. She saw me and she saw Drustan. I ensured few words were exchanged. I relieved the lady of the key and told her not to return, for her own sake as much as anything. I'm certain Alpin never knew.'

Faolan listened, mute. There was movement around the clearing: birds were coming in to settle on the bending boughs of elders, in the crowns of elms, not a flock that belonged together but many birds of different kinds. As he watched, a tiny wren darted across to make a neat landing beside the two others that had remained still on their branch near Deord: a crossbill and a hooded crow. Faolan's horse was restless, twitching its ears, moving its feet in the undergrowth. Above them in the branches of a young oak wider wings moved, and a swathe of tawny plumage blazed momentarily in the sunlight. A hawk, its eyes piercing bright, now rested there, staring down at them. The smaller birds seemed oddly oblivious to the danger. Faolan felt the hairs stand up on the back of his neck.

'Her visit disturbed Drustan greatly,' Deord was saying. 'His moods are volatile. It distressed him. I don't want him upset again. You can't talk to him. I gave the lady what information I could, the second time.'

'Second time,' echoed Faolan. 'When was this?'

'A while back, not long after she met him. She threatened to expose our secret if I didn't give her the full story. She was shocked that Alpin would condemn his brother to a lifelong incarceration. Women have soft hearts. They don't understand such matters.'

'Ana threatened you? That can't be true.'

Deord was gathering up the chain and shackles; he appeared ready to depart forthwith. 'Nonetheless,' he said, 'that is what she did, and I believed the threat real or I would not have given her what she wanted. I do not know the lady as you do. Drustan told me she slept in your arms on the journey from Breaking Ford. Perhaps her threat was no more than a bluff.'

'Drustan told you . . . ?'

'Your secret is safe with us,' Deord said grimly. 'Drustan sees what others cannot. You did what you needed to do; the nights are chill here in the north. We both have dangerous secrets, you and I, and now we are privy to each other's. Maybe Breakstone does bind us to mutual aid, but I won't pass you information if it's going to put Drustan at risk. I ask you to go now. Your own survival depends on it. So does mine, and his. If you get the opportunity, ask the lady to keep away. He dreams of her. That cannot help him.'

'How could he know –?'

'Go,' said Deord, his features suddenly forbidding. 'Go now, Gael. Your presence here imperils all of us.'

That eldritch sense again, of eyes around the clearing, watching, waiting, tense with anticipation. Faolan realised he was holding his breath. He opened his mouth to speak, then flinched back as, with a susurration of graceful wings, a sudden powerful dive, all beak and scythe-sharp talons, the hawk swooped down a handspan before his face. Faolan put up his hands involuntarily, shut his eyes and took a step back. The horse whinnied shrilly. When Faolan opened his eyes again there was a second man standing beside Deord. The hoodie and the crossbill sat unperturbed on their branch. The tiny wren he had seen before now darted up to settle in the wild auburn locks of the newcomer. Of the hawk there was no sign at all. Faolan sucked in a shaky breath, unsure if what had just occurred was a freak of his imagination, a piece of clever trickery or something he had never believed possible: a manifestation of real magic. He was without words.

'Sit awhile, Drustan,' Deord said calmly. 'Get your breath back. As you see, we have a visitor. He's no threat to us. In fact, he was just leaving.' Then, turning to Faolan as the red-haired man subsided onto a fallen branch, long legs stretched out in front of him, 'Best if you go. He'll be weakened and confused awhile. He won't be able to talk to you. This takes a lot out of him. As soon as he's recovered we must go back. I ask you once more to leave. As a Breakstone man, you must understand how precious these times of liberty are for us, and what it would mean to lose them.' Deord bent to lay a hand on Drustan's shoulder, to murmur reassuring words. The red-haired man was shivering, a fast, febrile vibration that coursed right through his body, but his eyes, when he raised his head and turned to look at Faolan, were piercingly bright and full of an intelligence that was almost frightening.

Faolan could not summon a single word. His mind was doing its best to explain what had occurred here, to put the pieces together in a way that allowed this to fit into his own model of the world. Memories came to him: Bridei's charm of concealment, a spell summoned to get the two of them out of a fortress unseen late at night; a chill visit to a place known as the Dark Mirror, and the very odd emergence of a small dog from deep water. This was not, in fact, his first encounter with forces beyond the readily explicable. But this went far beyond those lesser manifestations. Frenzy, crazy spells, fits of madness: those, he could understand. But a bird that became a man? That was the stuff of fanciful tales, ancient ballads of wonder and sorcery. He knew his share of those; in the lore of his birthplace there were accounts of princesses turned into swans, of a fair lady who was bewitched into a fly, of creatures that were part one thing, part another entirely. But this, this here, now, right before his eyes . . . One revelation was quite plain to him: whatever this was, it was not madness.

'I'll wait,' he said, and crouched down beside the red-haired man. Drustan was making an effort to get his breathing under control and to work off cramps, stretching his limbs, moving his fingers, rolling his shoulders cautiously. Faolan had a momentary stab of sheer envy: what man has not dreamed of flight?

'You are her companion of the journey,' Drustan said. His voice was soft but compelling; it sounded to be under perfect control, though he continued working on his body, flexing arms and legs, easing his neck as a man does after vigorous exercise. 'Her protector of the little campfires in the night. Part musician, part spy, part killer. You guarded her well.'

'Drustan,' Deord's voice held a warning note, 'we must make haste. Faolan here has left your brother's hunting party by stealth and must return to it before he draws undue notice. You and I must be within the walls before anyone comes looking.'

Drustan glanced at him, then turned his head towards the two birds perched nearby. 'Go,' he said, and in an instant both had arisen to fly off into the shadowy reaches of Briar Wood. He looked at Faolan. 'They will bring warnings, if warnings are required,' he said. 'My smallest one here,' motioning to the wren which still nestled in his hair, 'will go with you. You took a risk.'

'As do you and your keeper,' Faolan said, wondering how it was that anyone could believe this gently spoken, courteous man crazy. 'The word goes that Alpin decreed you were never to be let out. That you are chained night and day.'

'When he sees me, I am chained. When he sees me, I am within those walls he set around me. What do you want from me, Faolan?'

'You already know my name. I suppose I shouldn't be surprised by that. You seem to have seen a great deal more than should be possible. What are you, some kind of mage?'

Drustan smiled; his face became a thing of rare beauty, transformed by a light that was almost otherworldly. Faolan was not in the habit of weighing people or objects by standards of loveliness, with perhaps one single exception. He generally judged his experiences solely by their position on the scale of risks and opportunities for whatever mission was his current responsibility. He had once valued beauty; at a certain point in his life, it had ceased to have any meaning. For all that, this man's features were arresting; they caused one, for a little, to forget to draw breath.

'I am no mage. I possess certain abilities; I see through more sets of eyes than my own. I journey, in a fashion, even when confined within prison walls. When Deord allows it I snatch my times of flight; I enter the other place only on those occasions. To change my form within the tight barriers of the enclosure my brother made for me could be disastrous. We agreed, Deord and myself, that we would avoid such a risk. These transformations are fraught with danger. If Deord were less compassionate he would not allow them. Then I would indeed run mad, for they are as much part of me as mind or heart. I would ask you a favour, Faolan.'

'A favour?' Faolan could not imagine what that might be; he was still struggling to reconcile the fact that his own existence and that of this bright-eyed, softly spoken being, part man, part creature, could stand side by side in the same world. 'Please do so. I, in my turn, have some questions for you.'

'If I can, I will help.' Drustan rose to his feet, swaying a little. He was head and shoulders taller than Faolan; indeed, he had a look of his brother, who was a very big man. But everything that was coarse and rough and thick in Alpin's appearance seemed subtly different in his brother's: Drustan's eyes were larger, clearer, his nose narrower, his mouth more finely drawn. His exuberant mane of hair, tawny red where Alpin's was a dull brown, seemed to capture the sunlight, shining with life as it fell across his broad shoulders. Although tall, he was not a bulky man like Alpin, but well proportioned and athletic in build. Those muscles were impressive; Faolan wondered how a man who had been imprisoned seven years had managed to develop them.

'What do you wish to ask?' Drustan went on. 'We should be quick; Deord's warnings were well considered.'

Deord had gone quiet now, ceasing his protests. The balance of power had changed here with Drustan's first words; there was no doubt in Faolan's mind that it was the red-haired man, now, who controlled the situation. That gave him pause.

'You wish to ask me about my brother?'

The fellow was a little too astute for comfort. In fact, there was another question that was crowding out the others. 'I saw what just happened; the way you changed. If you can do that at will, man to bird, bird to man, what on earth possesses you to stay here? Why don't you just fly away beyond your brother's reach? Nobody could possibly track you.'

Drustan's expression changed; his features seemed to close in on themselves. 'I cannot,' he said. 'The thing I did was done when I was in that other form. Sometimes I do not recall those times clearly when I return; sometimes, when I am in the other place, I have only hazy memories of my human state. To risk a repetition of such an ill deed would be irresponsible. I cannot go free. Not beyond the brief times Deord allows me.'

'You possess sufficient awareness to return to Deord, and to do so promptly, if I understand right. Perhaps you underestimate yourself.'

'I have developed better control, that is true,' said Drustan.

'But I will not risk the safety of the innocent for the sake of my own freedom. I killed once and returned with no memory of it. What man can say with authority that it could not happen again? Besides, I am not a wild creature, I am a man who possesses a certain – difference. I cannot live my whole life in that other form.'

'I see,' said Faolan, torn between admiration for Drustan's strength of will and astonishment that he could have made such a choice.

'That was not the question you wished to ask,' said Drustan.

'About Alpin,' Faolan said. 'He agreed to a treaty. You know of the situation between Fortriu and Dalriada? You would have been captive at the time Bridei won the kingship . . .'

Drustan nodded gravely. 'I know how matters stand. My own territory of Dreaming Glen, in the west, is strategically located in relation to the Gaelic holdings. That makes my brother a popular man. Both Dalriada and Fortriu have cause to woo him, to offer him incentives.'

'Indeed,' Faolan agreed, relieved that his instincts had been sound; this man did indeed possess an awareness of what he had lost when his brother declared him mad and shut him away. 'A rare incentive this time: a young woman who carries the royal blood of the Priteni, meaning Alpin's son could one day become king of Fortriu. Your brother has agreed to a treaty in return for this bride. An undertaking not to attack Bridei from either of the two territories, Briar Wood or Dreaming Glen, and in addition not to ally himself with Gabhran of Dalriada.'

'That's what anyone would have expected,' put in Deord. 'It's clear where the threat to Bridei lies: from the western anchorage.'

'The Gaels have been here?' asked Faolan straight out, for time was passing; it only took so long to corner and kill a boar and carry the carcass back to camp. 'They've made an offer in their turn?'

Deord and Drustan exchanged a glance.

'I'm unable to give you that information,' Drustan said. 'Alpin is my brother. Blood commands a certain loyalty. You would not ask that I expose him to attack, I hope.'

'If any emissary has come here from Gabhran,' Deord said, 'it's been done covertly. Alpin's not stupid.' The look in his eyes invited Faolan to interpret this carefully phrased speech however he wished.

'I see. You understand, I need to be sure Alpin will hold to his word. I will not leave Lady Ana here until I'm certain he'll keep to the terms of the treaty.'

'*You* will not?' Deord queried mildly.

'I am Bridei's emissary,' Faolan said. His instincts told him he could rely on Deord's word; the word of a Breakstone man, sealed by suffering. He'd have to take a chance on Drustan. 'Circumstances led Ana to provide me with another identity on arrival here; Alpin gave us no cause for confidence. She believed my life to be at risk.'

'As it is right now if you don't get back to the hunt,' Deord said.

'Alpin sets harsh rules for those who are merely visitors to his house.'

'If I told you,' Drustan's voice was very quiet now, and he no longer looked Faolan in the eye but stared out into the forest, 'if I told you I thought my brother likely to make his choices in complete disregard for any sworn promises, what would you do then? Would you take Ana away from Briar Wood?'

'Drustan –' Deord attempted to interrupt, but Faolan's attention was on Drustan's face: the look there had become, quite suddenly, that of a desperate man. He felt a chill down his spine.

'If I were certain that was true, I would make sure the handfasting never took place,' he said carefully. 'Yes, I would take her back to White Hill. I would not see her sacrificed for an alliance that was nothing but a sham.'

'Sacrificed . . .' Drustan's tone had shrunk to a whisper.

Faolan said nothing. He would not confess, even to a Breakstone man, that a small part of him wanted Alpin to be a turncoat, wanted the treaty to be worthless, so there would be a reason to stop this marriage. He would not admit how much he longed to take Ana safely home, home to a place where she could smile and laugh and sing, home to a bed she need not share with that big, crude oaf who would only hurt and degrade her. Those thoughts were never to be spoken aloud, for they made a mockery of the mission Bridei had set him. And, in the end, his loyalty to Bridei was the only thing that mattered.

'You love her,' Drustan said, his bright eyes now fixed unnervingly on Faolan's.

Faolan felt the words like a cold hand around his heart. For the first time he saw a look on Drustan's face that was quite plainly dangerous.

'Tell the truth,' Drustan said. 'We will not aid you if you lie to us. We have no patience for such games.'

Faolan drew a deep breath. 'I'm a hired bodyguard,' he said, glancing at Deord. 'I work for my keep; Bridei pays me. I undertook this journey as the lady's protector and as the king's personal emissary since, oddly, he seemed to think me best suited for the job. For a man such as myself to harbour feelings of the kind you mention, especially when the lady in question bears the royal blood of the Priteni, is . . .' He was not sure what word suited best: laughable? Pathetic?

'Is the truth,' said Drustan. 'You have your own reasons for wanting this marriage stopped. Your instincts are sound. But I will not tell you my brother is a liar. I wronged him terribly; I will not compensate him by sticking a knife in his back.'

'Has it ever occurred to you,' Faolan ventured, anger rising in him that the other had, in effect, exposed a raw wound in a part of him he had believed untouchable, 'that it's very convenient for your brother that you're considered incapable of managing your own affairs? That it suits him extremely well to have you removed from the world of strategy and trade and alliances? How useful for him to be in control of that well-situated landholding on the west coast as well as his own wide territory and substantial fighting force! No wonder powerful men court him with gifts. Does that trouble you when you wake at night, Drustan?'

Drustan gazed at him, eyes clear as forest pools under an open sky. The anger was gone. 'I long to return,' he said. 'For all to be as it was before. But the past cannot be unmade. Once we love, our hearts do not shrink in on themselves again. Once we kill, our spirits bear the stain of it forever. I'll never go back to my home in the west. I have banished it from my dreams.'

The hoodie flew in, passing close; Faolan managed not to flinch. It landed with a neat folding of the wings on Drustan's left shoulder.

'Go now,' Drustan said, 'and you have time to rejoin them unseen. Wait longer and Alpin will surely notice your absence and your return. Do not risk that. He is a violent man.'

Faolan did not ask what silent communication had passed between man and bird. This went far beyond his powers of comprehension. He mounted his horse, then remembered something. 'You said you had a favour to ask of me,' he said to Drustan.

'I ask that you do not tell Ana what you saw here today,' Drustan said, his eyes suddenly bleak. 'I don't wish her to know of this . . . malady.'

This was unexpected and more than a little odd. 'I'm unlikely to have the opportunity to say anything of consequence to the lady,' Faolan told him, 'since Alpin takes exception if any man so much as looks at her the wrong way. I haven't seen her alone in all the time we've been at Briar Wood.'

'Do not tell her. Give me your promise.' Drustan's tone was suddenly iron-hard; the change was alarming.

'Very well, I promise. If she's to live here as your brother's wife she must find out some time, and I don't see why this is important . . . But yes, you have my word.' He could hardly offer less, since Drustan had provided better answers than he might have hoped for. All the same, the whole encounter had made him uneasy, and it was not solely the utter strangeness of what he had witnessed that caused him concern. 'You said murder sets a stain on a man,' he said, drawing a deep breath. 'You implied that being shut up for life was a fair punishment for what you did. I spent a few moons incarcerated. Before Breakstone, I had only ever killed one man. Only one. But what I did destroyed a whole family; it put an end to all that had given my life its meaning. It was a crime of the most unspeakable nature. Your own misdeed is a small thing beside it, Drustan. And indeed, my sojourn in the Uí Néill prison was not for the act of murder, but simply for a failure to cooperate. Your keeper here,' he nodded to Deord, a sign of respect and recognition, 'understands all too well from the experience we share how easily a man can fall foul of the powerful chieftains of Ulaid. I bear the mark of what I did. It changed me forever. It did not stop me from living some kind of a life. Perhaps you judge yourself too harshly. Perhaps your brother is less just than you believe.'

260

'Go,' was all Drustan said. 'Go while you still can.'

As he rode away into the wood, Faolan's heart was pounding like a war drum. He fought to slow it, to calm his breathing and ready himself for an unobtrusive reappearance amongst the men of Alpin's hunting party. He struggled to push his ghosts back into the locked part of his mind, the part that had been so long unopened he thought perhaps he had begun to forget. Today was the first time in all these years that he had spoken of that day, the very first time, and now they were all here beside him, his mother ashen-faced, his father silent, Áine wide-eyed and terrified in her nightrobe. And Dubhán. Dubhán smiling and saying, *Do it,* and then the blood.

They were on the way home at last, the carcasses of two wild boar carried triumphantly with them, all gaping, long-tusked mouths and rank, blood-crusted pelts. Ludha had come up alongside her mistress, riding a sturdy pony. Her young features wore a look of concern.

'You're very pale, my lady. Are you unwell?'

What with the hideous, yelping spectacle of the killing, the daubing of hot blood, afterwards, on the cheeks and brows of every man who had taken part, and the undeniable onset of cramps in her belly, Ana thought it unsurprising that she looked less than her best. It was fortunate her bleeding had not yet started; she would at least be able to get back to the fortress before the pain became debilitating. 'I'm fine,' she said and, as Alpin turned back towards them, she summoned a guileless smile for her future husband.

'There should be a fine feast tonight, my lord,' she observed.

'Partial to roast boar, are you?' The smears of blood on Alpin's broad features were drying to a brown that almost matched his beard. 'Yes, it'll be a grand night of festivity. Pity it can't end in a little personal celebration, just the two of us, a warm fire in the bedchamber, a cosy blanket or two, a jug of spiced mead . . . For that, I'd gladly forgo the roast pig and the trimmings. What do you say?' He reached across from his horse and placed a big hand on Ana's thigh, squeezing. She managed not to yelp in pain.

'It sounds . . . pleasant, my lord. Unfortunately I fear I will be indisposed; I feel the onset of cramps in the belly. Just the usual thing . . .'

'Uh-huh,' grunted Alpin, clearly embarrassed. 'Shame. If you have to miss supper, you'll miss the music. Your bard – where is he now, ah, there, with the other servants – has promised me a fine account of today's chase and killings, all sung to the accompaniment of the harp. It's been years since we had such entertainment here. Not that I wouldn't prefer the other. You're a lovely woman, Ana. I wish that confounded druid would get here; I'm getting tired of waiting.'

'I will make an effort to be in the hall for supper,' Ana said, not liking the look in his eyes. 'Your courage in the hunt deserves no less. It's clear you excel in this.'

Alpin grinned widely and slapped his thigh. 'Indeed I do, my dear. And you'll find out soon enough it's not the only pastime I have a particular talent for. Eh, lads?'

Ana scarcely heard the men's laughter. There was little room in her thoughts for Alpin or the wedding or the treaty that was so important. For all Deord's calm assessment of Drustan's situation, and Drustan's own acknowledgement of guilt, she still could not make herself believe he had done such a thing. Ana had ever believed herself a balanced person, one who made her choices in a calm and considered manner. She knew she was thinking like a foolish young girl who tosses away her whole life for love, or for what she imagines to be love. Yet she could not stop thinking about it: Drustan, the murder, that strange day . . . There had been a witness. That old woman, Bela, had been there. If only she could be found . . . If Bela confirmed Alpin's account of that day, Ana would accept it. She would settle down and marry Alpin and bear him the sons he wanted; she would have exactly the sort of future she had always known awaited her. If Bela told a different story . . . Ana shivered. Her future was immovable. Drustan's guilt or innocence had no bearing at all on marriage or treaty or the undeniable fact that some time soon the druid must arrive, and there would be no excuse to delay the handfasting any longer. If somehow Drustan was proven innocent, he would be freed from imprisonment; that would gladden her heart. But it would not change her own future, could not do so. She must stop thinking of the other future, the sweet, tantalising, wonderful future she saw in her dreams, and had done since Alpin's brother first captivated her with his gentle voice and bright eyes. With his fine body. Such thoughts were perilous indeed; she must banish them.

Chapter Ten

King Bridei and his druid Broichan celebrated the feast of Midsummer at White Hill, and folk spoke of that ritual afterwards as one of the greatest and most stirring a man or woman was ever likely to see. What better time of year to summon the strength for war than the day when the Flamekeeper reached his peak and the form of the ritual honoured all men in their bravery, wisdom and vigour?

That ceremony completed, the year turned all too soon towards the festival of Gathering, but it was the old men, the lads and the women who would bring in this season's harvest. From every corner of Fortriu, groups of warriors began slow, meticulously controlled moves in the general direction of Dalriada. It was like a gradual tide flowing westward, regulated with what subtlety its various leaders could apply, for the longer the Gaels remained in ignorance of Bridei's plans, the more likely the chances of a stunning success when at last the two old enemies came face to face.

The scope of Bridei's endeavour was enough to give even a seasoned war leader pause. Carnach led a massed force out of Caer Pridne, ancient seat of the kings of Fortriu. His own men-at-arms from his holding at Thorn Bend, on the Circinn border, were amongst those under his command, but a number of other chieftains had come to join him, bringing well-trained warriors of their own. These men had needed only the sharpening-up provided in the northern camp to render them battle-ready. Wredech, a cousin of the old king, rode out by Carnach's side, with a band of exceptionally fine archers wearing his colours.

Talorgen had returned to his home at Raven's Well, down the Great Glen on the shores of Maiden Lake. At the designated time, he took his personal army in the opposite direction from that the Gaels might have anticipated, striking out a little to the northwest across deserted passes and lonely glens towards a certain coastal holding where a chieftain named Uerb had been preparing ships and training men to sail them. In the wild lands north of the Great Glen stood the high crags called the Five Sisters. From a remote encampment in those parts Fokel of Galany, deposed chieftain of a territory now held by the Gaels, despatched his far smaller force on a mission of its own. These warriors had developed particular skills during their long years in exile: skills in hunting and tracking; the ability to cover long distances and difficult terrain with speed and secrecy; a knack for finding original solutions to seemingly impossible problems. Some called Fokel's methods questionable. His results spoke for themselves.

Bridei left without fanfare. There would be a time for stirring speeches and heroic actions, and when it came he would summon both; a king must be ready for that. From the moment he made his decision and gave the order to set the advance in motion, he became more war leader than monarch, and he rode away as a seasoned campaigner does, with a minimum of fuss. The major part of Fortriu's army was already on the move; the king set off with a company of twelve men-at-arms, many of them old friends from Broichan's household at Pitnochie, and a number of other men with special skills. As his personal guard, Bridei took Breth. The Pitnochie men could provide backup. Garth had pleaded to go, putting forward the arguments that his combat skills were wasted at White Hill, that he had given more than five years' loyal service, that any red-blooded man of Fortriu owed it to the gods to be part of such a grand endeavour. That his sword arm was itching for a Gael's neck or three. Bridei pointed out kindly but firmly that if Garth went as well, there wouldn't be a single one of his most trusted men left at White Hill to guard Tuala and Derelei. He could not proceed in confidence unless either Breth or Garth stayed to perform that duty, at least until Faolan came home, and nobody knew when that would be. There was no need for Garth to ask why Breth had been chosen to go and himself to stay. He had a wife and children; Breth had neither.

'I trust you as a friend. I know you are the best man for this special task,' the king had said quietly. 'Guard my dear ones well and look to your own.'

'Yes, my lord.' The bodyguard had given his monarch a quick, hard embrace; they were old friends. With that, it was done.

The slopes of White Hill were thickly wooded below the sheer walls of the king's fortified compound. From the point where Tuala stood with her son in her arms, watching dry-eyed as her husband rode away to the dangers and uncertainties of war, the path could only be seen for a short distance down the hill. She saw Bridei look up towards her and lift a hand in salute and farewell. He smiled. A moment later he was gone, his horse, Snowfire, becoming a pale blur amidst the green. Ban ran from one part of the upper courtyard to another, whining in distress. It was clear that every part of him yearned to disobey his master's command and follow. His heart, far bigger than his diminutive body, would have had him run by Bridei's side into the heat of battle.

'Papa,' said Derelei conversationally, wriggling to be set down.

'Papa's gone,' Tuala said. 'We'll go indoors now, shall we?' And without waiting for an answer, she turned abruptly and headed off across the courtyard, bearing her son with her.

'She won't let herself weep in front of anyone,' Fola remarked to her old friend Broichan, who stood beside her watching as the last of Bridei's party rode out of sight under the shadow of the pines. 'Ferada should be here by this afternoon. I sent for her; she's riding across from Banmerren with an escort. It's not good for Tuala to keep everything bottled up. She needs a friend.'

'Mm,' murmured Broichan. It was evident he had not heard a word his companion had said.

'You surprised me.' Fola's tone was neutral.

'What?' Now he was listening.

'I was certain you would go with him. It's your dream he's bringing to reality here as much as his own. This venture is every-thing you were working for all those years when you were bringing him up. You rode to battle often enough at the side of Drust the Bull, and gave him your good counsel. A king needs his druid at such times.'

'Years have passed since Drust was king, and still more years since he rode to war,' Broichan said with finality.

'And yet,' Fola replied, resting her small, neat hands on the parapet wall before her, 'you are not an old man.'

Broichan remained silent, staring out over the trees. He had ever been a man of tight controls, whose thoughts and feelings were locked away even from those close to him. There were few such people; his foster son, Bridei, was one, and Fola was another.

'If you had made it known earlier that you were not to travel at his side,' the wise woman said, 'the druids could have found a younger, fitter man to take your place.'

'Fitter?'

Fola regarded her old friend. Her dark eyes were shrewd; not much escaped her notice. 'I think it is not age that prevents you from being part of this heroic push to the west,' she said quietly, 'but something else; something you have kept even from Bridei and are reluctant to acknowledge publicly, for you see it as a form of failure.'

Another silence. Fola noticed the slight tensing of Broichan's hands on the parapet.

'We've known each other a very long time, my dear,' she said. 'If you are ill you should tell me. I might be able to help. We have a highly skilled herbalist at Banmerren. I wish Uist were still with us. His healing hands were unparalleled, save by your own.'

'I'm quite well. Don't fuss, Fola.'

'Fuss?' she echoed, brows raised. 'When have I ever fussed? I'm simply suggesting you acknowledge what's becoming clearer every day to me and to Tuala, and take steps to do something about it.'

'Tuala? What has this to do with her?'

'Don't bristle, Broichan. Haven't you made your peace with the girl even now, after all these years?'

'I was not aware we were at war.'

Fola sighed. 'Tuala mentioned to me quite some time ago that she thought you might be in pain; that perhaps your health was failing. She was aware that you wished to conceal it from Bridei. She has not spoken of it to him.'

'There were certain words between us concerning Derelei and the prospects for his training. It seems she understood me better than I realised at the time.'

'I wonder why, even now, the two of you cannot trust each other. Why you cannot become friends.'

'There's no need for that. We are worlds apart.'

'Nonsense,' Fola said briskly. 'You fear one another, not because of that, but for a reason that is entirely the opposite. There is such talent in her; I saw only the first glimmerings of her potential when she was with us at Banmerren. Because of her position here, she won't allow herself even the slightest use of her powers in public, and that I fully understand, for she must protect both herself and Bridei from the corrosive influence of gossip and innuendo. Because of you, she won't use her abilities in divination and augury even behind closed doors and among trusted friends. And that, I fear, may deprive us of a tool that could make all the difference to the future.'

'Rubbish. What of yourself and the abler of your priestesses at Banmerren? What of the forest druids? Why would we need the intervention of a . . . of one of the Other Kind?'

'Even I cannot summon the visions of the scrying bowl at will,' Fola said. 'My choice lies only in the interpretation of what is shown me. Tuala's skill goes far beyond that. There is a certainty in it that is beyond question. One might think her, at such times, a direct conduit for the goddess herself.'

Broichan folded his arms; his bony features formed an implacable mask. 'It's a raw talent,' he said, 'uncontrolled, untutored and dangerous. I recognise her loyalty to Bridei and to the child; I do not deny that bond. But one cannot get past the fact of her origins. She is not one of our kind. Unpredictability is her very nature. One might as well trust the visions of a will-o'-the-wisp as hers.'

'Where do you think Derelei got his uncanny abilities from, Broichan? Why is it that you are able to find room in your heart for him, not to speak of allotting him a significant part of your time each day, when you dismiss his mother with words of disdain? If Tuala is ill-tutored, whose fault is that? We had her at Banmerren for less than one year. You had her in your household for close to thirteen. Just think how much you could have taught her.'

After a moment the druid said, 'What I can impart would be wasted on a girl. They soak up learning for a while, then lose interest when they're old enough for a man and children.' His tone was dismissive.

'Talorgen's daughter has already proved you wrong,' said Fola evenly. 'She has ambitions for her school and for herself, and is busily making up for lost time. She has builders at work now and expects her first students by autumn. Ferada could have married, and married well. She has chosen another path.'

Broichan's brows rose in scorn. 'Were I the kind of man who lays wagers,' he said, 'I'd bet you a handful of silver pieces to a cornstalk that Ferada will accept a proposal from some likely chieftain before two years are out and abandon her entire plan for ladies' education. If I'd believed she'd stay the distance I'd never have given my consent to her plan. All young women are the same: at heart, it's hearth and family they want most.'

'That was not what I chose.'

Broichan inclined his head courteously. 'My argument excludes those who enter the service of the Shining One, of course. Besides, Ferada is not only well connected, she's young and comely.'

There was a pause.

'You've such a tactful way of expressing yourself, Broichan,' Fola said. 'Believe it or not, in our youth Uist and I came *this* close,' she held up a hand, thumb and first finger a hair's-breadth apart, 'to abandoning duty for love. We were all of us young and comely once. Even you, I suppose.'

He made no response to this, but after a little he said, 'You spoke of opening the heart. What better reason need I for teaching the lad than that he is Bridei's son?'

Fola began to speak, then halted. She gathered her cape around her shoulders as if preparing to depart.

'What?' Broichan's tone was sharp. 'What were you going to say?'

She sighed. 'Something best not spoken. Come, it's a chill breeze. We've seen him on his way. The venture is in the hands of the Flamekeeper now.'

'Fola,' said Broichan, 'what were you going to say?'

'Something you won't want to hear.'

He waited, tall and pale in his black robe.

'Very well. He is Bridei's son. He's also as like you as two peas in a pod, for all his brown curls and fey light eyes. He mimics your gestures as if the two of you were one being. He copies the inflections of your voice while still too young to form the words; he even sits the same way you do. This resemblance will become closer as the child grows older, and other folk will begin to comment on it, folk less perceptive than Tuala or myself.'

Broichan neither spoke nor moved. It was almost as if he had not heard her.

'I knew you wouldn't like it,' Fola said drily. 'Bear it in mind, that's all I suggest. It may not be such a bad thing if the child decides to become a druid. Court may well not be the best place for him. I've no doubt his early promise will flower into a prodigious talent: a talent something akin to your own. He'll need to be protected.'

And, seeing that the druid was not going to make any comment at all, Fola turned and strode off briskly to her allotted quarters, wondering if she had just set a taper to something that could in time become a raging wildfire.

'There,' said Tuala, blowing her nose on a square of linen. 'I've cried enough tears for one evening. We all knew this time would come; really, I am so proud of what Bridei is doing it's ridiculous to weep over the fact that he has to go away. Ridiculous and selfish.'

'Not at all,' said Ferada, who was seated opposite her friend in the king's private quarters. Before the hearth, Derelei sprawled on a sheepskin mat examining a rattling ball on a string, which he had inherited from Garth and Elda's twins. 'It is absolutely natural for women to grieve when their men ride off to war. Even more so when the woman in question possesses uncanny powers of foresight. I suspect you have seen something in Bridei's future that troubles you, and that you are trying quite hard not to mention it to anyone.'

Tuala managed a smile. 'Does it show so clearly?'

'Only to your friends. It's all right, you need not tell me. I know you wish to present yourself to the good folk of Fortriu as an ordinary woman, the same as any wife and mother, with not a special talent to your name. And, as an ordinary wife and mother, you're entitled to a few tears when your husband sets off on such a perilous expedition. It makes me extremely glad I have no man to bite my nails over, unless you count my father, and he's survived so many battles I've got out of the habit of worrying about him. I thank the gods that my brothers, at twelve and thirteen, are as yet too young to go to war.'

'There is a particular danger to Bridei this time.' Tuala spoke very quietly. 'I don't know what it is, but there is a strong possibility that the driving out of the Gaels will be achieved at the cost of his life. I saw that in an augury Broichan cast; yet I also saw victory.'

'Did you speak of this?'

'I told Bridei. Nobody else.'

'And still he went ahead?'

'He values the freedom of Fortriu far above his own life. I must trust that the Shining One will hold him safe in her hands and bring him home to us when this is done.' Tuala glanced down at her son, who was holding the wooden ball very still in his hands; the thing was rattling away merrily. 'Tell me what you've been doing, Ferada. How's the building progressing?'

'Very well, thank you. Oh, and that reminds me – I brought Derelei a little gift. Let me fetch it from my bag.' Ferada rose, walking over to the bundle she had stowed on the chest by the narrow window opening. Her clothing was more utilitarian than her elegant gowns of former times, and her auburn hair was dressed more plainly, but Tuala noted with a smile that her friend's grooming was as immaculate as ever, her posture quellingly upright. The new students would be too intimidated to set a foot wrong.

'Here,' Ferada said, fishing out a small object from the inner recesses of her bag. 'I thought he might like this. Garvan made it. He's working on some carvings for Fola just now, and he didn't want to waste the little pieces of leftover stone. Can I give it to Derelei?'

'Of course.' Tuala watched as her friend got down on her knees on the floor and hid the tiny horse under her skirt, making it appear and disappear until Derelei, the rattling ball abandoned, seized it in triumph with a cry of 'Doggy!' Perhaps, after all, the students would not be so cowed by Ferada, not once they got to know her.

'It's beautifully crafted,' Tuala observed, 'in keeping with the skills of the royal stone carver. Look at the little saddle cloth, all covered in tiny symbols. And the quirky expression: it reminds me of old Lucky. The creature looks as if it's about to cackle with amusement. I had no idea Garvan possessed such a sense of humour. Nor that he had any spare time to fashion playthings for children.' She glanced from the child and his new toy to Ferada, still on the floor. Ferada was wearing an ornament on a fine cord around her neck: a tiny fox carved in intricate detail. Not stone, this, but dark wood, perhaps heart of oak. Tuala was quite certain Ferada had never worn this charming miniature to court before. In the past, Talorgen's daughter had favoured jewellery in fine silver, set with precious stones.

'Has Garvan taken up wood carving as a sideline?' Tuala asked.

Ferada's fingers came up abruptly to cover the little vixen, then she set both hands in her lap. 'Don't make assumptions, Tuala,' she said with severity. 'One can have a friend who happens to be a man, surely, without the need for folk to gossip about it.'

'Who's gossiping?' Tuala said lightly, smiling. 'I won't say a word, I promise. What is he making for Fola, statues of gods and creatures?'

'He's carving symbols on an archway we've made linking the main Banmerren garden with the outdoor area of the new wing,'

Ferada said. 'My wing, that is. The major part of the stone masonry is already finished. Garvan and his assistant are doing the decoration. And some statues. It's a big job.'

'Mm-hm,' Tuala said.

'Don't do that!' Ferada snapped. 'I'm too busy to think about men. I never wanted them and I still don't. I have far better things to expend my energy on.'

'I'm sorry,' said Tuala. 'Really. And I didn't mean men, just one particular man.'

'If you mean Garvan, the only woman he was ever interested in was you, Tuala. After you turned him down, he chose to put his energies into his work.'

'Turned him down? I was barely thirteen at the time; I count myself very fortunate that Fola provided me with an alternative to marriage. At the time I thought Garvan a kindly man, and perceptive, though he could never be considered handsome.'

Ferada grinned. 'Tactfully expressed, Tuala. He's a plain-looking man; Garvan himself would be the first to admit that. Our friend Ana would say it's not looks that count, it's what's inside.'

'And what do you say?'

Ferada did not answer. Her attention had been caught by Derelei, who now lay on his stomach on the rug, both hands stretched out towards the little stone horse. Beside him, the rattle whirred quietly to itself, showing it was not quite forgotten, but the child's attention was on the carven creature. As he beckoned, it lifted one delicate hoof, then another, tossed its head and whinnied softly, then began to nibble experimentally at the sheepskin.

'He will do these things,' said Tuala in tones of apology.

'Did Broichan teach him this?' breathed Ferada, staring as the little creature set off at a trot around the rug.

'Broichan is giving him the tools to control his natural abilities,' said Tuala. 'Whatever I might think of the man, I recognise his wisdom in seeing the need for that. What Derelei does, he does without thinking first. He may have exceptional skills in this craft, but that doesn't change the fact that he's less than two years old.'

Ferada watched with rapt attention as the tiny horse completed its circuit of the sheepskin and returned to the child's side, nuzzling at his cheek. Derelei chuckled. A moment later his hand moved in a controlled gesture that was startlingly not that of an infant, and the little steed was once again no more than a wondrously carven artefact of smooth stone. 'Tuala,' she began cautiously, then stopped.

'Let me offer you a cup of mead,' said the Queen of Fortriu. 'I've a very fine brew here, put by for special occasions. I'll give you a crock to take home with you. You might share it with the stone carver; I imagine a long day with the chisel and mallet gives a man a powerful thirst.'

'Stop it!' Ferada got up to seat herself on her chair again. 'Yes, let's share a drink, there's precious little of it at Banmerren. Your son reminds me of someone, but I'm not sure who.'

'Bridei, I imagine. His hair is just the same.'

'It's more an impression, not anything so obvious. He may have inherited Bridei's curls and calm disposition, but it's what comes from your side that's intriguing; the skills you seem anxious not to make too public. When he's older, Derelei's going to ask you about his origins, Tuala. What are you planning to tell him?'

Tuala was pouring the mead into a pair of fine blue-glass goblets which had been a gift from a visiting southern chieftain. 'I have no answers for him,' she said. She had never told Ferada about the pair of Otherworld visitors who had both consoled and plagued her in the years of her late childhood; how they had promised she would discover the truth about her parentage, and had snatched away that prospect when Tuala made the choice to stay with Bridei and forsake the world beyond the margins. They had been much in her thoughts of late, since she had overheard her son prattling to what seemed to be invisible companions. Derelei had few words as yet: Papa and Mama, Broichan, a handful of others. There were two new names she had heard him use with increasing frequency, names that his infant tongue rendered as Gomma and Wooby. These, Tuala had recognised immediately. They were evidence that the Good Folk, who had toyed with her life and Bridei's with cleverness and cruelty, were already interfering in her son's. Derelei was only little; for all his prodigious gifts, he was entirely vulnerable.

'I must trust Broichan to protect him while he's growing up,' she told Ferada. 'Garth is here to keep away dangers of the worldly kind, and Faolan should be back soon. The king's druid has the power and the skills to deflect the other sort of threat. But I do worry about my son. I'm all too aware that I have set him on a most difficult path in life. His eldritch gifts come through me. Because of my choices, he must make his way in the human world. As the king's son he will be much in the public eye. Folk will talk.'

'You'd best send him off to the druids if you want him to be invisible.'

Tuala frowned and hugged her arms around herself. Derelei had rolled onto his back; he seemed to be drifting off to sleep. 'I don't want him to go away,' she said. 'Bridei needs his family here. We are his strength. Even Broichan prefers that Derelei has his education at court. He actually seems quite fond of him. Almost like a grandfather. I'd never have believed him capable of that.'

'Interesting,' said Ferada. 'Perhaps it will all become easier when you have more children.'

'Not if they are like this one.' Derelei was singing to himself now, a wordless crooning in his infant voice. Although they had not seen it move, the stone horse had assumed a sleeping posture, lying down with legs tucked up and eyes closed. The rattle was vibrating softly, a handspan from Derelei's outstretched arm.

'Well, you know what I said before. Any small girls you and Bridei produce will be very welcome in my establishment. If their talents prove to be more magical than scholarly, I'll pass them over to Fola.'

'You might have one or two of your own by then,' said Tuala, grinning.

'Want that mead down your neck?'

'I'd much prefer to drink it. I promise not to speak of such matters again; not tonight anyway. It's such a delight to see you happy, Ferada, I can't resist teasing you just to watch that spark in your eye, the one you had in the days before . . . before it all happened.' Tuala was abruptly solemn.

'Yes,' replied Ferada soberly. 'It's very odd to be saying this, but I suspect that if she could see what I'm doing now, my mother would be quite proud of me. I'm not sure if that makes me feel glad or scared.'

'You are not like her,' Tuala said. 'At least, only in good ways. In your strength and determination. And in your unerringly fine sense of style.'

Ferada's hand was closed around the little wooden fox. 'I was so afraid of her,' she said, expression suddenly bleak. 'If I ever had a daughter, how terrible if she felt like that about me.'

Tuala did not reply. Derelei was almost asleep; she picked him up and bore him off to bed. When she returned, Ferada had refilled the two cups and was looking calmer.

'You know,' Tuala said, 'that is the very first time I've ever heard you speak of motherhood as even a remote possibility.'

'I wasn't serious. I plan to grow old happily alone, like Fola.'

'Uh-huh. You'll make your own choices, that much is certain. You shouldn't be afraid of becoming like your mother, Ferada. You are so much yourself: strong, good, clever. A true friend.'

'Thanks,' said Ferada after a moment, in a tone of genuine surprise. 'I suppose it's Ana who will be producing children next. I wonder if she'll come back and visit us some time, with her handsome northern chieftain by her side and a brood of miniature Caitt warriors about her skirts.'

'I see Ana with daughters,' Tuala said, staring reflectively into her mead.

Ferada glanced at her sharply. 'You mean, because she's the soft, feminine kind of girl? Or have you actually seen something in her future? Do you know if she is happy?'

Tuala hesitated. 'I don't know. A glimpse, something strange . . . I can't tell, really. I don't do this any more.' She would not meet Ferada's eye.

'Because of what you might see? For Bridei?'

'It's more complicated than that. I catch little things sometimes, by accident. I'm very concerned for Ana. Those glimpses I have had show her weeping, anxious, afraid. Of course, these images could be of past or present or times yet to come. And . . . and I saw Faolan playing a harp.'

Ferada gave a snort of laughter. 'Now *that* I refuse to believe as anything but a figment of the imagination. I put it down to too much mead. Clearly it's my duty to help you finish this jug. Let's have a toast, shall we? To absent friends: may the gods watch over them and bring them safely home.'

'May the Shining One give them good dreams tonight; may the Flamekeeper brighten their waking,' said Tuala, but there was a shadow in her eyes: how many such wakings might there be until the time of war, when Bone Mother walked the field of blood and pain, gathering up her broken sons for the longest sleep of all?

Faolan might as well have been playing the music of war, for the drumbeat of his heart was in keeping with such martial entertainment. His skin was clammy with nervous sweat; his fingers would be hard put to pluck the harp strings cleanly. The tight codes with which he had learned to rule his behaviour and rein in his feelings all through the long years since the night his life changed forever were not going to be of the slightest use tonight. The moment he set hands to harp, the moment he opened his mouth to sing, he would lay himself bare again. How could he possibly get through even one song, let alone sufficient to last the lengthy duration of a festive after-hunt supper?

Ana was gazing at him. She did look ill; the pallor was more pronounced now, the cheeks hollow, her lovely mouth set as if she were attempting to control pain. She nodded to him gravely. Faolan saw in her eyes an acknowledgement that she had erred in her judgement and the recognition that it was he who would suffer for it, though she could not understand the full extent of that, since he had never told her his story and now never would. He saw that she was sorry and forgave her instantly. He bowed his own head in response; it was the courteous gesture of servant to mistress, stiff and formal, calculated not to offend Alpin in any way. Then Faolan cleared his throat and began.

They liked the hunting song. Gerdic, true to his word, picked up the rollicking chorus and led the assembled crowd each time it came around. Faolan had been extremely careful in his research; nobody in the hall could have guessed he had not, in fact, been present when Lord Alpin's own spear had pierced the first boar's heart, or when the second creature had unexpectedly erupted from the undergrowth and come close to gelding Briar Wood's assistant chief huntsman before the dogs moved in. By the end of the song – a long one, twelve verses in all – Alpin was singing along with the best of them, and Ana's expression could only be described as stunned.

The hunting song had been delivered unaccompanied, save for rhythmic stamping and clapping. Faolan felt the sweat dripping down his neck; it was as if he had fought a battle all alone. In a way, that was exactly what this had been: a battle against himself. He was uncomfortably aware that the real test was yet to come.

'Let's hear the harp, lad!' shouted Alpin, beaming. The chieftain was well pleased; the fact that he had not called Faolan 'Gael' proved it. 'Give us a little something for the ladies. What about a love song? You'd like that, my dear, wouldn't you?' He patted Ana's graceful hand with his own massive one.

Faolan made himself breathe slowly. He set the harp on his knee; took his time fiddling with the tuning, although it was already perfect, for he had checked and rechecked it before entering the hall.

'Faolan,' Ana's voice came clear and soft across the crowded space, 'I am fond of that ballad about the man who fell in love with a fairy woman, you know the song I mean?' She turned to Alpin. 'Of course, it's in Gaelic, but you won't mind, will you, my dear? I do enjoy the melody, even though I can't understand the words.'

She thought she was helping him, providing him with a song he already knew, since she had heard him humming it at the ford. Thought, perhaps, that it was the only other piece in his repertoire.

Alpin made a gruff comment that indicated reluctant consent and set a heavy arm around his betrothed's slender shoulders. Faolan's hands moved; paused; moved again in a confident, sweeping flourish across the strings. The sound rang out, bold and true, silencing every tongue in the hall. His heart quivered and trembled with the harp's frame, a sudden flood of emotion threatening to unman him completely, so long had it been since such powerful feelings had been set free within him. He must do this; this time he could not hide, he could not run away. Faolan drew breath and began to sing.

She did understand Gaelic, of course; enough of it so that, if he had not needed every scrap of his strength to prevent his memories from overwhelming him and making him break down, he could have used this opportunity to speak to her, to warn her, perhaps, that Alpin was quite probably a liar and that they might need to make a hasty departure; to praise her beauty and courage; to tell her what he could never tell her outside the safe confines of a fantastic tale of passion and heartbreak. As it was, Faolan let the harp speak for him, conveying in its delicate tracery of notes the wondrous love of Fionnbharr for Aoife, the maiden of the *sidhe*, and the aching void he felt within him when he lost her. The singing seemed to happen despite him. If his voice cracked once or twice, his audience scarcely noticed. Goblets were arrested between table and mouth, pork bones held unmoving in greasy fingers. Serving people stood rooted to the spot, laden platters in hand. By the far wall a short, bald man with big shoulders stood listening intently, eyes calm, mouth displaying a small, ironic smile.

Eventually it was over. Wild applause broke out, with shrill whistles and table-thumping. Gerdic came over to slap Faolan on the shoulder, almost dislodging the harp; another man thrust a brimming cup of ale into his hand.

'Drink up, then let's have another. Not one of those tearful, slow things, for all the ladies lapped it up – look at my wife there, she's sniffling as if her mother just died. Give us something with a bit of a beat to it, a marching song or suchlike. And then that first one again, we know the tune now.'

'Bard!' Alpin called out. 'No more of that soft Gaelic rubbish, I've no patience with it. Let's have words we can understand, for pity's sake. And give us a tune fit for men, for we've shed a boar's blood today and we need entertainment fitting to the occasion. Play us something bold and stirring.'

Faolan took a mouthful of the ale, set the cup down and began again. Finding the right sort of tune was not difficult; he knew hundreds of them. Playing was no real challenge, even though his fingers had been untested at the task for more years than he liked to remember. The techniques came back to him readily enough, and the neglected harp stood up remarkably well to the challenge. If Faolan could have shut himself off from the painful return of the heart's knowledge, he might have done as he was asked and emerged with nothing worse than blistered fingers. He laboured on, glad that the company showed a marked preference for rousing, cheerful songs, for it was the sorrowful and profound that were most likely to undo him.

At a certain point in the evening Ana made her excuses and retired to bed. It was clear to Faolan she was struggling to hide her astonishment and, he supposed, relief: the last thing she would have expected was to find him entirely competent as a musician. They allowed him a brief rest during which he was plied with food and drink. He spoke with Gerdic and some others. Later, he could not remember a word he had said. He tried breathing in a pattern, which was a thing he had observed Bridei doing at times of stress, and found it helped slightly. The flood of memories still surged in him, but he was able to hold back its physical manifestations: shaking hands, unsteadiness of voice, furious tears. The long evening finally drew to a close; Alpin called for one last song.

Faolan had not decided, as his fingers moved to the strings once more, just which piece he would give them. His common sense dictated something brief, bland and cheerful to send them to their beds smiling and give them pleasant dreams. At the last moment he chose to disregard his own good counsel and began the introduction to a far grander song, an account of a heroic battle, Gael against Gael, in which a great leader inspired his forces to unlikely victory. He did not sing in his own tongue but in that of his audience, and instead of a red-headed chieftain of Ulaid his hero was a young king of Fortriu newly come to his throne, a man whose token was the eagle, and on whose great endeavour the Flamekeeper gazed with benevolent warmth and heart-deep pride. He did not actually name Bridei, but there would be neither man nor woman present in the hall who would mistake his meaning. He told of how old men laid down their walking sticks and ale cups to cheer as the young leader came by; how men in their prime rode off by the hundreds to join him; how youths scarce old enough to leave their mothers' skirts took up the rusting swords of dead grandsires and marched away to pledge themselves to the new king's service. He sang how, in this young leader, the courage, wisdom and strength of the original ancestor, Pridne, seemed reborn.

The piece ended with a stirring melody on harp alone, and a single bright note from the highest string. It hung in silence for a count of five, then Faolan bowed his head as applause thundered around him. He had performed the whole song without conscious thought; it had seemed to flow, not because of him but almost despite him. Once, when he was young and struggling with technique, he would have given much for such intuitive creation. Tonight he was only aware of how he felt now it was over: as if his body had been dragged over stones. He felt bruised, battered, like a beaten cur, his heart cowering within him, cringing from the assault it had suffered, for he had opened a door long closed and bolted, and had let in more than he could rightly hold.

'Come here, bard.' Alpin was standing, ready to retire; benches scraped on the flagstones as the household rose with him.

Faolan's feet made the necessary moves, carrying him across the hall to stand before the Chieftain of Briar Wood. He found that his knees were not prepared to bend; the pretence of subservience no longer seemed to be possible. He managed to bow his head, for if he had tears in his eyes, he surely did not want this man to see them.

'You surprised me.' Alpin's tone was not inimical, merely curious. 'The last thing I expected was that you could actually play. The lady was not lying after all.'

Faolan looked up, tears forgotten. 'Lady Ana does not lie,' he said coolly.

Alpin scowled. 'Maybe you play prettily,' he said, 'and sing wittily, and maybe you did provide good entertainment, but if you're a court bard, I'll skin the next cat that crosses my path and eat it for breakfast, bones and all.'

'Yes, my lord.' Faolan's hands clutched themselves around the harp frame.

'I'm for bed,' Alpin said. 'The lady's unwell; I might look in on her, see that she wants for nothing. I hope she's not going to be sickly. I need sons, bard. No amount of pretty singing is helping me get those. Off you go then. By the Flamekeeper's manhood, you look as pasty in the face and shaky in the knees as your mistress. What is it with you southerners? Gerdic, get this fellow off to the sleeping quarters, will you, before he passes out and drops that instrument. We need him in one piece, and the harp; no doubt the womenfolk will be wanting more fancy ballads tomorrow. Goodnight, lads. The Flamekeeper bring you dreams of wild beasts slain and battles won. And an accommodating armful of a woman in your bed.'

There had been a time, more than five years ago, when Faolan had spent a long wakeful night by Bridei's side. He remembered how Bridei had retched his stomach dry; how he had fought a trembling that possessed his body; how he had managed to stay quiet and to hold back tears. They'd all been there for him that terrible night of the Gateway sacrifice, himself, Breth and Garth, and they'd tended to their soon-to-be king out of love as much as duty. Tonight Faolan himself was the one in danger of falling victim to an excess of dark emotions, and if there had been a comrade nearby to offer support, he would have shrugged him off. Indeed, he did not believe a man like himself could have such a thing as a friend; he was of his nature undeserving of it. There wasn't a soul in the world he would allow to witness his weakness. There wasn't a man living to whom he would confess his full story. Not even Bridei. What he had revealed to Drustan and Deord was the merest sliver of the truth, and even that confidence he regretted. Such things were best left where they were, locked inside, not to be spoken. Almost, but never quite, forgotten.

So he made his excuses to Gerdic and the others, who were keen to take a supply of ale back to the sleeping quarters and continue the evening's celebration. Faolan made his way alone up to the selfsame small courtyard where he knew Ana sat in the afternoons with her embroidery. There were guards on the walkways, and they were keeping an eye on him, as indeed they should, but they did not attempt to halt his climb up the narrow stone steps. He held back his demons – ah, Dubhán, best of brothers, and the hot blood spurting, dyeing his own hands scarlet – until he reached a shadowy corner where the light from torches set here and there in iron sockets would not fall on him. There he crouched down, put his arms up over his head like a lost child and, in silence, wept.

'You're looking better this morning,' Alpin said through a mouthful of porridge. Ana had begun to take breakfast with him again as soon as her bleeding had passed and her belly was free from cramps. 'Touch of rose in the cheeks, that's more like it. I've had some news.'

'Oh?' Ana helped herself to bread and cold roast mutton. She wished to convey an appearance of relaxation and wellbeing, though her heart was thumping with nerves. She had a question to ask her betrothed, and she was not sure if he would care for it.

'Yes, that druid's likely to be here within the next couple of days. He was sighted coming down the hill path from Storm Glen yesterday, and one of my people sent a runner in to tell me. Not long to wait now.'

The look in his eyes made her shudder. 'Oh. Good,' was the best she could manage. Two days. So soon. The fact was, however many days it was until this wedding, it would always be too soon for her. She could hear Drustan's soft voice in her head: *I don't want you to marry my brother.*

'Smile,' Alpin said, regarding her closely. 'Convince me you're pleased.'

Ana was startled; was her mood so transparent? 'I am pleased,' she said, but could not find a smile. 'I suppose I am a little nervous. I apologise if that shows in my manner, my lord.'

'You've been here long enough to have settled in by now, surely.' Alpin sat with legs apart, arms folded on the tabletop, leaning towards her. 'And you've had a chance to get used to me, and to the idea of marriage. You need to relax a bit; there's no need to be so prim and proper when you're alone with me. Come here; sit by me, that's it. Closer.' One great arm came around her shoulders and the other hand, suddenly, had pushed up her skirt and was insinuating itself with some boldness along the inside of her thigh. Ana gasped.

'Hush, hush,' Alpin said as if reassuring a nervous animal. 'Bit of practice, no harm in that . . . It'll make it all that much easier on the night, I promise you . . .' The hand had rapidly reached a point where she was going to have to make it stop. The other hand had moved up onto her breast, squeezing most uncomfortably, and his lips were on her neck, nuzzling, sucking. His breathing had quickened. Ana felt rigid distaste throughout her body. She was to marry him in two days, *two days*, and if he did not stop this she would scream or be sick, she couldn't help herself. Duty held her still and silent as disgust washed through her in chill waves. She tried to think what Ferada would do in such a situation, but nothing came to her. It was clear Ferada would never have allowed matters to progress to this point. If Ferada ever let a man touch her thus, it would be some fellow she had selected herself after rigorous testing.

Alpin's fingers were stroking, pressing, probing; he was easing aside the fabric of her smallclothes . . . Ana wriggled a little, trying not to wince as his fingers brushed across the naked flesh of her intimate parts. She edged away, making herself kiss him on the lips, a quick but not too maidenly effort, for she must not let him know just how this distressed her. Then she slid away from him on the bench, tugging her skirt back down.

'If you would have me at my best, my dear,' now she managed a smile, 'you must allow me to finish my breakfast.'

Alpin laughed. Now it was his face that was flushed. 'By the Flamekeeper's manhood, lass, who'd have thought two days more would be so long to wait, after all this time. I hope you know how hard this is for a man. I hope you know how much I want you. There's some fine nights in store for you, I promise. Here, have a handful of this.' He grasped her hand and, before she realised what he was doing, placed it firmly between his legs, pressing down so the alarmingly forthright shape of his manhood stood up hard against her palm. 'They say I'm built like a bull,' Alpin commented smugly, releasing her and applying himself once more to the porridge. 'I'll give you sons aplenty. And pleasure such as you never dreamed of. There'll be a few bruises here and there two nights hence, but they'll be good ones. Eat up. You're right, we need our strength.'

If he thought to reassure her, he had done a bad job of it. For a little they ate in silence, then Ana took a deep breath and began. 'I hope you won't be annoyed with me, my dear, but I have a request to make of you.'

'Oh, yes? And what's that?'

'I am still somewhat . . . distressed about the family situation here. About your brother, and the way he's locked up but still here in the house. It seems to me that casts a kind of sadness on Briar Wood, a shadow from the past that falls over all of us. I worry about that, Alpin. You speak of sons. I worry about my children growing up in a place with such a terrible secret.'

Alpin continued to eat; she took that as a good sign. 'What do you want me to do?' he asked. 'Send him away?'

'Oh, no, I don't mean anything like that,' Ana said hastily. 'I just want to understand the situation better, and perhaps mend a few broken ties. I'm told you dismissed most of the folk who worked here at the time . . . at the time the terrible thing happened.'

'You were told. Who told you?' There was a new note in his voice, one she didn't like.

'I spend every afternoon sewing with the other women, Alpin. Women do gossip.'

'Hmph. They'd be better to keep their chatter for more appropriate topics. It's none of anyone's concern who I keep here and who I dispense with.'

'I heard there was an old woman who looked after you and your brother and sister when you were children. That she lives somewhere out in the forest, all alone.'

'Uh-huh.'

'It seems rather sad that you do not keep such a faithful old retainer under your roof. Isn't it dangerous for her out there on her own?'

Alpin gave her a searching look. 'What is it you want?' he asked.

'I'd like to go and visit her,' Ana said, palms clammy with nervous sweat. 'Talk to her; try to get some understanding of this family I'm marrying into. If your sister were here, or if your mother were still alive, I would ask them. If Orna were prepared to talk, I would ask her. But she won't say anything about it.'

'You can't visit Bela.' Alpin picked up his knife and set it down, took a drink of mead, refilled his cup. 'Nobody's seen her for years. She could be dead, or gone away.'

'Doesn't she have a cottage? A hut? How does she survive all by herself?' Ana pressed doggedly on, unwilling to accept that this last hope of proof might come to nothing.

'I've no idea.' Alpin gave her a sharp look. 'Why this sudden interest in old Bela?'

'I . . .' Ana thought quickly. 'I was thinking of our own children, the ones we will have. We'll need a nurse, and since this is a trusted family servant . . .'

'She's a crazy old crone,' Alpin said dismissively. 'We'll get a new nurse for our own boys. Someone young and energetic. Can't have you wearing yourself out, my dear. I want you fresh and eager. Gods, it feels as if I've waited a lifetime for this. If you please me well, you'll find me a good husband, I swear it. There's nothing I won't give you.'

Ana could not meet his eyes; she stared down at her platter. 'I hope I will please you, my lord,' she said through gritted teeth. 'As you know, I am entirely inexperienced in matters of the bedchamber.'

'Just what a husband expects of a new wife,' Alpin said easily. 'You'll learn. I'll show you what to do and I'll teach you to enjoy it. It's like anything new: riding a horse, flying a hawk, using a bow. Nothing to be afraid of. But you are afraid, aren't you? Now why is that?'

She could hardly tell him his touch unnerved and disgusted her. 'I'm a little upset today,' she said. 'Sad that none of my own people will be here for the wedding.'

'You've got your bard.'

'A servant is no substitute for one's family,' Ana said, glad that Faolan could not hear her.

'I'll make it up to you,' said Alpin. 'In time we'll travel and visit them. And invite them here. There'd be advantage in that, great advantage.'

'I think we should try to find Bela,' Ana said, 'so that she can be properly provided for. Could someone be sent out to look, perhaps? I would like to speak to her, Alpin. There's almost nobody left here who can tell me about the old days.'

His eyes narrowed. 'And why would you want to know about them?'

'I just . . . I suppose it is to do with Drustan.' She hoped her voice did not reveal the sudden rush of warmth she felt as she spoke this name. 'About his malady. I thought his old nurse might be able to tell me about Drustan as a boy. If I am to bear your children I must know how this illness manifests itself.'

'So you can do what? Put them down like weakling pups?'

Ana flinched. 'No, of course not. But, at the very least, seek the early advice of a physician.'

'The best hunter at Briar Wood won't find the old woman, Ana. She went to ground. There's no cottage. There's no hearth fire to send up a revealing plume of smoke. Nobody knows where she is, and these woods are a tangle of trickery.'

'Oh.'

'As for Drustan, his story is quickly told. He was different even as a small child. Wilful. Odd. Difficult. We couldn't have him here. He went to our grandfather's when he was seven. He grew up there in seclusion, where he could not endanger my sister or me. Our grandfather died when Drustan was twenty. He left him the entire holding at Dreaming Glen, including the waters of a deep, sheltered inlet. That was an act of supreme folly, as by then my brother's madness was approaching its most florid. He was indulged there in his own place; it had been an error to let him go. Years passed. My sister married and went away. My father died and I became master here. I saw Drustan very seldom, and that suited me well. I had almost come to believe my life could follow a steady course; my marriage only strengthened my growing conviction that it would be so. For a little I was happy; happier than I'd ever been. Then Drustan came here, ostensibly to discuss the use of his deepwater anchorage by my forces. And it happened.'

Ana willed herself calm. 'He killed your wife,' she said. 'For nothing. Just like that.'

'Just like that. He pursued Erisa through the forest to Drift Falls, where the stream plunges down to the lower parts of the forest, into a place where the trees grow so thickly there are no paths in and none out. She slipped on the rocks at the cliff edge and fell. Within a heartbeat of her fall, Drustan was gone from sight.'

'He –' Ana bit back the words. *He says he can't remember.* 'I cannot understand why he would do such a thing.'

'You're seeking explanations where none exist.' Alpin sheathed his knife with an abrupt movement.

'Just one more thing.' Ana saw Alpin's thick brows angle into a scowl; she must bring this to a swift conclusion. 'How was it Erisa managed to outrun Drustan on the way to this place – Drift Falls? She was heavily pregnant. He was . . . I presume . . . a fit man like you. He could have overtaken her, surely.'

'He didn't want to overtake her.' Alpin's tone was leaden. 'He wanted to drive her off the edge of the falls. And that was exactly what he did. Bela was there, and that was the tale she told me before she vanished into the forest. Drustan has never denied it.'

A cold hand fastened itself around Ana's heart.

'I don't enjoy telling the story,' Alpin said heavily. 'But you're right; since we're to marry, you deserve to hear the whole of it. You're upset; I understand that. If you want me to send him away once we have bairns of our own, I will. It seemed more fitting to have him here; he is my brother, after all. I can keep a close watch on him this way.'

'You must do as you think best,' Ana said, hearing the tight, wounded sound of her own voice. It did not make sense. How could Drustan be two people, the gentle man she knew and this other, violent and unpredictable? But why would Alpin lie about such a thing?

He was saying something; she had not heard him.

'What was that?'

'I said, better have a quiet day; we don't want you tired out for the wedding.'

'That's a good idea, Alpin.'

'We might have a wee supper this evening, just the two of us.'

'I'll look forward to it,' Ana lied. What to do now? Take the easier, crueller option and simply never speak to Drustan again? Never go back to the little courtyard, the place of whispers and secrets? Or use the afternoon to speak to him, to tell him . . . what? That the only witness was not to be found, and that she was forced to believe him guilty for want of any proof to the contrary? One thing was certain. Once she was married, there could be no more of those covert dialogues, the sweet, longed-for times of shared song and story, the tender interchanges. His birds must cease to come to her with their bright eyes and their little gifts. She would restrict her embroidery patterns to dogs. And yet . . . and yet she still loved him . . . There, it was said, foolish, ridiculous, dangerous, yet truer than any truth. It seemed he was a killer, subject to the gods only knew what fits of frenzied rage, and still he was the only man in the world she would ever love, the only man she wanted to touch her as a husband does his wife . . .

Ana closed her eyes a moment and drew a deep breath, letting it out in a sigh. She was being unfair to Alpin, terribly unfair. He had lost his wife and son. Maybe he was rather crude and a little too ready to raise his fist, but all he wanted was another chance for a family. That was entirely reasonable. She'd been sent here for the sole purpose of marrying him and had put up no arguments about it. If she had fallen in love with another man, the most unsuitable man she could possibly find, that was her own folly. She should not ruin Alpin's chance of happiness for something that was never going to be; for a love that had no future. Most women wed without love; most marriages survived. A woman had her children, after all, and her household to run. Tolerance and friendship were adequate grounds for a lifelong partnership. Not everyone could be like Bridei and Tuala, who had those things and true love as well.

But for all that, for all those sensible, practical arguments, it was Drustan who filled her heart and her mind. She wanted him, she needed him, she longed for him. Nothing was going to change that, not even her marriage to his brother. The future, she suspected, held not the cosy domesticity she had once craved, but a nightmare of broken promises and shattered hearts.

Faolan had put a system in place whereby he was informed of any comings and goings at Briar Wood. There was a kennel hand who had no particular reason to love Alpin, having borne the brunt of

his anger after saving a pup that was less than the perfect specimen the chieftain sought for his breeding stock. The lad had not
drowned the creature as ordered but raised her covertly, and now
she followed him everywhere like an adoring acolyte. Dovard
had been happy to be Faolan's eyes where the small exit alongside the kennels was concerned. All that was required in return
was to scratch his hound behind her drooping ears and comment
on what a handsome creature she was.

So Faolan heard, even before the master of the house did, that
a certain visitor had arrived unexpectedly: a pale, hooded man
with the appearance and accent of a Gael. Dovard did not know
his name, only that he had been to Briar Wood several times
before, and that the rule was that nobody but Alpin or Dregard
was to know he was here. The visitor would follow his usual
patterns, Dovard said: he'd wait in the chieftain's chamber and
hold a private meeting when Alpin returned from his morning
ride. Later in the day, the fellow would slip away unseen.

A Gael. Faolan wished momentarily for some power similar to
Drustan's, which would allow him to become a fly or beetle on
the wall of Alpin's council room and listen to their conversation.
This might reveal the very information he needed to turn the tide;
to declare the marriage contract and the treaty a sham, and bear
Ana away from Briar Wood before it was too late. The druid was
expected tonight; tomorrow, Ana would become Alpin's wife and
there would be no going back.

No going back . . . He did not want to go back, not to that part
of his own history that was full of blood and terror and impossible choices. But White Hill offered him a place and a purpose. He
had been with Bridei more than five years now, and knew his
bond with the young king went far deeper than he had ever
planned to allow. Now this wedding was almost upon them, and
if it unfolded as Bridei had wished, in two days Faolan could be
on his way back to White Hill to report the treaty concluded,
Ana bedded by her oaf of a husband, and a mere matter of the
loss of the entire escort to balance that indubitable success. What
evidence did he have, after all, to suggest Alpin's ready promise
of peace was less than it seemed? He'd done his best to ferret out
what information there was over the course of two turnings of the

moon, and he was good at what he did. But all he had were the words of a man supposed to be quite out of his wits, telling him Alpin would make his choices with scant regard for treaties, and the subtlest of hints from Deord, a man who only talked when it suited him. It was not enough. Bridei needed this marriage; he needed Alpin tied to him by bonds of kinship. The thing could not be halted without good reason. It could not be stopped without hard evidence, and Faolan was forced to admit that there didn't seem to be any. He'd had plenty of time to dig out the truth, if truth was to be found. He would swear that, if Alpin intended to betray the King of Fortriu, nobody here knew of it save the chieftain himself. If such a plot existed it had been expertly concealed.

Until now. A Gael, a covert meeting, one of several. There had to be something in it. Unfortunately even the most able spy in all Fortriu could not insinuate himself into Alpin's private chamber past a heavily armed guard. There was the other door, of course, the one that led to the hidden apartments of Deord and Drustan. Faolan considered attempting a variant of the exercise he had planned once before, a spot of wall-scaling, an entry through the grilled roof of their enclosure and a request that Deord allow him to eavesdrop through that little door. He discounted it. There were too many guards about today; the ramparts were bristling with them. Besides, the women would likely be up there with their handiwork in the afternoon; he could just imagine how they would react if he suddenly popped up over the wall of their secluded courtyard. The plan was too risky. There was not even any certainty that he'd be able to hear from in there. He cursed quietly to himself and bent to pat the hound, which seemed to have taken a fancy to him, gods only knew why.

'She likes you,' observed Dovard, who was chopping meat on a slab, preparing a meal for the hunting hounds. In their enclosure at the rear of the kennels they milled about making anticipatory whining sounds.

'She tolerates me,' Faolan said. 'You're the sun and moon for her.'

'Ah, well,' it was evident this comment had both pleased and embarrassed the boy, 'she's a good dog.' With a shrug, Dovard turned his back and moved over to the rear enclosure, to be greeted with a frenzy of excited barking. His own hound edged across and filched a strip of meat from the slab. The look in her eyes begged Faolan to appreciate this act of cleverness.

'I'd best be gone,' Faolan said. 'Thanks for your help. Keep an eye on this feast, or there'll soon be none left.'

As he went out into the courtyard, it came to him that another variant on the plan was possible, one that required only that Deord decide to come out to the hall and go back to his quarters at least once before the secret meeting commenced; that, and an opportunity to have a word with him alone. Simple; perfect. He could get the information he wanted with no risk to anyone. And if what he really wanted was for Bridei's treaty to fail so that the loveliest woman in all Fortriu need not wed that coarse bully, nobody but himself need ever know that. It was a thought unworthy of the king's emissary. Whatever future Ana faced, the man standing by her side would not be himself. He was nobody; he was just a tool for carrying out other people's business. Ana had shown him his shield was not impervious; he had no control over his dreams. But he had ever governed both words and actions expertly and he must do so now and put the marriage, put her, to the back of his mind.

Chapter Eleven

The King of Fortriu was at Raven's Well, Talorgen's holding by Maiden Lake. The nature of their own particular mission meant they would be the last piece to slot into place in this great game of war. While Talorgen himself joined Uerb in a seaborne assault on the coastal settlements of Dalriada, Ged would combine his force with Morleo's, heading for the south by stealth to circle around and attack Gabhran in the heartland. The main mass of Priteni warriors, under Carnach's command, had already moved westward and broken up into smaller groups. By now they should be encamped in the hills, ready to descend on the smaller fortresses and settlements of the Gaels between Gabhran's stronghold at Dunadd and his northern borders. Bridei himself would wait until the time when all the others should be in place. On a designated day, counted out from Midsummer, his party would sally forth to Galany's Reach to link with Fokel's fighters and retake the fortified encampment which had been the scene of a youthful Bridei's first taste of battle, more than five years before. From there they would move southward to meet up first with Talorgen, then with Carnach. The complement of Caitt warriors mustered by Umbrig would join them on the road. No warriors had come from the Light Isles; Bridei's vassal king had ignored his request for aid. Another hostage would be required. Nonetheless, by the time the army of Fortriu marched on Dunadd, it would be a mighty force indeed.

Bridei stood in the yard at Raven's Well, looking down between the dark pines to the cool gleam of Maiden Lake. A shiver ran through him: the recognition of time passing, and the knowledge that within the great circle of birth, life, death, rebirth there came other circles, other repetitions. If one did not learn something from them, one was surely doomed to a life wasted. He had stood here in this selfsame spot once with an old and true friend, a friend who, not long after, had died in Bridei's place. The guilt of that was something he had not been able to shed. He had sent Faolan away; Faolan, the only one who had come close to taking Donal's place in his life. He remembered telling Faolan he expected them to become friends, and the Gael's cool response that he did not have it in him to be more than a man who did a job and received a payment. It was Bridei who had been right, though Faolan had never acknowledged that. He had accepted the mission to Briar Wood as a servant accepts an order; his distaste for it had been plain. Bridei wondered why he had made Faolan go. True, he had wished to spare the Gael a choice between fighting his own people or failing to protect his king and employer. The real reason had probably been to preserve him. There was a very real chance, on the perilous course facing the men of Fortriu this autumn, that the king's personal guard would fall in his master's service. Perhaps, Bridei thought, his own motives had been quite selfish. He shrank from adding the burden of another friend's sacrifice to that he already bore.

All the same, right now he wished Faolan were here. Breth was effective, strong, good at his job. In his way he, too, was a friend. But it was the Gael who had seen Bridei at his weakest, his most exposed. When they were away from home, in the men's world of campaigning, he did not have Tuala at his side to listen to his fears and problems and offer the grave, wise council on which he depended so strongly. At those times it was Faolan to whom he opened his heart when doubt and uncertainty plagued him.

294

Faolan's responses could be dry; he often seemed a man incapable of emotion. But he could be relied upon to be completely truthful. It was ironic that his stock in trade, as a spy, was concealment and subterfuge. With Bridei, Faolan was scrupulous in his honesty.

Bridei's sharp ears caught a movement down the hill: someone approaching on foot, two men or three. Breth had been standing guard at a slight distance, knowing Bridei wished to be alone. Bridei signalled him over. Together they looked down the hill in the moonlight, but could see little.

'It's late for anyone to be coming in,' Bridei murmured.

A moment later the dogs began to bark, the guards called a challenge and voices answered from the track under the dark pines.

'Messengers from Umbrig of the Caitt!' one shouted. 'We come peacefully; wolves delayed our arrival. I am Orbenn, my companion Hargest, both of Umbrig's household. Can you shelter us here?'

'Come up to the gate!' the guard commanded. 'Closer. Stand in the torchlight. Now drop your weapons. All of them. Turn around. Now kneel and don't move until you're told to.'

It was standard procedure. Raven's Well being only a stone's throw, so to speak, from the borders of Dalriadan territory, spies frequented the lands to the west. It was rare for visitors to Talorgen's stronghold to be admitted unchallenged.

Bridei and Breth made their way indoors to the council chamber. It was not long before the guards brought in two young men. Two very young men; Bridei would have called them boys, save that these lads were so big and ferocious that one would hardly dare insult their manhood thus. They wore the skin cloaks favoured by the Caitt and their fresh, beardless faces were already decorated with the first of their warrior tattoos, the intricate detail in the pattern work identifying the wearers immediately as the northerners they had said they were. One lad was broad-faced, broad-shouldered and muscled like an ox. The other was marginally slighter. Both of them were glaring; it seemed to come naturally.

Bridei was wearing no signs of his status, neither circlet nor torc nor silver clasp. Nonetheless, as they saw him each of the young men bent his head respectfully. 'My lord king,' the two of them mumbled together. It had been well rehearsed.

'A difficult journey, from the sound of it,' Bridei said. 'Did you mention wolves?'

'Yes, my lord.' The slightly less massive youth squared his shoulders and tugged his tunic straight. 'I am Orbenn of the household of Umbrig. I'm to give you his message and then go back to where he's camped. My lord said you'd know where that is.'

Umbrig, then, was already moving into position. 'And your friend here?' Bridei asked. 'Is the message so weighty it requires two to carry it?' He had hoped to lighten the mood, for the bigger of the two youths seemed wound so tight he would snap if touched. The boy's cheeks flushed red at the remark, and Bridei regretted it.

'I am Hargest,' the young man growled. 'I'm here – I came here to –' His fists were clenched. His eyes, of an unusual light blue colour, were narrowed and inimical.

'He came along uninvited,' Orbenn tossed in, provoking a furious scowl from the other.

'I can speak for myself,' Hargest snapped. Then, taking a deep breath, 'I apologise, my lord king. I can explain myself.'

'Then do so,' Bridei said coolly. 'It's late and we're busy. You must understand, surely, that in such times as these a household cannot welcome with open arms any man who happens to turn up at the door. Why have you come here?'

'I would – that is to say –' The young man shot a glance at his companion, looked at Breth, armed and dangerous by the king's right shoulder, gazed around at the men-at-arms who were posted strategically about the council chamber. 'I don't wish to speak before all of *them*,' Hargest blurted out, cheeks reddening still further.

'You think the king a fool?' challenged Breth. 'He doesn't give private audiences to complete strangers, not even in times of peace. Now state your business or you'll be put out to try your luck with the wolves again. Stop wasting the king's time.'

'My personal guard, Breth,' Bridei explained mildly. 'What he says is true. However, I think we can arrange to feed you while you talk to us. Imposing as the two of you are, you're surrounded by the best-trained warriors in all Fortriu here, and I'm sure they relieved you of every one of your weapons before they let you in here. Enfret?' He addressed one of his own guards, a Pitnochie man who had come in his personal escort. 'We need some food for these travellers; see to it, will you? And have the men stand back just a little; give them room to breathe.'

Once they were seated on a bench, with bowls of mutton-fat porridge in their hands and ale cups beside them, the young men's demeanour relaxed slightly. Orbenn's message was not secret, and he delivered it quickly between large mouthfuls of food. 'My Lord Umbrig says he'll meet you as planned, and he says if you want a number, it's three hundred and twenty, give or take a few.'

Bridei's eyes widened. Three hundred and twenty fighting men: that was a sizeable force and, under Umbrig's leadership, one to be reckoned with. 'Thank you,' he said calmly. 'Anything more? Did he mention any other chieftains?' There had been talk of Umbrig linking up with Fokel of Galany; each had expertise in transporting men and supplies over seemingly impassable terrain. Bridei had hoped, as well, that by now Alpin of Briar Wood might perhaps be part of the plan, though he would not say so, not to this youth of whom he knew nothing.

'No, my lord king,' Orbenn said, and took a long draught of ale. 'By the Flamekeeper's manhood, that's a good drop. Those were the only words in the message. You're referring to Fokel of Galany? You expect him to join you?'

There was an awkward silence.

'For a young fellow who's still wet behind the ears,' Breth said, 'you seem to think you know a lot. Who are you to be asking the king such questions?' On occasion, when Bridei's bodyguard spoke, folk said they could hear the scrape of a drawn sword in his voice. This was one of those times. Orbenn's hand stilled with the ale cup halfway to his lips.

'You understand,' Bridei said, 'such matters are for private councils amongst chieftains and druids. As a messenger, your job is to bring the words and pass them over accurately, no more, no less.'

'I know that,' Orbenn muttered, setting the cup down.

'This'd be the first time Umbrig's trusted you with such a job then?' put in Enfret with a grin.

There was no reply. It could not quite be said that the messenger sulked; for all his youth, he was too formidable a figure for that. He simply seemed to close in on himself.

Bridei waited until the two of them had eaten their fill. Then he sent Orbenn off with Enfret to find a corner of the sleeping quarters that could accommodate the travellers. Hargest he retained with a small gesture of the hand.

'Now,' he said, 'let's hear what this is all about. You'll have to speak up in front of Breth here; he's my personal safeguard and stays by me at all times. The others aren't interested, believe me. Who are you and why are you here? I've no wish to anger Umbrig just because you've taken it into your head to have an adventure. What's your position in his household?'

'I'm a fighter.' This was spoken defiantly, as if expecting derision or at least challenge.

'Mm-hm,' Bridei said. 'You've the build for it, no doubt of that. So, you're one of his men-at-arms?'

Hargest looked down at his boots. 'In a manner of speaking,' he said indistinctly.

'Why did you come? Protection for a friend? Safety in numbers?'

The boy did not reply.

'Speak up!' Breth folded his arms, glaring. 'If you can't provide an explanation for your presence here we'll be obliged to lock you up until we can find out the truth. Right now I can't think of a single reason to trust you.'

Hargest looked up again. He had regained some of his composure, but his eyes were angry. His manner had something in common with a young bull's, aggression and uncertainty mixed. 'I want to do a job,' he said. 'A real job, one that will test me. I want a job like yours,' glancing at Breth, who stared back in genuine surprise.

'In what capacity?' Bridei was torn between amusement at the lad's boldness and a real admiration for his approach. As a warrior, Hargest would surely be the one to charge in first, heedless of his own safety. 'If you're the fighter you say you are, don't you already have a job with Umbrig?'

A flicker of emotion passed across the young man's broad features. 'He won't let me fight,' Hargest said. 'One small skirmish, that was all, and then he put me back in my old job. Looking after the horses.'

'So you are no warrior, but a stable boy?' Breth grinned.

'You think I can't fight?' Hargest snarled. 'Just try me!'

'Ah – no need for that,' Bridei said calmly. 'Tell me, Hargest, how old are you?' He wondered if the boy would lie, and if he would be able to tell.

'Fifteen, my lord king.' That, surely, was the truth, even though the lad was almost as tall as Carnach and twice as broad.

'And what exactly is your place in Umbrig's household? I don't think you told us that.'

'I was fostered there, my lord king. I am a kinsman of Umbrig. A sort of kinsman.' The flush entered Hargest's cheeks again; it made him look younger.

'A sort of kinsman. Born out of wedlock?' Such matters were delicate, though common: men acknowledged their natural children but rarely bestowed land or other privileges on them. A place in the household was generally considered enough.

'Yes, my lord. My father is Umbrig's second cousin. He fathered me when he was just fourteen. I was sent away to Storm Crag at seven. It was thought best, since he – my father – was to marry. I was viewed as an embarrassment.'

'I see.' Bridei, himself a foster child, knew all too well the loneliness, the confusion, the feelings of loss such a decision could bring. Being brought up by Broichan, admirable as the druid had been in instilling learning into his small charge, had not made for the warmest of childhoods. 'And now Umbrig employs you as a stable hand?'

'I like the horses,' Hargest said simply. For the first time he sounded natural, as if he had temporarily forgotten his protective screen of aggression. 'I'm good with them. He wouldn't have brought me on this expedition if I wasn't. But I'm better with a sword or a staff or with my fists, and that's what I want to do, my lord king. Be the best warrior in all the lands of the north; prove I can outlast any challenger.' The young eyes were fierce, the back very straight.

Bridei waited a moment, noting the genuine courage behind the fighting words, and then he said quietly, 'Prove to whom? Your father?'

Hargest seemed to deflate a little. 'Maybe,' he mumbled.

'I don't think you mentioned his name,' Bridei said.

'Alpin,' said Hargest. 'Alpin of Briar Wood.'

'Ah.'

'You know him?'

'I know something of him,' Bridei said. 'Do you go back there, now that you are old enough to move beyond fostering? Do you see him often?'

'No, my lord. Umbrig said I could stay at Storm Crag, and that's my choice. It suits my father. He prefers me out of the way.'

'Really? A fine young man like yourself?' Breth's tone was not quite mocking; in truth, this was a lad any father would be proud of, a physical specimen akin to a prize ram or boar.

'He has his reasons.'

'Hargest,' Bridei chose his words with care, 'you mentioned Alpin's marriage, when you first went to Umbrig at Storm Crag. I've reason to believe he may be marrying again, perhaps this very summer. Have you heard any news of that? An invitation, maybe?'

'Huh!' Hargest snorted in derision. 'I'm the last person he'd want at his handfasting. It's true about a new wife. Umbrig was invited, but the wedding was delayed and now he can't go, since he's in the field. Hope my father has better luck than last time.'

'Last time?'

'His first wife was murdered. Killed by my mad uncle. Briar Wood's a cursed place, that's what my mother says. Everything goes awry there. Nobody in their right mind would want to stay.'

Bridei felt a chill in his heart. He hoped very much that the lad was exaggerating. It had been hard enough to despatch Ana to an unknown husband; he had known his sweet-natured, honourable hostage deserved better. He hoped this realm of madmen and curses was the product of an aggrieved young man's too-fertile imagination.

'Where is your mother now?' he asked Hargest. 'Does she still live in Alpin's household?'

'No, my lord. She left soon after I was sent away; she went back to her home settlement in the west and married an old sweetheart. I get messages sometimes, and I send them. I know she's well.'

'Good,' Bridei said. 'Now tell me, what will Umbrig think of this defection? If your friend Orbenn goes back alone with the news that you are staying here, won't your foster father be angry at such a desertion? Who's going to keep the horses in prime condition on the long ride south?'

'There are other stable hands, my lord king.'

'But he'll still be angry. You owe him better; he's provided you with a home and security.'

'He won't be angry if Orbenn tells him you've offered me a position amongst your men, my lord king.'

The effrontery of it caused Breth's jaw to drop. Bridei was momentarily without a reply.

'And what position would that be?' Breth's tone was quelling. 'By the Flamekeeper's manhood, you have more than your share of –'

'Thank you, Breth,' Bridei said. 'Answer his question, Hargest. You're evidently qualified as a stable hand. I don't suppose that job would appeal to you. You'll need to be precise.'

'I wish to serve you, my lord.' Hargest startled them both by dropping gracefully into a kneeling position. For such a big man, he showed a remarkable quickness and fluidity of movement. 'To train as a warrior; perhaps to learn at the hand of just such an able man as your bodyguard here.'

'So you do acknowledge you may still have something to learn.' Again Bridei was torn between amusement and admiration, for, at fifteen, this lad had a certainty that spoke of bright things to come, if he were only given the right opportunities.

'I'm a good fighter, my lord. Good but raw; I know that. Your men could provide the polish I need, the refinement, the tricks of the trade. Let me stay. Let me ride into battle with your forces.'

Bridei regarded the flushed face, the shining eyes. 'If Umbrig wanted you in battle,' he said, 'he'd have placed you amongst his own warriors.'

'He doesn't see that I'm a man now –'

'I suspect you're wrong about him. I imagine your foster father simply wants to keep you safe. To see you survive to manhood and make something out of your life. Foster fathers care about their foster sons, Hargest, though sometimes we don't see it.'

'We?'

'I was the same as you. Only mine was a druid. That made it even more difficult. I was eighteen before I marched into my first battle.'

'Can I stay? Will you have me?'

Breth gave a little cough.

'We'll see,' Bridei said coolly. 'Both you and Orbenn may lodge here at Raven's Well a night or two. I need time to consider this. And you must come to terms with the fact that, by running off thus, you will have caused Umbrig serious concern. That in itself tells me you have not yet reached years of manly maturity. No –' as Hargest, still kneeling, made to protest, 'it is true, and in time you'll realise what you have done. It may not be until you have sons of your own, but it'll come like a thunderbolt, believe me. Now up you get and off you go to your bed; one of the men will show you where. We rise early here. Make sure you're ready for what the new day brings.'

'Yes, my lord.' Hargest's face was full of hope, the dark glare quite gone. 'May the Shining One give you good dreams, my lord king. And you,' dipping his head to Breth, which was something of a surprise.

'May the Flamekeeper light your waking,' Bridei said, and watched as the youth was ushered away by the men-at-arms.

'All that muscle and manners too, when he remembers them,' observed Breth. 'All the same, I wouldn't be too hasty with a decision if I were you. There's more to that one than meets the eye.'

A cartload of fresh rushes had just been delivered, and Faolan found Gerdic with two of his fellow serving men engaged in clearing away the soiled remnants of the old ones prior to laying their replacements. On the tabletops prowled, crouched or reclined a number of cats, black, white, striped, patched, all of them showing rapt interest in the upheaval. At the far end of the hall a familiar robed figure could be seen bundling a quantity of the newly cut rushes with a length of rope.

'Need any help?' Faolan asked Gerdic, glancing around to ensure the absence of men-at-arms or anyone else likely to be observing him with any degree of interest.

They were used to him now; he had cultivated a reputation as an eccentric, in keeping with his bardic profession, and most of the serving men accepted without surprise that he would set his hand quite willingly to the most menial of tasks simply to fill in the day. It was amazing what snippets of information folk let slip while cleaning fish, digging privies or kneading bread dough.

He worked his way gradually over to Deord, pitchfork in hand, rolling the malodorous layer of soiled rushes ahead of him. Clouds of small insects arose, and he felt a constant prickling around his ankles. At some distance behind, Gerdic went over the same area again with a millet broom before a third man strewed the clean rushes. The reason for the cats' attention was soon apparent: Faolan's fork uncovered here a mouse, there a rat, there a family of dark-carapaced beetles scuttling for cover. For the feline population of Briar Wood this was a feast day.

Next to Deord's feet, Faolan bent to loosen a clod of decaying material caught in the tines of the pitchfork and made his request in as few words as possible. 'Gael, today, visiting Alpin. I need a report.'

Deord fiddled with the fastening on his bundle of rushes. 'Playing with fire,' he muttered.

'I need this,' hissed Faolan. 'Tonight, if you can.'

'You should go home. Get right out of this.' Deord hefted the substantial bundle onto his broad shoulders and turned his back. 'I'll do what I can.'

Faolan's steady work with the pitchfork resumed as the other man walked away.

'Odd fellow, Deord,' remarked Gerdic, who had made up ground during the interchange. 'Must be the worst job in the world, that.'

'I can think of a few to rival it,' said Faolan, scratching his leg and eyeing the filthy tidemarks where rush carpet usually met whitewashed stone walls. 'What do we do with these, carry them out and burn them?'

'The lads'll do that when we've finished. Here, take a turn with the broom, it's easier on your back.'

'Gerdic?'

'Mm?'

'This wedding; I'm supposed to provide entertainment for suppertime, I've got that prepared. But what else happens during the day? What's the order of it? Ritual, feasting, dancing?'

'You'd be better to ask Orna; the women are the ones who take pleasure in such festivals. It's a long time since we had anything like it here. Lord Alpin's not one for music and flowers and dressing up. I know the men'll have their own celebration in the morning, plenty of good ale and some sport and games. That gives the women time to put the finishing touches on the feast and to make themselves look their best. In the afternoon the handfasting takes place. If it's anything like my sister's wedding that's when you'll get your prayers and suchlike. And dancing later on; dancing and feasting. That's when they'll be needing you, Faolan. Thought you'd know all about it. You must have played for weddings before.'

Faolan continued to sweep. 'Well, yes,' he said. 'But not amongst the Caitt. Folk here have their very own way of doing things.'

'Drustan?'

'Ana?'

'I've come without Ludha. I wanted to talk to you alone.'

He was silent a little. Light rain had begun to fall; Ana, crouched on the stones of the upper courtyard, put her shawl up over her head. Today she had not even attempted to unpack her work basket.

'It is the last day,' Drustan said. 'Tomorrow you marry my brother.'

There was a lump in Ana's throat; it made speaking difficult. 'Yes,' she said. 'The druid is here. There's no more reason to delay. He's putting the terms of the treaty in writing and it will be signed in the morning.'

He said nothing.

'Drustan, I had hoped . . . I wanted to track down that old woman, Bela. Ludha said she may still be out in the forest somewhere. I'd hoped she might tell me . . .'

'What, Ana?'

'If we could find her . . . if she's still alive . . . I thought she might tell me the truth. That you didn't do it. I can't believe you were capable of such an act, not even if you were in some – some state of mind that made you unaware of what you were doing. But nobody knows where she is, and it's too late. And now I have to marry Alpin, even though . . . even though . . .'

'Tell me, Ana. What is wrong?'

'Even though his touch disgusts me.' It came out in a very small voice; she was ashamed to be saying it aloud. 'I cannot bear his hands on me. I don't know how I can . . . I don't know how I will be able to . . .' She had not intended to tell him this, not Drustan of all people, but it had come out despite her.

'Don't do this, Ana.' Drustan's voice was fierce.

'I must do it.'

'He will hurt you. And I will not be able to help you.' This was a whisper.

'Drustan?'

No reply.

'I cannot speak to you of what I really want. But, if I must wed your brother, I wish you would just go, when Deord next gives you the chance. Run away into the forest, leave Briar Wood behind, seek a life elsewhere. Even if . . . even if you did do what they say, you should not be condemned to be shut up forever. How can I live here knowing you are just beyond the wall, in chains? At least if you took the chance to flee, I would know you were out there free, happy, even though I would never see you again.' She sniffed and fumbled for a handkerchief. On her cheeks, tears mingled with the soft rain.

'I would rather be in chains and close to you, dear heart,' Drustan said, 'than out in the forest, free and far from your side. Besides . . .' A darker note had entered his voice, making Ana shiver.

'Besides what, Drustan? You should seize your chance to get

away. How can you choose captivity? That is . . . well, it's madness, and nobody has managed to convince me yet that you are out of your wits, though they've certainly tried.'

'If I did that deed,' it was the first time she had ever heard him express the slightest doubt on the matter, 'I cannot go free again. If I killed one innocent, I could kill another. That is a risk I dare not take.'

'So it would not be love that held you close to me after all,' she said, 'but fear. Fear of yourself.'

'Do not say that I do not love you. You are my moon and stars, my spring and my summertime, Ana. I knew that from the first moment we saw you by the ford, so alone, so brave. You are the constant in my world of whirling chaos.'

'Is that how it feels?' she whispered. 'Whirling chaos? And yet, when I asked you what it was like, the . . . the frenzy, you spoke of it not as a fit, but as a kind of journey, almost the same as druids undertake in deep trance, when they travel from one world to another. Are you so unhappy, every moment of the day? I'm sorry, that's a stupid question. Any man shut away as you are must be half out of his mind with frustration.'

'To stay sane under these conditions requires a certain strength of will. It helps to have a guard like Deord. Such men are rare. Ana?'

'Yes?'

'If you had found her – Bela – if you had found her and she had told you the tale was a lie, and that I was innocent, you would still be bound to wed my brother. Does not this treaty hang on that?'

'Yes,' she said miserably. 'But . . .'

'But what? Tell me. It cannot be long before Deord returns, he has only gone to fetch rushes and clean water.'

'I shouldn't say it. But I will say it. If I thought there was the least possibility that you and I might – that there might be a different sort of future for us, some day, then I would do all I could to avoid this marriage. You know I don't want to marry him. From the first I have shrunk from his touch and been wary in his company. You know what I really want.'

'What you wanted,' he said softly, 'until you found out what they say of me is true.'

306

'No!' Her denial was louder than she had intended, and she put her hand over her mouth; she'd been in danger of forgetting where she was. 'No, Drustan. Even if it's true, even if you did what they say you did, it would not alter the fact that . . .'

'Say it.'

'That I love you. That, for me, you are the only man in the world.' She had said them at last, the sweet, perilous words.

'Ahh . . .' His sharp intake of breath held more pain than delight.

'I want you to have hope, Drustan. Hope that you can be proven innocent. Hope that you can be out in the world again. Trust your own goodness; it shines from you.'

'If you marry my brother I will never have hope again.'

'It's too late to change that.' The rain drizzled down, wetting her shawl and her hair and beginning to pool by her skirts. 'There's no way out, not if Bridei's treaty is to hold. And I don't think I can come here and talk to you again, Drustan. I think this is goodbye. I will keep trying to find out the truth for you, I swear it . . .'

'Ana, don't . . . don't do it . . .'

'Goodbye, my love. Have hope; don't let go of that. Oh gods, I can't do this, it's too cruel . . .'

'Ana . . .

'You'll always be in my heart, every moment . . . Goodbye . . .'

If he replied, she did not hear it, for she stumbled blindly to her feet and made for the steps, dashing the wet hair back from her face. A shadow moved, a sudden dark flicker further down as of a figure darting out of sight. Ana froze. A sound, perhaps a furtive foot on the stones. Was someone there?

'Ludha?' she called as the rain became heavier, not a shower now but a downpour, enough tears to drown a woman. 'Is anyone there?'

The steps were empty. As Ana made her way, hurriedly now, along the path to the sewing room, she could see no sign of life, though the door was ajar when she reached it and she was certain she had shut it behind her. Inside, Orna, Sorala and two other women were at their work. A small heap of cats drowsed before the fire; the atmosphere was tranquil.

'Not the best day to be out of doors,' Orna commented, her gaze running over Ana's saturated shawl, her bedraggled hair, the rain-darkened hem of her skirt.

'It came on quite suddenly,' Ana said. 'We had fine weather for our morning ride. That seems to be the way of it in these parts: smiles, then tears. I'd best go and change my things.'

'Left your work basket behind.' Orna's tone had an edge to it now.

'Oh – oh, dear, so I did, how silly –'

'Don't worry, my lady, I'll send a lad up for it. There was a boy here a moment ago, you might have seen him? You go off and get out of those wet clothes. It wouldn't do to catch a chill on the day before your wedding. You'll need to be at your best; Alpin will be wanting that.'

The rest of them gave knowing smiles, and Ana felt cold run through her, a deep, icy sensation that had nothing at all to do with the rain. 'Thank you,' she managed, and fled.

When Drustan's brother came to visit, the rules had to be seen to be in place. At other times it was unusual for Deord to shackle his charge. Today there was no choice. Deord recognised with some reluctance that, as a Breakstone man, he felt obliged to provide the report Faolan had asked for, though he could see nothing coming from it but trouble. On a good day, he could have left Drustan for as long as it took to eavesdrop on a private meeting and bring back the gist of it. Drustan, he suspected, had found a new way of amusing himself in the afternoons. Once or twice he had heard the sound of a whispered conversation hastily concluded as he approached; sometimes a thread of song had made its way down to their dark quarters. It seemed to Deord that, at such moments, Drustan was more than happy to be left alone.

Not today. Deord had been delayed earlier, bringing back the rushes and their other supplies, by one of the men-at-arms wanting his opinion on a new bow, and when he'd got back Drustan had been working up to one of his wilder moods, thumping his fists bloody on the stones and shouting his need to change the way things were. It was garbled, but the name Ana was in it, and

308

Deord cursed again the coming of this highborn bride and her Gaelic henchman to stir the captive's forlorn hopes. The fact was, Drustan was his own worst enemy. After seven years it was of no matter to Deord whether his charge was guilty or innocent. He saw only that, if the incarceration lasted much longer, there would come a point when even his care, his controlled breaking of the rules to allow those short times of sunlight and exercise and the rarer opportunities for this strange creature to perform his transformations, would not be enough to hold Drustan back from the line between gifted oddity and complete madness. He should let him go. He should let him fly away and simply take the consequences, which would no doubt be dire, Alpin being the man he was.

He'd calmed Drustan down as well as he could, but it wasn't easy. There'd be no going out to use up some of that terrifying, pent-up energy in combat practice or in flight. There were visitors at Briar Wood and a wedding tomorrow; it was no time to risk attracting attention. Drustan was not beating his hands on the stone now, nor seeking to wrench the iron gate apart, but his eyes were bleak and his features pinched and lost-looking. There was a shivering in his body, rapid and constant, and a sheen of sweat on his skin. Deord had seen something of the same look in wild creatures trapped and anticipating death. He had never left Drustan alone before unless he was at least reasonably calm.

He explained why he had to go out again, and Drustan submitted to the shackles without protest, holding out his wrist while looking in the opposite direction, as if it mattered little.

'You did not believe, surely, that she could ever have been for you,' Deord said quietly. 'That's a thing that could never happen.' Drustan swung towards him with the speed of a striking predator, his eyes bright with sudden fury, the fingers of his free hand curled claw-like, striking towards Deord's face. The hand halted just in front of his eyes; Drustan lowered his arm.

'I've a modicum of common sense, if you haven't, lad,' Deord said, summoning his customary calm. 'I'm concerned for you.' He studied the length of chain by which Drustan's iron bracelet was attached to the stone bench. 'Unfortunately I'm bound to the task I must undertake now; what we share makes that bardic fellow a kind of blood brother, and I must honour his request. Those who come out of Breakstone are few enough; that place eats up men. We who survived it owe it to one another to help, if we can.'

'Go then.' Drustan was pacing now, jerking rhythmically on the chain. 'You think me not fit for her; you ridicule the very notion. You and most of the world, no doubt. She bids me hope; you bid me hope. In the same breath, both of you condemn me to despair. Go on, don't be late.'

'I'll need to change this.' Deord moved to unlock the bracelet again. 'I won't leave you with the full chain, not for so long. Do you want to be inside or out? The rain's getting heavier.'

'I don't care. Put it on if you must. You think I would slip this around my neck and somehow make an end of things?'

'You've given me a few frights before,' Deord said grimly, attaching the shackles in a different way so that his charge was now held closer to the wall with the chain doubled up to reduce its length. Drustan could sit on the stone bench; he could see through the little window. He could not move far, nor could he loop the chain around his neck.

'I'm sorry, lad.' He left Drustan standing with his back turned, staring at the wall. Doing this kind of thing had been no easier the fiftieth time than the first, nor the hundredth time than the fiftieth. But he could not take the risk of leaving his charge free in the enclosure, not when this mood was on him. The birds were in hiding, their huddled forms scarcely visible on their high ledge.

Alpin's meeting with his Gaelic visitor took longer than Deord had anticipated and left him with a crick in the neck and a feeling of impending disaster in his belly. This was trouble indeed: trouble for the bard, trouble for the lady, trouble, he suspected, that would soon embroil everyone here at Briar Wood. Once he brought this news to Faolan, the bard was sure to need another favour, one that would be a great deal more difficult to provide. Deord cursed silently as he made his soft-footed way back through the storehouses and along the sunken pathway to the enclosure. The bard was in danger. If Faolan didn't play this right his life would be worth no more than a scrap of straw on the midden. Of course, if what that fellow had told Alpin today was true, Faolan probably deserved whatever he got. But Deord was bound to help him. The pity of it was, there was no way to warn him. If Alpin did as Deord anticipated he would, the bard would be under lock and key before suppertime.

Drustan was still standing by the wall. The iron bracelet was bordered, now, by a broad, oozing welt where he had chafed and jerked at the restraint, flaying the skin from the underlying flesh. There was blood everywhere. Drustan's eyes were red, his face stained with furious tears. The birds were perched on his shoulders, the little sounds they made eerie in the quiet shadows of the dim enclosure. Deord unlocked the restraints without comment.

'I think I'm going to need your help,' he said. 'I need you to be yourself, Drustan: calm, clear-headed, quick-thinking. If I tell you the lady and her bard may both be in danger, I suspect that will make it easier for you to listen to what I have to say.'

'Danger? Ana in danger? What?' Drustan gripped Deord's arm then, wincing, let go.

'Come inside, I'd better bandage that for you. You need to hear this story. I don't know how we can warn him. But I do know the only place he's going to be able to turn for help is here.'

The harp would probably do more work in the next couple of days than it had for years, Faolan thought as he sat in a corner of the yard working his way through the repertoire required for the festivities associated with a wedding: five or six ballads, ten or twelve drinking songs, an assortment of other narrative pieces and a wide range of dances, though he suspected the instrument's voice would hardly be heard in a hall full of Caitt warriors and their women making merry. Merry. It would hardly be so for Ana. Unless, on the very eve of the treaty's signing, Deord brought him news he could use to declare it a sham, she would marry that man tomorrow and he must spend the day making music for celebration, music for gladness, music for lovers. Poor harp, he thought as his fingers brushed across the strings, to tell such bitter lies when music should be for the deepest truths of all, the most profound of sorrows, the most inspiring acts of courage and goodness. Well, soon enough this instrument would fall silent once again and he would be gone from this place.

The easier way, of course, would be for Deord to come back with nothing of significance. Then the marriage and the treaty could be sealed forthwith and he would set off to take the news to White Hill. A success of sorts, if bitter on a personal level. The alternative was fraught with difficulties. If Deord uncovered treachery, how would he take the next step? This chieftain wanted his royal bride. The look in his eyes, his roaming hands showed simple lust was part of it; the respectability she would confer no doubt a bigger part. They were in his fortress, guarded by his men, surrounded by a wilderness of forest whose paths, if one could call them that, were treacherous and whose rivers would still be running high and fast. Beyond the wall there were neither horses nor supplies to be had. As he hummed his way through a repetitive drinking song, Faolan's mind was working very quickly indeed. His concentration was intense; he did not see Alpin's men-at-arms coming until they were right beside him and laying ungentle hands on his shoulders.

'Whoa –' Faolan protested as the harp went over sideways; he managed by instinct to grab it and set it safely on the bench by him before he was hauled bodily to his feet. 'What is this? There's no need to bruise a man –'

'Save your words, bard. Lord Alpin wants you. Now.'

'But –' It seemed appropriate to continue protesting, as a mere musician might under the circumstances, while they hustled him into the house again and up the narrow steps to the family apartments. There could be only one explanation: Deord had been discovered listening and, when confronted, had implicated him. What else could this be?

'What do you think you're –?' His words were stopped by a ringing blow across the mouth, delivered by a gauntleted fist. He tasted blood, and was silent. With his jaw on fire, he fought to prepare an explanation: insist that Deord was lying; no, he could not betray a Breakstone man, even if Deord had done so to him; give them the truth, perhaps, or something close to it, that Bridei had bid him ensure by every means possible that Alpin meant what he said. That Ana had not known he was more than a bard. Alpin wasn't going to like that, but there was a chance he would believe it.

312

There were four men in Alpin's chamber: the chieftain himself, his adviser Dregard, a grey-clad druid and another man, pale, unremarkable looking, dressed in a hooded robe. Faolan could feel the hostility in the room. At a barked command from Alpin, the guards released their captive and retreated; by the inner door one man already stood guard, legs apart, sword and dagger in his belt.

Faolan took a step towards the table where the four were seated. There was a parchment lying there, its corners held by stones. A jug and goblets stood ready on a tray, but nobody was drinking. All eyes were on Faolan. A chill spread through him; the look on these men's faces did not bode well.

'My lord,' he said coolly, clasping his hands lightly behind his back and doing his best to appear untroubled.

'Don't speak until you're spoken to, bard,' snapped Alpin, whose broad features were flushed. 'I want an accounting from you, and you'd better take care with it. I'll have no more lies here.'

'Lies, my lord?'

'Shut your mouth. I don't like your glib manner. I have a story to tell you and you'll keep silent until you've heard all of it. But perhaps you can guess what it is.'

Faolan said nothing. He had taken one glance only at the hooded man, a glance that had left him with the disquieting impression that he'd seen the fellow somewhere before. He would not look again.

'Answer me!' Alpin demanded.

'I cannot guess, my lord.'

'Tell him what our guest here told us earlier, Dregard. I've no appetite for going over it again. Such duplicity sickens me.'

Dregard cleared his throat. 'We've reason to believe –' he began.

'Just tell it, will you?' Alpin was impatient, his voice tight.

'My lord has been informed that, far from being the lady's household musician and ignorant in matters of policy and strategy, you are in fact very well versed in both and highly skilled in a number of other areas that have little to do with music,' Dregard said.

'I have certain abilities.' Faolan kept his tone calm. 'Lord Alpin knows already that I can sharpen knives and use them. I think I've demonstrated, also, that my talents as a musician are at least passable. I am a bard. The lady told the truth.'

'Our friend here tells us you travel rather widely; perhaps more widely than any other member of Bridei's court.'

Now the chill was around his heart. He did not let his alarm show in his eyes. 'It's in the nature of a bard's profession to do so,' he said. 'I've worked for a number of patrons over the years, both within Fortriu and beyond.'

'And now you work for the lady.' Alpin rose to his feet, folded his arms and fixed Faolan with a penetrating stare.

'Yes, my lord. Of course, after the wedding, I will –'

'Be silent! Let me tell you this tale. It concerns a young man who seemed to be one thing and was in fact quite another. A fellow whose bardic talents provided a convenient excuse for entry to the halls of kings and princes, chieftains and druids. A man who was handsomely paid by the patron he worked for, whether that was the young King of Fortriu or a lovely lady who liked music and was a hostage at White Hill.'

Faolan stood silent. Not Deord, then; this had come from that hooded man, the same, he assumed, that Dovard had said was a Gael. A spy. A man like himself with a talent for being unobtrusive. Perhaps only one of his own kind had the ability to expose another. He calculated how to answer.

'So, you are Gael, musician and spy. Bridei sends you here with a set of instructions. So far, so good. No harm done, you say, perhaps you lied a little, but the lady is here, the treaty is ready to be signed,' Alpin motioned to the parchment, 'and then you can be on your way. You've done your job, I've got my bride, Bridei has his agreement and no harm done at all.'

There was a silence of anticipation in the chamber; Faolan cleared his throat but did not attempt to speak.

'Perhaps you've gathered a little information while you've been enjoying my hospitality,' Alpin said. 'Troops, armaments, plans . . . Any self-respecting informant could not fail to seize that opportunity.'

Faolan maintained his bland expression; it was a skill he had perfected long ago.

'However, there's another part to this tale,' Alpin went on. There was a still intensity in his stance now that suggested a wild-cat about to pounce. 'You were seen at Dunadd, barely a season ago. I'd been thinking you reminded me of someone; it took my friend here to point out who it was. There's a certain nobleman of the clan Uí Néill who bears more than a passing resemblance to yourself. This man,' nodding towards the hooded Gael, 'observed the two of you in covert conference on more than one occasion. Close enough to be that of blood kin, the likeness is: cousins, maybe, or uncle and nephew. I would conclude you've been there more than a few times, and taken away some handsome pay-ments for the information you brought them; information only a man close to King Bridei would be likely to have. Being kin to the Uí Néill makes you kin to the King of Dalriada, bard. It makes you Bridei's sworn enemy. Taking silver from the lords of the Uí Néill makes you a traitor.'

The word hung in the air like the sound of a whiplash. That it was a lie made it hurt no less. Crazily, the thought uppermost in Faolan's mind was that the hooded man deserved congratu-lations; he wouldn't have believed the most able spy in the world could have discovered this. He had covered his tracks meticulously.

'Ah,' said Alpin with a savage grin, 'at last you have nothing to say for yourself.'

'Not so, my lord.' From some deep reserve of strength came the courteous words, the cool tone. 'I had already severed the bonds of kinship before I left my home shore years ago. I possess no allegiances of blood. If this man has led you to believe other-wise he was mistaken.'

'You deny that you were at the court of Dalriada in spring? My friend here is a reliable source of information. He has never played me false before.'

'Then your lordship is indeed fortunate,' Faolan said. 'Carrying false intelligence is part of any informant's job. It's how cleverly he uses it that marks his talent for the profession.'

There was a little silence.

'May I ask a question?' Faolan ventured.

They looked at him.

315

'Why is this man present?' He nodded towards the grey-clad druid, who was listening calmly, his head turning towards one or another speaker, his old eyes bright with interest.

'As an impartial witness,' Dregard said. 'You should be glad of his presence, bard, for it means a true account of this meeting can be conveyed elsewhere without any cause for one to accuse another of twisting the facts.'

'Conveyed elsewhere. What do you mean by that?'

'Where would we start?' Alpin spread his hands as if to take in the whole world. 'With Bridei, perhaps?'

Think, Faolan ordered himself. How to make this an opportunity; how to seize control so he had a chance of getting her away. How to find out exactly what this was all about and employ it to his own end. This was like balancing on a wire. He must pick a course with delicacy; he must use all the expertise he had, for Alpin was enraged, his eyes were like a fighting boar's; it was something else that had sparked this anger, surely, something they were not discussing here. 'Of course,' Faolan said to the chieftain, 'every leader worth his salt has a skilled informant at hand in these times of turmoil. Yours has me at a disadvantage, my lord. Interesting that he, too, is a Gael.'

'Ah,' Dregard seized on this, 'so you do know him.'

'Even silence can speak to those of us who know how to interpret it.'

The druid nodded at Faolan's speech; he seemed to appreciate the sentiment.

'Tell me,' Alpin said, seating himself once more, 'why is it a man who has relinquished ties of kinship is so greedy for silver that he must accept payment from two masters at once? I'll wager there's a poor old mother tucked away somewhere, an impecunious sister or two in need of a dowry. Or have you conveniently rid yourself of them as well?'

A red fury welled up in Faolan and he could not stop himself from surging forward. A moment later he was on the floor, his head ringing from a blow, his ribs aching from a boot thrust as two of the Briar Wood men stood over him. The pain was nothing beside the awareness that, in all the years since he walked away from his home and kin, he had never before lost control thus. He could not afford another error. More lives than his own hung in the balance here.

'I touched a nerve,' Alpin said, sounding genuinely surprised. 'The best spies aren't supposed to have those. Perhaps you're losing your edge, Gael. Get up, and wipe off that blood, it's getting in your eye. We can't have our bard spoiling his pretty face, not with the wedding tomorrow. Now give me one good reason why I shouldn't chain you up like a dog and send a messenger to Bridei's court right now telling him the spotless bride he despatched to me was accompanied by a stinking turncoat in the pay of both Fortriu and Dalriada? Why shouldn't I do that? I'm signing an agreement to support this king, after all – there it is before you all written down, just waiting for my mark and the lady's.'

Alpin was starting to enjoy himself, Faolan thought, angry or not. He must be supremely confident of his authority if he could use this argument while a Gaelic spy sat by him at his council table.

'I see where you're looking,' the chieftain of Briar Wood said, curling his lip. 'I remind you that there is not one Gael amongst us tonight, but two. And one of them is a servant of two masters. Don't I owe it to Bridei to warn him you're a danger and should be stopped?'

Somewhere in Faolan's head a hammer was banging on an anvil. His vision blurred; the candle flames danced. 'I have an answer, my lord. It is an answer best suited to private conversation, just you and I in confidence.'

'Hah!' Alpin's brows shot up in disbelief, and Dregard laughed aloud. 'I don't think so, my fine friend. Those dancing fingers of yours are quick enough with a knife to make that most unwise.'

'Have your men bind me if you prefer. Retain one guard here if you must, as long as he can be trusted to keep his mouth shut; you may not want any of your men to hear what I have to say. I won't speak before the Gael, nor this druid, nor your councillor there.'

'It's not for you to start dictating terms –' Dregard protested.

'Lord Alpin is nothing if not astute,' Faolan said quietly. 'Like any leader of ability, he understands the importance of timing. And of exploiting opportunity when it offers itself. Tie up my wrists and ankles. I am not so prodigious in my talents that I can fly across the chamber and attack a man with my teeth.' He had seen the spark in Alpin's eye, the awareness that something was on offer that perhaps he could not afford to let pass.

'The druid stays,' Alpin said. 'He's my safeguard where the lady is concerned. The rest of you leave us. Yes, you too, Mordec, after you've bound this fellow securely. Goban, stand outside the door and don't let anyone in.'

Dregard, muttering, ushered the hooded man out as the two warriors tied Faolan's arms behind his back, somewhat more tightly than was required, and twisted a length of rope around his ankles. He attempted a joke about hoping they'd be able to get the knot undone and was rewarded with an eye-watering blow to the kneecap. The door closed behind them. At the table the druid sat calmly, his demeanour one of polite attention.

'Get on with it,' Alpin said. 'I don't expect a confession; I think we both know what my informant has told me is correct in its main material, and that as a result you are in quite an awkward position. Does Ana know? Is she complicit in your treachery?'

Faolan turned cold. There had been something in Alpin's tone as he spoke her name that was truly frightening. If this simmering anger was for her, though Faolan could not imagine why that might be, the need to get her away quickly was even more pressing than he had imagined. 'She knows nothing,' he said levelly. 'She's entirely innocent of any wrongdoing. This is offensive –'

'Still your tongue, bard. Keep to the facts. The lady is, as it happens, a great deal less innocent than you so touchingly believe. Ana has made me very, very angry. Her behaviour's been not only devious and ill-considered, I suspect it's been on the verge of wanton. Hardly what I wished to discover on my wedding eve, and neither was the realisation that I'd harboured a two-faced spy in my household in the guise of a meek harpist. And yet her manner is so virginal; she had me completely convinced. Was that simply a ploy designed to distract and mislead me until I discovered on the wedding night that Bridei had traded me soiled goods? Eh? What do you say? You travelled alone with her; perhaps I was right about you the first time I saw you. Maybe you sampled the wares yourself.'

Breathe slowly; think of tomorrow. 'Not so, my lord. Ana is quite untouched, I am certain. You malign her with what you suggest.' Faolan managed to keep his tone even. He must not lose control again.

'We'll see what she has to say on the matter. She's certainly not above a little deception. Never mind, I'll beat that out of her if I must. A man who can't control his wife is not much of a man. Now, Gael. Time's passing. What is it you need to say that cannot be aired before my closest adviser? What is it you particularly don't want my friend from Dalriada to hear?'

Faolan found that he was shivering and commanded himself to stop. 'You told me a story,' he said. 'Now I wish to tell you one. Your friend from Dalriada did well in discovering certain facts about me. I can do better.'

'It'll need to be good, Gael. It would be simple enough for me to make you disappear. I could tell the lady you decided to make an early departure for White Hill. The tracks in these parts are notorious; travellers go missing all the time. Go on, then.'

'It concerns a man who was fortunate enough to control a pair of territories which were both particularly well positioned. On one side, give or take a few neighbours, was the kingdom of Fortriu and on the other Dalriada; this man's lands lay between the two and included a very useful anchorage, deep, sheltered, with a clear passage to the shores of that latter territory, the king-dom of the Gaels. No wonder powerful leaders courted him with gifts: silver, cattle, a woman, not just any woman but a bride who would give him a stunning opportunity, for through her he could become a father of kings. Everyone wanted to be his friend.'

'Get on with it,' said Alpin, but he was leaning forward, eyes narrowed, listening intently.

'He had to make a choice,' Faolan said. 'War was imminent; he had to throw in his lot with one side or the other. An informant can accept the payments of both Priteni and Gaels; it's a require-ment of the job that a man has no conscience. A chieftain, eventually, must align himself somewhere. How was he to choose? One offered a royal bride. The other held out something he wanted just as much: the opportunity to ally himself with those who he believed in time would rule not only Dalriada but all the lands of the Priteni. They wanted exclusive use of his anchorage; they wanted the support of his substantial fighting force, renowned throughout the north for its excellence. All the other leader wanted was a mark on a sheet of parchment.' He paused. This was a perilous course to take, based on guesswork and rumour and his own estimate of where Alpin's preferences would lie. Why should this chieftain place any trust in him?

'You think that?' Alpin asked him, rubbing his beard and frowning, not so much in anger now as in concentration. 'That the Gaels are destined to rule the whole of the north? We of the Caitt would never surrender our territories. An alliance is one thing, an abject ceding of control quite a different matter.' He might have been speaking to Dregard or another of his advisers. The druid shifted slightly as if to remind them of his presence.

'It is my considered opinion,' Faolan said quietly, 'that Gabhran's ambitions extend only to the northern borders of Fortriu, not beyond. I'd be surprised if his overtures to you and your fellow chieftains ever went further than a request for assistance against Bridei. They will, of course, want use of the waterways at Dreaming Glen. If I were you I would not be concerned about a possible threat to your own holdings. The reputation of the Caitt makes that unlikely.' He did not add that there was little in the territories themselves to recommend them to an invader, unless someone was after trackless wastelands in which to lose himself. 'As for the other matter, in time Dalriada must prevail. I am convinced of it.' It was an argument he had heard many times at the court of Dunadd, and once or twice elsewhere. He did not, in fact, agree with it, but he did know how to make it persuasive.

'Gabhran's folk are already well settled in the southwest of Fortriu; the more pragmatic of the native chieftains have welcomed them. They farm those territories and father children on Priteni women. If they do not move further up the Glen in Gabhran's time, they surely will under his successor, or under the next man. Bridei does not see this. He is passionate in his adherence to the gods,' here Faolan gave the druid a placatory nod, 'having been druid-raised. He sees only the day when all Fortriu will be returned to the ways of his forefathers.' The words tasted bitter, like a betrayal, even if it was Bridei's work he was doing here.

'Interesting,' Alpin said. 'And inconsistent. These sentiments hardly ring true from the lips of a man who, not so long ago, was singing lavish and apparently heartfelt praises of the leader they call . . . what was it?'

'The Blade of Fortriu, my lord. You forget, perhaps, that I am a bard, and a good one. It is a necessary part of my skill to be able to make any patron into a hero.'

'You devious little toad,' said Alpin. He might have been speaking in distaste or in admiration, perhaps both.

'Yes, my lord.'

'Go on, then. Where is this leading? Forget your storytelling. If you have something to offer, state it plainly.'

'My lord, I am entirely at your mercy. I'm in your custody and trussed up like a roasting chicken. As if that were not enough of a disadvantage, the secret of my duplicity has been laid open before your adviser and this druid. By tomorrow it may be revealed more widely. You could, as you said, send a messenger to White Hill to let Bridei know that not only is the treaty signed and the lady wed, but that one of his party thought to knife him in the back, so to speak. It is clear that, in this confrontation, you possess all the weapons.' *Feel your own power,* he willed Alpin. *Relish my submission. Be convinced you have total control. Then I'll give you a reason to let me go.*

Alpin waited.

'I've given you my informed opinion on the future of the region,' Faolan said, choosing his words carefully. 'Of course, you may already have heard this from other sources. You mentioned that I reminded you of someone. Can it be that you yourself have been a visitor at the Gaelic court of Dunadd? Which Uí Néill chieftain was it you met with? Black Conor? Fionn, known as the scourge of the north? Ruaridh the Elder of Tirconnell? You may be close to the ear of any of those powerful clan leaders. Or is it possible there may be some information in my possession that your tame Gael didn't pass on to you?'

Alpin cleared his throat noisily. He was red in the face.

'Your man did well enough, my lord. But I am the best of my kind. Allow me to prove that to you.'

'I think,' Alpin said, rising to his feet and laying a hand on the druid's shoulder, 'that after all we need not detain you in this meeting any longer, Berguist. You've had a tiring journey and tomorrow will be a busy day. Goban!' The door opened; the guard looked in. 'Escort my druidic guest down to the hall for some food and drink, will you?' And, at Goban's scowl of protest, 'I'll be quite safe, unless you fellows have lost your skill in tying knots. When you've done it, come back and wait outside the door until I call for you.' Then, when he and Faolan were alone, 'I cannot believe this. You have the gall to offer me your services after coming here in Lady Ana's escort.'

'Yes, my lord.' The fish was nibbling at the bait; he must pull him in with utmost care. He made himself breathe slowly. The bindings were beginning to hurt quite a bit; they had been tied with no regard to the prisoner's comfort. Fleetingly, Faolan thought of Drustan and his iron shackles. 'Odd as it may sound, I do set some value on staying alive.'

Alpin had regained his composure; he sat down and took a mouthful of his ale. 'I expect you have a substantial store of silver set away by now; your two masters must pay you handsomely if you're as good as you say you are. What if I can't afford what you have to offer?'

'The price is not so high. I want my life and my freedom. Send me back to White Hill as everyone expects. Send me with whatever information you want Bridei to hear. I will undertake to deliver it faithfully.' He did not mention that, by the time he was likely to get there, Bridei would be long gone.

'Why should I trust you? What possible reason could I have to do so?'

Faolan smiled. It was something he did rarely, and always with calculation. 'Once I give you the information I have you'll know that I'm not lying. I am closer to Bridei than you imagine; I have his ear and am privy to all his plans. He counts me among his close friends and has done so these five years. You can use this how you choose: to strengthen your ties with Gabhran or merely to hold to yourself until such time as you need a lever. The treaty remains. I suppose it will be signed. I do wonder, since it seems you have a tame Gael of your own, whether you intend to honour it.'

'By the Flamekeeper's bollocks!' Alpin stared at him. 'What are you trying to do here, bard, get yourself summarily executed?'

'It's the nature of my profession to be comfortable with risk, my lord,' Faolan said coolly.

'What about the lady? I could have sworn your devotion to her was genuine. You discard her now without another thought?'

'Lady Ana is a trade item of high value. I've delivered her here intact. I've completed my job. Bridei can hardly ask for her back when you've bedded her, my lord. Allegiances change; borders change. You will still have your royal sons, whatever happens between yourself and Fortriu. By the time your children are grown, Bridei's time of power may well be over.' His own words sickened him, but he kept his gaze steady and his features calm. 'To put it crudely,' he added, 'you'll be wanting the bride without the baggage attached.'

Alpin gave a low whistle. 'You astound me,' he said.

'Thank you, my lord. I do have a certain regret that she's been traded at less than her true value, but when all's said and done, she's only a woman. Have we perhaps reached the point where my ankles might be untied?'

'Not until I hear the information you mentioned. I want timing, routes, numbers. I want it now. Make good your wild promises and I might consider what you're asking for. It's dependent, I presume, on my ensuring Bridei doesn't learn the truth about his back-stabbing friend. Should I agree, and that is very much conditional on the quality of what you deliver, there'd be a rider on it. I'd want you to gather certain intelligence at the other end and bring it back here. White Hill and Dunadd both. You did say you were a traveller.'

'You want me to work for you?' Faolan could hear a note of shaky triumph in his own voice, and hoped it had passed the chieftain by. 'At that point, we'd need to start discussing a fee.'

'Not so fast,' Alpin said. 'Substantiate your extravagant claims or I'll have no hesitation in getting rid of you this very night. There are one or two of my men who would enjoy executing that order, slowly and with as much artistry as you give to your soulful ballads.'

'A veritable poetry of death,' murmured Faolan.

'Tell me then. What exactly is Bridei up to?'

As assassin and spy, Faolan was indeed accustomed to taking risks. He could not remember a time when the risk had seemed as high as this. He must provide information that was new to Alpin, detailed, and utterly convincing. It must be as close to the truth as he could reasonably make it. If he played this right, his lies would get him out of Briar Wood, and Ana with him. He must calculate with precision just how far he could take this without endangering Bridei and the armies of Fortriu. It was odd that, as he set it out for Alpin, the early advance, the routes to be taken, the numbers, he did indeed feel like the basest of traitors. He wanted to curl up on himself as a hedgehog does or, slug-like, creep under a stone and be forgotten. But he kept his tone detached and his eyes calm. When he had said that he was the best, he had told the truth.

When it was all out, Alpin put his hands together, fingers pointed upwards, and sighed. 'So he really is ready to move so soon,' he said quietly. 'Setting off at Measure, eh? I'd suspected it when the message came advising me of this bride's imminent arrival. But I hadn't quite thought it possible. Taking a risk with the season, isn't he? Maybe that druid of his plans to put in a prayer for fine weather.'

Faolan said nothing. The fish was on the hook.

'Tomorrow,' Alpin said. 'You'll need to be seen; to go about your business as folk expect. You must be present when this thing is signed; you must provide entertainment in the evening. I want my people to believe you're no more than you seem. I want you to depart as planned, the following morning, with the good news for Bridei. That way you can confirm for the King of Fortriu that the marriage has been consummated. I'll even give you a look at the sheets.'

Faolan's jaw tightened; his hands became fists, bound as they were. That Alpin had not spoken, this time, to goad him into anger but was simply making a coarse jest did not alter his fury. *Just set me free*, he thought, *and your sheets will stay virgin pure; she'll be out of this place and away from your filthy hands before the sun sets on your wedding day.*

'I'll need to keep you locked up tonight,' Alpin went on. 'One or two of the fellows overheard our earlier discussion and they're not happy. I need time to fill them in, that's if you're to have a full complement of fingers for the wedding dances. There's a locked enclosure in the kennels; comes in handy when we get a mad one. Happens from time to time: flaw in the breed. Keep your mouth shut when you're in there. Look at this as earning a bit longer to live. We won't look beyond that yet, to bags of silver and a handy smallholding to settle on when you retire from the business. You'll need to prove yourself first.'

'Thank you, my lord. You won't be disappointed.'

'Mordec!'

The door opened and the designated guard came in.

'Untie him,' Alpin said. 'He's a spent force. Take him to the kennels, covertly, you understand, and lock him up like the mongrel cur he is. Don't hit him too hard. There's a wedding tomorrow and we're short on harpists.'

Chapter Twelve

na spent the rest of the afternoon alone. Ludha had not come to her chamber and she had no inclination to go looking for the maidservant, since that meant being seen around the house with her nose running and her eyes swollen with crying. She had done the right thing, she told herself as she stood by the narrow window, watching rooks about their business atop the elms beyond the wall. The rain continued unabated, a steady, soft fall that turned the forest to a misty grey tinted with silver. There had been no choice but to sever the tie; to bid him goodbye. Her wedding dress was laid out on the bed. A pair of kidskin slippers sat neatly by the embroidered hem. To keep on talking to him, to cling to those brief interchanges that were the heart of her existence here was to endanger Drustan himself. That, she could not do.

Ana shivered, moving across to the bed and kneeling to run a hand over the exquisite work her maid had done on the gown. A band of embroidery went around the high-waisted skirt, formal in style as befitted the occasion, regular patterns of fronds and leaves in shades of green and soft blue. Here and there was a delicate flower; here and there, too, were little round-eyed creatures, for like all true artists Ludha had been unable to keep her personal touch from her work: vole, marten and salamander, siskin, frog and dragonfly could all be found half hidden in the ordered sprays of ferns and greenery. The fabric itself was pale fine wool, spun and woven by Sorala, who was the most skilled of the Briar Wood women in these crafts. The gown had a modest cut – Ana had insisted on that – with long, narrow sleeves and a round neckline. The skirt fell in soft folds from a band of blue-dyed wool just below the breasts. She knew it was a lovely thing and that she looked well in it. All the same, she felt a shiver of revulsion as she gathered it up, folded it carefully and put it in the storage chest. The gown represented Alpin; she could not look at it without imagining him undoing the fastenings, peeling it off her shoulders and then doing what he had to do to her, tomorrow night. How could she bear that? How could she pretend? And how could she stop this flood of weeping, which seemed fit to drown her right here where she stood?

She lay on the bed awhile, attempting to fix her mind on happy things. Half-asleep, she drifted in a realm that was not quite the home of her childhood and not quite the garden at White Hill, but some mixture of the two in which she walked and played and laughed with a pair of little children. She was of this scene and at the same time apart, as is the way with half-dreams: at the same time Ana was one of the small girls, and yet she was watching them from a distance. Their game was elaborate, featuring a pair of well-loved woollen dolls, grimy from many adventures, who were made to scale a drystone wall before embarking on a daring raid across a field full of cows. The children's skirts were muddier than the dolls'.

It's my turn, Ana.

No, it's mine.

I had it first.

I'm the eldest, you have to do what I say.

Do not!

Then the child that was Ana gave a push and her sister fell, her tunic and arms instantly coated with the dark, heavy mud of the cow field. Breda began to wail. Back home: Auntie getting out the willow switch, Ana shrinking back against a wall. *Put out your hand.* The urge to say, *It wasn't my fault, she made me,* as she heard Breda sniffing and sobbing out in the kitchen and being mollified with honey cakes. Choosing not to say anything. The back straight, the head high, the hand held out firmly, not a tremor in it. *I am a princess.* Then the blow . . .

Ana sat up with a start, blinking. Outside the light was fading; she'd fallen asleep. It was nearly suppertime and there was still no sign of Ludha. She'd have to wash and change by herself, make herself beautiful for Alpin's intimate feast for two. Gritting her teeth, she made her way out to the privy that served the family quarters, noting a guard outside Alpin's door and a second at the head of the stairs. This did not trouble her. She had become accustomed to the close presence of armed minders during her earlier years as a royal hostage. Her trips to Banmerren had usually been in the company of four large men; wasted, as it turned out, since her cousin, the King of the Light Isles, had made not a single effort either by force of arms or by diplomacy to win her freedom. And now she was reduced to this: tying herself to a husband she despised, and living a stone's throw from the man she loved and could never have.

Back at the door of her chamber, the tall figure of Orna stood waiting. 'You'll be wanting help to dress for supper.'

'Where's Ludha?'

'Taken a little poorly. She won't be here tonight.' The housekeeper had gone into Ana's chamber and was making herself at home, opening the chest and hunting for suitable clothing. She lifted out the wedding gown carefully, setting it aside. 'Which of these do you prefer, my lady? The blue?'

Ana was inclined to stamp her foot childishly and say she would have none of them. 'The grey, please,' she said politely. 'What's wrong with Ludha? She seemed quite well this morning.'

'Nothing much. A few aches and pains, that's all. Are you sure about the grey?' Orna held the tunic up, frowning; eyed the matching skirt. Of all the outfits that had been provided for Ana, this was the plainest.

'Yes.' A girl had brought warm water; Ana washed her face and hands in the bowl provided, dried herself and, turning her back on the housekeeper, took off her outer clothing. She stood still as Orna slipped the grey tunic over her head; she stepped into the skirt and submitted to the fastening of its girdle by the other woman. When it was done, Ana looked into the bronze mirror that stood on her shelf, seeing her image dimly in the flawed surface, unsteady candlelight adding to its ghostly vagueness.

'I'll dress your hair for you, my lady.'

'No, I'll do it, Orna.' It felt wrong, somehow, for this dour servant, little more than a mouthpiece for Alpin, to perform such an intimate task. Orna said nothing, but began sorting and folding the discarded garments. Ana brushed and plaited and worked her abundance of flaxen hair back with cruel discipline into a ribboned net; not a wisp was allowed to escape. The blotched and reddened features that stared back at her from the bronze were not those of a bride happy in anticipation of sweet time spent alone with her beloved. She looked wretched.

'You can't go in to him like that,' Orna said bluntly. 'The clothes are bad enough; you might as well have a wise woman's robe on, you're so covered up. Well, it's your choice. But you'd best leave your hair loose, at least, or he'll see in an instant that you've spent your afternoon weeping.'

She was right. Ana pulled out the pins she had jabbed into the tight weaving of plaits, removed the net and let the long, gold flow of her hair fall down her back instead, with one narrow, plaited strand across her brow. Her eyes were still ugly and red, but it was not at them Alpin would look first.

'Aye, that's better.' Orna's tone was not unfriendly. 'A word of advice, my lady; I hope you won't take it amiss.'

'If you've something to say, Orna, best just say it.' Ana did not care to be bullied, and this had felt remarkably like it. And she was worried about Ludha, who had shown no signs of illness earlier.

'We can all see you're not happy,' Orna said. 'That you're not settled yet. There's one lesson we all learn here at Briar Wood, my lady, if we're to stay safe and peaceful. That's to keep our mouths shut on certain topics. That way we can get on with things and no harm done.'

'What are you saying, Orna?'

'Just that. Give him the answers he wants and you'll make him happy. And if he's happy we all are.' The housekeeper's grim expression did nothing to convince Ana that this was sound advice. Indeed, it made her deeply uneasy.

'Orna,' she said, 'you were here when Lord Alpin's first wife was still alive, weren't you?'

'I was.' Orna went to the door, ready to whistle for a lad to clear away the bowl and jug.

'What do you think happened on that day? The day she died? Do you believe –?'

'Hush!' Orna's tone was a sharp hiss. 'Don't make this any worse, my lady. He's told you the tale of it, I'm sure, and that means you've no need to hear it again from me. It's in the past, and the past's best forgotten.'

'Even if it means a man might be falsely accused and wrongly imprisoned?' Ana's heart was thumping.

Orna closed the door abruptly. 'I know you're not foolish, my lady. You just haven't grasped our ways here. This is a matter that's not spoken of. Not ever. You'd best follow that rule, for your own sake at least. He's not in the best of moods tonight, I heard him shouting earlier. My advice is to do whatever you need to do to win his favour. Please him if you can. Now I'm away, I've other things to do. He's expecting you as soon as you're ready. Be careful, that's all I'm saying.' And with that she was gone.

The boy came and cleared the washing things. There was nothing to stop Ana from going next door; Alpin would be waiting, perhaps impatiently. There had been no reason for Orna to give this gratuitous advice. Ana was to marry the man tomorrow. Of course she had to please him. She should go now, right away, and make a start on it. But her feet were reluctant to move. She lingered by the window, her brow against the cool stone, her eyes closed. *I love you,* she said in silence. *More than home and family, more than beauty and wisdom and goodness, more than life itself. Forever and always.*

A small fluttering of wings: she opened her eyes. The wren, which he had called Heart, was perched on the sill by her hand. As she breathed its name the tiny bird flew up to her shoulder. With its gold-brown colouring it seemed quite at home shielded by the bright flow of her hair.

'No,' she murmured, reaching up to take the creature in her hand; it made no attempt to evade her. 'Not tonight; I can't take you with me.' She put her hand out the window, releasing the bird into the pale light of the summer evening. It fluttered just beyond the opening, and when Ana stepped back it flew in again.

'Go,' she said. 'Go home, go back to him. If he somehow hears your voice, if he can see through your eyes, tell him I love him; I will love him forever. Show him my tears. But don't stay with me. Alpin mustn't see you.'

She put the bird on the sill. It perched there, watching her, a fragile slip of feathers, eyes bright with a wild knowledge she could never understand. 'Tell him,' she whispered, and went to the door and out before the wren could follow. Then it was chin up, shoulders straight, back held like a queen's as she walked to Alpin's door. The guard let her in.

Her courage lasted only until she looked into her future husband's eyes. For all the festive supper laid out on the table, the candles in their silver holders, the fine glassware and ornately decorated spoons, there was something in Alpin's expression tonight that chilled her to the marrow. 'You took your time,' he said. 'Sit down, I'll pour you some mead. I'm getting hungry.'

'My maid has been taken ill. It took me a little longer to dress.'

'Taken ill, is she?' Alpin passed a goblet across to her, then leaned back in his chair, legs crossed, hands clasped around his own cup. His knuckles were white. 'I suppose that's one way of putting it.'

The chill had deepened. 'What do you mean? What is wrong with Ludha? What are you telling me?'

'Your maid required chastisement once again. She's become quite lax in some respects since we gave her over to your control, so much so I think we may have to dispense with her services. A little unfortunate, as I understand the girl has no family to go to. But there it is.'

'Are you saying someone has hurt her? That she's been beaten? This is completely unacceptable! I told you I would mete out any punishment myself – what's she supposed to have done anyway? She's behaved perfectly in every respect. She's spent days and days on the wedding gown –'

'I would be careful if I were you.' Alpin rose to his feet, his voice dangerously quiet. 'Very careful. Perhaps your serving girl has not committed the more common sort of offence such as stealing or slovenliness or lechery. But she's guilty of something far worse than those; she's broken one of my rules, *my* rules, the ones by which this entire household is governed. If a beating is all she's incurred for it, the girl should count herself fortunate.'

'What rule?' Ana fought for a steady tone.

'Let's not discuss that just yet. I've an appetite for this fine supper, though I must say I was hoping I might at the same time enjoy the sight of my lovely betrothed with the fair skin of her shoulders and arms, and perhaps a hint of bosom, set off by a delicate gown suited to her wedding eve. Your blue, perhaps; you look fetching in that. What I see before me is the moon veiled by clouds. You look like a widow in mourning.' As he spoke he was passing her a platter of baked fish, another of onions and cheese, as if this were an ordinary occasion. Mute, Ana helped herself from both, then sat staring down at her hands. She did not feel like the moon, nor like a widow. She felt like a creature caught in a trap, alone and terrified.

'My lord –' Her voice came out as a croak. She cleared her throat, sipped her mead and tried again. 'My lord, I can hardly settle to enjoying a meal when I've just been told my maid has endured a beating. And –' She hesitated, knowing it was ill-considered, then plunged ahead, suddenly unable to hold back the words. 'I'm uncomfortable about the rules you maintain in the house: the subjects that one cannot discuss, the restrictions on going outside the walls. If I'm to be mistress here, I must have workable arrangements with the serving people. I'd have welcomed the opportunity to speak to Faolan once or twice, as he is the only person I have here from home. Alpin, I . . . I think it's odd that your brother's crime is so shrouded in secrecy. That suggests to me an . . . irregularity.'

'Go on,' Alpin said. His voice had gone quiet.

'It would be dreadfully unjust if Drustan had been locked up all these years for a crime he didn't commit.'

His brows rose. 'What alternative theory do you propose?'

'I have no theory.'

'Are you accusing me of lying? Is that what this amounts to?'

'No, my lord,' Ana said, flinching before the cold strength that had entered his eyes. 'As you were not present when Lady Erisa died, your own account must rely on others. I'm sure you believe it is true, as do the other folk I have spoken to.'

'What other folk? This is forbidden territory for my household. Who's been talking?'

Ana swallowed. 'I asked Orna. She did not tell the tale, only said your version was the one folk considered accurate. There is nobody else here to ask. Your old servants all seem to have gone away.'

'You find that odd, do you?' Now Alpin, too, had abandoned his supper.

'Unusual certainly.'

'I want as few reminders of that dark day around me as possible.'

'But you keep him here.'

'Him?'

'Your brother. You keep him here at Briar Wood.'

Alpin's stare was intense. It seemed to Ana that he was trying to read her thoughts; that he would wrench her secrets out of her if he must.

'I wonder,' he said quietly, 'how this idea got into your head, the idea that there might be another story. The notion that the madman might not be guilty of his crime. Do you feel so little for me that you spend all your energy on going over my personal tragedy, raking up the half-forgotten anguish of my past? Has it somehow escaped your attention that we are to be married tomorrow?'

'Indeed not, my lord.' His behaviour was scaring her, and she could hear the wobble in her own voice. 'That is my reason for raising these matters now. There should be trust between husband and wife. Trust and honesty. I'm concerned for the future –'

'Rubbish!' Alpin thumped a fist on the table; he was no longer quiet and controlled. 'You're not concerned about anything of the kind. It's Drustan who fills your thoughts and consumes your energy. Why would you entertain this obsession with his guilt or innocence unless someone had given you another story to believe? Most women would shun him; most brides would be glad he was shut away where he can do no more harm. Not you. Explain yourself!'

She took an unsteady breath. 'I have no idea what you mean, my lord.'

'You're lying.' Alpin rose to his feet, striding around the table to her side where he stood over her, hands on hips, legs apart, glaring down. 'He's put this into your head, the crazy man, the wild man – he's spun a web of falsehoods and you've been caught in it fair and square. I can just see it, you with your ladylike manners and your gentle ways, you'd have a soft spot for every stray dog or injured creature or miscreant with a tale of injustice. He always had a beguiling way with him; he'd twist words to mean whatever he wanted. Me, I'm a plain thinker and a plain talker. No wonder you shrink away when I try to touch you.'

Ana made to protest; the look on his face held her mute and still.

'No wonder you think I'm not good enough for a lady of royal blood. It's all him, isn't it? That wretch has poisoned your mind and turned you against me. He's wheedled his way into your affections; he's out to ruin my chance of a future yet again. Tell me! Tell me!' Alpin seized her by the arms and dragged her to her feet. His grip was painfully strong.

'That's not true,' Ana whispered. 'Let me go, you're hurting me.'

The grip tightened, and she could not suppress a cry of pain. 'It is true,' Alpin growled, his bearded face close to hers, anger flushing his skin to a mottled purple-red. 'I know it's true. I know about your little sewing afternoons, your private sojourns up in the courtyard with that maid of yours, and the conversations you've been having. A flaw in the construction of his prison, apparently; how could I have overlooked it?'

Ana had not believed she could be any more frightened, but she looked past Alpin as he said this and saw a tiny bird fly in to land on the windowsill, a brave small presence in cream and brown. She turned her gaze away quickly. 'Sit down, my lord, please,' she said, remembering Orna's advice.

'Don't presume to give me orders in my own home.' He gave her a shake; her head reeled. 'Certain information came my way and I sent a boy up there today to verify it. He heard you. You're a cheat and a liar, and you're certainly not the pure princess you make yourself out to be! How dare you play the part of lady, putting me through hell with your pretence of modesty, when every day you've been murmuring love talk to my brother? Answer me, by all the gods, or I'll have it out of you another way!'

'Please let me go. You're scaring me.'

'Tell me, curse you!' He shook her again; her teeth seemed to jar in her head, and she could barely find her voice.

'I did speak to him, yes. Not what you say. Just idle talk. I felt sorry for him. It is a long time of solitude. Since he speaks like a rational man, I thought . . . I believed . . . Is this why you've punished Ludha? Did she tell you . . . did you make her . . . ?'

'Agh!' With an explosive sound of disgust, Alpin threw her back down to her seat. 'That cur, that godforsaken excuse for a man! I should have made an end of him seven years ago; I should have had the courage. The ties of kinship are no more than fetters when such atrocities are committed. If he'd not been of my blood he'd have been disposed of within a day, his head displayed over my gate, his corpse left for crows to feast on. How could you listen to him? How could you be so stupid?'

Ana rose to her feet. She tried to summon the queenly dignity which had proved so helpful in the past when she was distressed or afraid. The cold terror did not relinquish its grip on her heart. 'I don't intend to remain here being shouted at and manhandled,' she said with as much hauteur as she could summon. 'Before I retire tonight I wish to see my maid, to ensure she has not been mistreated. And I want to see Faolan.' Her voice shook on his name. 'I wish to see my bard without you present; I am happy for another to be in attendance, perhaps the druid.'

'Not so fast.' He came to stand before her again. Ana calculated the number of steps to the door, and wondered whether there would be any point in running to her chamber and locking herself in. 'You're in no position to begin making demands,' Alpin went on. 'What my informant heard up there wasn't just passing the time of day. He described it as a great deal more than that. What he told me made me unhappy, Ana. Very unhappy, and more than a little angry.'

'You no longer wish to go ahead with this marriage?' The

question trembled between the recognition of strategic failure and a wild, impossible hope.

'What, and ruin King Bridei's treaty? Hardly. Besides, what a waste of all that sewing. Shame your maid won't be here to see you in the confection she fashioned for you. But I'll see it. I'll see you smile in it, and make your promises in it, and I'll watch the look on your face as I strip it off you and take what you don't want to give me because the man you save your sweet words for, the man you're lusting after, the man you're panting for is that accursed lunatic Drustan!'

'How dare you!' The bitter injustice of it filled her heart, and for a moment fury took the place of caution. 'Your brother is a hundred times the man you are!'

His fist came across like a thunderbolt, cracking into her jaw, and she fell across the table, her head and neck a red hot ball of pain. As she staggered back to her feet, the wren flew across to her shoulder, its small, twittering voice blending strangely with the harsh sound of Alpin's laboured breathing.

'I said to you once,' Ana gasped, 'that if you raised a hand to me I would not marry you, treaty or no treaty. Fetch the druid, and send for Faolan. I'll have no more of this.' The bird had made no attempt to conceal itself. She willed it to fly away.

'You're a whore, even if it's only in your mind,' Alpin said, his tone rough. 'You were heard, and your defence of my brother proves it. You're in no position to dictate what should or should not unfold.'

'You forget, I am the one who must sign the treaty on Bridei's behalf.' Her whole body was shaking. 'I want to see Faolan. I will not –'

'Stop right there.' Alpin's eyes were on the bird. Ana took a step back. 'For you, there is no "cannot", no "will not". You've broken the rules. You've talked to my brother; you've allowed him to insinuate his way into your heart and, if he were not safely behind locked doors, no doubt he'd be in your bed as well, making up for all those years when women only featured in his crazy dreams.'

'I won't listen to this. If Faolan knew you had hurt me, he would –'

'Shut your mouth!' His fist came up again, and she fell silent; her courage did not stretch quite as far as that. Trying to run would be futile, since it was plain he could outpace her. And it was his guard who stood beyond the door. Did these people all know what Alpin was? Perhaps, in the world of the Caitt, such behaviour was quite normal.

'Faolan, you will find, is unlikely to be of much assistance to you tonight,' Alpin said. 'As for you, my dear, there's no backing out of the treaty, or the marriage, at this late stage. Wanton as you are, liar and dissembler, you do bear a certain blood line, and you will bear sons for me. I don't care if that's to your taste or not. Maybe you can think of Drustan while I'm having you; that should help the juices flow. And you'll sign. Your bard will be leaving the day after tomorrow to take the news back to Bridei. It's all arranged.'

'I won't do it.' Ana spoke through clenched teeth. *Fly away. Now. Fly back to him.*

'Yes, you will,' said Alpin, and with a snatch as rapid and expert as that of a cat pinning its prey, he reached out and took the wren from her shoulder. In his big fist its body was invisible; Ana could see only the delicate beak, the bright, terrified eyes.

'*Please –*' A strangled whisper broke from her.

'You will do it. You will do precisely as I tell you, and you won't run to your tame Gael or to anyone else with tales of woe. You'll stay away from my brother from now on. No songs, no whispers, no visits from his wretched creatures.' He glanced at the trapped bird; Ana saw its head move frantically as it sought escape, but the hand held it fast. 'You'll sign the treaty, you'll go through the handfasting without any show of reluctance and you'll open your legs for me when, where and how *I* choose.'

'No –'

'Yes,' Alpin said. 'Because if you fail to do any of those things, I'll squeeze the life out of Drustan as quickly and surely as *this*.' He fixed her with his gaze, cold and calm now, and tightened his fist.

The wren died without a sound. It was Drustan's cry that echoed through every corner of Briar Wood at that moment, the wrenching scream a man utters when a piece of his living heart is torn from his body.

Alpin tossed the little corpse into the fire and wiped his hand on his tunic; a fragment of wispy feather floated gauzily in the air. Ana was without words. Somewhere inside her a child repeated, in a sobbing whisper, *Let this be a dream, let me wake up now.*

'Sit down,' Alpin said.

She sat. After that chilling cry of anguish, there was only silence outside.

'Change of plan, I think. We might sign the treaty now; all parties should be available. I've lost my appetite for this cosy supper. And you can see your bard. I think it appropriate that he witnesses the signing, since he's to bear the document back to King Bridei. A chance to say your final farewells. The druid can be present, just as you requested. But I will also be there. I don't trust you, Ana, and after this I probably never will.'

'You are an evil man,' she said. 'Cruel and barbaric. Why do you hate Drustan so?'

'You ask that only because you refuse to recognise the truth. Drustan killed what I loved best. Of course I hate him. He was flawed from the start; he should have been drowned at birth. He was never like the rest of us. He shouldn't have come back here.'

'If he had not,' Ana's voice was quivering with shock and rage, and with the chill knowledge of defeat, 'you would not have gained control of his waterways at Dreaming Glen. And he would never have been locked up.'

'We won't discuss that.' Alpin spoke without emphasis. His eyes were cold. 'I'll expect you to keep your mouth shut from now on where matters of warfare, strategy or alliance are concerned. That is men's business and best confined to men's gatherings. You know what to expect if you disobey me.'

'It seems your wife will be silent most of the time, her conversation limited to the anticipation of roast beef for supper or a discussion of the weather.'

'As long as you oblige me in bed, I've no problem with that.' Alpin went to the door, summoned his guard, made a hurried, quiet request. He closed the door again and stood with his back to it, watching her. There was a smell in the room like meat charring. Ana felt sick.

'When Faolan sees this mark on my face,' she said, 'he will

know that you hit me. What kind of news is that to take back to White Hill?'

Alpin's brows rose. 'They don't discipline their women in Fortriu?'

'I would swear Bridei has never raised a hand against his wife; such a thought would not enter his mind.'

'Uh-huh. A little odd herself, isn't she, from what I've heard? One of the forest folk. That could be a weak spot in a man's armour.'

'Tuala is of another kind,' Ana said quietly. 'She's one of my dearest friends.'

'Got a penchant for the exotic, have you? I can't conceive of anyone wanting my brother as a lover; such a notion is perverse. His condition has been a source of deep shame to our family since Drustan was a child, long before he decided to turn his hand to murder. And you expect the household to discuss it openly. You're a fool.'

Ana said nothing. From now on, she thought dully, there would be many silences. If they were required to prevent another sacrifice, she would hold her tongue, and weep on the inside.

Faolan came in with a tall guard at his back and a thickset one beside him. There were red marks around his wrists as if he had been bound. Above one eye was crust of blood, and a purple bruise marked his jaw. Beneath these signs of blows, his face was white. The shutters were down as they had so often been at White Hill, his features wearing the bland, indifferent look of a man who desires not to attract attention. He said not a word.

'Faolan,' Ana managed. 'You are well?' The courteous question hung in the silence between them, and behind it all the things she could not say, the things she would never say.

'Yes, my lady.' The voice level, toneless. The eyes now looking anywhere but at her face, where no doubt a florid bruise was spreading to match the fierce aching in her cheek and jaw. Then, as if he could not help himself, 'You've been hurt.'

There was a small metallic sound as Alpin shifted a knife on the tabletop.

'A clumsy accident,' Ana said, looking at the floor. 'My maid opened a chest just as I leaned over. These things will happen.' His wrists were livid; there were marks on his legs, too, revealed above the worn shoes they had given him to wear. She found she was staring and made herself look away. 'My lord tells me you're leaving for White Hill the day after tomorrow. So soon.' Her voice was shaking; she must try to be strong, for if they had hurt him they could do so again. They could hurt him, and they could hurt Drustan. She must govern every word, every look, every gesture.

'There's no need for further delay,' Faolan said. 'I understand the treaty is to be signed tonight; the handfasting occurs tomorrow. After that I'll be straight off, since I'm no longer required here.'

'You must do as you think best, of course,' she said tightly. 'What would I know of such matters?' They were all watching and listening, Alpin, the men-at-arms, that fellow Dregard who was always at Alpin's right hand, the druid, who had entered the chamber with a quill and ink pot. She longed for a few moments alone with Faolan, even though she could not tell him the truth, not with Drustan's safety in the balance. If the others were not here, she could at least clasp his hand, wish him well and thank him for his courage and friendship. She could tell him he had done a good job. 'Safe journey, Faolan,' she said quietly. 'I don't suppose there will be time for us to talk tomorrow. Please give my warmest good wishes to Bridei. And to Tuala.' Tears were close; she swallowed them. 'And hug Derelei for me. I miss him.'

'Yes, my lady.' Still the stubborn refusal to meet her eyes. Was he under the same pressure as she was? Acting a part, not to bring down Alpin's wrath?

'Well, now,' Alpin said, 'we're all here, so let's get down to business. I will ask you to be seated – not you, bard, you can stand where you are – and perhaps Berguist will do us the courtesy of reading the terms of the treaty, just so we're all sure of what we're agreeing to.' He directed a patronising smile towards Ana; she stiffened her spine and gave a polite nod in return. She seated herself and waited. By her hand, on the table, a brown feather stirred in the draught.

The druid, Berguist, set out the terms of the treaty clearly and simply. For him, at least, there was no reason to be anything but calm. It had all been rendered into Latin and set down on the parchment, which he offered to Ana to read over in case he had made any errors. She scanned it, but such was the desolation in her mind that the thing could have been a stock list or a Christian prayer, so little of it did she take in.

'My future wife is something of a scholar,' Alpin was saying. 'Clever as well as beautiful; every man should be fortunate enough to find such a paragon, eh? Finished, my dear?'

'It seems everything is here, my lord,' she said. 'Even the reference to Dreaming Glen which Faolan and I requested. You've been thorough.'

Alpin's eyes narrowed. 'Sign, then,' he said.

She took the quill and, in the place the druid indicated, wrote her name: *Ana daughter of Nechtan, Princess of the Light Isles.* And beneath it, *for Bridei son of Maelchon, King of Fortriu.* Alpin, impatient, seized the pen from her fingers before the ink was dry and placed his mark beside hers. The druid took the parchment back to record Alpin's full name above the cross he had made, and to append his own details as witness. It was done.

'Ah,' Alpin said expansively as the druid sprinkled sand from a little bag onto the document to hasten the drying of the ink, 'a most satisfactory ending to a particularly trying day. And won't King Bridei be pleased? This could make all the difference to his future plans.'

'A great achievement, my lord,' said Dregard.

'Will you provide Faolan with a guide as far as the borders of your territory, or maybe further?' Ana asked Alpin. 'I imagine Breaking Ford may still be impassable. And there are your warlike neighbours –'

'That need not concern you,' Alpin snapped, his mood abruptly altered. 'It is –'

'Men's business, I know.' Careful, careful; watch every step. 'I simply wish to remind you how important it is that the news does reach Bridei. Bear in mind that, although we've been here two turnings of the moon, word has not yet been sent advising him that our escort was lost. And that his emissary was drowned,' she added hastily, unsure if that earlier lie counted for anything after what had come about today, but anxious to help Faolan get home safely. His demeanour troubled her. He did not seem himself tonight.

'We'll see your pet Gael safely off the premises, don't worry,' Alpin said. 'We've reason enough to want him gone. Of course, it may not be for long.'

The atmosphere changed subtly; there was a chill in the room. 'What do you mean, my lord?' Ana asked.

Alpin seemed to be savouring in advance what was to come; he had that air again, the gathered tension of a wildcat about to pounce. 'I could tell you,' he said. 'But I think we'll get the bard to do that himself. You've been solicitous of his welfare from the first. You may as well know from his own lips what a two-faced piece of scum you brought inside my walls. His account of himself will make a change from those sickly love songs he likes to entertain us with. Go on, bard! Tell her!'

'Faolan?' she asked. 'What is this? What is he saying?'

'My lord –' Faolan turned to Alpin, protesting.

'Tell her!' Alpin barked.

Faolan cleared his throat.

'Come on!'

'I . . .' Faolan appeared to be unable to go on. He stared at the floor. The chamber fell silent; it was clear nobody was going to help him. A look passed between Alpin and his men-at-arms: a look that said quite plainly, *If that's what it takes, hit him.*

'Faolan,' Ana said, 'please tell me, whatever it is. What does Lord Alpin mean, two-faced?' She had seen Faolan without defences before, after the ford, but never quite like this. 'Tell me,' she said again, fighting the growing fear.

He looked up then, and the eyes that met hers were as of old: cool, detached, as if nothing much mattered to him. She heard him take two deep breaths before he spoke.

'Lord Alpin received information,' Faolan said. Another careful breath. 'A man saw me at the court of Dunadd last spring. What he saw led him to believe I'm in the pay of both Bridei of Fortriu and Gabhran of Dalriada.'

Ana sat mute, waiting for more. A lie; this had to be one of Alpin's tricks.

'The deduction was that I work for Bridei only to the extent it suits me,' Faolan said levelly. 'Being of Gaelic origins myself, I must, of course, owe some allegiance to Dalriada: to my own kind. Nonetheless, Lord Alpin is generously allowing me to return to White Hill with an account of our journey and its successful conclusion.' He glanced at Alpin. 'Is this what you wished me to tell, my lord?'

'It isn't true.' Ana was shaking with anger. 'This must be a mistake!' Faolan, who had been Bridei's right-hand man, his trusted bodyguard and sounding board these five years – Faolan, a Dalriadan spy? It was nonsense. She knew he had been at Dunadd; where else could he have gathered the information that had brought her to Briar Wood? But Faolan in the pay of Gabhran – that was impossible, and it offended her to hear it. 'I cannot believe it, my lord,' she said to Alpin, who had an amused smirk on his face. 'Just because Faolan is of Gaelic origins, there is no need to leap to conclusions –'

'It's true, Ana.' Faolan's tone was flat.

'What?' she whispered.

'What I said is true. I've been working for Gabhran since before I came to the court of Fortriu. I carry information both ways.' He looked her straight in the eye. She could have sworn he was telling the truth. 'It pays well.'

Ana struggled to find her voice. 'It can't be – Bridei – Bridei trusted you – I don't understand . . .' In her mind were the things Faolan had said, at White Hill and on the terrible journey; his strength, his reluctant kindness, his capable handling of crisis after crisis. The way he spoke to Bridei and watched so tirelessly over both him and Tuala; his wretchedness at the ford, believing he had failed in his mission. This must be an act, part of some strategic plan on Faolan's part, requiring him to lie thus for Alpin's ears. Or . . . 'Faolan,' she made herself ask, for all Alpin's intimidating stare, 'have you been beaten into saying this? Has this false confession been wrung from you by force?'

'Would I indulge in such treatment of a guest in my home?' asked Alpin lightly. 'After all those ballads? The information was freely given after the Gael knew he was cornered.'

Ana's jaw still ached from his blow; she could still see his fist squeezing, squeezing the last scrap of life from the tiny captive. 'I don't believe you,' she said, her heart hammering with fear.

'No?' Alpin did not seem perturbed. 'Then it's just as well we have a witness. Berguist, please confirm for the lady that this fellow's account of himself is accurate.'

The druid was looking most uncomfortable. He had, after all, come to Briar Wood only to do a little scribing and call down the gods' blessing on a marriage. 'My lady,' he said quietly, 'I regret to inform you that the Gael confessed to this quite readily once the informant's tale was out in the open. Faolan here was not under duress. Although one cannot condone his past actions, it is to his credit that, at the end, he chose to tell the truth.'

'That will be all,' Alpin said crisply, and Faolan inclined his head without so much as a glance at Ana then, flanked by the men-at-arms, turned and left the room. 'What a shame,' Alpin went on, reaching for the mead jug. 'Such a fine harpist too. Once the word gets around, I imagine he'll find it difficult to secure any kind of patronage.'

'Excuse me.' Ana was not sure if her legs would carry her as far as the door. 'I will retire now. Tomorrow is a busy day.'

Alpin rose courteously to his feet. 'Goodnight, my dear. You need your beauty sleep, of course. Will you require assistance undressing?' He curled his hand around the back of her neck and kissed her on the cheek, a lingering pressure of the lips. Ana recoiled; every part of her seemed to freeze.

'Not a personal offer, much as I'd like that.' His tone had lost its affable quality. 'But as your maid is indisposed, another servant perhaps?'

'No, thank you.' Chin up . . . back straight . . . It had never been more difficult to remember who she was. She wanted to scream, to run, to hide, to be anywhere but here. 'I wish you all goodnight. May the Shining One give you fair dreams.'

'May the Flamekeeper light your waking.' The druid murmured the formal response. A little frown had appeared on his brow.

Back in her chamber with the door bolted, Ana changed into a nightrobe and lay down on her bed, staring up at the cobwebs on the ceiling. She felt hollow, empty. The future stretched ahead like an endless, shadowy path with not a single light to show the way, a future of bullying and blows and desperate lies. A future in which friends became foes and innocent lives were snuffed out on a whim. This was the man whose children she must bear. And Faolan, Faolan whom she had come to trust, in whose arms she had sheltered in the great darkness of the wild forest, Faolan whose songs were so full of heartbreak and yearning and hope that they brought tears to the eyes of hardened warriors – could he truly have betrayed Bridei so? How had her life turned into this wretched thing with not a scrap of truth left in it? She had wondered, in the past, how anyone could choose to make an end of themselves, for life was the gods' precious gift to each man and woman; it fell to each to walk the path with courage and goodness, and to follow it for its allotted span, until Bone Mother gathered the weary traveller home. Tonight, in the darkness, the prospect of a sharp knife, a quick, bloody ending almost made sense.

The pale, cool light of the summer night crept through the narrow window. The silver fingers of the Shining One brushed the stones and, as if carried here in the goddess's gentle hand, two small forms appeared on the sill. With a whisper of wings they flew across to the chest by her bedside. Then, as Ana sat up, they moved one, two, to her shoulders, the crossbill on the left and on the right the heavier weight of the hoodie.

She could not go. Drustan needed her. And she needed him, even if she could not see him, even if she never heard his voice again. She was bound to him as surely and completely as these creatures were, and if she left him, whether to journey in this world or another, she would be torn in two and broken beyond mending. This was a heart-deep truth; it shone with constancy in a web of shadows and deceits. While Drustan lived, she must stay at Briar Wood, no matter what she had to endure. She would find the truth, however long it took. Somehow she would set him free.

The floor of the kennels made a hard bed, though Faolan had endured worse. In any event, his thoughts kept him awake.

Knowing he could not afford distractions, he dragged his mind from the look in Ana's eyes as she heard his confession – wounded, betrayed – and worked on his plan, such as it was. There was only one thing in his favour, and that was the tradition Caitt men observed of spending the best part of a wedding morning in uproarious celebration. Gerdic had told him about the copious flow of ale, the games and tests of strength and skill, the dogfights and boar-baiting and other activities that accompanied this event. When the games were over, which would be around midday, the handfasting would take place in the courtyard; druids preferred to conduct the ceremony outside, so the eyes of the Shining One and the Flamekeeper could look down on it directly and ensure the promises were made with goodwill.

Faolan thought through each obstacle in turn. He must move when most of Briar Wood's men were in the courtyard absorbed by the morning's entertainment. His hands were not bound; that was a start. There was a bolted iron grille to get through, Dovard sleeping with his mongrel in the corner, the guard keeping watch by the small back entry to the fortress. It would be necessary to walk straight across this man's line of vision at close quarters. Then he must get across the packed courtyard, pass more guards in the family quarters and face the possibility that, even if Ana were in her chamber, she might have her door locked. If Gerdic's predictions were accurate she'd be getting dressed for the handfasting. There might be women in attendance: what to do with them? Felling an armed man was one thing. It was another to despatch a hapless maidservant with a well-aimed tap to the skull. Judging by Ana's reaction to his words earlier, she would probably be unsurprised to see him leave a trail of blood and death behind him, and that was only fair; certain missions in his past had required exactly that.

So far, so good; in his mind, they reached Alpin's quarters and the little locked door. He'd heard nothing from Deord. Possibly the guard did not know where Faolan was. How much had Deord managed to hear, and just how far could the unspoken bond between Breakstone men be stretched? Would it get them into the madman's quarters and out beyond the wall? If not, they were in trouble. As for what he would do once they were out, think too carefully of that and he might be in danger of letting this chance go: this one chance. He could not do that. He would get her out and safely home if he died in the attempt. He would sooner chop off his own right hand than see her marry that wretch. The fact that Alpin was a cheat and a liar who had no intention of honouring Bridei's treaty seemed almost secondary.

Briefly, Faolan forced himself to rest. He'd be no use to anyone with his edge blunted by weariness. It was summer and dawn came early; with the first lightening of the sky the hounds awoke and began a restless pacing, eager to be let out. Their yipping and squabbling roused Dovard, who went out to splash his head under the pump before coming over to the grilled gate of the little cell reserved for dangerous dogs, the ones that went feral.

'Hungry?' the kennel boy asked. 'I'm making up feed for them and I'll put a pot of gruel on; you're welcome to share. Sorry I can't let you out. I'd be in trouble.' Already Dovard was fishing around in bins and sacks, finding the makings of a fire, giving a black-crusted pot a desultory wipe. The dogs' clamour intensified.

'Thank you,' Faolan said, eyeing the ring of keys that hung from a peg by the outer door and trying to work out which was the one he would need. 'Seems I'm the one who's in trouble right now.'

Dovard was poking sticks and wisps of straw into the pile of wood he had laid on his central hearth. 'What did you do?' he asked without great interest.

'Got something wrong. Made Lord Alpin lose his temper. He's letting me out again later; nobody else to sing and play for the festivities. If there's breakfast going, I won't say no.' Faolan rubbed his hands together, blowing on them for warmth. His wrists and ankles ached from last night's bonds.

'Got to take them out for a bit first,' Dovard said, and swung open the gate of the main enclosure. A river of hounds poured forth, shoving, pushing, falling over their own feet in their haste to stretch their legs and taste the sun. A bowl of water went flying. 'I'll be back soon; just a run around the courtyard. Best get it done before too many folk are stirring.'

Silence fell on the kennels once again. Faolan stared at the keys. How to do this without hurting the boy or bringing down

Alpin's anger on him . . . no, that was stupid. He was thinking like a woman, all good deeds and sympathy. He could not afford scruples today, not with the stakes so high. The only thing that mattered was getting Ana safely away.

When the bird flew in, it took him a moment to react. It alighted on the rail above the hounds' enclosure, eyeing him, then flew with two neat flaps of its dark wings to perch on the peg that held the hanging keys. Faolan stared as the hoodie began, with delicate, controlled movements of its strong beak, to work one key off the ring. He reminded himself that this was the place where he had seen a bird become a man, though that, now, felt almost like a dream, something he had only imagined. The iron ring on which the keys hung had a small gap in it through which more could be added. The bird was working its chosen key around to this spot, a difficult task because of the weight of those others, which the hoodie must keep clear. Faolan found he was holding his breath as he willed the creature to get the job done before Dovard returned with his exuberant pack. *Come on, come on, you've almost got it* . . . A jangle as the keys dropped to the bottom of the ring. His heart sank; surely there wasn't time to start again. Then a beat of wings and the hoodie was at the door of his cell, the prize borne proudly in its beak. Mute, Faolan put up his hand and the bird placed the key on his palm. A moment later the crow was gone, and Faolan's freedom was tucked away, invisible, in the pouch at his belt.

He ate the gruel; Dovard's cooking left something to be desired, but at least the watery brew was hot. Then came a wait that felt like days, enough time for his mind to fill with unwelcome thoughts: the risk he was taking, not so much for himself as for her; the others who might be drawn into peril by his decision, innocents like Dovard; Deord, whom he had compelled to help him; the inscrutable Drustan, not yet clearly identifiable as friend or foe. The future: a future in which, whatever happened, Ana would undoubtedly wed a man who was not himself. There was nothing more certain than that. What was he, a fool? He had the chance to go freely, to leave this sorry place behind and ride unhindered back to White Hill. In this, he had seen that for once Alpin meant what he said. He could be out, and be safe, and get on with his life, such as it was. What he was planning could get them all killed, and for no reward at all. If Faolan succeeded today and snatched Alpin's bride from under his nose, he'd be spending the rest of his life waiting for a knife in the back. He'd be seeing the fellow's evil face every night in his dreams. He began to wish that Bridei had authorised him not only as emissary and spy, but also as assassin.

At last, increasing sounds of activity from outside told Faolan the men were gathering in the courtyard for their morning's fun. Dovard was evidently tempted, for he went to the door several times, but he did not go out.

'The games are good, but I don't like the dogfighting,' he muttered. 'That fellow, Cradig, I won't let him keep his creatures in here, not even in that corner you're in. His animals are rubbish; he's trained them to hate, and that's something a dog doesn't do, not naturally, they don't have it in them. If his beasts so much as stick a nose in here, it upsets the hounds; gives them nightmares.'

'I bet.' Faolan was listening intently now, not to the kennel boy but to the noises from outside; he was waiting for his moment. There was still a stream of folk walking by the kennel doorway. He must not make his move until something held all their attention. Remembering a certain suppertime, he suspected it would be dogfighting that did it.

When the time came it was unmistakable, for the crowd began to scream and bay and hoot as if some madness had entered them. Dovard's dogs, on the other hand, fell remarkably quiet. The kennel boy busied himself cleaning the pack's hunt collars and murmuring quietly to his own hound which sat at his feet, shivering as the noise from the courtyard came in waves; these men had the scent of blood in their nostrils, and it had released a hunger in them that must be satisfied.

'There, now,' Dovard said in soothing tones, 'there, girl, we'll have a little walk on our own later, when it's all over. Poxy Cradig,' he added, rubbing grease into the leather with some violence. A moment later he toppled from his stool, an expression of surprise crossing his face before he surrendered to unconsciousness. He had heard neither the key turning in the lock, nor Faolan coming up behind him with a length of firewood in his hand. The dog, distracted earlier by the noise from outside, belatedly began a frenzied barking, and the rest of the hounds chimed in. On an ordinary day the kennels would soon have been full of guards. Today, this hubbub was drowned in the roaring from out there.

Faolan dragged the kennel boy into the small enclosure and locked him in. The dog bared her teeth at him, but when Faolan growled back at her she retreated, and when he went to the outer doorway she took up a station by the iron grille, watching her unconscious master anxiously and whining from time to time. Dovard would wake with no more than a bad headache. With luck he would not come to himself for a while.

Faolan peered cautiously outside. The crowd was gathered in the centre of the courtyard; the guards up on the ramparts had eyes only for the bloody spectacle below. Faolan looked the other way, towards the living quarters. The man who had been guarding the little back entrance, the one beside the kennels, had come out from his secluded post and was watching, craning his neck to see above the press of men. He was standing right where Faolan needed to go.

There was no time to think. Faolan judged the distance, then left the kennels at a run, three strides before he launched himself at the fellow, sending him sprawling back into the narrow way through to the gate, out of sight. A brief but difficult struggle ensued. The guard had the advantage of greater height and weight, a pair of daggers and a leather jerkin. Faolan had the element of surprise on his side, at least briefly. He had experience. And he had a harp string ready in his hand. He performed the killing quickly and, because of its nature, quietly. This man was harder to drag to concealment; Faolan folded him up as best he could and stowed him in a dark corner. He helped himself to the daggers and crept back to the courtyard.

The dogfight was nearly over; the quality of the shouting had altered to a combination of victory cheers and catcalls. There were other dogs out there waiting, held at the end of taut ropes by sweating servants. There would be time, if he moved fast.

Nobody in the vicinity of the living quarters; they were all intent on the fight. He sprinted across the open yard, from shadow to shadow. Now he was inside, traversing the passage-way that led off to hall and kitchens on the right, and up to Alpin's private apartments at the end by broad stone steps. A guard at the top. Faolan pressed himself back against the wall. A woman at the bottom, carrying a basin of some kind; she did not see him but went off towards the kitchens. The guard turned, ready to pace the length of the upper hallway again. Bored, no doubt, and wishing he could go out and join the fun. Fun. By all the gods, who but the Caitt would choose such sport as this to celebrate a wedding day? Faolan palmed the stone he had con-cealed in his pouch and began a silent ascent of the stairs. He was in full view of anyone who might cross the lower hallway. Timing was everything here, that and an accurate hand.

He reached the top as the guard was finishing his short walk to the far end of the passageway, beyond the door to Alpin's cham-ber. The man turned. The stone caught him precisely in the centre of the brow; his hands had been reaching for his weapons even as Faolan hurled it. The guard sank to his knees, dazed. Faolan closed in, using a dagger in one quick, sure thrust to the heart; it was tidier than throat-slitting. The longer it took for anyone to spot his trail the better.

Outside Ana's door Faolan hesitated, working through the possibilities: it might be locked, requiring him to make a noise and perhaps alert the women downstairs or other men-at-arms. She might not be there. There could be a whole group of them inside, ready to scream and run for help. There were courses of action to deal with each of these chances, but he didn't particu-larly like any of them. No time for scruples. He reached out and gave the door a push.

It was not bolted. It swung partly open, well oiled and silent, and through the narrow gap he saw her standing by a window, gazing out beyond the wall. Time stopped for a moment. Faolan knew this image would stay with him always; it would never lose its power to grip his heart. Her hair was unbound, its silvery-fair waterfall tumbling down her back, touched to a thousand glint-ing points of light by the morning sun. She was wearing what must be the wedding dress; its lines curved around her shoulders and clung to her breasts before falling in graceful folds that gave subtle hints, here and there, of the shapely figure beneath. Her ash-pale face was illuminated by the sunlight; Faolan's eyes drank in her delicate brows, her sweet mouth, the perfect lines of cheek and chin. The livid bruise that stained her skin did nothing to diminish her beauty, but it made his heart sick. Her grey eyes, once so serene, now looked out on the world with a desperate sadness. And yet she held her back straight. It was this that struck him most deeply; delicate creature as she was, there was an iron discipline in her. She might seem some princess of fantastic story, but Faolan saw in that moment those qualities that had first made him love her: her courage and her honesty. He recognised that in all the world he would find no other woman to equal her.

'Ana,' he said quietly.

She whirled around; she had been far away.

'Hold the door open for me.'

Startled into compliance, she did as he told her, her eyes widening as he dragged the dead man in and stowed him behind the door. There was no concealing the bloody trail on the flagstones.

'We're leaving,' he said. 'Now, straightaway. No time for talk. You need boots, a cloak.'

'What?' She stood rooted to the spot, staring first at the corpse, then at Faolan himself, who had now opened the storage chest and was rummaging through the contents. 'Faolan, what is this? What are you doing?'

'Boots!' he snapped. 'Get them, put them on and come with me. Quick!'

'Come with you?' Ana backed towards the window. 'Don't be stupid!'

He found a cloak, spotted her outdoor boots at the foot of the bed, seized both. 'We're going home,' he said. 'Trust me, Ana. Now move, will you?' He reached out a hand; she pressed back against the wall as if afraid of him. 'I'm taking you back to White Hill. But we have to go now or there's no chance of getting away.'

'I'm not going.'

'What?'

'I said I'm not going. It's my wedding day, Faolan. Now get out of my room before the guards come.' Both of them glanced at the fallen man.

'This is crazy!' Faolan's whole body was tense with the awareness of time passing, time they could not afford to waste. 'You're not telling me you actually *want* to marry that oaf Alpin, are you? If it's the treaty that's bothering you, forget it. Alpin has no intention of honouring it. Come now. Quick!'

'I'm not going, Faolan. I can't.' Her tone was cold; there was a strength in it that told him this was no token protest.

'Ana, don't be foolish –' He made to take her by the arm, to drag her out if he had to, for there was no way he would let her stay here; this was utter madness.

'Don't touch me!' She shrank away, and he froze. What was this? Surely she did not actually believe he was a traitor? 'I'm not going, I told you! I must stay here! I can't leave him, I won't!'

Faolan made himself take a controlled breath. 'I assume it's not Alpin you're referring to,' he said as a strange feeling came over him, the sensation that everything was about to turn upside down.

'Faolan, just go, will you?'

'You won't leave him.' He could not let this go, though time was passing. 'Who?'

'Drustan,' she whispered, and he saw something in her eyes that terrified him beyond the thought of Alpin's brutish threats and a flooded river and packs of armed guards pursuing them: he saw the implacable determination of a woman in love.

A man experienced in the professions of assassin and spy is accustomed to performing tasks that may be displeasing on a personal level but are necessary to the mission. It was ironic, Faolan thought, that having entertained so often, in his dreams, the delight of touching Ana in passion, he now took hold of her by the shoulders before she could dodge, before it occurred to her to scream, turned her around and, with his forearm across her throat, applied an expertly calculated amount of pressure for just as long as it took to render her senseless. He made sure he had the cloak and boots, then manoeuvred her up over his shoulder as if she were a sack of grain and made his way to the next-door chamber: Alpin's chamber. He was not altogether surprised to find the little secondary door unlocked. He edged through, balancing Ana's weight as he ducked below the lintel, using a foot to close the portal behind him. In the semidarkness of the storage chamber where he stood, something stirred. He started, unpleasantly aware of how vulnerable he was, thus burdened; how helpless she was, and would continue to be unless she gave up this foolish determination not to be rescued. How far could he hope to progress if she were unwilling? It was a long way back to Fortriu and the terrain was not easy. He had counted on her help.

The thing moved again, whisking across into deeper shadow, and he saw that it was a cat. He followed it through a maze of narrow passageways and out to a path sunk between high walls, where the creature sat down and would go no further.

Ten paces along the path he met Deord coming the other way. The bald-headed man seemed to take in the situation at a glance. He showed no sign of surprise.

'She's injured?'

'No. She wouldn't come with me. Can we get out this way?'

'Go on ahead. I'll lock up behind you.'

The gate to the gloomy enclosure at the end of the path stood open. Within, the tall figure of Drustan could be seen moving about restlessly. Today, even the pretence of security seemed to have been abandoned. At the sight of the blood-spattered Faolan with the limp figure of Ana over his shoulder, Drustan sprang forward, and Faolan began to wish Deord had not left the place so welcomingly open.

'She's hurt! What have you done?'

Then, almost before Faolan could take a breath, Ana's weight was gone from his shoulders and she was across Drustan's lap as he sat down on the bench, one arm supporting her body, the other hand curved to cradle her head against his shoulder.

'Ana!' Drustan's voice was edgy with anxiety. 'Ana, wake up!' Then, looking up at Faolan with accusatory eyes, 'What happened?'

It was not the response of a distant acquaintance concerned for her wellbeing. The fierce tone, the glare, the way Drustan's fingers moved against her skin and her hair, all spoke the feelings of a lover. Faolan wondered how this could have happened; how he, the best spy in all Fortriu, had managed to miss it.

'Don't wake her up,' he said. 'She refused to come with me; I need her like this until we're safely away.'

'You hurt her. What is this bruise?'

Faolan sighed. Where had Deord got to? They must move on quickly; it could not be long before someone found the evidence he had left behind. 'She'll wake with a slight headache and she'll be angry. I had to, Drustan. As for the bruise, that's not my doing. What's it to you anyway?'

Drustan ignored the question. He had stopped trying to revive Ana; his arms, instead, had gathered her tighter, and he pressed his lips to her hair, closing his eyes. 'You're taking her away,' he murmured.

Faolan hated him. He hated Drustan's hands, holding her with the confident touch of one who has every right to do so; he hated Drustan's assumption that he could do what custom and duty would never allow for Faolan himself. He had dreamed of caressing her thus. Drustan did so without even considering how wrong it was. 'Since the alternative is for Ana to marry your brother,' Faolan said tightly, 'yes, I'm taking her away. The treaty is worthless, Alpin admitted it. And she's afraid of him. He hit her. I won't have it. We must leave this morning; I was hoping Deord –?'

'He has supplies packed for you.' Drustan had not opened his eyes. He was rocking Ana in his arms; Faolan heard her breathing change, a sign that she was regaining consciousness. 'We did not expect that you would take her. It is too dangerous. Alpin will come after you with dogs. How can you keep her safe?'

'The longer we delay, the less likely it is that I can,' Faolan snapped. 'Am I right, is there a way out from here, somewhere I can slip past the guards?'

'Answer me,' Drustan said, and although his eyes were still closed, his tone commanded a response.

'Ana is more resourceful than you seem to believe,' Faolan said. 'She saved my life on the way here at risk of her own. Just help us get out; we'll do the rest.' It came to him that this was a perfect opportunity for Drustan, too, to make his escape. Watching the captive's hands, threaded into Ana's golden hair, Faolan held his tongue.

The iron gate creaked and slammed shut. Much to Faolan's relief, Deord strode into sight, moving quickly, but calm as always.

'I can give you provisions, a weapon, a pair of boots. You won't get far in those,' eyeing Faolan's cracked, ill-fitting shoes. 'Can't help with a horse. You may do better on foot anyway. But the lady – I wasn't anticipating that.'

'How much did you overhear yesterday?' Faolan asked as Deord fetched a small, neatly strapped pack from the sleeping quarters and handed him a pair of well-worn but serviceable boots.

'Enough. Alpin found out your secret; perhaps put pressure on you to betray Bridei. For some reason he decided to lock you up for a while. It was anyone's guess whether you'd cut and run or do as he wanted. Being a Breakstone man, you did what I'd have done under the circumstances. In the end, we answer only to ourselves.'

'You answer to Alpin, surely,' Faolan said, glancing around the gloomy enclosure. On the bench Drustan sat motionless; Ana's bright hair made a shimmering cloak over his shoulder and chest. He looked bereft, as if he were about to lose the one good thing in his world.

'Alpin's given me work and a place to live,' Deord said. 'No more than that. If I've stayed, it's not been because of him. Faolan, you can't take her with you. You don't stand the slightest chance of getting away.'

'I'm taking her. That's why I'm going. She's not marrying that man; I won't allow it.'

'*You* won't?'

'There's no time for this.' Faolan shrugged the pack onto his back. 'Where's the way out, the place where you two get into the forest? I killed two men this morning and stunned another; I need to be off. Here,' moving to Drustan, 'I'll take her now.'

Ana let out a moan and rolled her head from side to side; she was coming to. Drustan's fingers moved against her hair, stroking gently. He murmured words of reassurance.

'I have a draught,' Deord said with some reluctance. 'We use it on our worst days. A little of that will keep her thus for some time longer; long enough for you to reach a deeper part of the forest.'

'Please.' The thought of drugging Ana was repugnant to Faolan, but Deord was right: the chances of getting away were slight at best and he must seize what help was available. He waited while Deord fetched a tiny vial from indoors, uncorked it and administered what seemed a very small dose indeed.

Drustan's features tightened. 'It gives long slumber,' he said. 'And disturbing dreams. She will awake confused and afraid.'

Faolan did not reply, simply knelt by Drustan, ready to take Ana on his back once more. She was silent now, the drug already beginning to do its work.

Drustan looked up. 'Deord,' he said, 'you must go with them. Aren't you bound to aid this man? To make sure he remains free?'

A silence.

'I can't,' Deord said flatly. 'I can't go off and leave you on your own.'

Drustan gave a joyless smile. 'My brother will find me another guard. I want you to do this. Faolan's right, Ana must go home. She must not marry my brother. Take her and run. The two of you together can do it. Go, Deord. I want you to go.'

'You know what you're saying?' Deord crouched down by Drustan, looking him in the eye. 'This will enrage your brother. He'll be off after Faolan like a wildcat on a rabbit's scent. If I go too, and we escape him, the one who'll bear the brunt of his anger is you. I'm responsible for you, Drustan. I have been these seven years. I'm not abandoning you to that.' Then, glancing at Faolan, 'Unless . . .'

Faolan had to force the words out; the words he knew were right. 'Why don't you come too, Drustan? Go free; leave Briar Wood behind.'

Two pairs of eyes turned to him. There was a brief silence.

'After all, why not?' said Deord quietly. 'Fly away; never come back. That was the dream of every Breakstone man. Fly away and make life anew. Few of us achieved it.'

'I can't do that.' Drustan's tone was flat.

'We've all killed, some of us more than once,' Faolan said. 'You've paid the price. More than a fair price; your brother imposes harsh punishments. You'd be a fool to stay on.' Then, when neither of them replied, 'You must decide now, the two of you.'

'What if I go, and kill again?' Drustan was looking down at Ana; her lids were heavy, her face pale save for the livid bruising on cheek and jaw.

'You once said,' Deord reminded him, 'that you would never hurt her. Was that true, or wasn't it?'

'I would never harm Ana. She is my hope.'

'Then come with us. Alpin will chase us by the known paths, difficult as they are. Those are the paths his hounds will follow. But there are other ways, ways better known to stag and buzzard, hare and fox. You can lead us; you can show us how to evade him.' And as the red-headed man looked up with something new in his eyes, 'You can save her, Drustan.'

Drustan glanced around the familiar enclosure as if in panic. 'She would know, then. Know what I am.'

'I can't spare time to debate the issue,' said Faolan crisply, lifting Ana onto his shoulders. 'Show me the way out.' He thought for a little that Drustan would not give her up; his hand held hers until the very last moment.

'She needn't know,' Deord said quietly. 'Go in your other form. You have the changes under control now. There's no need to show yourself. This way, Faolan.' Moving to the sleeping quarters, Deord looked back over his shoulder.

'You go, Deord,' Drustan said. 'I will follow if I can.'

'Make sure you do,' Deord said. 'I don't want your death on my conscience. Don't delay too long.' He took a bag of his own from a shelf and slung it on his back. Then, to Faolan, 'Best let me carry her; I've broader shoulders. See there, our rabbit hole to the outside; we knew you'd be coming, so it's open. Keep your head down.'

'Will he come?' Faolan asked, looking back as he clambered down into the underground passage.

'He'd better,' said Deord. 'If he doesn't, he'll be making me into a deserter, a man who abandoned a friend. If he stays behind his brother will kill him. Silence now, until we're well into the forest. Wait for my sign before we run for it. I know the patterns those guards keep. Ready?'

'I'm ready,' said Faolan.

Chapter Thirteen

I t was said, amongst those few who had the knowledge, that a man who survived incarceration at Breakstone Hollow lost his capacity for fear: the nature of the place was such that terrors faced in later life paled into insignificance. A Breakstone survivor was tough in body and mind; he had to be, or he'd be dead or mad before he could bear his mark of brotherhood out into the sunlight again.

Fear, nonetheless, sped Faolan's flight through the forest that day, fear not for his own safety but for Ana's. It didn't take much imagination to guess how Alpin would treat her if they were taken. As for his own survival, since that was critical to her return unharmed to White Hill, he must ensure he evaded capture and retained his ability to protect her. There was no time to think beyond that. It was one foot after the other, running on uneven paths, clambering up rocky slopes, ducking behind boulders or bushes before a punishing sprint across open ground. Sometimes Deord carried Ana and sometimes, feeling bound to do his share, Faolan bore her on his own shoulders.

Deord's potion must have been strong. They ran on, driving themselves as hard as they could in the rapidly shrinking time before Alpin's inevitable discovery that his bride had flown, and still Ana lay heavy-eyed and supine, unable to help them or herself. Unable to protest; and thank the gods for that, Faolan thought grimly, glancing across at Deord's tireless figure as they made their way downhill under a stand of oaks. All the same, he'd be relieved when she opened her eyes, even though her first words would likely form an angry protest.

As for the mysterious Drustan, he had not made an appearance. Faolan thought of certain men he had seen in the Uí Néill prison, men who had been as desperate for freedom as he, yet who would not contemplate the prospect of escape; men for whom the cruelty and degradation, the grinding daily routine had become, somehow, a safer prospect than the terrifying dream of the outside world with its multiplicity of choices. Prison could do that to a man. If he stayed there long enough, the place could rob him of his judgement, so that liberty became a thing to be feared, too wondrous and too difficult to be given credence even when the way was open. Such men stood at the door looking out on sun and green fields and wild mountains, then retreated into their dark cave. Faolan had seen the panic in Drustan's eyes as he faced the prospect of leaving his enclosure, of leaving Briar Wood forever. Seven years was a long time.

He'd better not hesitate much longer. Chances were the alarm had already been raised. No doubt Alpin would search every corner once he found Ana's chamber empty. Faolan and Deord would be marked men. And Drustan, if he lingered, would bear the brunt of his brother's fury. Faolan could not bring himself to wish the bird-man would join them, for all that. Following Deord down the slope to a shallow stream, grimly wading in to walk in the other man's steps – with luck this would put the dogs off their scent – he was seeing in his mind Drustan's hands on Ana's body, Drustan's lips pressed to her golden hair; he was hearing Ana's defiant voice: *I'm not going.* It was ridiculous, impossible. The man might not be crazy, but he was – he was what he was, an oddity, one of a kind, and the further away from him they travelled the happier Faolan would be. It wasn't that he wished Drustan ill. He just hoped the fellow would fly away in the opposite direction, home to his estates in the west. Faolan glanced skywards through the green canopy of the spreading oaks.

'No sign,' Deord said, pausing to shift Ana's weight on his broad shoulders. Her hair, which they had tucked into the cloak, was coming loose now; the long locks dipped into the stream, pale as summer wheat. The guard was calm as ever, but there was a bleakness in his eyes.

'It's his choice.' Faolan came up behind him, reaching to help the other man. He gathered Ana's hair and stuffed the strands as best he could under the cloak fastening. 'He wanted you to do this. And he's a grown man.'

'We need him,' Deord said. 'Alpin has the advantage unless we can find paths he doesn't know. Pray that Drustan reaches us before his brother does. Are you done?'

'Mm,' grunted Faolan. It was his ill luck, he thought as they splashed on up the stream, that where Drustan's hands had stroked and caressed those silken strands, his own were limited to bundling them out of the way with clumsy speed. Ana was ill-dressed for this venture; the borrowed tunic and trousers of their outward journey had been far more suitable. He must try to obtain things for her on the way; borrow or steal from farm or settlement. She couldn't run in a wedding dress. And the nights were cold. To offer to keep her warm as before, with his own body, now seemed unthinkable.

Deord was out of the water, starting to climb a wooded slope where oak gave way to silvery birch. Small birds were darting about up above, calling to one another in chattering voices. Fragments of bark or twig, dislodged by their activity, fell to the forest floor by the men's feet. Something rustled in the undergrowth: only a creature foraging. Then, from a distance, came a new sound: the baying of hunting hounds. Deord paused, looking back at Faolan. 'We might need to go back in the water,' he said. 'Can you swim?'

'If I have to. I can't speak for Ana.'

'Where's Drustan when we need him?' muttered Deord as they moved across the rise, finding a place where they could scramble up supporting Ana between them. By the time they reached the top the wedding dress was more mud-brown than cream. Her hair was loose again and catching in everything. Deord took his knife from his belt and, with three swift, expert slashes, cut the long fair locks off level with her shoulders. Faolan was speechless.

'Put this in your pack,' Deord said. 'We may not outrun the dogs, but we can at least avoid laying a trail for them. Don't just stand there, do it. Now come on. Pick up the pace.'

They ran. Deord found ways Faolan could barely see, muddy channels overgrown with clinging foliage, narrow divides between great stones, precipitous tracks more suited to goats than men. They picked paths across stepping stones and, where there were none, waded knee-deep through gushing streams. They squelched across boggy hollows and balanced on tenuous log bridges. Deord had not been joking when he ordered a faster pace: even with Ana on his shoulders, his speed and endurance were formidable. Faolan closed his mind to distractions and concentrated on keeping up.

They reached the shore of an isolated lochan, beyond which sheer slopes rose to a formidable line of peaks. Their crowns were pale, bare stone; they seemed as implacable as a brotherhood of ancient gods. On the near side the lake was fringed by pines; the water sparkled in the sunlight. Not far from where the two men had emerged from the trees, a high waterfall tumbled in a graceful ribbon of white to spill across stones to the lochan. The roaring of the fall did not quite drown the insistent voices of Alpin's hounds; they were closing fast, no doubt followed by men on horseback.

Picking a way along the stony shore would be too slow. Where a man could go, a dog could follow; besides, any track around this expanse of water was destined to end in a slope too steep to be climbed. The lake lay in a deep bowl of rock, with only one approach: the way they had come. The way Alpin was coming.

'Now where can a man go that a dog can't?' muttered Deord.

There was a moment's pause, punctuated by a moan from Ana. The two men looked at each other. Together, they turned to the waterfall.

'Halfway up a cliff,' Faolan said as the bray of a hunting horn sounded in the forest behind them. 'Or better still, halfway up a cliff and underwater.' The two of them began to run. 'By all that's holy . . . if this story ever gets told there'll be two madmen in it, and neither of them will be Drustan . . .'

'Save your breath,' grunted Deord.

Ana was regaining consciousness; she was making weak attempts to struggle and groaning as if her head were on fire. Deord clamped his arms firmly around her knees and back as she lay across his shoulders. Pretty soon, Faolan thought, it wouldn't matter how much noise she made. By the sound of that barking, the hounds would have them in sight before a man could count to five times fifty.

They fought their way over stones and through thick grasses. The noise of the waterfall was deafening; its voice sang a powerful challenge: *Assail me at your peril!* At the base was a pool and, for all the remoteness of the place, offerings had been tied to the bushes there, strips of linen, tattered ribbons, fraying lengths of wool. Who would not wish to placate whatever savage deity claimed this violent flow of water as its own? Faolan shivered. The memory of Breaking Ford stirred in his blood. For Ana's own sake, he prayed she would remain oblivious yet awhile.

'Up,' said Deord. 'Up and under cover before they come out into the open. Here, take her.'

Faolan looked upward. High on the cliff, partly obscured by a swirling mist of water droplets, he could see birds flying in and out; there was, perhaps, a cave or hollow behind the plunging torrent. The way up was precipitous, the rocks slick and moss-coated. He could hardly refuse to carry Ana in his turn. But up there? What did Deord think he was, a squirrel?

'Quick! Go!' Deord eased Ana's body onto his companion's back. Faolan raised his arms to hold her steady; how was he going to climb? 'I'll help you up the first bit,' Deord said. 'Hold her with one hand, climb with the other. You can do it.'

It seemed impossible. Faolan gritted his teeth, adjusted Ana's limp form to lie across one shoulder, her head hanging down behind, and began a slow ascent. It was insane. The whole day was insane. There was one moment when his foot slipped and his weight and hers skewed sideways, leaving him teetering over the precipice, water gushing, his heart pounding. Deord's hand came from behind, balancing Ana and correcting Faolan's own position in one sure push. They reached a ledge and Faolan drew breath.

'Go on,' Deord shouted over the roaring of the falls. 'Up there. Should be a cave. Hide and wait.'

'Till they starve us out?' Faolan joked grimly, peering upwards and trying to convince himself he could see a cave somewhere beyond the mass of flying water.

'No need for that.' Deord had let go and was heading back down. 'I'll lead them astray; give the dogs a different scent. If I'm not back by sundown, go on without me. My advice would be to head on up and look for a track across those hills.'

'What –?' It was suicide. The fellow was completely crazy.

'Go on, Faolan.' Deord looked back, his eyes steady, his expression calm. 'Without this, we'll be stuck here like rats in a trap while they wait for us to give up. Now get up there before they see you. You can do it. Look after her well, bard. Give Drustan my greeting, if he comes.'

Faolan was dumbstruck. Before he could summon a response, Deord had disappeared down the cliff, and it was too late to say thank you, or farewell, or anything at all.

Faolan executed the remaining climb almost unaware of what he was doing. He had no room in him for fear of falling, or for anything save the automatic adjustment of balance or grip or position that would move him upwards without dropping Ana or losing his hold. He did not look down. He did not look to see what Deord was doing, nor did he listen for hounds or horses or men out hunting. At a certain point, considerably higher, there was a broader ledge that curved around into a deep hollow beneath a sharp overhang. The water fell across this jutting stone, and the cave beneath was filled with the sound of its falling. The space was rock-floored and not entirely wet. Within, Faolan looked out on the white sheet of descending water, sunlit from beyond. The voice of the falls was deafening. He lowered Ana to the ground, wincing at the pain in his back, his knees, his abraded hands. The light in the cave was ghostly, a pale gleam through moving water; it turned Ana's wan features sickly white. She was stirring; shivering. Her gown was soaked, his own clothing no drier. He went through what practical steps he could: undoing his pack, looking for something warm and dry – what had Deord put in here, a cloak? Ah, a tightly folded blanket – and wrapping her in it. He made sure she was positioned safely so she would not roll straight over the edge if she woke confused and afraid. All the time the image of Deord was in his mind, Deord going back down, Deord hunted through the forest, Deord, in effect, giving himself up so they could be safe. Why? The man hardly knew them. The Breakstone link did not demand such sacrifice. He shouldn't have let Deord go; he should have insisted . . . But then they would all have been taken, even Ana. Perhaps Deord knew what he was doing. Wait until sundown, he'd said. Sundown was still a long way off. They could have done with some help. Where in the name of all the gods was Drustan?

As if in answer to the unspoken question, a small, neat form appeared, flying in through the curtains of water to land, shaking the droplets from its red feathers, on a protruding stone. Not the hawklike creature they needed; only the crossbill. Faolan glanced at it with dislike.

'Faolan?' Ana's voice was weak, but he heard her through the water's powerful music. 'Faolan, where are we?'

As simply and clearly as he could he explained, while Ana sat with pinched features and shadowed eyes, huddled in the blanket. He did not tell her how much it had hurt that she had believed he would betray Bridei. He did not speak of that at all, only of the treaty scorned and the need to get away before she was committed to her mockery of a marriage. He apologised for rendering her unconscious. He explained that Deord had helped them, and that now Deord was gone.

'Why do you look like that, Faolan?'

'Like what?' He was squatting close to her, keeping an eye on her, for the shadow of drug-dreams still haunted her eyes, and he feared she might make a sudden bolt for freedom. Here, nowhere was safe; the cave itself was the best refuge they had. In front of them, where the water hid them, was a fall to sudden death. Outside on the cliff they would be in full view of Alpin's men when they emerged from the trees. They might be in range of his arrows.

'As if you could feel Bone Mother's cold breath,' she said.

'I . . .' He hesitated, disturbed that she could read him so easily. 'I can't see how Deord could survive it,' he said, knowing she would want the truth. 'Alpin's out there with hunting dogs. One man, however able, is not going to outrun his hounds and his mounted warriors. Eventually they must take him. Then they'll kill him or they'll try to extract information from him, which in the long run is the same thing. Why would he do it?'

He expected no answer and Ana did not offer one. She had her head bent now, her shoulders slumped in defeat. The crossbill flew from its perch to alight on her shoulder and she started violently. 'Oh!' She glanced around the cave as if there were ghosts in its corners. One hand released its clutch on the blanket and came up to stroke the little bird; this seemed to calm her. All the same, Faolan maintained his watch on her. In this state, it seemed to him she might do anything.

'I'm sorry about your hair,' he said. 'Deord cut it. I couldn't stop him.'

Ana's fingers moved from the bird to the ragged ends of her shorn crop. She barely seemed to register the assault on her beauty. 'Faolan, I need to go back,' she said, staring at the curtain of rushing water as if she would indeed leap out that way if it were her only choice. 'I had such dreams . . . such cruel dreams . . . When I woke up, and we were here, I thought maybe . . .'

'What?' he asked quietly.

'I – I thought maybe it was all a dream; that perhaps we were still in the days after the ford . . . Out here, sheltering where we could, and everything wet . . . I saw so much death, death and blood and cruelty . . . I can't seem to remember what is dream and what is real, Faolan. It scares me.'

'It's the draught Deord gave you. It does that. The confusion will go away as the effect wears off.'

'Why did Deord . . . ? Oh. Oh yes, I remember. I wouldn't . . . and you killed a guard . . . Faolan?'

'What?' Now she would ask, and he must swallow the hurt and find an answer.

'I can't go with you,' she said flatly.

'Why not? Because you believe I would stab the King of Fortriu in the back?'

'No, I . . . Maybe for a moment I believed it. You did say it was true.'

'You must have a very low opinion of me if you would so readily believe me a traitor.' He could hear the tight sound of his own voice.

There was a pause, then Ana said, 'I dismissed the thought almost as soon as it came to me, Faolan. I'm sure you have a good explanation for what you said.' She was holding the crossbill between her hands now; Faolan wondered if Drustan could feel it when her fingers caressed his creatures thus. Of him, she had asked nothing at all.

'Bridei knows all about the work I do for Gabhran of Dalriada,' he said. 'Gabhran, on the other hand, is not aware that I am Bridei's man. To refuse Gabhran's payment would be to arouse his suspicion. It's been a useful arrangement for Fortriu. Now that Alpin's found me out, it will have to cease.'

Ana regarded him gravely; her look reassured him. 'I understand,' she said. 'The need for such subterfuge and dishonesty is unfortunate, but my own position has made me all too aware of the games that must be played by kings and their powerful advisers. I would not want such an occupation as yours, Faolan. Bridei asks a great deal of you.'

She had surprised him again. 'And of you,' he said. 'What did you mean, you must go back? You can't be telling me you'd still consider marrying Alpin? After this?'

'I thought . . . I thought I could go back alone. I can tell him you abducted me. It's the truth. You can go home to White Hill. I need to be at Briar Wood, Faolan. I told you before. I meant what I said.' A wave of shivering passed through her. The skirt of her gown was dark with water; she must be freezing. The blanket she wore was the only dry thing he could give her. If he couldn't do better, she'd die of a chill before they got as far as the borders of Alpin's land. Curse the Caitt. Curse this place.

A dark thought came to him. If he lied to her, he could make her give up this mad idea. All he had to say was that Drustan had decided not to join them; that he had bid Faolan take Ana home, and had chosen to fly off to his holdings in the west when freedom was offered. No, not fly, he could not say that. Drustan had bound him not to tell her that particular truth and he would honour his promise. But if he could persuade Ana that the bird-man

367

preferred to enjoy his new-found freedom alone, she'd have no reason to rush off on some ill-conceived rescue mission. It might even be true. If Drustan had intended to come after them, why wasn't he here? It did look as if the fellow had turned his back on her. If this had been another woman, that is what Faolan would have told her.

'Faolan?' Ana was regarding him closely. 'You understand, don't you? I can't leave Drustan. If Deord has abandoned him, he's all alone now. Drustan won't leave Briar Wood. He's convinced he'll harm someone if he is set free. He has nobody, Faolan. Can you imagine how that feels?'

He heard the change in her voice when she spoke Drustan's name; saw how she lifted the bird to touch its bright plumage to her cheek. At that moment he felt a murderous hate for Drustan. But he could not hate Ana. 'Deord only left because Drustan told him he should,' he said. 'Both Deord and I tried to get him to come with us. He seemed to be finding it difficult to make up his mind. He said he would come later. He's not so much of a fool that he would have stayed to face his brother's wrath alone, surely. If you went back you'd walk straight into Alpin's arms. Into Alpin's bed. If that's what you really want, I've seriously misjudged you.' It was crude, maybe; he had to shock her out of this somehow. 'All for nothing, if Drustan is already gone.' There was no point in enumerating the other reasons why her scheme was foolish and ridiculous: that her clothing was wet, that she did not know the way, that it was late in the day. That the terrain had been a challenge even for Deord. He knew she would take no heed of such arguments.

'He might not leave, even so,' Ana said slowly. 'He believes in his own guilt. He's afraid of what he might do. He lacks faith in himself.'

'But you don't.'

'I don't what?'

'Your faith in him is astonishing. Evidently you've decided he is innocent, for all his own doubts on the matter.'

There was a silence.

'He'd be here by now, wouldn't he?' Ana's voice was small. 'If he was coming, he'd be here.'

'Who knows? The decision was not ours but his. We left the way open.'

'And if he isn't here, it's because he didn't want to come with us.'

Faolan said nothing. He watched as tears began to fall, dripping from her pale cheeks to the blanket. He remembered Drustan's mouth against her hair and hardened his heart. 'I couldn't say. I hardly know the man. I do know that if I'd been in his situation, I'd have been out and away the moment I got the chance. I've no idea how Drustan's mind works. They say he's crazy. Maybe it's true. Maybe he prefers being locked up.'

'No,' Ana said, sniffing. 'He loves the sun. He loves the forest and the open air. Nobody could prefer a dark, damp place like that. Why hasn't he come?'

'Maybe he thought sending his creature was enough.'

She said nothing. Her eyes were desolate.

'Ana?'

She looked at him.

'How did this come about? You and him? Deord told me you met the two of them. But that was only once. How –?'

'There's a place. A place where you can whisper and hear each other. I used to talk to him. We found it by accident, Ludha and I. Ludha . . . Faolan, we have to go back! Alpin punished her. She's in danger and it's my fault!'

Faolan thought of Dovard lying senseless in the kennels, another innocent victim who would likely get a beating or worse for letting the prisoner escape. 'There's nothing we can do,' he said. 'They're all under Alpin's thumb. Try to intervene now and he'll just add you to his list of miscreants to be dealt with. I'm sorry.'

'But –'

'Use your wits, Ana. You can't go back. What we must do is wait for Deord, and then try to get home to Fortriu. Deord can help us; he's strong and capable. Once we're beyond Alpin's reach it should be easier to procure supplies. It's time to go home.' He thought of Bridei, who might by now be on his way to Dalriada; Bridei, who did not know that Alpin was already in league with the Gaels.

'On foot?' Ana asked. She took the crossbill on one hand and used the other, as a child would, to scrub the tears from her cheeks.

'Now you know why I insisted on the boots,' Faolan said. 'It'll be slower, but easier in a way; we can use tracks Alpin wouldn't think of.'

She said nothing. Perhaps she heard the truth behind his briskly confident words: that it was a long way over difficult terrain, and that the only path he knew was the one they could not take. That the man who could be of most help to them was the one he hoped would never come back.

'Ana?' He couldn't hold his stupid tongue; he had to ask her.

'What?'

'You and Drustan; what did . . . how is it . . . how did you . . . ?' Gods, he sounded like a stumbling youth of fifteen, half out of his wits over some village sweetheart. He wished he had never clapped eyes on her. She had made him care about her; she had made him feel again. She had left him exposed and wretched, weakened by the crack she had opened in his heart. She had woken his darkest memories and made him weep, and hate, and love. He wanted to be the old Faolan again, the one folk described as hard and heartless, a man incapable of emotion.

'Forget it,' he said. 'I'd better take a look outside. If anyone decided to come up, we wouldn't hear them over the water. Chances are Deord hasn't fooled the whole of Alpin's party; if they've split up, they won't have much trouble following our tracks. I don't suppose you still have that knife I gave you?'

Ana grimaced. 'It wasn't something I anticipated needing on my wedding day, Faolan.'

Despite all, he found himself smiling. 'I can think of a few good uses you might have put it to. There's another here, smaller. Take it. With luck there's nobody out there. But you need to be prepared.'

She eyed the little knife in its leather sheath, drawing it out to reveal an immaculately clean blade that looked lethally sharp.

'Deord's,' Faolan said. 'Now don't do anything stupid, I need your help with this.'

'Stupid,' she echoed. 'Such as slashing my wrists, you mean?' There was a silence; only the water gave voice. Then Ana said,

'You don't really know me very well, do you, Faolan? I honour life, even when it brings cruelty and sadness. Go on then. If you must look outside, look. And try not to get yourself killed. It seems as if you're the only friend I have left.'

It seemed to Broichan that he could feel a poison working its way through his body, devouring it as a canker does a rose or a worm an apple, from the inside out. It was a long time since an enemy had struck at him with a clever dose of toxic ingredients, a brew even the king's druid had not detected until the symptoms began: crushing headaches, a voiding of the bowels in watery flux, crippling pain in the joints. He had endured these privations without complaint, for he was strong in self-discipline. It was the fogging of the wits that was the hardest. In those first days after that long-ago attempt on his life, his mind had been unable to hold its concentration for more than a snatch at a time. No sooner had he grasped a thought, an idea, than it was gone. He'd struggled to remember even the learning that lay deep in his bones, hard won over the nineteen years of the novitiate: the druidic teaching, the tales, the prayers and ritual. Even tree lore had deserted him in that dark season when he'd fought the alien substances in his body and begged Bone Mother not to take him yet, not with Bridei's education scarcely begun and Fortriu's very future dependent on it. The goddess had heard him; she had spared him to return to Pitnochie and his small foster son. Bridei was a man now, with a son of his own. He was King of Fortriu. And Broichan knew Bone Mother had not revoked the sentence of death all those years ago, merely delayed it.

Death, of course, should not be feared, but awaited with a certain wonder. To die was to step across a threshold into a new world, unknown, unimaginable. There was a whole realm of learning to be had in the experience. This journey should be greeted with hope and anticipation, especially by a druid. Broichan remembered the old man, Erip, who had tutored Bridei in more worldly matters than those covered by the druid's own lessons. Erip had been ready to die; he had seemed to step through the doorway even before his last breath left his body. And Erip, though a scholar of some erudition, had been no druid. He had faced Bone Mother fearlessly; she had taken him with kindness. His had been a gentle passing.

Broichan could not see such an ending for himself. The pain that racked his body might perhaps be dulled by soporific draughts. The mist that rose to enshroud his mind, to deny his intellect its true exercise and to cripple his control of the craft of magic, that was the element truly to be feared. These symptoms were familiar to him. It seemed to him the poison administered long ago had not left his body but had lain dormant all these years, biding its time before it struck again. So he believed; he could not think of any other possible cause for his malady, and he was learned in the healing craft. He would take no draughts; he had ordered Fola sharply to stop trying to be helpful. He must keep the last spark alive. He must not lose what fettered powers remained to him. There was a child to be taught. And there was Bridei, far down the Glen now with no seer by his side to advise him.

That had been the hardest cut of all: to watch his foster son, the young king he had made, ride out to war and not to be there by his side, ready to protect him in ways the most able of body-guards could not. Who but the king's druid could cast an augury on the eve of battle to determine whether to advance or hold back? Who else could employ the tools of divination as they travelled, and pass down the wisdom of the gods? Without that guidance, the great victory over the forces of Dalriada depended entirely on the judgements of men, and those were unreliable even when the men were good, clever, courageous and steeped in lore, as Bridei undoubtedly was.

It was pride that had held Broichan back from summoning some other druid from the forest to take his place by Bridei's side: pride and a pathetic hope, for up until the day of the king's departure, he had prayed that he might be well again and strong enough to go with them. Because of that, Broichan had sent the man he loved like a son out to face the Gaels without proper safe-guards. He had undertaken to watch from afar, using the tools of divination. He had not told Bridei, or Fola, or anyone that even this now seemed to be beyond him.

He bolted the door of his chamber from the inside, lit a lamp from the candle he carried and went to the oak chest for his scrying mirror. It was a fine piece, a gift from his old teacher: a disc of polished obsidian bordered with creatures wrought in silver: owl, marten, frog, otter, dragonfly. A lovely thing. He planned to show it to Derelei soon and see what the child made of it. If the boy possessed Tuala's raw talent as a seer, he should soon begin to be guided in this art, so its development would be gradual and controlled. He was so young . . . *How long,* the druid thought, *just tell me how long I have, so I can plan for him. A year? Two? A season only?* It was unthinkable. Not to see Bridei achieve his great victory, not to see the true faith restored throughout Priteni lands, not to see his small charge grow and flourish and learn . . . How could he bear it? But bear it he must, if it was the gods' will. Obedience was at the core of Broichan's being. Obedience had seen him enact the Gateway sacrifice year after painful year until Bridei declared an end to that observance. Obedience kept him on his knees night after night, listening for the voices of the gods while cold and pain turned his body to a living hell. Obedience stopped him from seeking help . . . Perhaps not. He could hear Fola's crisp voice, saying something about pride, about arrogance, about thinking he knew best. To seek help was to discover, perhaps, that he was beyond help. This he feared above all.

Broichan unwrapped the mirror from its covering of soft woollen cloth and held it between his palms, not touching the polished surface. He slowed his breathing, willing it not to catch in his throat. The deepest breaths made his lungs burn like a blacksmith's fire; he made his body relax into the pain, let agony flow through him unheeded. He gazed at the dark obsidian with eyes unfocused – that, at least, was not difficult today – and let his mind drift. He banished, one by one, the thoughts and images that tangled and twisted in his head: Bridei; the battle to come; Derelei growing up at court without him, so vulnerable, so easily exploited. All the things he had not done, and now would not have time to do . . . He breathed them away into oblivion, out of the shadowy chamber where the lamplight was barely sufficient to cast a faint glow on the equipment of his craft, set out precisely on stone shelves: his herbs and remedies, his scrolls and inks, his oaken staff standing in a corner. And the more secret objects, those he could recall the child Bridei staring at in wonder the first time his foster father had let him enter the private chamber at Pitnochie. Part of Broichan wanted to pack it all up and go back there now. There, he could stop pretending and just let it happen. Mara would tend to him; his cook Ferat would try to tempt his failing appetite; Fidich and the others would accept the druid's presence calmly and continue to ensure the smooth running of household and farm. At Pitnochie he could die in his own place, amongst his own folk.

The lamp flickered, making Broichan blink. It was a reminder. Put Pitnochie out of his thoughts. Put all of it out . . . Float . . . Let the conscious mind go . . . Let vision blur . . . Forget the ever-present fear that today, yet again, his power in this would fail . . .

He sat there a long time. In upper corners of the chamber spiders spun webs, and in lower ones beetles fossicked. Within the walls mice went scurrying about their business. A vision came at last, not on the dark surface of the mirror itself but straight to his mind, a vision that was the clearest he had been granted for many moons. He had hoped to see Bridei or the other Priteni leaders, or the Gaels, or a pattern of events or objects that might be construed in a way that was useful. What came was unexpected.

A man was running through dense forest. He made good speed, remarkable speed for one of such stocky build. The runner was broad of shoulder, deep of chest and bald as an egg. There was a pack of hunting hounds on his trail, and following them a group of horsemen armed with bows and spears and knives. They were uniformly big men, with heads of shaggy hair and beards to match; they wore fur cloaks and their broad faces bore intricate tattooing. Warriors of the Caitt. The fugitive was marked with battle counts on one cheek, done in the same mode as the others. He was one of their own. He bore knives at his belt but no other weapons. His features showed nothing of the terror of the hunted: he appeared calm and controlled. Broichan could tell he was regulating his breathing, husbanding his strength for the confrontation to come. Someone had given this man remarkable training.

The vision changed and changed again. Always the runner:

374

now balancing on a log across a deep gorge, now hurtling down a steep, rocky slope at a pace that put limbs in danger of snapping and brought a shower of stones after him. He did not seem over-cautious about making noise; it was almost as if he wanted to draw the pursuit after him.

Dogs and horsemen closed on him; their leader found another way around the gorge and a path that bypassed the steep incline. The hounds sighted the runner and gave voice. The leader raised a horn to his lips. In this man's eyes Broichan read a thirst for blood and, although he could not hear, the druid's mind could guess what this chieftain was shouting to his men. 'Hold back the dogs! He's mine!'

They cornered the bald-headed man against a rock wall; he had seized a fallen branch and was sweeping it before him at waist height, this way, that way, in a savage arc. The dogs could not get near him, and their keepers went in at the chieftain's command to fix ropes to the baying hounds' collars and drag them, slavering, away. The warriors made a loose semicircle around the trapped man, keeping their distance from that swinging branch. The man's arms were corded with muscle; Broichan recognised the phenomenal strength required to hold a thick length of damp timber at that height and control it thus. He watched as the leader gave another command and four of his company set arrows to bowstrings.

The druid opened himself to the voices in his vision. There was no sound in the quiet chamber where he sat with his mirror, for this was an image in his mind only, conjured by his readiness for what the gods offered him at this particular moment. The mirror he used as a tool to detach the mind from the myriad thoughts that crowded it, to clear it of distractions, the better to make room for the visions he might be granted. To hear as well as see required a deeper level of concentration; slowing his breathing further, Broichan found it.

'Where is she?' demanded the leader of the hunting party, his voice harsh with fury. 'Where have you taken her?'

It was clear the cornered man had no intention of replying. He simply continued to fend off the attackers with his branch, while keeping an eye on the archers.

'Hold off!' the leader barked at his men, and the bows were lowered slightly. 'I need his answers first, then you can have your sport. Put that thing down, scum, and speak to me! Where's Ana? Where's the wretched Gael, and where's my brother? By all the gods, how could you set Drustan free? Haven't I provided you with food and shelter and a steady supply of silver pieces these seven years past? I trusted you, and you let that murderer out!'

The branch continued its steady sweeping motion; it was the only thing separating the fugitive from his attackers. He spoke now, levelly, as if he had not just run the race of his life. 'I'm ready to fight. Set your men against me one by one, or two by two. If you want to make an end of me, let it be in fair combat. Would you hunt a man down like vermin?'

'Vermin is what you are, and it's I who will choose the manner of your death. Answer my questions and you can have your fight. It'd need to be three at a time, I think; the men know your reputation. Fail to answer and your end will be slower. And it will hurt more. Now tell me! Where's Ana? Where's her godforsaken turncoat bard? And where's my brother, you treacherous apology for a servant? Where's he flown off to?'

When there was no response, the leader gave a nod to his archers. A red-fletched arrow left the bow, whirring across to skim the trapped man's shoulder, for he had ducked just in time. Another nod; a second missile, this one more skilfully aimed in anticipation of a move. It took the quarry in the left arm, lodging deep in the well-developed muscle. The fugitive grunted; he could not reach to draw out the shaft without putting down his makeshift weapon.

'Where are they? Where have you hidden them? Speak up, my patience is running short.'

'Somewhere in the forest,' the fugitive said calmly. 'If you search for long enough, you may find them. Or they may slip from your grasp, Alpin. I care nothing for any of them. Weakling bards, golden-haired ladies, what are they to do with the likes of me? As for your brother, he's served his penance, poor wretch. I doubt you'll ever see him again.'

'You're lying. You helped them escape. We found your cunning little tunnel and your clever concealment. You helped the Gael get away; you helped him steal my wife. He wants her for himself, I saw it in his eyes from the first. He's probably out there having her right now, and Drustan's standing by waiting for the leftovers. When I find the bard I intend to take him apart. Limb by limb. Out with it, Deord! Tell me where they are and I'll let you die like a fighting man and not like a rat in a hole.'

The man called Deord looked at the other, eyes untroubled. The branch he held ceased to sweep before him; he lowered its outer end slowly to the forest floor. 'Whatever I do between this moment and the moment of my death,' he said as blood from the arrow wound spread a slow stain across the sleeve of his shirt, 'I won't betray a trust. Don't think you can prevail by threatening me, Alpin. I've seen your tactics too many times. Your brother's gone. He's free. As for the others, they are none of my concern.' As the leader drew a long knife from his belt and took a step forward, Deord added, 'I've often thought the quality of a man can be judged by how well he dies. I intend to make my end a measure of what I am, as a man.'

'A man does not scream and whimper and plead for release,' Alpin said. 'Believe me, before I'm finished with you, you'll be doing all three and soiling yourself to boot.'

Deord did not reply but, as Alpin drew closer, he turned in a sudden whirl of movement, his right leg coming high behind him in a powerful kick that sent one man sprawling at full length on the ground, while a punishing blow from the undamaged right arm caught another in the chest, winding him. Alpin, who had stepped back out of reach, clicked his fingers. Arrows whirred and thumped, and Deord, rising from his turn, received them in shoulder and thigh, each quivering shaft lodged deep. He staggered, then steadied. A knife appeared in each hand.

'Tell me the truth!' Alpin snarled. 'Tell me now or pay the price! Where have you taken my wife?'

Deord gave no sign of having heard him. His stance, legs apart, knees slightly bent in readiness for whatever move was required, was that of a seasoned fighter; the barbs that he carried in his body seemed no more than a minor inconvenience. His eyes remained calm. Around him the semicircle of hunters drew tighter, but there was a certain margin beyond which none of them would advance, not even their leader. To Broichan, watching with the eyes of a practised seer, it seemed the hand of the Flamekeeper himself stretched out over this lone fighter, imbuing him with a kind of purity that stripped away all trace of fear and made him an instrument of deadly force. What man, so outnumbered, could face his enemy with such fearless equanimity, save one favoured by the god himself? The Flamekeeper honoured courageous deeds; he loved the fire that burned in the hearts of his dauntless sons. Perhaps he had marked this one for a place at his right hand. The scene in Broichan's mind could not be destined to end in triumph for this fighter, not against such odds. The druid found that he was holding his breath, willing into being what could not happen. He made himself relax and pace his breathing once more, for if he lost control thus, he risked losing the vision entirely. It had been sent for a purpose. He must watch to the end, the bloody, inevitable end, and then hope he could make some sense of it.

Alpin called back those who held the dogs straining on their ropes; he ordered those who bore spears to move up. The archers set new arrows to their strings, one, two, three and four. Deord stood poised, fresh blood staining his clothing at shoulder, arm and thigh.

'Last chance,' Alpin called over the anticipatory voices of the hounds. 'Give me what I need and I'll give you the end a fighting man wants. Just tell me which direction, which track. They've found a bolthole somewhere, no doubt; the lady's hardly up to running far in this terrain. Say it and your death need not be protracted and painful. It need not be a thing of shame. North? East? Which way did they go?'

'Bring on your dogs,' said Deord. 'Bring on your spears. I'm ready for them.'

Broichan found himself praying the end would be quick. It mattered little that the visions precipitated by the scrying mirror could show matters past, present or future, or merely a symbolic representation of some inner truth. The immediacy of this was compelling. He sat immobile, willing the gods to deliver this warrior a swift and merciful ending.

It was not to be. The odds were impossible; the man must

know it. Nonetheless, he made of his last battle a thing of beauty, a poem of control and grace, his body moving faultlessly to his command in block and thrust and turn, in the calculated deployment of damaged limb and whole one to best advantage. It was like a great shout of courage; a celebration of what it was to be a man. It made Broichan's heart stand still.

In the end, of course, Deord could not prevail against so many. Failing to wear him down by their assaults with sword, spear and knife, and seeing both dogs and men strewn in a torn and bloody circle around the furious, almost magical figure of the lone warrior, Alpin's men took to arrows again, spiking their quarry so full of shafts that at last he began to slow, to stagger, weakened by the loss of blood. No missile had taken him in the heart, or in the eye; none on its own had delivered a death blow. Deord wore leather beneath his shirt, and he was expert at fluid dodging and ducking, even trapped as he was.

It was a long time; too long. Broichan observed the paling of the fighter's face; Deord was grey-white now, his body running with sweat, and his hands could barely grip his weapons. He saw the three wounds become seven, ten, twelve; he watched the blood run until the fellow's clothing was all over scarlet. He saw Deord, at last, drop to one knee, wheezing; he saw the look in the warrior's eyes, calm, eerily calm, and recognised in that sublime control something of the skill he himself had striven to achieve back in the first years of his druidic training. Such discipline. Such a marvel. The god must soon summon this favourite son to his side, must reward such perfect self-possession with highest honour in the place beyond death. It was as if the man would be burned away by the flame of his own impossible courage.

At the end, Broichan could hardly bear to look, for the vision was both beautiful and harrowing beyond belief. Deord was down. He was spent, but he lived; the light of a fierce will shone in the tranquil eyes. Any of them could have taken him then but, oddly, the hunters stood back, apparently each hesitant to be responsible for the final, fatal blow. It was their leader, the chieftain named Alpin, who approached the fallen man after a period in which Broichan sensed an uneasy silence broken only by the faint, uneven rasp of Deord's breathing. Then, overhead, birds began a conversation, an exchange of chirrups and whistles, and beside the fallen man Alpin took out a small, narrow-bladed knife.

'I said you would beg before the end.' His tone was cold. 'The end is not yet come. What part of your flesh is yet untouched? I need a memento: a trifle to take home with me, just in case anyone else in my household decides disobedience is in order. Goban, Mordec, get him upright. Come on, he can't hurt you now, he's done for. Erdig, Lutrin, see to our dead; put them on the horses and prepare for departure.' Two burly men-at-arms seized Deord on either side and heaved him to his feet. He made a valiant effort to shake them off, but they held firm, their hands and arms soon slick and dark with the wounded man's blood.

'No answers, then.' Alpin spoke quietly, his eyes on Deord's. 'You're not just a traitor, you're a fool. Some of my brother's malady must have rubbed off on you. Well, no matter. I've lost my appetite for this. I'll just make a little cut *here*,' his hands were at Deord's groin, and Broichan winced, 'and *here*, and take myself a small trophy, and we'll be on our way. Thanks to you, a dangerous madman is at liberty in these woods. Thanks to you, a spy has slipped through my fingers. Thanks to you, I'll be spending my wedding night alone. But tomorrow,' he raised his gruesome prize before Deord's blanched face, 'tomorrow I'll hunt them down. Tomorrow the Gael will swing before my fortress gates. Tomorrow I'll get a son on the wife who betrayed me with my own brother. And tomorrow, when I find that killer Drustan, I'll punish him as I should have done seven years ago: with death.'

Deord had endured the mutilation without a sound. His features were those of a skull, shadow and bone. Broichan heard his hoarse whisper. 'You'll never find him. He will outpace you, outfly you, outwit you. My only regret is that he did not seize his chance sooner.'

'Wretch!' Alpin's fist came up, striking the other a jarring blow on the jaw. Deord's head snapped sideways. 'What must I do before your arrogant tongue begs for a merciful end? What?' He delivered a matching blow to the other side; blood trickled down Deord's chin, red on white.

'Merciful?' the warrior breathed, eyes steady on Alpin's. 'You

don't know . . . meaning of . . . mercy. As alien to you as . . . love
. . . duty . . . courage . . .'

Alpin's knee came up, catching the captive between the legs,
where blood already flowed from his crude surgery. Deord could
not hold back a sudden, anguished exhalation of breath.

'Beg!' Alpin shouted. 'Grovel, you wretch! You are flesh and
blood like the rest of us!' Another blow, this time with a boot.
Deord bit back a cry. 'Scream!' Alpin commanded. 'Go on, let it
out! Does this hurt? And this? And this?'

With every fibre of his being, Broichan willed the gods' intervention; with every scrap of breath he urged Bone Mother to step
forward, to fold the warrior in her dark cloak of sweet oblivion
and draw his spirit away. The druid prayed for the Flamekeeper
to call, *It is time. Bring my son home to me.*

The blows continued to fall, but there was no further sound
from Deord, and after a little, Alpin seemed to tire of this pastime
and drew back, his clothing spattered with blood. One of the other
men spoke, perhaps asking if he should administer the final, the
most merciful blow. But Alpin was mounting his horse; around
him, those of his warriors who had survived this uneven combat
had already loaded the bodies of their fallen comrades across
their saddles and were ready for a sombre departure.

The two men who had been propping Deord upright let him
go. He collapsed to the ground where he lay curled up on his side,
a still heap of bloody rags. Broichan let out his breath; the gods, at
last, had seen fit to take pity. At a word from their leader, the
horsemen touched heels to their mounts and were gone through
the forest. The sun was low over the crowns of dark pine and
silver-barked birch; birds sang high fluting songs as they flew in
to rest in the branches.

Broichan knew the vision was close to its natural end. He
could feel it in his fingers and toes, in his back and neck, in the
gradual return of his body to the clay form of everyday. He could
not hold this much longer. As the images began to blur and
darken in his mind, he saw movement where he had thought life
extinct. The fallen man's hand, reaching out, clawed into the dark
litter of the forest floor. Deord's eyes stared, half blinded by pain, up
beyond the canopy of green to the open sky. He rolled, struggling

across the ground until he could prop himself, half sitting, against a knot of roots that formed a low arch. He sprawled there like a discarded doll. His blood oozed and seeped and flowed from myriad wounds. The earth received it silently. The birds continued their song, an anthem to life, to beauty, to freedom, and Deord, dying, listened with eyes bright with pain, yet steady and calm. As the vision clouded and vanished, it came to Broichan that the warrior was waiting, but for what, he did not know. Maybe even this bravest of souls did not want to die alone.

Chapter Fourteen

The poppy draught had hit Ana hard. As the day wore on she drifted over and over into uneasy slumber, her head awkwardly pillowed on the damp pack, to wake each time with a start, eyes full of confusion. At each new dawning of consciousness she seemed less willing to talk. Faolan watched over her, a growing tension gnawing at his belly. Deord had not returned. Faolan did not want the death of a Breakstone survivor on his conscience; it had more than enough to carry already. The urge to go off searching was stronger with every passing moment as, outside their hiding place, the sun moved westward and somewhere a brave man put his life on the line for the sake of a pair of virtual strangers. Never mind that for Faolan to go after him was the last thing Deord would want. Faolan knew that if he did not act he would regret it to the end of his days.

'If you want to go, just go,' Ana said with uncharacteristic crossness after he had gone outside and come back in for the twentieth time. She was lying prone, forearm up to shield her eyes, as if even the filtered light in the cavern hurt them.

'I can't,' he said flatly. 'Go back to sleep. You'll need all your strength in the morning.'

There was a short silence.

'I'm being a nuisance, aren't I?' Her tone had changed. 'I'm holding you back.'

Faolan could not bring himself to contradict her, although their current predicament was hardly her fault.

'Just go, Faolan, for pity's sake. You're making me feel even worse.'

'My job is keeping you safe. Of course I can't go.' He was wound tight as a harp string, every part of him on edge; his imagination was full of blood and death. Deord wasn't coming back. He knew it. He wasn't coming back unless someone went out searching and found him quickly, before Alpin made an end of him. Faolan tried to be still, to focus his attention on keeping Ana comfortable. Before long he got up again, compelled to check outside one more time.

The spray from the waterfall made it hard to get a clear view, but he did his best to scan hillsides, forest, lochan, searching for the least sign of anything unusual. There was only the green of the pines, the pale sheet of water, the bare, daunting peaks that rose to north and east. He judged from the sun's position that the day was well advanced; if Alpin was still out hunting, he'd need to call it off soon to get his men home by dusk. There was enough time left for a rescue, but only just. And he couldn't go. How could he leave Ana on her own?

A sudden harsh sound above and behind him made Faolan start. His foot slipped on the rock ledge and he grasped at a clinging creeper, his heart thudding. Another *craaa* and he saw the hooded crow perched on the slender branch of a tiny, stunted willow that had lodged its roots in an improbably small pocket of soil. The little tree's slender leaves were silver with moisture. Above the hoodie, on a ledge, perched a larger bird, tawny gold-brown, its eye bright, its curved beak formidable. Its gaze was fixed on Faolan.

'At last,' he muttered, relief surging through him for all his reservations. 'Where in the name of all that's holy have you been? Well, no matter. Ana's there, in the cave . . . Gods, I'd better be right about you and not be talking to some wild bird that's decided to pay us a visit in passing. I need to get to Deord. You must guard her; keep her safe.'

The hawk did not move. Its steady stare was disconcerting.

'I haven't told her,' Faolan added. 'About you, I mean. Somehow she'll need to be persuaded that this is acceptable; that birds are an adequate safeguard. That's unless you plan to favour her with the truth.'

No response, but when Faolan ducked his head and went back into the little cavern, both hawk and hoodie flew in after him, coming to rest on either side, where the contours of the rock allowed precarious perches. The crossbill was already in Ana's hands; even when sleeping she had held the creature cupped safely between her palms.

'Ana,' Faolan said, squatting down beside her, 'I'm going now. There are three birds here, see? You should be safe. I need to find Deord.'

She looked perplexed. 'Three . . . but . . .'

'Crossbill, crow, hawk,' Faolan told her, watching as her eyes went to the largest of the birds and widened. 'They all seem to be Drustan's creatures. What wild bird's going to come in here with us of its free will? That thing has a lethal beak and a good set of talons. He can defend you if need be.' He hoped it was true. 'Stay in the cave and wait for me. I'll be back before dark. Don't go too near the edge.' He looked at her more closely. 'I'm sorry,' he said. 'Truly sorry.'

'Go.'

Her voice was drowned by the falling water. He remembered Breaking Ford, where she must have believed she was all alone with the rushing river, alone in a world turned to madness.

'Go, Faolan,' she said. 'Find him while there's still time.'

In the event, Faolan continued to follow the trail until far past the time when he needed to turn back to complete his journey by daylight. At last he found Deord in a small clearing, lying sprawled at the foot of a venerable oak. He seemed already dead. Blood had soaked his clothing and spilled to stain the earth in a wide circle around him. His limbs were slack against a tangle of roots. Moving closer, dropping to his knees beside the limp figure, Faolan heard the faint, rasping sound of Deord's shallow breathing and saw, between the slits of his eyelids, the familiar stare of his calm eyes.

'. . . you . . . here?' Deord whispered. 'Away . . . should . . . away.' Then, 'No . . .' as Faolan made to move him to a better position, '. . . no point . . .'

Faolan cursed under his breath, running his eye expertly over what he could see of the fallen man's wounds through the wreckage of his shredded clothing. Deord had taken many blows. An arrow, its shaft roughly broken off, was lodged deep in his arm; others lay snapped on the ground by his legs. There was evidence of a monumental struggle: bushes crushed, undergrowth trampled, the soil gouged out by the movement of booted feet and horses' hooves. A spear lay in two pieces; a broken sword had been cast aside into the bushes. In the undergrowth Faolan spotted the inert forms of several hounds.

He reached for the water flask he carried; put an arm around Deord's shoulders and lifted him slightly. Deord's skin was clammy; he smelled of blood and sweat. His breath caught in his throat as Faolan touched him.

'Drink,' Faolan said, 'just a sip. Good,' though nothing had gone down; Deord was beyond swallowing. 'Now, where's your pack?' He found it, pulled out some kind of garment, spread it over Deord's chest and shoulders.

'. . . lady . . . ?' Deord asked. His voice was a wisp of sound.

'Drustan's with her. I came as soon as he arrived. Gods, man, you surely led them a chase.' Faolan kept his tone light; no point in burdening Deord with his own bitter regret. It was starkly clear that he had arrived too late.

'Drustan . . . good. Faolan . . . ?'

'What is it?'

'Drustan . . . could be . . . something. Get him away . . . away safe . . .'

'After today,' Faolan said, 'my sword has Alpin's name on it. First I complete this mission, then I turn from hunted to hunter. That scum can't be allowed to live.'

'Drustan . . . important, Faolan . . . look after him . . . and her . . .'

Faolan could not suppress a scowl.

'Your word now . . .'

'All right, I promise; I'll get the two of them out if it kills me. A pox on the gods of Fortriu, they're cruel and unjust. A Breakstone man should be given the chance to make something of his freedom. You deserve more time than this. Why did you do it?'

Deord was shivering convulsively now; the smile he attempted was a rictus of death. 'Did . . . make something . . . good . . . ending . . .'

'For us. For strangers.'

'You . . . now . . . you go on . . . make good . . . self . . .'

'Me? I threw away my chances of achieving anything long before I entered Breakstone. I'm the one who should have acted as decoy.'

'Nonsense . . . Faolan . . . ?'

'Tell me what you want.'

'Message . . . home . . .'

'Where is home?'

'Tell . . . family . . .'

'Where, Deord?'

'Cloud . . . Hill . . . near place of kings . . .'

'In Laigin?' A chill ran through Faolan; what was he promising? 'But –?'

'Sister . . . wed one of your kind . . . Tell her first . . .'

'She wed a Gael?'

'Tell them . . . sorry . . . Say . . . ended it . . . well . . .'

Faolan nodded. His throat was tight; it was hard to speak.

'Faolan . . .'

'What, Deord?'

The bald head was lying against Faolan's shoulder now; one hand came up to touch his sleeve. 'Sing,' Deord whispered. 'You . . . sing . . .'

So Faolan sang. He sang as the sun went slowly down behind the trees and the light in the clearing faded from rose to violet to the dusky pale grey of the summer night. He sang and a multitude of birds sang with him, bidding their own farewells to the day on which this warrior had fought his last and bravest battle. He sang a stirring tale of war whose words were all of the fine deeds of men, their courage and nobility, their selfless sacrifices for the greater good. Deord lay against him, heavy and limp, a small twitching of the fingers now and then, as a spasm of pain passed through him, the only sign that he still clung to life. That, and the eyes; closed to mere slits, they were on Faolan's face as he made his music with tears streaming unabated down his cheeks; tears that were not solely for the waste of a fine man, but for all the inmates of Breakstone, those who had been destroyed there one way or another and those who had survived to make their damaged paths in the world. And because he, too, was a Breakstone man, some of his tears were for himself.

Towards the end Deord's breathing began to catch more frequently, as if blood were welling in his lungs, in his windpipe; and pain made his body tense and shudder. Faolan held the big man as if he were a child, with firm, gentle hands. Since there wasn't much else he could do, he kept on singing. Another man than Deord, at such an extreme, might have begged his comrades for a sharp knife and oblivion. Deord endured, teeth clenched, fists balled, silent save for the laboured breath.

From somewhere deep in his memory, Faolan found the remnants of a lullaby. Its sweet, simple melody set a quiet on the clearing that stilled even the birdsong as night fell and Bone Mother held out her arms to bring her lone warrior home at last.

Sleep, my child, so brave and bright
Fair dreams wrap you all the night.

A solitary owl hooted deep in the woods. Deord moved his head a little, settling against Faolan's arm.

Night birds sing your lullaby
Beneath the blanket of the sky.

Deord's white-knuckled fists relaxed; his breathing slowed. Somewhere beyond the oaks, the pale light of the rising moon set silver on the edge of the sky.

Danu take you by the hand
Lead you to the shadowland.
Rest tired limbs and weary eyes
And to a bright new day arise.

Faolan's voice cracked. He looked down; Deord was smiling. A moment later the calm eyes grew fixed, the features slackened, and he was gone.

For a little, Faolan continued to hold him and to sing. Then, for a long time, he sat in silence. It seemed fitting that a kind of vigil be kept here: who else was there to acknowledge this man's heroic passing but himself, the turncoat spy who slit throats for a living? Later, when the moon had risen higher, he did what he could to prepare Deord for burial, wiping his face, straightening the wreckage of his garments, taking appalled inventory of the damage Alpin's hunting party had inflicted. Then he dug out a shallow grave, using the broken sword for a shovel. He laid the warrior down with arms crossed on chest, his knives by his side, and covered him with his own short cloak. He did not say prayers, for Faolan set no credence in gods, nor did he know which Deord himself had honoured. If Breakstone did not convince a man that deities either did not exist or did not care, it tended to do the opposite: made a prisoner believe in them to a degree bordering on obsession. Men died in there still scream-ing for divine intervention; Faolan had heard them. Deord, he suspected, was the former type of man, a man not dissimilar to himself, though he would never have done what Deord had done today. He'd be prepared to die for Bridei. He would put his life on the line for Ana. But he would never sacrifice himself for strangers. And that was odd. Not so long ago, he had considered his life of no worth at all. He had gone on with it simply because it seemed weak to take the other alternative. Something had changed. Perhaps it had been changing for a while. They had all played a part in it: Bridei, Ana, Deord. And now Faolan had more missions to fulfil than he had ever wanted. Keep wretched Drustan safe; get Ana home; make an end of Alpin. Report to Bridei, or to his representative at White Hill. Go back to Laigin and tell a woman her brother had been hacked to death so that a pair of strangers could live and be free.

In the midnight shadows of Briar Wood he blanketed Deord's still form with earth then searched for stones by moonlight and laid them in a rough cairn to keep scavengers from the body. He stood guard over the makeshift grave, waiting for first light so he could begin the long walk back to the waterfall; to Ana, whom he had entrusted, all night, to the mercurial Drustan. In the long, long time from deep of night to first whisper of dawn, Faolan thought of loyalty and honour; of choices made and chances taken; of blood and betrayal. With sheer terror in his heart, he thought of home.

Fola had returned to the house of the wise women at Banmerren. Bridei was far beyond reach. Uist no longer wandered in the same world as his old friends, but had gone on before them to the place beyond the margins. Aniel, astute as he was in matters strategic, had no grasp of the stuff of visions and portents. There was nobody Broichan could talk to. There was nobody he could tell. The urge to share what he had seen was great. Indeed, it was his duty to do so, if those images of a man enduring an unspeakable death with god-given courage might prove in any way helpful to the future endeavours of Fortriu's king and his army. But he could not tell; not until the interpretation became clear to him. It boded poorly for the alliance with Alpin of Briar Wood. It seemed disastrous for the royal hostage, and perhaps also for Bridei's right-hand man. But Broichan knew well enough the deceptive nature of such visions, their skewing of time and place, their jumble of the real and the symbolic.

Curse this illness! His head was fogged with uncertainty and his limbs ached from so long keeping still, holding the vision. Once, he had been able to kneel through the night, arms outstretched in pose of meditation, and arise at dawn with not a trace of cramp. Once . . . that was before the malady began to overtake him again. The Shining One aid him, he felt like an old man in his dotage, weak and sore and confused. It was not to be endured. Had this vision been sent solely to tell him he must accept death gladly? That he must face it without regret, as that lone warrior had seemed to do?

Suddenly desperate to fill his lungs with fresh air, Broichan unbolted his door and walked out into the garden. It was a shock to find the sun shining, to see its light touching the orderly rows of vegetables, herbs and medicinal flowers with warm benevolence.

On the patch of grass beside the lavender bed, Derelei sat playing with his little stone horse, his infant features solemn with concentration. Opposite him sat his mother, cross-legged and straight-backed, watching the child with eyes as big and mysterious as an owl's. She might have been a sister to Derelei, Broichan thought, so young did she look and so slight. A frisson passed through him, a fleeting, unwelcome chill that was part memory, part foreboding. What Fola had said about the child was nonsense; nobody with any intelligence could credit such a notion. Derelei's parentage was evident in his curling brown hair and candid blue eyes – Bridei's, both – and, a more mixed blessing, the pallor and the unusual talents he had inherited from his mother. And if it were Bridei's own parentage that was in question, that, too, was beyond dispute. Anyone who had known Maelchon of Gwynedd would read his imprint in Bridei's strong-boned features and upright stance, and see something of Maelchon's powerful presence in his son's mastery of men. The king of Gwynedd had been a born leader; Bridei was that and more. Besides, Anfreda was not the kind of woman to betray her husband. All the same . . . all the same, there was a deep unease in Broichan's mind as he walked towards Tuala and her son and saw both faces alter as they turned towards him. Tuala's features became wary, guarded; Derelei held up his arms, beaming.

'May I join you?' Broichan settled on the grass, dark robe spread around him. Then, following a sudden unlikely impulse, 'Tuala, I've a favour to ask you.'

'Me?' she queried, clearly taken aback. 'Of course, if I can help.'

Without stopping to think too hard, he gave her an account of what the gods had shown him. She sat quietly, grave eyes fixed on him as he spoke of the running man, the hunt, the impossible last stand. Derelei was making the little horse jump over his outstretched arm.

Tuala did not speak until the tale was finished, the warrior sprawled, dying, alone in the forest. Then she said, 'A grim vision indeed; it is no wonder you look so pale. I had thought you ill. This is deeply disturbing. Alpin, you said? And he spoke of Ana. This cruel hunter who mutilates dying men is the chieftain we sent her away to marry. Can it be a vision of the present, do you think? Or is it perhaps what might be if we do not take steps to forestall it?'

'I would welcome your own interpretation.'

'I . . . if you wish.' The reason for Tuala's hesitation was plain; in all the years since she had been placed in his household as a newborn babe, Broichan had never once asked for her opinion on such a matter, although he knew well what talents she possessed. 'Of course,' she said, 'I did not see these images myself. That means I must interpret at second-hand, through your eyes. Had I been by your side, using the same scrying tool, my eyes would perhaps have given me the same vision, but in the way the gods intended me to see it. That would be more useful.'

'Tell me anyway.' Broichan clicked his fingers; the stone horse turned its head towards him.

Still Tuala hesitated.

'What is it?' he asked.

'I must say this, even if I offend you. If I speak, you would not . . . you would not use it against me? There are folk here at court, and beyond, who would grasp at any means available to undermine Bridei's power, especially now, while he is away. I need to be careful, Broichan.'

'I ask this only for myself, Tuala.'

'Fola would do it better.'

'You are here and Fola is not.'

She cleared her throat nervously. Could it be that, grown woman and queen as she was, she was still afraid of him? Derelei had moved over to Broichan's side now and the little horse had followed, lifting its stone hooves in orderly sequence.

'It sounded very – immediate,' Tuala said. 'The forest, the light, that seemed akin to the place where Ana was going and to the current season. I don't know who this warrior was. Perhaps he is not a real person, more of an embodiment of the ideal of manly courage. After all, the Priteni ride to war this summer. The gods may be telling us many must fall before we gain our victory. But . . . you heard this chieftain, Alpin, speak of Ana; that she had run away or been abducted . . . That she had betrayed him with his own brother . . . That cannot be true. I know Ana. She holds duty and propriety above all things. She is the last person to act so impulsively and in such disregard of the conventions of society. Alpin mentioned a Gael. That could be Faolan, though surely the escort would be well on the way home by now . . .'

'He said the Gael was a bard,' Broichan mused.

'So, not Faolan then. If this was a true image of present or near-present, something has gone terribly awry for Ana. I fear for her; for all of them. And . . . if the marriage has not taken place, that could mean Bridei's treaty has not been signed. That Alpin of Briar Wood never agreed to it. That is dangerous news for Bridei.'

'You do not see the vision as purely symbolic then?' Broichan felt the tension in his own body, and made himself breathe more slowly. 'A message about, say, the nature of death and dying?'

There was a long silence while Tuala's wide, strange eyes regarded him solemnly. 'Why would the Shining One send you such a message?' she asked eventually.

The answer came out against his better judgement. 'To instruct me that I should accept what is in store for me,' he said. 'That I should not continue to beg her for more time. Pain, I can endure; I've taught myself how to disregard it. But this is too soon. I've so much more to do . . .' Derelei had climbed onto Broichan's lap and was playing with the long braids of the druid's hair, twisting and knotting them together. Broichan curved his arm around the child's slight form and looked across at Tuala. What he saw on her face was not shock or sorrow, nor even the satisfaction of observing an old enemy weakened. Instead, her fey eyes now blazed with determination and her delicate jaw was set as firmly as any warrior's.

'It is a vision of true things,' she told him, 'and most probably taking place now, which is bad news for the fallen warrior, but better news for you. The Shining One entrusted you with Bridei's upbringing and, in a sense, with mine. The goddess considers you a favoured son and a conduit for her wisdom. You should not forget that, as a druid, you are the servant of the gods. And since we are speaking of trust, I have entrusted you with my most precious treasure: my son. You owe it to the gods and to me to survive until you have taught Derelei those things he needs to know. Without that learning, his path in life will be perilous indeed. It was very hard for me to give you that trust. You need to play your part in the bargain.'

She had surprised him; she was tougher than he had believed. It could have been Fola speaking. 'Unfortunately,' he said as Derelei's arms came up around his neck and the child snuggled his head against his shoulder, 'I cannot hold back the effects of a poison that was administered to me years ago, and which has damaged me. It works in me now; my days are indeed numbered.'

'What help have you sought for this malady?' Tuala asked. 'I know you are sick and in pain. It has become ever clearer to me as the season has progressed. You wanted to go with Bridei, I could see that. I tried to ensure he did not know the truth, since that would have weighed heavily on him during the campaign. He would have liked you to go.'

Broichan held the child close and did not speak.

'Has Fola offered help? Or the druids of the forest?'

He did not answer.

'Very well. You asked me for help, and I will help. But you must accept that, in this case, you may not be your own best physician.'

'I asked for help in the interpretation of a vision. Not for this.'

'You are the king's druid. Why would you need me to explain the messages of the scrying bowl to you?' Her tone was gentle; he heard in it that she already knew the answer. Suddenly it became possible to speak truly, and it all came flooding out: the headaches, the temporary blindness, the gradual dulling of his powers so that even the simplest tasks of the craft often seemed beyond him. The terror that, all too soon, he would lose his gift entirely.

Tuala listened quietly; he realised how good she was at that. There was no judgement in her eyes. When he was quite finished, she drew a long breath and said, 'How frightening for you. You must have felt so alone.'

'I'm accustomed to being alone.'

'All the same. Now, will you let us help you?'

'Us? I don't want this to become public knowledge, Tuala. That can only alert Bridei's enemies to a weakness in his court. It must be believed that I am still capable of exercising my full role here.'

'Only those you trust need know. Fola, certainly, and her expert healers. Aniel, perhaps, since he can cover for any absences. And me. I know you've never trusted me, but you've told me now, and Bridei would want me to help you.'

He scrutinised her small, heart-shaped face with its snow-white skin and large, lustrous eyes. 'You offer this on Bridei's behalf?'

'And on my own,' she said. 'You saved Derelei's life. He needs you. We all need you, Broichan. If we put up the best fight we can, all together, maybe this malady can be defeated. Today's vision is a good sign, surely. Your account of it was lucid and detailed.'

'It is a long time since such images last visited me; longer still since the interpretation sprang to my mind promptly and truly. I'm the most skilled healer in all the lands of the Priteni, Tuala. If I haven't been able to hold back the course of this illness, who can?'

'I don't know,' she said. 'Perhaps what you need lies beyond the efforts of one man, whether he be king's druid or no. I just know you are worth saving, and that if we can, we will do it. Maybe the vision was telling us simply that: be strong, be brave, be the best you can be. And not to give up hope, even in the darkest moment.'

His heart was beating fast; he felt as if he had leaped from a high cliff and landed, to his astonishment, in safe hands. He could feel the blood coursing in his veins; beyond the sward where they sat, druid, young woman and child, the flowers of White Hill's garden bloomed in colours that seemed, all of a sudden, brighter and more real than any he had seen before.

'All the same,' Tuala added soberly, 'we should send a message to Bridei. He needs to be warned that all is not well in the north.'

'You think of everything.'

'Not quite,' she said. 'As the king's wife, I am still learning. Now, I'm going to send for Fola. Or, better still, I think we'll go to Banmerren and pay her a visit.'

Ana had been wreathed in a wonderful dream, a dream in which she had lain in Drustan's arms, his body warming hers, his hands moving on her skin with a passion and tenderness that awoke sensations of surprise and delight, soon followed by an urgent, throbbing desire. The aching unfulfilment of this remained with her now as she awoke at first light in the little cave with its curtain of rushing water. The power of her physical feelings astonished her. Surely, if the body teetered thus on the brink of release, something of it must show on one's face, in the eyes or in the flushed cheeks. Thank the gods Faolan was not here to read her thoughts. There were only the three birds on the rock ledges of the cave, the crossbill preening its scarlet feathers, the hoodie using its beak to probe some small creature out of a crevice, and the other one, the one that was some kind of hawk, though unlike any species Ana had seen before, simply fixing her with a bright, unwavering stare.

The dream faded; reality came flooding back. It was light. It was day, and Faolan had not returned. That could mean only one thing: Alpin had found him before he caught up with Deord. The two of them were captured, injured or dead. She was all alone in the forest with miles of unfamiliar territory on every side, clad in a damp wedding dress and with only Deord's little knife to her name. And the birds, of course, but it seemed to Ana that they were unlikely to be of much assistance if Drustan himself was not close by. Their main role had always been as messengers; as extensions of the man himself. Without him, what could they do to help her?

She shivered, hugging the small blanket around her shoulders and trying to think practically. She could attempt to get back to Alpin's fortress. Following the course of a stream should lead her, eventually, to the lake close by those stone walls. She could throw herself on his mercy. At least there would be warmth and shelter there. Alpin . . . Alpin who had brought that trapped expression to Faolan's face as he forced him to tell her a half-truth he believed would turn her against her trusted friend; Alpin who had hit her; Alpin who would be very, very angry with her. Alpin who, it seemed, had no intention of honouring Bridei's treaty, but intended to father sons on her anyway. She muttered to herself, going over the choices as the light brightened outside the cavern, presaging sunrise and a day on which she must leave this temporary haven one way or another, for one thing was certain: she'd no intention of starving here like a rat trapped in a hole.

'Drustan's gone, isn't he?' She addressed her question to the three birds, since they were the only available audience. 'Gone back to the west. He loves that place, Dreaming Glen. It was his only true home; the only place where folk did not reject him. Of course he's gone there . . .' Cruel; so cruel, after that vivid dream, which had felt utterly real. Had she been foolish and naïve, deluded by her notion of what love was? She had believed Drustan's sweet words of passion and desire. She recalled Deord's dry comment, *He's a comely man*, and Faolan's wordless perplexity as he tried to ask her how it had happened. 'I thought he loved me,' she whispered to the birds. 'I thought he meant it. But he's not coming . . .' She swallowed the tears that threatened to overwhelm her. There was the day to be faced, and all the other nights and days of an impossible journey back to White Hill. Somehow she was going to have to do it alone.

'Ana?'

Faolan was at the cave entry, his clothing smeared with blood, his face white and exhausted. Relief flooded through her, and with it a terrible misgiving. 'Faolan! Are you hurt? What about Deord? And . . . Drustan?'

His gaze flicked towards the birds, then back to her. 'There's no gentle way to put this. Deord's dead. Alpin's hunting party made an end of him.' And, at her murmur of horror, 'I reached him too late to be of any help; all I could do was sit with him while he died.'

'How –?'

'You don't want to know, believe me. He died bravely; he took a number of Alpin's men with him. Are you all right? I couldn't get back last night, he was a long way off –'

'I'm safe and well, Faolan. Of course you needed to tend to Deord. It is terrible; so sad. He was a fine man.' She remembered how quick Deord had been to protect her when Alpin would have laid violent hands on her. She recalled him sparring with Drustan in the forest, a wondrous image of strength and grace. 'I've often wondered what his past was and how he came to be at Briar Wood. I suppose we'll never know now.'

Faolan said nothing. He had a small pack, Deord's presumably, through which he was rummaging now, setting out what he found: a flint, a roll of linen for bandages, an oiled bag that might hold compressed tinder, strips of dried meat, a water-skin. A leather glove, thick and strong.

'Did you see anything of Drustan?' Ana had to force herself to ask; it would hurt so much to hear him say no.

'Deord was convinced he had left the fortress,' Faolan said, glancing quizzically at her. 'He asked me to help Drustan get away safely. And to look after you. He thought of everyone except himself. He died because of us, Ana. A cruel waste. Alpin will pay for this.'

She had never seen him quite like this before. There was something frightening in his eyes. 'Not entirely a waste,' she told him, 'if we do our best to use the opportunity Deord has given us. To get away safely, and to live our lives with courage and goodness. To live them for him as well as for ourselves.'

'In time, perhaps I'll learn to be philosophical,' Faolan said tightly. 'You didn't see what Alpin did to him. Now come on, we're leaving. I've no doubt Alpin will be out on the trail again this morning with his henchmen, and by the time he reaches here I want to be well away. I suggest you tuck up your skirt or, better still, rip it off short, so you can climb. We're heading up the cliff, and then over those hills.'

In silence Ana took the little knife and used it to cut around the delicately embroidered skirt of her gown at a level two handspans above her ankles. She rolled up the damp strip of fabric and stuffed it into the pack; he did not need to tell her no evidence should be left behind. Without a word, she followed him out of the cavern.

'You wear this pack,' Faolan said. 'It's lighter. I've put most of what we need in mine. Best if you go first, then I can catch you if you fall. Don't rush it. The rock's slippery.'

'How will we know where to go, without Deord?' Ana was gazing upwards; the precipitous cliff face loomed above her, its dark, slick surface softened here and there by tiny pockets of greenery. The air was full of fine spray.

'I'm hoping we already have a guide,' Faolan said as cross-bill, crow and hawk flew one by one from the cavern to spiral upward before them, leading the way. 'At such an extreme, you have to take some things on trust. Up you go, then. I'll be right behind you.'

The rest of the day passed in a blur of climbing and scrambling, balancing and jumping, running over scree and rock, down muddy forest tracks and through dark, squelching patches of bog. When she thought she could go no further, when her chest ached with each snatched breath and her knees shook with every step, Faolan would find a place of concealment and allow her a brief rest, a mouthful of water and a bite of the detested dried meat, all too familiar from their last journey across country. For all the alarming look in his eyes he found kind words, words of praise and encouragement. Without those, Ana knew it would have been impossible for her to keep going at such a pace. Surely they must have left Alpin and his men far behind. Surely they must be able to camp tonight and not be in fear of attack.

The hawk flew ahead. Faolan followed the tracks it chose even when they seemed less than promising. They journeyed on high ground; the pockets of woodland lay far below them now, and their way was exposed to view as well as to the wind that blew chill across the hillsides even in these days of summer. Tiny flowers bloomed in crevices, raising jewel-bright faces to the sun. The shadows of high clouds danced across the bare flanks of the hills, and pale grasses bowed before the breeze. In the distance, daunting peaks arose, purple and grey and deepest blue. There was no sign of human habitation, but deer and hare had left their traces on the hillside. At night there might be wolves.

As the sun passed over to the west and the shadows lengthened, the hawk led them downhill again and back into a tract of pine forest. For the first time, Ana saw Faolan hesitate as hoodie and crossbill followed the bigger bird into the ever deeper shade of the tall trees.

'Are we beyond the borders of Briar Wood here?' Ana gasped, taking advantage of the brief pause to catch her breath.

'I don't know,' Faolan said. 'I'd sooner not be back in the wildwood; maybe it offers concealment, but it feels uncomfortably like Alpin's home territory. I've seen how quickly he traverses this terrain with his hunting party. He knows his way about.' Ahead of them, the hoodie gave its familiar *craaa* sound, and the crossbill darted from bush to bush. The hawk could not be seen. 'I suppose we have to trust him. Ready to go on?'

'Him?' she queried.

'The bird. He's all we've got. Come, take my hand. You're doing well. Now run.'

There was no making fire that first night. They sat close, but not touching; they slept little and listened to the sounds of the forest: rustling in the undergrowth, squeaking in the foliage, the fey, hollow voices of owls and once, in the distance, a chilling howl. Neither of them offered a suggestion as to what that might be.

The three guardian birds remained nearby. The crossbill was generally on Ana's shoulder, the hoodie perched on the branch of a rowan, and the largest bird could be seen in the needled canopy of a dark pine. Whenever Ana looked up she met its bright, disconcerting gaze. It was an odd substitute for the one Drustan had lost, the tiny, soft-downed wren. She wondered where they came from; whether he was able to conjure them when he needed them or exert his charm on the wild creatures of the forest to draw them under his spell. As he had done with Ana herself . . . Maybe he'd only been playing some kind of game with her. Men seemed to enjoy that sort of thing: look at Alpin. Maybe Drustan had never seriously considered that the two of them might have a future together.

'Are you crying?' Faolan's voice was quiet, almost diffident.

'Of course not.' Ana sniffed and wiped her nose on her sleeve for want of anything better. 'Why would I be crying?'

'I could enumerate five or six reasons.'

'I just . . . I just don't understand why Drustan wouldn't come with us,' she blurted out, unable to help herself, for her mind was going over and over it. 'I know he thought he might hurt someone if he came out . . . But if Deord was right, if Drustan left Briar Wood freely, why hasn't he reached us yet? I thought he would want to . . . I thought he cared about me . . .' It sounded pathetic; she bit back more words, but she could not stop the tears. 'I hope he did get away,' she said shakily. 'What if Alpin caught him too? What if he's –'

'Stop it, Ana.' Faolan did not sound angry, only very tired. 'Just think of getting home and starting again. And be glad you're still alive. There have been too many lost on this ill-fated mission of ours. If it helps, I don't believe your precious Drustan is one of them.' He glanced at the hawk, and it stared back at him, eyes intent. 'My instincts tell me he survived and got out of Briar Wood. What he decided to do from that point on is none of my business.'

There was a silence; his tone had been somewhat quelling.

'It is your business, Faolan,' Ana said eventually. 'And mine. Didn't Deord ask you to make sure Drustan was safe? He passed on his own responsibility to you. To us.'

Faolan's voice was tight. 'What are you suggesting we do? Go back to Briar Wood and check on him? Walk straight into Alpin's welcoming arms?'

'What's wrong with you, Faolan? Drustan is a fine man, a good man; I've never believed him guilty of the crime he's accused of. I know he wouldn't do such a thing. You were ready enough to go back for Deord, whom you knew no better. Drustan is in real danger. He could be wandering alone in the forest, with Alpin after him.'

'Just as we are,' Faolan pointed out. 'And if he has any sense, he'll get out of Alpin's reach as fast as he can, just as we're doing. I'm certain he's safe, Ana. I think he knows how to look after himself. He's probably a lot more self-reliant than you imagine.'

'Faolan?'

'Mm?'

'When you saw him – when you and Deord left the fortress – did Drustan say anything? About where he would go, or . . . Did he say anything about me?' She could imagine what Faolan would think – that she was obsessed, besotted – but it was impossible not to ask.

Faolan took his time about replying. 'It would be better if you put this behind you,' he said at length. 'You should try to forget it.'

'Just answer the question, Faolan. If Drustan said nothing of me, it's best that I know, isn't it?'

She heard his sigh.

'He was thinking of you above everything. He didn't want to let you go, but he did, because what he wanted most of all was for you to be safe. He more or less ordered Deord to come with us.'

'Oh.'

'I wasn't sure if Drustan would come out of Briar Wood. It seemed to me he was almost afraid to leave his confinement. Long imprisonment does that to some men. Deord seemed confident Drustan would make his escape, and Deord knew him far better than either of us did.' His manner seemed awkward, as if he were reluctant to tell her this, and from time to time he glanced at the birds.

'Are you worried that he'll hear you?' she asked.

Faolan stared at her, eyes narrowed.

'I mean,' said Ana, 'there have been times in the past when he sent his creatures out and, when they returned, he knew what they had seen. I didn't realise you knew about that.'

'I've seen it,' he said. 'It's a strange sort of gift.'

'Faolan?'

'Mm?'

'You don't like him, do you? Drustan, I mean.'

'I don't know the man,' Faolan muttered. 'I know that Deord is dead and that you are bitterly unhappy. Drustan has played his part in both those things. What cause would I have to like him?'

'You could keep an open mind,' Ana said. 'Don't blame Drustan for what's happened to us. The fault is Alpin's. He should have refused the treaty and sent us home. That would have been the honourable course of action, if you're right and he really is in league with the Gaels.'

'Tell me,' Faolan said, 'if Drustan turned up now, how would you expect the future to unfold? Remembering, of course, our flight from his brother's fortress under dubious circumstances, Alpin's betrayal of Bridei's trust and the fact that we've no doubt earned this powerful chieftain's lifelong enmity. Last but not least, there's the small fact that Drustan is . . . different. Markedly different from other men. You realise that when we get back to White Hill, Bridei will be looking for another chieftain or petty king to offer you to? Of course, he'll be more careful next time.

But there's sure to be some worthy leader of strategic interest looking for a royal bride, even if she now has a reputation for getting herself in trouble.'

She drew a deep breath and let it out before she replied. 'I can't help what happened between Drustan and me, Faolan. You sound as if you despise me. All I did was fall in love.'

This appeared to have silenced him.

'As for what you asked,' Ana went on, 'if Drustan came here now I'd be so happy I wouldn't have room in me for anything else. But even if he doesn't come, even if he chooses to leave me and go to the west, I'll never consent to an arranged marriage. Not now. It just isn't possible any more. I'd have to tell Bridei I couldn't do what he wanted.'

'You think Bridei would agree to your union with a – a –'

'A what, Faolan? A madman? A murderer? Drustan isn't either of those things. I'm certain it was all lies, or a misunderstanding.'

'Do you remember what you told me on the way to Briar Wood?' he asked her. 'That you wanted to go home, but that duty must always come first, because you bore the royal blood of Fortriu?'

'I was wrong,' she said, wondering what it was that made him so cruel tonight. 'Back then, I didn't know what love was. I didn't realise it would change everything. I thought it only happened in stories; finding the one person in the world who is your perfect complement, the one who makes you whole. But it's true. How could I reject that, if I were fortunate enough to have him come back for me? I don't expect you to understand. I just hope that, one day, you'll be lucky enough to meet someone who makes you feel like this.'

'Wretched and tearful?'

'It's hard to explain. Yes, I feel terrible right now, as if my heart's been shredded. But I could never wish I hadn't met him. I couldn't wish it had never happened. Even if those few whispered conversations were all we had, it was worth it.'

Faolan said nothing.

'Faolan? Are we still friends?'

After a little, his hand came out and closed over hers, warm and strong. 'Always,' he said. Above them in the tree, the hawk moved, lifting its tawny wings restlessly in the darkness.

'Were you really a bard once?'

'Mm-hm.'

'You surprised me.'

'There won't be any repeat performances. I did what I had to. But no more.'

'Why?' she asked him. 'Does it hurt so much to put your feelings on show? Your singing is so beautiful; and the harp, that was some of the loveliest playing I ever heard. It is sad not to share that with folk. Surely it is a better calling for a man than . . .'

'Than spy and assassin?' His tone was bitter. 'What I do suits me. It suits the man I am now.'

'But you've shown me you are also that other man, the one who conjures magic with his fingers. The one whose voice makes hardened warriors weep.'

'That man is gone. I played a part for a little, because it was necessary. I've no intention of doing it again. And yes, it hurts. It weakens me. I can't afford that.'

They sat in silence for a little, and then he said, 'Ana, you should try to sleep a little. We need to press on at dawn and you're exhausted.'

'I don't want to sleep. It's cold and dark and . . . and I don't want to dream.'

'You had nightmares? The drug may still be affecting you –'

'They were good dreams,' Ana said. 'It's the waking up I don't like. Don't worry about tomorrow. I'll do what I have to. Just now I'd rather talk than rest. But I'm not being fair; you must be weary yourself. I don't suppose you got much sleep last night.'

'I'm used to doing without sleep, remember?' She sensed his smile in the darkness and was reassured by it. 'Talk if you want. It helps the time pass.'

'Deord told me once I should ask you about prisons.' Ana tried to settle more comfortably on the hard ground, tucking her legs up under her woefully shortened skirt. Any attempt at propriety was ludicrous. She was glad the shadows hid, for now, the length of calf that was on show above her boot top. 'What did he mean?'

'It's not something I talk about. He and I were both incarcerated in a place called Breakstone Hollow, back in Ulaid, though not at the same time. Let's just say it's highly unusual to get out of the Hollow in one piece. Deord was the only other survivor I've ever met. There was a bond, whether we liked it or not; an obligation to help each other. Deord took that to an extreme. I did not ask him to die for me.' His tone was bleak.

'Why were you imprisoned?'

'I fell foul of a certain influential family. The two branches of that clan are in a state of more or less constant feud; I was caught in the middle. I refused to perform a certain task; as a result, I was sent where they believed I would no longer pose a threat to them.'

Ana hesitated. 'You told me once that something happened to you . . . something terrible that changed you for ever. Was that what it was, being locked up in that place?'

'No.' He shifted restlessly. Ana wished he would sit closer and put his arm around her shoulders, for it was cold and her clothing was still damp. She hugged the blanket tighter; Faolan had refused her offer to share it.

'So there's another story? Was it when you were a bard?'

'It's a part of my life I choose not to revisit,' Faolan said. 'I hadn't touched a harp since . . . since before. I will not do so again, and I'll thank you if you don't mention my musical abilities when we return to White Hill. Playing, singing . . . they awaken memories I can't afford, not if I'm to go on with my wits intact.'

'Will you tell me what happened? It can't be good for you to keep it all locked away . . .'

'I agreed to talk, not to have my darkest memories laid bare. This is not appropriate for your ears; it would sicken you. Your own life has been one of privilege and protection, for all your status as a hostage. This was . . . it was unspeakable.'

'Privilege and protection,' she echoed. The words had stung; it was as if, now they had left Briar Wood, he had once again relegated her to the category of spoiled princess. She had thought he knew her better. 'Maybe that's true. I can't help the fact that my mother bore the royal blood of Fortriu. Nor could I help it that both my parents were dead before I was five years old, nor that I was taken away from home before I was eleven. I haven't seen my little sister for nine years. Breda could be married and a mother by now. She could be the next hostage. I was all she had, Faolan; I was mother and father to her. Then there's this: Alpin, and what's happened here . . . and D-Drustan . . .' Gods, she was going to cry again and show him just how weak she really was. 'I don't enjoy talking about those things. I could try to forget them, I suppose, because they make me sad and guilty and angry. But they're part of me; they've made me who I am.'

Faolan was silent a little. He was still holding her hand, which she took as an encouraging sign.

'I –' He faltered, then tried again. 'That night, the first night I played the harp, it all came back. All of it, every sound, every smell, every hideous moment of it. The men wanted to celebrate after you and Alpin had retired. They'd have had me playing all night. You want to know where I was?'

Ana waited.

'Curled up in a ball like a frightened child, hiding in the dark. Weeping myself into a sodden, gasping mess. A man who does the job I do can't afford such weakness. It lays him wide open to his enemies.'

'I'm not your enemy, Faolan. We're alone in the forest with only birds and insects to hear what we say. Perhaps, if you do tell this, the memory will not weigh you down so heavily.'

'It would . . . it would be unpalatable for a lady. Shocking . . . distressing . . . I can't.'

'Would a lady wear her skirt so short, not to speak of the hair? Think of me as your friend, a good friend who can be relied upon to keep confidences. Tell it as a tale, if that's easier. As another man's tale, the way you would if you made it into a song.'

'This would be the most wretched of songs.'

'Maybe so. Maybe you only need to tell the story once. You are a good man, Faolan, no matter what lies in your past. We've stood by each other in some frightening times. If you're ever going to be free of this, the time to start is now. Come on, try.' She put her other hand on his knee; he started violently as she touched him. He was wound so tight tonight, Ana did not think she could move closer than this. Then, in a low voice, he began to tell the story.

'There is . . . there is a powerful clan in my homeland known as the Uí Néill; you've probably heard of them. Both the high kings at Tara and the kings of the Gaels in this land come from that family. It has two branches, one in the northwest and one concentrated in the east. There are many chieftains and many feuds over land and dominance. The story concerns a . . . a sub-branch of the family, closely related to a warlike chieftain by the name of Echen, but led by a man whose main desire was to keep his kin and community secure and peaceful. He didn't want any part in the territorial wars. He was what we call a *brithem*, a practitioner of the law; an elder in his settlement and much respected. He had a large family: his wife, her elderly parents, two sons and . . . and three daughters. The family was quite prosperous. Their region had managed to avoid involvement in the Uí Néill disputes for long enough to become almost complacent. Children played out in the open; young women gathered berries and milked cows with no need for armed guards to watch over them. Young men learned crafts and trades other than war.'

'Such as music?' Ana ventured softly.

He glanced at her. 'The *brithem*'s younger son had a talent for it. When he reached a certain age his father found a master bard who needed a lad to train, and the boy went off to polish up his skills on the job, for, of course, it's in the nature of a bard to travel. He was gone quite a few years. When he next came home to visit, he was not a boy but a young man. And things in the settlement had changed.'

In the darkness, lit dimly by the moon hanging low beyond the trees, Ana saw his face as a pattern of shadow and bone, the eyes dark hollows. She tightened her grasp on his hand but did not speak.

'The – the father had made a judgement that went against Echen Uí Néill,' Faolan said. 'One of the chieftain's henchmen was found guilty of several crimes, their nature doesn't matter, and as a result Echen believed he'd lost status in the region. The guilty man was exiled. He'd been useful to Echen, and the chieftain resented his removal. The Uí Néill practise swift vengeance. Things began to happen, cruel things. A house was burned down. Cattle were stolen, sheep slaughtered and left lying in the fields. The lawman's wife lost five of her prized breeding cows. Then the husband of the eldest daughter was found hanging in the barn. Some folk said he'd killed himself. But he wouldn't have done that. She was expecting their first child. She lost the baby; the shock was too much for her.'

'But . . . didn't you say these people were Uí Néill's own kin? How could he –?'

'That only made it worse. Echen couldn't believe my – the *brithem* would pass a judgement unfavourable to his own. Some men have no understanding of the principles of law; of honour and fairness. My – this *brithem* was scrupulous in such matters. That was what made it . . . that was . . .' He faltered.

'Did the family take action against Echen after the acts of violence? Didn't the community rally in support?' Ana asked, trying to help him.

'Imagine Echen as a man like Alpin, one who uses fear as his primary tool. A man with complete control within his own territory. If Alpin encounters opposition, he simply cuts a man to pieces and hangs him up as a lesson to anyone else who might be foolish enough to challenge him. Echen was the same. But the territory he commanded was many times larger than Alpin's. What chance has one local *brithem* against such power? Nonetheless, the family did not lie down and accept the inevitable. They took a stand.'

'How?'

'The – the – I don't think I can go on with this.' He was shivering. Ana took off the blanket and laid it around his shoulders.

'No,' protested Faolan. 'You'll get cold –'

'Then share it with me. It's only common sense.' He looked up then, towards the hawk still perched unblinking in the high branches of the tree. 'You feel awkward, telling this in the presence of these birds?'

Faolan's mouth twisted. 'Oddly enough, the only people who've ever heard me refer to what happened are Deord and Drustan. I must hope Drustan will not judge me, if he can hear.'

'Tell me the rest of the story. What did this family do?'

'By the time the younger son came home, the men of the district had already formed a ragtag force to guard their land, their possessions and their loved ones. Their weapons were scythes and pitchforks. What fighting skills they had were those they'd picked up in friendly bouts of wrestling on fair day. The elder son of the *brithem* was their leader. He was clever, and he was angry. He'd seen the despair that was overtaking his father after the loss of what would have been the first grandchild. This young man, he . . .'

'What was his name, Faolan?'

'Dubhán.' He had to force this out; the word was harsh with pain. 'He executed a coup. They heard Echen was to visit the district, to extract tenancy payments from the farmers who worked his land. While Echen was being entertained to supper by one of the wealthier local landholders, the young men stole ten fine riding horses from his encampment, as well as some weaponry. One guard was killed, the other trussed up and left for his master to find. Dubhán was his father's son; in return for one life, that of his brother-in-law, he took one life. A subtlety lost on Echen, unfortunately. By the time the Uí Néill's men came out searching, the horses had been spirited away out of the district. It was a triumph, audacious, clever, in keeping with what folk knew of Dubhán. He was always . . . he was . . .'

'The younger brother looked up to him?'

Faolan nodded, momentarily unable to speak.

'I know this must end in tragedy, Faolan. Will you tell me the rest?'

His voice had become a halting monotone. 'Echen pulled in some of the young men of the community, those he suspected might have had a part in it. His methods were brutal. Eventually one of them broke and named Dubhán as the ringleader. That night . . . that night the family was gathered around the hearth, as was their habit, for singing and storytelling. Mother, father, brothers, sisters, old folk. Echen came with armed men, a great many men. They laid rough hands on the *brithem* and on his elder son. Accused of the offence, Dubhán did not deny responsibility. He stood tall and attempted to set out Echen's own crimes against his father; to use logic against vengeful fury. His father, held by a pair of thugs, watched him with tears of pride in his eyes. The younger brother, whose hands were more apt to pluck harp strings than to use a sword, whose voice was sooner raised in song than in valiant defiance, longed at that moment to be Dubhán, for it was a demonstration of true courage. Then Echen's men beat Dubhán in

409

front of his family, his weeping mother, his younger sister screaming protest, his father tight-lipped and grey. The younger brother
did not know which was strongest in him: fear, hate or pride.'

Ana squeezed his hand, not saying anything.

'Dubhán would not grovel. Bruised and bloody, gasping for
breath, he would not give Echen the apology he sought. It must
have become evident to Echen that his tactic wasn't working. So
he began to threaten the others.'

A chill ran through Ana.

'Not what you might think,' Faolan said, 'that he might hurt the
father, or another of the family, if Dubhán did not apologise.
Perhaps he saw, in all their eyes, the integrity which was the very
backbone of the upbringing their father had given them, the core of
what made this quiet family so strong. And perhaps he saw a . . .
a weak link. Echen's followers moved in. Suddenly an armed man
stood by each of them, the grandmother, the young widow, the
little sister; knives were held across throats, daggers poised to enter
hearts. There was no weapon aimed at Dubhán himself; he was
kneeling in the centre of the chamber, hands bound behind his
back. There was no weapon trained on his younger brother, the one
who had gone away to be a bard and come home to a nightmare.
Then . . . then Echen stepped forward to address the musician. He
put a knife in the young man's hand. He . . . he offered him a
choice. Dubhán, Echen said, was marked for death; an example
needed to be made, so nobody else got it into his head to defy the
Uí Néill, thinking he could get away with it. The question, therefore, was not whether the miscreant would die or not, but how
many he would take with him. Echen's eyes went around the
chamber as he said this. The young bard followed the chieftain's
gaze, seeing his mother's ashen face, his grandmother with her
neat clothing rumpled and her white hair dishevelled, a man's big
fist gripping her cruelly by the shoulder. His older sister had her
hands over her face; a red-faced fellow was holding his younger
sister, fourteen years old and quivering with rage and shame as the
wretch's hands groped her through her demure gown. The grandfather was trying to stand tall, his gaze on his distressed wife. The
father's jaw was set, his eyes dark with the premonition of horror.
Perhaps he had seen before any of them what was coming.

410

'"It's not my choice, lad," Echen said to the younger son, "but yours. Slit your brother's throat and I'll order my men to release every person in this chamber and do them no more harm, provided your family never meddles in my affairs again. Refuse and I'll do the job for you. Then my men will make an end of all the others."

'The mother gave a terrible cry, a moan from deep in the belly; the grandfather cursed, and was rewarded with a cracking blow to the jaw, which sent him crumpling to his knees.

'"Perhaps not all," Echen added, his eyes on the younger sister, sweet and rosy as a new season's apple. "We'll take *her* to keep us company tonight; pity to waste such obvious promise. And we'll spare you, of course," his gaze on the young bard who stood trembling by his brother, the knife shaking so violently in his hand that he could scarcely have used it even if he'd had the will to. "Kill him, and you save their lives. Balk at it, and you'll watch them die, one by one. You'll live on to see it, over and over, every night in your dreams. Show us what you're made of, pretty boy."

'The bard looked wildly at his father, seeking guidance, but his father had closed his eyes. The wisest *brithem* in all the world could not make such a judgement. Tears were rolling down the lawman's blanched cheeks. His lips moved in a prayer.

'"Don't do it, Faolan!" the young sister shouted. "Don't give that scum the satisfaction!" Then she, too, was silenced with a blow.

'The bard looked down at the knife. He could not hold it still; it jerked and shuddered in his hand as a wave of nausea went through him.

'Then his brother spoke. "Stand behind me. Set the point of the knife below my left ear. Draw it across in one steady stroke, and make sure you press hard. You're strong, Faolan. You can do it."

'"But –" All the bard could manage was a strangled croak. His throat was tight, his head felt as if it was going to explode, his heart was hammering fit to split asunder. His palms were slick with sweat. His mind sought desperately for solutions: attack Echen instead, try to run for it, turn the knife on himself . . . It was evident none of these things would save his family. But this – this was Dubhán.

411

'"Hurry up," Echen said, and he gave a little nod towards one of his men. A moment later the grandmother slumped to the ground, a knife protruding from her ribs.

'"You're a man, Faolan," Dubhán whispered. "Do it now."'

Ana had her teeth clenched so tightly her head ached.

'The bard . . . the bard looked into his brother's eyes, bright with courage. Dubhán was his hero. He would have followed him into the gates of hell. What his brother asked of him, he had always done. So he tightened his tenuous grip on the knife and drew the blade across Dubhán's throat. The blood spurted hot and red over his hands. He heard his sister's scream; he heard the sound his mother made. His father was silent. The young man stood there in the centre with his brother's body by his feet, and waited for Echen and his men to go.

'But Echen wasn't quite finished. His men released the family when he bid them, standing by with weapons drawn as the women tended to the dying grandmother. For Dubhán, it was already too late.

'"Search the house," the Uí Néill chieftain said lightly, as if it were an afterthought. "Look for our missing knives and bows, and bring out anything else of interest, will you?"

'The family was frozen, silent. They waited. The grandmother's blood drained out into the cloths they pressed to her chest. The grandfather held her hand against his cheek. In a little, Echen's men came back, holding between them the third sister, the one who had gone to bed early that night . . . Áine, the youngest, a child in her long nightrobe, eyes dark and scared, hair tumbling down over her shoulders.

'"Ah," Echen said, and his smile was cruel, "hidden treasure. We'll take her; I recall promising to spare all in this chamber, nothing about the rest of the house. A little pearl. How old is she, twelve? Fresh. Tantalising. Fetch the poppet a cloak, Conor, we can't have her catching cold. Farewell, *brithem*. I think your son here has a future, and it's not as a musician." His expression as he glanced at the bard was of surprise, almost of admiration; it was clear the result of his experiment had not been the one he expected. He turned back to the father. "Don't let me hear of you again. I'll be less magnanimous next time."

'As they left, dragging the girl along with them, the young man hurled himself across the chamber after them, desperate to make it right somehow, to save his sister at least, though the nightmare would indeed be with him for ever. Echen laughed; I can hear it now. Then someone struck the lad a heavy blow on the head, and for a little there was the relief of unconsciousness.'

There was nothing Ana could say. She sat paralysed a moment, then put her arm around him and leaned her head against his shoulder. 'Faolan, that's . . . it's unthinkable. Nobody should ever have to . . . nobody . . .' And, a little later, 'What happened afterwards? What did you do?'

'I was possessed by hatred.' He had given up the pretence of telling someone else's story. 'When I came to, all that was in my mind was rescuing my sister and plunging a knife into Echen's heart. But that was not allowed me. I came out from the sleeping quarters to find my parents waiting. My mother had packed a little bundle with food and drink for the road. My father gave me a ring he had had from his grandfather, silver with a stone in it. My harp was ready in its bag. I was to go; to go away and not return. They didn't say much. I saw on my mother's face that, after what I had done, she did not want me in her house. My father was suddenly an old man. I protested; who would save Áine if not I? Father forbade me to try. He said the violence had to stop. He said it would already be too late for her. There was a distance in his tone that I had never heard before. My other sisters did not come out when I left. Before the sun had risen I had walked beyond the borders of Echen's land. I gave my mother's bread and cheese to a beggar by the wayside, and tied the cloth to a yew tree, though it was no offering to the gods; from that dark night on I would trust neither gods nor men. I traded my father's ring for a passage to Fortriu. I left them all behind. I have heard nothing of them since. But they are never far away. When I play the harp I see my little sister in the hands of those men. I hear my mother's scream. When I go to sleep at night, I feel Dubhán's blood on my hands, and I hear my father speaking to me as if I were a stranger.'

'Oh, Faolan . . . I'm so, so sorry . . . I can't think what to say . . .'

'There's nothing to say. What I did was unforgivable. I made the wrong choice. I destroyed my family just as effectively as Echen Uí Néill would have done with his armed band.'

'Why didn't you ever go back? Didn't you want to make your peace with your folk? To find out what had happened to them?'

Faolan's tone was bitter. 'I worshipped Dubhán. He was my big brother. I obeyed him to the very last. And I obeyed my father when he told me to go away and not to come back. Since then I haven't earned my keep by playing music, but by the two things I proved I could do that day: following orders and slitting throats.'

The self-hatred in his voice silenced Ana.

'I have been back,' Faolan said. 'Not home, but back to Laigin. Echen's henchmen tried to recruit me. He'd heard, perhaps, that the pretty boy had developed certain useful skills. I refused. Hence Breakstone. Men died of despair in that place. I lived. I was already beyond despair; I'd lost any capacity to feel. That made me a worse bard but a better killer. I didn't work for Echen, but I did work for everyone else: the chieftains of the Uí Néill, both northern and southern, the princes of Ulaid, the King of Dalriada. And now, for Bridei.'

'You haven't lost the capacity to feel,' Ana said. 'Nor to awaken feelings in others. What about your music? Even Alpin's huntsmen had tears in their eyes.'

'Until I met you,' he said quietly, 'I had lost it. I won't play again. It's wrong for me to set my hands to music when they're tainted with my own brother's lifeblood.'

'What utter nonsense!' Ana snapped before she could stop herself. 'You said before that you made the wrong choice, but, Faolan, there was no right choice. As a lawman, your father knew that. Whatever choice you made, it had to end in sorrow and death. You were very young. That man had no right to set such a terrible burden on you.'

'I should not have told you. Now you, too, will dream of this.'

'I have my own troubling dreams. I'm glad you told me, Faolan. It took courage to put this in words. You are the most courageous man I know.'

He made no reply to this.

'Faolan?'

A nod.

'You need to go back. You know that, don't you? If you're ever to come to terms with it at all, you need to make your peace with them.'

'It's not a fairytale.'

'I'm not saying the memories will disappear, or that all the hurts will be instantly mended. I understand it's too complicated for that. What I do know is that they would want to see you: your father and mother, your sisters . . . A long time has passed since you left. The way you tell it, they sound like fine people, strong, just people. They will understand, by now, the impossible choice you faced, and why you did what you did. You were bound to it by love. You need to go back. Your long absence will have hurt them, your father especially.'

'I'll never go back.'

'Then you are less courageous than I thought. The greatest courage is to go ahead and do what you must, even when the prospect of it turns your insides to jelly.'

'Was that how it felt when you pulled me out of the water at Breaking Ford?'

Ana shivered, remembering. 'For a bit, yes; once I saw you, there didn't seem to be any choice in the matter. I had to salvage the one thing left, the one good thing. If I were a crueller woman, I would say you owe it to me, as well as to Deord, to come to terms with the past. To give yourself a future.'

'I have a future. I am still Bridei's man.'

'Without this, you will never be true to yourself.'

'When I told you my story, I wasn't expecting instruction on how to live my life.' He edged away from her, releasing her hand.

'We're friends, Faolan,' Ana said quietly. 'True friends. I will never instruct you. But there is a path I want to see you take, so you will not be eaten up by self-loathing. I see the man beneath the armour of indifference. I want the world to see him too. I want you to be fulfilled and happy.'

In the moonlight, she saw his twisted grimace of a smile. 'You ask the impossible,' he said.

'I thought,' she whispered, 'that you might be the kind of man for whom nothing is impossible. I'm hoping that, in time, you'll prove me right.'

At the end of a third day's searching, Alpin called off his hunting party and headed back home. There, he filled a pack with supplies for a man travelling alone a fair distance, and put the affairs of his household in the hands of the capable Orna. He left certain instructions with Dregard, and others with Mordec, who headed his men-at-arms. He took his sword, his knives and his crossbow, and he headed back into the forest alone at dawn next morning. Where a hunting party with dogs and horses could not easily go, a skilled man on foot might travel quickly and quietly, tracking another. The Gael and the royal bride might have slipped beyond his borders, and his brother vanished into the concealment of the wildwood. But Alpin was not yet defeated. He wanted Ana, soiled goods as she'd likely be by now. She was his; she'd been sent to him to be his wife and he'd have her by whatever means it took. He owed it to himself to enact vengeance on that freak Drustan, and on the wretched turncoat Gael, and, ultimately, on the upstart King of Fortriu who had sparked this off with his ill-considered attempt to woo Briar Wood to his alliance.

Well, the alliance would keep, Alpin thought as he made a good pace along the treacherous tracks of the deep forest, retracing his own path to the place where Deord had died, observing with a certain amusement the care with which the fellow had been laid to rest, then picking up a new trail back towards the high tarn below the waterfall, a place his hunting party had dismissed as without any exit a woman might essay. He had them; he was on to them.

It would take time to track the fugitives down and to move in on them by stealth. No matter. He could afford to be absent from home for a while. There was no longer a need to mobilise his army, his fleet, his considerable forces; not yet. Perhaps not at all. The answer to that problem, he sensed, was not in an armed assault but in his alternative plan, the one he'd put in place some time ago: the deployment of the secret weapon nobody knew about save himself and Dregard and his most trusted men-at-arms. And, of course, the son who had, against the odds, finally proven to be of some use to him.

It had become increasingly clear as first Ana, then Faolan had spoken of Bridei's powerful presence, his leadership, his iconic status to his people, that the success of any Priteni venture against Dalriada depended heavily on this one man, this so-called Blade of Fortriu. Too heavily, in Alpin's estimation. Remove Bridei and the whole thing would come tumbling down, he was sure of it.

So he'd sent the young king a little present; how convenient that the lad had already attached himself to Umbrig's forces. Hargest had been only too willing to oblige; the boy was desperate for Alpin's approval. He probably saw himself as the rightful heir to Briar Wood. The way things had worked out with Ana, at the moment he *was* the only heir. That would change soon enough, Alpin thought grimly. He'd have his royal bride and he'd keep her. She'd give him as many sons as he wanted, and through those sons he'd wield a power unrivalled in all the lands of the north.

Chapter Fifteen

'Quite an entourage,' remarked Fola as Tuala's party dismounted before the gates of Banmerren. The queen had brought not only a waxen-faced Broichan, but also the bodyguard Garth, his wife Elda and their twin sons, as well as a young maidservant. And, of course, Derelei, now being helped down from the cart that had conveyed nursemaid and children. 'You've remembered, I hope, that druids are the only men permitted in our sanctum?'

Tuala smiled at her old teacher. 'How could I forget?' she said, recalling a time when Bridei had scaled the wall on a rope in order to visit her. Was that really only five years ago? It seemed a world away: the two of them high above the ground, perched in the oak tree, and that first kiss . . .'I was thinking the rest of us might be lodged in Ferada's domain. I'll go and speak to her while Garth and Elda unload the baggage.' As she turned down the little path skirting the high stone wall, she saw Fola take Broichan's arm and lead him through the gate to the wise women's sanctuary.

Down the pathway the wall had been extended to shelter a new enclosure where a long dwelling house stood within a fledgling garden. An iron gate set in the wall opened at Tuala's push; across a grassy sward, an archway in the side wall opened through to the grounds of Fola's school. Tuala walked quietly into the new garden. She was not alone there; Ferada was sitting on a bench with a little book open in her hands, and by the archway could be seen the brawny figure of the royal stone carver, Garvan, who was balanced on a wooden platform beside a huge slab of rock, doing something delicate with a chisel. A youth, apparently his assistant, was sorting tools on a bench. It was a fine day; the quiet, industrious scene was bathed in warm summer light. In the grass small flowers made bright points of pink and blue. Ferada's feet were bare and she had one leg drawn up under her on the bench while the other foot dangled. Her hair was unbound, flowing down her back in a fiery stream. Garvan, a man whose features had something of the look of an untouched lump of stone themselves, was whistling under his breath as he worked.

'I'm sorry to disturb such a peaceful scene,' Tuala said, advancing across the grass with a smile. 'I'm afraid you have visitors: four adults and three rather active small boys. We'll try to keep them away from the tools.'

There were no easy ways between Briar Wood and White Hill. Where there was not trackless forest, there were high fells and craggy peaks across which chill winds laid a constant scourge even in summer. Where there were not broad streams and rushing falls to get across, there were cliffs and ravines and crumbling escarpments. There were bogs. There were wild pigs. At night, there were wolves.

Once Faolan was confident that Alpin had lost their trail, he allowed a small fire at night. He had not long finished laying and lighting the first of these, while Ana used her knife to divide up a strip of the dried mutton that was their only food, when the hawk flew off awhile, returning in the twilight with a fat rabbit dangling from its talons. Faolan wondered how much Drustan understood when he was in this form; whether he had a full comprehension of human speech, whether he formed opinions, felt joy or sorrow, planned and strategised and dreamed in the same

419

way as a man. He wondered how much Drustan would remember when he changed back. Right now, he was more use to them in bird form, able to fly high and seek out tracks where a man could not, able to hunt with no weapons beyond beak and claws. When would Drustan decide the time had come to show himself to Ana? To reveal to her the full truth about himself? Was he really so frightened of her rejection that he would hold back all the way to White Hill? A lover who could not trust seemed to Faolan to lack something essential. Still, it was an odd thing, a bizarre thing. There was no telling how she might react when she knew.

Ana did a competent job of cooking the rabbit on the fire. She left a portion raw, putting it on a fallen tree where the bird could take it easily. The hawk ate with precision, the haunch of rabbit held in one foot as the fearsome beak tore off the flesh a strip at a time. Hoodie and crossbill watched from a distance; for them, hunger did not seem to be an issue. Faolan imagined the slow pace of human feet gave the two of them plenty of opportunity to forage on the way.

Once or twice, as they went on and one day began to merge into the next, Faolan was tempted to catch the hawk on its own, to trust that it could understand and to suggest to Drustan that he tell Ana the truth and put her out of her misery. Once or twice, he got out the single glove Deord had carried in his pack and tried it on his right hand. But he took the idea no further. Why rush things? The longer Drustan left it, the likelier it was that Ana might see her feelings for him as infatuation rather than love; the impulsive generosity of a woman who finds it all too easy to pity the unjustly treated. The longer it took Drustan to reveal his secret to her – if he ever did – the more time Faolan had alone with her. And while his mind understood all too well that there could never be more than friendship between them, his heart cherished these precious days as a flower welcomes the sun's warmth. Never mind that the two of them were filthy, cold and exhausted; that home had never seemed so far away. For now, for this small span of time, he had her entirely to himself. He was warier now, not trusting himself to lie by her at night, but he could look at her, talk to her, store up every moment for a future in which, as surely as the sun set in the evening, their paths would go separate ways.

He had opened the darkest part of himself to her, the part he had thought would remain locked away for ever. She had accepted his offering; even knowing the terrible thing he had done, she had remained his loyal friend. If this fragile happiness must be shattered by Drustan's return, let it be not yet.

Ana was doing well, keeping up, not complaining even when her feet hurt her. When she took off her boots and he saw the blisters, Faolan ordered a day's rest. She protested; he insisted. It was clear to him that they would not be back at White Hill until summer was over. He hoped Drustan knew what he was doing. Perhaps he was playing a game of his own.

Bouts of rainy weather had slowed their progress and the season was passing swiftly. It did not help that their guide had a disconcerting habit of disappearing without warning, leaving them to wait for a day, two days, until he flew back and the journey recommenced.

They had been two nights in a derelict shepherd's hut on a high corrie, waiting for the hawk's return from one of these absences. Faolan had little idea of which path to follow, and the terrain was perilous. Nonetheless, he was close to losing patience completely and assuming the role of guide himself from this point on. Ana had been growing increasingly withdrawn, and he had noticed a hollowing of her features and a change in her eyes that disquieted him. She had become markedly thinner, unsurprising on the diet of one meal of meat a day. The hawk had left them a brace of hares before it vanished this time, as if it knew it would not be back awhile.

'We'll wait one more night,' Faolan told Ana as they sat in the shelter of a boulder, looking out over the hillside under the strange half-dark sky of the summer night. 'If he's not back by then, I can find a way for us. Head roughly southeast and we must strike the coast near Abertornie eventually.'

'Faolan?'

'Mm?'

'It's going to take a long time, isn't it? To walk all the way back, I mean.'

Faolan considered all the things he hadn't told her: the difficulty of providing food without bow or spear; the fact that the dried meat would last, at best, another seven days; the undeniable truth that, even in summer, there would be broad rivers to cross. 'It will be slower than riding, of course,' he said. 'But we'll manage. How are your boots?'

Ana showed him. The left was holed right through the sole; the right was splitting apart where the upper met the heel. No wonder her feet were sore. The wedding gown was stained and tattered to rags. His own garments were hardly better.

'Mm,' he said. 'A pretty picture we'll make walking into White Hill, the two of us.'

There was a silence, then the unmistakable sound of suppressed weeping. 'Sorry,' Ana muttered.

'It's him, isn't it?' Faolan asked flatly. 'Drustan. You're still crying over him. A pox on the man.'

'I can't help it, Faolan. I want him to be here, with us. With me. I hoped . . . I had so hoped . . .'

Faolan observed that her belt was so loose on her now that she had to wind it several times through itself to keep it around her waist. Her lovely hair fell in lank, lifeless strands to her shoulders; she no longer held herself as straight as a queen. He ached to put his arms around her and hold her close.

'I worry about him, Faolan,' she said in a small voice. 'He's so vulnerable. If he's gone back to his own place, Dreaming Glen, he could be imprisoned again, even killed. Alpin's men are in control there now. What if –?'

'Ana,' Faolan said, 'we can't do anything about that. Trust the man; he can sort out his own problems.' Privately, he was beginning to doubt this. He had no idea at all where Drustan was right now, or what he was playing at.

'I wanted to help him.' She was staring up at the night sky as if it might provide answers. 'I still want to. He's terribly alone. Wherever he chose to go, whatever he chose to do, I wanted to be with him, by his side, so he need not be alone any more. It must be both a blessing and a curse to be born different. His grandfather understood that. It seems nobody else did. Deord, maybe.'

'Different?' Faolan wondered exactly what Drustan had told her.

'Like a seer, I think. These spells he has, what Alpin called frenzies or fits, it seems that when they come upon him Drustan experiences a kind of vision, walks in a different world for a while. He had them even as a child. Some people can't tolerate such oddity.'

'Indeed,' Faolan said, thinking she had no idea of just how odd the man really was. How would she feel about the prospect of bearing children who might at any moment sprout beaks and feathers?

'Faolan?'

He waited.

'Every day we travel, every step towards the east, I feel as if my heart's being torn apart just a little bit more. I thought after a while it might start to dull, not to hurt so much. But it keeps on getting worse. How could I leave him behind? Something's wrong. He wouldn't have gone away without me. He was telling the truth when he said he loved me, I heard it in his voice. Why would he lie about something like that?'

'Men do,' Faolan said. 'They do it all the time.'

'Not Drustan.'

'A paragon.' He could not conceal his bitterness.

'Stop it, Faolan. Anyone would think you were jealous.'

There was a silence. The longer it drew out, the more intense was Ana's scrutiny of his face and, at a certain point, he had to look away to stop himself from some kind of foolish response, a lying denial, a declaration of his feelings, a withering riposte that would hurt her. There was no point in saying anything. It was quite plain to him that, at last, she understood what was in his heart.

'I'm sorry,' she said eventually, her voice low and warm. 'I'm so sorry, Faolan.'

'Ah, well.' He attempted a smile. 'I'm only a hired guard, after all. It's not my place to entertain personal feelings. Forget it. Your life is complicated enough already.'

'You are my dear friend,' Ana said, 'and my loyal protector on the road. I should have seen this earlier; I can't imagine how I missed it. You know I trust you, Faolan, and respect you, and rely on you . . . I never thought to find such a friend, and I thank the gods you have been by my side through all this. But . . . what

I feel for Drustan is quite different. It is too strong to be denied. It's like a – a wave, a tide –'

'Destructive, you mean.'

'Maybe. He's gone, and I feel as if I'm breaking apart. I'm sorry it's making things difficult for you. When I spoke of him, and of how I felt . . . that must have hurt you terribly.'

Faolan's mood softened at her words. Even at such an extreme she remained a lady through and through. 'I want you to try something for me,' he said.

'What?'

He reached for his bag; drew out the heavy leather glove. 'Put this on and stand up.'

'Why?' She did as he requested, expression mystified.

'Now call him. The hawk. Call him to you.'

'I don't know how. I don't know what kind of sound I should make.'

'Can you whistle?'

'Not very loudly. I can try; just don't look at me or I won't be able to do it.'

The sound she made was tiny in the immensity of the folded hills that spread before them; a little two-note tune, falling, falling. It was the kind of call a lady might make to a beloved kitten or well-trained lap-dog. She paused awhile, listening, then tried it again. It was as if the night hushed around her, holding its breath.

Then, a movement of wings in the half-dark, a subtle shifting of air, and the bird flew out of the night to her hand, talons gripping the glove, wild eye meeting Ana's, bright, inscrutable. She held her arm strong, supporting the hawk's weight; her own eyes were full of wonderment. 'He came back,' she breathed. 'How did you know he'd do that?'

'Call it a hunch,' said Faolan, noting the change in her voice. Did she sense the truth? 'Intuition.'

Ana's fingers came up to stroke the hawk's plumage, the long, strong wing feathers, the downy covering on the chest. Her hand was perilously close to that rending beak; it did not seem to have occurred to her that the creature had the capacity to rip her hand apart. Faolan held his tongue. He wouldn't be putting his own fingers in harm's way if he could help it, but he knew this bird would never harm Ana.

'This means we can go on,' she said. 'We were running out of food, weren't we?'

'I would have provided for you, one way or another,' Faolan said, not looking at the bird in case the dislike was too evident in his eyes. Ana was right, of course; it was Drustan's presence that would see them safe home.

'I feel a little better,' Ana said, putting her cheek against the creature's feathers for a moment. 'If all three of them are with us, it means Drustan hasn't quite forgotten me, even if he can't be here. If they stay together, I think it must mean he's still alive and safe. I'm going to try to sleep now, Faolan.'

'Goodnight, then.'

'May the Shining One give you good dreams.'

'You wish the impossible for me. You, I suppose, will dream of one thing only.'

She was settling herself on the ground under the rudimentary shelter of a small overhang, the blanket around her shoulders. The three birds stayed close to her, perched on the rocks, a trio of miniature custodians conjuring visions from some mythic tale of magic. There was silence for a while, and he thought she was asleep. Then she spoke again. 'Don't mock my dreams, Faolan,' she said. 'Apart from the birds, they're all I have left of him.'

'I'm sorry,' he said, but Ana did not reply.

Much later, when he knew she had fallen asleep, Faolan picked up a stone and weighed it in his hand. He listened to Ana's breathing, slow and steady. Hoodie and crossbill were huddled by her, immobile, heads tucked under wings. The hawk kept watch, perched a handspan from her shoulder. Faolan considered the possible trajectory of his stone; judged speed and distance. If he were quick, it could be over in an instant. He'd never have to watch the two of them together; he'd never have to see the fellow's hands on her and stand by as if it were none of his business. Darkness welled in his heart; his fingers closed around the missile.

Ana sighed, turning in her sleep.

'Tell her,' Faolan said, dropping the stone to the ground. 'Tell her the truth; let her make her own decision. You can't leave things like this. You'll break her heart.'

The hawk regarded him, its eye unreadable.

'Change back. Show her what you are. If you don't have the courage for that, you don't deserve her. You may as well fly off and leave us. We'll cope. We did before and we can again.'

No response save that unwavering stare, a look that seemed to Faolan profoundly dangerous. This man was a wild creature. He carried peril in his very nature.

'What are you waiting for?' Faolan challenged. 'She's here, she loves you, she's the most perfect woman any man could hope for. What's holding you back?'

There was no reaction; no sudden start of surprise, no transformation. The bird turned its head away.

'You're afraid, aren't you?' Faolan said. 'You're afraid that once she knows, she'll turn her back on you. So you punish her, you put her through torture worrying about your safety, your future, why you've abandoned her, even as she wears herself out walking and fades to skin and bone for want of proper nourishment. If you're really a man, act like one. Trust her with the truth.'

Alpin was built like a bear. Still, growing up at Briar Wood had given him a number of skills unusual in such a big man; the forest provided good hunting, and he had learned early to move in near silence and to cover difficult territory quickly. He had learned to pick up a trail and not to lose it, though Deord's solitary flight across the forest had diverted him awhile from this particular scent. Now he had it again, and he moved after the fugitives quietly, efficiently, with deadly purpose. As he ran and climbed and waded to the northeast, his mind was not on the terrain or the weather or the signs of human passage; he absorbed these clues without thinking. Instead, within him a fierce, furious anthem of vengeance played, a song of hatred, of lust, of the will to torment and to obliterate. He saw Ana spread-eagled with his brother on her, and then the Gael, and then wretched, deviant Drustan again. If she had a child in her belly when he got her home, it would have to be put down; his heir must be indisputably of his own blood. By all the gods, she'd better give him sons after all this trouble. He'd beat the defiance out of her soon enough. He'd make sure . . . On the other hand, he'd have to stay his hand awhile. He'd need to moderate his anger after the initial punishment Ana would endure on their return to the fortress. He'd lost his temper with Erisa once too often, and look what had happened. The stupid woman had tried to run from him, and when she fell she'd killed his son as well as herself. If his freak of a brother hadn't happened to be there to provide a neat alibi, he could have lost everything. Drustan . . . Gods, why had he been so generous to the man? He should have got rid of him straightaway, and not let the blood tie hold him back. Now Drustan was out, and if he remembered, if he told . . . No, that was fanciful. Folk knew Drustan as a madman; nobody would believe him. There was nobody left at Briar Wood who could give him support, nobody who remembered the time when he was rational. Old Bela had fled as soon as it happened. She was probably dead by now, and the rest of them were gone, all but Orna, who knew how to keep her mouth shut. Alpin had been thorough. All the same, he wouldn't be content until he set his hands around his brother's neck and heard the last breath gurgling out of him. As for the Gael . . . The Gael was not to be trusted. He could have been useful as a spy. All the same, it would be necessary to get rid of him now. Alpin pondered the exact manner in which he would do this as he made his way up across an exposed stretch of fell, stopping to examine signs of recent habitation in a ruined hut. Ashes from a small fire; strands of fair hair; the bones of a little creature, gnawed clean. They'd been here. Not long now. His hands were itching to inflict punishment. He would take the two men first. Then he'd have Ana where he found her; there was another part of him with an itch, and there was only one way it could be satisfied.

Bridei had learned caution early. The first attempt on his life had been made when he was a small child, and Donal had foiled it. Years later, when those who opposed his rise to kingship tried again, Donal had died in his place. The third time it had been

Faolan who had pulled him back from the brink. He had learned not to trust too quickly, even when his instincts inclined him towards friendship.

He liked Hargest. He could see something of himself in the boy's uncertainty and in his constant striving to excel. Caught between a father who had been all too ready to send him away and a foster father who had perhaps been overcautious in his treatment, Hargest seemed to Bridei to be balancing on a narrow bridge to maturity and manhood. The lad was a mass of contradictions: the desire to please, the terror of appearing weak or inept, the will to prove himself superior. Under it, there was a desperate need for love: a father's love.

Bridei had Breth and the others include the young man in their daily combat practice and take him out on their sorties to the fringes of Dalriadan territory. Hargest was always closely supervised, although they did not let him know it. He was never alone with Bridei, but the king made a habit of including him in conversation and often asked after his progress. Gradually, over the time they stayed at Raven's Well, Hargest became accepted amongst the men, and they ceased to speak of him as if he were an outsider. One or two of them observed that, should Hargest march to war in their company, he'd be quite an asset. To start with, he'd be twice the size of any Gael in the field. And that sword arm of his was something to be reckoned with.

Bridei had sent a message back with Orbenn, and in it he had asked the opinion of Hargest's foster father as to the lad's readiness to go to war. Umbrig's answer, when at length it came, left the decision up to Bridei himself. If he thought the lad would be useful, he should take him. If not, he could despatch Hargest back to Storm Crag to cool his heels. There was no mention of Hargest returning to his father at Briar Wood, even though he was a young man now.

So it was that, when summer was drawing to its end and they marched forth from Raven's Well on the first stage of the long advance, Hargest took his place in the small personal force of the King of Fortriu, a proud, square-shouldered figure standing a head taller than most of the men and bearing his spear, his sword, his bow and quiver as if this were something he did every day and was quite at home with. Breth, riding by the king's side, had an edgy look about him. He had never fully trusted the boy, and he made no secret of his unease at Hargest's rapid acceptance into the ranks of Bridei's men-at-arms. There were whispers that the king's bodyguard felt threatened. Hargest, some folk said, was the obvious choice – young, fit, keen, strong – to step into the role of Bridei's most trusted minder.

Bridei had heard all of it and considered it nonsense. Breth knew his position was as secure as any man's can be who is heading into armed combat. As for Hargest, Bridei had him on a tighter leash than anyone recognised. The boy's desperate wish to please him was the most effective control he had; he would use it to stop the lad getting killed before he had a chance to grow up and learn what he was made of.

So, at last they were in motion, traversing the selfsame territory through which Bridei had marched as a lowly foot soldier in Talorgen's army on his way to his first taste of what war does to men. He could expect Hargest to be deeply disturbed by it, for all his bravado. Bridei hoped he would have time to talk to the lad afterwards, to listen as Hargest worked his way through what he had seen, what he had done. What he had been obliged to do. War could bring out the best in a man. Unfortunately, there were those in whom it awakened cruelty, and others who simply cracked under the terror of it. If this great venture went the way they'd planned, perhaps there would be no need to put the men of Fortriu through it again for a while. Perhaps there would be long years of peace, the Gaels gone from Priteni shores, Circinn ready to talk sense and men able to tend stock, plant crops, ply awl and tongs and hammer in the practice of their trades once more, not waiting for the rap on the door and the call to arms. He prayed it would be so, not for himself, not for his own glory, but for the good of his people. Defeat the Gaels and he could turn his attention to the other great task the gods called him to: uniting Circinn and Fortriu in the practice of the old faith.

As Bridei's forces made their way westward to the fringes of Gabhran's territory, from every side of Dalriada other bands of Priteni warriors were closing in on the Gaels. Gabhran and his chieftains could never have imagined such a massive and complex attack, such unity of purpose, such precision of timing.

Bridei and his war leaders had taken measures to increase their chances of remaining undetected until the last moment. They had made allowances for delays: a sickness, inclement weather, an ambush. Each chieftain had another man who could step up to lead in his place, should he be slain or taken. The trap in which they planned to catch the Gaelic king was like a clawed hand closing around Dalriada. Each finger must be in place; each relied upon the others to leave no gap, no weak spot through which Gabhran and his chieftains might escape. Bridei's leaders and their forces were days' travel from one another, and yet each depended on the others, in the end, for the successful closing of the trap. Bridei had been fostering their bonds of friendship for five years now. They knew one another well; they were a band of brothers, each proudly independent, each very much his own self, from wild Fokel of Galany to level-headed Talorgen, from flamboyant Ged to reserved Morleo, each part of a team dedicated to the future of Fortriu and to their king's great purpose. They had been vanquished by Dalriada before; the older chieftains, Talorgen and Ged, had seen many battles over the years. This time it seemed to be different. Even as they spoke of fall-backs and contingencies, they had the light of sure victory in their eyes.

Bridei shivered. It was daunting, sometimes, to see that and to know that a great deal of it was down to him. He was the king; he was chosen by gods and men to guide Fortriu to victory. These men, these seasoned, cautious leaders believed he could do it. They believed Bridei himself was the difference between another grinding defeat and the final, longed-for overthrow of the invader. He had tried to give them what they expected. He had made the plan as watertight as it could be. He believed, when he prayed to the Flamekeeper at dawn or to the Shining One at dusk, that the gods still smiled on him. All the same, it was a great weight to carry, and there were times when the longing to be at home was so powerful his heart ached with it. He wanted to sit by the fire with Tuala, watching as she brushed her hair in long, even strokes. He wanted to hold his son in his arms and to see Derelei's odd little smile, his wide eyes full of secrets. He wanted Broichan close by, Broichan whose grave advice had so often helped him find his way through one or another perplexing quandary. But he was the king, and he was riding to war, and it would be a long time before he saw them again: his home, his dear ones. It would be long past the feast of Measure, even if all went well. He wondered if his son would remember him.

They camped a night in the woods above Fox Falls, waiting for Fokel of Galany to join them. After they had eaten – a kind of broth that included hare, wood pigeon and hedgehog – Bridei walked around their campsite with Breth, speaking to as many of the men as he could. They did not need stirring speeches now; if they were feeling the way he did, what they'd be wanting was friendly words and reassurance. He listened to their concerns with courteous attention, giving each one of them his time and leaving each, he hoped, with the knowledge that he had the king's trust. It grew late, and most of the men fell asleep rolled in cloaks or blankets. Those on watch stood about the perimeter of the camp, silent shadows under a waxing moon. Bridei and Breth returned to the small shelter that had been erected for the king, where one of the Pitnochie men, Uven, was standing guard.

'Breth, you sleep now,' Bridei said. 'Let Uven take first watch here. I must make my peace with the gods before I lie down. I won't be far off.'

'If you're sure.' Breth had been stifling a yawn.

'I am. Go on now. Once Fokel arrives, and that may well be tomorrow, rest will be in even shorter supply. Wake him when it's time to change over, Uven.'

'Yes, my lord.' The Pitnochie men had all known Bridei since he was a child of four. Their manner towards him was almost proprietorial, but never lacking in respect. He had earned the loyalty they showed him.

Bridei walked up to a little hillock not far from the camp, a place where the light of the Shining One filtered through the broad reaching arms of the oaks to illuminate dimly a patch of mossy stones and the heart-shaped leaves of a low plant that crept along the crevices in the rock. Here he knelt in prayer, and Uven, respectful of the bond between king and god, stood back beyond the light, spear in hand, eyes watchful.

For a man druid-educated and weaned, so to speak, on the

ancient lore, Bridei made his prayer simple enough. Tomorrow and the next day and for many days after, on all sides of Dalriada, men would die because he had decided it was time for war, men like the good souls he had been talking with tonight. As king, it was he whose confidence was pulling them to the west with the light of a quest on their ordinary, honest faces. Many would not return. There would be wives, mothers, children whose time of waiting would last a lifetime. There were those who would receive back only a broken wreck of a man. Even if the forces of the Priteni achieved a great and noble victory, it would be thus, for war is cruel and impartial. In the heat of battle, on the field, there are no good men and bad men, simply two armies of fathers, sons and brothers who put their lives at hazard because their leader convinces them it is right. He, Bridei, was that leader.

He did not ask the Shining One to take away the burden he bore on his shoulders, a load that would grow heavier with each day of conflict. He simply asked her to make him strong enough to bear it. He did not ask her to spare his special friends, Breth, Talorgen, the Pitnochie men, only that, if they died, they might die cleanly and with purpose. As for himself, he hoped he would get home to White Hill and hold his wife and son in his arms again. But he did not put this in his prayer. He would not request for himself what he knew could not be granted to every man in his army. He prayed that the way he had chosen was a good one. He commended Tuala to the goddess's care; he asked the Shining One to send his little son sweet dreams. Then he knelt awhile in silence, arms outstretched, making his breathing calm.

Something stirred just behind him. In an instant Bridei was on his feet and reaching for his knife. A moment later, Uven hurled himself across the clearing, spear at the ready.

'It's all right, Uven.' With an effort, Bridei held his voice steady. 'It's only Hargest. By the gods, lad, you're soft-footed for such a big man.'

'What do you think you're playing at, sneaking up like that?' Uven addressed the young man in a furious snarl. 'Another instant and I'd have run you through!'

'An instant is long enough for an assassin to strike,' Hargest observed, pointing to the knife in his belt. 'My lord king, your bodyguards aren't up to the job.'

'You little –'

'Never mind, Uven,' Bridei said. 'I'll have a word to Hargest about manners; no harm's been done. If I didn't hear him, you certainly wouldn't; I was trained by Broichan. He'd be ashamed of me tonight. Come, Hargest, I'm finished here. Come back to the camp and talk to me awhile.'

They stood by the little fire that burned near Bridei's tent: Uven tense with irritation and unease, Hargest with folded arms and a belligerent expression, Bridei maintaining a well-practised calm. Hargest did not offer an apology. Perhaps, Bridei thought, he did not realise how close he had actually come to a knife in the heart. If so, the boy had learned less than he should have during his time with the king's men-at-arms.

'Hargest,' he said quietly, 'it's not wise to test the reactions of my guards by approaching me stealthily. Not only are they on orders to kill, but they've trained me to defend myself. My foster father taught me to use my ears as a wild creature does. Had I not been deep in meditation, I would have stabbed you in the heart before I had a chance to identify you.'

'When you are at prayer, then, your guards should be doubly alert.'

'Don't blame Uven,' Bridei said with a sigh. 'He was doing his best to balance discretion with vigilance. My men know me well, Hargest. There are times when I do need to maintain the illusion of solitude, if only for my own peace of mind.'

'They say you love the gods. That the Flamekeeper views you as his favourite son.'

'I hope all men here love the gods. As for favourite sons, I can only trust that the Flamekeeper supports our venture and considers me worthy to lead it. Now tell me, why are you here and not sleeping with your allocated group? Why did you approach me as you did? Not solely to draw attention to a weakness in my personal defences, I assume.'

'I want to talk to you alone.' Hargest's voice was a growl; he glared in Uven's direction. 'Private business.'

'No chance,' Uven snapped.

'He's right,' Bridei said, eyeing the young man's clenched fists and set jaw. 'In view of what you've just told us you must think your king a fool, that he would dismiss his single guard and conduct a private conversation at night in the woods with a man he's known for only – what – one turning of the moon? Not even that, I think.'

There was an awkward silence.

'Please, my lord?' Hargest's voice had quieted marginally. He was looking at his boots.

'Take a few steps away, Uven. Now, Hargest, what is it? Are you concerned about the battle? Have I made the wrong decision, permitting you to join my fighting force?'

'No, my lord.' The young man squared his shoulders. 'I'm fit to serve; I'll take my place. It's afterwards I want to speak of.'

'Afterwards? Afterwards is another battle, Hargest, and another march, and then another battle. That's what war is about. It's bloody and sickening. We do it because we must. Believe me, gods or no gods, this is not at all to my taste. When it's over, if you're lucky enough to survive, you'll go back to Storm Crag and you'll recognise that every day of peace the gods grant you is a precious gift.'

'I would . . . what if . . . ?'

'Whatever it is, say it, Hargest. It's late, and I must at least go through the motions of resting tonight or Breth will be displeased with me.'

'There's a chance one of your personal guards may be killed or wounded in the battle. If that happens, is there a possibility you might . . . ?'

Bridei could not suppress a smile. 'We've refined your combat skills at Raven's Well; the men are full of praise for you. It seems we haven't trained you in diplomacy. Are you so keen to take on the duties of bodyguard? They tell me it's a thankless job: little sleep, constant anxiety, no time to yourself. And the pay's no better than average, unless you've something special to offer. My principal guard, the one who's off in the north, is an expert translator and has a number of other skills. As for Breth, I will not challenge the gods by predicting his fate in the battle. I've several other men I can call on, such as Uven here. Trusted men.'

'You can trust me, my lord.' Hargest's voice was croaky with eagerness. He sounded very young. 'I've seen what you are to these men: a king, a leader, a friend. They see you as their brother, their father. They look in your eyes and see the gaze of the Flamekeeper. You know I'm a good fighter, my lord. I'm fit. I'm quick. I'm fearless. Give me a chance and I'll prove how good I can be as a bodyguard. I'll be better than any of them.'

'I don't require that,' Bridei said levelly. 'I'm more than satisfied with the men I have. They've proved their worth over a long period; in the case of Uven here, almost a lifetime.'

'Everyone has to start somewhere, my lord. Give me a trial, please. You won't regret it.' The youth's voice was shaking with feeling. So young; so full of passion.

'One of the required attributes is the capacity for icy calm in the most testing of conditions,' Bridei said.

'Put me to the test, then.'

'You're bold, that much is plain. Too bold, my advisers would tell me.'

'Please, my lord king. I will prove myself. I swear it on the Flamekeeper's manhood.'

'Let us take Galany's Reach first,' Bridei said, wondering if this explosive package of youth, ambition and hero-worship would be broken on the day of his first real battle, or survive to win the future it seemed he craved. 'Let's see how you acquit yourself there, and maybe I'll consider giving you a trial. You'll need to deal with Breth's disapproval.'

'Yes, my lord.' The young man's eyes were alight with hope, and a grin of pure delight curved his mouth, replacing momentarily his customary demeanour of sulky belligerence. 'Thank you, my lord. I swear you won't regret –'

'Let us survive Galany.' Bridei was suddenly weary. 'I don't in any way undervalue what you are offering, Hargest. Be clear on that. I honour your courage and sincerity, and I hope the Flamekeeper holds you in his hand when we advance into battle. You do need to learn a modicum of tact when dealing with my men. You should also remember that I am King of Fortriu. Breth and Uven and the others use a certain familiarity in private when they speak with me. They have earned the right to do so through many years of faithful service. Perhaps, in time, you too may earn that right. Goodnight, now. May the Shining One give you good dreams.'

'Goodnight, my lord king.' Hargest sketched a bow. As he straightened, his crooked grin was that of a mischievous son enjoying a private joke with a stern but loving father. It was more than Bridei could manage not to smile back.

In the long dusk of a summer night, Faolan and Ana made camp on the fringes of a pine wood, high above the glen of a long, lonely lake. They had seen a pair of eagles flying over earlier in the day, heading for the bare peaks that rose beyond the fells, and Ana told Faolan this was an auspicious sign.

'It is Bridei's token of kingship, and a pair is an especially potent message from the gods,' she said as they gathered wood for their little fire and dealt with the hawk's evening offering, a fat bird of some unidentifiable kind. Crossbill and hoodie looked on unperturbed as Ana plucked and gutted the kill; another indication, she thought, of their profound difference.

'Mm-hm,' grunted Faolan, striking a spark with knife on flint. 'I'd be happier if I knew exactly where we are, and how far we still have to go. If the gods want to be helpful, they might tell us that. Our guide there is leading us on a circuitous dance; it's almost as if the creature doesn't want us to get home. Maybe it's time to dispense with his services.'

'That wouldn't be a very good idea if you don't know where we are, Faolan. Besides –' Ana broke off. He was not in the best of humours, and she knew it annoyed him when she spoke of Drustan. Drustan . . . his absence hurt more with every step she took away from Briar Wood. Time was not healing that heart wound.

'Besides, the birds are all you have left of him, I know, I know.' Faolan blew on the flaring tinder, began to place twigs on top. 'They can't be with us forever. And they're not helping much; we're surely too far north here, and likely to lose ourselves if we must go through this woodland on our way to the coast. I'm half inclined to seek out the path myself; to let them go.'

'How would you make them fly off? Surely they answer only to Drustan.'

'I would tell them to leave. Or better still, you would tell them. Think how the hawk comes to your glove, obedient as a well-trained hunting bird. Order him to go and I'll wager the three of them will be away the same day.'

Ana said nothing. The hawk's trophy, skewered on a stick, was ready for cooking; her hands were a mess of blood, entrails and feathers. If she ever got back to White Hill, she'd do so with skills she had never expected to develop. As for their three guardians, they had become so familiar, each day shaped by elegant flight from glove to sky, by the soft touch of downy feathers on cheek or fingers, by the little sounds they made at night and the mysterious knowledge in their wild, bright eyes, that she knew her life would be incomplete now without them. They were her companions and friends. If the hawk was leading them in a roundabout way there must be a reason for it. Perhaps there was danger on a straighter path; perhaps there was no shorter way save the one they could not take, the one that led across Breaking Ford. The land of the Caitt was every bit as difficult as the tales told, all deep vales and daunting mountains, thick, dark forests and broad wind-whipped lakes. It was grand, vast and, for the most part, empty of human settlement. Here, the echo of a cry for help might ring on forever unanswered. Here, stag and boar and wolf lived and died never knowing the fear of the huntsman. If the hand of any deity stretched out over this great wild place, Ana thought it was surely that of Bone Mother, goddess of dreams, guardian of the ancient earth. She shivered, moving closer to the fire. Bone Mother governed the portal between this world and the next; her choices determined the span of a life. In the vast lonely sweep of this northern land, the goddess could snuff them out as easily as a pair of candles by the bedside. They would simply vanish, their passing unmarked, their bodies never found. Their flesh would darken and crumble and turn to soil under these trees and their bones would be scattered, crow-pickings.

'What's wrong?' asked Faolan, glancing at her as he balanced the skewered bird over the fire.

'Nothing,' Ana muttered. In the distance a cry rang out over the woods, a greeting and challenge: the uncanny music of wolves. From time to time, during the last few days, Ana had had

437

the sense of being tracked, watched. She had not heard the pad of feet, nor cracklings in the undergrowth, but she had felt it nonetheless. She hoped Faolan would make one of his reassuring comments, such as, 'They're further off than they sound,' but he said nothing.

On these summer nights the hillsides were bathed in a pale, cool light until nearly midnight, and the time of darkness was brief. Usually Ana was so exhausted by the end of the day's walking that she fell asleep soon after they had made fire and eaten. The discomfort of a bed made on rock or earth or forest floor was no longer enough to hold back the dive into a dark well of sleep. She knew she was much thinner; she felt the pressure of her hard bed on knees and elbows, on hips and shoulders that had lost the protective padding of their healthy flesh, and she was glad there were no mirrors here. She saw in Faolan something of the same. Hollow-cheeked, dark-bearded, he had acquired an edgy, dangerous look, the look of a man who fears he is losing control of the situation.

Tonight sleep was not going to come. The bones of their meagre supper gnawed clean, they sat close to their fire and listened to the howling. There was a pattern in it: a call, an answer. A summons, a consent. The pack was drawing nearer. The moon hung low in the sky, near full, a pale presence more guessed at than seen against the cold grey-blue of the summer night. The pines seemed darker, taller, more ominous than any Ana had seen before; the spaces beneath them were secret hollows, gaping mouths tenanted by unknown presences ready to swallow any intruder. Ana glanced up at the birds. The hawk perched high; he was restless tonight, moving about on the branch, a pair of eyes, a shadowy swathe of feathers. Hoodie and crossbill huddled close together like a pair of nestlings. From deep in the woods she imagined she could hear rustling, growling, the pad of many feet.

'We should build up the fire.' Faolan's tone was commendably steady. 'We need enough wood to keep it burning until first light. You'll need to stay awake and help me keep watch.'

Without a word, she got up to help him gather fuel, not venturing too close to the forest's edge. As they moved about, their boots making twigs crack and undergrowth rustle, the woods seemed to hush and the wolf voices fell silent. When Ana and Faolan returned to the fireside, their task complete, the creatures took up their hunting song again, and it was closer.

'What if they –?' Ana's teeth were chattering; she clenched her jaw to stop them.

'The fire will hold them back.'

'But if they come; if they attack?'

'Knife in one hand, fire in the other – grab hold of a brand, like this –' He snatched a flaming stick, gripping the unburned end. Ana saw that he had laid the fire in a way that provided a ready supply of these. He was expecting it, then, for all the calm demeanour. He, too, thought they would move in tonight.

'I suppose we could climb a tree,' she said, not altogether joking.

Faolan eyed the tall pines, their trunks devoid of useful branches to a point well above his head. 'From the looks of this forest,' he said, 'I think I might prefer to take my chances with the wolves. Ana?'

'What?'

'Something's moving down under the trees, behind you. Stay calm. Reach down for a brand; when you turn, hold it up in front of you. Remember, it's the barrier between you and the wolf. Don't be tempted to run. Keep the campfire at your back. Don't use the knife unless there's no other choice. Ready?'

Ready? How could one ever be ready for this? 'Yes,' she said, and turned, and saw them. Moving warily under the trees, not twenty paces away, they could be discerned as eyes touched to shining points by the firelight, forms merging with the layered darkness of the night wood, a hundred shades of grey. She tried to count them and, sickened by terror, found that there were too many to number, shifting, passing, grouping and separating like so many dancers in an elegant parade of long-limbed, sharp-toothed grace. The hawk gave a harsh scream in the branches above them and the wolves retreated a pace or two, then moved forward again in silent, expectant concert. The hawk swooped, a blur of sudden movement, and swept a handspan before the leading creature's startled eyes, talons extended. The wolf snapped its jaws; feathers flew. The bird went up and out of reach, then dived again.

'They're moving around behind us.' Faolan was by her side, his own fire stick in his hand. 'Just remember –'

'Keep the fire at my back,' Ana muttered, fear clawing at her gut. An instant later, one of the long, grey forms made a feinting run towards her and she thrust forward with her fire-brand, the knowledge that she actually was going to have to fight for her life warring with the unreality, the nightmarish quality of it all. The bird swooped, and this time its talons found a mark. There was a scream of pain and the wolf that had attacked her fell back.

She couldn't see Faolan. Behind her, on the other side of the fire, she heard him stumble and curse, and then he began to shout, as if he might keep the creatures at bay with his voice. Another made a dart at her, jaws snapping, and she swung the brand across, fighting to keep her balance and to maintain her position so they could not slip between her and the fire. The hawk had flown up out of sight. Hoodie and crossbill were nowhere to be seen.

Ana yelled something, anything, stabbing forward with the fire stick and hearing how small and shrill, how utterly ineffectual her voice was. It was the little squeak of a mouse before the owl swallows it; the squeal of a rabbit as the jaws of the hunting dog fasten on its fragile skull. Whirl, jab, shout; dodge, lunge, scream. First there was one, then two, then three of them coming in turn against her, quicker and quicker, a snap, a run, a bite, a jump . . . Gods, if one of them went for her throat this would all be over in an instant. The rank, wild smell of the creatures was all around her, their growling filled her ears. She could feel the thundering of her heartbeat in every part of her body; her knees were weak as water. Duck, turn, thrust, shout . . .

A great roar, and Faolan was at her side, sweeping his own fiery brand across and sending three of the wolves cringing back as the trail of flame singed them. Then he was gone, and she heard the sounds of his own particular game of attack and defence behind her. Ana drew a gasping, choking breath and shifted her grip on the wood. It was burning fast; soon, somehow, she'd need to find a moment to snatch another. Already the three were advancing on her again, slowly, their every movement a masterpiece of harnessed tension. Their voices united in an eldritch, snarling growl.

Faolan made a sound, a strangled curse, and she knew immediately that he had been hurt. She couldn't turn; she couldn't even look, let alone help him. She poked her brand at one, then another, and slashed wildly with the knife. On the outer edge of the circle wolves were running now, many wolves; the trap was closing. Ana could hear the sound of her own breathing, shallow, rasping, no longer strong enough to support a shout of defiance. No longer even enough for a last desperate prayer. She dropped to one knee, knife point held outward, and snatched a new brand from the fire. The leading wolf bunched its hindquarters, ready to spring.

'Drustan! Get out here and help us!' roared Faolan, moving into sight again and hurling something – a rock? – in her attackers' direction. 'Be a man!'

There was no time to ponder the oddity of this. He had won her the moment she needed to get up, to face the wolves with new fire. She waited, brand before her, as they jostled and dodged and moved again into pose of readiness.

'Drustan!' Faolan's voice was a powerful shout from deep in the belly. 'Do it! Do it now! Come out and help us or we're both dead! What price your scruples then, you fool?'

And then, oh, then . . . Suddenly from nowhere there was a third figure running, swerving, turning, a firebrand in each hand, dazzling the wolf pack into open-eyed stillness with his rapid, fluid sequence of movement, a tall, broad-shouldered figure with a mane of hair as wild and red as the fire he bore in his hands. Faolan's words had conjured him out of nothing. Ana's heart turned over; her breath stopped in her throat. Drustan was here. He had come back, and the world was made anew.

He did not halt the creatures long. They moved again in their circling ritual, teeth bared, voices a rumble of menace. But with three by the fire, it was much harder for the wolves to choose a target, to feint and to strike. Before the onslaught of whirling fire, of changing forms in the flickering light, the hunters drew back, some slinking up the hill to crouch beside an outcrop of shadowy stone, some moving down into the first shelter of the pines where they spread out in a line, waiting.

'Take a new brand.' Faolan's voice was tight. He seemed to have been injured in both leg and shoulder. 'They'll be back soon.' He glanced at Drustan, who was standing a little way off, bent over, catching his breath. 'You took your time,' Faolan said.

Ana's heart was so full she had no room left for fear. No time now for questions: where had he been? How had Faolan known he was close by? Drustan was alive and he was here. Nothing else mattered. She moved to his side; he straightened. She reached up a hand, a curious shyness overtaking her, and touched his cheek. Drustan brought her fingers to his lips, a moment only, then released her and stepped back. In the unsteady light from the fire, it was not possible to confirm her suspicion that he was blushing.

'More wood,' Faolan snapped. 'Build up the fire. If you can find anything else that will burn, bring it. Ana, stay by the fire; don't present yourself as a target.'

'I want to help.'

'Rest while you can, Ana,' Drustan said. Her name on his lips was the sweetest balm to the heart. She met his eyes and smiled. His mouth curved in an oddly tentative response before he turned away to help Faolan in the search for fuel. The two men together were able to drag a heavy pine branch up to the fire; it would burn long. They set more sticks ready for use as brands; they cleared the ground nearby of obstacles that might cause a man or woman to trip and become vulnerable. Wolves target the weakest; in Ana's mind there was no doubt at all that this was herself.

'Now we wait,' Faolan said, returning to her side. He had a hand clasped over his shoulder and he was trying to disguise a limp.

'Faolan, you're hurt! Let me see –'

'It's a scratch. I won't die of it. But they'll have scented blood. That will keep them here, fire or no fire, until the sky begins to lighten. Just stay calm and be alert. Now that our friend here has decided to grace us with his presence, we have some chance of surviving until morning.'

His manner was strange, almost offensive. 'You called him here yourself,' Ana said.

'I see them moving,' Drustan murmured. 'Ana, I don't want

you trying to fight. Stay behind me; I'll make sure they don't harm you –'

'Don't give her orders.' Faolan's voice was cold as stone. 'She's capable of helping us; let her do it.'

A little silence. Ana peered downhill in the half-dark. The shadowy forms had made ground; she could see the red glint of the flame in their eyes. Fear flooded back. It was a long time until morning. 'Please don't argue,' she said in a small voice, and stooped to take another stick from the fire.

The leader of the pack surged forward, baying, and it all began again. She lost the awareness of time passing. It felt endless: a cacophony of growling and whining, the curses and shouts of the two men, her own pathetic attempt to deter the attackers with a voice grown hoarse and breathless. The heavy, splintery feeling of the fire stick in her hand; the heat scorching her face; the sight of Drustan, not far off, a brand in each hand, tossing them up and catching them in a whirling display that seemed to send the animals around him into a daze. Of the three, he seemed least in danger of attack. Ana edged around to Faolan's side of the fire. Three wolves confronted him, long muzzles, bared teeth, slavering tongues and tense, anticipatory bodies. Faolan was standing awkwardly, favouring one leg, sweeping his firebrand two-handed before him. The wolves watched it closely; they seemed to be calculating the moment for a strike. Ana thrust her own brand forward, squinting against a shower of sparks. Her nose hurt, her eyes stung, her vision was blurring.

'Leave him alone!' she screamed at the attackers. 'Get away! Go! Go!' and swept the fire stick across one way and the other. The eyes of the wolves moved to her, intent, thoughtful and quite without pity.

'Best do what he said,' Faolan's voice was a gasp. 'Let him defend you . . . best chance . . .'

'You're injured,' Ana muttered. 'You can hardly stand up.'

'Go . . . other side . . . Drustan . . .'

'Stop it!' she snapped. 'We're friends, aren't we? Partners. Just keep going. The sun has to come up some time.'

For a while it seemed as if they might perhaps do that, main-tain the fight until dawn came to their rescue. Sometimes the wolves fell back and there was a chance to catch the breath, to push the log further into the fire, to snatch a new brand. But those brief respites grew shorter and less frequent. Faolan was struggling more and more, his breathing harsh and laboured, his injured leg less steady as each wave of assailants came forward. Drustan looked weary; his face was chalk white in the moonlight, his eyes shadowed. Ana felt exhaustion dragging through every part of her body. It was an effort to breathe, hard to stand up, a trial to summon the strength even to lift a stick from the fire. Beyond the circle of light cast by their small blaze, the number of wolves seemed greater every time she looked. Was the sky beginning to lighten? She told herself there was a tinge of warmer colour in the slate grey of the summer night. She knew it was not true.

They had gathered themselves for another onslaught when rain began to fall: the light, drizzling rain that bathed these hills once or twice on most days even in summer. The fire started to hiss. Within the forest, birds made restless sounds from their myriad perches. The wolves began to move in again, padding closer on every side, a hungry grey tide. To die like this would be cruel indeed. The gods were playing a strange sort of game with them. Why had she and Faolan survived Breaking Ford, why had Drustan escaped his brother's grasp, why had they been allowed to love one another if they were destined to die bloodily and painfully, for no purpose but to provide some creature's supper?

'This can't go on,' Drustan muttered, taking a new brand from the fire. 'There must be another way.'

'If the three of us could fly,' Faolan said bitterly as the rain grew heavier, 'no doubt there would be. Failing that, we must fight on as best we can.'

Drustan eyed him. 'We can't keep this up if the fire goes out,' he said. 'I'm going to try something else. Give me your fire stick.'

'What –?'

Before Faolan could say more, Drustan had seized the flaming brand from his hand and was striding off alone, down towards the forest, straight into the ring of wolves.

'No –!' Ana screamed, launching herself after him and coming up short as Faolan grabbed her arm.

'Don't,' he hissed. 'If he wants to get himself killed, fine, but he's not taking you with him.'

She could hear, then, her own wordless sobbing; she could feel the hard grip of Faolan's hand around her arm as, from every side, wolves began to move. They streamed after the red-haired man as he made his way towards the trees, juggling fire with his graceful hands. What was he doing? Surely he would not sacrifice his own life so she and Faolan would be safe, just as Deord had done? What could provoke a man to such reckless courage?

They watched until Drustan's tall form almost merged into the shadow of the pines. Despite the rain that was dousing their fire, his torches still flamed as they rose and fell, the pattern of them now a wheel, now a web, now a flower, dazzling and strange. The wolves were gathered all around him; Ana could hear their growling. She waited for the first to leap, the others to follow. She waited for the man she loved to be torn apart before her very eyes. When they were done with him, they could take her; she would no longer care.

The wolves sensed what was coming before Ana heard or saw anything. The growls changed to a thin whining; bellies were lowered to the ground, ears flattened. There was an eldritch sound from the forest, an immense stirring and rustling as if the very trees were about to lift roots from the soil and march forward. A moment later, flying out from the dark pines, came birds: a great, dense flock of birds, more than any Ana had ever seen gathered together before, even at the spring arrival of geese to the wetlands by Banmerren. They were a whirring cloud, a chorus of shrill voices, the perilous sweeping of a sorcerer's cloak. They dipped low over the heads of the cowering wolves, making a fluid circle whose centre was the man standing with fire in his hands, the man who, somehow, had conjured this strange army of owl and swallow, dunnock and siskin, thrush and redstart to his aid.

Faolan's hand released its vicelike grip; his arm came around Ana's shoulders, perhaps for reassurance, perhaps merely so he could keep his balance. As she stared, stunned into silence, the birds swept once more in their circle and vanished back into the depths of the wood. In the darkness down the hill, she could

445

see Drustan returning, his torches smoking in the rain. Of the wolves there was not a sign. She looked the other way, up the hill to the rocky outcrops where more creatures had sheltered, ready to attack. Nothing stirred; the silence was absolute.

Then, sudden as the sun peeping from parting clouds, two small forms flew out of the night to alight on Ana's shoulders: crossbill on the right, hoodie on the left. She waited for the hawk, but it did not come, only Drustan, walking up to the dying fire with raindrops on his auburn hair. His shoulders were stooped with the weight of utter exhaustion.

'They're gone,' he murmured and a moment later his tall form folded up on the ground, head in hands.

'Drustan! Are you hurt?'

'No, Ana. I need a little time, that's all.'

The rain was passing over, and the pine log was still smouldering. What to do first: tend to Faolan's wound, try to build up the fire, stay on guard in case the wolves came back? Begin to ask Drustan all the questions that tumbled through her mind, or simply put her arms around him and thank him for saving their lives?

'The fire,' Faolan muttered as if reading her thoughts. He took his arm away from her shoulders and made to shift the log, to stir up the embers that sizzled in the rain. Ana heard his gasp of pain as he squatted down. The firelight touched the bloodstains on his ragged clothing.

'Were you bitten? How bad is it? We should try to clean the wounds, bind them up –'

'It's nothing.'

'Show me.'

'Fire first,' Faolan said. 'If it goes out, they'll surely return.'

They tried to shelter the heart of their dwindling blaze from the worst of the rain. After a little, Drustan got up and went to fetch more wood from down the hill, near the edge of the forest where it might be drier. This time Ana made no move to stop him, just watched him go with wonder. 'They didn't even try to hurt him,' she said.

'He's a dab hand with fire, I'll give him that.' There was a dour note in Faolan's tone; she could not put it down entirely to the fact that he was in pain.

'You called him,' Ana said. 'I heard you. You called him and all of a sudden he was here. How could that be? Where did he come from?'

'I'm not the one you should be asking.' Faolan had rolled up his trouser leg and was inspecting the wound in the fitful light; a dark bruise stained the flesh of the inner thigh, along with a mess of drying blood. Ana felt sick. Dog bites were difficult to deal with even if one had clean water and healing herbs at hand. Ill humours commonly entered such wounds, and the fever that accompanied them was generally fatal.

Faolan must have seen her expression. 'I've had worse than this in my time,' he said. 'Forget it. It's stopped bleeding. I can still walk. Be glad we're alive. That was too close for comfort.'

'Faolan?'

'Mm?'

'What did you mean, you're not the one I should be asking? You must have known he was nearby, to call him thus. Have you been keeping something from me?'

'Ask your precious Drustan. I think you'll find he hasn't been entirely truthful with you. Now he's here, you've got what you want, and it's time for him to give you the full story.'

This was odd; but perhaps not so very odd, save that it meant Faolan had knowledge of Drustan that he had kept from her. A suspicion was creeping up on her, one that was strange and wondrous, and made sense of a great many things.

There was a little silence as they watched Drustan approaching in the dwindling rain, the moon touching his damp curls to silver. He bore a heavy armload of fallen branches.

'He's strong,' Faolan observed. 'That'll come in handy.'

'You're so angry. I can almost feel it. He just saved our lives.'

'Ask him for the truth. Ask him where he was and why he didn't make an appearance until we were looking death in the face. Ask him if that's what a man puts a woman through if he really loves her.'

Drustan came up to them, dropping his load and stooping to help with the fire. 'We must keep it burning,' he said. 'I don't think they will come back. But you have no warm clothes, Ana, and the two of you look half-starved and worn out. Here –' He

447

shrugged off his tunic and the fine wool shirt he was wearing beneath, passed the shirt to a wordless Ana, slipped the tunic back over his head. 'Wear this, please. Your gown is ruined. You must be freezing. I'm afraid there's still a long way to go.'

'You know the way?' she asked him, feeling again that curious tension between them which was partly the stirrings of physical desire, not wholly dulled by hunger, cold and shock, and partly a kind of reticence, a shyness that held back the words she longed to say. To speak what was in the heart, what awoke every moment in the body, seemed somehow dangerous. It was too soon.

'I can guide you to the east coast,' Drustan said. 'I can lead you to a meeting of two rivers, from which it will be easy to make a way south to Bridei's court. I will find shelter soon, good food, warm clothing. In these parts there is nothing. I'm sorry.'

Ana snuggled into the shirt, which was still warm from his body and long enough to cover her almost to the fraying, cut-off hem of her tattered gown. She looked up at Drustan; his bright eyes regarded her, solemn, a little wary. 'Thank you,' she said. 'This is wonderful. And thank you for saving us. I don't know how you did that, but it was . . . it was like magic. Beautiful and mysterious.'

'You have something to tell the lady.' Faolan glanced at the other man. 'An explanation.'

Drustan was staring into the fire now. 'That is for tomorrow,' he said quietly. 'It is for a place other than here; for a place of safety, in sunshine, when Ana has rested and eaten. I will tell her. But not tonight. Not yet.' He reached out and took Ana's hand in a firm grasp, drawing her down to sit beside him, next to the fire. The rain had abated and the blaze cast welcome warmth on her chilled hands and face. Opposite them, Faolan seated himself awkwardly, stretching his injured leg out straight. Drustan's arm came around Ana's shoulders. She felt his touch all through her body, she who had for so long been too tired and sad and hungry to desire anything beyond the next day's meagre supper, the next night's uncomfortable sleep. The blood surged to her cheeks; she laid her head against his shoulder and closed her eyes.

'Drustan,' Faolan said, 'I have to tell you that Deord is dead. Alpin killed him. He fell bravely.'

Drustan nodded, as if he had known this already. 'A grievous loss,' he said. 'He deserved a life; he deserved the freedom he won for us.'

After a little, Faolan said, 'You mentioned guiding us to the coast. Does that mean you don't intend to come all the way to White Hill with us?'

'It depends.' Drustan's voice had gone very quiet.

'On what?'

'On what Ana wants. It depends on tomorrow.'

Ana took a deep breath. The two men seemed lost in some cryptic game of which she had no understanding. There was nothing for it but to speak quite honestly. 'I want you to come with us, Drustan,' she said. 'I don't ever want you to go away again.'

A wave of tension ran through him, startling in its intensity. Then he said, 'If you can say that tomorrow as we sit by our fire and watch the birds fly in to roost at nightfall, then I will tell you yes, I will never leave you, not in all the days and nights of my life. If you cannot, I will guide you to the safe path southward, and then go home to Dreaming Glen and tend to my land alone. No –' as she made to protest, 'say no more now. We are all weary. Let us wait for the sun, and then we should move on to a place of shelter. A place where wolves cannot reach us.'

At dawn they quenched their fire and moved on. Crossbill and hoodie accompanied them, darting off from time to time in their usual manner. Ana did not ask where the hawk was. She had gone very quiet; Faolan wondered what she was thinking and how much she had guessed at.

They did not go far. After that night of fear and struggle and no sleep, they were all weary. Faolan's injured leg had stiffened alarmingly and he was finding it difficult to walk. Ana's stumbling progress suggested she was asleep on her feet.

They followed a stream that gurgled through the forest, and in a clearing where sunlight filtered down through the interlacing of alder and willow, they stopped to rest. Faolan's knee did not want to bend, and when he had eased himself to the ground, he found that the others were both staring at him. 'It's nothing,' he snapped.

'All the same,' said Drustan, 'a poultice of healing herbs can relieve this greatly. We still have a long way to go. Along this stream there's likely to be found a number of useful plants, including something to stave off fever.'

'There's no rush.' Faolan winced as he reached to remove his pack; the shoulder was a mass of fiery pain.

'You need this now, Faolan,' Ana said. 'Don't be foolishly brave about it. Let Drustan help you.'

'You know what's required?' Faolan eyed Drustan sceptically.

'I have sufficient knowledge not to harm you, yes,' Drustan said, smiling. 'Rest now; I won't be long. When I return I will stand watch awhile. Of us all, my need for sleep is least.'

He walked off, footsteps silent on the forest floor. Ana and Faolan settled as best they could. It should be easy enough to stay awake until the bird-man got back, Faolan thought. This pain was sufficient to keep the most placid of men on edge. He listened to Ana's soft breathing; glanced across at her still form, head pillowed on hands, eyes closed, the small blanket spread over her. He looked up into the canopy of leaves; saw hoodie and crossbill perched together, utterly still. A moment later, he was asleep.

Faolan woke to a pair of hands at his throat, squeezing; a man kneeling astride him, a hoarse whisper, 'Now die, Gael!' and, through the miasma of sleep, a sudden fierce urge to stay alive. He twisted, his heart thudding, his knee in agony. He bucked and kicked even as Alpin's furious face swam in and out of focus above him. Unconsciousness was close; he had been slow to wake. Beyond those mad eyes, that contorted mouth, he saw movement: Ana waking in silence; Ana getting to her knees, eyes wide with shock; Ana seizing a piece of fallen wood and lifting it to strike . . .

Faolan made himself suddenly limp; against all instinct, he rolled back his eyes, then closed his lids. An instant later his assailant let go, jumping to his feet and out of the way of Ana's makeshift weapon.

'Oh, so *you'll* fight me now?' Alpin sneered, turning towards her. 'Well, your Gael's done for and my brother's nowhere to be

450

seen, so it's just you and me, my dear. By all the gods, I've waited too long for this –' And as she swung the branch again he seized the other end and tore it from her grasp.

Faolan, behind him, reached out for his knife. His knee would not take his weight; he could not get to his feet, and he would not be able to fight. The moment Alpin turned and saw him, he was dead meat. The knife was by his pack, close, so close . . . He could not reach it without sliding along the ground, making a noise . . . If Alpin heard him, if Alpin killed him, Ana was lost. *Run*, he willed her. *Don't try to fight, run. Find Drustan. Get away.*

She ran. It had been a waking from too little sleep to sudden terror, and she stumbled. For a moment Alpin stood with hands on hips, laughing at her, and then he set off in pursuit. Faolan rolled to his side; stretched out his arm. Just a little further . . .

'You!' It was Drustan's voice, the tone astounded, and Faolan, his fingers closing around the weapon at last, saw Drustan emerging between the trees, a sheaf of foliage in his hands, a bird now on each shoulder. He was staring at his brother as if struck by a dark revelation; as if looking into an abyss.

In the middle of the clearing, Alpin reached Ana, seizing her from behind, one arm around her waist, the other across her neck. 'Make one move, bird boy,' he said, 'and I'll snap her in half.'

'You . . .' Drustan was frozen, his expression that of a seer in a trance. 'It's the same as Drift Falls,' he breathed, 'just the same . . . shouting . . . Erisa running . . . you after her . . . *I saw you* . . .' Abruptly, his eyes became focused, his expression ferocious and his tone a war cry. 'By all that's holy, it was a lie! *You* killed her. I saw you. Let Ana go! Let her go at once or I'll strangle you with my bare hands, brother or no brother!'

'No, you won't,' Alpin said, backing away with Ana still captive in his arms. 'You won't kill me because, if I die, I'll take her with me. As for Erisa, you'll never prove that. Who'd take the word of a mad freak against mine? A delusion, that's all it is.'

Drustan took a slow, deliberate step towards him, and another. His eyes, now, were deathly calm. *Back him up towards me*, Faolan willed him, *give me a clear target.*

'You think I wouldn't do it?' said Alpin. 'I don't want her as much as that, little brother. Not after the two of you have been there before me. If you come any closer I'll just tighten my grip like *this* –'

Drustan launched himself forward, hurtling through the air with hands outstretched like talons.

A brother should not kill his brother. That stain sits too heavily on a man's spirit. Faolan threw the knife. Before Drustan could touch him, Alpin crumpled to the ground, the weapon protruding from his back and Ana pinned beneath him. For one chill moment, Faolan thought his knife had pierced her body as well. Then Drustan rolled his brother's limp form over and, shakily, Ana got to her feet. There was a red stain on her gown.

'I'm all right,' she said before either of the men could speak. 'Gods . . . How did he . . . He came from nowhere . . .' Then, clapping a hand over her mouth, she staggered to the clearing's edge and retched up the contents of her stomach into the undergrowth.

'A clean kill,' Faolan said, managing to stand and hobble forwards, his knee on fire. 'Better than he deserved. More merciful than he meted out to Deord. I must offer you both an apology. I fell asleep on watch. I have no excuse.'

Alpin's eyes were open. Even in death, their baleful glare was disturbing. Drustan knelt and closed them, gently enough. 'Any one of us would have killed him,' he said. 'For Deord; for Ana; for Erisa . . .'

'What did you mean?' Ana had returned, wiping her mouth on her sleeve. She looked wretched, sheet-white, with eyes like saucers. 'About Drift Falls, and Erisa? You remembered at last? Did you say *he* was responsible?'

'He lied.' Drustan was still kneeling by his brother's side, as if unsure what should come next. 'All those years, he lied to save himself. When they called me,' glancing at the two birds, 'when I came back and saw him running after you . . . it was the same, just the same . . . They argued, and she ran from him, and he pursued her . . . and then she fell. He did not intend murder. Even he would not wish to kill his unborn son. It was an accident. But his doing. His, not mine . . . Gods, to remember now, after all those years . . . He's right. Who will believe me? There is no way to prove my innocence.'

'Oh, yes, there is,' Ana said. 'Find the old woman, Bela. Hear her story. With Alpin gone, she may be prepared to tell it. Do that and folk will at least listen to you.'

'A remarkable tale,' said Faolan. 'I'm sad Deord cannot hear it; he believed in you, Drustan. He said you could be something. This death,' he touched the body with the toe of his boot, 'will make things still more complicated for you.'

'What do we do now?' Ana asked shakily. 'Go on? Go back?'

The two men looked at her.

'We bury him,' Faolan said. 'Then we go on. You and I do, at any rate. Wild horses couldn't drag me back to that place. Drustan's choice is up to him.'

'I will accompany you to the coast, at least,' Drustan said. 'For now, nothing changes. For the future, everything changes. It is too much to come to terms with.' He had taken his brother's lifeless hand in his. Faolan saw in his pose both love and disgust, relief and anguish.

'At such times,' Faolan said, 'practical work is useful. I still need those herbs; my knee feels as if it's about to split apart. Ana probably knows how to make a poultice. She was educated by wise women, after all. You and I must dig a grave. And Ana must rest before we go on; indeed, we all should do so. You may wish to say prayers; to speak formal words of farewell. I don't know. I don't know if you are a man of faith.'

'I would have killed him,' Drustan said, getting up. 'If you had not acted in that moment, my brother's blood would be on my hands.' His odd, bright eyes were fixed, unwavering, on Faolan's.

'Exactly. Be glad one of my trades is that of assassin,' Faolan said.

'And I would have killed him.' Ana's voice held both horror and a certain pride. 'If I had been a little stronger . . . We're all responsible for this. I think we must bury him, say a prayer and be on our way. A tale might be told later, at Briar Wood, of our discovering his body in the forest. Folk suffer mishaps in these parts all the time.'

Faolan was astonished at her coolness, her presence of mind. 'This journey has surely changed you,' he said. 'You're suggesting Drustan lies about it?'

'Not exactly,' said Ana, putting her hand on Drustan's shoulder.

'There are times when not all of the truth need be told. Times when it's best to get on and let certain things go. If Alpin had followed that advice he would still be alive.' She shivered. 'You don't think he has others with him, do you? A hunting party, so far from Briar Wood?'

'One would have thought that likely,' said Faolan. 'But it seems not, or they'd be here, surely. All the same, your advice is sound. We'd best get this done and move on.'

After that, little was said. Drustan dug out a shallow grave; Ana and Faolan collected stones. If prayers were spoken over the fallen man, it was done in silence. Then Faolan submitted to the application of herbal poultices for knee and shoulder. Later, Drustan said, he would brew a draught as well, to stave off fever and allow Faolan to rest. Not now. They no longer wished to stay in this place.

They did not walk much further that day. It was clear to Faolan that he was holding them back, and he gritted his teeth and did his best to maintain a steady pace, with limited success. When they had reached the far side of the woodland, where an open valley lay before them and rocks provided shelter from the wind, they halted. Drustan made fire and, true to his word, brewed a herbal concoction of bitter taste and muddy appearance. He stood over Faolan until it was all gone.

As drowsiness crept over him, mingling with the dizzy, hot feeling in his head, Faolan wondered what Drustan's choice would be: let Ana go hungry, or reveal his other form so he could hunt and provide for her. Before there was a chance to find out, Bridei's right-hand man sank into sleep.

The next day the sun shone, the clouds vanished and the travellers made their way down into the valley. Drustan seemed tireless. The herbal remedies had eased Faolan's discomfort, and he could walk more freely. All the same, today he would almost have welcomed the pain; anything to distract him from the sight of Drustan and Ana together. He watched them as the day wore on and they came to a sheltered stretch of lake shore, where sunlight bathed the pale trunks and glinting foliage of birches and spread its warmth over the silvery water like a blessing. With every step they took, it seemed to Faolan that the distance between himself and the two of them increased, a distance not to be measured in strides or steps, but in something far less tangible. Drustan and Ana were walking in a different world from his, a world in which everything was good and joyful and easy to understand. They did not talk much; they did not walk hand in hand; they did not embrace. It was the smallest things that spoke to him: the not-quite-accidental brushing of fingers together, the brief touch of bodies in passing, the way Drustan's hands lingered at Ana's waist as he helped her down a steep drop. The colour in their cheeks and the brightness in their eyes. Their drowning glances.

Once or twice they did move on ahead of him, for his leg was still slowing him down. Crossbill and hoodie stayed close to Faolan. He wondered if, when Drustan was not keeping an eye on him, these two were bound to perform that duty. It was a good thing, Faolan conceded. Despite the dark jealousy Drustan aroused in him, accepting the fellow's help was a lot better than being left behind for the wolves.

Late in the afternoon, Drustan and Ana went ahead along the shore to look for a place to camp, for Drustan had suggested they stop their day's walk early and rest. It was evidently plain to him that Faolan could not manage much more. It was a bitter feeling to become the weak link. Faolan hoped his wounds would mend quickly. He was still Bridei's emissary. It was bad enough to be returning to White Hill with news of a mission turned to disaster. He would rather not be carried in burning with fever and owing his survival to this strange bird-man, this creature who was even now taking Ana away from him, step by inevitable step. No, that was foolish. She could never have been his. He was a Gael. He was an assassin, a man whose very existence relied upon his personal obscurity. He had destroyed his family; he had shattered all he held dear. And he was kin to the King of Dalriada. Like it or not, he was an Uí Néill. It made an impressive list of reasons not to think of her the way he did. Unfortunately, the heart took no account at all of logic. The heart whispered that, when he had had the opportunity, he should have thrown that stone.

Faolan came around a stand of birches and saw the two of them by the water, close together but not touching. Both had taken off their boots and were standing ankle deep, soaking weary feet. They had been talking, but they fell silent as he approached. He tried to minimise his limp.

'Look, Faolan,' Ana said, smiling, 'along the lake, that way – there's smoke rising. Drustan thinks there's a little settlement there. We'll be able to clean up your wounds and sleep under proper shelter. It's been so long, I can hardly remember what that feels like. Are you all right? Does it hurt badly?'

He shook his head, observing with wonder the change in her. Though gaunt and weary, her face was suffused with happiness and her eyes had regained all their old serenity. Even her stance was different, her back straight, her shoulders held proudly. It was Drustan who had worked that magic; Drustan who now stood by her side, a flush in his cheeks and something of the same quiet radiance about his own bearing.

'Let's rest here awhile,' Drustan said. 'You should take the weight off that leg. I thought I saw some hazelnuts higher up; we could procure a meal of sorts.'

'As long as they are fit for men and not only for birds.'

'They are fit for men, Faolan. Would I try to poison you? You have been Ana's friend, her guardian, her lifeline. But for you, she and I would not be together. I honour you as a brother.'

Faolan was wordless. The weight of Dubhán's death, and Alpin's, and a lifetime of might-have-beens hung in the air between them, stilling his tongue. He looked across at Ana, who had settled herself on the grass of the lake shore, the scarlet-feathered crossbill perched on her hand. She was stroking its head with a finger and whistling softly. Her cropped hair, for all the lack of care, gleamed dark gold in the afternoon sunlight. She was cross-legged, her pale, bare feet showing below the long shirt Drustan had given her. There was a rosy colour in her cheeks; her lashes screened her eyes as she turned her attention to the little bird.

Something shifted in Faolan. He recognised that her happiness outweighed everything. She loved Drustan; at least, she loved the man she thought he was. Hope of a bright future had restored her to herself: the brave, serene, lovely woman who had captured his own heart before ever they came to Briar Wood and found themselves embroiled in this strange tale of brother against brother. He had been on the point of challenging Drustan again, for the day was advanced, the sun was shining and they were close to shelter. The words had been on his lips, *Tell her the truth now*. He could not say them. He could not shatter her newfound joy. How could he bear to see that little smile fade, the rosy cheeks grow pale, the proud shoulders droop in despair?

'I'll go in search of nuts,' said Drustan absently.

The hoodie flew to his shoulder as he headed off under the trees. Ana's heart was in her eyes as she watched him walk away. For a little there was no sound but the calls of birds overhead and the distant roaring challenge of a stag high on the hillside across the water. It was an unsettling reminder of how far advanced the season was; had they indeed walked away the remainder of the summer in these endless mountains?

'Faolan,' Ana said quietly, 'he told me.'

He stared at her.

'He told me the truth. About the – the changes – how he's been with us all the time, since the waterfall, and how he can go between forms. I already knew, really. The hawk had his eyes. The truth had been creeping up on me a while.' She looked at the little bird on her hand, frowning. 'I can't believe Alpin did what he did; that was so cruel and wicked. To lock his brother up for his own misdeed, to keep up the lie, to let Drustan believe himself guilty . . . Worst of all, to call such a god-given ability madness . . . I can't understand that. At home, it would surely be seen as something rare and wondrous, like the transformations druids spend years and years learning to do, but so much more powerful, and so natural . . . There were others in his family with similar talents, long ago; that's what he says . . . Did you know Drustan first did this at only seven years old?'

'You accept this so easily? You're not . . .' His words trailed off. It was quite evident she was neither shocked nor afraid. It was clear she cared not at all if her children were a strange blend of bird and human, as likely to fly off in search of fat mice to eat as to attend to their nurses and tutors. She would never cease to surprise him.

457

'Why are you smiling, Faolan?'

'There's a song in this, that I can say with confidence.'

'Don't put me in any songs until I have a comb and some hot water and something more than rags to dress in,' Ana said, grinning.

'You're perfect just as you are,' he told her quietly. 'But I won't be making any songs; my barding days are behind me.' This song would be deep inside him, in the hidden recesses of the heart, both utmost joy and deepest pain. No one but he would ever hear its sweet words of love. No one but he would weep as it played out its tale of need and silence and loss. And that was just as it should be. 'I wish you every happiness, Ana,' he said.

She said nothing, and soon after, Drustan returned bearing a broad leaf on which was piled a small harvest of nuts. It came to Faolan that the other man had left him and Ana together just so they could speak thus. He swallowed resentment that he must add tact to all Drustan's other virtues.

'Why did you keep flying away?' This question had to be asked, now the secret was out in the open. 'Why did you abandon us without any warning? And why did you take so long to reach us after we fled Briar Wood? Deord was out there all alone, fighting a whole hunting party.'

'Would he have prevailed had I been by his side?' Drustan asked, his tone sombre.

Faolan was obliged to answer honestly. 'In my opinion, no. You'd both have been killed. He wouldn't have wanted any of us to be there. But I'd have thought you'd want to help him.'

'I could not help him. The changing is not always easy for me. I was distressed and confused, wanting to leave, afraid to leave, desperate to be with Ana, terrified of what I might do if I went free. In that other form, my mind is different. I do not see or hear or think quite as a man does. Sometimes I do not even remember. It was thus with Erisa's death. I was in my other form. I saw them, but once I returned to myself, the memory was gone. Until yesterday. So, after you left, I made a choice: Ana over Deord. That's what he would have wanted. In the end, I caused his death.'

'We all had a part in that,' said Faolan grimly. 'And the other times?'

Drustan cleared his throat; he sounded nervous. Faolan found himself oddly in sympathy. 'I cannot maintain one form or the other too long without . . . without becoming unsettled. Distressed. The need to change builds in me and must be released.'

'You become violent?'

'Faolan –' Ana protested.

'It's all right, you need to know this,' Drustan said. 'You need to know all of it. Violent . . . Only if I am confined and prevented from doing what body and mind call me to do. Alpin's barred enclosure was a particular form of torture for me; he knew how such restraint tormented me. Deord saved me. He understood the need to let me fly free. But there were long times when we could not go out. Deord shared his own skills with me; kept me occupied, kept me moving. Sometimes it was not enough.'

'Did you ever attack him? Or others?'

'I came close once or twice with my brother. Hence the shackles. If I am restrained at such times I hurt myself, nobody else.'

'What about before?' Ana's tone was gentle. 'Before Alpin imprisoned you?'

'At Dreaming Glen I came and went as I pleased. It is my own place; my people know me. I moved freely and easily from one form to the other. I taught myself to retain the understanding of human speech even when I walked in the other world. Some skills I lost in captivity, but I am regaining them. I was afraid to trust you with the truth, Ana.' He gave her a shy smile. 'I misjudged you. So, when it was time to be a man again, I flew off into hiding. There was no way to reassure you; to let you know I would return.'

Ana slipped a hand into Drustan's. 'I think we will need all the days from here to White Hill,' she said, 'to choose the right words for presenting this tale at court.'

Chapter Sixteen

trategists say that if no more than one in three fighting
men is lost in securing an objective, the action can be considered a success. Between them, Bridei and Fokel lost
less than this proportion in the final decisive battle for
Galany's Reach. The ancient banner of Galany was raised above
the settlement, this time to fly in perpetuity; a ritual of thanks to
the Flamekeeper was conducted on the conical hill where once
a mighty carven stone had stood to mark this land for the Priteni.
That night Bridei made his own prayers in silence, and the man
who guarded his solitude was Elpin, formerly of Broichan's
household. Bridei had allowed Uven a time of rest, a time he
knew this warrior of middle years would spend with the other
men, working through the sights and sounds of today's conflict,
speaking of the friends lost, listening to the strange mix of grief
and anger and bravado, of determination and courage and uncertainty that must attend such a gathering.

As for Breth, he would never stand guard by his king and
friend again. One in three; it could be the turn of any man to fall to
a swift arrow, a slashing sword, a final, insistent spear. Bridei had
lost his keen-eyed archer somewhere in the midst of the bloody

maelstrom before the palisade of Galany's Reach, and found him sprawled limp and open-eyed amid the human wreckage strewn there after Bone Mother had swept the field, bearing the spirits of Fortriu's fallen sons away. Bridei had first met Breth in an archery contest when Bridei was still a child; that child had made a choice to lose, and thus allowed the warrior to salvage his pride before an audience of fighting men. One in three; a victory. It did not feel that way, not even with Galany safe in Fokel's hands.

When he had said his prayers, Bridei sent Elpin off to rest and sat awhile with Hargest, whom he had summoned some time before. He knew he must soon go back to the settlement, find words of strength and hope for his army and make decisions quickly: who would stay to keep the new-won territory secure, who would march on to the next objective. He must determine the best way to deal with the Gaelic captives, the women and children, the old men. He would do it. But not yet. Not just yet.

'I'm sorry, my lord,' Hargest said quietly. They sat together by the rowans atop the neat hill which had once housed the Mage Stone; by day, there would be a sweeping view of the valley, the settlement, the field still littered with Gaelic dead, the pale waters of King Lake not far off, spreading westward to the sea. 'About Breth, I mean.'

'Mm.' Bridei thought about how young Hargest was, far younger than he himself had been when he had his first taste of war, here in this selfsame proving ground. 'They tell me you acquitted yourself bravely today. Did more than your share.'

Hargest said nothing.

'It's a grim business,' Bridei said.

'They are Gaels. They deserve to die. My heart beat more strongly with each one I slaughtered.'

Bridei regarded him quizzically. 'We must do all we can to prevail, that much is true,' he said. 'When you are older, I doubt if you will see it in terms so black and white.' It would be easier, no doubt, if one could think as this boy did; it would lessen the pain. He had never possessed such certainty himself. Questions of right and wrong, justice and fairness had plagued him since the day of his first engagement with the enemy. He did not doubt the rightness of his god-given mission to drive the Gaels from Priteni shores. It was

461

the falling of each man, be he of Fortriu or Dalriada, the knowledge of each loss that weighed on him. Breth had been a good man, loyal, honest, a true friend. But who was to say the death of this warrior who happened to be dear to himself was of any greater or lesser account than that young Gael with a spear in the belly, or that dark-bearded archer from Fokel's company? Because a man did not love the ancient gods of the Priteni, because a man's father happened to be born in some place other than Fortriu, did that make his death any less of a sacrifice? Bridei thought of Faolan, and knew in his heart that a good man was a good man, whatever his origins, whatever his convictions, whatever his occupation.

'My lord king?' Hargest was regarding him closely, a little frown on his broad brow. 'What are you thinking? You seem . . . distracted.'

'Dangerous thoughts, Hargest. I must put them away until this campaign is done. What about you? Were you not troubled by the sights you saw today? It's a big step from keeper of Umbrig's horses to a warrior in the first line of advance.'

'Troubled? No, my lord. War's war. Folk die.'

Bridei nodded. 'I have something to say to you, and although it seems too soon, I'll say it now before we go back down and are surrounded by men with questions. You're a brave lad, and able. I've lost Breth; it's a sorrow to me but, as you so bluntly put it, folk die. We're headed for much bigger action now and the experienced men are going to want to be in the thick of it; they're not going to take kindly to an assignment that requires them to put their king's personal safety before their own chances of accounting for the enemy.'

Hargest sat silent, waiting.

'I can't offer you Breth's job,' Bridei said bluntly, for the bright anticipation in the boy's eyes was unnerving. 'You may have the skills, but you lack experience.' He did not add that it was still early days; too soon to trust a young man who had attached himself to the king of his own choice, and who was known amongst the warriors for his volatile temper. 'I plan to share Breth's duties amongst the Pitnochie men. We'll need one more or they'll be too short on sleep. I want you to join them. No solitary guard duty; they generally work in pairs, as you know. Your assistance will allow me to free them from time to time to concentrate on fighting without needing to keep a constant eye on me. Will you do it, Hargest?'

'Yes, my lord.' The youth's grin was ferocious. One look at him and any would-be assassin must surely have second thoughts.

'Come,' said Bridei. 'We've work to do tonight. There's another march ahead of us, and another battle. You'll be on first shift with Enfret.'

'Yes, my lord king.' Hargest's voice was raw with feeling, not the doubt and fear and edgy excitement that were the expected aftermath of battle, but anticipation, determination and a note of pride that was almost smug. 'You won't regret this, my lord.'

'We'll see,' Bridei said. Fifteen. Was he being foolish, trusting the boy with such responsibility? Hargest was naïve, he was impetuous, he had a lot to learn about men and what drove them. But he was a good lad at heart. All he needed was someone to guide him; to watch over him until his childish judgement caught up with his manly physique. For all Hargest's clumsy manners and insensitivity, Bridei liked the boy.

As they walked the spiral pathway back down the hill, Bridei thought again of Faolan, a man who was a great deal slighter than this burly youth, and who had so much more to offer; Faolan who could be told anything at all and knew whether to give his unique brand of blunt advice or simply to listen in silence. Faolan who was almost like a brother to him. Faolan who was a Gael. A puzzle; a quandary. He must set such considerations aside until the peace was won. Donal, his old friend and tutor, had told him once that a warrior could not afford to see the enemy as a man like himself, or he would never succeed in battle. At the moment of engagement one must be transformed into an efficient killing machine, cold and deadly. One must indeed convince oneself, at least until the war was over, that one in three was a good result. The gods forgive him for what must unfold; he did not think he could ever forgive himself.

Tuala had planned to stay at Banmerren only as long as it took to assure herself that Broichan would not walk out the door before

Fola and her women could so much as begin to help him. He made no secret of the fact that he doubted their ability to effect a cure; if he could not do this himself, how could they? Tuala had needed to present arguments concerning both Derelei and Bridei before the druid conceded, with great reluctance, that he was prepared to try.

Ferada had made her visitors very welcome, housing them in the accommodation that stood ready for the autumn influx of students; plain, bright chambers that opened to the newly planted garden. Tuala knew, all the same, that Ferada was counting the days until she had the place to herself again. Garvan would be moving on soon, his work at Banmerren complete and a new assignment awaiting him in the south. Ferada said nothing, nor did the stone carver, but Tuala could read their silences.

She told Garth and Elda to be ready to ride home in a day or two. It would be good to be back at White Hill, where she could watch over things in Bridei's absence. Banmerren was full of memories, sweet ones, frightening ones; the spreading canopy of its great oak seemed full of whispering voices. She hurried along the path, trying not to hear them.

Broichan and Fola were sitting in a chamber without windows, a place lit by lamps even now when the sun was high. The walls were lined with stone shelves on which the materials and implements of Fola's craft were arranged in orderly fashion. On a central table was an object concealed by a thick cloth of black-dyed wool. The ewer that stood nearby revealed to Tuala what it was and what they had been doing, and she took a step back.

'Please,' Fola said, 'do come in. We need to talk to you, Broichan and I. We won't trap you into anything; we understand your decision to shun the scrying bowl. It will remain darkened unless you decide otherwise, Tuala.'

Tuala came into the chamber, closing the door behind her. Knowledge of what lay under that dark swathe of fabric made her jittery and nervous. Even through the thick covering, the scrying bowl called to her, filling her with the longing for knowledge. She had become accustomed to averting her gaze from rain puddles, to avoiding lakeside walks. The truth was, her seer's gift was so powerful it was more torment than blessing.

464

She spoke to fill a silence that felt alive with danger. 'I'm planning to leave in a day or two. I need to be at White Hill. There's so much to do –'

'You would not consider leaving Derelei here awhile?' Broichan's voice was quiet; he looked weary, the lines showing deep and stark on his face.

Tuala had not considered what her departure would mean for the druid. 'Derelei needs to be with me,' she said. 'He's still very little; his lessons can wait until you are better, surely.'

It was but rarely that Broichan allowed folk to see anything on his features beyond a mask of stern calm. Now, suddenly, he looked bereft.

'The child is weaned now, isn't he?' Fola put in. 'You could leave him here with the nursemaid. If you're worried about his safety, they could all stay, Garth and his wife too.'

'And leave Ferada with three little boys running around just when her first students are about to arrive?' Tuala managed a smile, but she felt a deep unease. What had they seen for Derelei, these two wise visionaries? 'He's in danger, isn't he?' she blurted out. 'You've seen something. Tell me!'

Broichan sighed. 'I spoke to you of one vision, a powerful and disturbing one. But my command of the scrying mirror is not what it was. That moment of clarity was like one bright flower in a field of dead and drying stalks. I see fragments, moments, fleeting and impenetrable.'

Tuala looked at Fola.

'Unfortunately, the Shining One has not chosen to send me what I need of recent times,' the wise woman said. 'She has drawn a veil across her fair face and left me in shadow. Tuala, we two old friends together have discussed the limited knowledge the gods are allowing us. What we have seen concerns us deeply. We have grave misgivings. But we are powerless to act unless the scrying bowl yields up more answers than we are able to summon.'

Tuala had to force herself to ask. 'If you've seen danger for Derelei, you must tell me. I can set more guards in place, I can –'

Fola's expression brought the flood of words to a halt. 'Broichan asks for Derelei to stay here chiefly because he can't bear to let the child go,' the wise woman said quietly. 'Broichan will mend better if he has Derelei close by and can continue teaching him. But you're the child's mother; you must decide. It's not Derelei who concerns us. It's Bridei.'

A cold hand closed around Tuala's heart. 'Tell me,' she said.

'As I explained,' Fola went on, 'the images are vague and disjointed. Both Broichan and I have believed for some time that there is a shadow over Bridei, a threat of some kind beyond the usual dangers of war. Because we cannot summon exactly what we need to the scrying bowl, we cannot go further than that. I saw a huge wildcat stalking him; Broichan glimpsed a strange bird of prey swooping down on him. In another vision I saw Ana with a burning brand in her hand, fighting a pack of wolves.'

'What?'

'Unlikely, and more the kind of fantasy a new young student of the craft will imagine she sees in the water than an image that would reveal itself to these old eyes, I know. When I add that she was clad in a very short gown and had an improbably beautiful young man by her side, you will no doubt tell me I am in my second childhood. But there it was.'

There was a brief silence.

'If we can find out what the danger is,' Broichan said, 'we have at least some chance of intervention. You know this, Tuala. You and I together have taken action to save him once before.'

She nodded. It had been the only time the two of them had shared any sort of understanding in all the years of Tuala's growing up in Broichan's house at Pitnochie.

'You want me to do it again.' She heard the fear in her own voice, and the longing.

'It will be quite safe here,' Fola said. 'You're in a place of sanctuary, behind closed doors, with old friends. Powerful old friends. Nothing of this will be spoken by either of us outside these walls. If we need to tell Aniel or Tharan, if we need to despatch a messenger, we will say the vision was Broichan's. I know you haven't attempted this since the day Bridei rode to Pitnochie to fetch you back. I think the time has come when you must attempt it again.'

Tuala nodded, eyes pricking with tears. 'I saw that there was danger for him,' she said. 'Before he left, when Broichan cast the augury. Victory or death: those were the possibilities. I explained it to him. He chose to go.'

'Why didn't you tell me?' Broichan's voice was a shocked whisper.

Tuala looked at him. 'There was no need for both of us to shred our hearts with worry,' she said. 'What the augury told was like your visions, fragmentary, unspecific. He will take extra care. He'll make sure his guards are vigilant. I could not tell him what the danger was, the source of the threat or when it might come. There was nothing any of us could have done.'

'I should have gone with him,' Broichan muttered.

'No,' Tuala said gently. 'Your best place is here with Derelei, and with me.' She took a deep breath. 'All right, I'll do it. Just this once. It's so long since I've tried, I may have no more success than you, but . . .' She drew the cloth away from the bowl, which was already full of clean water. The chamber seemed to darken further, but the vessel itself was filled with light, with colour, with a dazzling confusion of images. Tuala bent to look.

The vision consumed her immediately. She was barely aware of the others moving to stand by the table, each of them taking one of her hands and joining their own to make a circle around the copper bowl. Fola's hand was small, warm and relaxed; Broichan's long fingers were cold, the joints bony, but his grip was reassuringly strong. In the water Tuala could see him in a younger form, a dark-haired druid in his prime, walking deep in the forest with his oak staff in his hand and his eyes distant, as if he were in a trance. Tuala could not be sure if what she witnessed was a spirit journey, a voyage of the mind carried out during long meditation, or a physical venture into the wildwood.

She knew the place. It was above Pitnochie, near a waterfall called the Lady's Veil. The season was early spring; the freshest of green leaves sprouted on the bending boughs of the beeches, and on the great oaks buds were still swelling, awaiting the releasing touch of warmer days. The light slanted down between the trees, dappling the druid's white robe and setting a gleam on his dark plaited hair. White. When had Broichan ever worn white? This must be the time of Balance, and the druid going off for his three days of lonely vigil under sun and stars, the secret days of his spring equinox observance. Broichan had done this faithfully for year after year. Exactly what the practice entailed, none but druids knew. Privation, fasting, endurance: all would likely be part of such a solitary rite.

But in this vision, Broichan was not alone. From behind the beeches, half concealed in that pattern of light and shade, someone was watching him. Tuala caught a glimpse of a pale gown, a delicate white hand, a drift of dark hair; there was a shimmer, a ripple, a shifting of the air. The druid was suddenly still, halted in his tracks, listening. After a moment he went on and, as he vanished along the path under the trees, someone darted after him, someone small and slender yet womanly in shape, someone with locks as black as soot and eyes wide and light as the touch of the sun on a forest pool. Someone who bore a disconcerting resemblance to herself.

Before Tuala had a chance to blink, let alone begin working out the implications of what she had just been shown, another set of images took the place of the first. The bowl was suddenly full of twisting, tangling bodies, of cutting and thrusting, blocking and evasion, of mouths stretched wide in scream of agony or primitive challenge, of sword and spear and club, swift arrow and deadly knife. A great battle; the pattern of it was ever-changing, a swirling, capricious, devouring tide, and the most able strategist in all Fortriu would have been hard-put to say what orders the men followed, or which of these two armies had the upper hand.

Tuala was in no doubt that she was witnessing the great culmination of Bridei's venture, an engagement of massive scale and decisive strategic importance. She had asked the goddess to show her a true picture and to reveal the nature of the threat to Bridei. Past experience told her the Shining One would show her what she needed or nothing at all.

There were familiar faces to be glimpsed here and there in the melee: Uven with a bandage around his arm; Carnach on horseback, shouting orders; Talorgen wielding a great sword two-handed, with blood on his tunic. Enfret lying wounded and Cinioch trying to drag him to the shelter of a small grove of willows. The battle raged up and down the banks of a broad, shallow stream; many of the struggling, grappling men were up to their knees in the water. Tuala saw at least one man finished off when his opponent simply held his head under. The stream flowed red. The warriors fought on a carpet of fallen comrades. Later, there would be great fires. Tuala muttered under her breath, 'Bone Mother, take their hands. Grant them peace,' although there was no knowing if what she saw had already taken place, or was even now unfolding. Perhaps it was yet to come.

At last she saw Bridei and her breath stopped in her throat. He was down; wounded, perhaps already dying. The conflict swirled around him, but there was a little space where he lay, as if the King of Fortriu had fallen unnoticed and might perish in the midst of the field of war, the goddess taking him with no more ceremony than she did any other combatant. But Bridei was not quite alone. A young man with a look of the Caitt, a very big young man with piercing blue eyes, was kneeling over him, an arm behind Bridei's shoulders. His guard, helping him up. Or holding him as he died. It was hard to remember this was only a vision, both less and more than simple truth. She must breathe; she must concentrate. She must not lose sight of him.

The water seemed to swirl, and suddenly Tuala was looking at the two of them from the other side. Bridei was white as chalk, his hands clutched at his chest, and the young man was trying to move the tight fingers, he was trying to check the king's injury, he was . . . Tuala turned cold. The youth had a knife gripped in his own hand and the point was at Bridei's breast. The guard was not helping his patron, he was killing him. Bridei's fingers were clutched around the other's wrist; the pallor, the strained expression were those of a man pushing back against certain death. The moment his grip weakened, the knife would pierce his heart.

Tuala gasped in horror, and the image on the water began to fragment and disappear. 'No . . .' she whispered. 'Not yet . . .' and sought desperately to fix on something, anything that would give her the *when* and *where* and *who* without which there would be no way at all to save him. A group of trees, a contour of distant peaks, a cloak, a banner, the colour of eyes, of hair . . . The water settled once more and the vision was gone.

The others released her hands. Without a word, Broichan set the dark cloth back over the scrying bowl. Fola slid a stool in place behind Tuala and helped her to sit. Broichan set a cup of water before her. Then they waited. Each had long experience in this craft and knew not to rush the seer, even when the knowledge she had to impart was of vital importance.

Tuala could not stop shivering. After a moment she blurted out the tale, not the earlier part with Broichan, for that could wait, but all she had seen of battle, blood and murder. She forced herself to recall the scene in as much detail as possible, for if they could at least fix on the place, that might provide a clue to the time. As for the man who had held a knife to her husband's heart, the youth with strange light eyes that hardly seemed to see his victim, she would remember him for the rest of her life.

'He looked like a bodyguard,' she said. 'He wore a tunic with the royal colours, just as Breth and Garth and Faolan do when they go into battle by Bridei's side. It seemed . . . it seemed to me that he was someone Bridei trusted. That would explain how he had got so close. And then . . .'

'You say this young man was of the Caitt? One of Umbrig's men?'

'He had that look. He was certainly young, but powerfully built. He looked very strong. Bridei has immense strength of will, but I don't think he could . . .'

'This may well be yet to come,' Fola said quietly. 'It's early yet for Bridei's forces to be engaging in such a major battle. Did you say Talorgen was there? That must surely not come yet, but a little later, for Talorgen was to move in by sea. Bridei must first take Galany's Reach and another settlement to the south. I think we do have a little time.'

'If they kill him,' Tuala said with a feeling like a heavy stone in her belly, 'the armies will lose their spirit. Carnach is an able leader; so are Talorgen and the others. But you know, and I know, that none of them can take Bridei's place. He is the Blade of Fortriu. He is their hope and their inspiration. They trust him. They will ride into the jaws of death for him.'

'So,' Broichan said, 'we have an enemy who is either highly intuitive or who has been given some intelligence that he's putting to effective use. Someone's decided the simple way to defeat the Priteni is to remove their leader. Someone's recognised just what Bridei is. The Caitt, you say. I don't see Umbrig letting a traitor slip into his ranks. The fellow's astute. A bodyguard. Surely Bridei wouldn't put a new man in at such a critical time. Where was Breth, I wonder?'

Neither of the women offered an answer, for the likeliest explanation was one nobody wanted to voice.

'Can we reach him in time?' Tuala's mind was racing, searching for possibilities. It was a long journey down the Glen, and the place of this engagement seemed beyond King Lake. She thought she had glimpsed a great body of water in the distance, a shining expanse that must be the western sea. The scene in the vision did not match what Bridei had told her of Galany's Reach, which would be the place of their earliest encounter with the enemy. 'I know a man cannot walk or ride there easily, and that finding them could be difficult. And dangerous. But perhaps there is another way.' She glanced at Broichan.

'Curse this weakness!' the druid said bitterly. 'There was a time when I could have made the journey in the space of a day, travelling by paths unknown to ordinary men. I could have employed charms of concealment and transformation. Now I am reduced to a powerless shell of what I was. I cannot even attempt it, Tuala; I doubt such skills will ever be within my reach again. And Uist, alas, is no longer with us. Of all the brotherhood, the two of us were the only men who ever achieved mastery of such journeys, save for the one who taught us, and he is long departed.'

'Fola?'

The wise woman spread her hands helplessly. 'I may be quick for an old crone, but not so quick as that. Ordinary walking is the best I can manage, and I don't have the ear of wild creatures as some do. If we had Uist's mare, now that would be a solution. But Spindrift vanished when the old man left us. Wherever she went, she's beyond our summoning.'

'Tuala,' Broichan said, 'have you any source of help you can call on that we might not know of? This is beyond the abilities of men. The quickest message Aniel or Tharan could despatch would not reach Bridei in time unless this is to occur much later than I believe it will. We must act immediately. If you know any other solution, I hope you will tell us.'

Tuala swallowed. 'I hadn't planned to speak of it,' she said. 'But I see that now I must. I did have some . . . visitors . . . when I was younger. Two of them; folk from beyond the margins, a girl and a boy. They came often, but not at my bidding. They played a dangerous game with us, me and Bridei; both of us came close to death that night at Pitnochie when Bridei and Faolan brought me home from the forest. We talked about it later. We thought maybe it was all for the purpose of testing our strength: his fitness to be king, mine to stand by his side. I suppose we passed the test.'

Broichan said not a word, only watched her, his dark eyes unreadable. After a little, Fola said, 'And now? Do they still visit you? Would they help you if you asked?'

Tuala felt her lips twist in a bitter smile. 'They've never done my bidding before. I think they are more friends than foes, to the extent that their kind can understand such concepts as friendship. I haven't seen them for years. Sometimes I hear whispers. They were in the oak tree, just before. But perhaps that was only my memory playing tricks.'

'They no longer come to you, you say.' Broichan's tone was almost hesitant. 'But they visit Derelei.'

Tuala nodded, a lump in her throat. 'I think so, yes. I've heard him trying to say their names. How did you know?'

'My powers of observation are not so dulled that I cannot detect what is clearly one half of a conversation, even if the speaker has not quite mastered language. The invisible presences to whom your son speaks are not imaginary friends but real ones. At least, one hopes very much that they are friends.'

'He needs protection from their cruel tricks.'

'They may intend the best for him, as it seems they did for you and Bridei. I have already begun to teach him such safeguards as he is able to employ. Such folk are ill-attuned to human ways. Their purposes can seem obscure. Often enough, they do the work of higher powers. The Shining One has had a hand in Bridei's future, no doubt of it.'

Tuala glanced at him, thinking of the vision she had seen, the one she had not spoken of. An idea was simmering somewhere in the back of her mind, a crazy idea she could not quite dismiss. Perhaps the goddess had had more of a hand in matters than anyone had ever realised. 'I can't summon them,' she said. 'They only come when it suits them, not at my call.' She remembered that terrible journey home to Pitnochie, all by herself at Midwinter, a flight whose ending would have taken her out of the mortal world forever, leaving Bridei behind. How had Gossamer and Woodbine ever persuaded her to consider that? 'But I can try.'

'Then try,' Fola said quietly. 'For it seems that if you cannot send these strange messengers down the Glen to warn him in time, Bridei is lost, and the war is lost with him.'

As summer became autumn and the trees of the Great Glen turned to scarlet and gold, ochre and yellow, the armies of the Priteni swept southward through the lands of Dalriada, and as they moved they linked and merged to form a single, monumental force. Bridei had set strict rules for the conduct of the action and its aftermath. He did not want victory to descend into an orgy of burning, pillage and rape, leaving only a charred and ruined wasteland where once, before the coming of the Gaels, had been thriving Priteni farms, staunch fishing communities and well-protected outposts. He had made his expectations for the business of war clear over the five years of his kingship, rules every one of his chieftains was bound to instil in his fighting men. One could not expect flawless obedience, but those who erred knew they would be punished. It made for an orderly advance; for the conquered, it eased the pain of defeat. As Bridei moved through, he left behind men who would maintain order and control, men who understood the rules he had set and were strong enough to enforce them.

They pressed on. Elpin fell in battle at a place called Two Rivers. In the same action, Uven sustained a deep knife wound to his left arm, which he bound tightly and ignored, riding on with his comrades. He could still help with horses and supplies and arms, but he would not be guarding the king, nor doing much fighting for a while.

It became clear that the carefully planned strategy was a stunning success. The Gaels, not ready for such an early move by the armies of Fortriu, nor for the massive scale and complex nature of the onslaught, began to scramble into defensive positions once word of the first attack spread across Dalriada, but it was too late to summon powerful help from abroad, too late to call upon northern chieftains such as Alpin of Briar Wood, and too late to save each small settlement, each outpost, each regional fortress that fell before the disciplined advance of Bridei's combined forces. The Dalriadan fighting men perished in their hundreds.

Sometimes there was surrender, and when that occurred Bridei gave the Gaels a choice: submit to the authority of his own regional chieftains and to the ultimate rule of the throne of Fortriu, and they might stay in their settlements and live their lives in peace. The alternative must be death for the men and exile for the women and children beyond the borders of Priteni lands.

He had not intended to be quite so magnanimous, and it was clear both defeated Gaels and victorious Priteni were somewhat taken aback by it. That the gods required this of him had become clear to Bridei when they entered the settlement at Two Rivers, on the way south towards the Gaelic stronghold of Dunadd. Without it the western lands would lose their heart.

There was a man at Two Rivers whom the Priteni had spared, for he was no fighter but had the look of a scribe or teacher, being dressed in a long robe and without weapons. As the people of the settlement gathered on open ground for the formal surrender, Bridei saw this man draw a woman and children close to him, as if to offer what shelter he could against the overwhelming tide of Fortriu's army. He saw that, although the man had the broad features and ruddy hair typical of so many Gaels, his wife was slight and dark, a woman of Priteni blood. The little girl's curious eyes gazed, innocent yet of the knowledge of death, at the tall strangers who had marched into her home with the light of conquest on their stern faces. She was like her father, a rosy, red-haired Dalriadan; her brother, older and more wary, was as lean and dark as any son of the Flamekeeper. The wife clutched her husband's arm; he held the boy's hand and cradled his daughter in his other arm, bending his head to murmur words of reassurance against her bright curls. At that moment, the gods whispered in Bridei's ear that he must compromise. If he swept every Gael from this western shore, he would destroy the fabric of community, part mother from son, husband from wife, set this land back to a time of chaos and uncertainty. The Gaels had been settled in these territories through the lives of son, father, grandfather; these were one people. His plan must change, starting now.

So he spared those who agreed to peace, but made certain it was understood any attempt at revolt or uprising would be met with iron. Each community was left with a small force of armed men and an assurance that, once Gabhran relinquished the kingship of Dalriada, they might return to their old lives. Only one thing would change: each region would be governed by a chieftain of Fortriu. Bridei did not tell them there must be no public observance of the Christian ritual. Time enough for that when the last battle was won.

So they moved on, and by the eve of the feast of Measure they were in the Dalriadan heartland. Intelligence had come in that Gabhran had ridden forth from his fortress at Dunadd with what remained of his forces, and was heading north to meet Bridei's army in the open field. Perhaps the Gaelic king already saw that the Blade of Fortriu would cut him down sooner or later, its edge honed by the bone-deep certainty of a mission ordained by the gods. Or perhaps Gabhran believed, foolishly, that he could still defeat them; that they had entered his domain like minnows swimming into a net, and that he need only close their escape and draw in the catch.

Bridei met with his war leaders for what might well be the last such gathering before the decisive battle. Around them their combined force was encamped, resting in preparation for the morning. They had reached the fertile lowlands near the southwestern coast; each chieftain had his own tale to tell of the journey there, the encounters won, the men left by the wayside, their own buried hastily, the enemy piled and burned or left to crow and gull.

Talorgen's sea force had taken the coastal stronghold of Donncha's Head by surprise, standing off until dusk, then sweeping in to sink the Gaelic fleet before the enemy could launch a counterattack. That had been almost too easy, with the outpost undermanned; by then Gabhran's fighting men had been called southward to form a defensive shield before Dunadd, for the news that the Priteni were coming in force was spreading to every corner of Dalriada, and the safeguarding of the king held high priority.

As for Bridei's own protection, Hargest was taking an ever-increasing share of the duties, with Cinioch and Enfret the only Pitnochie men still uninjured. The boy's strength and endurance made him an asset on the long marches, though Hargest had not yet achieved his fervent desire to stand by his king in battle. By night, two of the three guards stood watch while the third slept. So close to victory, the king must be protected with utmost vigilance. Who knew what the Gaels might try with a skilled assassin?

Hargest complained that Bridei hardly needed a night guard at all, since he barely slept; why didn't he lie down and rest properly, instead of spending the precious time of respite in prayer or meditation or conversation with whoever else was awake in the darkness? Uven, frustrated that his injury had relegated him to a secondary role, reprimanded the boy for being too outspoken, but Bridei merely smiled. The boy could not understand what it meant to be druid-raised, nor how the responsibilities of a king robbed him of the capacity to surrender to sleep. For Hargest life was a great deal simpler. He reminded Bridei of a wild creature, perhaps a hunting cat. Enemies existed to be killed. If good men fell in the process, that was the way it was. Eat, sleep, move on, kill again. In all these long days of marching, Bridei had not managed to persuade Hargest that there was more to it than that.

Tonight the chieftains of Fortriu gathered within a protective circle of their personal guards and finalised their strategy for the last assault. Alongside Carnach, Ged, Morleo, Wredech and Talorgen were Fokel of Galany and the huge, fierce figure of Umbrig. Bridei had approached the Caitt chieftain earlier and obtained his consent for Hargest to remain with the king if he wished; Umbrig had seemed more relieved than concerned, admitting that he'd begun to find the boy's attitude trying of recent times. Hargest chafed at the restrictions of his foster father's household while remaining reluctant to test his father's goodwill by requesting a return home to Briar Wood. The lad's talents were best suited to work with the horses, Umbrig was sure of it, but that was just what Hargest least wanted to do. If Bridei wanted him he could have him. As for seeking Alpin's permission, there was no need of that. The truth was, the lad's father had lost interest in him long ago. A pity, that. Umbrig thought what Hargest needed was the firm authority best given by a father. He'd tried to do it himself, but the boy was difficult: difficult to discipline and difficult to like. Bridei had thanked the Caitt chieftain and refrained from comment. He hoped very much that, when all this was over, he might be able to make a mature man of this volatile young warrior. Time, patience and good example would surely bring out the best in Hargest.

They made three plans: one for an encounter on open, level ground; one for an uphill assault on a fortification – it was greatly to be hoped they would not need this – and a third for a downhill attack, in which their well-practised pike-block formation could be utilised to devastating effect. In an open situation, which Carnach believed Gabhran would favour, they would commence with a mounted charge, complete with banners. Once the front line of the Gaelic force had been broken by this, the Priteni warriors massed behind the horsemen would march in on the enemy. The sheer size of Fortriu's consolidated army allowed the possibility of moving on Dalriada from three sides, provided they could glean advance intelligence of where Gabhran's force was mustering.

'The men are hungry for this,' Talorgen said. 'They're weary, of course, after so long on the march and so many lost. But they scent victory. They know the end is close.'

'If we can make it quick,' Carnach said, 'so much the better. Use the spark they have now to seize the upper hand. If we can take Gabhran himself, that will give us the leverage we need to call a halt. I believe his chieftains will be prepared to negotiate.'

'What is there to negotiate?' Ged's tone was blunt.

'The life of the Dalriadan king is surely worth something,' put in dark-bearded Morleo. 'What do you plan, Bridei? Will you make an end of him if he does not perish on the field?'

Bridei had an idea of how it might fall out; his long nights of hard thinking and his silent conversations with the gods had borne some fruit. He was not sure he wished to put it in words, even before his most trusted war leaders. 'Let us see how he conducts himself,' he told them. 'Do not doubt that, if it is necessary, I will order Gabhran's death. Do not doubt that if I must execute that order to secure capitulation, it will be done immediately and without hesitation. I wish him to kneel before me and renounce the kingship of Dalriada. He must surrender and withdraw his fighting men beyond our borders. Should he agree to that, I will give consideration to his future and that of the Uí Néill princelings who support him. There won't be any wholesale slaughter of captured warriors unless there's no alternative. They have a fleet; let them sail back to their home shore and never trouble us again.'

Talorgen cleared his throat.

'In fact,' Carnach said, 'since Uerb and Talorgen engaged in a little seaborne warfare of their own, there's not much of the Gaelic fleet left. Still, they'll have a few ships in the south. I expect they could get back home, given the right encouragement.'

'What if Gabhran decides to turn tail and hole up in Dunadd?' Ged asked. 'It could be a lengthy siege, and we're far from home.'

'At least there are plenty of supplies to be had,' said Umbrig. 'It's good farming land in these parts; wouldn't mind a little holding myself. The cattle down here are twice the size of the ones at home.'

'Let us see how this unfolds,' Bridei said. 'I'll deal with Gabhran and his chieftains first, then we must establish our own base here and ensure these lands remain stable and productive. Certainly I will be looking for chieftains who possess both authority and sound judgement, for I need strong leaders here in the west. We'll talk of this when the war is won. Talorgen, what is your best guess of time and place for this encounter?'

'Soon,' Talorgen said with grim satisfaction. 'I reckon we'll meet them within three days. As for the place, it's likely to be somewhere Gabhran can't find himself hemmed in by our much larger force. There's a valley a day's march southwest of here. In times past the place was known as Dovarben, but no doubt it now bears some Gaelic invention of a name. There is a stream, broad and slow-flowing. There's not much cover save at the far ends of the strath. If I were the Gaelic king, that's the place I would choose. We'd need to pass that way to reach Dunadd. To execute the strategy we prefer, we'd have to be in position well before they made an appearance, and we'd somehow have to avoid detection by Gabhran's advance scouts. With a force of this size, that's near impossible.'

In the half-dark by the small fire Carnach's man Gwrad had made for them, Bridei's chieftains avoided one another's eyes, and the silence drew out as each of them sought a solution. An open plain, limited cover, the Gaels now forewarned of their coming and of the size and makeup of their combined force, assuming Gabhran's spies were doing their job: it added up to a significant challenge.

'Ah, well,' Ged sighed after a little, 'the Flamekeeper delights in setting tests for us, each one a little harder than the last. I hear the Gaelic archers aren't bad. Given enough warning, they'll pick us off before we get near enough to touch them.'

Fokel of Galany gave a little cough. The others fell silent. All eyes turned in his direction. Unlike Ged, Fokel rarely spoke in jest; in fact, he did not speak at all in such councils unless he had a vital and usually startling contribution to offer. 'One of my fellows happened to go out that way a couple of nights back,' he said casually. 'All being well, he should slip back later tonight with information for us: Gabhran's location and the possibilities for getting in behind him or, at least, finding a position from which we can launch a flanking strike. With your agreement, Umbrig and I will take our men forward under cover of darkness and go to ground in readiness. I've other people out there with the express purpose of disabling the Gaels' forward scouts and sentries just before we move. I may not be able to get word back to you of precisely where we are, but we'll be in place to assist your frontal assault, you have my promise on that.'

Bridei looked at him, brows lifted. Such enterprise was typical of Fokel; nobody could call him anything but bold. If he did not quite respect the rules of team play, his tactical flair was brilliant. Umbrig was beaming with satisfaction.

'Well done,' Bridei said. 'I don't need to tell you that the enemy must not be allowed to detect your presence so close to his final position, since that would endanger not only your men but ours as well. Surprise has been at the heart of our success thus far.

I know also that your men are highly skilled in what they do, able to undertake this independently and to endure days and nights on scant supplies and little rest. You drive yourselves hard. The Flamekeeper smiles on your courage. Let me know when the messenger comes and when you are ready to leave. Gods willing, this will be the last battle of the campaign. Your men should go forward with the blessing of the gods in their hearts and the exhortation of their king fresh in their minds.'

When the time came, he spoke to them as King of Fortriu and as comrade in arms. In the darkness they gathered around him, the lean, sharp-eyed fighters of Fokel's troop and the hulking Caitt warriors, all spiked weaponry, shaggy beards and skin cloaks, and he spoke to them as he would to a brother, honestly and with passion. Their wild appearance no longer gave him pause; it had become familiar on the long marches, the tense, uncomfortable nights and gruelling, bloody days. Bridei had seen the men-at-arms from Pitnochie and Raven's Well and Thorn Bend grow more gaunt and dishevelled themselves as the campaign drew on. He knew that if he bent to examine his reflection in pond or stream he, too, would have something of the same look. His chin bore an unkempt beard, his hair was down to his shoulders and he smelled no better than the rest of them. Discipline kept weapons sharp, blades clean, arrows in good repair. It kept boots maintained and leather armour supple. Such niceties as combing, shaving and donning fresh small clothes must be set aside for the time when this army might once again cross the home threshold and embrace wife, sweetheart or children.

He kept his address simple, and the men welcomed it. When it was done, he made a prayer, asking the Flamekeeper for victory. On the men's behalf, he prayed also for survival, and for those to whom that could not be granted, an honourable and merciful death. Then, in the firelight, each man came forward to a place Bridei had designated and each set down a small stone. By the time all of Fokel's men had stepped up, as well as those of Umbrig's force who were to take part in this covert sortie, a cairn had been erected in the clearing where they were assembled. When the main force moved on they, too, would place markers here, each man in his turn. Later, on the homeward journey, those who had survived would each take back a stone. All knew that, when this was done, a smaller cairn would still remain. Each stone left behind would be a son of Fortriu. This glade would hold their memory through summer and winter, until the sapling birches grew up to shade the monument and moss and fern crept gently over to blanket it in soft green. When men ceased to tell of these losses, when the story of them was forgotten, the trees would shiver, remembering. The little stones would hold it deep within them, each to its heart.

Two days later the main force moved on towards its final battle. The weather was fair and the signs were good. One of the swiftest of Fokel's men had run back to inform them that the Gaelic army was moving up to position itself just where Talorgen had predicted, and that the Dalriadan numbers were considerably more substantial than Bridei and his chieftains had believed likely. Had intelligence somehow come to Gabhran early enough for the Gaelic king to summon aid from his Uí Néill kinsmen across the water? Bridei could have sworn Dalriada knew nothing of the timing of his advance until the first Priteni attack on a Gaelic settlement not so very long ago. Faolan had been expert in the spreading of false information at the court of Dunadd. How could they have known?

It was too late to ponder this at length. The army of Fortriu was committed to battle, deep in enemy territory, with such great gains behind them that they must now dare all and finish this one way or another. The men were full of spirit, their eyes alight with the anticipation of triumph even as their faces betrayed the exhaustion of the long, hard campaign. They had rested well, camped for two nights in the shelter of birch woods. They were as ready as they'd ever be, and Bridei knew in his heart there was no choice but to go on.

He rode surrounded by the Pitnochie men, Uven with his arm still strapped, Enfret and Cinioch watchful. At the rear, Hargest sat straight and proud. All of them, Bridei knew, could feel the presences of Breth and of Elpin like shadows riding beside them.

481

The survivors wanted vengeance. They wanted Gaelic heads in payment for their slain comrades. At such a time, the place for a true son of Fortriu was out there in the thick of it, striking his blows for the Flamekeeper and the return of the ancestral lands. Bridei knew he should not deny them that opportunity in what might be the final conflict. He would let them fight alongside Carnach's mounted men, each in turn. It would be foolish to take only Hargest into battle at his side, but the lad could surely share that duty with either Enfret or Cinioch. It was time to give him his chance.

His instincts told him the lad would survive; if anyone was big and fierce enough to frighten off a Gael or two, it was this formidable young warrior. Once they got through this, once they were back at White Hill, Bridei planned to put the boy's training in Garth's hands. Garth would add self-discipline to the strength and skill Hargest already possessed. He himself would try to educate Hargest in the art of considered debate and in the many shades of grey that existed between black and white. He'd ask his old tutor, Wid, to help with that.

'You'll ride with me tomorrow,' he said now as Hargest, mounted on one of Umbrig's solidly built hill ponies, came up alongside him. 'Enfret and Cinioch will be part of the mounted charge. We need their skills on horseback. After that they'll take turns backing you up as my personal guard, depending on how the course of battle unfolds. You know your role: stay close, warn me of the unexpected, put my survival before the opportunity to take Gaelic heads yourself. We'll both be part of the fighting, nonetheless. I've been through many battles with Breth and my two other personal guards, and we've accounted for a respectable number of opponents between us. I don't stand back and let my men die in my place. Yours is not an easy job. You'll be wanting to charge in and forget all about me. You can't do that, however strong the urge. There's a symbolic importance attached to the king's survival.'

'Yes, my lord king.' The look on Hargest's broad face was arresting. His eyes, ever striking in their odd, light colour, were now full of a strange exaltation that seemed out of proportion with the opportunity Bridei was offering him. What young warrior would not prefer to be let loose in the battle proper, to test himself fully against the Gaels as Cinioch and Enfret would be doing? Bridei was struck by those eyes, which seemed almost blind in their fervour; by the fierce determination in the set of mouth and jaw. The boy was not even of Fortriu itself, but of Caitt descent; his devotion was almost frightening.

'Relax, Hargest,' Cinioch said. 'Save that look for the Gaels, it'll have them in screaming retreat before they get a chance to draw their swords.'

'I'll do what I'm called to do.' Hargest's tone matched his look; he sounded as if he'd as likely take to Cinioch himself with his knife as he would a Gael. 'Pay attention to your own mission and leave me to mine.'

Bridei did not intervene. The men were keyed up, on edge. The Flamekeeper filled their veins not simply with surging blood, but with an excess of burning aggression that would carry them into battle with the name of Fortriu on their lips and in their hearts.

His own thoughts were more complex. Had he not longed for such a day since the Dark Mirror first granted him its wrenching vision of cruelty and courage? Tomorrow Gabhran of Dalriada might kneel to him on the field of war and forfeit his territories in the west. *Fix on that*, Bridei told himself as Snowfire carried him steadily southward, and around him his longest-serving and most trusted men and his newest and youngest guard rode in stern-eyed formation. *Triumph. Victory. The will of the gods.* But what he saw was that cairn, and a silent line of warriors, bloodied and bruised, filing past, each to take one stone in his hand; men whose eyes were full of the memory of comrades lost, of desperate small struggles, a hundred moments of fear and horror and helplessness, a hundred blows to heart and mind and spirit. Their fingers reached to touch other stones: *This was set here by my brother, this by my friend; the man who laid this down is never coming home.* Bridei closed his eyes a moment, bringing Tuala into his mind, Tuala who had told him with grave calm that for himself, death would hover so close he would feel the beat of its dark wings. He heard her voice: *Do not lose faith, dear one. The gods smile on you. Go on bravely and win your war for Fortriu. A candle burns for*

*you at White Hill. When this is done come home, and weep your tears,
and be comforted.*

It was autumn when Ana and her companions walked into
Abertornie, a trio of weary and dishevelled wayfarers brown
from the sun and worn to the bone with long journeying on scant
supplies. They had obtained this and that along the way. Ana was
clad in the serviceable homespun garments of a farmer's wife.
She had been relieved to discard the threadbare remnants of what
had once been a delicately embroidered wedding gown. Ged's
household was shocked enough at her reappearance and the tale
she had to tell. At least she had not had to make her entrance
in rags.

At Abertornie she borrowed a somewhat better gown at the
insistence of Ged's wife Loura, and submitted to being thoroughly
bathed by a pair of energetic maidservants. It felt odd to be clean
again. Her hair had grown back to below shoulder length. After
rinsing with chamomile water and strenuous, painful brushing, it
turned to a wild nimbus of gold threads. She looked at her reflection in Loura's bronze mirror and did not recognise the strange
woman who looked back, skin tanned, figure so lean the gown
hung in loose folds around her, eyes wary and quizzical. This
capable-looking person was not the bride who had ridden out
from White Hill in springtime. Ana thanked the servants and
went out into the garden. After so long living in the open, it felt
uncomfortable to be long indoors.

The household was subdued, for it had been necessary to
break the news of the loss of her escort, the girl Creisa amongst
them, and a family was in mourning. Ged himself was long gone,
and his fighting men with him. Bridei's army would be well into
Dalriadan territory by now. If everything had gone to plan, the
war would be all but won.

Ana felt a certain reluctance to reach the journey's ending, now
they were so close. At White Hill she would have to explain what
had happened in full. She would have to tell Broichan and Aniel
and Tharan that the mission had failed and there was no alliance
with Alpin. She would have to face the strong possibility that the

powerbrokers of Bridei's court would hatch new plans for her, plans that would involve another chieftain, another marriage. Perhaps she had acquired some courage on the journey; perhaps she had learned to stand up for herself. All the same, the temptation to put off the day when she must tell them she would no longer do their bidding was strong. She longed to stay here awhile and rest. She longed for time alone with Drustan.

Ana walked under the shade of a double row of pear trees, the sward soft under her borrowed slippers. The day was warm, the sky cloudless; the song of birds filled the garden, and insects chirped and buzzed in every corner. A hoodie poked about in the roots of an ancient tree, fossicking for beetles. A scarlet-throated crossbill perched in the branches, watching Ana with its head to the side. The men had been shepherded away by an ancient servant when she was conveyed to her bath; they should be ready by now.

Her thoughts went to Drustan and how difficult it would be for him at White Hill. They'd need to stay there until Bridei came home, at least. Longer, probably. Apart from obtaining the king's consent to their marriage, they had other decisions to make. With Alpin dead, it would soon enough become imperative for Drustan to return to the north and establish a new order for Briar Wood and Dreaming Glen. She had thought of the possibility of going home, right home to the Light Isles. There, the two of them could settle amongst her kin and make a life for themselves free of the burden of Alpin's crime, and free from the doubt and suspicion that must face them at Briar Wood. She did not suggest this to Drustan. Later, they would visit and she would see her sister at last. She knew Drustan must face his demons first and lay them to rest. They would find Bela. They would prove Drustan's innocence before all his people.

He would find the court of Fortriu a challenge. He had spent the best part of seven years in close confinement, with only one other for companionship. To be placed in the midst of that circle of powerful men, of intrigue and gossip and manoeuvring, would be quite a shock. She'd have to explain for him; to tell Tuala and probably Broichan about the changes, about the talent that made Drustan the exceptional man he was, and to explain that he needed to be free to move between worlds. She'd have to tell them a princess of the royal blood of Fortriu intended to marry a shape-shifter.

'Ana?'

She whirled around, startled out of her reverie. It was not Drustan standing there under the trees but Faolan, clean-shaven, his dark hair combed and tied back, his plain, borrowed garb revealing how thin he had become. The afternoon light deepened the lines of illness and exhaustion that marked his face. He had his expression under expert control, but Ana saw both sadness and concern there. He had a bag on his back and outdoor boots on his feet. She met his eyes without saying a word.

His smile was crooked, self-mocking as he took in the changes in her appearance. 'This is not the image I will remember,' he said.

'What do you mean?' She was filled suddenly with misgiving. 'I'll be at White Hill and so will you, Faolan.'

He looked down at his hands, no longer prepared to meet her gaze. 'If you're there with him,' he said, 'then I cannot stay at White Hill. I'm going ahead now. I'll break the news of what's happened to Broichan and to Tuala. You stay on here awhile with Drustan. He needs to get used to being amongst folk again, and that will be easier here than at court. Come on when you're both ready. I'll make sure I'm gone by then.'

She was dismayed. 'But, Faolan, what about Bridei? You can't go, he needs you. I understand how awkward things are, but we're still friends, aren't we? We've made a long journey together, the three of us. You can't leave White Hill.'

He was persistent in looking away. His features were forbiddingly closed; he wore the same mask as in early days, when she had believed him a man incapable of feeling. 'You mean to marry the man, don't you?' he asked her. 'That's if you can persuade Bridei it's a good idea. You intend to stay at court until Drustan's ready to go back west and reclaim his lands. That means I must leave, Ana. If it means quitting Bridei's service, that's what I'll do. When it comes to it, I'm a sword for hire and can earn my keep anywhere. One master's no different from another, as long as he pays in good silver.'

There was a brief silence, then Ana took a step towards him

and clasped his hands in hers. 'We've done this, haven't we?' she asked as a bitter sense of loss filled her heart. 'Drustan and I, we've driven you away. This is terrible, Faolan, cruel and wrong. I know what Bridei is to you. You mustn't let what's happened destroy that bond. Your own brother died, and in the manner of his death he took away a piece of your spirit. Don't let your anger rob you of a friend who is as close as any brother could be. Perhaps you feel you have failed this mission. Bridei won't agree with that. At least wait at White Hill until he has the chance to tell you so.'

Faolan detached his hands gently from her grasp, hitched the pack higher on his back and turned away. 'Some things shouldn't be put in words,' he said. 'Sometimes it's best to keep silent. I must go now. I feel an urgency to this, a need to get back to court quickly, even though Bridei will be away. That compels me even more than . . .'

'Even more than your distaste at seeing me and Drustan together?' she asked him straight out.

'What pair of lovers welcomes a constant observer?' His tone was bitter. 'I wish you well. Goodbye, Ana.' A few strides away under the trees and he was gone from sight before she could draw breath to form an answer, though indeed she did not know what that answer might be.

She waited for Drustan, sitting on the grass with her hands around her knees, trying not to confront the growing conviction that, unless both Drustan and Faolan were somewhere close by, she would always be missing some essential part of herself. Her mind shied away from this: it couldn't be right, it was out of tune with everything she had expected, an irregularity in a future path that should have unfolded exactly to pattern. She had never believed she would be fortunate enough to find a man she could love as she loved Drustan, with a heady, thrilling passion that drove all else from her mind. Almost all else. There was Faolan: her dearest friend, her constant, strong companion, her counterpart. He had held her steady when the path crumbled before her feet. His music had made her weep. His arms had kept back the dark. His eyes had told her . . . His eyes had told her he loved her as Fionnbharr loved Aoife, the fairy woman, with a deep and steadfast passion. She had known this since that day in the forest when she had accused him of jealousy. It was the strength of her own feelings that seemed new and shocking. Something had crept up on her unawares, something whose full significance she had not realised until now, when he was gone. The goddess had played a trick. She had brought Ana not one, but two men to love. And, painful though it was to acknowledge it, it seemed to Ana that she needed both of them. Such a thing plainly could not be. Faolan was right. In this cruel game of three, one must be destined to walk on alone.

'Ana?'

This time it was Drustan coming along the way between the pear trees, clad in a borrowed tunic and trousers of fine wool dyed in the many-hued fashion of Ged's household, his cascade of bright hair tied back, not altogether successfully, with a cord. His smile drove doubt from her heart in an instant; she jumped up and ran to him, and his arms closed around her, strong and warm. She felt the wild thudding of his heart against her, an echo of her own.

'I missed you,' he whispered against her hair. 'You smell like spring flowers, and your hair feels like thistledown.'

'Mm,' Ana murmured, savouring the moment; they had been circumspect on the journey, respecting Faolan's presence. To be as close as this was to set loose a feeling like a fire kindling, a heat in the body that would all too quickly grow so powerful there would be only one way to quench it. She lifted her face to his, and a moment later his lips met hers, hesitant at first, touching lightly, a feather-soft imprint. Then touching again, this time more deeply, his hand coming up to her neck, his lips parting as hers did, and the primal sensation of his tongue sliding against hers, sending a thrilling shiver through the depths of her body. Her limbs felt weak; her heart was doing its own crazy dance. Her hands moved against his broad back, pressing him closer.

The hoodie cawed. Remembering, Ana drew her lips away and brought her hands around to place them over Drustan's heart. 'Drustan?'

'Mm?' He took her right hand in his, bending his head to kiss her palm, to circle there with the tip of his tongue, making her tremble.

'You'd better stop, I can't think straight when you do that.'

He was suddenly still. 'What is it, Ana?'

'Faolan. He's gone ahead by himself.'

Drustan said nothing.

'And he told me he won't stay at White Hill if we're there. He would leave the life he's made there, turn his back on Bridei, his patron and dear friend, go off and seek a living as a mercenary, a killer for hire. He mustn't do that. Not now, not now he has sung his songs and told his story and begun to come alive again. It's . . .' She stumbled to a halt. She could not put into words what a terrible waste that was, nor how desolate it made her feel.

'You weep for him.' Drustan's tone was as gentle as the finger he lifted to brush the tears from her cheek.

Ana nodded, still unable to speak.

'He loves you; his passion has grown so powerful he can no longer hide it from you. He tried his best to conceal this.'

'You knew?'

'Since I first met him; since I saw the look on his face as he spoke your name. Come, let me hold you. I, too, can exercise restraint when I must, though this flame that burns in me is a cruel delight. There, weep. What shall we do? I had hoped for some days here, a few at least. He left, I think, because he thought that we would . . . because he did not wish to be here when . . .' Abruptly, he too was lost for words.

'You're embarrassed,' Ana said, the spectacle of his blush sufficient to bring a smile through the tears. 'It's all right, Drustan, I'm not shocked. You must surely know the selfsame fire burns in me. Your every touch fuels it. True, I was once a girl who followed rules: obedient, dutiful and correct in every way. That girl would never have considered anticipating her wedding night, especially before she had obtained the king's consent to the match. She'd have been unable to make such a speech as this without turning as red as you are.'

Drustan smiled. 'I see a becoming shade of rose in your cheeks, Ana. You look like springtime; like the fair All-Flowers in mortal guise. If I blush like a nervous boy, it is because this is quite new to me and I cannot know how you will answer.'

'Answer? What is the question?'

Clearly he was somewhat abashed by what he had to say; he shuffled like an awkward lad of sixteen, and Ana reminded herself that he had been shut away for seven years and was yet unused to going amongst folk.

'You want to go after Faolan, don't you?' he queried.

'I'm sure that wasn't what made you blush, Drustan, but yes, I do. We can't let him slip away from court and disappear from our lives. We owe it to him to help him face the past and accept the present, even if it means he must accept friendship and love and pain. It's time he admitted he's a man, with a man's weaknesses as well as his strengths. He needs to accept that love hurts, and that it heals.'

Drustan regarded her gravely. 'Then we will borrow horses and ride after him straightaway,' he said.

'That's what we should do.' Ana heard the uncertainty in her own voice; Drustan's hand was on the back of her neck, stroking the skin beneath the fly-away softness of her shorn hair, and the delicious sensation of this was making it hard to concentrate. 'Straightaway. He won't be pleased, but . . .'

'So,' Drustan murmured, taking her in his arms again, 'not tonight, then?'

She couldn't speak. Every corner of her was crying out for him; the hunger in her was potent, frightening.

'I will do what you want, Ana,' said Drustan, and his hands slid lower, one to her waist, the other to her buttocks, pressing her against him at breast, belly, groin. The hard shape of his manhood was startlingly evident, and still more startling to Ana was her own response, a throbbing heat awakening between her legs, making her strain against him in a manner she would not so long ago have thought shockingly unseemly.

'This isn't fair,' she gasped. 'You know what I really want . . . but . . .'

'Ana,' Drustan said, 'I will ride out now if you wish it. This journey has bound the three of us together, you and I and Faolan. We'll never escape that, whatever we do, wherever we go. We must do as you suggest. We must follow him, find him and dissuade him. I had entertained sweet thoughts of our sojourn here at Abertornie, I won't deny it. But I can wait. In seven years, I should at least have learned to do that.'

'Mm,' Ana said, disengaging herself with some reluctance to sit on the grass once more. 'You know, it is not Faolan's arrival at White Hill that is the issue, but his departure. He did offer to break the news to Broichan for us. He must stay at court three or four days to confer with Bridei's councillors. That is the least they will expect from him. Besides, although Faolan would never admit it, he was so exhausted he must surely make camp quite soon for tonight, and not ride on until the morning. That means . . .'

'It means we could delay our own departure until tomorrow and still catch up with him, my princess.'

Ana grinned at him. 'Princess? I didn't feel much like a princess in that rag of a gown, with wolves all around me; nor do I now, bath or no bath.'

'To me, and to him,' Drustan said solemnly, 'you were never anything less. Will you stay for a night?'

She nodded, suddenly shy.

His eyes were very bright, his expression altogether serious. 'Will you be my wife?' he asked her.

She stared at him; he had surprised her. 'That wasn't the question I expected either,' she said.

'Tell me what you expected.'

Ana cleared her throat. 'Will you . . . will you lie with me tonight?'

'Yes,' said Drustan immediately.

'My answer is also yes. Loura will be shocked.'

'I doubt it,' he laughed. 'I think she believes the worst of us already; I was shown the sleeping quarters they prepared for us, and there is a door between. Oh, Ana. Such happiness is more than I am worth. I want to shout, to sing, to fly high and cry it out so the whole world can hear me. Such joy I could burst with it.' His face was radiant. It seemed to Ana the hurts, the reversals, the cruelties of the last seven years had been wiped out in an instant. She had done that. She had turned his world upside down and made him whole again. There had been a cost. Tomorrow they would borrow horses and ride out to do something about that. Tomorrow.

'You honour me,' she told him a little shyly.

'Ah, no,' Drustan said. 'If you agree to be my wife, you grant me a gift above honour.'

'I have already agreed.'

He startled her by dropping to his knees, wrapping his arms around her and laying his head against her like a child; she felt a tension in his body that was new. 'He may not consent. Bridei. He may not think me suitable. You are my princess. You are also a princess of the Priteni, a bride of immense value to the kingdom. What if . . . ?'

'Drustan.'

A silence; his face was against her, and she could not read his eyes.

'Drustan, look at me. That's better. I love you, dear heart.' She stroked the exuberant cascade of his bright hair. 'More than sunrise, more than moonlight, more than birdsong or light on the water or a warm fire after long journeying. I love you with all my heart, forever and always. I want my children to be your children. I want us to grow old together, still full of delight every moment we look on one another. I dreamed of a child, did I tell you? She had your head of hair, your beautiful eyes. She was ours, Drustan. I know this is meant to be. If Bridei will not give his consent, I will leave court with you anyway. The gods will understand that the bond between us runs deeper than any druid's handfasting can make it.'

'And Faolan?' His tone was a whisper.

Ana sighed. 'Faolan is dear to me. In another world, if I had never met you, perhaps . . . No, I cannot say that. Faolan has more journeying to do on his own path. I think there is a quest he must undertake, and with that we cannot help him. I don't deny I would prefer to have him close by. But I think his destiny lies away from ours.'

'And that makes you sad, even at such a moment of joy.'

'A little sad, but I will put that aside until tomorrow. In the morning we'll go after him and try to make him see sense. Until then . . .'

Drustan rose to his feet. 'How long do you think it is until sunset?' he asked her, smiling.

'Not as long as it will seem,' Ana said. 'I suppose we can wait until then, after all this time. I hope you will take off that outrageous tunic before bedtime. It is more than a little dazzling.'

'Do you remember,' Drustan said softly, 'a long time ago, I asked you if it would please you to undress before me? I think I recall your answer was yes. Or perhaps you said maybe.'

'Fairly soon, you'll find out,' Ana said, tucking her arm in his and turning back towards the house. 'Perhaps you should show me these adjoining bedchambers. I won't ask where Faolan was supposed to sleep; I hate to think what Loura had in mind. She must be more observant, and more broadminded, than I gave her credit for. But then, she's Ged's wife. I suppose she's seen everything.'

Chapter Seventeen

Tuala had seen them coming in her scrying bowl. Since Fola and Broichan between them had made her break her promise to herself, she had begun to seek its revelations every day. Her head had no room for anything but Bridei; as she paced the hallways and chambers and gardens of White Hill, she was making his journey with him, across the valleys and passes and farmlands between here and Dalriada, through battle and respite and battle again. She slept little, knowing Bridei would be lying awake weighing the cost of this man, that man. The territories won, the advantages gained would, for him, never be quite sufficient to balance the human cost.

She had made the difficult choice to leave Derelei at the house of the wise women for a little, with Broichan. The maidservant would tend to him lovingly, and both druid and infant might be the better for the peace Banmerren could provide. Tuala herself was too distracted to give her son the time he needed. She would bring him home soon enough. In the meantime, Bridei's little dog, Ban, had taken to following her about, settling at her feet when she sought the visions in the water, trotting by her side as she paced restlessly.

Tuala knew a subtle watch was being kept over her. Aniel had set his own guards to maintain a discreet protective presence. Tharan would appear from time to time to enquire with grave diffidence if she were well. These two, the senior councillors, knew what the scrying bowl had revealed. She had sought their advice the day she came back to White Hill, hoping beyond hope that there was something she hadn't thought of, some way the distance between here and the south of Dalriada might be traversed in time. Their grim faces had soon quenched that hope. Even supposing a messenger could make his way to Dalriada unscathed, he would not reach Bridei before autumn was well advanced. Tuala knew in her heart that this would be too late. As for her attempts to summon the folk of the Otherworld to her aid, those had been futile. As she'd suspected would be the case, her pleas had fallen into silence. Gossamer and Woodbine and their kind only came when it happened to suit them. Whatever the solution was here, it lay in human hands.

There had been no repetition of her other vision, Broichan in the forest in springtime and a woman of the Good Folk watching him. Who knew what druids did on their long, lonely forest vigils at the festival of Balance? The goddess commanded their obedience in mind and spirit. And in the flesh: did not they of the brotherhood hang for days in the forks of the oaks, wrapped in ox hides, inviting prophetic visions? Perhaps there were other ways a fit man's body could be called to the Shining One's service. She wanted to know what year that image had belonged to. She suspected it was the year Broichan travelled to Caer Pridne and nearly died of poison: the year of her own birth.

The scrying bowl yielded no further glimpses of Bridei, but this morning in the clear water Tuala had seen Ana riding home, Ana strangely altered, as if she had been through a furnace and emerged stripped of all but her essential core. Tuala's friend was painfully thin and her lovely hair had been cropped oddly short. In the vision she rode by Faolan's side down a familiar track, the main way from Abertornie. Faolan looked wretched: sick, defeated. Something had gone terribly awry, that much was plain. There were just the two of them, no escort, no guards, just the man, the woman, the two horses. And . . .

And the hawk. Ana wore a single heavy gauntlet, and on it was perched a creature whose magnificent plumage held every colour from deep oak brown to fiery red to ripe barley gold. Its eyes were piercing, knowing, dangerous. The bird was of a species unknown to Tuala, its rich colours and noble bearing seeming to mark it out as something exceptional, one of a kind. Ana carried it easily despite its size, her arm and shoulder relaxed. Her grey eyes had ever possessed a deep serenity; she had always appeared calm but somehow sad. There was an expression in those eyes now that Tuala had never seen there before. For all the manner of this return, a clear sign that the mission to Briar Wood had not fallen out as Bridei had wished, Ana's eyes were alight with a transcendent joy.

Tuala made a judgement that this was a vision of the present time and set preparations in place to receive the two of them later that day. The light in the image was that of early afternoon, a warm glow shining on the foliage of the beeches, the sun brushing the forest paths and turning Ana's hair to a bright splash of gold amid the green. Already the leaves were showing the mellow hues of autumn. The war in the west might be nearly over. If Bridei lived. If the gods spared him. If a big young man with a knife in his hand and a mission in his eyes were somehow stopped in time.

Tuala sighed. The gift of the seeing eye was a cruel one. Life, after all, was full of chances and dangers and quick decisions. If a man did not die of the assassin's blade, there was still no saying he might not perish in some other way the next day, or the next. Seek to intervene because the water showed something unwelcome and one risked setting in train a whole sequence of events that might, in their way, be more disastrous than the vision. On the other hand, the Shining One sent Tuala these images for a reason. And this was Bridei: not simply her husband, her beloved, her dearest friend and the father of her child, but also the King of Fortriu, his people's great leader. What was that vision but a call to act?

With this dilemma tumbling through her mind, Tuala now stood by the rampart on the upper level of White Hill with Aniel, looking down the slope for any sign of riders approaching. Ban was at her feet, small body tense with expectation. Tuala had called Aniel as soon as she saw Faolan in the water, for there was some small hope in his return. Had not Bridei's right-hand man always been able to fulfil the most challenging missions and find answers to the most perplexing puzzles? Faolan was bold, inventive and capable. Perhaps he would discover a solution where even Broichan had been unable to discern one. Tuala kept to herself her disquiet about Faolan's appearance. She would let these travellers tell their tale before she shared hers.

It was close to dusk by the time the riders came into view. When she saw them Tuala stifled a gasp of surprise.

'I thought you told me Ana and Faolan were alone,' commented Aniel, narrowing his eyes for a better view. 'So who is *that*?'

His tone reflected Tuala's own response. Not only were Faolan and Ana now accompanied by a third, but he was sharing Ana's horse, supporting her with an arm as she sat across the saddle in front of him, her golden hair tangling with his own mass of wild russet locks. The two of them were like an image from an ancient tale, a picture so lovely and so arresting it stopped the breath in the throat.

'That's no guard,' Tuala said. 'I can only suppose it's her husband, Alpin of Briar Wood. It looks as if she's done rather better for herself than anyone expected.' Ana's companion was, without a doubt, the finest specimen of manly beauty that had ever visited White Hill. Even Tuala, who considered Bridei the most perfect man in all Fortriu, was obliged to concede this. Belatedly she recalled the vision Fola had recounted, which included a battle with wolves. It had seemed unlikely at the time. Then she noticed the hooded crow that was riding on the fellow's right shoulder, and the smaller red bird on his left. Ana's glove was gone, and so was the hawk. There was something decidedly odd about all this. Ana leaned on the young man as if he were her home, her hearth, her sanctuary. His supporting arm curved with delicacy and tenderness around her thin frame in its too-large clothing. Perhaps the mission had been a success after all.

'Come,' Tuala said to the councillor. 'We must go down and receive them properly. They have a tale to tell, and I expect it will be a strange one. Come, Ban.' The little dog followed obediently, but his ears were drooping. Tuala's heart bled for him. 'Be patient,' she whispered, bending to pat the small creature's head. 'He will come home.' *The Shining One grant that it be so*, she added in silence. *The gods bring him home alive, and well, and victorious, so we need not do this again awhile. Let my next child be born into a world at peace.*

It was indeed a strange tale and a sorry one, for eleven men from White Hill had died at Breaking Ford, and their kinsfolk must be told the shocking news. Tuala sensed that Faolan, who was doing most of the talking, had not given the whole story. He had introduced the stranger as Alpin's brother, and Ana had told them with quiet assurance that the chieftain of Briar Wood had proved a great deal less than they had hoped for. Alpin, she said coolly, was now dead as the result of an unfortunate combination of circumstances. With the king's permission, she would be marrying his brother instead. His brother: this bright-eyed, fine-looking stranger whose manner teased at Tuala, reminding her of something she could not quite identify. The two birds stayed close to him even here in the council chamber where the travellers had gathered with Tuala, Aniel and Tharan to give their account of themselves. Drustan held Ana's hand quite openly. The two of them glanced at each other often, as if they could not bear to keep their eyes away. Save for a courteous greeting, Drustan had not said a word. There was a mystery here, but it must wait.

'What news of Bridei?' Faolan asked. 'Where is he? How far has the force advanced?'

Tharan cleared his throat. Aniel glanced pointedly at Drustan.

'We need to speak with you alone, Faolan,' said Tuala. 'There's a grave and urgent matter we must put before you. We're hoping very much that you can help.'

'What matter?' His tone was sharp.

'In private,' Aniel said firmly. 'Lady Ana, you'll be weary after the ride from Abertornie. I'll arrange some refreshment, and a chamber for your –'

'They should stay,' Faolan said. 'This concerns Bridei, doesn't it? You can speak openly before the two of them, indeed should do so. Ana can be trusted with your secrets. Drustan is a friend and ally.'

The two councillors stared at him. What he suggested was a total breach of protocol. There were sound reasons for such rules, especially in time of war. Faolan, of anyone, must know the risks that lay in spreading sensitive information.

'I have no allegiance in this conflict and never did.' Drustan spoke quietly. 'My brother took it upon himself to employ my territory as a base for his seaborne forces; that will change when I return to Dreaming Glen. Now that Alpin is gone, Briar Wood will also fall under my custodianship. Ana's friends are my friends. I stand outside the war.'

'Tell us,' said Ana. 'What is it? Has Bridei's venture gone wrong?'

'I'm sorry.' Aniel's tone was suddenly forbidding. 'Such matters are for private council. Whatever Faolan's opinion might be, the decision, in the absence of both the king and his druid, is for myself and my fellow councillor here to make, with the queen's advice. A man does not gain entry to such meetings on the strength of a few moments' acquaintance, or a presumption that he may at some time in the future be judged an acceptable suitor for a royal hostage.'

A look appeared on Faolan's weary features that could only be described as frightening. His hands tightened into fists.

'Drustan,' said Ana calmly, 'you and I will retire awhile. Aniel's right, I am tired, and besides, I want to show you the garden before it gets too dark. And introduce you to Derelei. Come, shall we?'

'Thank you, Ana,' Tuala said. 'I'm afraid Derelei's not here; he's at Banmerren with Broichan. I will come to see you as soon as we're finished here.' And, as Ana and her extraordinary young man went out, still hand in hand, 'Faolan, sit down, please. We have no time for arguments amongst ourselves. Bridei's in danger. We need your help.'

He sat, tight-lipped.

'You tell him, Aniel,' Tuala said.

Aniel set it out: the vision – he did not specify whose – the battle, the struggle, the large young man with the knife. Tuala watched Faolan's cheeks grow pale and his jaw tighten as the account progressed.

'We believe,' put in Tharan gravely, 'that this must take place soon, if indeed it has not already occurred. Broichan tells us he has not the power to make a rapid journey to the west, as his kind have sometimes been known to do; indeed, there is now no druid with that capacity alive in all of Fortriu. We've despatched riders, of course. But we are convinced they will not reach Bridei in time. The weather is particularly balmy just now, unseasonably fine for autumn. The description of this scene, the light, the colour of the trees, all suggested such conditions. Our estimation of this battle's location fits with the plan of Fortriu's war leaders. We think it's imminent.'

'Broichan's augury, before Bridei left here, contained a warning of death.' Even in this setting, with all of them trusted advisers, Tuala was careful not to mention her own role in any of it. 'This is desperate, Faolan.'

'I should be there,' Faolan muttered. 'I should have gone with him.'

'We were hoping,' Tuala said, 'that you might be able to think of something we couldn't. I cannot believe the gods would sacrifice him so easily, nor that they would grant this vision if there were no way to intervene. We must save him.'

'There is a solution,' Faolan said. 'It lies with Drustan: the man you don't trust. You'd be asking him to put himself in peril. You'd be asking Ana to put her hard-won future at risk. Even with Bridei's life at stake, that sits ill with me.'

'You speak in riddles,' said Tharan. 'How can this man help us? He's a stranger. He's Caitt; he's the brother of a man it seems may have been in league with Dalriada. How could we trust him, even assuming he can do the impossible?'

Faolan did not answer.

'Faolan?' Tuala ventured. 'Time is short. What should we do?'

'I will speak to them.' His tone was reluctant, his gaze averted. 'If they want to help, it is for Ana and Drustan to explain to you, to tell their story. He can reach Bridei in time. Whether we should lay this task on him is another matter.'

⁊⁊

They waited only until daybreak. Drustan, reticent and nervous now that he was among strangers, did not wish to effect his transformation in public. Ana herself had observed it for the first time only a day or so since, and it had been evident to her that he still saw his ability as both gift and burden, something that would always mark him out as different, odd and, for some folk, threatening. She had thought it wondrous and beautiful to watch. When he had made love to her, she had sensed his dual nature in the vibrant power of his body, the feather-soft touch of his hands, the fluid, restless elation that possessed him afterwards. The energy of their coming together had been such that, at dawn the morning after, he had been compelled to enter his other world, to become his other self awhile, and she had marvelled at the sight of the tall man standing in a clearing, arms outstretched in a pose like that of prayer, bright eyes open to earth and tree and pale sky, and then, in a whirl of sudden movement, the hawk soaring upwards to the endless expanse of blue. He had come back to her in that other form; she had gentled him with her voice, with her soft hand, and had borne him home on her glove with such pride and awe and tenderness that her heart had no room for misgiving.

Now, bidding him farewell in the privacy of a little courtyard at White Hill, she wrapped her arms around him, willing herself to believe this was not the last time. She made her voice as strong as she could. 'Fly safe, my heart. Fly true and find him. I'll be here waiting.'

Drustan's lips were against her hair. He said nothing at all, his body already moving towards that state where he would have the energy, the capacity for the transformation. He held her a moment, then released her and moved away. Ana watched in silence as he turned once, twice, the edge of the rising sun drawing fire from his tawny hair; watched as the wide pinions of the bird swept out and up, and a single bright feather drifted down to settle on the flagstones by her feet. He wheeled above the summit of White Hill and winged away southwestward towards Dalriada. In the time it took for Ana to stoop and pick up the red-gold plume, and for hoodie and crossbill to appear from nowhere to alight, one and two, on her shoulders, Drustan was gone from sight.

Ana stood in the courtyard, reluctant to retreat inside for all the chill of the early morning. She knew Drustan's unease with this mission; sensed its cause, although he would not speak of it. He was only a messenger. All the same, he was flying into the middle of a war, to find a man who might be fighting for his life. And there had been something more, a look in his eye as they described the assailant to him. She did not know what it was, but she knew he was no fighting man, for all the skills Deord had taught him. Drustan had no will for vengeance or punishment. All he wanted was wife, home, freedom.

She could not make herself go indoors. If she were here where she had seen him, held him, spoken her farewell, then the distance to Dalriada would not seem so long, nor the many dangers that lay between White Hill and the battlefields of the west so insurmountable. A bird was such a fragile thing, a miracle of bone and feather and quick-beating heart. Even a great hunter such as an eagle or hawk was vulnerable to storm, to cold, to an arrow or hurled stone. Besides, he had not only to fly that long distance, but to find Bridei when he got there; find him in the midst of a land in conflict, dotted with encampments of warriors. Perhaps he would need to find him in the turmoil of battle. Bridei was king. Bridei, however, wore none of the trappings of his status into war. How would Drustan know where he was? How would he identify who he was? This was indeed a desperate mission. No wonder Faolan had been so reluctant to put it to them.

Drustan had listened calmly as Tuala gave the most detailed description she could of time, place, the king's appearance and that of his would-be assassin. He had asked questions about the young Caitt warrior, such as the style of his hair and the colour of his eyes – a pale, unusual blue – and had simply said yes, he would do it. He would warn Bridei.

Ana knew why he had agreed without hesitation, for all the risk. Perhaps there was a general wish to aid them, to repay Ana and Faolan for their friendship and trust. The other reason was more powerful and could only be put into words when the deed was done. To speak of it too early seemed to mock the gods. But Ana had seen it in Drustan's eyes, in that glance that went straight to her face the moment Faolan told them what Tuala and the others wanted. Drustan was doing this for his own future, and Ana's. He hadn't wanted to reveal the full truth about himself so soon after reaching White Hill. When it came to it, there had been no choice.

Now he was gone, and the sun was rising, and as the day grew gold and bright, shadows crept into Ana's heart. Perhaps she had presumed too much, wanted too much. Had her sudden decision to abandon duty set the gods against her? Perhaps, this very day, Bone Mother would rob her of her wondrous gift, her great adventure, the vibrant creature with the power to fill her every breath with happiness. Ana did not think, if it came to it, she would have the capacity to be stoical. If she lost him, her world would turn to ashes.

'You're sad.' Faolan had come up the stone steps to the upper court; she knew he had been waiting below, watching Drustan go, keeping back so the two of them could say their farewells. As he approached, the two birds flew off to perch on the wall. 'He will be safe. He's strong.'

'I hope so, Faolan. And I hope he will be able to warn Bridei in time. I wonder if our lives will always be like this: a moment of safety, then suddenly plunged into terror again, the gods testing us and testing us.'

'Maybe,' he said, coming to stand by her and look down over the dark pines that clothed the hillside below. For all the brilliance of the morning, there was a chill breeze; the year would soon turn to the dark. 'For me, that has long been the expected pattern. I hope your own path will be smoother. The two of you have challenges to face before that can come about. It won't be easy for Drustan to regain his lost territories.'

'As you said, he's strong. And we can afford a little time for him to recover and to come to terms with all these changes. I don't think we will stay here at court, Faolan. We'll seek a home elsewhere until he's ready to go back. I've already asked Tuala if Broichan would let us stay at Pitnochie in his absence. Drustan is not comfortable in enclosed spaces, nor amongst large gatherings of folk. It's possible that may never change.'

There was a pause.

'You would not leave court because of me, I hope,' Faolan said.

'My reasons are all good ones, based on love,' said Ana, laying a hand on his arm. 'Please don't go yet, Faolan. Bridei's in such danger. If he is killed, everything will change here; it will change for all of us. You're badly needed. Your strength means a great deal to Tuala. And if Bridei comes home safely, he will expect you to be here waiting. He relies on you. You know how few true friends he has.' She could hear the wobble in her voice; her throat was constricted. She did not look up, but felt the weight of his gaze on her.

'At such a moment you concern yourself with me?' Faolan's tone was both incredulous and tender. Ana could no longer stop the flow of her tears, and after a little she felt his arms come around her, and she laid her head on his shoulder and wept. And whether he embraced her like a friend, or a brother, or like a lover who understands this is the one and only time he will ever hold his heart's delight so close, was a thing she never told anyone, not for the rest of her life. When she had shed her tears, Faolan wiped her cheeks with his hand, his eyes on hers, and she sensed he was drinking his fill, storing up memories to sustain him in lonely seasons to come.

'I . . .' he began, and halted, his mouth twisting in a grimace.

'Shh,' Ana said, touching his lips with her fingers. 'Don't say it. I know already. Now I'm going inside. It's getting cold, and Tuala's been down in the garden keeping an eye on us since before Drustan left. Just don't go away right now. Just wait a little and think about it. Promise me, Faolan. At least stay until we know they are safe, Bridei and Drustan.'

He gave a crooked smile. 'I find myself unable to refuse you,' he said. 'I will stay at White Hill until Bridei gives me leave to go. That much I promise.' And he lifted her hand, but did not kiss it, simply held it against his cheek a moment, then released her and stepped away. Ana knew she would remember his expression forever: the mouth drolly self-mocking, the eyes desolate.

'Ana! Faolan!' Tuala's voice came up the steps, carefully light, though she of all of them had most at hazard in this desperate time. 'I thought we might have an early breakfast in the garden; will you join me? With Derelei gone, I just can't get used to the quiet.' It was a brave attempt at calm; Ana saw through it immediately. Tuala was desperately worried, and feeling very alone.

'Of course,' Ana said, descending the steps to link her arm through her friend's. 'Drustan is on his way; we must wait now until news comes back to us. Faolan and I have more to tell you. Yesterday's account was only the first taste of it. I'm afraid you will be quite shocked at me, Tuala. I went away one person and have returned an entirely different one.'

Tuala and Faolan exchanged a glance. Ana could not quite read it.

'That's not the way I'd put it, Ana,' Tuala said quietly. 'It seems to me more that you have discovered who you are.'

'We are all changed,' Faolan said. 'Forged in the fire; stripped bare and made anew. Our sinews stretched into harp strings, our hearts made beating drums. Fate plays a different tune on each of us. Love, loss, betrayal, fulfilment.'

Tuala's eyes widened. 'You speak like a bard, Faolan,' she observed.

'We are all stronger for what we have been through,' Ana said. 'Now we must pray that Drustan is strong enough for this journey, and that the gods still smile on Bridei.'

So they went down to the garden, the three of them, and the long time of waiting began.

The army of Fortriu moved on the Gaels at dawn. Gabhran's forces were massed along the southern flank of a wide strath down which flowed a stream of considerable size, broad, stony and swift, but for the most part no more than knee-deep. It was inevitable that this watercourse would see the heaviest action. Bridei's men had moved up in darkness and at first light they began a frontal assault: a mounted charge, a quick withdrawal, then a steady onslaught by men on foot, holding the pike-block formation. The opposition, who had still been scrambling into defensive positions when the line of spear-wielding riders had galloped towards their encampment, suffered heavy losses in that first attack. The pike-block assault that followed was disciplined and deadly, the front rank with shields held in a solid defensive wall, the thrusting spears of the second rank jutting over the shoulders of the first like the prickles of a hedgehog, and the third rank equipped with throwing spears to hurl over this formidable barrier into the mass of enemy foot soldiers.

Carnach and Bridei, seated side by side on their horses and breathing hard after that first heady charge and retreat, watched the triple line of men make a steady progress forward, the roar of their challenge, 'Fortriu! Fortriu!', punctuated by the purposeful tramp of booted feet, the splintering crunch of iron spear on wooden shield, the whirr and thud of Gaelic arrows loosed too late to turn this relentless tide.

Hargest had ridden at the king's side, along with Cinioch, and despatched his first Gael with an efficient sweep of the sword. The mounted charge over, Cinioch had gone to change places with Enfret, down where Carnach's horsemen were regrouping. Hargest waited now, every part of him tense with battle fever, while Bridei and Carnach surveyed their progress and reviewed their strategy. The Gaels were re-forming up the rise near their camp. They had not been caught unprepared. The Priteni advance had simply come somewhat earlier in the day than they antici-pated. It would not be long before they gathered themselves into a spirited defence. Their numbers were substantial.

'At a certain point we let them push us back to the river,' Carnach was saying. 'Still agreed? Our men should advance no further than the stone wall up there or they risk being trapped, that's if Gabhran's chieftains know what they're doing. We must give the Gaels the advantage, lure them forward.'

'But not too readily,' said Bridei, his eyes on a particular point where a banner had been raised, perhaps that of the King of Dalriada. 'It must look convincing. This could take a while, Carnach.'

'We'll weather it.' The chieftain of Thorn Bend threw a glance Hargest's way. 'Guard the king well, boy. This will be ugly before the morning is over.'

'I know what I'm doing!' Hargest snapped.

Carnach ignored him. 'The Shining One protect you, Bridei.'

'The Flamekeeper shield you, friend.'

They rode, then, in opposite directions. Carnach, shadowed by his own guard, Gwrad, followed his foot soldiers forward into the fray, where the pike-block had now broken up into small attack units of six or seven men working together to press the tactical advantage against a confusion of Gaelic warriors. Once they got close to the wall, Carnach would order a retreat; the men had been alerted to this likelihood and would recognise in the wording of their chieftain's command that a particular piece of strategy was now in play. The requirement to obey instantly had been drummed into them, for it would go against instinct to respond to this order; they had the bit between their teeth now and were edging forward almost faster than Carnach wanted.

'This way!' Bridei ordered, guiding Snowfire back towards the mounted warriors who had survived the first charge and were now assessing the damage to men and horses while the foot soldiers in their turn clashed with the enemy. Many had fallen to hastily loosed arrow or barbed spear. One horse lay thrashing on the ground, a foreleg snapped. In tears, a big warrior stroked the creature's neck with his left hand as his right readied a knife. Uven was applying a makeshift bandage to a young fighter's arm; Cinioch had dismounted and was tending to a riderless horse. And Enfret . . .

'We lost Enfret, my lord.' Uven looked up as Bridei rode by, and delivered this news levelly. 'Took an arrow in the neck; he went down fighting. I saw him open a Gael's chest with his sword.'

Another one. 'The Shining One grant him rest,' Bridei said. 'Be strong, men. Hold fast. We'll win this for him, and for all the lads we've lost. We're close to the end now and we're going to do it.'

'My lord?' There was a furious grief in Cinioch's voice, audible over the sounds of death that assaulted the ears from all sides at once. 'You'd best keep me by you. It's as messy as a sheep's guts out there. You're not safe with just *him*.' He jerked his head towards Hargest, and Hargest scowled at him. 'But . . .' He dashed a furious hand across a face streaked by dirt and tears.

'But your friend has fallen and you want to avenge him,' Bridei said. 'I understand. Cinioch, we need every seasoned man in action here, yourself included. You're the last able-bodied Pitnochie man left; you must represent Breth and Elpin and Enfret in this last battle. Uven, I know you too will make a valuable contribution, one-armed though you are right now. Do us proud, men. Think of it as a reward for all those years Broichan kept you cooling your heels at Pitnochie, guarding a small boy who liked to wander about in the forest. Under the circumstances, I'll make do with my one guard. It's Gabhran who'll be a sitting target; I can see his banner from here.'

'All the same —'

'Don't argue, Cinioch, move. When you hear Carnach's order, be prepared for the Gaels to surge towards us; they'll believe we're in full retreat. Make sure our own spear-holders don't damage you as they draw back. Go now. Uven, do your best to protect these wounded men. May the gods be with us all.'

Bridei had explained his own role to Hargest on a morning when the first rays of the sun had awoken a jittery restlessness that was part excitement, part fear in the younger and less experienced warriors. All were now battle-hardened; the north of Dalriada had not been won without heavy fighting, and all had seen their share of blood and death. This, however, would be the decisive battle. Each army set its king in play today. For Hargest, who had already proven himself in feats of arms, it was a new challenge. Without Bridei, Fortriu would be leaderless, cut adrift, no longer held safe in the Flamekeeper's hand. It mattered little that others could step up and take the king's place as battle leader. Bridei was more than merely monarch of Fortriu. In his plain leather breast-piece and unadorned helm, his tunic and trousers of grey wool and his serviceable boots, he might have looked to a stranger much the same as any warrior of six and twenty summers; a young man in his prime, determined and strong. The only mark of his identity, other than the kin signs graven on his face, which a Gael could not interpret, was his square wooden shield bearing the symbol of the eagle in blue on white. His eyes echoed that blue; they were the eyes of leader and scholar, fighter and peacemaker, for Bridei strove to be all these things. Blade of Fortriu. He wondered, often, what he had done to deserve such a title. He was flesh and blood. In the midst of a battlefield he was as vulnerable as any of them, and as anonymous.

His desire to appear a man amongst men set his bodyguards a difficult job. Both Breth and Garth had remarked, at different times, how much easier it would be if this king wore a gold helm or silver torc on the field; if he bore his banner beside him or went protected by a shield wall of hand-picked warriors. It would at least make losing sight of him less likely. Faolan had commented drily that, as this king went under the protection of the Flame-keeper, their own presence was superfluous anyway. He, however, was the most skilled of all of them at sticking to Bridei's side in the midst of battle.

Hargest did his best, but in the milling whirl of action Bridei felt the youth's slicing weapon several times come perilously close to his own head. Once, only Snowfire's evasive dance to the side prevented the lad from cleaving his master's skull in two. A moment later the sword went sideways, chopping, and a mounted Gael who had been readying an axe for flight toppled to the ground instead, clutching his side. Hargest grinned; Bridei saw it and looked away. Then there was another Gael, and another, and it became clear that Carnach had called the retreat, for a flood of men surged back from the Dalriadan lines, making for the river, Priteni and Gaels together locked in a hundred small, desperate combats. Men fell; booted feet tramped over them, hooves struck heads and the ground turned to a hideous stew of mud, blood and body parts. Hargest sat steady on his stolid pony, his bulk protecting Bridei and Snowfire from the worst of the human tide. From time to time he reached down and jabbed with his dagger or slashed with his sword; the action seemed to Bridei almost arbitrary, like swatting flies or slapping off midges. He wondered what went through Hargest's mind when he killed.

The Gaels were gaining ground. They sliced and clubbed and chopped their way down towards the river. Drive the Priteni back to the far side of this watercourse, Gabhran's chieftains would be thinking, and hold them at that line, and the day was won. Carnach's forces were in as orderly a retreat as could be managed. Here and there a rank of six shields or seven still held fast as men maintained their formation even while the spears of the enemy jabbed and flew into their ranks.

The mounted warriors were on the flanks; an elite few, they used their advantage of height and mobility to edge in, deliver a crushing blow and wheel away. The hill ponies of Fortriu, trained over long seasons in such manoeuvres, were sweating and wild-eyed now, for no amount of rigorous drilling can teach a horse, or a man, to be ready for the sounds and sights of a scene such as this. The screams, the groans, the straining of metal on metal and the hideous crunch and smash of bodies breaking under the onslaught: it took a strange kind of creature not to be affected by it, not to dream of it over and over, night after night in the time of peace. Hargest, Bridei thought, was that kind of man. The lad almost seemed to be enjoying himself. Perhaps the reality of it would hit him later. For himself, Bridei counted every Gael he slew; he looked in each man's eyes and struggled to see the enemy who had stolen his homeland and set the creeping threat of the new faith in the hearts of his people. He saw only another man doing a job as best he could. All the same, Bridei used his weapons effectively, as his old tutor Donal had trained him to do. He could hardly expect his men to fight if he were not prepared to do the same. All the time he watched for that banner. Gabhran. He wanted the King of Dalriada alive.

They were at the river. The Priteni forces were bunched together in a mass, some in the water, some on the bank, holding fast as the Dalriadan troops pressed closer. On the flanks, Ged's riders and Morleo's fought fiercely with the mounted Gaels. Dalriada had far greater numbers of horsemen and was using them to devastating advantage. Ged's men were under pressure; Bridei watched as their rainbow-clad forms toppled and fell, one by one; he watched the riderless horses bolt back across the shallow river and make their foam-flecked, staring-eyed escape. He scanned the melee for Ged himself and saw him on his stocky, dark horse, grim-jawed and white-faced, hacking a steady path forward. Talorgen he could not see, but the forces of Raven's Well were holding their ground between centre and flank, preventing the enemy from coming around to circle the Priteni foot soldiers and trap them at the river crossing. Carnach yelled another order; his captains relayed it in voices like braying trumpets, and the main mass of warriors stepped up the pace of their retreat across the water, relaxing the pressure against the pursuer. 'Back!' Carnach shouted. 'In the name of the Flamekeeper, back!'

The Gaels gave voice, scenting the kill. Horns shrilled; men screamed: 'Dalriada! Dalriada!' and like an angry tide they surged forward, driving the Priteni before them.

'Pray that this works,' muttered Bridei, halting Snowfire a moment to look behind him. 'Pray that Fokel and Umbrig are as good as their word, or we've lost the advantage.' As he spoke, two mounted Gaels approached at a gallop, one with thrusting spear at the ready, the other wielding a club. There was no time to think. Donal's training asserted itself and Bridei guided Snowfire in a deceptive movement one way, the other way, evading the man with the club while, out of the corner of his eye, he saw Hargest block the spear with his sword, then execute a deft, powerful action that levered the opponent from saddle to muddy ground in a ripple of movement. The club-wielder was circling Bridei, coming in again. Snowfire snorted and tossed his head; Bridei rolled from the saddle, hanging low to the side, and passed close to the enemy unscathed, then rose with dagger in hand as Snowfire executed a tight turn. Before the Gael had time to realise what had happened, Bridei's knife was in his neck and the lifeblood was pumping scarlet across his tunic. He fell; his horse halted to stand trembling amid the maelstrom that surrounded them, perhaps shocked into stillness, perhaps simply waiting for instructions that would never come.

Bridei dismounted and bent to retrieve his weapon. Not far off, Hargest, too, had got down from his horse. As Bridei watched, the youth plunged his sword into the chest of the man he had unseated, not once, but over and over until his opponent was a crushed mass of bloodied flesh. When Hargest looked up, his face was linen-white, his eyes glittering like moonlight on deep ice, a strange, unsettling blue. A frisson of unease passed through Bridei. It was too much. He must call a halt to this for a while at least; get the boy out of it before he lost control completely.

'Hargest,' he said firmly, 'that man is dead. Get back on your horse and follow me.'

To find a space within this confusion of struggling men and scything weaponry was difficult. Bridei led his bodyguard a short way along the river bank and up a slight rise to a patch of level ground amongst rocks. A group of stunted willows grew there, and the body of a Dalriadan warrior, his head lolling at an

unlikely angle, lay sprawled on a darkened patch of grass; otherwise the place was empty. The battle raged on below; between the
trees it was possible to see something of the flow of it, and this
provided Bridei with justification for leading Hargest off the field.

'Your eyes are younger than mine,' he said to the young Caitt
warrior, not mentioning that his own eyes were druid-trained.
'Look down and tell me if you see Fokel's men or Umbrig's. This
is finely balanced; a turning point. If they don't appear soon
Gabhran will drive our forces right back across the water.'

'Why are you looking at me like that? Why don't we stay down
there and fight?' Hargest's voice was very young and strident
with arrogance. There was something else about it that set
Bridei's nerves on edge: an odd tone, the tone of a man frustrated
beyond endurance. The boy sounded ready to take desperate
action, to jump off a cliff or smash a precious treasure.

'Because you were enjoying it too much,' Bridei said flatly.
'You're only fifteen. I am responsible for you. I asked more of you
than I should have done. You've already accounted for your share
of Gaels today.' He was gazing down the hill, seeking the banner
of Dalriada and finding it by the water's edge where the press of
men was thickest. So many had fallen now that their still forms
bridged and dammed the water, which ran red around them.
'Where's –?' Bridei began. The words were lost in a wheezing
exhalation as a powerful arm seized him around the chest. A
moment later he was flat on his back with his assailant kneeling
astride him and a dagger pointed at his heart. Instinctively he
grabbed the attacker's wrists, slicing his own palm open on the
blade, and held on grimly, pressing away so hard he felt the strain
of it in his back, his thighs, his clenched jaw, his head. There was
no point in calling for his bodyguard. Staring, incredulous, up
into those avid, pale eyes, Bridei wondered how long Hargest had
been planning to kill him.

'What –' he started, but the knife pressed down harder, and
he knew he could not waste his breath in speech. Hargest was big,
he was fit, he was young. Even if Bridei yelled at the top of his
voice, who would hear him above the din of battle? In the space of
a few laboured breaths he was going to die; in each inhalation, in
each instant of resistance a small farewell . . . Tuala . . . Derelei . . .

Broichan . . . *Save me*, he prayed with every scrap of his will. *Save me for them, and save me for Fortriu . . .*

'It's time to pay your dues,' said Hargest in a small, cold voice, and Bridei felt the youth's grip shift on the knife, easing the pressure momentarily. 'You've evaded my blade too many times, you weak excuse for a king. Now it's time to die. You're a fool if you can't see the inevitable: it's the Gaels who will triumph here. They'll be all over the Glen by the time I bear this news back to my father. Your reign is over, *King* Bridei.'

Then, as Bridei arched his back and made to twist out from beneath him, Hargest pushed down again and the tip of the blade entered flesh. Even as it came to Bridei that there was a technique Faolan had once shown him, a trick he could have used if he had been ready in that moment's respite, he felt a piercing pain in his chest and, no longer husbanding his breath, he sucked air into his lungs and yelled, 'Help me! In the gods' name, help!'

Hargest smiled; the knife bit deeper as Bridei's arms, the muscles straining in painful, trembling spasm, began to lose their strength. Bridei sensed the wings of the dark goddess beating above him. Her chill breath touched his sweating brow, her eldritch lullaby whispered in his ear . . . Then a flash of movement, something brushing his face, feathers, claws, beak, a wild eye and a scream to match his own, the cry of a great bird of prey. Hargest, too, shouted, the pressure of his hands suddenly slackening as the hawk's talons raked across his face, drawing a pattern of bloody lines. Bridei, a man druid-raised, did not waste time in pondering the strangeness of this intervention. He seized the moment's advantage, rolling, sliding, making himself like a snake, an eel, a salamander as the bird flew upward, still calling its harsh warning, then dived once more to send Hargest reeling back, arms up to protect his lacerated face. Bridei scrambled to his feet, intent on the knife still clutched in Hargest's fist. The youth was standing; blood was trickling into his eyes. He was breathing hard, but he held the weapon steady and his feet were planted square.

'Come on, then!' he challenged, glaring at Bridei. 'Take it, come on, take it off me!' Then, 'Cursed creature!' slashing wildly as the hawk made another sweeping pass, threatening to topple him.

513

Save me for Fortriu . . . Bridei dived forward, seizing Hargest's wrists, and as the hawk swept by once more, making the young man stumble and curse, he shoved with all his remaining strength.

Hargest fell. The sound of it was something Bridei dreamed about later; something he would have given much to be able to erase from his memory. There was a hideous, crunching finality about it. Nonetheless, after a moment's horrified stillness, Bridei bent to check as the hawk settled on the rocks nearby. He managed to contain himself, though his gorge rose as he looked. He reminded himself of Broichan's old dictum that there was learning to be had in everything. Yes, even in the sight of a boy who was full of promise lying with his head smashed in like an overripe fruit that has fallen from the tree. Hargest had been unlucky. Perhaps the gods had placed that stone there, intending the young man to die when his head struck it. Perhaps this was their all-too-simple answer to Bridei's prayer.

He knelt to cross Hargest's arms on his chest; to place the knife by the boy's side. The open eyes gazed up at the sky, wide, blue, blank. Bridei searched for a prayer. For the moment, he could not think of one. All he could think was, *Why?* All he could hear was the thud of his own heart, a drumbeat of anger and grief, shock and hurt.

'My lord! Bridei! What –?'

A small company of men, then, suddenly there beside him, Cinioch and three others, all on foot with swords drawn and white faces. A moment later there was a rustling movement behind him, and as he turned he caught a glimpse of something wondrous and unsettling, the wild-eyed, tawny-feathered hawk changing before his gaze to a tall, broad-shouldered man with eyes bright as stars and a mane of hair that same vivid gold-red.

Cinioch shouted again and the men surged forward, weapons lifted to strike. One stumbled over the body of the dead Gael, still lying on the sward. The red-haired man put up his hands; he bore neither sword, knife nor bow. 'I am a friend,' he said with admirable calm, then staggered as if weary to exhaustion and put out a hand to steady himself against the rocks.

'Hold back, lads,' said Bridei. 'I'm safe. This man came to my rescue. But Hargest is dead.' He could not find it in him to explain further; indeed, he could not begin to understand what had happened.

'Bridei, you're bleeding.'

Cinioch came forward, and as Bridei looked down he saw a spreading bloodstain on his own shirt, through the slit Hargest's dagger had made in the leather breast-piece. His hand was dripping blood where the same weapon had sliced it; his mind showed him a small image of Hargest seated by the fire at night, sharpening the blade with a concentration that set a frown on his young brow and a narrowed intensity in his eyes.

'It's nothing,' Bridei said, but submitted as Cinioch checked the damage and applied makeshift bandages, saying Bridei had indeed been blessed by the gods, for a little deeper and he'd have been off in Bone Mother's arms before he had a chance to know it. One of the other men was rolling the dead Gael over, removing the man's weapons, giving him a token kick. Save for the presence of the red-haired man, there would have been no need to speak of what Hargest had done. But this stranger had witnessed it. He had intervened as if in response to Bridei's prayer. As a bird. A messenger from the Flamekeeper? This man was kneeling beside Hargest now, handsome features sombre. He reached out long fingers to close the boy's eyes. His hand was not quite steady.

'Who are you?' Bridei asked him.

'A messenger. Sent by the queen, your wife.'

'By Tuala? But –'

'There was a vision; your friends at White Hill knew you to be in deadly danger, with none able to reach you in time. I was there. I offered to come.'

Now the other men were staring, distrust mingling with wonder on their faces.

'You are a druid? A mage?' Bridei asked, hearing from down the hill a change in the sounds of battle and knowing they had little time for explanations now.

'I am Drustan of Dreaming Glen and Briar Wood; I am neither mage nor druid. I see my brother's hand in this: Alpin, who was to have wed your royal hostage. I have to tell you that my brother is dead, and that he never planned to honour your treaty.'

515

Bridei was silent a moment, glancing from the stranger to the fallen youth and back again.

'This is his son, isn't it?' Drustan said, eyes bleak. 'Hargest. I haven't seen him since he was a child, but I'd know those eyes anywhere. The queen described the assailant to me. Even then, I knew.'

'He was your kinsman,' Bridei said, and the words *mad uncle* were somewhere in his mind. 'I'm sorry; that was a choice no man should be asked to make.'

'But, my lord king,' Cinioch protested, 'what are you saying? That it was Hargest, your own bodyguard, who –?'

'Enough for now,' Bridei said. 'We've a battle to win, and I think I hear Umbrig's ox-horn trumpets in the midst of it. Drustan, you should take this Gael's weapons; he has no use for them now. Whether you mean to stay here or fight alongside us, or . . .' He glanced skyward, but did not put the third option into words, 'you'll need to be able to defend yourself. I owe you my life. I won't leave you to be slaughtered by the first group of warriors to find you, be they Gaels or men of Fortriu.'

In silence, Drustan accepted the weapons, setting the sword belt around his waist and shouldering the crossbow. 'Thank you,' he said. 'I will ride with you. Since it seems my kinsmen have betrayed you twice over, it must fall to me to make amends.'

'You a fighting man?' Cinioch asked him bluntly.

'I can get by,' Drustan told him, taking the reins of Hargest's horse. The animal was nervous and wild-eyed; Drustan set a hand on its neck and murmured in its ear, words in a language Bridei could not understand. 'I will not seek out Gaels to kill, but I can ride by the king's side and help to protect him.'

'Why would you be wanting to do that when you could just wait it out?' one of the men challenged. 'If you're kin of *his*,' glaring at the fallen Hargest, 'and he's responsible for this attack on Bridei, you must be crazy to think we'd trust you with the king's safety.'

'Give us one reason why we should,' put in Cinioch, glowering.

'I have given one already,' Drustan said, mounting the horse in a fluid movement. 'I make amends for my kinsmen's treachery. I will give two more. I am a friend of the king's chief bodyguard.

Since Faolan cannot be here where he most longs to be, I will take his place. And that which I long for most in the world is in King Bridei's gift. If I harm him, or let him fall foul of Gaelic swords, I lose my moon and stars, my joy and hope of the future. Believe me, I will protect him well.'

They stared at him, for the moment silenced. Then Bridei said, 'We must wait to discover what this treasure of yours is; while we debate here, the battle's being lost and won. Men, where are your horses? Down under the trees? Find them and get back down there. I will trust myself to Drustan's guardianship. A man who journeys the length of the Great Glen to provide me with a warning can hardly be less than a friend.' He glanced at the red-haired man. 'Ready?'

Drustan nodded gravely. 'I am, my lord king. Let us ride.'

It came to Bridei, as the two of them emerged from their cover and headed straight for the seething mass of warriors by the stream, that the man by his side might almost be the Flamekeeper himself in human form, so well-made and comely was he, so compelling of expression with those piercing eyes and that flow of exuberant fire-bright hair. When Drustan had first appeared, a creature, then a man, Bridei had wondered for an instant if the god of warriors had chosen to answer his cry for help in a particularly personal way. Wherever this man went, folk's eyes would be drawn to him. If not a druid, what was he? Human, surely, if he was brother to Alpin of Briar Wood. But what ordinary man possessed such a wondrous power of changing? No time to ponder this further now; it was back into the fray, though with some caution. His wounded hand was a liability in battle, the loss of blood from the shallow chest injury likely to weaken him. The enigmatic Drustan was an unknown quantity. From this point on, Bridei knew, his own survival must take precedence over the capacity of the two of them to contribute as fighting men. He must hope this bird-man could provide him with adequate protection.

The tide of the battle had changed again. The highly trained forces of Fokel of Galany and the Caitt chieftain Umbrig had been lying in wait since before the Gaels reached the strath, quietly picking off any Dalriadan scouts who happened to come

517

close to their hideouts in the wooded areas further along the broad valley. They had chosen their moment well, moving up the river banks from either end while the Gaels were engaged in countering Carnach's advance, and reaching the action just as both Gaels and Priteni were concentrated down by the water, where the staged retreat had drawn the enemy. Umbrig's men set their massive ox horns to their lips. Fokel's warriors let loose a howling, chanting, screaming battle cry that set a chill even in Bridei's bones, for it was like a message from Black Crow, a call from beyond the grave. Carnach's forces, who had a moment ago been in full and rapid retreat, ceased their flight, turned, planted their legs and raised their weapons, eyes blazing with a new zeal.

Talorgen rode up to Bridei, his own personal guard at his side. The Chieftain of Raven's Well looked grim; there was blood on his face and on his clothing but he sat tall in the saddle. 'Now?' he queried, looking at Bridei, then glancing sideways at Drustan with a little frown.

'Now,' Bridei said, a strange sense of calm coming over him even as the scene before him erupted into a new spectacle of clashing metal and shouting men.

Talorgen's guard, Sobran, opened a bundle strapped alongside his saddle, deftly removed a roll of white cloth and three short, socketed poles and assembled the banner with an efficiency born of long practice. It was time, at last, for the King of Fortriu to make himself known.

'Raise it up, Sobran,' he told Talorgen's man. 'We'll all go forward together.' And as the white banner was lifted and the wind from the western isles whipped it out to reveal, in blue, the crescent and broken rod of the royal line and above them the eagle that was Bridei's chosen token of kingship, a sudden quiet fell over the men who were closest. Then Bridei raised his arm, clenched fist held skyward in honour of the Flamekeeper, and cried out in a great voice that seemed to come from beyond the earthly realm: 'Fortriu!' And from a hundred, five hundred, a thousand mouths parched from the long morning's work, a thousand bodies exhausted from the fierce tests of mortal combat, a thousand minds in which the sights of death and loss and pain would linger for years to come, a cry went up that set terror in the heart of every Gael in that place: *'Fortriu! Fortriu!'*

The men of Dalriada fought bravely and hard, but they were marked for defeat from that moment. The flame that Bridei had seen in a vision, long ago, still burning in the poor remnants of a defeated Priteni army, now roared and crackled and exploded in these weary men, and he thought he saw the god's radiance shining from the face of each and every one of them, from battle-hardened chieftain to humblest spear-carrier. Each of them was a beloved son of the Flamekeeper, held in his hands, trusted and cherished. It was the lot of some to fall and not to rise again. Others would die of their wounds, for they were far from home. Many would live to ride, victorious, back to their settlements and the welcoming arms of their dear ones.

Talorgen and Bridei rode forward together. Sobran bore the banner. Drustan, somewhat to Bridei's surprise, was a whirlwind of motion, executing a number of highly efficient, unusual and deadly moves. As a result, not a single Gael got close enough to challenge the king, although Talorgen had cause to employ his sword more than once before they cut a way through to the river, and did so with the skill and determination one would expect from a seasoned warrior chieftain.

Choices lay before the King of Dalriada, as with all leaders at the point in a conflict where defeat becomes inevitable. Some prefer annihilation on the field, the sacrifice of a whole army of men, to the bitterness of surrender. Some weigh the options carefully, even in the moment or two fate allows for this as their men lie dying around them, and think beyond the time of humiliation to a future in which negotiation, diplomacy, regrouping and new alliances may yet make victory from defeat. At length Gabhran's decision was made, and a messenger despatched to carry it through the turmoil of struggling men and the debris of fallen ones to King Bridei, now waiting coolly under his banner with a group of mounted warriors around him. The messenger wore a white cloth knotted around his brow, over his leather helm, a sign that he should be allowed to go unmolested. By the time he reached Bridei and gasped out his message a stillness was creeping over the scene of battle, for the sight of the King of Fortriu waiting there, his blue eyes blazing, his grey horse proud and quiet amid the carnage, and the movement of the white-crested messenger, drew the men's eyes down the stream to a place where another king now waited under the red and gold banner of Dalriada, a look on his face that went beyond exhaustion into dignified resignation. At that, the hundred small battles began to cease; combatants backed off, sheathed swords, lowered spears, not without maintaining a careful eye on their opponents. The Gaels began to drift in the general direction of their original encampment and were halted by an implacable line of Fokel's men who had come around to block their retreat. They were surrounded. If Gabhran chose to pursue this fight to the death, he'd take every one of them along with him.

There was another figure who drew the eye. As King Bridei rode forward and his escort moved with him, the men of Fortriu stared and blinked and stared again, and more than one of them muttered a childhood prayer, for it seemed just possible that the bright-eyed, flame-haired figure who shadowed the Blade of Fortriu might be none other than their beloved Flamekeeper made flesh, he who had long valued this young king, his devout nature and his commitment to his lands and people. That this exceptionally striking-looking man seemed to have come from nowhere added weight to the theory.

Bridei reached a certain point, dismounted and waited for the Gaelic king to come to him. By his side, Talorgen now held the royal banner, and through the subsiding chaos of the battle rode other leaders, Morleo, Carnach, to join the king's party.

Gabhran approached on foot, his standard-bearer behind him, two chieftains flanking him. There was hardly a need for words. He came within four paces of Bridei, unbuckled his sword belt and laid it, complete with weapons, on the muddy ground. He spoke briefly in Gaelic.

Bridei waited. He understood well enough, but caution had ever made him less than forthcoming about his grasp of this tongue. He regretted, once again, the absence of Faolan.

'You require a translation,' someone said in the tongue of the Priteni. A slight, tonsured figure stepped out from the ranks of the Dalriadan king's supporters.

'You!' Bridei could not help exclaiming at the sight of Brother Suibne, religious adviser to Drust of Circinn and a man who had played no little part in his own election as king. 'You're everywhere!'

Suibne smiled. 'Only God is everywhere,' he said. 'My place at the court of Circinn has been taken by another. A powerful wind drew me to the west, harbinger of a great awakening to light, a new dawn of faith. The king wishes to hear your terms for his surrender. He is hoping you may be magnanimous and spare the lives of those of his men still standing.'

'I will not ask how you yourself walked through this battle unscathed,' Bridei told the Christian cleric, 'for I know already what your answer will be. Tell King Gabhran I'm prepared to talk. He must order his men to relinquish their arms immediately, to place them on the ground as he has done and to step back. I, in my turn, will give the command that my forces do no more than patrol the perimeter of this area until we reach agreement. Your men may tend their wounded; mine will do likewise. One false move and we finish this not in peace but in blood. Be sure Gabhran understands that.'

Suibne relayed this accurately to the Gaelic leader and obtained grudging assent. A series of orders was issued and conveyed to all quarters of the field. One might have expected a certain reluctance to obey. It sits oddly when one has just been locked in a sweaty, bloody duel to the death to see that same opponent unarmed, no more than a couple of arm's-lengths away, and not to seize the opportunity to finish him off. The battle cry had not long left their lips; the heat of the god's inspiration had not yet burned down to ashes in their breasts. As for the Gaels, how could they trust that, once relieved of their weapons, they would not immediately be slain by the victorious Priteni? From an ancient enemy, a promise is hardly to be taken on face value.

This, however, had been only the last battle in a war that had stretched over almost a full turning of the moon. The men of Fortriu had endured a long and gruelling march to reach Dalriada. As the warriors of Raven's Well and Storm Crag, Pitnochie and Thorn Bend, Abertornie and Longwater began to spread out across the gentle slopes of the valley, bending here and there to examine a broken body, crouching to lift a man who still seemed to have some life in him, and as the Gaels, more cautiously, moved to start the same process, it became evident that these armies had had enough. For the Priteni, weariness and anguish were beginning to seep through the elation, for their losses had been substantial; for the Gaels, survival took the place of victory as the outcome most to be wished for. They would tend their fallen and then, gods willing, at last they could go home.

Chapter Eighteen

B ridei had thought, once, that the moment Gabhran knelt to him and surrendered the kingship of Dalriada would be the fulfilment of his dreams. The Gaelic king was in a weak position, with the northern part of his territory already reclaimed for Fortriu and the remnant of his army at risk of wholesale slaughter if he did not agree with Bridei's terms. As it was, Gabhran was so calm and dignified in defeat that Bridei wondered what the man saw in the future that he could not.

The leaders of the Priteni set out their requirements. Brother Suibne rendered them into Gaelic and delivered Gabhran's response, while beyond the small pavilion where the chieftains had gathered, in what had formerly been the Gaelic encampment, the dead and dying were tended to and the wounded patched up as well as was possible. Talorgen had brought his household physician; at present, this man was tending to Ged. The news had come to Bridei just before this formal meeting that the chieftain of Abertornie had been sorely wounded on the field and was not expected to survive. Carnach, too, had an expert in his party, one with skill at bone-setting. In the event, Priteni surgeons worked on Gaelic casualties and the reverse, though not without a certain degree of doubtful muttering from the men.

Bridei secured Gabhran's agreement to relinquish the title King of Dalriada and to withdraw with his Uí Néill chieftains to Dunadd, under armed escort. In due course all must quit Priteni lands. The elders who controlled the various settlements of Dalriada, the leaders who governed fortress and fishing port must all step down; any dissension and they faced exile or death. The ordinary folk, those called to arms solely for this particular war, might return to their homes and pick up their lives once more, as long as they understood the west would be under the rule of Fortriu from this day on.

Gabhran consulted with his chieftains, then, grim-jawed, set his sign to the document Bridei had had prepared some considerable time ago.

'And,' Bridei said, 'it goes without saying that the practice of the Christian ritual will cease throughout these territories. Your priests will return to their homeland. The people will not observe the festivals of the new faith, nor join in public prayer to the Christian god. This must be understood.'

Brother Suibne leaned forward and spoke in an undertone to the Gaelic king, and Gabhran responded.

'Ahem,' Suibne cleared his throat. 'I know you are well aware of the presence of our holy men in Circinn. The king asks if you also know that the Light Isles provide shelter for a number of Christian clerics, who are treated with tolerance and courtesy by the king there and by his people. King Gabhran seeks assurances that the members of that peaceful community will be neither molested nor driven out. We understand the King of the Light Isles is subject to your overlordship.'

'I have no comment on that matter,' Bridei said. 'It falls outside the scope of these negotiations and beyond Gabhran's authority.'

'Then,' said Suibne, 'I will inform you of another complication.' He did not wait to consult Gabhran this time but appeared to offer the information on his own account.

'Go on,' Bridei said.

'What of the western isles?' the Christian asked mildly. 'You wish all Gaels in residence there, and there are several hundred spread across a number of small settlements, to quit those shores entirely? Will you set up local leaders there also? Those villages, and the farms and fishing boats that sustain them, are marginal even with the number of folk who dwell there now.'

There was a pause.

'Why do you ask this?' Bridei was cautious; he knew this man from the past. From Suibne, these could not be idle questions.

Suibne exchanged quiet words with Gabhran once more. 'A promise was made,' he said, turning back towards Bridei. 'It concerned a very small island, barren, windy, of no significance at all. The old name for the place is Ioua.'

'Yew Tree Isle. I know of it.' Bridei's childhood lessons in geography had been extremely thorough. 'A place of great beauty, I was told; wild, light-filled, remote. What promise?'

'My lord king had an approach from a certain man. From an outstanding man, Bridei, a priest whom even you, should you be fortunate enough to meet him face to face, would acknowledge as powerful in faith and radiant with grace. His name is Colm; they call him Colmcille, which could be translated as "dove of the Church".' There was a glow on Suibne's unprepossessing features and a warmth in his tone which Bridei could not fail to notice.

'What promise?' asked Carnach, features set. 'Get on with it. You know our opinion of this faith and the damage it has already wrought in Priteni lands. It's divisive and dangerous.'

'Brother Colm seeks a refuge, a quiet place where he and a small group of brethren may establish a house of prayer, a hermitage, away from certain influences at home. King Gabhran has promised them sanctuary on Ioua. It's a speck of an isle.'

Carnach hissed; Talorgen grimaced; Morleo clenched his fists.

'Ioua is not in King Gabhran's gift,' said Bridei calmly. 'As of today, he holds no power in Priteni lands. The western isles are under my control, and I will decide who comes and who goes. Fortriu wants no more zealous Christians poisoning the minds of its good folk.'

Suibne translated this and Gabhran gave a measured, grave response.

'The king says this great tide will hold back for no man. Not even the Blade of Fortriu can halt it,' Suibne said. 'He's right,

Bridei. If you would know what we mean, invite this priest to your court at White Hill. See him, talk with him. I know you as tolerant and open-minded, a man who forms his own opinions. Hear Brother Colm at least. None can meet him and remain unchanged.'

'What is this fellow trying to tell us?' Talorgen was becoming restless. 'He's here to translate, surely, not offer you his personal advice.'

'We are friends of a kind,' Bridei said. 'But you're right. Brother Suibne, tell the king I have noted this request. We are done here for now.' He addressed Gabhran direct, while the Christian translated in a low voice. 'My war leader and kinsman, Carnach, will arrange an armed guard for you. He will escort you personally to Dunadd and see to arrangements for the future. We've some work to do here first, men to bury, a ritual to perform and some decisions to make as to which of your warriors will accompany you and which may return to their communities here. I've no quarrel with any man who has a genuine desire to settle in these territories for good, as long as he respects Priteni law and Priteni faith.'

'My lord king –' Fokel was at the entry to the pavilion. His face was white and his tunic was covered in blood.

'I must leave you, my lords.' Bridei rose to his feet and made a courteous bow. 'A dear friend is dying; I must speak to him while I still can. You, too, will have farewells to make. Do so swiftly. I want you out of this place before day's end.'

Ged was lying on a makeshift stretcher, the terrible wound he had sustained covered by a bright cloak laid over his torso by one of his household men-at-arms. All around him other injured warriors lay; the surgeons were working in a welter of blood and flesh. The men who were helping them were grey-faced and silent. There was little equipment at hand; they needed saws, braziers for cauterisation, healing herbs. In this land which had become a foreign country, there was only the scant supply each physician had carried in his saddlebags. The men with lesser wounds might be conveyed to a Dalriadan settlement and get reasonable attention there. Many would die here; this was the nature of a war fought on the march.

'Ged,' Bridei said, coming to kneel by his friend's side and taking Ged's hand between his. 'This is grievous news.' There was no point in pretence; Morleo had described the wound to him earlier as they prepared for their council with Gabhran.

'Bridei . . .' Ged wheezed. 'Good fight, wasn't it? Fellows did us proud . . .'

'They did, my friend. Tell me now, is there anything I can do for you? Messages to convey?'

Ged tried to smile and managed a contorted grimace. 'You're a king, not . . . errand boy . . . But, Bridei . . . my boy, Aled . . . He's only twelve, too young to take over Abertornie yet awhile, and the little ones are all girls . . . Loura shouldn't have to run the place on her own . . . Could you . . . ?'

'I'll talk to your wife. We'll put something in place for her, don't distress yourself on that account.' Bridei could hear a change in Ged's breathing and see a filmy quality stealing across his eyes. Bone Mother was a hair's-breadth away. 'We're all here, Ged,' he said quietly. 'Talorgen, Morleo, Fokel and a good contingent of your own fellows, too. They fought as you've trained them to do, with heart, with guts, with inspiration. The Flamekeeper breathe his warmth into your spirit and shield you on your journey.'

'Ah . . .' Ged breathed. 'It hurts, Bridei. It hurts more than I thought it would. Hard to draw breath . . . But it's good. We won it . . . We won our place back . . . If anything's worth dying for, I think . . . it's that . . .' The eyes glazed and became sightless; the chest ceased its shallow rise and fall. A thin trickle of blood came from one corner of Ged's mouth to lose itself in the scarlet and yellow and green of his covering.

'Bone Mother cradle you gently, old fellow,' Talorgen said, turning aside to wipe his eyes.

'Blessed All-Flowers bring you dreams of the comeliest girls and the brightest gardens in all Fortriu,' said Fokel, bending to touch the dead man's brow with his lips.

'The Shining One light your pathway until you march forward into a new dawn.' Morleo knelt and closed the staring eyes; Bridei moved to cross Ged's arms on his chest, where blood had soaked all through the borrowed cloak. He could find no more words.

There was nothing to be done here. Ged's men would keep a vigil, though only until dawn, for there were many to bury, and nobody wanted to linger in these parts. For himself, there were things to do yet, people to see, news to pass on. It would be a long time before he could be alone and begin to weigh this.

He found Cinioch, drew him aside and told him that the matter he had seen unfold between himself, Hargest and the mysterious red-headed stranger was to be kept strictly secret, for now at least. He was to make sure the other men who had been with him understood this.

'Already told them,' Cinioch said. 'The only thing is, I did speak of it to Uven. Had to; he was all questions about our unexpected visitor. He knows to keep it to himself. Did you hear he killed three Gaels one-armed? Didn't lose a single one of the wounded.'

'Uven's not lacking in courage,' Bridei said. 'As for you, I heard you acquitted yourself more than ably.'

'What will you tell Umbrig, my lord?' Cinioch asked baldly. 'You going to let him know the boy he sent you as a bodyguard turned out to be an assassin?'

'Hush, Cinioch. What I choose to tell Umbrig is my own business.' Bridei saw the genuine concern on Cinioch's face and relented. 'In fact,' he added, 'I'll be telling him the truth.' Once before he had come close to being slain by a friend turned foe, and he had lied to that man's father to shield him from hurt. Talorgen had almost certainly guessed the truth, but the lie had helped him and his two younger boys to deal with their grief more easily. Bridei would not lie this time. 'But there's no need for the entire army to know as well. I'm going to find Umbrig now. And where's –?' He glanced around the area where the Pitnochie horses had been tethered. A number of men he knew were seated, resting, tending to minor wounds or repacking gear. Someone had made a small campfire and was cooking what smelled like porridge.

'Drustan? The bird-man?'

'That, too, should be kept quiet. Is he still here, or has he flown off while we were making our terms for peace?'

'He's up yonder, my lord. Looks as if he hasn't the strength for any flying; not yet anyway. By the Flamekeeper's manhood, though, that fellow can fight more cannily than any warrior I've seen in the field. He's got a rare talent. I'd like to learn a few of those moves. For a while there, I almost thought . . .'

Bridei managed a smile. 'Perhaps we all did. But this is a mortal man, in my judgement; the fact that he claims to be Faolan's friend seems to prove it. Offer him some food, will you? He's come a long way in a hurry to help us. Ask him to wait until I come back. I wish to thank him. And I think he has a request to make of me.'

Umbrig surprised Bridei by shedding tears, and then by stating that he'd been worried all along the boy would turn bad; his father had a mean streak, and there was always the suspicion Hargest might revert to type. As for the news that apparently Alpin, too, was dead, Umbrig took that calmly. The Caitt chieftain opined that, if Hargest had attempted assassination, it would be Alpin who'd put him up to it. Umbrig suspected the two of them might have met, once or twice, during those long expeditions the boy liked to make on horseback, ostensibly to build up the stamina of newly trained mounts. The boy's public disdain of his natural father had never quite meshed with his desire for recognition and for a place in the world.

'A desire for love, I think it was,' Bridei said quietly, feeling his own failure as an ache in the chest. 'I tried to help him. I could have done much for him if he'd given it time. Hargest had promise; all he needed was good guidance until he recognised his own humanity.'

'I did try, Bridei,' muttered Umbrig, wiping his face on the cat-skin border of his massive cloak. 'I tried over seven years. There's bad blood in that family. Strange stories; dark history.'

'You know the boy's uncle, Drustan, is here? That it was he who brought the news of Alpin's death?'

Umbrig stared at Bridei. 'The mad uncle? Really? What side was *he* fighting on?'

'He intervened to save my life. You'll see wounds on your foster son's face. His uncle inflicted those. But the mortal injury was my own doing. I didn't mean to kill him, Umbrig. I sought only to prevent him from piercing my heart with his knife. I would give much to have that time again, to turn him from his mission and to guide him into a future of bright possibilities.'

'You're not a god, Bridei, for all so many folk come close to thinking so. You can't get it right every time. Maybe it was meant for Hargest to go today. The lad was eaten up by rage and frustration. Perhaps he'd never have been satisfied. Perhaps he'd never have accepted the fact that he wasn't Alpin's legitimate son and heir. Who knows? We lost scores of good men on this field today. In the long run, the boy's just another casualty of war.' Tears were flowing freely down the broad, tattooed features.

'Thank you, Umbrig,' Bridei said, bowing his head. 'This places me in your debt, and I will honour that when you need it. Just tell me quickly: this mad uncle we spoke of, has he earned that description through temperament or infirmity? Drustan does not seem to me addled in his wits.'

Umbrig grimaced. 'Haven't seen him for years,' he said, 'not since the lot of us were children. He was all right then, bit of a dreamer, but nothing unusual. Tale goes that he killed Alpin's wife and child, and his brother declared him a danger and locked him up for safety. Seven years ago; that's just after Hargest was sent to me. So he's out, is he? That'll be interesting. You realise Drustan owns the anchorage in the west? The one Alpin's been using for his seaborne forces? And I suppose Briar Wood will go to him now as well. That's going to make him one of the most powerful chieftains in the north.'

'Interesting,' said Bridei. 'I must ask Talorgen if there were Caitt ships amongst those he sank on the way here. But first, I will seek out this uncle and put some questions to him. Farewell, Umbrig. Again, I can't tell you how sorry I am about the lad.'

'You don't need to,' Umbrig grunted. 'It's written all over your face. Go on then. I've men to bury. I'd best start now and get it done with.'

Drustan was alone, standing at some distance from the campfire Uven had made. It had been a very long day. Dusk was falling now and the breeze had dropped to a gentle westerly, bearing the salt smell of the sea. Many birds flew overhead, calling to the coming night, and the red-haired man was gazing up at them. His arms were wrapped across his chest. As Bridei approached, he saw that Drustan was shivering and that his jaw was set tight as if to keep his teeth from chattering. A metal bowl of food had been set on a flat rock nearby; it appeared untouched.

'Drustan?' Bridei kept his tone soft. He had not come alone; Cinioch and Uven were close by and watching out for him. While he had never quite shed his desire to be able to move about without constant protection, he accepted that today was somewhat exceptional. He had chosen to trust Hargest, and Hargest had almost killed him. Today, his army had won Dalriada back; the peace depended on him.

'My lord king.' Drustan unfolded his arms and inclined his head courteously. His voice was not quite steady.

'You seem unwell. Shall we sit?'

'I am well enough. To change my form takes some toll on me; to ride straight into a conflict after what had occurred tested me severely. Besides . . .' Drustan hesitated.

'Come, sit.'

They settled on the ground, side by side. This field provided few comforts.

'As you doubtless saw, I have been trained to fight,' Drustan said, 'and to do it capably. I've been a prisoner, seven years locked up with just the one guard. To pass the time and to keep me from madness and despair, he taught me what he knew. The moves, the skills, those I enjoy. It is good to exercise body and mind. Riding into battle and employing those skills to maim and kill is alien to my nature. It troubles me. And I am unaccustomed to being amongst folk. I offer my apologies. Your men must have thought me churlish and ungrateful.'

Bridei absorbed this speech, which contained several surprises. Things being as they were, he was unlikely to have time to get to know this intriguing man very well, for a while at least. 'Drustan,' he ventured, 'I have a number of questions to ask you. Indeed, I scarcely know where to begin. Umbrig told me you were locked up by your brother for a serious crime. A heinous crime.'

'You wish to ask if this is true? Why would you believe me over Umbrig, whom you already know?'

'Umbrig tells only what he has heard. You are in a position to tell the truth.'

'I am innocent of that crime.' Drustan turned his lambent eyes on Bridei. 'Do you trust your man, Faolan?'

This was unexpected. 'With my life,' Bridei said.

'He knows I am innocent. He will speak in my support. So will Ana.'

Something in Drustan's tone caught Bridei's attention. 'You refer to the royal hostage, Ana of the Light Isles, whom we sent to wed your brother?'

Drustan lowered his eyes. A little smile curved his lips. 'She never doubted me,' he said. 'Even when I myself was unsure, she trusted in my innocence. They have been true friends to me, the two of them.'

'You surprise me. According to Faolan, he doesn't have friends.'

'You and I know that he does.'

'I think you'd better tell me the whole story,' Bridei said. 'We don't have much time; in the absence of my druid, I must conduct a ritual before nightfall. And I have a request to make of you, but it depends on your answers to my questions.'

'I wish to ask a question of you, before I tell our tale: mine and Faolan's and . . . Ana's.' There it was again, the name spoken with such delicacy and passion that one could not hear it without a jolt to the heart.

'Ask, then.'

'You fought and killed today as we all did. You took your place amongst your warriors and led by example as a true king should. Indeed, it seemed you chose to set yourself at hazard, to conceal the signs of your royal status until the very end, taking your chances with the rest of your men. You were courageous, decisive. Now you appear calm and controlled. But I saw in your face that you relished the shedding of blood no more than I did. This interests me. Your Faolan speaks of you almost as if you were a god . . . No, that's wrong, he is not a man who places much trust in things spiritual. He sees you as a leader without peer, and as a man whose example is outstanding in every way. He sees you also as a friend, although he will not acknowledge it.'

There was a silence. Then Bridei said, 'What is the question?'

'How do you reconcile these things?' Drustan asked, placing his arms around his knees. 'How can you bear it?'

Bridei managed a smile. 'At times like this,' he said, 'with considerable difficulty. I was raised by a man who understood what a king must be; he prepared me well. I have folk at White Hill, and chieftains here in the field, who support me with all they have to give. And there's my wife. Without Tuala I couldn't make sense of any of it. She is my anchor, my still centre, my heart and my gift.' It felt odd, yet strangely right, to be confiding this to Drustan, whom he had known for so short a time. In a curious way, the bird-man reminded him of the old druid, Uist, who had ever seemed full of an Otherworldly radiance and wisdom, even in the darkest times, as if he stood outside the ordinary rights and wrongs of human business.

Drustan was smiling. 'Thank you,' he said. 'I honour you, and I pity you. Each of us has his own shackles. I escaped mine with the help of remarkable friends. But you can never escape.'

'You misunderstand me. I love the gods and I love my country. The duty of leadership has called to me from the first, and I follow this path willingly.'

'Love sustains you. Tuala is a remarkable woman. I will tell my story now.'

His account was long, dark, and stranger than anything Bridei could have anticipated. Ana's role seemed utterly out of keeping with what he knew of her nature, and some of Faolan's choices surprised him, but the tale was compelling and he believed it. He listened in silence until Drustan brought his story to a close with Tuala's request that he act as messenger. 'And I knew,' the red-haired man said, 'I knew in my heart that this assassin was none other than my brother's son. As soon as the queen spoke of his eyes, I knew. I did not tell them. For Faolan in particular, asking me to intervene in such a situation would have sat very ill.'

'Why for Faolan especially?'

'There is an event in his own past, an experience I cannot share with you, for the account of it was given in confidence. Faolan would be loath to ask a man to put the life of a kinsman at risk. That was always possible, even though, as far as we knew, all I had to do was deliver a warning. I did not wish to reveal my blood bond with Hargest to him.'

'I'm sorry. Had I known –'

'It could have made no difference, my lord. I made a choice. Your survival outweighs Hargest's many times over. You are the Blade of Fortriu. He was . . .'

'Just a confused and angry boy? I can't see it that way, Drustan. It seems to me a man is a man, and each small passing deserves an equal share of tears. I could have helped that lad; he could have been something, I know it. Now another friend has entrusted his son to me, and I fear I will botch the task all over again. Outstanding example? At times like this, I feel as if I'm blundering along in the dark.'

'You need your wife beside you. You need to shed your tears, as we all must, and recognise your own weaknesses, and take time to recover your courage. But you have no time.'

Bridei stared at him. 'How can you know this? How can you understand so well?'

'Perhaps because I came close to despair myself, despair, violence, self-destruction . . . Without Deord, I could not have survived that. Without Faolan, I would not have escaped. Without Ana . . .'

The flow of words ceased. From beyond the campfire, someone was calling Bridei's name. 'Go on,' he said. 'I imagine you wish to make this request of yours.'

Drustan gave a sigh. 'I will not ask you. Not now. Let it wait until your work is done here and you are returned to your home hearth and the ones you love. Such matters are best not spoken in such a place of death.'

Bridei nodded. He was reluctant to make his own request, for it seemed too much to ask. Drustan, for all his openness and understanding, looked drained by exhaustion. He said instead, 'What are your plans for the future? White Hill is open to you, if you wish to remain with us awhile.'

Drustan smiled. 'Thank you, my lord. The queen also offered the hospitality of your court. I need time to come to terms with what has happened. But I must return to Briar Wood before too long, and then to the west. I wish to clear my peaceful waterway of my brother's fighting ships.'

'Drustan –'

'I will bear the news of your victory home in the morning,' said the red-haired man, forestalling Bridei's question. 'At dawn I will go. By evening your people will know that you are safe.'

'I don't know what to say.'

'Say nothing. I saw the look in your wife's eyes. With every breath, she was willing your survival. Besides, I have my own powerful reason for a swift return to White Hill.'

'Drustan?'

'Yes, my lord?'

'There's more to this than you've told me, isn't there?'

Drustan was silent a moment. Then he said, 'The facts, as I know them, I have set before you in full. But there were three of us on this journey. Each of us has a tale to tell. Seek Faolan's accounting of it when you return home. That's if he has not departed by then.'

'Departed? Where?'

'I believe you will find him much changed, as indeed are Ana and I. He has unquiet spirits to set at rest before he can move forward, and a broken heart to mend. He does not wish you to see him thus unmanned. Ana bound him to stay until your return, but he may not have the strength to abide by that promise.'

'You alarm me, Drustan. Are you sure we're both speaking of the same man?'

Drustan nodded. 'It is the same, only changed. He will try to flee from his friends; even from you. Tread carefully with him. We don't want to lose him.'

'We?'

'Ana and myself.' This spoken softly and with pride.

'I see,' Bridei told him, guessing that there was at least one fact Drustan had not yet shared with him, and that it closely concerned the princess of the Light Isles. 'I hope I will be home within a turning of the moon, but there is much to be done here in the west. If you can, please ask Faolan to wait for me. Tell him it's important. There's a matter I wish to put before him, one on which he is better qualified than anyone to advise me.'

'I will, my lord king. Have you other messages for me to convey?'

'Tuala knows my heart without the need for words. Just tell her, in private, that I miss her and Derelei, and am counting the days until I reach home again. And thank her and Broichan for their wisdom in sending you to save me.'

'I did not meet your druid. He was elsewhere, and so was your son. But I will pass on these words.'

'You may tell Ana, unofficially, that I am glad she returned home and did not wed your brother. It goes without saying that this message should be delivered in private.'

'Thank you, my lord.' The smile now was less tentative, the eyes very bright.

'There have been losses here. I will wait until our return to relate those to the household; I will not burden you with such sad news. Now I must go; they're calling me. Will you attend our ritual for the dead?'

Drustan shook his head. 'I hope you will excuse me. I'm best alone tonight; I will rest and prepare myself for the morning. I wish you well, my lord king.'

'You'd best call me Bridei. After all, you're Faolan's friend, and that's what he always does.'

'Goodnight, Bridei. You are a fine man, deserving of our people's loyalty.'

'I suppose, in the end,' Bridei said, 'all we can do is our best, and trust that the gods will find it sufficient. Goodnight, Drustan. The Flamekeeper guard your journey. And, from the bottom of my heart, thank you.'

It was indeed a turning of the moon and more before the King of Fortriu rode back to White Hill, accompanied by the contingents from Pitnochie and Abertornie and a group of men-at-arms from the court itself. There was no challenge at the gates, not today. They stood open and, in the courtyard beyond, the entire household was assembled to welcome Bridei and his warriors home. The bad news had arrived much earlier, by messengers despatched to every place that had lost men in the war. That spared the families of those men who had laid down their lives in

536

the Flamekeeper's service from having to watch the return of each small band of travel-stained survivors, hoping beyond hope to see a well-loved face amongst them, and at length realising that a certain son, father, husband or brother would not be coming home.

For all those losses, it had been a great victory. Now, riding proudly at the front of the line, Cinioch bore the royal banner high. One of Ged's captains carried the bright standard of Abertornie in tribute to his fallen chieftain. In time a formal celebration would be held, and all those leaders who had played a part in the reclaiming of the west would be invited to White Hill, each to be honoured in his turn. That would not take place now until spring, for this return was late in the season and the approaching winter already set chill fingers on the land. Soon travel would become dangerous or impossible. Besides, Carnach and Talorgen were still at Dunadd, seeing to the departure of Gaels deemed a risk, and establishing secure rule in those territories. Fokel and Umbrig were in the north of Dalriada performing similar work, Fokel at his own ancestral home of Galany's Reach and Umbrig at the fortified coastal settlement of Donncha's Head, which he had taken a particular liking to. There would be a time for all things, even rejoicing. Without saying it aloud, the leaders of Fortriu had shared a conviction that the losses were too raw, the changes too overwhelming to make this appropriate yet. It was going to take some time even to come to a full realisation of what they had achieved.

It was close to the festival of Gateway and the shades of the dead were only a cold breath away. Winter allowed space for reflection; it was the spirit's fallow time, in which the seeds of wisdom began their long, slow generation. No need for cheering and music, feasting and celebration. It was enough to know that, when it was time, a new spring would come.

This, then, was not so much the triumphal entry of a king as the return of a family. First out the gates to meet the riders was the little white dog, Ban, yipping a frenzied greeting, his body trying in vain to keep up with his frantically wagging tail. Snowfire, steady as ever, walked into the courtyard with this miniature whirlwind performing a welcome dance around his feet. Then, as each rider came in and dismounted in his turn, he was surrounded by his loved ones, wife, mother, children, until the courtyard was alive with tears and smiles, embraces, friendly claps on the shoulder and, here and there, the sight of young fathers greeting newborns for the very first time. Men whose families lived away from court received kisses from maidservants and kitchen women who had nobody else to welcome. There was laughter aplenty.

The king, of course, must conduct himself with somewhat more restraint in public, even when his dignity is compromised by a small dog jumping up and trying to lick any part of him he can reach. Bridei's own welcoming party stood on the steps: Tuala, grave and still, with Derelei in her arms. The child looked doubtful, as if he were not quite sure who this grim and weary warrior might be. There stood Aniel, wearing a rare smile, and Tharan, tall and watchful. On Tuala's other side was Broichan. There were Ana and Drustan, unabashedly hand in hand: by all the gods, they made a handsome pair. Bridei saw Garth, bearing a thrusting-spear and a broad grin. There was no sign of Faolan.

Bridei took a step forward, and Tuala stepped down, and in an instant he abandoned decorum and wrapped his arms around his wife and son, for he had dreamed of this moment every night he was away, and now he could not hold back. Derelei froze; he opened his mouth to wail in fright.

'Papa's home, Derelei.' This was Broichan's voice from behind them. It seemed so much the kind of thing Tuala would say that Bridei was startled. The child blinked, closed his mouth and, a moment later, leaned his curly head on his father's shoulder.

After a little, Tuala stepped back and scrubbed her cheeks, smiling ruefully. 'You'd best greet the others, Bridei. There have been sad losses; your messenger brought us the news. Breth gone, and both Elpin and Enfret . . . And Ged, such a lovely man . . . That was grievous. His children are still young.'

Bridei nodded. 'He wanted us to help them, and we will. It's so good to see you; just how good, I cannot tell you in such a public place. Aniel, Tharan, greetings to you both. Many of our chieftains have remained behind in the west; there's much to be done there. Tomorrow I will convene a council and give you all the news.'

'A great victory, Bridei,' Aniel said with satisfaction. 'You walk in the light of the gods.'

'Broichan.' Bridei clasped his foster father by the arm and was momentarily lost for words. The druid looked at the same time far more worn and frail, and yet far more his old self, the dark eyes clear and formidably questioning. 'I hope you are well. I have you to thank for Drustan's intervention. Between you, you saved my life.'

Broichan shook his head. 'The credit goes not to me but to your wife,' he said quietly. 'It warms our hearts to see you back safely, Bridei.'

He said nothing more, and that in itself was clear evidence that something had changed. No mention of the victory? No mention of the routing of the Gaels and the triumphant reclaiming of the west? This had been Broichan's great vision. It was for this he had devoted fifteen years of his life to preparing Bridei for the kingship.

'Tomorrow,' Bridei said, 'if it suits you all, I'll place certain matters before you. You won't like all the decisions I've made as to the future of Dalriada. There are questions I need your advice on. That fellow Suibne, who was spiritual adviser to Drust the Boar, turned up at Gabhran's side. He gave me some disquieting information.'

Broichan nodded. 'Tomorrow,' he said. 'We have waited long enough for news; we can wait a day more, while you take a little time to rest and recover.'

Garth was leading Snowfire away; the other men were taking their own mounts to the stables, and the crowd was starting to break up.

'No formal feast tonight,' Tuala said. 'The household has been told the day of arrival is for private reunions, each to his own. Our quarters are barred to visitors until suppertime at least. And there's hot water ready. A bath and a change of clothes will be welcome, I expect.'

Bridei nodded. His eyes went to Drustan, standing by Ana on the steps. 'I don't see Faolan anywhere,' he said.

'He's been much away.' It was Ana who replied. 'And, of course, we did not know the exact day of your return. He will be back. He promised.'

'He'll keep his word,' Drustan said.

It was unsettling. Bridei had expected his friend to be here to greet him, sombre-faced and efficient, keen for news and ready with practical and ingenious advice. He had missed Faolan greatly, and to find him absent from this homecoming was disconcerting. 'Very well,' he said. Then, in a different tone, 'Come, Derelei. Let's take Ban up to the garden. I suppose you can run faster than he can now. Why don't you show me?'

As dusk fell beyond the window of the royal apartments, Bridei lay on his bed with Tuala drowsing in his arms and let his mind drift, the contentment of this day balancing, for a little, the doubts and quandaries that accompanied the aftermath of his great conquest. His wife's warm body curved against him, slight and graceful; her cloud of dark hair fanned across his chest, and he felt the small stir of her breath against his skin. His performance had been somewhat less than satisfactory, desire having got the better of him and rendered their love-making brief and explosive rather than tender and gradual. He and Tuala had laughed about this and promised each other next time would be a masterpiece of control. Derelei, worn out from chasing the dog and then from the novelty of splashing his father in the bath, was sleeping soundly in an adjoining chamber under the watchful eye of a nursemaid. Ban kept guard at the door.

'Bridei?' Tuala was stirring.

He curved his hand around to cup her breast. Desire had not yet reawakened fully, but he loved her body in its neat, small perfection; to touch her was like coming home all over again.

'Mm?'

'I have something to tell you. I don't know what you'll think about it.'

'That sounds intriguing. What is it?'

He felt her draw a deep breath, as if she needed to gain courage to speak.

'Bridei, this is going to seem . . . crazy. I really don't know how to say it, so I suppose I'll just have to come out with it. Bridei, I think maybe Broichan is my father.'

He took a moment to react. 'Your . . . ? But . . .'

'There is some logic to it. I suspect Fola has the same idea. I saw a vision. I cannot imagine any other reason the goddess would have shown me this. And it explains . . . it explains his bond with Derelei. Watch the two of them together, their movements, their expressions, the inflections of their speech. Such a similarity is not simply that of tutor and small student. It's the likeness of blood kin.'

'But . . .' Bridei began, not quite able to take in what she was saying, for it opened a view of the past that was darker and more troubling the more he considered it, 'if this is so, who is your mother? Broichan doesn't – I mean, he wouldn't – He's a druid, Tuala. How could he –?'

'A druid is a man, for all he gives his life to the gods. If the Shining One demanded of a man an expression of love that was carnal and worldly, as part of the conduct of a ritual, would not that man be bound in duty to obey? I know little of a druid's practice during the three-day retreat at the time of Balance. I know only that Broichan's habit was to go into the woods alone. My vision showed him as a man in his prime, walking the forest paths in springtime. There was a woman there, one of the Good Folk. One of my own kind.'

'How can you know –?'

'I can't. Only Broichan could tell me. And I haven't been brave enough to ask him. He would be deeply disturbed by such news. Disgusted, probably.'

'But, Tuala, if this is true, surely he must know? He must have known all along.'

'Perhaps not.' Her voice was small and calm.

'Of course he would know. An experience of that kind in spring, and a baby appears on his doorstep at Midwinter – no man with his wits about him could fail to make the connection. If you are right, it means that, knowing you were his own flesh and blood, he still treated you as a danger and a threat. He still would have cast you out –' He was sitting up now, the languor gone, his heart thudding with shock and outrage.

'I shouldn't have told you.' Tuala slipped out of bed, reaching for a robe. 'Bridei, be calm. I'm quite certain that, if it's true, he's never thought of it. You'd be surprised how blind people can be to truths they don't want to consider possible. I expect Broichan has shut the whole experience away in a forgotten corner of his mind. The last thing he would want acknowledged publicly is that he has me as a daughter. One of the Good Folk; his nemesis; the child he was forced to shelter in his house, for fear of offending the goddess or antagonising the foster son on whom all his hopes rested. Poor Broichan. It would be kinder not to tell him. But there are rumours; not of this, but of a possible irregularity in your own birth, or in our son's. The older Derelei grows, the more such rumours will be given credence. That worries me. These foolish tales can undermine your authority as king. To tell the truth, painful as that might be to Broichan, would clear the air and ease the burden on you and on our son. Sons, possibly.'

'You are saying –' Bridei looked at her, meeting her wide, strange eyes, the eyes that marked her out as something more than humankind.

'All being well, we will have another small son or daughter by early spring.'

'Tuala! Truly? This is wonderful news!' He got up and took her in his arms, feeling tears spring to his eyes. 'How long have you known?'

'Before you left I had a slight suspicion, no more. I have become surer as your absence grew longer and my fear for you deeper. I'm glad you are pleased, and still gladder that you will be at home when the child is born. I hope there are no more wars yet awhile.'

'I, too. Tuala, this talk of rumours disturbs me. Who has been saying such things? Aniel and Tharan should have taken steps –'

'Hush, dear one. There's no real danger, not yet.'

'But you must be upset –'

'A little. But I'm the queen; I can deal with these things. What's important is how I go about it.'

'I'll speak to Broichan, if you prefer that. If this is true, he must be brought to account.'

'No, Bridei. It's for me to talk to him. Strangely enough, I don't seem to be afraid of that any more, just a little awkward about it. Broichan's been seriously ill. He should really be at Banmerren

542

now; Fola has him under strict supervision. But he knew you would be home before Gateway and he insisted on travelling here to welcome you.'

'Tuala?'

'Mm?'

She had tied the robe's girdle around her narrow waist and had begun to brush out her hair. Bridei watched the steady, graceful movement, the ripple of the long, dark strands. He wondered how he had been able to bear being away so long. 'You're so wise,' he said.

'Maybe that's yet more proof that my theory is correct,' she told him with a grin.

Ban gave a warning bark and, a moment later, Garth's voice came from beyond the door. 'My lord?'

'What is it, Garth?'

'Faolan's back.'

Bridei looked at Tuala; she met his gaze and said, 'Don't look like that; we'll have plenty of time for ourselves later. You'd best see him now. He hasn't been himself since they came back.'

'Thank you, Garth,' Bridei called. 'Ask him to wait, please.' Then, as he began to dress, 'How not himself? I've heard an account of what happened from Drustan, but it was abundantly clear that was only part of the story. What does Ana have to say?'

'Less than you'd imagine. She and Faolan seem deeply changed by their journey. Since they came back here, the three of them have formed a tight little group. Faolan, of course, is performing some of his old duties, which Garth certainly welcomes. But I'm always coming upon them sitting in corners, conducting private conversations. Between Ana and Drustan, it's undoubtedly the concourse of lovers. But I'm just as likely to discover Drustan and Faolan deep in intense debate, or Faolan and Ana standing in complete silence, side by side, looking out over the forest. Faolan is restless. He doesn't want to be here. I hope he will talk to you.'

Faolan was waiting in the garden, where lanterns had been lit against the dusk. He wore riding boots and a heavy cloak, as if newly returned from a journey. Bridei walked across to grasp his forearm and draw him into a quick embrace. For a moment Faolan returned it, then he stepped back.

'I missed you,' Bridei said simply.

Faolan nodded. He was avoiding the other man's eyes. There was a small pack by the wall nearby, neatly strapped, and it came to Bridei suddenly that his friend was not arriving but leaving.

'Faolan,' he said, 'what is this?'

'It warms my heart to see you home safe,' Faolan said. 'But I wish to be released from your service.'

Shock, hurt and concern rendered Bridei incapable of response.

'My lord,' Faolan added belatedly.

Bridei drew a deep breath. 'As you know, it's not so easy,' he said. 'I imagine you'll be wanting what I owe you. Before I can pay you, I need an account of the mission. That's a requirement, Faolan. Will you come indoors and share some mead before the fire? It's cold out here.'

'No, my lord.' Faolan's voice was tight. 'No point in prolonging this. I don't need the silver; I've more than enough put away. As for the account, Drustan's told you what happened. The mission was a disaster. I lost the entire escort on the way. Alpin unmasked my role at Gabhran's court and threatened me with public exposure. I was forced to give him information about your advance that was perilously close to the truth, though I managed to convince him you were moving at the end of autumn, no earlier. The treaty was signed under false pretences. I got Drustan's loyal guard killed. Is that enough?'

'It seems, however,' Bridei maintained a level tone, though Faolan's bitterness alarmed him, 'that in bringing Ana away and thus invalidating the alliance, you did all of us a favour: Ana, Drustan and, in the longer term, myself as King of Fortriu. It seems Alpin would have been a perilous ally.'

'Indeed. Had I not been almost certain he had already deduced your advance was to be before winter, I would not have taken the risk of skirting so close to the truth with him. Ana's safety was the issue; I gave Alpin what I believed would buy me the time to get her away. I didn't like doing it.'

'Well,' said Bridei, 'Ana is safe and the war is won, though not without some grievous losses. You and I have both fulfilled our missions, one way or another. It seems our royal hostage may wed the Chieftain of Briar Wood after all.'

'Indeed.' Faolan was looking fiercely at the ground; his voice had changed again, the emotion back under tight rein.

'What is this all about, Faolan? Like you, I mourn those lost. But you've done well. You've saved Ana from a very dangerous situation and brought her home. She seems well pleased. I find no fault in your conduct of the mission. A flood is an act of the gods; to take personal responsibility for that seems more than a little arrogant. Do you no longer wish to work for me? Where are you intending to go?'

'Anywhere. Just not here.'

Bridei drew a deep breath. 'You know,' he said, 'I've never heard you sound childish before, Faolan. And I didn't think you would lie, not to me, your friend. I will not release you from my service until you answer two questions to my satisfaction.'

Faolan raised his head. 'Ask them,' he said.

'Why can't you stay here, and where do you want to go? I want the truth.' He wondered if Faolan would simply refuse to answer. He knew, as Bridei did, that he could simply turn and walk away from White Hill, and that, short of exercising force against a trusted friend, Bridei could do nothing to stop him.

'You'll be shocked at my weakness, Bridei.'

'Try me.'

'I can't stay because I can't bear to see the two of them together. It's a slow torture. I'm only here now because she – Ana – extracted a promise that I would wait until you came back.'

'The two of them – you mean Ana and Drustan? But I thought the three of you were very close. Tuala said –'

'We are close. We are friends. She loves him. He loves her. I love her. That is the simple truth, and I beg you to let me go.'

This from Faolan, of all men? Faolan whom people were apt to describe as devoid of human feelings? 'I see,' said Bridei, too astounded to summon a more meaningful response. 'And the second question?'

'I'm going home,' Faolan said quietly. 'Back to Laigin. A man died because of us, a fine fighting man with a spirit of exceptional generosity. He laid it on me to bear the news to his kin. Believe me, I have no desire at all to go back. But this is a duty I must fulfil.'

'And reconcile your own past?'

The dark eyes narrowed. The thin lips tightened. 'Who spoke to you of that?' Faolan snapped.

'Drustan told me there was a matter that still troubled you. He gave no details, saying it was told in confidence. I had thought you might want to visit your kinsfolk.'

'Ana would have me do so.'

'I see.'

'A lady of the royal blood of Fortriu, a Gaelic assassin, yes, of course you see. You see before you a deluded fool who couldn't keep his own feelings out of the king's mission, and botched it as a result. You should be glad to be rid of me.'

'Really?' Bridei said. 'Is that really what you want, for me to tell you, very well, go, and for the two of us never to meet again? To walk away and leave all this behind? Drustan and Ana will not stay here forever. And, to put it bluntly, she's not the only woman in the world. You're a mortal man, Faolan. This malady does befall men, and in time they recover from it.'

'I will not ask if you would have spoken thus had you lost Tuala that night in the forest. You wish to cheer me; I thank you for that. I don't deny I have missed your company and that this is no easy decision. I think I must go, Bridei. At every turn there seems a new reason for me to travel back. I know I cannot remain here. If I do so I will descend into a dark pit of destructive jealousy. I love her; I can't do that to her.'

'I can hardly believe it is so short a time since you were strong in your condemnation of this lady as a spoiled princess with limited riding skills, the guarding of whom was entirely unworthy of your talents,' Bridei could not help saying. 'What did she do to change your opinion so drastically?'

'Showed herself to be of true nobility: strong, courageous, selfless and wise.' There was a silence. Then Faolan added, 'Let me go, Bridei.'

'Tell me,' Bridei had been thinking fast, 'what if I were to offer you a new mission, one that would take you close to where you intended to go, but on my business and in my employ? Tuala and I would do our best to settle Ana and her companion somewhere further afield before you returned to White Hill. I know already that court life cannot be to Drustan's taste.'

'What mission?'

'You are prepared to listen, at least?'

'I've agreed to nothing. You can tell me what it is.'

'Faolan, have you heard of a Christian cleric, a compatriot of yours, by the name of Colm? He's sometimes called Colmcille, which translates as –'

'Dove of the Church.'

'You know of him?'

Faolan nodded. 'He has a reputation. Strong. Influential. Difficult. He's kin to the High King in Tara. He got himself in strife recently over a secular matter, put his oar in where it wasn't appreciated during the course of a territorial war. The man sounds like trouble. They were all talking about him at Dunadd last spring. What have you heard?'

Interesting, Bridei thought, how Faolan's voice changed and his eyes came alive when he forgot his troubles and addressed a new challenge. 'Gabhran offered him an island,' he said. 'One of ours. Several folk have told me this man Colm is the spearhead of a great Christian push beyond the shores of your homeland; it's said in Dalriada that he's a force nobody can hold back. On the other hand, it sounded as if all the fellow wanted was a small bit of turf to call home, and it's already been promised. Ioua's an out-of-the-way place. And that cunning man, Suibne, pointed out to me my own inconsistency in letting missionaries settle in the Light Isles while I push them out of the west. I want to know more about what this Colm is up to. Whether, if he's given a straw, he'll take the whole haystack. Whether these Christian brethren are a new invasion in disguise. Their relationship with Circinn. Anything you can bring me.'

There was a long silence and then, in the deepening dusk, Bridei saw Faolan smile.

'I expect you were good at fishing as a boy, were you?' Faolan asked.

'Not especially. Why?'

'You know just what bait to use and how to pull them skilfully in.'

'Maybe. My aim is not to kill but to harness a man's talents to their best use. Will you do this for me, Faolan?'

'I'd planned to go now, right away –'

'In the dark, with winter closing in? Come on now, credit me with a little intelligence. Wait until morning and take time to say your farewells. That way I can give you a full account of all I've heard, and we can reach agreement as to the scope of the mission and the time of your return.'

'And the payment,' Faolan said, the fleeting smile returning for a moment.

'That, too,' said Bridei. 'And if you need to take time for your family business while you are there, that can be accommodated. You cannot accuse me of being inflexible as a patron. In fact, I'm doing my utmost to hold onto you while trying to maintain a modicum of dignity. I've already lost Breth. I don't want to lose you as well.'

For a moment, as he stood by the great gates of White Hill waiting for the guards to let him out through the smaller door at the side, Faolan almost broke one of his own most sacrosanct rules: never lose control in public. He made the mistake of looking back. He could gaze into Bridei's eyes with equanimity; he was sorry to be leaving his friend and patron so soon, but they understood each other well enough. Bridei had given him the means to depart with dignity and purpose. Faolan would repay this, in time, with the flawless execution of his new mission. And by coming back. He wanted to come back. Just as long as they were gone.

He could look at Drustan and keep his features calm. One could not hate Drustan, despite the gnawing jealousy, the constant awareness of the impossibility of matching up to such a man's example. The fact was, Drustan had taken from him the only woman he had ever been able to love. Drustan had stolen his treasure and, despite that, he could not help liking the man. It was a conundrum, and he'd be glad to see the last of it. That farewell was not so difficult.

548

But Ana . . . Ana at dawn, holding his hands in the chill of the upper courtyard, the glint of tears on her cheeks. Ana trying to tell him something that began with 'if only' and stopping herself with the back of her hand over her mouth to block the words, dangerous words. If only what? If only a woman were allowed to love two men? If only they had turned back at Breaking Ford and never come to a place where love and loss awaited them? Or merely, if only Faolan had not sung a song, and crossed a river, and given away his heart despite himself? He would never know what she had wanted to tell him. He only knew he had to go away, for all their sakes; for the three of them.

So, looking back now as the little door by the gate was opened and there was no longer any excuse for delay, he met her gaze as she stood by Drustan, and he made no effort to conceal what was in his eyes, but let her see his love and his sadness and his hope for the future; her future and Drustan's. And what he read on her face brought a sudden hot rush of tears to his eyes, but he did not let them fall until his back was turned, and he was through the doorway, and his feet were carrying him on a path westward; westward to Laigin and a place that had once been home.

Author's Note

The Bridei Chronicles are based on real history; Bridei himself, his mentor Broichan, and the various territorial kings who appear in these books were all real people. Bridei became King of the Picts (Priteni) in 554 AD, and approximately five years later he led his people against the Gaels of Dalriada, inflicting a crushing defeat on the forces of King Gabhran.

The details of Pictish daily life, religious observance, military organisation and political structure in these books are based loosely on the existing evidence. However, that evidence is quite slim as the Picts did not leave any written records of their own. Historians are reliant on the writings of other cultures such as the Romans, who were scarcely unbiased, and Christian clerics such as Adomnan, who penned his *Life of St Columba* approximately one hundred years after the events in these books took place (the *Life* was written well after Columba's death and is more hagiography than history). Pictish artefacts such as the famous symbol stones give us further clues about their culture.

My notes at the end of the first book in this series, *The Dark Mirror*, discuss the use of imagination and informed guesswork to fill in the gaps in the known history of the period. A more detailed version of those notes can be found on my website at www.julietmarillier.com under the link *Bridei Chronicles*.

The political story of *Blade of Fortriu*, concerning the first major military campaign of Bridei's kingship, is broadly based on history, as is the gifting of the island of Ioua (which got its current name of Iona through a slip-up in penmanship) by the Dalriadan king to the Irish priest Columba. Gabhran's generosity led to later complications when the staunchly pagan Bridei won back the territories of the west.

For readers new to this series, the geography of the books is that of the Scottish Highlands. However, I have taken some liberties with distances and locations in the interests of better storytelling. The notes on my website include a description of the method I used for inventing place names appropriate to the period and culture.

This is a work of fiction, not a history. The story of Faolan, Ana and Drustan has little basis in historical fact. I imagine most powerful leaders of the period needed someone like Faolan at hand to deal with those situations calling for swift, silent solutions. The Caitt were a real tribe (Caithness in the far north of Scotland gets its name from them) and they were known as wild, independent and warlike. Ana's situation at the court of White Hill is based on fact: it is documented that Bridei kept hostages in order to control his vassal king in the Light Isles (Orkney).

For readers wanting to find out more about the Picts, my website includes a bibliography of reference books I found useful.

Coming in 2007: *The Well of Shades*
(Book 3 of The Bridei Chronicles)

In the seventh year of Bridei's kingship, he sends his chief assassin and spy, the Gael Faolan, back home to Ireland to investigate reports of a powerful Christian cleric whose charismatic leadership may prove a threat to the stability of Bridei's pagan kingdom of Fortriu.

Years before, the action of a cruel chieftain caused the young Faolan to deal a shattering blow to his own family, forcing him to leave home for good. Now he must return and face his demons. Without this resolution, his future looks bleak; the woman he loves is to marry another man, and he has lost his hard-won ability to distance himself from human emotions.

Back in his home province of Laigin, Faolan encounters surprises on two fronts. The path his family has taken after the terrible events of the past is not the one he expected. A side trip to break the news of a brave warrior's death to his kin results in Faolan's return to Fortriu, not alone, but accompanied by a young woman for whom he has suddenly become responsible. There is no telling whether the volatile Eile is friend or foe. The only certainty is that she seems to create trouble wherever she goes.

At Bridei's court of White Hill, the queen, Tuala, wrestles with questions of identity and calling, for it is becoming increasingly evident that by choosing not to use her gifts in the craft of magic, she may be limiting Bridei's ability to foresee danger and to stand strong against the encroaching presence of the Christian faith.

For Bridei himself, questions of faith, belief and choice loom large in this time of relative peace. Flawlessly loyal to the pagan gods of the north, he responds to the intelligence Faolan brings by inviting Colmcille, the powerful Irish cleric, to travel up the Great Glen to the court of Fortriu. In the presence of the king's advisers and friends, a confrontation occurs between Christian miracle and pagan magic that embroils the powerful druid Broichan, Tuala and her small son, and threatens Bridei's lifelong quest to reunite all Priteni lands under the old faith.

The Well of Shades covers a two-year period from the date of Bridei's great victory over the Dalriadan Gaels.

Juliet Marillier
Foxmask

Seeking to uncover the truth about his father, Thorvald makes a
perilous journey north to the forbidding Lost Isles. With him travel
his childhood friend Sam and an unwelcome stowaway, Creidhe.

On the isles the weary travellers find the Long Knife people, ruled by
a cruel tyrant. Suspicious and frightened, the islanders will not explain
why Creidhe must cover her golden hair, or why there are so few
children amongst them . . .

When a baby is born, Creidhe discovers the horrific truth of the curse
the vengeful Unspoken tribe has placed on the Long Knife people –
and the only solution. But there are deeper secrets in this battle for
survival, secrets that Thorvald, Sam and Creidhe discover when it
may be too late . . .

'Foxmask and Wolfskin are examples of just how wide the appeal of
fantasy novels can be. An artful blend of history and mythology, with
a hint of magic'
AUSTRALIAN BOOKSELLER & PUBLISHER

'To say what happens . . . would be to deny readers the excitement of
the story's resolution. There is tragedy here together with the risk and
power of sacrificial love'
SYDNEY MORNING HERALD

'[Marillier] disdains the Galahadian-type hero
and creates characters rich in emotion and
heart that have a life of their own'
HOBART MERCURY